I0760806

Darkness Defined

Order of Light

The Knights of Nyx

S BOLANOS

SERIES

Paranormal Stories

War on Darkness

Darkness Defined (MM)

Order of Light (MM)

Knights of Nyx (MM)

Moons of Mystery

Sara's Moon (MF)

Charline's Solstice (MF)

Diana's Eclipse (MF)

Kisin Novels

Courting Death (MM)
Death, Love, & Tacos (MM)

WAR ON DARKNESS

Fated Mates
Truth in Exile (MM)

Contemporary Romances

Ulwich Preparatory Academy

Our Last Fall (MM)

Our Secret Winter (MM)

Our Epic Spring (MM)

Oak Haven Romance

One Brave Thing (Enby/M)

All the Hype (MM)
Any Which Way (MM)
A Thin Line (MM)

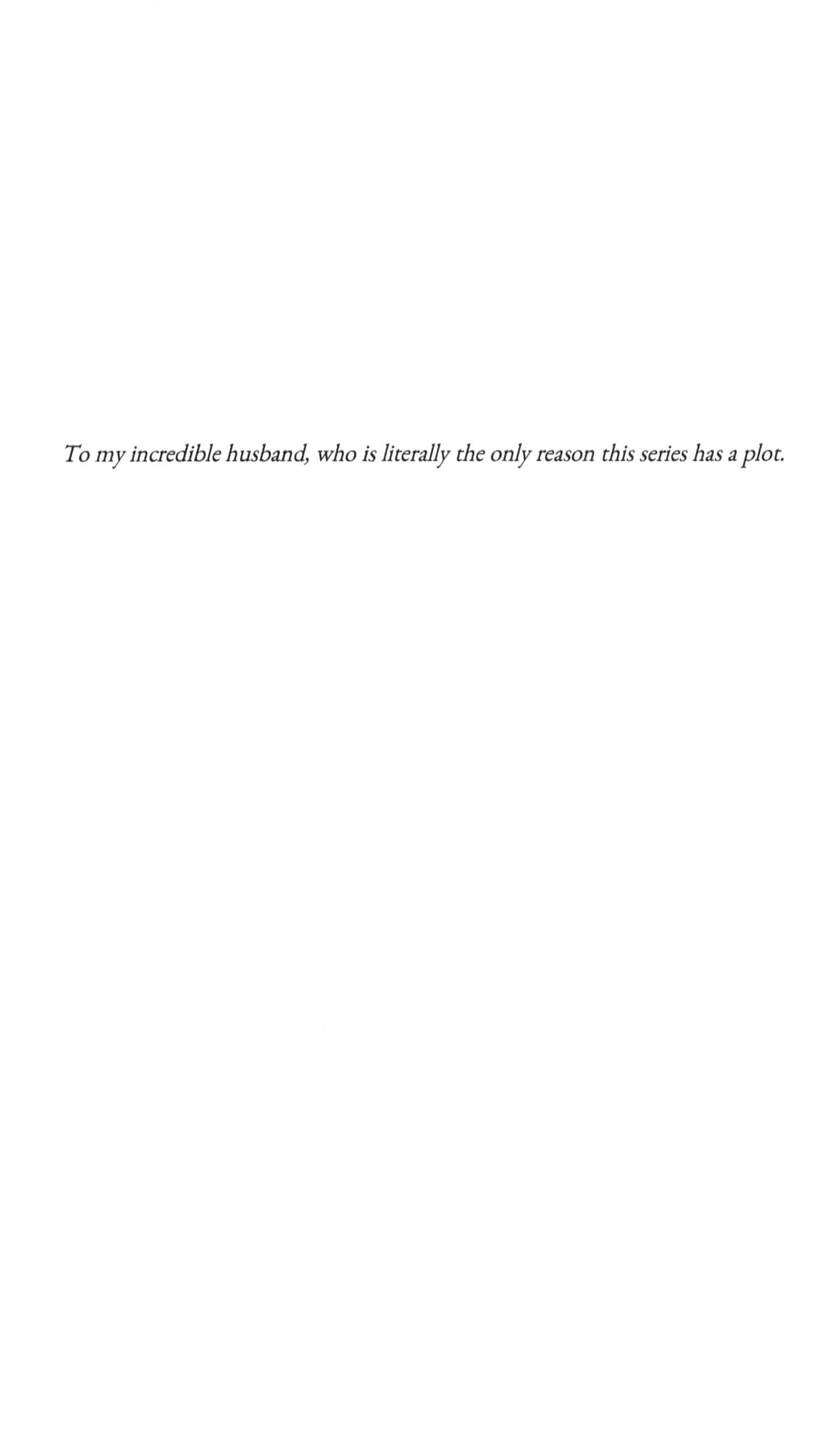

To my incredible husband, who is literally the only reason this series has a plot.

BOOK ONE

DARKNESS DEFINED

S BOLANOS

CONTENTS

Chapter 1
Superno House

Matt

A faded green door with age-spotted glass opened and the jerk that had hauled me out of the half-way house shoved me unceremoniously into an office. "Administrator Smith will see you now."

I ripped my arm free of the unnecessarily tight hold and glared at him as he retreated out the way we'd come. The door snicked shut, then I turned my attention to the room's occupant.

A portly man seated behind a metal desk paused his perusal of open files to give me a once over. His thinning, gray hair was combed over in a vain attempt to hide the balding, and the dark circles under his eyes spoke of a persistent exhaustion. Add to that the frayed edges of his coat and it was clear he cared more about his job than his appearance. Still, his eyes were borderline vacant as he took in my bedraggled appearance.

I fought the urge to shrink as his empty gaze took stock of me from my too small shirt that didn't quite cover my stomach and frayed shorts with more holes than cloth, down to my worn-out shoes.

"Matthew Duncan." Whatever insecurity I'd been nursing vanished with his monotone use of my full name. He gestured at the lone chair across from him. "Have a seat."

I did my best not to sneer and begrudgingly sat. I'd been off of the streets for three hours—max. Immediately stirring up trouble with the guy in charge wouldn't endear me to anyone, not to mention it would guarantee they put me on a shit list.

The administrator grunted at my lack of response and looked back at the page before him. "I see you've had a rough go of things."

Understatement of the year.

He lowered tiny, round spectacles from their perch on his forehead and resumed his inspection of the folder. "Let's see... in the system since you were born. No luck with foster families or adoption agencies. Numerous incidents of running away, disrespecting authority, and physical violence. I guess we should be glad you're not a fire demon with that sort of temper." He sighed and set the folder on his desk. "Still, a demon is a demon."

I waited for the half-hearted laugh to emphasize the sorry joke. Instead, he went on as serious as he had started.

"You'll need to understand that this sort of behavior," he jabbed his index finger onto the hefty folder, "will not be tolerated here. Superno House may be a home for wayward supernaturals, but we run a strict campus."

I frowned, but he either didn't notice or didn't care.

"We have cared for everything from your standard witch with budding powers to demons of the highest carnal class. When I say this will be your last stop, I mean it. However, your stay here can be much more pleasant if you," he peered through his glasses at the report again, then flicked his gaze back up to me, "could enlighten us as to your particular demon class."

I crossed my arms, leaned back in the uncomfortable chair, and propped my feet on the edge of his desk. "I don't know what the hell you're talking about."

"Language, Matthew."

My feet flew off the desk and landed with a thud on the floor... except no one had touched them. I searched for some kind of clue for how he could have done it with no more than a flick of his fingers.

Smith let out a long sigh. "While yours might be the most enigmatic, I've dealt with tough cases before. We will determine what kind of demon you are." He removed his glasses and started cleaning them. "Though with no physical manifestations to provide guidance, the discovery may be less than pleasant."

I bristled. I'd been called a lot of things over the years, and honestly, "demon" wasn't new. Whatever he called me, all I needed was ten months. Ten months until I could no longer be considered a ward of the state. It was the only goal that mattered: freedom. I ignored the bait and simmered in silence, tuning out the nonsense he was spewing about how things were different here. It was all lies. Superno House would be no different from any of the seven orphanages.

Orphans had their own hierarchy. Those that had been around the longest typically occupied the top of the food chain while the newcomers landed on the bottom—or were made to. Funnily enough, it was those attempts that usually resulted in me getting kicked out of whatever place I'd been dropped. I smirked to myself. It wasn't my fault the other boys couldn't hold their own.

"Are you paying attention?" Smith huffed. "Listen here, Matthew-"

"I go by Matt."

His eyes narrowed. "I will not tolerate rudeness. We may not know what kind of demon you are yet, but we will. When we do, this untouchable status you think you've cultivated will be gone. The children here are not the easy pickings you're used to."

My dislike of the man solidified. I was not a bully.

Unexpectedly, the tough teacher act dropped and Smith sagged in his chair, exhaustion pulling him deeper into the dilapidated cushion. "I understand how frustrating being passed around can be. Once we're able to determine how best to help you with your abilities, then the anger will fade. You have my word."

I stared blankly back.

"Has anyone explained why you're here?"

I snorted and crossed my arms. "Got caught after running away from the last place."

Smith shook his head. "That's not quite what I meant. Do you know why you're here specifically?" He tapped his desk for emphasis, and I rolled my shoulders to ease my increasing discomfort. Smith studied me for a moment. "You really don't know, do you?" He paused as if unsure how to proceed, then said slowly, "Superno House is... special."

"Whatever. I've heard that before." If I was anymore disgusted with this ridiculous charade, I might actually spew all over his desk. "As for 'abilities', last time I checked, having a bad temper and being a target for bullies wasn't an ability, it was a nightmare. Not to mention I've been tested for practically everything under the sun... multiple times. So, please, spare me. The results are always either a flat out nope or 'inconclusive'." I tightened my arms across my chest. The tests had been less than pleasant.

"I'll ignore the attitude for now, because I genuinely believe that you do not know about your true heritage. I'd love nothing more than to provide some insight, but without proper testing..." He spread his hands. "Given your—colorful—record, I'd hazard that you belong to the Chaos Class. We have a few of those here. Though, given your obvious anger management issues, it's possible you're a type of elemental. Either way, you are a supernatural, Matt. There's no doubt about that."

I scoffed. "Are you for real? You can stop blowing smoke up my ass. We both know the only reason I'm here is because the age of majority in Nebraska is nineteen. Less than a year, and I'm gone." It didn't take a fantasy to explain why I was angry. Being abandoned at a Catholic church less than a month old then passed from one awful place to another did that to a person.

Smith sighed and leaned back in his chair, rubbing his temples. "It's worse than I suspected." He visually regathered himself and smacked the arm of the chair. "Let's start with a tour of the facilities. That should put things in perspective." Smith stood and walked to the door. He opened it, then waited for me to follow. When I didn't, he added, "You're welcome to stay here, but meals are only served in the cafeteria and that sofa isn't nearly as comfortable as it looks."

I eyed the questionable orange couch that by no means looked comfortable, then pushed myself up from the chair and trailed obediently behind him. I didn't really need a tour; one orphanage was much like another.

Beyond the door, a pair of kids were running full-tilt down the hall. I shook my head. Yep, exactly the same as all the others.

When the kids caught sight of Smith, they ground to a halt just shy of crashing into us. The girl looked to be a few years younger than me and the boy younger still. They looked similar with iridescently dark skin, pinched faces, and decidedly pointed ears.

The girl sneered. "What are you supposed to be?" Her doll-like face twisted into something eerily savage. I half expected to see serrated teeth peeking between her thin lips.

"Now, Mercy, don't be rude. Matt is the newest addition to the home. I expect you and your brother to make him feel welcome," Smith tacked on, his voice stern.

"He doesn't belong here," the boy piped up. His equally delicate features remained perfectly impassive, as if they were carved from black marble.

"Christian!" Smith admonished.

"He's right," Mercy added while her brother's face remained unsettlingly blank. "He's dangerous."

I snarled at her, and she shrank back. Smith gave me a nervous look, but didn't comment. I supposed next to these frail children and with my reputation, I was the bigger threat, but no one would ever peg my five-seven as imposing at first glance.

Smith cleared his throat and angled himself between us. "A specialist will come out next month. She's been recruiting for an exclusive school for... unique demons. It's possible that our recent addition may not be with us long." He gave me a sidelong glance that I was pretty sure I wasn't supposed to notice, and swallowed.

Mercy stepped closer to her brother. "Good riddance."

"Yeah, all demons do is cause trouble. They're just a bunch of bullies," Christian echoed.

I was fully aware that I'd been branded a troublemaker, but that didn't make me a bully. And what the fuck was all this demon shit about?

"That's enough." Smith pointed down the hall. "Off with you, and I better not catch anymore running. We wouldn't want a repeat of last month's incident, now, would we?"

The two shared a menacing look, then continued down the hall. All of two steps later, the peculiar kids vanished from the hallway, leaving two bright points of light where they'd been. I blinked to clear what I assumed was an afterimage, but the glowing balls stayed hovering above the ground. Then, just as suddenly, they zipped down the hall.

I staggered back and looked at Smith, my eyes in danger of falling out of my head. "What the hell was that?"

"Sprites." Smith shook his head. "Intuitive and mischievous to a fault, but they're never wrong." He finished locking his office and took off down the hall. "It's an unfortunate fact that most of the children that end up under our care are Fae or Demonic. There's the occasional elemental, but their own kind keep a closer watch on them."

I remained rooted to the ground, still struggling to make sense of what I'd seen. Except it wasn't possible. No way those creepy kids had turned into tiny balls of light and flew. Was flew even the right word? Whether it was or not didn't matter because it wasn't possible in the first place.

Smith glanced over his shoulder, not really slowing. "I told you these kids would be different. Come on, the cafeteria is this way."

I debated making a break for it, then recalled how Smith had somehow knocked my feet off my desk without touching me. If he could do that, then there was no telling what else the people in this place could do. I shuffled to catch up, equally concerned about being too close to the administrator and not really wanting to be alone.

As we walked, I examined every kid we passed for any signs of weird. Mostly I saw the usual curious faces, a couple more hostile expressions, but other than that, nothing extraordinary, and certainly nothing like I'd seen earlier. A couple of turns later, I was ready to chalk up the whole encounter to low blood-sugar. It was as likely as anything, given I couldn't remember the last time I'd eaten.

Suddenly, Smith stopped and looked over at me. "Do you smell burning?"

I blinked back at him. Now that he mentioned it, there was the faint smell of burnt popcorn, but that shouldn't be unusual in a place full of kids. Suddenly, a stream of fire blasted out into the hall of an adjoining corridor.

"Oliver!" Silence met Smith's bellow. "Oliver, I know that's you. Get out here right now."

A boy about my age stepped out, his shoulders hunched and his vibrant red hair sticking out in every direction as if he'd stuck his finger into an electrical socket.

I wrinkled my nose. The kid reeked of sulfur and had burned sleeves.

"What's your problem? Haven't you ever seen a fire demon before?" He bared his teeth at me. "I suggest you wipe that look off your face before I do it for you."

My hands curled into fists at my sides.

"Oliver." The boy flinched at Mr. Smith's tone. "How many times have we talked about fires inside?"

Oliver tore his angry glare away from me. "It's not my fault! Rufus started it." He gestured behind him and a column of fire shot from his hand.

The fear I'd been doing my best to ignore prickled along the back of my neck. Actual fucking fire had come out of his hand. If he could do that, it was entirely possible the creep twins really had turned into light.

What the hell is this place?

"Shit," Oliver hissed, shaking his smoking hand, which seemed like a terrible idea to me.

"Language," Smith admonished.

"I'm telling you. It was all Rufus." Oliver shot me a glare, and I quickly wiped the panic from my face.

Logically, I realized that getting into a fight with this kid could likely be the end of me, but if he started something, I'd finish it. The fire would be tricky, but I'd gone up against guys twice my size and come out unscathed. I was too close to freedom to let some brat intimidate me.

Smith crossed his arms while a scowl pressed into his full face. "That's enough, Oliver. You and Rufus can go see Miss Mary Ann. I'm sure she'll be able to sort this mess for you and perhaps remind you about the importance of being careful."

Oliver groaned and turned to the open door. "Come on, Rufus, you heard him. Time to go see your girlfriend."

Another kid poked his head out. He was smaller than Oliver, with sun-starved white skin and a dark mop of unkempt hair on top of a spindly frame with a thin neck like some kind of creepy bobble head. The observation was reinforced by the fact that his eyes were abnormally large and couldn't seem to hold still. Together, they trudged down the hall.

Smith rested a hand on my shoulder and I about near jumped out of my skin. "I'm sorry. It's a never-ending battle around here. Adolescence is hard enough. When you add to it budding powers, things can get a bit dicey. Safety is our number one concern, though. Fighting is strictly prohibited," Smith finished pointedly.

I frowned. That was often easier said than done in most cases. Smith nudged me along until the hall opened onto a massive room. Where I'd been expecting the usual sterile white walls, the room was a warm cream decorated with all sorts of art. It made an odd contrast to the standard metal tables with attached benches and the pristine—and currently empty—buffet.

"Meals are promptly at eight, noon, and seven. Though there are snacks available. No junk food, but plenty of fruit." Smith gestured vaguely down a wide corridor. "You'll find the sleeping quarters that way. Girls on the left, boys on the right. A fresh set of clothes should await you on your assigned bunk. Lights out at nine. Now if you'll excuse me, I think I'll be joining Miss Mary Ann in dealing with our fire-starter." He spun on his heel, leaving me standing all alone at the entrance to the cafeteria.

I glanced at the analog clock on the distant wall. Two hours 'til dinner. My stomach growled at the prospect of food and I was half a step away from making a beeline for the snack table. An apple sounded like a fantastic change from the scraps I'd been able to snag over the last couple of weeks. And yet, I hesitated.

A quick glance down the opposite direction Smith had gone showed a hall shockingly devoid of people. I chewed my lip and debated what to do. I could grab some food and even the fresh set of clothes, but that would waste precious time. Both Smith and whoever Mary Ann was were occupied. The path to the main entrance was wide open and after what I'd witnessed, I had no desire to stay here.

I made my way down the hall, careful not to appear rushed or like I was doing something I shouldn't be. The path stayed clear all the way to the remarkably mundane double doors leading to the street and freedom. I smiled to myself and didn't bother looking back as my pace quickened. With any luck, the doors would be unlocked.

I reached for the push bar and suddenly found myself walking back the way I'd come. My worn-out shoes squeaked as I came to an abrupt stop and looked around. With a frown, I spun around and aimed for the exit with more conviction… only to end up even further down the hall instead of outside where I should have been. I growled and tried again… with the same result.

"What. The. Fuck?" I glanced between the door and the hall where I kept ending up. Before I could second guess myself, I sprinted for the door.

"When you've tired yourself out, I'll take you to the showers where you can get cleaned up."

I jumped at the unexpected voice and turned to find an imposing woman leaning against the wall. She had dark hair pulled up into a bun, was easily a head taller than me, had greenish skin, and, yep, those were tusks. I swallowed hard and took a step back.

"You must be Matt."

"What the hell are you?"

She flexed an imposing pair of biceps as she straightened. "Smith mentioned this was new to you. We'll address the impropriety of asking someone 'what' they are later. For now, I'm more concerned with getting you into clothes that don't look like they're going to disintegrate. Come with me." She turned and began walking down the hall toward the cafeteria and the dormitories beyond, clearly expecting me to follow.

Though she hadn't bothered to introduce herself, I had a sneaking suspicion I'd just had my very first run-in with the infamous Mary Ann. She glanced over her shoulder and I hastened to catch up. Maybe I could stay a little longer.

CHAPTER 2
DANIEL

Alexi

"I've already told you, Daniel, I'm not interested." My gaze wandered around the room in search of my suitcase, pointedly avoiding anywhere near my *ex*-boyfriend.

I finally found it hiding behind the cracked door. That was one mercy. At least I wasn't trapped in a closed room with him. That would undoubtedly be trouble if my history with Daniel was anything to go by. Of course, my mother's strict rules about no boys in the room also didn't hurt, not that he was following them. I moved the luggage and opened the door until it touched the wall.

"Don't be like that, Alexi," Daniel said, sitting on the bed and nearly undoing all of my efforts to organize my packing.

I heaved an exasperated sigh and saved a stack of shirts before they could officially topple to the floor, a move that brought me dangerously close to him. Thanks to my absolutely zero self-control, I couldn't help but breathe in the sharp cedar of his cologne.

Getting ahold of myself, I sped up my movements before he could take advantage of my proximity. Sure enough, I caught a sigh of disappointment and looked up just in time to see his fingers pass right *through* my arm. I quickly put more distance between us. Fortunately, while beautiful, Daniel wasn't the brightest. Hopefully, he'd assume that I'd simply been out of reach and not incorporeal.

"Why are you even here?" We hadn't spoken in weeks, not since we'd broken up—again. It had been our lot the last few years to be that notorious on-again-off-again couple.

"Your mum let me in. And I couldn't very well let you go traipsing off to some fancy Uni I've never heard of without a proper goodbye." The wicked gleam in his eye left little doubt what kind of goodbye he had in mind.

Daniel knew he was classically good-looking with his square jaw and dark hair, not to mention a physique that would make Michelangelo drool. He was our small English town of Denham's uncontested resident charmer and my own personal kryptonite. He was also a lying, narcissistic jerk that had never managed to win over my mother, who liked pretty much everyone. Which begged the question: how had he gotten past her in the first place?

A glance back at him showed he was playing with my clothes, most noticeably the underwear. I leaned over and snatched the teetering stack, plopping it into the now open case before he could stop me.

Daniel looked at me with that smug grin, his dark hair falling in his eyes, then seemed to flow up off of the bed. For a human, he was surprisingly graceful, especially since he was even taller than my six feet. Once, it had been nice to be with someone who could literally cocoon me with their embrace. Now it was just suffocating. Daniel stepped forward until he'd invaded my personal space.

My spine stiffened, but I refused to back down. "Like I said before. Not interested," I reiterated in blatant disregard of my already racing heart. This is what Daniel did, what he always did, but I was determined not to make the same mistakes.

"Come on, Alexi, no one knows you like I do. No one can touch you like I can." Daniel's voice was practically a purr.

Desire pulled at me, undermining my resolve. He leaned in just enough so I could feel his breath on my lips. One last hurrah, that's what we would call it. Something to remember him by when I finally left for Arminius and could put all of this behind. But I knew what would really happen. We'd go out, have an amazing night, end up back at his place, and in the morning, I'd wake up feeling used—again.

"I think we could really make the long-distance thing work." His slick words were barely more than a suggestive whisper hovering over my lips.

I barked a laugh. "Are you serious? Long distance? Daniel, we couldn't even make down the street work." This time, the laugh was bitter.

"It'll be different," he argued.

"You mean you *won't* cheat on me?" I fired back.

"Clarke hardly counts, and we were drunk anyway, so it definitely doesn't count."

I looked at him in total disbelief. "Do you even hear what you're saying?" I scoffed to myself. One of us knew better. "You know what? I'm done entertaining your ego. I want you out of my house."

Daniel reached for my arm.

I ripped it out of reach, still not trusting myself if he actually laid a hand on me. "Now."

His arm dropped, and he looked at me entreatingly. "Lexi."

I pointed to the very open door.

"Baby," he cooed.

I stood firm. After what felt like forever, he rolled his eyes and stomped out, every inch the petulant ass who hadn't gotten what he wanted. I waited until he crossed the threshold of my bedroom, then slammed the door shut and locked it for good measure.

I rested my head against the door, still struggling with the contradictory impulse to race after him. It wasn't like I hadn't dated other guys. There was just something about Daniel that kept me coming back like a glutton for punishment. I grabbed a random book off the desk by the door and chucked it at the far wall.

Why am I so weak? How does he still have any hold on me? He cheated on me, for God's sake.

"Honey, are you alright?" a delicate voice asked through the thin wood.

"I'm fine, mom."

"If you're so fine, then open the door."

I stared up at the ceiling in search of divine intervention. When none presented itself, I unlocked and opened the door. On the other side was my mother, a full foot shorter than me, and tapping her foot impatiently.

"Why did you let him in?" I asked heatedly.

She inspected the room before deigning to answer, most likely searching for signs that we'd been fooling around, despite the very clear no fooling around rules. "Frankly, I was hoping it would help you pack faster. Though I see that hope was in vain."

I blinked, taken off guard. "What? I thought you didn't want me to go?"

She let herself into the room and walked over to the bed, where she placed three stacks of clothes in the open suitcase before sitting down in the now empty space. "Oh, sweetie, you know I love you, but truth be told, we both know I can't handle your powers. You need proper schooling with people like yourself. While you've done great blending in with the humans around here, you aren't one. You should be spending more time with your own kind."

I shook my head. "Mom, demons tend to be solitary."

"But not you, Lexi. You're social and vibrant, always have been. Or at least you were until..." Her face twisted as she looked at the door Daniel had walked through shortly before.

I was fully prepared to launch into yet another defense of my decision to continue dating Daniel over the years when she continued.

"This school opening has been the best thing that could have happened. Just think, if we had never joined the Arminius Community Forum, then we wouldn't have even known about the special classes and you would've had to wait another year, maybe even two, before you could enroll. The world hardly knows anything about Shadow Demons. This is your chance."

"The world knows to fear us. Half of the supernatural community here won't go anywhere near me since the Rebellion, and that ended ten years ago. I was eight for crying out loud. What did they expect me to do?" The words tasted as bitter as they sounded.

"I know it hurts, sweetie, but that doesn't mean you shouldn't learn about your powers. You still face the same risks that all untrained demons do. Alexi, if you lose control..." she trailed off. We both knew how dangerous that could be.

"I won't. I'm not some newbie who just learned they had powers. I've been practicing for years." I reached out and gave her hand a quick, reassuring squeeze. "You made sure of that."

She heaved a sigh. "But is it enough? What about your potential? We don't even know what you're fully capable of. What sort of world will open up to you once you start learning more?"

"Honestly, I'm probably close to peaking. I bet I'm years ahead in study from the rest of the class. After all, I've read every resource book on Shadow Demons we could find." Not that there had been many, or that they'd been easy to find, in a world that had no clue supernaturals existed.

"Lexi, I can't help but feel you're making an argument not to go at all."

Her hand settled on mine and I realized I'd steadily been unpacking as we talked. I groaned in despair.

"You were so excited about this last week and now it's like you're dreading it."

I looked over at her, taking in the tight ringlets of sandy blonde hair falling around her petite face that was nothing at all like my own jet black. My heart hurt more at the thought of leaving her here alone than it did at the idea of never seeing Daniel again. My mother was a lovely woman, and it was a shame she'd never remarried. I knew why though. She'd loved my father more than anything, and when he'd left her with nothing more than a swollen belly, she just couldn't move on.

I'd never seen so much as a picture of him before. But from what she said, I was the spitting image of a man that had stolen her heart eighteen years ago.

It must be true, because I didn't look a thing like her. Except for my eyes, those were definitely hers—a bright green that shone like spring.

"I'm going to miss you," I finally said.

"I know, honey." She lifted her hand to cup the side of my face. "But I'm only a call away. I'll be fine. My goal has always been to see you succeed, and you can't do that here." She released me and placed another stack in the case, smoothing out the wrinkles on top. "Now, Alexi Roman, I need you to dig deep and be the strong person I know you are." She stood up and gave me a hug.

Her arms wrapped tightly around me, and I carefully returned the embrace. Demonic strength had not been a fun thing adjusting to growing up.

"Enough of this." She pushed me away, surreptitiously wiping a tear. "You need to stop dawdling and finish packing. Orientation is in a week and you still have to collect your things from the community center."

"Yes, mom." With a smile, she patted my cheek and left me to my task. I turned back to my mess of folding.

I don't need much, it's just school after all. It's not like I expect to meet the love of my life.

Now that I was focusing, the suitcase steadily filled. It was hard to believe that, in just a few days, I'd be in Austria at a prestigious university for the supernatural. I briefly considered packing my poster of Arminius University, but dismissed it as childish. After that, it was official. Everything worth packing was.

I flopped onto the bed, causing it to groan in protest and reached to feel beneath. When my fingers brushed a binding, a smile spread across my face. I promptly pulled it out and settled back against the wall. The book was one of the few my mother had found over the years. By some miracle, she'd known what my father was and had known to look out for the same traits in me. That knowledge had saved both of our lives.

As I thumbed through the worn pages, I couldn't help but wonder if Shadow Demon's antisocial nature was a product of our own making or biological. Hopefully, this new school—class really—could finally answer those questions. While I wasn't exactly enthusiastic about Vera Scry being the one to lead it, since she was the reason the supernatural world feared people like us in the first place, it was better than nothing.

I stopped on a page with an illustration of a shadowy woman reaching toward a knight in full armor. The passage on the other side described the scene.

The darkness itself took shape and reached out. Eyes blacker than night drank my soul. Such a creature could put fear into the evilest of man or beast. Would that my Light had not abandoned me. That cursed torch with the power to beat back this monster and preserve my essence.

I felt the darkness encircle me and draw my breath. The Daemon approached, the promise of death in its kiss. Words escaped me as the night stole the very breath from my lungs. My only mercy was that it didn't speak.

A mercy short lived as words like that from a fallen angel poured forth and drew me close, wrapping around me, a lover's embrace. My will was robbed, and I walked forward to fall into oblivion...

The rest of the passage was too obscure to make out. The creature described had all the makings of a terrifying monster and a timeless love. This was where the original owner of the manuscript and I had differed.

Notes in the margins declared the belief that this man was fighting for his immortal soul against some nameless demon and losing. I, on the other hand, believed that while the man had originally set out to slay the creature, he instead had found himself captivated, falling madly in love with his worst nightmare, that the reference to "a lover's embrace" wasn't a typo or poor translation. Even the illustration looked more like a man meeting a secret love than succumbing to pure evil.

I sighed and set the book down. It was pointless to speculate. As far as the rest of the supernatural world was concerned, we *were* evil. Vera Scry had seen to that. I still wasn't sure how I felt about going to a school she'd started. Just because she and the rest of her military unit, self-dubbed the Shadows, had switched allegiances, didn't mean we could automatically trust them.

Who's to say they won't be just as bad or worse than the Regency?

It was a fact that Shadow Demons were rare, just like it was a fact that I'd never met another one, not even the infamous Vera herself. The prospect of meeting her now was simultaneously terrifying and exciting. Not just because of who she was, but because of *what* she was—a level two. Contrary to how most things in the human world were rated, demon classes followed more of a pyramid structure when it came to levels. The lower the number, the higher you were on the general power scale, with level ones, or originals, being right at the top.

I didn't even think it was possible for someone like her to exist so far removed from a direct lineage of power. The stories said that her level was a freak accident, absolutely unprecedented. And yet, the existence of this class at all said that Shadow Demons were primed to make a comeback from the brink of extinction.

I held out my hand and called to the darkness with my essence. As thick fog pooled in my palm, I could feel it straining against my control. My mother had a point. I had no idea what I was really capable of beyond parlor tricks and half-baked theories. What *could* a trained Shadow Demon do?

I guided the substance by force of will across the room to turn off the lights. Instantly, my realm of influence extended. Controlling my tiny bubble of shadow at once became easier and infinitely more difficult. Without the light to destroy it, maintaining the shadow was a piece of cake. However, now that darkness was all around, it echoed my call, reaching for me as much as I reached for it.

It glided along my skin, intimate and gentle, like a lover's caress. That was the main reason I believed the man in the book had been seduced. The night could be full of terrors, but it could also be full of passion. I released the shadow to join its essence—my essence.

I am the darkness, and the darkness is me.

The resonance inside of me intensified as I continued to extend my control. As I reached for the night, the night reached back for me, igniting a longing that went deeper than a mere need to be touched.

I let it go, sinking back to the normal realm of sensation. Someday, I'd find someone who could make me feel as alive as the darkness did, who would understand what I could never hope to explain. I shook off the romantic thought and sighed into the gloom, still struggling with my own mixed feelings. What *would* it be like to meet others like myself? If I was being honest, I was absolutely terrified at the prospect. It was too late to back out now, though. In eight days, I'd meet an entire class full of people just like me.

I smiled into the darkness.

Well, maybe not just like me.

Chapter 3
The Newcomer

Matt

Beneath the strict supervision of Miss Mary Ann, I got cleaned up and into clothes that almost fit. Then I wandered around Superno House while I waited for dinner, doing my best to stay out of the way. The more I saw, the less I understood. Calling these kids different was a nice way to put it. And somehow, somewhere along the line, someone had gotten convinced that I was one of them. A supernatural.

I grabbed a tray and made my way to an empty table by an oil painting of a forest, determined to lie low. If I could stay out of trouble long enough, this place could be my last stop before I was finally free to decide about my own life. A girl sat down at the far end of my previously unoccupied table. I glanced over as she tucked her hair behind her ear. A light smile tipped my lips. She was pretty and there was no reason the wait had to be totally intolerable.

I was about to call over to her when I saw the horns poking up through her straight black hair. Air went down the wrong way and I struggled to cough through it without drawing attention to myself or dying. Thoroughly put off of pursuing anything with someone at Superno House, I focused my attention on my tray. Given how sporadic my meals had been the last few weeks, I didn't care what the food looked like; it smelled edible, and that was good enough.

I took a bite of what I hoped was meatloaf and almost immediately had to smother a moan. Whatever it was, it was good. I fought the urge to shovel all of it into my mouth as fast as possible, already debating about trying to sneak back for a second helping. No amount of going slow would make it last, though. In record time, my plate was clean and the only thing I had left were my thoughts, and boy, did I have plenty of them. Most of the people I'd seen appeared normal enough, but like the girl at my table, I suspected they were all far from it. Even

Oliver had looked like any other scruffy orphan and he'd shot fire out of his hand.

I looked down at my hand. He'd called himself a fire demon. I examined both sides of the appendage and imagined what it would be like to do what I'd seen earlier. Unsurprisingly, nothing happened. I scowled, disappointed in my juvenile fantasy, and let out a huff. The way everyone said "demon" made it sound like there was more than one kind. If that was the case, how many kinds were there? Had I met any before? Was it possible Smith was right, and I was a demon? But if I was, then how did he know? And why didn't he know what kind?

I sagged beneath the weight of doubt. Per usual, I had more questions than answers. My stomach gave a small growl, drawing my attention to the more important question right now—could I snag another helping without getting caught? I was about to try my luck when the hairs on the back of my neck stood up.

"I think we should give the new guy a proper Superno House welcome. What do you think, Rufus?" a voice that sounded suspiciously like Oliver said beside me. A quick glance without moving my head confirmed it.

"I think that's perfect," the guy who I assumed was Rufus responded. "Khima?" The girl with the horns looked over.

I blanched as I realized the rest of her was also sporting barbs.

"I'm game," she responded without hesitation.

I swallowed hard. So much for not making waves. Another glance up showed that Rufus was practically on top of the table leering at me. His bug eyes wiggled incessantly, and he smiled, revealing alarmingly pointy teeth. My eyes widened slightly. Behind him, Oliver stood, holding a steady flame in his hand. There was no pretending anymore. These guys definitely weren't human.

Rufus's head cocked to the side and the queer sight of it almost made me lose my dinner. "Carter is coming," he whispered, lowering himself to sit on the bench.

The flame in Oliver's hand disappeared into a closed fist just before a man that looked more like a gorilla than a children's care attendant walked by.

I held my tongue and tried not to look panicked. If I called for help, they'd only find me later and it would be so so much worse. Once he was gone, someone grabbed the back of my shirt and pulled me to my feet, not caring when my legs got tangled between the table and the bench.

Oliver's manic smile filled my vision. "Good, you made it, Scylla."

My optimistic belief that I could take him now seemed stupid and short-sighted. He might be the ringleader, but there was no way I could take four of them on my own.

"Wouldn't want to miss this." The owner of the voice bared a striking resemblance to the kids I'd met in the hall, though she looked meaner and older and was porcelain pale where the others had been dark. Resemblance or no, it didn't make a lick of sense how she could drag me off of the table like it was nothing, not with her light frame.

"Get moving, meat." She shoved me toward a side door. I had no idea where it led. I also didn't have any options, so I walked.

"Meat," Rufus chuckled. "It's funny because he's practically human. I mean, look at him. How did he even get in here?"

"They let in all sorts of weirdos these days," Khima said, pulling up on my left. Who was she calling a weirdo? The girl in the hall had called me dangerous, but compared to this group, I was inclined to agree with Rufus.

Strangely, or maybe not strangely at all, no one seemed interested in five kids working their way to an obviously off-limits metal door. I attempted to drag my feet.

Maybe that gorilla-thing will come back and stop this whole mess before I end up in a pulverized puddle.

The door got closer.

Where did he go? Where are all of the adults?

I intentionally stumbled at the threshold, one last desperate attempt to buy time.

"Hurry up," Scylla hissed, and forced me through the opening.

To my dismay, the door shut with a whispered hiss of air. A quick glance around showed that we were now in some sort of courtyard, or maybe it was a playground, with a high brick wall to our right. I squinted in the darkness and was able to make out basketball hoops and a jungle gym. What I didn't see were witnesses.

My jailer gave me another shove, and I stumbled a forward. I spun around, wanting to keep all four of them in sight. Fat lot of good that did. The group spread out to encircle me, driving me further from the only escape route I knew of.

"He looks scared," Khima snickered, her horns back-lit by distant lamps.

Oliver stepped forward to separate himself from the ring. "He should be." The world took on a sudden light as two pillars of flame shot up from Oliver's hands. I instinctively bent my knees and sank into the ground. I didn't know what to expect, but it didn't take a genius to know that I didn't want to lose my footing.

"Aw, is the little baby crying for his mama?" Scylla crooned to a chorus of cackles.

"I can't hear anything. Maybe I should get closer." Rufus sped toward me as if he wasn't even touching the ground, his teeth glinting in the unnatural light from Oliver's hands. Panic twinged in my chest as the reality of what I was seeing struck home. That freak had wings.

The thought barely had time to form before I had to dodge out of the way. I spun around to search for him, only to be sucker punched by Khima in the gut. The hit ejected all the air from my lungs. I struggled to drag it back in, but it wouldn't come, almost as if someone was simultaneously pulling it back out. I searched my attackers frantically for the source until I saw Scylla's feral smile. She made a pulling motion and I put it together.

Sprite, that's what she is, just like the kids from the hall. Mischievous and what? Intuitive.

Mercy and Christian had called me dangerous, but how could I possibly compare to something that could literally steal the air from your lungs? Then again, Smith had said sprites were never wrong.

I gave up trying to draw air, and the resistance vanished. Scylla stumbled back as if I'd let go of a rope she'd been pulling. I turned to face Oliver. Chances were that if he went down, the others would back off... hopefully.

"What's the matter, Ollie? Too afraid to face me yourself?" I wheezed.

The red-headed demon's face lit with fury. "That's it, step back. I'm going to show this miserable wretch what a real demon can do."

"Hey," Rufus whined.

"Shut up. You're a lower class and you know it." Rufus withered at the onslaught and Oliver turned his attention to the Sprite. "I heard Mercy and Christian talking. He's supposed to be something worth fighting. What do you think, Scylla? Is he worth my time?" Tiny flames licked up and down his fingers while he spoke. It was easy to see how his cuffs had gotten burned. Unlike the fabric, though, his skin didn't seem to react at all.

Her smile looked evil in the lurid light of the flames. "I think all the power in the world doesn't mean shit if you don't know how to use it."

"My thoughts exactly." Oliver's eyes narrowed as his attention returned to me. "You're nothing special. You're just some overgrown toe rag no one wanted, and a coward to boot."

My anger grew as the insults hit me, pulsing like a living thing, eager to escape and tear him apart.

"Scared little chicken shit is what you are."

The world went black.

Where other people saw red, I saw darkness, pure and all-consuming; it was everywhere; it was everything. The first time it had happened, I'd freaked. It had only lasted a moment, but it had been enough to leave me shaking and terrified. That had been a long time ago, and I wasn't the same scared little kid. My focus zeroed in on Oliver. He thought he was tough shit because his hands were made of fire, but he'd have to catch me first. I didn't wait to see if the others would listen to his high-handed command. I rushed him where he was too busy gloating to realize I'd moved.

"What the fu-" Oliver started in disbelief.

Out of the corner of my eye, I saw Rufus flying towards me. He almost sideswiped me, but instead ran into Khima on the other side, who I hadn't even realized was approaching.

Pay attention. This is no time to lose track of people.

Oliver braced himself for impact, the flames on his hands growing into large spheres that encircled his fists. At the last second, I changed my course, heading for Scylla instead. She'd already proved she didn't have to touch me to hurt me. If I even had a chance of taking down Oliver, she'd have to go as well.

Scylla's eyes lit with panicked rage when she finally saw me coming. Before she could react, I was behind her. She seemed genuinely startled, but it was too late. I grabbed her by the arm and flung her back. She soared across the courtyard to slam into the wall back by the door.

For a moment, I almost lost my concentration. I'd never thrown anyone that far before. Then Rufus was bearing down on me again, those unnerving teeth ready to tear me apart. I searched the ground for something to put between me and his mouth of razors.

Then I spied it. In the dark, it looked like only a shadow, but it was definitely club-shaped and that worked for me. It was cool to the touch as I wrapped my fingers around it and fell into a batter's stance. Once Rufus was in range, I swung with all I had. As the miraculous club slammed into his mouth, confusion exploded across his face.

Time stretched as the momentum of his assault met the force of my swing. Then he, too, went flying. I didn't see where he landed. Oliver's head swiveled around like he couldn't believe what was happening while Khima tried to get back to her feet. In the distance, it sounded like Scylla was also recovering. I was running out of time.

I renewed my run for Oliver, my feet pounding on the pavement. He looked far less confident now. Shame it never occurred to him he couldn't see anything with all that fire in his face. Ironic really.

Abruptly, my steps slowed as if I was trudging through molasses instead of open air. That had to be Scylla. I pushed through, determined to finish Oliver before she could finish recovering.

I should've hit her harder.

The resistance vanished as suddenly as it appeared and I sped through. Oliver was thoroughly alarmed now and searching among his fallen friends for help.

Who's the chicken shit now?

When it was clear no help would come, he squared off, his flames growing to outrageous heights. With the fire blinding him, there was no way he could see I wasn't running up the middle anymore. I smiled to myself. This had almost been fun. They'd lasted a lot longer than most.

I couldn't even see Oliver anymore amidst the orange and red plumes, but it didn't matter. A few more feet and this whole thing would be over.

Without warning, the two of us rose off the ground like giant hands had picked us up. I struggled to no avail against the unseen hold. Oliver shouted and his flames went out. The night instantly plunged back into darkness.

I blinked several times to eliminate the afterimage from his inferno. When my vision finally cleared, there were two figures by the door we'd come out of who knew how long ago. As they stepped forward, I saw one was Smith, and the other was a woman.

For a second, I thought she might be another menacing Mary Ann, but something told me she didn't belong at Superno House any more than I did. Whoever she was, she was definitely the reason I was hanging six feet off the ground, unable to move a finger. And she was just like me.

"Smith, what part of 'don't let the demons fight' sounds complicated to you? It's basic preservation." Her words dripped with sarcasm and the barest hint of a Southern accent. "The place may be warded, but all it would take is one curious pedestrian."

"We only sent the missive yesterday when we realized we couldn't identify his race. You weren't supposed to be here for another month," Smith protested.

"I'm a Shadow Demon, Smith. Try to remember that. Not some snot-nosed brat you can tread all over. When I asked for your cooperation, I had no idea I was resigning myself to work with an incompetent, self-righteous, pompous, son of a..." Her tirade snapped off and she took a deep breath. "Let's try this again. Does he know?"

"Know what?"

"For Nyx's sake, Smith. Does he know what he is?" she asked, the essence of put-upon exasperation.

Smith darted an anxious glance toward me and wrung his hands. "According to him, no. I suspected he might be lying, but he seemed genuinely shocked by everything here. Honestly, I don't think he knew about supernaturals at all before this afternoon."

"And yet, he single-handedly took out an Ick Demon, a Sprite, a Spiculo, and a Fire Demon. Impressive." She gave me an appraising look while I tried to parse out what the hell she was talking about. "Do you mind?" She gestured to the air in front of her.

"Mind what?" Smith echoed.

"A light, Smith. As you can imagine, that's not really my forte." I could practically hear her rolling her eyes. "I want to get a better look at my latest recruit."

A sickening tone of subservience replaced Smith's previous combativeness. "Sorry, Miss Scry." He waved a hand and muttered something I didn't catch. Then a bluish light blossomed overhead, illuminating the speakers in high-relief. To my shock, the woman was much younger than I would have expected for someone commanding so much authority. Old or not, her eyes were sharp and ruthless and she looked meaner than a pissed off copperhead.

I glanced around from my suspended perspective. Now that there was a proper source of light, the damage was clear. Oliver's gang lay strewn about the courtyard. Only Scylla had found her feet while the other two looked comatose.

"Good heavens!" Smith exclaimed, taking in the havoc I'd wrought.

I snickered, and he shot me a look while the woman stared at me as if assessing something I couldn't see. I glared defiantly back, and she cracked a smile. It was gone before I could decide if it was sinister or sincere.

The woman waved a dismissive hand at the apoplectic Smith. "Cool your grits, they'll be fine. The damage is minimal, nothing a healer can't set to right."

"Minimal? He could have caused actual harm! And in case you didn't realize, we don't exactly have the funds to maintain a fully trained healer on staff," Smith snapped as he walked over to help Rufus, the club I'd shoved in his mouth, now gone.

"He's an absolute natural." The woman's smile definitely seemed genuine now. "I dare Gabriel to top this one. He's easily above a ten, maybe even as high as a seven. Hard to tell now, though, with no training."

"Ten!" For a second, it looked like Smith might actually faint. "He could've killed them!"

She rolled her eyes. "Please. Did you miss the part where I stopped them?" She gestured at where Oliver and I hung a few feet apart in the air. "As for a healer, I'll send you mine if you're that worried, but we both know they each got what was coming to them. Besides, the injuries seem mostly superficial." She tilted her head to the side and Oliver plummeted to the ground. His resulting moan said he was fine, but in pain.

"Miss Scry, I really must protest at your abuse of my wards." Smith marched up to her, wagging his finger.

Her eyes went solid black, and the night seemed to warp around her. Chills crawled up my spine as the darkness tightened around me, causing me to wheeze. The color drained from Smith's face, and he dropped his accusatory finger.

"It's no less than what he deserves. We all know what he intended, dragging my ward out here." Menace laced the low words and goosebumps pimpled my skin. "It's a far cry better than what he would've gotten if I hadn't intervened. Matthew is clearly raw and untrained. If his record is anything to go by, his anger and control are both out of reach."

Without warning, I flew towards her. My eyes widened in panic and I struggled harder. This lady was without a doubt the most dangerous person out here, and after what I'd just felt, I had no desire to be any closer. My flight stopped as abruptly as it had started, leaving me mere inches from where she was standing.

"Do you have any personal effects here?" Vera asked, her eyes still obsidian.

I shook my head vigorously, fear momentarily freezing my tongue.

"Good. Smith, we're leaving. Next time you get even an inkling of a power level like this, you call me sooner rather than later," she ordered, her eyes still boring into me.

I swallowed and fought to keep from shaking uncontrollably.

"Y-yes, of c-course," the cowering administrator stammered.

"And Smith," she finally looked at him, "try to keep this lot under better control. If you need help, I'd be happy to send some... volunteers."

Smith went noticeably paler, an impressive feat considering how washed out everyone already was in the bluish light. Fear once again trickled down my spine.

She turned back to me. "Give me your hand."

I shook my head and tried to shrink away, for all the good it did me.

She rolled her eyes and grabbed my left arm. The world was sucked from around us. There was only darkness. Then I blinked, and we were standing on a sidewalk. A glance behind me revealed a sign with scrolling letters that read Superno House for Wayward Children.

I looked back at the woman, able to see her better in the yellow streetlights. Turned out she was dressed in nothing fancier than blue jeans and a t-shirt with wild red hair that looked like the fire Oliver had been sprouting minutes before.

"Who are you?" I blurted out.

At the question, her entire intimidating demeanor fell like she was dropping a mask. Then she put her hands on her wide hips and smiled. "Sorry about that. Some of these old fogies are still living in the last century. All they know is reputation and fear. Sadly, honey doesn't get you as much as it should these days, but I'm working on that."

She's absolutely certifiable.

"My name is Vera Scry. I'm the expert you were promised. Sorry I didn't find you sooner, but at least you were still here to find. Shadow Demons are a tricky lot, especially if they haven't really manifested. I confess, if I hadn't already been in the states, it might have been another month before I got here." She looked at me expectantly. "You know, you're not restrained anymore."

My leg twitched.

How far could I get?

"But I will say, if you're thinking of running, remember, you were running the last time I caught you."

My eyes widened. Was it possible she could read minds? Was that even a thing?

"Well?" she prompted.

"Well, what?"

She frowned. "Just because I've read your file, doesn't mean you shouldn't introduce yourself. That's just good manners."

Who is this lady?

"I'm Matt and I don't know what I am."

She smiled again and started walking down the sidewalk. When I didn't follow, she glanced back and waited. There was nowhere else for me to go and she'd already proved that running was pointless, so I joined her.

"I figured as much. Well, Matt, I have a proposition for you."

I looked at her out of the corner of my eye. "Proposition makes it sound like a choice." It definitely didn't feel like one.

"Observant, aren't you? I suppose technically it is a choice, though I really hope you say yes and don't make me persuade you."

There was no telling if the persuasion would be a pros and cons argument or torture. Something told me neither would phase her.

"I've started a school to help our kind, Shadow Demons." She glanced at me. "That's what you are, Matt. We're kind of a dying race and I may have created an atmosphere of fear over the last decade, making it especially unsafe for our kind." Her focus shifted to the ground and the loose pebbles she was kicking. "I'm trying to fix that. By bringing together young demons and training them properly, we simultaneously ensure that they embrace their demonic half and that they don't lose control and go on an accidental killing spree." Silence hung for a moment.

"You're insane."

She gave me a crooked smile and shrugged. "So, I've been told."

CHAPTER 4
THE OUTCAST

Alexi

The sun warmed my back as I approached the community center. To my surprise, hardly anyone was around the bleached white building, shining like a beacon in the middle of town. Then again, with it not quite being summer yet, the usual classes and events hadn't started, so that made sense. Of course, that didn't stop the bulletin board from being cluttered with pamphlets.

I chuckled to myself as I spent a few minutes rearranging the multitude of paper. How the heck people expected to get anyone's attention with everything overlapping like that was beyond me. I reached a cream-colored page that was hiding beneath an advert for a dog walker and paused. A small smile tugged at my lips as I freed it from the chaos.

The Denham Agrarian Poets Society has moved meetings to the private residence of Mary Elizabeth Parker. Please reach out directly for updated times and admittance.

I pinned the supposed "update" to a corner where others could see it. When my mother had uprooted us from Greece to this small parish in the UK, I'd never expected to find a community, let alone a community of supernaturals. Luckily, they'd recognized me as one of them and given me the rather vague advice of joining DAPS. Best decision ever.

I gave the board another once over, then dusted my hands and went inside, where I was immediately greeted by an older woman with a faded brown face and graying hair pulled up in a bun.

"Alexi! What brings you here?" Roberta Mannheim may have looked like a quiet old lady, but I was convinced she'd never had a quiet day in her life.

I smiled warmly and rushed to help her with the table she was currently relocating to the side of the room. "Nothing much, Robbie. Came to pick up a few things before mum and I head out."

She paused and straightened up, giving me a beaming smile. "That's right, your kiester got into that fancy early admittance program!"

I shrugged at her enthusiasm. That wasn't quite the case, but it was the story we were going with.

"Come here, squirt." She waved me over, and I obligingly stepped into her warm, grandmotherly embrace, or what I assumed a grandmother's hug would be like. "Ooh, I knew you were too smart for this little old town. But gosh, we're gonna miss you." Robbie suddenly pushed me to arm's length, her wrinkled face now serious. "Now don't you go gettin' yourself into any trouble, Alexi Roman."

I laughed and gave her another big hug. "Wouldn't dream of it."

"I mean it," she said with a sniff. "Mind all them boys."

"Robbie..."

"What? You're a good lookin'-"

I grabbed her hands and quickly cut her off before she gave me the birds and the bees lecture... again. "I'm going to learn, not for romance."

"Well, never say never, dear." She patted my cheek, then put her hands on her hips. "Suppose I better stop dilly dallying and get back to work."

"Anything I can do to help?"

"Oh, no, sweetheart, I've got this. Jerry should be along shortly. You go on about gettin' your things." She gestured toward the back of the room where a hall led to the storage closets and the kitchen. "Be a dear and make an old lady some fresh tea?"

"I'd love to, but how many times do I have to tell you? You're only as old as you feel."

Robbie snorted. "Says the eighteen-year-old. If that's the case, then I feel a hundred and twenty." I was about to offer to help again when the promised Jerry came in. "There you are, you lazy bag of bones. Come, give me a hand."

In the kitchen, I pulled out enough cups for everyone, then rummaged through the cabinets until I found Robbie's favorite tea. While the kettle warmed, I took out my to-do list, crossed off a few items, added a few more.

"Thought I heard you in here."

I swallowed and glanced up to find Nemo Santori leaning against the wall, large arms darkened from spending hours in the sun crossed over his chest. "Hey, what brings you here?"

"Work." Nemo's voice had the unfortunate effect of always sounding like a growl, making it difficult to tell whether or not he was angry. Considering he was a werewolf, it was best not to chance it.

"Yeah? Finally, get roped into helping Marge with the renovations?" I asked with a forced smile and as much positivity as a person could muster. Beside me, the kettle whistled.

He uncrossed his arms and walked over to the counter littered with cups. Then promptly poured himself some tea. "So, the rumors are true. You're headed off to that... school." He took a sip of the scalding liquid, his stern eyes staring at me over the rim. "Is it true that evil bitch is going to be leading it?"

I flinched. By "evil bitch", of course, he meant the notorious Vera Scry, who'd done her part in decimating werewolf packs across Europe. It didn't help that she was also a level two Shadow Demon. Hardly anyone had known about us until she showed up.

"Well? Wolf got your tongue?" Nemo gave me a toothy smile. Most of the town believed his wolf puns to be endearing and quirky. Some of us, however, were in on the truth.

"I... I uh..." I coughed to clear my throat. Vera had done a lot of horrible things while she'd been under the influence of the Regency, but most of them paled compared to the wrongs she'd done the shifter community. "I don't know. I mean, I'm not sure. The forum mentioned her being involved, but not to what degree."

Nemo's lip curled.

"I, uh, should probably finish getting my things." I took a tentative step toward the door, my tea forgotten. Nemo had once been a great mentor, practically a father figure to me, but the second Vera had rudely introduced Shadow Demons to the world, I became persona non grata. It hurt like hell to lose that, but even then, it might not have been so bad if his feelings on the matter hadn't spilled over into the rest of our small community of supernaturals. You'd think I was the one who'd done the Regency's bidding, then switched sides to join the Rebellion.

He grunted. "When do you leave?"

I swallowed and worked diligently to put on a brave front, ironically, something he'd taught me to do. "Our flight leaves in a couple of days. Then I'll be out of your hair for good. Except, of course, for holiday visits and break and... the like..." I trailed off.

Nemo nodded and set down his empty cup. "I best be getting back to work. Thanks for the tea, kid."

"You're welcome," I replied by rote, though I hadn't really made it for him.

He was almost out the door when he paused and glanced over his shoulder. "Alexi?"

"Yeah?" I hated how my voice betrayed my anxiety.

A smile I hadn't seen directed my way in years crinkled his eyes. "Stay true to yourself. You're gonna do great things." With that, he walked out the door, leaving me standing there with my mouth hanging open.

I took a minute to let Nemo's unexpected encouragement sink in. Maybe these last five years of stubbornly attending the secret supernatural community gatherings had paid off. Was it possible I'd really won Nemo back over despite sharing the genetic heritage of the most hated woman to ever wrong wolfkind? Figures it would be the second I was leaving town.

I rolled my eyes and finished organizing the teas. Once I'd delivered steaming cups to the ever-bickering couple, I disappeared into the back with my cup to finish what I'd come to do. The late morning turned to early afternoon as I rummaged through everything to make sure I didn't accidentally leave anything behind. A decision I was grateful for when I found my copy of Demon History sandwiched between dusty board games.

It might not have mattered so much if someone like Nemo found it, but if one of the decidedly human occupants of Denham had stumbled across it, that could have spelled trouble for all of us. Dubious about why I'd been so absent as to have left it here, I wandered over to the box I'd found that was now in serious danger of overflowing. I was finally putting the lid on when another voice called out.

"Alexi? Are you in here?"

My spine stiffened at the soft, timid voice. It took every ounce of decency I had to wipe the scowl from my face. I straightened up, dusted my hands, then turned to meet the second to last person I wanted to see, the last, of course, being Daniel. "What do you want, Clarke?"

They glanced from me to the box and back again. "I heard you were leaving town. Going to some school?" Their light brown eyes looked at me questioningly.

"You heard right." I might have been aiming for laissez-faire, but bitterness ate at my words. And, yet, despite knowing it wasn't entirely Clarke's fault, I couldn't seem to stop myself. "Is that all you wanted?" When they continued to stand there, I reached for the box.

Clarke surged forward, hand in the air. "No! I... uh... I..."

Sweet, merciful night. I did not need this right now. "Spit it out. Why are you here?"

"I was hoping we could clear the air?" They gave me a sheepish look.

I crossed my arms and couldn't help but compare us. Clarke was shorter and about as stereotypically white Protestant as a person could get. Where I was darker and all lean muscles, they were pale and soft. Was that what Daniel had really wanted? Someone he could easily overpower? Had he known that I wasn't human? Was that why he'd cheated on me? With fucking Clarke?

They took another step closer. "Please. I never intended to hurt you. We're friends." That was a loose definition if I'd ever heard one.

"Clarke..." I dropped my arms and scooped up the box.

"He said you were alright with it."

I fought the urge to throw the entire box at Clarke's head. It wouldn't have been hard, even if it was supposed to be heavy. Once my temper was under control, I tightened my grip and met their pitiful gaze. "Newsflash. He lied."

Clarke winced, probably not the least bit surprised.

I rolled my eyes and moved to go past them. Then another thought made me pause. I glanced at them. "Tell me one thing. Were you two even drunk?"

Clarke's face turned a bright shade of red, like they'd been out in the fields all day instead of inside having this awful conversation with me.

"That's what I thought." This time, I made it all the way to the door before I stopped again. Clearly, my conscience didn't care how much being around them hurt my heart. Deep down, I knew Clarke was gullible and naïve. I also knew Daniel was none of those things. "Hey, Clarke, when he comes crawling back—because he will—don't let him."

Clarke's choked sound was all the confirmation that I needed. Daniel had tried to woo me and when he'd struck out, he'd left my place and gone straight to Clarke. What was that saying? Oh right, no good deed goes unpunished.

I finished making my way out of the Community Center, sparing a wave for Robbie and Jerry, who were now enjoying biscuits with fresh cups of tea, and headed toward home at the edge of town. If I had been waffling about going to Arminius before, I wasn't now. I needed away from small town drama and cheating exes. A few years of focusing solely on my studies was the perfect diversion.

CHAPTER 5
THE HOTEL

Matt

I still had no idea what to expect from this "school" or what on Earth my new warden had done to make everyone so afraid of her. All I knew was that after we'd left the orphanage, we'd walked for what seemed like hours until we reached a hotel.

A man dressed sharply in a red coat, primly pressed with copper buttons, nodded in greeting from behind the counter. "Lovely to see you again, Miss Scry. I trust your visit has been productive?" If he wasn't in charge, he was at least important.

"I've told you before, Jeffery, call me Vera," my kidnapper tsked.

"Whatever you say, Miss Scry. Your usual room?" he asked, completely disregarding her demand. Maybe he didn't know what she was... what we? were.

I glanced at him, a little impressed, considering Administrator Smith had been cowering before her just a few hours ago.

"Yes, but I won't be staying. My adventures this evening have been quite..." her eyebrows lifted, "eventful."

The desk clerk's eyes widened slightly, and his face paled. Nope, he definitely knew. "Not too eventful, I hope." To his credit, his voice didn't shake.

Vera laughed like it was the best joke in the world. If it was, I certainly didn't get it. Then she turned his attention to me. "Jefferey, this young man is Matthew Duncan."

I grimaced at hearing my full name.

"For your sake, though, I strongly recommend you just call him Matt."

"Will Mister Matt be needing special accommodations?"

"Yes, but I'll see to them." Vera gave me a skeptical once over before heaving a sigh and returning her focus to Jefferey. "There's a chance he may try to bolt before I return. Caution the staff." My scowl went unnoticed as she continued.

"Other than that, please make sure he's well looked after. I'll be returning for him as soon as I can. There are several other stops I need to make before we can leave, and time is of the essence."

I stared at her in open disbelief. She'd basically kidnapped me and now she was leaving? Maybe I wouldn't have to wait the ten months after all. I could slip out the second I had an opening and that would be that. Fat chance she could find me again after I got lost in the city. Then again, that hadn't worked out so well for me the last time.

"As you say, Miss Scry." To my surprise, Jeffery didn't present her with one of those key-card things, but an honest to goodness key. Fancy and everything.

She rolled her eyes at his dry response and accepted it, then led the way to the elevator. I followed her in silence, soaking in the marble floors and impressionist art decorating the walls. Even the elevator doors were fancy. I glanced at her out of the corner of my eye, even more curious about how someone seemingly so young could just walk into a place like this. The doors slid shut, and I turned on her.

"How old are you? Where are we? Why did he treat you like... like..."

"Like I own the place?" she finished for me, raising an eyebrow.

I deflated a bit. "Well, yeah."

"Because I do. I own several hotels around the world. And to answer your very rude question, I'm twenty-eight. But don't let looks fool you. My husband has been around for a millennium and only looks thirty-five." She cocked her head to the side. "Forty on a bad day. As your powers develop and you truly embrace your demonic side, your aging will slow down dramatically. Trust me, I'm very aware that I only look twenty."

I choked. Like being twenty-eight, magically made it more reasonable that she owned hotels around the world and had men twice her age hopping to her every whim. "Who are you?" I asked once again.

She winced. "You'll learn that soon enough. The school I'm taking you to is actually for all kinds of supernaturals."

Yesterday, or even eight hours ago, I'd have snorted and told her she was off her rocker. Supernaturals weren't real. They were a story, make believe. Except, they weren't...

"Aside from learning how to use your own powers, you'll also learn about magical history, and that includes the history of demons." Vera paused, appearing genuinely anxious for the first time since she'd shown up out of nowhere and carted me off. "It's... not pretty, and you might not like me much once you know more about my role in... uh, recent events."

"You could just tell me now." I shrugged, because really, what did I care? I'd never met her before and she was leaving. It wasn't like who she was had any bearing on my life.

"I could." She stepped off the elevator and walked up to—surprise—another fancy door. A look around revealed very few extra doors, leading me to believe this had to be the suite level. She unlocked the door and stepped inside. "Come on in, Matt. Mi casa es su casa."

I frowned in response to her smile and walked past her into the room. Two steps later, I stopped dead. The nicest place I'd ever been was the Hiddleston house. They'd been a nice family, but their son had taken issue to sharing his parents' attention. I'd thought they lived in a mansion, that having my own room was the stuff of kings. It didn't hold a candle to this place. To be fair, I'd also never been in a nice hotel, or even a not nice one for that matter, so maybe my expectations were off.

Vera brushed past my shoulder, then walked over to lean against a couch so cushy it looked like it could swallow a person whole. "You'll have to stay here while I run the last of my errands. I apologize that I'll be leaving you on your own for a few days, but I trust Jefferey to take care of you." She gave the room a once over and turned back to me. "I also trust you don't need someone holding your hand to make sure you bathe and eat something decent?"

I finally put my eyeballs back in their sockets and turned to her. "You're really just going to leave me here?"

"Yep." She did a double take at seeing the utter disbelief on my face. "Matt, you're a capable young man. You'll be fine. I'll make sure Jefferey gets you a proper wardrobe and something for dinner."

"I already ate."

"Oh." She looked at her watch. "How the time flies. Well, I'm hungry, at any rate. I'll have something extra sent up, just in case." She hurried toward the door.

"Don't I get a key?" I called after her, causing her to pause in the opening.

Guilt flashed across her face. "You won't need one." She closed the door, and I raced over in time to hear the distinctive sound of a lock sliding home.

"Shit." I could still feel her on the other side, as well as a growing sense of something else. I waited until the sound of retreating steps was long gone, then tried the handle. The damn thing wouldn't turn. Rather than keep failing, I gave it up and wandered around the space.

This was certainly a suite fit for a king. It held two couches and a breakfast table, as well as several pricey looking decorative pieces. The plush beige carpet sank with each step, coating my footfalls in muffled silence. As I explored the rest of the room, I found an equally outrageous bedroom with a matching bath, each gilded to the extreme. If I could pry some of it off, I'd be set for life. But first, I had to get out of here. I glanced over at the sliding glass door.

The door slid open easily, revealing an extensive balcony complete with chairs and a small table. I stepped up to the iron railing. Overall, it was a spectacular view of downtown Omaha. The hotel wasn't overly tall, maybe only ten stories. Looking down at the street below, I immediately nixed any thoughts of getting out that way. It wasn't necessarily that I was afraid of heights, so much that I wanted to live. After taking a cautionary step back, I resumed taking in the sights.

I could just make out the Missouri River between some buildings, and of course, there were the parks. Despite the darkness, or perhaps because of it, the view was stunning. A noise behind me prompted me to look back inside. Room service was rolling in a cart, leaving the door wide open behind them.

Faster than seemed possible, I sprinted across the room towards freedom. The poor attendant looked a little alarmed at my frantic run, but didn't move to stop me. Just in case, I didn't slow down and was going full tilt when I ran into... absolutely nothing. I staggered back and reassessed the opening. It was empty. Nothing was there.

What the hell?

I held my hand up and met invisible resistance.

"Good evening, Mr. Matt. I trust you will find tonight's meal to your liking," Jefferey said as he stepped into the room completely uninhibited.

What. The. Hell?

I tried to force my hand through the opening, and again, met a perfect wall of resistance despite the lack of anything I could see. I slammed my fist against the barrier with enough force to crack wood and still nothing.

"If you are quite finished, your dinner is getting cold, and we have other matters to attend to."

"I already told her. I ate before." I turned to face Jefferey. How was it possible for him to get in while I couldn't get out?

"In that case, we'll skip right to our other task." The manager produced a thick yellow string and gestured for me to come closer. I took a tentative step forward and he draped the cord around my waist, pulling it tight.

"Get your hands off of me! What the hell do you think you're doing?"

"Mr. Duncan." I shot him daggers, and he held up a hand in apology. "Mr. Matt, I'm simply trying to obtain your measurements so that we can procure you an appropriate wardrobe."

I eyed the tape skeptically. Now that I was really paying attention, I could see the dashes marking inches and centimeters. "Oh."

"If you wouldn't mind?" He gestured to the center of the room. I dutifully walked over and held still. "Arms out," he commanded. I did as instructed.

The ribbon spanned the back of my shoulders and then was draped around my waist. This time, I was more prepared when he wrapped the cord around my middle. It didn't make me any more comfortable, but it wasn't nearly as bad as when he took the measurement for my inseam. I just barely didn't kick him in the face.

"See, that wasn't so bad. You will have a fresh set of clothes by morning. Though I imagine I should get you additional pants as well." He glanced at me and at the mark he had made on his notepad. "The new ones won't fit long."

I frowned, not following.

"At any rate, I trust you have found everything to your liking. If you should need anything, please ring. This room has a private line and the call will be answered almost instantly."

"I have not found everything to my liking," I snapped.

Jefferey's bushy eyebrows climbed toward his hairline. "Beg your pardon."

"Why can't I leave?" I gestured angrily to the still open door.

"Miss Scry made it very clear that you were to wait here until her return. Whatever holds you in this room is far beyond either myself or my staff."

"Who is Miss Scry, anyway?" Maybe he would give me the answers she had neglected.

He hesitated a moment. "A very respected and dangerous woman. You would do well to appreciate her generosity. Not all have been so fortunate. Goodnight, Mr. Matt." The statement didn't leave any room for further questions and he walked out before I could even try, leaving me once again all alone in the massive suite.

Not really sure what to do with myself, I walked over to the silver dome that presumably held dinner. Despite what I'd told them both, I was ravenous. The mysterious meatloaf had barely scratched the surface of my hunger, and the fight after hadn't helped.

Cautiously, I lifted the lid. I wasn't sure I trusted food from someone who casually abducted and locked up people. Then my stomach growled as the scent wafted into the open air from the steam drifting off of the massive burger. Upon closer inspection, there was both bacon and cheese, not to mention a healthy side of fries. My mouth watered.

Did it really matter if it was poisoned? Vera'd already proved that I wasn't going anywhere. That decided, I tucked into the meal. As I ate, I began to feel a little bad for my treatment of Jeffery. The meal was absolutely to my liking. Sufficiently stuffed, I wandered over to the bedroom, where I spent time languishing in the shower.

Steam clouded the entire bathroom, and I had to wipe the mirror to even see myself. I looked slightly better clean, but I was still every inch an oversized ragamuffin, as an old matron used to say. I swiped the image angrily and went to flop on the bed. The whole thing sank beneath me until it felt like it was literally hugging my entire body.

How do people sleep on such squishy things?

Apparently easily, because I passed out, robe and all, on top of the patterned comforter.

In the morning, breakfast and the promised clothes were waiting for me. I tried on the simple jeans and t-shirts that had been provided. Much to my amazement, everything fit perfectly. Jeffrey really knew his stuff.

There wasn't much to do in the room beyond stare out the window and watch TV. Not fond of either, I went in search of better amusement. Eventually, I found some pens and a notepad. The day slipped by as I sketched. I began with the creatures I'd met at the orphanage and kept going until I ran out of paper. Before long, there was a knock at the door and another attendant came in bearing what I assumed to be lunch, followed, of course, by Jeffery.

"I'm pleased to see that the clothes are to your satisfaction. You struck me as a no-frills type of lad, so I kept the options fairly basic."

I hadn't really thought much of it. A shirt was a shirt. He glanced around, no doubt checking to see if anything was missing or broken. His eyes passed disinterestedly over the sketches that littered the floor.

"When can I leave?"

"When Miss Scry retrieves you," he replied calmly, and left once more.

We repeated the same routine every day. The only exception was that Jeffrey began checking on me at dinner instead of lunch, and on the third day, an entire supply of sketch tools appeared. Even then, as nice and accommodating as this place was proving to be, I still tried the door every time it was opened and well after they left, all with the same lack of results.

A whole week had gone by when Vera swanned into the room unannounced. I might not have even noticed her sudden appearance except I always sat facing the door, ready to try my luck again. The freaky part was that she didn't come through the door at all. She walked through the wall next to it.

"You're certainly looking better," she said as she inspected my overall appearance.

I jumped up from my seat. "How did you do that? Where have you been? You can't just lock people up, you know."

"I believe that's exactly what I did. And I've already told you, I had additional errands to run. Still do, as a matter of fact. I just wanted to see for myself that you were doing as well as Jeffery claimed. He tends to exaggerate, but I see he was not regarding your artistic ability. I never could draw," she mused to herself.

"Wait, you're leaving again?"

"Of course. Oh, and these are for you." She dropped a bag that thudded when it hit the ground. It instantly toppled over, allowing several pamphlets and brochures to pour out. "I thought you might like to know where you're going."

"The only place I want to go is out of here." I kicked the bag, and she rolled her eyes.

"You don't have to read them, but there is no reason to be rude. I'll try to be quick. I'd hoped to provide you with some company, but things are not going well. All of my other recruits seem to disappear before I can get to them." Concerned confusion flashed across her face, then it was gone. "Anyway, I'll see you later. Mind Jeffery." With that, she was gone. She didn't even bother using the door or the wall. Not even a poof, just gone.

Chapter 6
Arminius

Alexi

Arminius University.

Looking around, you'd never know that a full tilt battle had taken place at the pinnacle of the Rebellion when the Regency had dug into their last stronghold. The reports that had filtered out to our tiny supernatural community had said parts of the campus had been virtually obliterated. Not that you could tell. Guess that was a benefit of being a supernatural college. They probably had many spells to undo damage or roll back time.

I ran a hand over the side of the admissions building as we walked in. It even felt old, which shouldn't have been possible. I knew for a fact that it had been completely restructured. The pictures of this place made it seem like a bomb had gone off. Come to think of it, it was entirely possible that one had.

"Lexi, do you know where we're going?" My mother's voice snapped me out of my reverie.

"Yes, the letter said to check in at Admissions. They'll give me my schedule and further instructions." I confidently led the way to the main desk, but as I got closer, my nerves took hold. They'd know why I was here, what I was. How welcome was my kind, really?

The attendant smiled at me from behind the curving mahogany desk. Everything was pristine, from the perfectly stacked admission inquiries to his checkered polo buttoned all the way to the top. Even his dark skin was flawless, providing a striking contrast to his short-cut, golden hair.

I took a fateful step forward. "Hi."

"Good morning. I'm Marquis, Administrator of Freshman Affairs. How can I help?" His eyes looked like stars. It was both eerie and fascinating.

"I'm Alexi Roman." I took a deep breath and handed him the letter. Everything he needed to know would be in there.

"Ah, excellent. You're here for Vera's class. That should be interesting." He gave me a knowing smile, and I glanced at my mom.

She gave my shoulder a reassuring pat. "Why do you say that?" she asked conversationally.

Marquis laughed as he put together my welcome packet. "Don't get me wrong, she's wonderful. You'll love her. Patience just isn't one of her strengths. It will be interesting to see how she does as a teacher. I mean, she did put her own teacher through the ringer to hear him tell it." He rapped the stack on the desk, straightening it to perfection, then put it in a folder and passed it to me. "There, that should be everything." He slid a map around to face us and pointed. "This is where we are. You'll be going across the campus to this area here. It's the newer of the old sections." He chuckled like it was a joke. "Orientation is not for a couple more hours, so feel free to take your time getting over there. We're all really glad you're here."

"Why?" I asked as I accepted the itinerary.

"Honestly? We were really afraid no one would show. There have already been several dropouts. The class is about half the size that it was originally. If this year goes well though, I imagine they'll re-register in the spring."

"Oh." I wasn't sure if I should be alarmed or not. "Um, what do we do about luggage?"

"That, you'll leave with me. They're waiting to give room assignments until orientation to make sure everyone can room with a classmate."

"I'll be rooming with another Shadow Demon?" The question didn't sound more believable out loud. Another supernatural, sure, but another demon? And a classmate on top?

"Vera wants you to have as much opportunity as possible to spend time with your own kind, something you otherwise may never have had the chance to do." Sadness clouded his features. "There are so few of you left."

"She's really thought this out." Rooming with another Shadow Demon. I could've gone my whole life without meeting another one and now I'd be roommates with one for who knew how long.

"You have no idea. This has been her project since the rebuild started. It's not right that Shadow Demons have been forced into seclusion. You all are surprisingly social for notorious loners."

"Told you," my mom whispered in my ear. "Now, let's go explore before I officially have to send you to school," she added, then promptly led me out of the office.

All around us, kids wandered around the campus. For summer, the school was surprisingly busy. If it wasn't for some of the more blatant uses of magic or strange appearances, Arminius could have been any college campus, and it was hiding in plain sight. We'd seen no indication in the neighboring town that they were even remotely aware of who attended this ancient school. I couldn't help but wonder how many students took summer classes just to be somewhere it was safe to be themselves.

Right in front of us, a group of girls passed a levitated book back and forth. A Frisbee spun overhead to be snatched out of the air by a tiny point of light that turned into a guy in his early twenties. Suddenly, I was very grateful that my very human mom had exposed me to as much of the supernatural world as possible. I still wasn't entirely sure how she'd found the supernatural community in town.

"Thank you, mom," I croaked out, my emotions dangerously close to overwhelming me.

"For what, dear?"

I smiled at the woman who had sacrificed so much for me. "For making me come and making sure I had a well-rounded childhood."

"That's what mothers do." She gave me a good squeeze, and I didn't even care that it was in front of half the student body. They didn't seem to, either. "Are you going to show me some of these haunts or am I actually going to have to use this thing?" She waved the map.

I laughed and chose a direction at random. "Okay, okay, let's start this way."

The campus was massive, and even with a couple of hours to burn, we wouldn't want to wander too much. I tried to point out the structures I'd dedicated to memory and offer what history I could. All around us, buildings rose up in various colors of bricks and stone, each one seeming more ancient than the last as we worked our way to the heart of the campus. It was incredible to see firsthand the sweeping banisters on some and turrets on others. The Witch's College even looked like a full-blown medieval castle plopped right on the green.

It was as though we were walking through a life-size textbook on the History of Architecture. Literally, the only building even remotely modern, in as much that it had clear glass versus stained, was the commissary. We skirted around it, preferring to marvel like tourists at the ivy-covered structures. Eventually, we worked our way over to the building Marquis had circled. It wasn't until we were right up on it, though, that I realized what it was. When I did, I couldn't help but laugh.

"What's so funny?" My mother looked around for the source of my humor.

"Marquis' joke makes more sense now. This part of the university was established three hundred years ago, officially making it the youngest section on campus. And this is Mysterio College. It was rededicated about fifty years ago to cover the more obscure arts. Fitting that Shadow Demons would be here." My gaze traveled up the moss-covered stone. "I wonder if they'll end up changing the name again."

Mom kissed me on the cheek and rubbed my arms. "I guess it's that time."

"You're not coming in?"

She shook her head, a small smile on her lips. "I think this is something you can handle on your own, and should." She let out a sigh and her eyes turned sad. "When did you grow up?" She brushed the hair back from my face. "Call me once you're settled and let me know how it went." She wrapped me in another fierce hug.

I nodded and carefully squeezed her back, fighting back a sudden rush of tears. "I will. I love you, mom."

She released me and I found her eyes equally misty. "You've got this, Alexi. I'm so proud of you." She fanned her eyes. "Whoo! I better go before I make a scene. Right. You be good, stick to your studies, don't forget to call."

"I know, mom. I won't."

She blew me a kiss, turned, and made her way to the main entrance of the university. I watched her go until she was an indistinguishable blur, then looked back at the building. Now that everything was real, I was nervous again. It was easy to forget my anxiety when I was playing tour guide, but now the moment had finally come. I was officially a student at Arminius University and was about to meet the most infamous Shadow Demon in the world.

I pushed the doors open into an empty foyer. Where I'd been expecting a welcoming committee or maybe a TA, there was only a nondescript sign that said to go down the hall to classroom forty-two. I followed the trail of signs around two curves before I found the room in question.

When I stepped inside, a woman behind a podium with a name tag that read Anne, Student Affairs, greeted me. She was petite, with a blonde bob and a friendly smile.

"Good afternoon. We're so pleased you could join us. Orientation will start in a few minutes. Could I get your name, please?"

Between the noise of too many people talking all at once and realizing they were all Shadow Demons, it took me a moment to realize she was talking to me. "Roman."

I'd heard about demons being able to sense each other, but this was a first for me. Disorienting was a mild way to put it. I could understand the insistence that we be made to bunk together. I was now absolutely sure I'd never run into another Shadow Demon before today.

"That's Alexi Roman?"

"Yes." My gaze continued to rove over the gathered crowd. The group was made up almost entirely of guys with only a few token girls.

"I've got you." Anne placed a decisive check on her clipboard. "Looks like you're the last."

"I'm sorry. I didn't mean to be late. We lost track of time while I was giving my mom a tour. I hope it hasn't been too much of an inconvenience."

"You're fine. I'll be surprised if Vera is on time herself. I mean, Miss Scry," Anne amended with a smile. "Don't worry, everyone has freaked a little. It's different being around someone of your own race, especially if you never have before."

It was mildly comforting to know I wasn't the only one who'd been taken aback.

"Honestly, only a couple of kids didn't react at all, including the first kid to get here. Poor thing. Vera dropped him off this morning, and he's been waiting all day. Anyway, take a seat or stand, whatever your preference." She scanned her list one more time, then set it down on the small podium and walked off.

I waited until the crowd obscured her, then scooted closer to her vacated post. A cursory glance showed over a dozen names. I double checked to make sure no one was watching me and gave the list a closer look. Beside many of the names were numbers, though not in any order I could discern, as well as a few question marks. My jaw might have actually dropped when I realized they were indications of possible power levels. I glanced around the room even more in awe. No one here was below a fifteen. There was enough power in this room to take out the entire building, if not a good portion of the campus.

I blanched at that and sought my name. The number nine stood out in bold. For a second, the entire room seemed to swim. I wasn't just strong; I was powerful.

I stepped away before someone could notice me snooping. I meandered closer to the crowd, still debating on whether to engage, when a couple of voices caught my attention. They stood off to the side and seemed to be looking at someone.

"Yeah, he was here when I arrived. Hasn't said two words to anyone." The comment belonged to a guy just shy of my height, with dull blond hair and an angular face. He sucked his teeth. "Probably thinks he's better than the rest of us."

His companion's face screwed into a scowl, highlighting his pronounced acne. "Wouldn't you if the most notorious Shadow Demon in history personally picked you up?"

The first guy smacked his sandy-haired friend's arm and pointed. "Look, George is going to get a piece of him." The two snickered. I looked around, but had no idea who George was or his intended victim. How was it they did? Had they met before coming to Arminius?

I was searching the vicinity the blond guy had pointed when a guy who I assumed was George stepped into my line of sight. His bulk was imposing, to say the least. He looked like one of those American football players you see in movies, and when he opened his mouth, he sounded like it, too.

"Hey, you. Who do you think you are?" George paused as if waiting for a response, though I still couldn't see who he was addressing. "Hey! I'm talking to you." His voice carried enough that it got most of everyone's attention, and several heads turned towards the commotion.

I slid around a few people to get a better look. Sadly, they moved as well. Now I could see George's profile, but not who he seemed to believe was slighting him.

"What was that? I didn't catch it." Another pause. "Are you dumb or something? I asked, who do you think you are?" He reached out and pushed whoever he was talking to, and the guy stumbled right into my line of sight.

My breath caught. He was gorgeous.

For a moment, my heart didn't even bother to beat. I swallowed, taking in every inch of him, from his dark, unkempt hair to the brilliant blue eyes that flashed with defiance. He was several inches shorter than me, and perfect in every way imaginable. My mouth went dry. Love at first sight was something for fairy tales, but I was two seconds away from being a full believer.

"I said, my name is Matt. I'm no one."

I seriously doubted that, considering my heart was still struggling to find a steady rhythm.

"That's right. You're no one." George pushed him again.

Matt scowled. "Do you have a problem with me?"

"Yeah, I do." George closed the distance he'd made. "Why did Vera bring you here herself? What makes you so special?"

"Nothing." Matt braced himself like he knew the guy was gonna take a swing at him.

George snarled. "Liar." George made to push him again, but Matt shifted and he missed. Wrong move.

I took a step forward, prepared to intervene, then paused. This wasn't like me. I didn't get into fights. Ever. Yet, even with all of my beliefs that violence wasn't the answer, there was no way I could just stand here and let this guy get pummeled.

"I am not," Matt insisted. "Leave. Me. Alone."

"Or what?" George countered.

Before George could actually hit him, I spoke up. "Cut it out. He didn't do anything to you."

They both turned to look at me. Matt appeared confused. George, however, realized almost instantly that Matt's focus had shifted. He took advantage of his distraction to give Matt another shove, this time hard enough to push the smaller guy off his feet.

I quickly closed the distance and barely caught Matt by the shoulders in time to prevent him from crashing to the ground. The second we touched, a current of electricity jumped between us, and I nearly dropped him.

Matt looked up at me, anger burning in his blue eyes. This close, I could make out more of his features. His face was surprisingly delicate. The rage that flashed in his eyes carried to his mouth to create the best pout I'd ever seen. In short, he was a damn work of art.

Eat your heart out, Daniel. Michelangelo has a new muse.

I stared down at him with a goofy grin. "Hi there."

Matt got his feet under him and pushed away from me. "Let go of me."

"I was just trying to help." My hands still tingled from where I'd touched him. I'd never felt anything like it before.

"I don't need your help." The words were sharp enough to cut, and my heart bled at the horrible thought that I might have just made an enemy of this stunning angel.

A woman's voice sliced through the babble of eager whispers, still curious if there would be a fight. "If we could please stop the juvenile behavior, I'd like to start."

I turned to find the source, hoping to glimpse the infamous teacher that had gathered us all here. To my disappointment, I didn't find some terrifying warrior, but a young woman with red hair pulled into a severe ponytail.

The woman continued her path across the room to the front. Instinctively, I gave way. Matt, however, did not. Instead, he watched her approach with an expression I could only describe as sour. After his reaction to George, I was beginning to think my angel might have a death wish.

She slowed as she got closer to where I was still standing beside the disgruntled Matt. "I swear, Matt, a couple hours, just a couple of hours," she hissed under her breath. His eyes narrowed, and she walked around him.

If I hadn't of been standing so close, I would've missed the whole exchange. I looked back at Matt, who was scowling even deeper now. My gaze flicked back to the woman making herself comfortable at the podium at the front of the room. This was Vera Scry? She certainly didn't look like a hardened murderer capable of wiping out whole towns. Night. She was barely older than the rest of us.

"Alright," she began, her voice filling the room. "I'm sorry I'm late. Apparently, nothing around here knows how to run without constant supervision." The undercurrent of resentment bordered on being an outright scathing rebuke. She stopped a moment, as if to check herself. Then, after a deep breath, she started again in a more professional tone.

"I would like to welcome you all to Arminius University. As many of you have either guessed or already know, I am Vera Scry. I'll be leading your classes for the most part. However, your curriculum will also include a variety of topics that go beyond just the study of your demonic powers. Your first semester will comprise Demonic History, Intro to Shadow Magic, as well as Battle Tactics." There were several high fives around the room.

I raised my hand.

"Yes?"

"Why? The others I understand. But why Battle Tactics? The Rebellion is over." I'd read it on the curriculum earlier and naturally assumed it was a mistake.

"I'm glad you asked. While we don't condone violence, we also recognize that each demon has their own strengths and weaknesses. As you'll learn, power levels with demons are broad with dramatic differences separating the levels, more so the closer you get to being an Original or level one. The priority of this semester is to determine where your strengths lie so that we can help them flourish.

Understandably, some of you may excel in practical applications, whereas others might need more... structure."

It could have been my imagination, but it sounded like that last bit was for Matt. A glance at him proved he believed so as well.

"Now, can anyone tell me why we're here specifically?" She gestured to the room itself.

"To learn how to be total bad asses," someone offered, followed by snickers around the room.

Vera's jaw clenched. "Any other thoughts?"

I waited to give someone else a chance, then raised my hand again.

"Yes."

"Mysterio College is for the study of obscure magicks. Shadow Demon lore has been outdated and misrepresented for centuries. In addition, we're here to learn control and make sure our kind don't die out because of unfulfilled potential." I might have read the brochure... a few times.

"Very well said. To be clear, while the study of your powers may have been what brought you here, you will still be expected to maintain grades in all of your studies. This will include standard scholastic topics as well. Battle tactics may be fun, but you still need arithmetic and linguistics to succeed in this world." There was a collective groan. "Yeah, yeah. You'll live. Probably," she added as an afterthought.

I blinked. Surely, she wasn't suggesting that some of us might die.

"I'm going to give you the rest of the day to get settled. Sadly, I wasn't able to have you all housed in the same dormitory. Best I could swing was having each of you room with at least one of your classmates. Your schedules will coincide to ensure that, no matter what, you have someone readily available to rely on. As your powers develop, they may also become more volatile and unpredictable. It's paramount to have a safety-buddy, if you will." She chuckled. Personally, I didn't think the fact that we were all at risk of going violently insane was all that funny.

"Anne will provide your room assignments," Vera continued, as if our possible demise was par for the course. "Once you know your destination, you can make your way across the lawn to the set of dormitories on the other side. Be advised, the dorms are co-ed and not exclusively demonic. I expect all of you to behave yourselves." Snickers rippled through the room. Vera pointedly ignored them and went on. "Student Affairs will take care of placing your things in your rooms. They should be waiting for you by the time you arrive. Thank you all for being here. I'll see you next Monday," she finished, stepped aside, and vanished.

Her disappearance was met with muffled surprise that rippled across the room. However, the aforementioned Anne didn't seem the least bit phased as she stepped up to take Vera's place. Anne held up a tablet and began reading. "Duncan and Roman, you'll be in room 2708 in Starling Hall."

Surprised to hear my name listed first, I glanced around in search of "Duncan". Sadly, no one besides me seemed to react to the announcement. I glanced back towards the entrance, curious if the attendee list was still there.

I casually made my way over, trying not to draw attention. Anne continued to call out assignments behind me, but I didn't care. I was on a mission. As I approached the podium by the door, I only had one desperate thought—please be Matt, please be Matt. At last, the list was within reach. But with only fifteen of us to be paired, I was running out of time fast. I quickly scanned the names.

I finally found the "Duncan" scribbled in at the bottom like it had been a last-minute addition. Even scrawled, the name clearly read Matthew Duncan. I could have whooped for joy. Suddenly, I realized Anne had finished and people were shuffling toward the exit. I stole another quick glance to see if he had a power level listed. My curiosity was rewarded with nothing more than a question mark.

The sound of people getting closer brought me back to reality. As close as I already was to the door, I had no choice but to be the first one out. I looked over my shoulder, hoping Matt was nearby and we could leave together. No such luck. Reluctantly, I exited the room solo. Despite my determination to wait, after several minutes of milling around the front of Mysterio College, it seemed like Matt was intentionally hanging back. With a sigh, I walked across the lawn to Starling Hall.

After a short flight of stairs, I found myself on the second floor of the dormitory. At first glance, I was reminded of an old hotel my mom had taken us to once. Deep green carpet flowed down the walkway like a plush river. I reached out and touched wallpaper far more intricate and, frankly, ancient than befit a college dormitory. Further down the hall, a door opened. A resident with a tail as long as they were tall emerged, ran three doors down, then disappeared into another. The only sound to betray the commotion was the door slamming home.

I continued on, eying each entryway. As far as I could tell, all the rooms had locks. The farther I went, the more concerned I was that I'd missed Anne mentioning where to get our keys. Maybe that's why Matt had held back. He'd actually been paying attention.

I smiled to myself, still a little amazed at my good luck. Now all I had to do was make sure he didn't hate me for interfering with George. My mind called up those incredible blues he had for eyes, recalling with perfect clarity the fires that had danced within. An angry fire—at my intervention. I grimaced. We hadn't even been properly introduced, and I was already making a mess of things.

Like you do everything, a voice that sounded suspiciously like Daniel added without mercy. I shook my head and refocused on the room numbers. Finally, I found it. On the outside of a door that looked positively ancient were two envelopes with the names Roman and Duncan written on them, respectively.

I grabbed mine, dubious about the wisdom of leaving our keys where anyone could take them, though both looked untouched. There was just enough time to register the thick vellum before the entire envelope vanished. A heavy bronze key befitting the antique lock fell with a muffled thud to the floor. Curious, I touched the other envelope. Nothing happened. Spelled envelopes, of course.

I retrieved my key from the carpet and turned it in the lock. The door swung open on silent hinges to reveal an interior that did not match the aged door, or the rest of the dorm, for that matter. Where I'd expected to find a traditional, cramped dorm room with barely enough room for two beds, there was instead what amounted to a modern apartment, complete with open living space, a kitchen at the back, and even a small breakfast table. No beds, though. I stepped deeper into the living room and the door swung shut behind me, the lock automatically clicking in place.

Note to self: don't lose your key.

A quick inspection revealed that the place was fully furnished with a red fabric couch, plates, silverware, pots and pans, and even a TV. My excitement surged at the increasingly pleasant turn of events. I doubted my mother had anticipated my having so much independence my first semester.

I glanced around for beds or somewhere that might hide beds. What I found were doors on either side of the space that each led to a bedroom with its own bathroom. My things were set up in the room on the left. Which meant the other luggage had to belong to Matt. Bit of a bummer that we didn't actually get to share a bedroom, but I supposed the killer apartment sort of made up for that.

I was inspecting the kitchen when the door clicked again. Time for damage control. I stole a moment to gather myself, then turned around to greet my college roomie, mentally crossing my fingers that I wouldn't bugger this worse than I already had.

Matt stood, holding his key and looking a little out of sorts. His uncertainty was quickly replaced when he caught sight of me. "It would have to be you, wouldn't it?" he said, blander than dry giouvarlakia. He tossed his key on the coffee table. It clattered a moment, then went still with a hollow thud. "Today just keeps getting better and better."

I frowned at the obvious sarcasm. "What's wrong with me?"

He gave me an incredulous look. "For starters, you stick your nose where it doesn't belong. Not to mention, you're an arrogant suck up who probably thinks they're great at everything." The words were unnecessarily hostile and clearly chosen to get a rise out of me.

I refused to give in so easily. Daniel used to say way worse when he was in a mood. Matt, I could handle. "Maybe that's just because you don't know me."

"How long have you been here?"

"A while," I answered honestly.

He crossed his arms and basically glared at me. "I bet you know this whole campus like the back of your hand."

I shrugged. He wasn't wrong.

"Privilege." He shook his head in blatant scorn.

"For the record, all of us were recruited." Taking a gamble, I added, "I heard Vera picked you up herself."

He gave me a searching look, but rather than answer, he asked a question of his own. "What's your name?"

"Alexi."

He stared blankly back at me. "That's a weird name for a guy." He looked away, and it seemed like that would be the end of our very brief, unusual conversation.

In a moment of inspiration, I said, "Then call me Alex." No one in my entire life had ever called me Alex, but if it made Matt comfortable enough to talk to me, then I would learn to answer.

"Okay."

Finally, we were getting somewhere. "You're Matt, right?" His guard immediately went back up. At this rate, I would never make any headway.

"Yeah."

I walked closer, gliding around the couch. This whole interaction was reminding me of the time I'd tried to encourage the neighborhood stray cat to follow me home. "How long have you known about the school?" I prodded.

"Two weeks," he replied while he looked around the space.

Only a couple weeks? No wonder he'd been penciled onto the roster. If that was the case, it begged another question. Which could either go really well or really poorly. "Um... how long have you known you're a demon?"

"Two weeks," he responded in the same flat tone.

Ho-ly. Shit.

"Well, that explains a lot." The words were out of my mouth before I could rethink them.

Matt's eyes narrowed, cutting the ice blue down to shards of glass. "What's that supposed to mean?"

"Nothing." I smiled to help play it off. However, the response only seemed to unnerve him further. "Demons tend to be more aggressive when they don't regularly use their powers. Like they're pent up... or something..."

"Are you saying I'm aggressive?"

Yes. A thousand times yes, you gorgeous, angry angel of a man.

"No. I'm saying you should lighten up, not take everything so seriously. I mean, look at this place. Aren't you even the littlest bit excited?" I chanced another smile, but it didn't seem to help.

He blinked and looked around again. It was almost as if he was taking inventory, either that, or looking for another exit.

"Oh, your stuff is in that room." I gestured to his right, my left, then switched directions. "Mine is over there. It was already set up when I got here, but the rooms are identical, so I don't think it really matters. Unless you're into Feng Shui or something, in which case, I don't mind switching."

Stop. Talking. You're rambling like some kind of tongue-tied preteen.

Matt eyed me, then walked over to his room. He hesitated before opening the door, as if he didn't trust what might be on the other side, then walked in. After another minute of silence, the door closed, and that was that, leaving me right where I'd started: alone in the living room with my foot in my mouth.

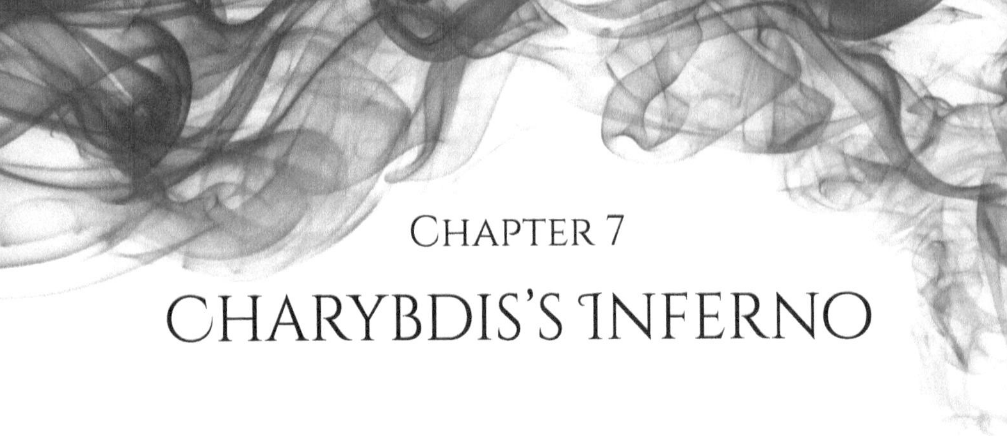

CHAPTER 7
CHARYBDIS'S INFERNO

Matt

I flopped onto the bed. It wasn't as nice as the one from the hotel, but it was still better than nothing. My roommate seemed nice enough, if a little too friendly. He clearly wasn't from the states. His cool, olive complexion and black hair reminded me of something, but I couldn't quite put my finger on it, not to mention his accent. British maybe? But that didn't really fit his looks.

At least he wasn't some bug-eyed creep or covered in thorns. I gave an involuntary shiver. This whole place was crawling with creatures right out of a storybook. It just wasn't possible. Yet here I was, lying on a free bed with my own bathroom at a university full of make-believe. All because apparently, I was a freak, too. No. Not a freak. A Shadow Demon. Whatever the hell that was.

I suspected that my roommate probably knew a lot about Shadow Demons, but over my dead body was I going to ask. I still wasn't sure why I'd told him the truth about how long I'd known. That was a rookie mistake. I knew better. Even thinking back on it, I was sure if he asked again, I'd reply with the same level of honesty. It didn't make any sense, except that he didn't strike me as dangerous—at least not in the way I was used to—not in the way the jerk at orientation was.

Recalling how easily that guy had pushed me around prompted me to get up. Now that I wasn't running from authorities, back-alley creeps, or trying to stay out of the next "well-meaning" home, I could finally start working out again.

The door didn't even creak when I opened it. This place might look ancient from the outside, but the inside was practically brand new. I wasn't even surprised to find Alex still nosing about in the kitchen, clearly at home in this world. It seemed cruelly unfair since I wasn't at home in any.

"I don't suppose there's food in that fridge."

Alex straightened up to his rather impressive height and glanced around in confusion until he spied me lurking by my door. "In the what?" He glanced at the refrigerator. "Oh, the icebox. No, but I found these." He held up two cards. "I think they're for the dining hall."

I frowned. "What's the point of a fridge if we have to eat in a cafeteria?" It would have been nice to make my own food for a change.

He cocked his head to the side, making him look like a bird. "There's a grocery there, too."

I rolled my eyes, and he went back to his perusal of the kitchen. From what I could tell, the place appeared fully stocked. I caught glimpses of plates and glassware as Alex continued to open and close various cabinets. The sound of the wooden doors shutting filled the roomy space until I couldn't take it anymore.

"Hey, you know this place pretty well, right?"

He turned back around and gave me a look. "I have a name."

Really? I got stuck with this guy? "Alright, Alex, do you know if there is a gym around here?"

"Why?"

"Because that's where you go to work out." I bit my cheek to stop myself from snapping. At the very least I'd be stuck with this smart ass for a few months, last thing I needed was to make him an enemy.

"I know why one would go to a gym," he said with a laugh. "I'm asking why you want to go."

"Look, just answer the question." Aaand... there went all my attempts at being calm. "Is there or isn't there?"

"Yes, but you don't need it."

"I think I know what I need a lot better than you."

"That's not what I meant." He seemed to flounder a second before finally asking, "You're going for strength training, right?"

I just looked at him. I didn't appreciate the assumption, even if it was true.

"That won't do anything," he added.

"Like hell it won't." I took in his excessively tall, lean form and pretty face. He'd probably never so much as thrown a punch, let alone stepped foot in a gym. All he had to do was smile and the world would give him whatever he wanted on a silver platter.

Alex smiled as he shook his head, which only emphasized my assessment. "Demons don't need to work out to be strong, we just... are. All it really does is make you look intimidating, bulky. If that's what you're into, then you do you. But you don't need weights to be strong."

"If you didn't want to help, you could've just said so. I'll find it on my own." I turned to make my way to the door. This was why I didn't talk to people. Useless waste of time. Now I'd have to waste even more time and probably get lost trying to find the damn place on my own.

"No, wait! I'll prove it to you."

I glanced back at him, curious despite myself. "How?"

"Take me for example. Do I look intimidating?"

"No."

His mouth fell open, then he closed it. "I'm going to choose not to be offended at how quickly you answered that. Come here." He waved me over as he sat at the table.

I continued standing by the door.

He stared back at me. A hardness that contradicted his obviously amiable nature flashed in his eyes. "Matt, don't be stubborn. Let me show you. If you're not convinced, I'll tell you where the gym is." He paused a moment, as if reconsidering. "Fine, I'll tell you anyway, but only after you at least let me try to make a point."

Begrudgingly, I walked over and sat down across from him. It was a little unnerving how excited he was.

"Give me your arm." He rested his right elbow on the table and held up his hand like we were going to arm wrestle.

I eyed his waiting hand. "You're joking."

"Are you going to let me show you or not? What's the worst that could happen? You lose?" One raised brow accompanied the edge of challenge.

I caved and placed my elbow on the table. Before I could change my mind, he snatched my hand. A jolt went through me as if there was one of those hand buzzers in his palm. In the shock of it, my hand almost got to the table. The muscles in my arm tightened and our joined hands stopped perfectly an inch above the surface. It was clear he wasn't trying very hard to hold it there. I felt the resistance lessen even more. His eyes sparked with triumph.

"You haven't proved anything," I said, at a loss to explain his unusual reaction or lack of apparent effort.

He smiled. "I know."

"This is stupid." I moved to free my hand.

"If you try to let go, I will win." The spark in his eyes made them look like they were gemstones, momentarily distracting me... again.

I frowned at my lack of focus and his weird attitude. "Fine."

"Try not to break my arm, okay?"

I didn't even have a chance to ask what the hell he meant before he pressed. I tightened my grip and pushed back. To my infinite surprise, nothing happened. We were in a perfect stalemate. I pushed harder and so did he. His grin widened.

I tried harder. Still no difference. My jaw tightened as I really laid it on. There was no way this lanky guy could match me for arm strength. I didn't care if he was freaking six feet tall and secretly ripped beneath that shirt. No one had ever come close to besting me like this.

I glanced at him. He wasn't even focusing on our hands. He was watching me, a smile teasing his lips and shimmering in his absurdly green eyes.

He's enjoying this.

The revelation only pissed me off further. I pushed past reason and gave it all I had. Finally, his arm slowly descended until it gave a decisive smack against the thin wooden table. Alex laughed as he rubbed his arm.

"What's so funny? You lost." I huffed and fought the desire to give my arm the same treatment. That had been hard.

He continued laughing anyway. "I don't think I've ever met anyone who could do that." He pushed away from the table and stood. "I'm telling you, Matt, you don't need a gym to be strong, but if you insist, there's a student gym not far," he said, then promptly disappeared into his room. Rude.

Before I could call him out for being a lying jerk, he returned holding a map. Guilt wormed around in my chest. I should know better than most not to judge people on appearances. Just because Alex was put together and seemed to take all of this in stride, didn't automatically make him a privileged know-it-all.

He laid the map down on the table where my arm was still resting. "This is where we are." He pointed to a cluster of rectangles. "This is Mysterio College." His finger swept across a wide swatch of open space to circle another square. "If you go this way," I followed the path he traced, "you'll run into the main dining hall. To the left is the student gym. I confess, though, I know nothing about it past that."

I stared at the map, trying to commit it to memory.

He slid it closer. "Take it. You're right. I have this whole place memorized."

"Thanks," I said, now officially feeling like an asshole for my behavior earlier. I folded it and stuck it in my back pocket. Then I made my way to the door, scooping up my key from the table.

"Hey, Matt."

I turned back. He was smiling again. Shocker.

"Thanks for not breaking my arm. You may not know it yet, but it wouldn't have been hard."

I shrugged, not knowing what else to say, and left. Once the door closed behind me, I took the map back out and made my way outside. In the early twilight, the campus spread out before me, a daunting arrangement of shrouded buildings and infinite unknowns. A tiny amount of fear wriggled up.

Pull it together. If you can make it on the streets, then you can make it here.

Except the streets didn't have expectations, and food, and a roommate that looked at you funny. I shook off the feeling and walked over to the nearest lamppost. In the dim light, I mentally traced the path Alex had pointed out, then glanced around. I oriented myself with Starling Hall at my back and set off.

The gym was at once closer and farther than I expected. I found the cafeteria no problem, and finally understood what Alex had meant when he said there was a grocery. Behind pristine glass doors were not only the expected food options, but at the back was what looked to be a small store. There was even a sign advertising fresh fruit.

In retrospect, I probably should have grabbed the dining card Alex had found. At any rate, I could always come back. Now that I wasn't locked in that hotel, I had all the freedom in the world.

I stopped in the middle of the sidewalk. I was free. Did the Nebraska age of majority apply over here? Even though Vera had failed to elaborate on where exactly here was, the brochures had mentioned Austria and a name with too many vowels and accent dots. I wasn't about to admit out loud that I didn't know where that was supposed to be, but it didn't take a genius to realize I definitely wasn't state-side anymore. Between the accents and languages I'd heard since I arrived, it seemed a safe guess that I was in Europe... somewhere.

I referenced the map again and looked around for the promised building. Now that I had found the cafeteria where Alex had said it was, I had faith that the gym would be as well. Except there was nothing. I spun around, searching the amber grounds for any kind of sign.

Finally, a discreet plaque far off to my right declared Campus and Recreation Center. I walked inside to the familiar sound of clanging metal and grunts of effort. At first glance, it looked like a typical gym, until you considered the odd assortment of patrons. Some appeared human enough, but others were decidedly not.

Lying on a bench was a rocky-looking creature, casually tossing up what looked to be hundreds of pounds in weights like they were nothing more than loaves of bread. In the corner, a man-sized lizard did flips up a Jacob's Ladder. And dead-center of it all was someone who looked human enough, except his legs were nothing more than a blur on the treadmill. Already these people were just as strange if not stranger than what I'd run into at Superno House.

How did this many types of beings exist and I'd never known? How was it even remotely possible that I was one of them? I didn't have horns, or wings, or a tail. Wasn't a demon supposed to? But then, Alex hadn't had any of those things either, and he was definitely... something. I thought about what he'd said as I walked the perimeter about demons being inherently strong. He seemed convinced that I could've broken his arm, but it felt like he'd held his own to me.

At a sudden shout, I tore my gaze away from a guy with static dancing in his hair to see a rail of a girl plummeting towards the padded floor. Horror rooted me to the spot as I realized she was totally going to splat. Why wasn't anyone doing anything?

Then, mere feet from the ground, she turned into a bright point of light that immediately zipped upwards. My eyes widened in alarm as I discovered another layer to this madhouse. Suspended forty feet in the air was a full gymnasium swarming with acrobats. These people were certifiable.

I shook my head and kept moving. As I skirted past a man with claws for hands, I caught sight of my reflection in the wall of mirrors and stopped dead. I barely even recognized myself. On the one hand, I was cleaner than I had probably ever consistently been and the weight I'd lost during my latest stint on the streets had come back. The hotel manager's comment that I would probably need new pants made more sense as I realized how much my body had changed. I may have been ragged and dirty before, but at least I had an edge. Now I looked... soft. Rage pounded through my veins.

Alex played me.

I glanced over at an unattended barbell. The last person had been lazy and hadn't removed the weights. I walked over, eager to see just how much strength I'd lost while I'd been kept like an overfed house cat. My hands were less than a foot from the textured bar when a thought occurred to me. Curious, I adjusted my stance and leaned down to pick it up one-handed, though it was substantially more weight than I'd ever lifted with two. But if Alex was right...

Still skeptical, my fingers wrapped around the cool metal. It rose effortlessly off the floor as if it weighed nothing. Shocked, I let go and gravity immediately reclaimed it. At the last second, I snatched it out of the air before it could crash. I looked around to see if anyone had noticed the scene I was making. Thankfully, no one seemed to care, being too busy with their own routines. I curled the bar up to get a better look at how much weight was supposed to be on it and quickly did the math. Ninety kilograms made it roughly two hundred pounds. Except that wasn't possible.

I carefully replaced the bar and shuffled off to test other weights, determined to prove that it was some sort of trick or faulty equipment. After going through pretty much every available weight, I started waiting for someone clearly struggling to finish before testing it myself. That earned me a few hateful glares. Once I'd pissed off the third meathead that was easily three times my size, I had to admit that maybe Alex really was right.

All of these years I'd struggled not to be the short, dumpy kid, to be strong enough to defend myself. And... none of it mattered. If what he said was true, then it was no wonder I'd thrown Scylla clear across a courtyard. I stared at my reflection as if seeing myself for the first time. Just what exactly did being a demon entail?

I immediately thought of two people I could ask. Neither struck me as appealing. If I asked Vera, then the entire class would hate me even more than they already did. All it had taken was the rumor that she'd picked me up to brand me as a teacher's pet. No doubt they all believed I had some secret "in" and was receiving special treatment. As far as I was concerned, getting abandoned in a mysteriously locked room for a few weeks did not magically make me her favorite. If they knew the truth—that I really was nobody—they probably wouldn't care at all. Strange part was, I didn't want them to know. Just once, I wanted people to like or hate me for no other reason than me.

The only other person I could think to ask was Alex. He'd already proved that he clearly knew a lot about being a demon, not to mention everything else in this wild place. But the thought of asking him was worse. The last thing I needed was the actual teacher's pet schooling me. And I certainly didn't want him to know that I was basically gutter trash, though I wasn't entirely sure why it mattered what he thought of me. Maybe it was because I'd have to see him every day.

I glanced up from my musings to see several offended gym junkies eying me unpleasantly, including the rock-freak. It seemed prudent to scoot out of there before one of them could decide to take my experiments personally. Outside, no one may have been giving me death stares, but there were still plenty of outrageously odd people. Everywhere I looked were wings, claws, teeth, scales or something I didn't even have a name for.

How am I ever going to survive this place?

"Hey kid," someone said behind me. It sounded suspiciously like one of the meatheads from earlier.

I turned around slowly to see the source and swallowed. Yep, definitely one of the guys from inside. He had to be pushing seven feet and looked like he ate linebackers for breakfast. I struggled to remember if I'd actually tested one of his weights.

"You look like you're looking for trouble." His voice tumbled and rolled like the beginnings of an avalanche.

I quickly shook my head. Enhanced strength or not, I had no desire to figure out how I would measure up against this behemoth of a guy. He laughed harshly, and I flinched.

"Nervous little thing, aren't you? I saw you back there." He pointed his thumb towards the gym entrance. "You must be new around here, but you look like you could handle yourself in a fight."

I eyed him. Given my new decidedly squishy appearance, it was a wonder he hadn't already clobbered me for no other reason than he could.

"It's clear what you're looking for isn't at a gym. I've got a better place for people like you."

I bristled. "What's that supposed to mean?"

His grating laugh set my already frayed nerves on edge. "Good, you've got some life in you, after all. Name's Otto. Follow me, I wanna show you something."

I refused to move. Big guys were usually slow. If I took off unexpectedly, I could probably outrun him.

"Here." He passed me a buck slip.

I squinted in the low light to make out what it said, then frowned. No way I was reading this right. I held up the small paper for a better look, but the words didn't change. It was clearly advertising an exclusive underground fight club. Who in their right mind fought on purpose?

"That's where we're going. We meet every Tuesday and Thursday. But we're having a kind of summer kick-off tonight."

"Show me." The outrageous demand flew out of my mouth unopposed. A downright menacing smile spread across his face. Then he turned and led the way across campus while I quietly followed in his wake, silently questioning my sanity every step of the way.

The red brick of the gym disappeared behind us, as well as several other buildings that I couldn't really make out in the growing dark. We walked in silence until he stopped unexpectedly on the perfectly manicured grass.

"This is the official boundary of the school. You see that door there?" I followed the path of his outstretched arm to see a small metal door that could have belonged to a warehouse and nodded. "That's where we're going. If we get caught fighting on school grounds, we could be suspended, expelled, or bound. Behind that door you won't find sympathy or healers. It's everyone for themselves. So don't expect your mama to come rescue you here. Got it?"

I didn't have a mom, and I had no idea what a healer was or what being bound meant, so I simply nodded again.

"Good. Now, we can't let just anyone in this place. What are you anyway?"

"A demon."

"I got that much at the gym. What kind? Some of you are a bit more trouble than you're worth. No offense." Otto shrugged, as if I should know what he was talking about. I didn't, so I answered honestly.

"Shadow Demon."

He gave a low whistle. "Neese is going to flip his shit. I heard y'all were getting your own class." He tightened his fist in triumph. "This year is going to be epic."

After a quick glance around that I echoed, and found what I suspected he had as well—a whole lotta nothing—he stepped toward the door. I followed a couple of paces behind, despite the fact that every logical bone in my body said I should run as far and as fast as I could in the other direction.

"By Tuesday, they'll have set up the gate key. That's when you'll need the password to get in."

I scoffed.

"Watch it, bub." Otto shoved a finger at my chest. "This place is no joke. I hope you're not suggesting it was a mistake I bring you here?" Even in the pitch dark, Otto looked intimidating.

When I failed to respond, he rapped on the door. Part of it phased out, and I heard someone ask for a password.

"Charybdis' inferno." Otto looked back at me. I gave a sharp nod to let him know I got it and we stepped in.

Noise hit me like a wall. There were people and things everywhere. Their shouts bounced off of dusty concrete floors and distant barren walls to create a bubble of sound that swallowed you whole. The collection here made what I'd seen thus far seem like a fluffy children's story. Where everyone before had been as normal as something with an extra set of arms can be considered normal. This group looked straight up like thugs and brutes. With dawning horror, it finally occurred to me why someone like Otto would invite nice, squishy me here—I was the bait brat.

"What do you have there, Otto?" The hissed question belonged to a guy with an iridescent bluish-green skin that seemed to ripple as he moved. I squinted in the uneven lighting and realized he had scales—like actual scales—covering his entire body. The only thing preventing him from looking like a human-sized snake was the fact that he was walking on two legs instead of slithering.

Otto grabbed me by the shoulders and squeezed. "This is our latest recruit. He's a Shadow Demon, Neese."

I shrugged off Otto's massive ham hands.

"No fucking way." Neese's slitted eyes turned on me. "You any good, kid? Ever been in a fight?" A forked tongue flicked out with each query. Maybe he was some kind of snake-thing. I frowned, and he laughed. "I'll take that as a yesss. You got a name?"

"Matt."

"Alright, Matt the Shadow Demon, let's see what you've got," he said, the S's dragging each time his tongue caught on the consonant. I repressed a shudder at the overall creepiness of it.

Without warning, he snagged my arm and flung me forward.

I stumbled through several people before stopping in what was clearly a ring. The circled crowd eyed me standing in the middle of the open space like an idiot. Logic finally caught up with me. I rushed to the edge of the informal ring as fast as I could.

"Oh, no, you don't," Neese hissed behind me. "Don't worry, the betting ssstarts next week. Tonight is just initiation." Snickers filled the room while wicked eyes seemed to pick me apart.

Fuck me.

"The kid's a little nervous," Otto called from the sideline. "Let's start him off easy. Is Granite here?"

What the hell kind of name was Granite?

I didn't have to wait long to find out. Less than five seconds later, the owner of the preposterous name stepped into the ring. He looked like he was made of solid rock. For a split second, I feared it was the guy from the gym. My gaze traveled up and up until I finally found what I hoped was his face. Not the guy from the gym. This one was definitely bigger. Looked meaner, too. Adrenaline shot icy cold down my spine as the reality of my situation sunk in.

I'm going to die here.

In a misguided attempt at self-preservation, I tried to backpedal, only to be hindered by Neese pushing me forward. I shook my head adamantly while my feet found no purchase on the grit-coated floor. There were no pads here, just unforgiving concrete. I didn't even care that the people gathered were jeering at my obvious unwillingness to face such an opponent. Despite my blatant refusal, Neese pushed me closer to the walking mountain.

At last, I found my voice. "You want me to fight that? What is he?"

"Oh, Granite? He's some kind of earth elemental or something like that." Neese shrugged like the answer was irrelevant. "Should be no problem for someone like you."

I did a double take. He hadn't advertised what I was. He'd said what he thought Granite was, but not what I claimed to be. He also said the betting started next Tuesday. Then it hit me. He didn't want people to know what I was. The only time you did that was when you were trying to get a jump on people, let them draw their own conclusions, make mistakes.

I reevaluated the gathered crowd as well as Neese's and Otto's reaction when they found out I was a Shadow Demon. Why were we so terrifying? Compared to the horned and thorned brutes here, I was a small fry. What did they know that I didn't?

"You just going to stand there, kid, or you going to come at me?" Granite looked behind me to Neese. "Really, man? I didn't come here so I could beat up little kids more likely to wet themselves than to throw a punch."

"Let's just see what he's got." Neese made to give me one last shove forward, only to fall on the ground for his trouble.

I'd had enough of being pushed around. If they thought I was some sort of terrifying creature, then maybe I was. At the very least, I could put up a good front. I walked closer to my opponent, who was literally made of rocks, without further prodding.

Neese looked up at me with anger seething in his eyes from where he was still lying in the dirt. "Give him hell, Granite."

I barely turned in time to see a fist that looked more like a boulder rushing towards my chest. Out of pure reflex, I twisted away, and the blow landed on my back. Pain radiated from the point of impact. By some miracle, I didn't fall beside Neese as all the air rushed out of my lungs.

The fist vacated my back, and I quickly dropped to the ground before Granite could take a swing at my head. When I came back up, I was behind him. He turned faster than anyone his size had a right to and started swinging. It took every ounce of concentration I had to stay ahead of the hits. But avoidance would only get me so far. Sure, I might eventually wear him out, but the longer we went like this, the better chance there was he'd get lucky, and I wouldn't survive a direct hit.

Right now, I couldn't feel my ribs thanks to the adrenaline, but that wouldn't last forever. I needed to knock him out first. How did you hit a rock, though? If I tried to use my fist, I'd just end up breaking my hand. I needed a weapon. Something small and light that could still break teeth.

I thought wistfully of the club I'd used on Rufus. Then, without explanation, it was in my hand. I grinned triumphantly and stopped side-stepping the attacks. My sudden shift in tactics made Granite hesitate. It was all the opening I needed.

The club landed with a resounding crack on the side of his face. The force of the impact traveled up my arm to jar my shoulder. Granite's eyes went wide as his head spun in slow motion. Then time caught up, and he fell to the ground in a mound of indistinguishable rubble.

A deafening cheer went up around me. Neese had regained his composure and was appraising me from the sidelines as Otto held up my arm. I had no idea what had happened to my convenient club or even where it had come from. All I knew was that I'd never felt more alive.

Then Neese was once again at my side as I was being shuffled out of the way for the next fight. He dropped a small bag in my hand and I glanced at him in confusion.

"Consider it a taste of things to come."

I frowned harder and pried open the bag to take a peek. It took a hot second for what I was seeing to register, then I snapped the bag shut.

A knowing smirk curled on Neese's reptilian face. "I suppose you could always just watch, but fighters get paid."

Oh, I was definitely coming back.

Chapter 8
Benchmark

Alexi

I shifted my pack higher up my shoulder and wound my way through the room to take a seat at an empty desk. The classroom itself was bigger than the number of students it contained. Still, there were more people than I would've expected for a summer class. Everyone from orientation was there, plus several others—most likely other demons.

I took a deep breath in a completely wasted attempt to temper my enthusiasm. Pen and paper found their way out of my bag and onto my desk. A quick glance around showed that I was one of maybe three who actually looked prepared. As I scanned my classmates, I noticed someone missing: Matt. I'd intended to suggest walking to class together since we'd already established he didn't know where anything was, but he'd already been gone.

There was a commotion by the door, and I turned, hoping it was my elusive roommate. To my disappointment, it was the teacher. Professor Hargrave was a bulk of a man that looked more like a dwarf than a demon. It just went to prove that we came in all shapes and sizes. I couldn't help but wonder if all earthen-type demons were like that.

"Good morn, class," Professor Hargrave said, his thick accent giving all the vowels a low rumble. He hobbled into the room, struggling to maneuver the hefty sack slung around his shoulders. "These be yer books for the term." He removed a leather-backed tome from his bag and passed it to the nearest student. Despite my concerns about being able to understand any of what he was saying during a lesson, I brightened.

I accepted my textbook as he walked past, making his way towards the front of the room. The book was weighty, with a faded blue cover and nearly indistinguishable lettering. My fingers coasted over the aged text reverently. This was it. History. Real demonic history.

I had a powerful urge to smell the worn pages, but promptly decided against it. Professor Hargrave was saying something at the front of the room, but I missed it, as I was too enraptured with my new treasure. I delicately opened the book as if it might crumble in my grasp at any moment. Instantly, my face fell.

Wait a minute.

Completely ignoring whatever instructions Professor Hargrave was giving, I reached down and dug through my pack until I found my red-backed demonic history. I sat it next to the one provided for the course and stared at them in disbelief. They were the same book. Unwilling to accept the truth, I flipped through, choosing a page at random. I quickly scanned the text. Aaand... they were exactly the same. I could have cried with disappointment.

A glance up showed the professor busy writing on the board. I slumped in my seat, my prior excitement thoroughly vanquished, and let my gaze wander. Picking out my fellow Shadow Demons was easy, not only because I recognized them from orientation, but because I could still sense them. Where I distinctly had a peculiar tickle of familiarity with them, I did not with others in the room. The guy sitting next to me was clearly a fire demon with those singed cuffs, but it was a pure guess, albeit an educated one. The brunette diagonal from me, however, I hadn't the faintest clue. Maybe something from the Carnal class? A succubus, or maybe a fastosus?

My gaze caught on a head of dark hair about three rows over, and I did a double take. When had Matt gotten here?

He turned around, as if sensing my stare. His crystal blue eyes held me captive.

All the moisture in my mouth evaporated and my attempt to swallow stuck in my throat. Damn, he was beautiful.

Matt glanced at my desk, blinked, and twisted back forward.

The break in eye contact snapped me back to my body. I dragged in a pained breath and turned to see what had snagged his attention. The only thing on my desk were the two books, a spiral notebook, and a couple pens. I hung my head in my hands. No wonder he thought I was an arrogant know-it-all. Could I be any more of a nerd? Had I been this much of an insufferable prat before?

What on earth did Daniel see in me?

A tiny voice in my head supplied the unpleasant answer. Nothing. That's why he cheated.

I angrily stuffed the redundant book along with the paper and pens back into my bag—I certainly wouldn't be needing them—and slumped in my seat. I cast a surreptitious glance back at where Matt was sitting. He had nothing to take notes with, but the book was open and he, at least, was paying attention. I let out an aggrieved sigh and turned to the appropriate page.

After class, I found myself once again attempting to catch Matt so we could walk to Battle Tactics together. In continuation of my disappointing day, I had zero luck. Whatever that guy did to get from place to place was making me think he might secretly be some kind of ninja. I shook my head at the preposterous thought and walked myself to class.

A guy that was maybe a year or two older than me was putting up a flier on the bulletin board in the hall a couple of meters away. He caught my glance and smiled. "Hey, you in Hargrave's class?"

"Yeah." I stuffed my hands in my pockets and ventured closer.

"I know that tone." The sandy-haired guy crossed his arms and rested his shoulder on the wall. "Let me guess, already read the book?"

I frowned. "How'd you know?"

He flapped a hand. "Eh, happens to a couple kids every semester. Those books have been reprinted a thousand times, but they haven't been updated in over a century." He held out a hand. "Name's Rubio. I'm a third year."

I accepted his hand and returned the smile, my funk momentarily lifted. "Alexi. And I'm pretty sure it's obvious I'm new here."

Rubio laughed and pinched his index finger and thumb together. "Only a little."

I tilted my chin at the bulletin board beside us. "What have you got there?"

"I run a tutoring business. The pay's not great, but it beats nothing." He shrugged, then glanced from the bulletin to me. "You're pretty familiar with the material. Would you be interested in being a tutor for the Demonic History classes?"

"Really? You'd trust me to teach other people?"

Rubio's eyebrows lifted, and he gave me a crooked smile. "Should I not?"

I chuckled and shook my head. "Okay, yeah, that was a weird question. I just didn't get... the best reception once my local supernatural community found out what I was."

"You're one of the Shadow Demons Vera scared up, right?"

I nodded and tensed as I waited for the inevitable rejection.

"That's pretty cool." Rubio straightened and pulled out a pen. "How about this?" He grabbed my hand and started scribbling on it. "Take some time to think about it and when you decide you'd be perfect for this gig, call me. Of course, you can call me for other things, too." He finished writing his name and number, even including a cute little heart over the "I," and gave me a wink. "See you around, Alexi."

"Uh, thanks. See you." I stared at my hand for a second, then reassessed him as he walked away. Rubio was maybe an inch or two shorter than me and had a pleasant face with dimples that popped when he smiled. His deeply bronze skin was intriguing, and he swayed a bit when he walked. Overall, he was pretty cute and friendly, which was a definite plus. I looked at my hand again, then at the flier advertising for affordable tutors. It couldn't hurt to have a little extra money while at uni, and it would certainly take some of the pressure off of my mom. Plus, I'd be able to put the hours I'd devoted to memorizing the textbook to good use.

Feeling a lot more hopeful, I tightened my hands around the straps of my backpack and set off for Battle Tactics class in Mysterio College. Despite my dalliance with Rubio, I still arrived with plenty of time to kill. Given this was the only Shadow Demon exclusive class, it wasn't like I had to wait for the room to be available, so I let myself in to wait.

With no chairs to choose from, I found a spot on the far side. My bag slid to the ground with an impressive thump. The wall was smooth against my back as I rested my head against the plaster and watched my classmates trickle into the room. I wondered if I would ever get used to sensing other demons like myself. Shadow Demons or not, though, some things never changed. Already I could make out the beginnings of cliques. There were your shy types, the gossips, and, of course, the bullies. My eyes narrowed as they fell on George and the two guys with him, the same two I'd eavesdropped on at orientation. I wasn't even surprised that those three had found each other.

On cue, Matt slipped into the room. Despite his unobtrusive appearance, George zeroed in on him like some kind of bloodhound. Cold caressed my back as it left the wall. My gaze flicked between the now advancing George and Matt.

Not again.

Matt glanced up, then back down to his backpack without acknowledging the pending threat.

I took a step toward him and hesitated, his rebuke from last Friday fresh in my mind. He hadn't said a word to me since that evening. With forced resignation, I stopped my advancement.

"Hey, pipsqueak," George said, now practically on top of Matt.

Matt's flinch was barely perceptible before he calmly straightened. Although George was taller than him, Matt met his gaze evenly, defiance written in every line of his body.

"Can I help you with something?" The question was eerily flat. Matt's presence seemed to swell, though he himself did nothing.

"Yeah. You still haven't answered my question. Who the fuck do you think you are?" George practically growled.

"I told you, I'm nobody. As for being special or the teacher's pet, I never met Vera before she showed up three weeks ago."

"I don't believe you." George pointed aggressively at Matt. "You're hiding something."

Matt's quiet calm evaporated in the blink of an eye. "How many times do I have to tell you..." Matt's words trailed off even as his fists clenched by his side.

George snickered at seeing Matt's reaction. "What are you gonna do? I'll tell you what. Nothing. Because you're a scared little chicken."

"Don't call me that," Matt gritted through clenched teeth.

"What? Chicken? Or Little?" George's snide response sent a wave of snickers rippling through the rest of the class.

Even from across the room, I could clearly see Matt's fury.

I have to stop this. I'll worry about him hating me later.

Just then, the door flung open and Vera herself waltzed into the room. She casually strode between the hostile pair, sparing Matt a disapproving glance. His furious gaze immediately switched from George to her.

Vera pointedly ignored his look and took a position in the center of the room. My classmates shuffled around her, thoroughly cowed now that a higher authority was here. "I have decided that in light of—certain circumstances," she began.

I frowned and glanced around at everyone else who seemed no more enlightened about these "circumstances".

"Rather than random assignments, each of you will pair with your roommate for training. I mean, class," Vera quickly amended. "Hopefully, the simple fact that you share living quarters will keep you from tearing apart your sparring partner."

My gaze slid to where Matt was still hovering by the door. He turned to look at me, and for the second time that day, our eyes met. Once again, my mouth went dry. Rubio was cute, but Matt was a dream. Maybe if he was forced to interact with me, I'd have a better chance at winning him over.

That's right. Forced. Because that's the only way a guy like that would ever talk to you. Daniel's voice was an unwelcome intrusion in my thoughts.

That's not true, I countered, doing my best to squash the insecurity. My efforts were met with a degrading chuckle that echoed in my head.

We both know it is, the voice insisted. *You aren't worth his time. You were barely worth mine.* The words stung, and I grimaced.

"What are you all standing around for?" Vera scolded when no one moved. "Pair up."

Mumbles rose as the cliques I'd been observing broke apart into room assignments. Vera walked through the class, pointing at where she wanted groups stationed from now on. Matt spared one final glare for George before rolling his shoulders and walking over to where I stood.

"Hey," I said in a greeting that he didn't return.

Instead, he crossed his arms and leaned against the wall in the same spot I'd been before.

"The nerve of that guy, right? I mean, is it really worth getting kicked out of school just to give you a hard time?" I laughed awkwardly.

Matt's gaze flicked to me, then refocused on a spot on the floor.

Vera clapped her hands, claiming my attention. "Good. Now that everyone is sorted, we will not be sparring today." A few disappointed murmurs greeted the declaration. "Quit your belly-aching. We'll get to that eventually. First, we need to figure out where all of you are developmentally."

I glanced at Matt out of the corner of my eye, fully aware that this would not help my case where he was concerned.

"We'll start simple enough. I want each of you to focus on the thing inside of you that is different. For some of you, it may feel like a still lake, or other body of water, others like the night sky. However, it appears to you, I want you to reach out and touch it. Nothing drastic, just like a get to know you hand shake."

Someone in the back made a rude comment, earning themselves a glare from Vera.

"The time to be juveniles is done. Whatever reasons brought you here, know this. Without this training, you will die." She scanned the suddenly pale faces, adding even more weight to the dire statement. "It may not be today or tomorrow, or hell, even in the next five years, but it will happen. Your powers, your potential, is raw and untapped. Without the proper guidance, they run the very real risk of taking over. Who here has heard fairytales of soulless demons?" She paused, giving the class a chance to respond.

A few hands, including mine, made their way into the air.

"That is what happens when your powers win. You become the monster everyone already assumes you are." Her gaze continued to travel the room. Eventually, she reached the part of the room where Matt and I were standing.

"Don't let them decide who you are for you." The statement was clearly directed at Matt, but I felt it just as pointedly.

I glanced back at where he was still stubbornly resting with his arms crossed. He shifted his shoulders as if her words made him uncomfortable. She let the warning sit for a moment, then went back to addressing the class.

"Now, with a little more give-a-damn if you please. Failure is not an option here. This is your life. If you can't take your classes seriously, then you have no business being in them. Am I making myself clear?"

I blanched.

Her eyes narrowed at the lack of response from the class. "Let me be crystal. If you fail any of your classes—I mean any—then you will lose your scholarship and be expelled from the university. I will escort you from campus and you will become someone else's problem. Just remember who is still responsible for cleaning up supernatural messes."

The threat was clear. Fail and be sent home where one day our nature would consume us. When that day came, she would be there to take care of us. Permanently.

I raised a shaky hand.

She acknowledged me with a curt nod.

"Perhaps meditation would be helpful?"

She let out an aggrieved sigh and stared up at the ceiling. Just like that, her entire fierce demeanor changed. "Well, that's a bet I lost. Fine. Meditation it is. Everyone, take a seat."

The class did as ordered, with substantial sounds of complaint, but I was officially shaken. I'd known there were risks for all demons when it came to mastering our powers. But this... this was something else. What horrors had Vera seen during her tenure with the Regency to make her this way?

I glanced over at Matt, kind of dying to know what he thought about all of this, especially since he'd only recently learned he was a demon. Where I'd expected to be captivated by his piercing gaze yet again, I instead found his eyes closed and face completely relaxed. I spent a minute appreciating the smooth angles of his slightly pink cheeks, the fullness of his mouth, and the delicate curve of his nose. I let out a wistful sigh at the sheer innocent beauty that was Matthew Duncan.

His lips parted, and he seemed to sink into his meditation. Then it hit me. My angel was asleep.

CHAPTER 9
PLAY BALL

Matt

I braced myself on the bathroom counter and let out a breath. Two weeks and I still didn't have a fucking clue what I was doing. School had never exactly been my forte. I'd never once considered pursuing higher education, maybe a trade school or on-the-job program, but never college.

Not for the first time, I considered walking out the door and right off campus. I wasn't afraid of Vera finding me, or powers I supposedly had, but couldn't use, destroying me. I wasn't even afraid of ending up in the hospital from a fight gone south. What I was afraid of was an empty belly, of getting caught in an alley by some creep, of never being able to have a decent night's rest again.

I shook my head and plunged my hands under the faucet that I'd left running. It wouldn't matter what I was or wasn't afraid of if I couldn't get my shit together. I believed Vera when she said she'd give us the boot if we fell behind. Considering my education had been a long series of stops and starts, with more time spent in trouble than in class, it went without saying that I was behind.

The door to the public restroom swung open behind me. I glanced into the mirror to see Alex's startled expression. Like every time I looked at him, I couldn't help but pick out his features. His strong, perfectly straight nose. His pronounced cheekbones that paired perfectly with his angular jaw. His lips that always seemed to be moving, even when he wasn't talking.

"H-hey." Alex held up a hand in greeting. "Fancy running into you here."

I blinked and turned off the water, then grabbed a paper towel.

Alex cleared his throat and shifted his backpack. "What did you think of that quiz in Demon History the other day?"

My jaw clenched. "Total bullshit."

"Yeah. Total." He shifted his weight, drawing my attention to his absurdly long legs. It wasn't remotely fair. Height, looks, and good grades? I didn't have to ask to know he'd aced the quiz. Not like my failing grade shoved into a crumpled mess in my bag. His gaze darted to the side toward the urinals.

I pushed away from the counter and swung my bag over my shoulder. "Don't let me stop you."

"Right. Yeah." He crossed the room and disappeared into a stall.

Shrugging off yet another weird encounter with my awkward roommate, I wandered outside. I was still drinking from the nearby water fountain when Alex emerged from the restroom after what had to be the fastest piss ever. He glanced around as if looking for something, then stopped when he spotted me. For some reason, that made me feel good. I wasn't sure if I'd ever been anywhere people wanted to see me. Most of the time, they pretended like I was invisible.

"You up for walking to class together?"

I crossed my arms. "What if I was ditching?"

Alex's face fell, and it was like someone kicked me in the gut. Maybe that was why people were inclined to give him whatever he wanted, because seeing him disappointed was physically painful.

I uncrossed my arms and licked my lips. "I'm not. Was just asking, you know..."

"Hypothetically?" Alex filled in with the beginnings of a smile that instantly made me feel better.

"Yeah, that." I waited for him to join me by the exit, and we stepped into the bright afternoon together.

"Well, hypothetically, if you were skipping, then I'd hope it was for a good reason."

I seriously doubted Alex would agree with my list of good reasons. We fell into an easy silence as we made our way across the quad. All around us, other students hurried to and from classes, shouting to each other, but it didn't quite touch our quiet little bubble. It was kind of... nice? Was that what having a friend was like?

I glanced over at Alex, curious if I should say something. That's how socializing worked, right? He said something, then I said something, back and forth until we reached our destination or ran out of things to talk about. Except, what could I possibly say that was even remotely interesting to someone like Alex?

"I joined a tutoring program," he said, taking the decision out of my hands.

"Oh?"

He flashed me a grin that somehow made his green eyes brighter. "Yeah, ran into this guy—his name is Rubio, he's older than us—but he started this tutoring business and invited me to join, seeing as how I've already read the whole Demon History text." He gave me a quick glance. "Did I mention it was for Demon History? Anyway, turns out there's a tremendous demand for tutors on campus. I already have a couple of clients. Can you believe that?"

I could absolutely believe that.

"I know the uni stuff is covered, plus we got those dining cards, but it'll still be pretty cool to have some extra cash. Don't you think?"

I nodded, because of course having money was great. I already had a bit stashed away from the couple of fights I'd done. Granted, Neese took his cut, but it was easily more than I'd ever earned.

Alex switched to talking about the day's lesson with a passion I'd never seen anyone show history, not even the professor.

I debated asking how much the tutors went for. Surely I could spare some of my winnings for a few sessions. There would always be more fights. But the words stuck in my throat. Alex was smart, really smart. Would he be interested in being friends if he knew I was struggling so badly? Even if I got a different tutor, he was bound to find out eventually.

"Oh, hey. We're here."

I glanced up at the moss-covered bricks and groaned. If I was bad at regular school subjects, I was worse at Battle Tactics. Which didn't make a lick of sense to me, considering I was holding my own at the club.

Alex's forehead crinkled in a frown. "Don't worry. You're not the only one having a tough time figuring out this shadowing business."

Great, so he'd noticed that. I walked toward the doors and he pushed them open.

"Seriously, did you see when Elle lost Cara's backpack in a pool of shadow? It took Vera half the class to fish it out. The whole time Elle kept apologizing. Meanwhile the rest of the class couldn't even figure out how she'd done it. You'll get it."

I hiked my shoulder in a noncommittal response and made my way over to the section of the room we'd been assigned. Instructions were already on the board to spend fifteen minutes meditating and basically connecting with our inner demon, then to move on to summoning enough shadow to fill your hand. A handful of our classmates were already getting situated, but there was no sign of Vera. Not surprising really. Sometimes she showed, but most times it was a TA.

"Really?" Alex groaned. "When are we going to do something else?" Grumbling to himself, he folded his legs and sat on the ground. Within seconds, an inky substance began swirling in his upheld palm.

I couldn't help but envy him. He made it look so easy. Like all you had to do was want it and it would come. I wanted it plenty, but I didn't understand how it worked. Why it worked and no one had bothered to explain that. Vera kept talking about all of this stuff like I was supposed to just get it. Alex clearly did.

The dark fog-like substance swirled around his palm, then ventured to curl around his wrist and twist slowly up his arm. For a second, I thought he'd lost control of the stuff, then I realized he had a light smile on his face. The darkness continued to move, intimately gliding over his body. I swallowed as it reached his shoulders and he tilted his head back so it could sweep over his throat. With his eyes closed like that, his body perfectly relaxed, Alex looked comfortable and completely at ease. No tension in his shoulders. He sat with his back perfectly straight, highlighting his tapered waist, which the shadowy substance was now encircling.

"Hey, Matt! Think fast!"

I tore my gaze off of Alex and his effortless skill in time to see Vera hurl a ball of something at my head. But it was too large to catch and too late to get out of the way. I threw my arms up to shield my face, bracing myself for impact. Except, when it came, it was dull, like it was far away.

I cracked an eye open and found a black shield hovering before me. Beyond it, Alex's mouth was hanging open and Vera had a smug expression on her face. I dropped my arms to get a better look at the timely shield, only to have it vanish.

"What was that?" I looked at Alex in the hope he had some idea.

He stood and walked over, eying the area in front of me. "I don't know. She threw something, and you… stopped it. Whatever she threw hit your shield and shattered." He looked at me with wonder and I stared at the empty space in front of us.

"But how?"

He blinked a few times and shook his head. "You've got me. I can summon shadow and make it do a few things, but I've never sustained anything of that magnitude."

I frowned. "But I didn't do anything."

Alex looked at me. "You definitely did something. I… felt it. Both what she did and what you did. Didn't you?"

Short answer: no. Not short answer: maybe?

Vera whistled. "Alright, enough gawking. Yes, it was a very impressive counter attack." She smiled at me and a tiny ember of pride burned in my chest. Then she spun to address the rest of the class. "Three guesses what we're doing this week."

A girl whose name I was pretty sure was Colleen held up her hand.

Vera pointed at her. "Yes."

"Making shields?" possibly Colleen guessed.

"Nope, try again."

A guy who I knew for a fact was named Kyle by virtue of the fact that he ran with George raised his hand, but didn't wait to be called. "Trying to kill each other?" He and his buddy Travis snickered and elbowed each other while George leered at me.

"Not quite." Vera held her palms out by her sides. "Come on, no one else?" After another empty pause, she snorted. "Fine, y'all are no fun. Today, we're going to play ball." She held up her hand and a much more reasonably sized sphere appeared above it. Unlike when Alex summoned shadow, hers was always just there. "Right, so here's the new lesson plan. You're going to work on making grapefruit sized spheres, like this one. From there, I want you to work on keeping its shape. You'll need to exert more influence than you do when simply calling it up."

For once the statement didn't seem to be directed at me, but at Alex. I felt him stiffen beside me, confirming that he believed so, too.

"When you're confident that the ball won't wink out of existence and rejoin the shadow plane, I want you to practice tossing it. Nothing complicated. Something like this." She illustrated by bouncing the ball in her hand, then juggling it to her other. "After you've got that down, then comes the hard part. You're going to take turns throwing your manifested shadow with your partner. Right. Those are your marching orders. Get to it." Her sphere disappeared, and she waved her arms for us all to get started.

Alex spared me a glance before putting some distance between us. To my surprise, I was disheartened he'd felt the need to move. Maybe we weren't becoming friends. It was probably my fault. With a huff, I focused on my hands and willed with everything I had for shadow to show up between them. Though how Vera expected me to do this when I couldn't consistently summon shadow in my palm was beyond me.

A solid back sphere flashed between my palms. I barked out a triumphant laugh, and it promptly disappeared.

"Motherfucker," I growled under my breath. Of course, Vera would choose that moment to walk up beside me.

"Relax, Matt. The power is there. You don't have to wrangle it into submission."

I huffed and dropped my hands. "Are you trying to tell me I'm trying too hard or not hard enough?"

A half smile tilted her lips. "Both."

I glared at her back as she walked away. "Fat lot of help you are."

Chapter 10
Sweet Dreams

Alexi

I set my bag down and sank into the couch. As far as sofas went, it wasn't too bad. The whole place wasn't too bad. But none of it was what I'd spent the last few months looking forward to. Sure, the apartment-style set up was nice, but whatever happened to cramped dorms? Or arguing over who gets what bed? Or, well, anything. What about the college experience?

Arminius had always been the ultimate destination for me, a place where I'd finally be able to appreciate who and what I was. But while I was physically on campus and technically enrolled, I still didn't feel like an actual student. My entire curriculum was basically Demons for Dummies. At least the tutoring thing had panned out. So that was something. Rubio was a super nice guy and the team he'd put together were equally friendly. I could already see myself becoming great friends with most of them, even if they were older.

Then there was Battle Tactics. My fears about the class had clearly been unfounded, as we had yet to do anything remotely battle-like or even complicated. Despite that, several of my classmates couldn't seem to grasp the simple mechanics of using their innate abilities. Namely, Matt.

I sighed and fiddled with the hem of my shirt. It was clear to me, at least, that without help, Matt would likely fall behind and would more than likely be sent home. I really wanted to help him, but he'd made it abundantly clear that he wasn't interested. He barely said more than a few passing words to me each day, and that was if I was lucky. What did I have to do to get him to stick around long enough to get to know me?

The small voice in my head that sounded eerily like Daniel spoke up. You're not worth knowing.

I tried unsuccessfully to push the cruel words away. But maybe he was right, maybe it was me. I sighed again, sinking deeper into my misery. This was going to be a very long summer at this rate. There had to be something I could do to show him I wasn't his enemy.

My heart still skipped every time I saw him, and I was starting to think that my uncontrollable yammering was why he was avoiding me. I couldn't really blame him; it was probably annoying.

What I wouldn't give, just to get him to talk to me.

I wanted to know about him—was practically dying of curiosity. Talking to people had never been something I'd struggled with before. Even when Daniel had been in one of his moods, I could still get him to open up, laugh even.

Absently, I pulled out my phone. I'd called my mom a few times since she'd dropped me off and her number was the only one listed in recent calls. I switched over to contacts and went through my options. While I loved my mom, it didn't really compare to talking to someone my age. It was a testament to my level of my desperation that I was already a click away from calling Daniel. I stared at my finger as it hovered over the call button.

It'll be a mistake. If I call him, only one thing will happen—he'll win.

Oh, there were lots of different ways he could go about it, but the result would still be the same. He could refuse to take the call to punish me for not spending that last day with him, only to call me back when I was asleep or in the middle of class. Of course, he could also answer, in which case, he would play so nice it hurt. He'd do everything he could to make me regret my choice to end things, pouring on the charm, no doubt all the while lying next to whoever he was using to ease his ego.

Angry at myself, I closed the phone. I didn't actually want to talk to Daniel. Nothing he said could make things better.

Maybe I should have given him one last day or a chance to at least try to explain.

I shook off the traitorous thought. The whole point of coming here early was to get away from him. No, who I really wanted to talk to was Matt. I longed for him to show more interest beyond ghosting around the dorm. I wanted him to see me.

I let out a sigh and tossed my head back to stare up at the beige ceiling. Who was I kidding? He was probably straighter than a fucking arrow.

"What's up with you?"

My body came a full inch off the couch at the unexpected question. I craned my head farther back to find Matt standing right behind where I was sitting. "You scared the crap out of me. How long have you been there?"

He simply shrugged and returned to whatever he was doing in the kitchen. "A while," he finally said. "So, is something bothering you or what?" I couldn't believe it; he was actually initiating conversation.

"Why do you think something is bothering me?" I asked, trying to hide the surprise from my voice.

He shrugged again. "Because normally by now you've already re-told me the entire lecture from class, quoted some dead scholar, or have given me a history lesson on why this is called Starling Hall." He pulled down a glass and glanced over his shoulder. "You haven't said a word since you got in."

I straightened up and stared, flabbergasted, at the door to stop myself from gawking at him. He'd actually been listening to all of that? "No, nothing is wrong." I wracked my brain for any hint that I might have overlooked that would have indicated he was already here.

"You sure?" The light concern in his voice had my heart doing those obnoxious somersaults.

I shifted to a more comfortable position and begged my hormones to be reasonable. "A little home sick, maybe. These last couple of weeks haven't gone like I expected."

"That's the truth." The faucet turned on briefly. "Anyway, I'm going to turn in early." He finished drying whatever he'd been rinsing, then a door opened and closed.

I swiveled around to confirm he'd truly left, then settled back with a disbelieving huff. Sleep was probably a good idea, considering I was clearly losing my mind. I looked over at my door.

Now to just motivate myself to get up.

I turned my attention to his closed one. Then again? Why should I? This was a common space and he'd already shut in for the night. I had every right to stay right here if I wanted. I nodded my head sharply, as if I'd just won an argument. I'd doze here for a bit, then maybe I'd feel more like relocating later.

That settled, I closed my eyes and tried to relax, beginning with my regular breathing exercises. In no time at all, I slipped into slumber's embrace.

When I opened my eyes next, the room looked strange, like it couldn't decide what shape it was supposed to be. Then I saw Daniel walking towards me and I knew it was a dream. Even in real life, he didn't look that nice.

Dream Daniel walked forward until he was kneeling over me on the couch. This version of him was much more like when we'd first met, all smiles and quiet confidence. When he kissed me, I let it happen. It was just a dream, after all. I didn't really miss him; I knew that, but that didn't mean I couldn't appreciate the dream of making out. At least here he couldn't be his usual arrogant, manipulative self.

I closed my eyes, letting memories fuel the feeling. Like the time we'd sneaked out to see a late movie. Or the time he convinced me to make out in the janitor's closet. I smiled to myself, remembering how much fun we used to have. Daniel hadn't been all bad. It was over time that he'd acted like he owned me. That was when all of our problems had really started.

This line of thinking was ruining what I was indulgently trying to enjoy. I reopened my eyes to get a handle on it. Where I expected Daniel's brown eyes, however, I was greeted with Matt's brilliant blue. I stared into them, getting lost. They reminded me of the clear crystal you see in pictures of the arctic. They were so bright that for a split second, I feared I was actually awake. Then he, too, leaned down and kissed me.

This dream just got a thousand times better.

I kissed him back, thinking of his natural pout.

He's probably an amazing kisser.

Shame you suck at it. I blatantly ignored the cutting remark.

Dream Matt sighed as my arms wrapped around him. This was everything and more than I'd hoped for in being roommates. The feel of him beneath my hands was pure extrapolation from the two very brief times we'd touched. He melted into me as only a figment could. I sank deeper into the fantasy. I had no doubt that Matt would be nothing like Daniel. Not that I had anything to base that on. I just knew.

My fingers tangled in his insubstantial hair, longing to feel the real thing. I felt a little guilty as I allowed myself to fantasize about what he would taste like. In the waking world, he was probably dead asleep less than twenty feet away.

It doesn't really matter.

I pulled the dream Matt closer.

It's not like he'll ever know.

I deepened the dream kiss and felt an echoing ache. How was it possible to want someone so much? A flicker of awareness said I definitely should not be having this kind of dream on the communal couch, but I was too far gone to care. I dug my fingers into my imaginary Matt's sides, desperately needing him closer.

There was a sudden sound outside of my wonderful bubble, as if something very large had hit the floor. I struggled to solidify the hazy illusion, unwilling to let him go. Not when it was getting good. A door slammed, and the dream shattered. I groaned in disappointment as the pieces fractured into the ether.

Finally, I cracked an eye to see what the commotion was about. What I found was not what I expected. Matt's face was a mask of panic as he stood outside his door, like he was trying to hold something back. I woke up a bit more when I realized he was only wearing pajama pants. After the dream I'd been having, it felt like the universe was finally taking pity on me. My fantasy didn't do him justice.

Perfectly smooth lines ran across his torso, creating a subtle definition. My hand twitched by my side, remembering how, only moments ago, we were dreaming about tracing the entire map of his skin. I swallowed hard. He was incredible. He also still hadn't seen me. Which meant I should probably stop ogling him before he noticed. It didn't take a genius to know I definitely should not be fantasizing about making out with my straight roommate.

"You alright?" I asked.

Matt looked up sharply, his eyes wild. At the question, his entire body seemed to simultaneously tense and relax. I did what I could not to gawk as the ripple made its way down his torso. Whatever was going on clearly had him strung out.

He looked around like he was searching for an answer. "I... I'm fine. I thought I heard something." Unexpectedly, he straightened up and walked over to sit beside me on the couch.

I quickly snatched a pillow that had fallen and moved it to my lap. He gave me a quizzical look, but didn't comment. Meanwhile, my hormones were painfully aware that if he was any closer, we'd be touching.

He sat in total silence, gazing off at nothing. I didn't trust myself to speak, so I held my peace as well. Mostly, I tried not to stare. His current state of dress, or lack thereof, was not helping my situation.

He abruptly stood and looked down at me. "Do you want a drink? Like a beer or something?"

"I don't really drink," I replied by rote, and could have immediately smacked myself. Was it possible for me to be any more of a dork?

"Don't really drink like you don't like the taste or don't really drink like you never drink?"

I thought about it for a moment, not wanting to squander the second chance to keep him talking. "Both I guess. Maybe a little more the second."

He nodded like this didn't surprise him, then turned to walk away. I couldn't help but let my eyes wander over his broad shoulders and where his back dipped in the middle. Then my gaze caught on something unexpected. The right side of his back boasted a mottled bruise that easily covered half his rib cage.

"What happened to you?" I asked without thinking.

He twisted in place to get a better look. "Oh that? Nothing," he replied nonchalantly, barely even looking back at me.

I desperately wanted to know the real story behind the bruise, but was not about to jeopardize our rapport by pressing my luck. If he said it was nothing, then it was nothing. But how the heck did you forget something like that?

"Do you ever drink?" Matt called from the kitchen.

"Occasionally, but I find I'm not keen on it."

"Keen," he repeated quietly to himself.

There was some additional shuffling and then quiet. When I looked back up to see where he'd gone, he was making his way back over with a beer in his hand. Sadly, he'd also put on a shirt. I just barely stopped myself from frowning.

"What have you tried?" He took a sip as he crossed his legs beneath him on the couch.

"A bit of this and that." I shrugged, at a loss for how to sound even remotely interesting at this point. "Maybe I'm just a picky drinker."

He held his beer out for me to try. "See what you think of this."

I stared at it obtusely while a bead of condensation trailed down the side of the bottle and splattered on the thin strip of couch separating us. Drinking from that was literally half a step away from an actual lip-lock.

"Don't tell me you're afraid of cooties." He wiggled the bottle and raised a speculative eyebrow.

"Cooties?" I echoed, not sure I'd heard him right.

He rolled his eyes. "You know, cooties, germs. Are you afraid of my germs?"

A laugh bubbled up and finally broke the spell, keeping me frozen. "I know what cooties are, and I'm definitely not afraid of yours, Matt." I accepted the proffered bottle and took a sip. It wasn't nearly as bad as I feared it would be. A little fruity even.

"Well?"

"It's better than I expected," I said, passing it back to him.

I will not think about how his lips were just on that. I will not think about how his lips were just on that.

My hormones clearly didn't care. Which is why the pillow remained firmly in my lap.

He smiled as he produced another bottle from behind his back.

My heart stopped altogether, and I forgot to breathe. I hadn't seen him smile once since we'd met. He was a completely different person when he did that. His entire face lit up and the shroud of anger he seemed to carry around like armor faded away.

I heard a pop and blinked. Then numbly accepted the fresh bottle. Had he really brought me one just in case? Failing to grasp what was actually happening right now, I latched onto the first question that came to mind. "Where did you get these?" The commissary definitely didn't sell beer or any other alcohol that I'd noticed.

He shrugged, taking another drink. "It wasn't hard. Hell of a lot easier than where I'm from."

I took an absent drink, mimicking his own. "Where are you from?" Another shrug. I was getting the impression that was Matt's way of saying he didn't want to say.

"Around, not really any one place. I moved a lot."

"Sounds rough. I didn't. Born in Greece, but grew up in a small-town east of London."

He snapped his fingers, startling me so badly I nearly spilled the beer. I quickly drank some to reduce the level.

"That's what you remind me of," he said.

"What?" I was spinning.

"You look like one of the people from a documentary my school made us watch. You know, with the wars and the gods causing all kinds of problems? Which god was it..." Matt mused to himself a moment, then his face brightened. "Apollo, that's the one." He gave me a considering look that I could feel. "Almost exactly like him. Except his hair was gold, and yours is black."

I choked on my latest sip, causing it to go up my nose. I leaned forward to prevent the liquid from getting anymore on me than it already was. He'd been thinking about what I look like? How long had he been trying to figure this out?

"Easy there. It's not air." Matt laughed. It was a rich sound, carefree and relaxed.

I looked over at him, still struggling with the breathing concept.

He tossed back the last of his beer, then his whole body turned blacker than night. In a blink, he was gone and back again. "Here." He passed me a dish towel, looking like himself again.

"How... how did you do that?" I asked as I began the embarrassing task of cleaning myself up. When had I become so damn awkward?

"Do what?" He cocked his head to the side and relieved me of my discarded beer. He finished it and set it aside.

"You shadowed," I finally managed, though it sounded more like a wheeze.

Pull it together, Alexi. You're going to blow this.

"Are you sure? I mean, all I did was go to the kitchen and come back."

I cleared my throat again. "Yeah, except really fast. I can't even do that yet."

He looked towards the kitchen and back at me. "How?" he asked, the picture of innocent curiosity.

I stared back. "You really don't know, do you?" The comment instantly made him bristle. "I don't mean anything," I rushed to explain. "It's just, most of the class can't do that on purpose and you just did it without even thinking. If anything, I should ask you how."

"I don't know. I wanted to be in the kitchen and you needed help. That's all there was to it."

"Well, thanks." I waved the towel and let it drop.

He settled back, but still looked uncomfortable, like he wasn't okay with the shift in topic.

"So... if you ever want, you know, a recap or something of the lessons, all you have to do is say so." I'd intentionally not used the word help. Something told me it was probably a trigger word.

Matt shifted around and brushed his hair back. Once again, my mouth went completely dry as I became enraptured by watching him move. He worried his bottom lip and seemed to debate whether he wanted to say something. It was positively maddening. I was now immensely grateful I'd had the foresight to snatch the pillow. If he was any cuter, I'd combust. He took a deep breath and had a couple of false starts.

What do you want to say and why is it so hard?

At last, he spit out, "Would you be willing to tutor me?"

"Yes," I replied a little too quickly, my enthusiasm clearly taking him aback. I forced myself to dial it down. He wasn't asking me on a date, he was asking for help with his homework. "Any subject in particular?"

"All of them," he mumbled.

"Okay."

He glanced up sharply, doubt swimming in his eyes. "Really?"

"Of course, that's what friends are for." I'd meant to say roommates, but apparently my brain thought intentionally friend zoning myself was a better idea.

He gave a slow blink as he stared back at me.

Suddenly, I had a different fear. Had I just scared him off altogether by calling us friends?

"Yeah," he finally said, the corner of his mouth tilting up slightly. He continued to stare at me while a smile teased his lips, then he blinked and he was right back to being awkward. "So, um, I'm going to go back to sleep. I guess we'll talk later?" The lilt at the end barely made it a question, like he still wasn't sure.

"Sure thing. I'll see you in the morning." The comment earned me an actual smile, though not the megawatt one that had sent me reeling earlier. He stood, gave me a half wave, then vanished into his room.

The moment the door closed behind him, I clutched my chest.

I think I'm having a heart attack. Can eighteen-year-olds have a heart attack?

The damn thing was in danger of beating right out of my chest. Had he heard it?

I looked back towards his room, afraid that he'd re-materialized and was witnessing my total freak out. Mercifully, the door was still closed. I now had zero doubts—I was one hundred percent absolutely in love with Matt.

CHAPTER 11
TUTOR 101

Matt

Alex rested his forearms on the breakfast table and looked at me. "Let's try a different approach. How about you tell me what you remember from class?"

We'd been at this for over an hour. It was clear he didn't know where to start, and I was starting to think this whole tutoring thing was a mistake.

"Hey, I can see you checking out over there. Focus. Here." He swiveled around a fat text book. "Demonic History. It's been a few weeks. What have you learned?"

I slumped in my chair while the sense of failure I'd been battling swelled. "I already told you, nothing."

"I don't believe that, Matt. You pay attention to everything."

"You're exaggerating." Alex was nice, but he was also overly optimistic about pretty much everything.

His eyebrow lifted in challenge. "You think so? Alright. What color is the dish towel?"

"Green."

"How many plates do we have?"

"Six." This was ridiculous. Why wouldn't I know how many dishes we had?

"How long does it take to get to the dining hall?"

"Seventeen minutes."

"Was the TA's hair up or down today?"

"Up."

"How many students were in class?"

"Nine. Three didn't show and Ellie had to leave early."

"What color shirt did I wear yesterday?"

"Blue."

"How many level ones are left in the world?"

"Five active."

Alex leveled a look at me.

"What?" I asked.

"You see and hear everything, Matt. You just need to learn to focus it." He smiled gently. "For the record, I'm assuming most of those were right answers. You tell me what would help. Everyone learns differently. We just need to find your way. Is it quiet study?" He held up the book, and I wrinkled my nose. "Do we need to turn it into a game with flashcards? Or do I just need to re-give every lesson?" None of those options sounded great.

"How should I know?" I'd never excelled in school. I'd always been occupied trying not to get pummeled at every turn. When you were a product of the system, the only one looking out for you was you. But it wasn't like that here, well, mostly. At Arminius, I was just another student. No one cared where I came from or who I was before. The only problem was that the classes were hard, like really hard. I felt like I was drowning. In class, everything sounded like white noise. How was I supposed to pass when I couldn't even hear or understand the lecture? For the first time, I actually cared. Besides, what good was being free, if I was only going to end up back on the street?

It had taken a while to sink in, but it finally occurred to me that this was a real opportunity to do something with my life. Asking my roommate to help hadn't been easy. Just admitting I needed help felt like admitting weakness. And he'd agreed, which I still didn't understand. No extra conditions or motives, wouldn't even take payment. He'd called us friends. I'd never had one of those before, had never been in one place long enough to try. And what was more, was that he seemed to genuinely care.

"I think we need a break. I feel like we're going about this all wrong." His head flopped on the table. If Alex couldn't help, I didn't know what I was going to do.

"It's okay, if you don't want to, you know," I mumbled. It wasn't fair to hold him on the hook for something so impossible.

Alex looked up at me from the table. "Did I say that?" He straightened back up. "Fine. No break. I want to help, Matt, but you have to give me something to work with."

"No, I think you're right. We need a break. Let's go down to the dining hall." Maybe food would help me focus.

He frowned. "It's raining."

"So, it'll take nineteen minutes," I countered.

He chuckled to himself and put the books away. We walked down to the front of the building together and stood staring out the glass doors. It wasn't storming anymore per se, but the deluge could resume at any moment. The rain had been constant since the thunder had woken me early in the morning, and now lakes of water obscured the normally clear lawn.

Alex glanced over at me, trepidation clearly written on his face. "You know we're going to get soaked."

"Yep."

"And we're actually doing this?"

"Yep." I looked at him, but he still seemed uncertain. "Race you." He barely had a chance to look confused before I was out the door. I heard the door behind me and knew he was following.

We were drenched in seconds, but kept going, laughing as we went. Other students gave us strange looks from beneath their umbrellas as we flew past. Water splashed up from each step. Running in the rain felt like being a kid all over again, except this time there was no mean matron to complain about puddles on the floor.

The dining hall came into view and I realized a fresh problem. I couldn't stop. My shoes and the ground were both too wet. I crashed into the building, skidding and sliding until I finally came to a halt. Alex had the same realization half a second after I did and came careening in behind me. I braced myself to catch him and we almost cracked skulls. Between his momentum and my soggy shoes, even hanging onto each other for support, we could barely keep our feet beneath us.

"That. Was. Awesome." I panted.

"We almost died!" He laughed, almost slipping again. I tightened my grip on his arms to steady him, and he cleared his throat. "Thanks."

"You sure you got it?" I teased. For someone always so confident, he didn't look it now. He looked nervous and he had water dripping in his eyes. I debated pushing his hair off his face so he could see, then his bright eyes caught mine. Just as quickly, he glanced away.

"Yeah, I'm good. But we're a mess." He wrung out the bottom of his shirt, lifting it enough to reveal that he was, in fact, ripped.

Mentally scowling to myself, I pushed the image of his damn near perfect abdomen from my mind and followed suit. "So what? Worth it. When's the last time you ran in the rain?"

He gasped. "Never." Then a light smile danced in his eyes. "I don't want to get pneumonia," he added.

"Can demons get sick like that?" Despite the obvious tease, now I was curious. I pushed my hair back from my face to stop the water dripping in my eyes.

Alex looked at me for a long second. I wasn't sure if he was considering the question or going to tell me I was overdue for a haircut. Then he blinked. "We should get inside before we find out."

We shuffled inside and he immediately bolted to the back of the cafeteria where the food joints and grocery were located. Meanwhile, I wandered around the periphery of the round room in search of a means to dry off. The rain must have been keeping people away, since the normally bustling space only had a few clusters of students occupying the round tables. It was by the restrooms that I chanced upon some unattended towels. Quest accomplished, I searched for Alex and found him at a table on the far side.

I tossed him the terrycloth as I walked up. "Look what I found."

"Awesome." He vigorously toweled his hair and wiped his face.

I laughed.

He glanced at me, frowning. "What?"

"You look ridiculous."

"What do you mean?"

I held my hands out from my head and he immediately started smoothing his porcupine hair. While he worked to tame his hair, I sat beside him and noticed he'd found some things as well. "What do you have there?"

He held up two small containers. "Oh. Peanut butter? Or cookies and cream?"

"Peanut butter."

He passed me the pint of ice cream and cracked open the other one for himself.

"I thought you were worried about pneumonia," I said around a mouthful of ice cream.

He waved his spoon at me. "There is always an excuse for ice cream. And I don't actually know if demons can get pneumonia."

I raised my chin to where he was decimating his pint of pure sugar. "Cookies and cream your favorite or something?"

He glanced down at the carton with a confused expression. "No. Why do you ask?" Now it was my turn to be confused.

"Because you gave me a choice and didn't care that I took the peanut butter. I just assumed that meant one or both were your favorite."

"That would make sense," he mumbled, taking a smaller bite.

"If neither one is your favorite, then why did you get them?"

He hesitated, as if he was really having to think about the answer, though it wasn't a complicated question. "Out of habit, I guess," he finally said.

I raised both of my eyebrows. That didn't make a bit of sense.

He caught the look and elaborated. "My ex couldn't ever really make up their mind, but always preferred the sweeter candy varieties. I just always got two different kinds in the hope one would work."

"That's really messed up." Alex's ex was an asshole.

"Yeah... it is." He absently stared into the frozen cream, his next bite forgotten.

I nudged him. "So... what is your favorite, then?"

"Strawberry." I laughed at the way he said it, like it was as much news to him as it was to me. He gave his own nervous chuckle and added, "I don't even know the last time I had it."

Rather than pursue what was obviously a painful topic for him, I shifted gears. "What do you know? You obviously have been studying demonology since before you got here."

"I know we got here in fifteen minutes," he said with a smile.

"No way." I looked up at the clock. He was right, and that included our near-death episode at the main entrance. "Alright, so we're fast."

"There's that. You already know about the strength."

Yep, it had proved quite handy on Tuesday when I fought another rock demon. "Okay, that, explain that to me more."

He cocked his head to the side. "What do you mean?"

"I get that there are levels and only a few of the highest left, but what does a power level really mean? How do they work?"

"You know, the lower the number, the stronger you are." I nodded, taking another bite, and he continued. "It's not just strength like being able to move heavy things, though, it's strength like overall ability. Most of us can do the same things, but how strong we are determines how well and how effectively."

"Can you get stronger?" It seemed like a logical question to me, but he made a weird face.

"To an extent. Eventually, though, you'll max out no matter what you do. You might get better at doing what you already can, but you'll never exceed it."

"I'm not following."

"Think of it like height. You can eat right and exercise all you like to get to your maximum height, but you'll never be able to go past it."

I gasped in exaggerated horror. "So, you're telling me I'll be short forever?"

He just stared at me a moment, then fell out laughing. His eyes squeezed shut as he laughed hard enough to make a few tears spill out.

"The secret is commitment... and platform shoes," I added belatedly, which only made him laugh harder. I enjoyed having a friend. "Okay, okay, let's see, what else?" I thought aloud as he sobered up. "What about that thing you can do?"

"What thing?"

"You know, the thing with the stuff." I mimed controlling something in the air.

"It's called shadowing. Well, technically, all of it is called that. It's not hard. See this?" He held up a spoon. "This is one of the first things I learned to do. On purpose anyway," he amended with a crooked smile. "Watch closely." The spoon turned black, as did his eyes as he focused on it. "Just stay relaxed and don't lose your concentration." The spoon melted down into a ball. "Hold out your hand."

"But I can't do that."

"I didn't ask if you could. Now hold out your hand." I did as he said and he dropped it onto my palm. "Keeping it in a different shape is called maintaining. Now technically, the spoon is just pure shadow right now with no defined shape beyond the one I'm giving it." At his words, the spoon morphed into a square, a pyramid, and then another ball covered in spikes. "What does it feel like?"

It returned to the perfect sphere, and I wrapped my fingers around it. "It's smooth, soft." Was this what it felt like when it twined around Alex's body?

"What else?"

"It feels a bit like holding fog, but like really thick fog, you know?" I looked up to see if that was the right answer. The sphere had spread out in my hand as if mimicking my description.

He smiled knowingly.

"What are you smirking about?"

"I'm not doing that. You are." The sphere dropped through my hand to the table where it was once again an inky black ball. "You're the only one standing in your way. Now turn it back."

"I don't know how."

"Yes, you do." His green eyes were intense as they held my gaze. "Remember, relax and focus. You know what it was before. Tell it to go back."

"If you're telling me to order this back into the shape of a spoon, you're a nutter."

He laughed again. "Not with words, Matt, with your mind. Will it back."

"That doesn't make any sense." Where were the rules? The logic?

"What did you say to me the other night? You needed to be in the kitchen? That's how it works. Need it to be a real spoon again."

"But I don't need it to be a real spoon again. I already have one." I held up my spoon.

He reached over and plucked it right out of my hand. "Now you don't," he said, using the stolen spoon to scoop another bite. "Go on. I would hurry, though, or your ice cream will melt."

"That's just rude," I mumbled, and he chuckled, still eating his stupid ice cream.

Guess I do need a spoon.

I picked the sphere up and thought about what it had been like before. Nothing happened. I looked at Alex and contemplated stealing my spoon back. "This is stupid. We already know I can't."

"Look at your hand."

I did as he said. Somehow, the spoon was back. It was still entirely black, but decidedly spoon shaped. "How?"

"You're overthinking it. Until you learn better control, everything is basically need based. If you need it, it'll happen. That's the thing that makes us so dangerous."

I thought about the mysterious club that kept showing up. "What about creating things out of nothing? Can we do that?"

"Of course. You basically just use available shadow and shape it to your will." He said it so matter of fact, it was hard to doubt him.

"But what if you're in a place that's really bright and there aren't any?"

"There is always shadow. Where there is light, there is darkness."

Suddenly, I felt a similar sensation to when Vera had intimidated Administrator Smith at Superno House. Like all the surrounding darkness was pulling into one space. I even felt a tug on myself, kind of like that night I'd woken up on the floor. All the while, Alex sat there with black eyes. In his hand, drifts of shadow spiraled into a new sphere. The pull on me got stronger.

My breath shortened and my hands sweat despite the container of ice cream I was holding. There was a pain in my chest, like something was trying to get out. My panic ratcheted up another level as I recalled a movie where an alien creature had done just that.

How could I not see how dangerous he is?

The spoon in my hand shifted to a miniature version of the club I'd used only last Thursday. There was inky black everywhere. The entire cafeteria had dimmed. My heart raced as I tried to determine the best way to make it stop. Meanwhile, Alex sat immobile, surrounded by night, then he closed his hand and the feeling stopped. His eyes returned to normal, and he looked back at me.

"That's what we are at our core—pure darkness," he said, once more his amiable self. If he could do that in a brightly lit room, what else could he do?

I swallowed my lingering fear and asked the only question that seemed to matter. "What happens if it's dark everywhere?"

"Then, depending on your power level, you could potentially exert control over everything."

I shivered and hoped he would blame the reaction on the ice cream. "That sounds like a nightmare."

"That sounds like how an entire race got a reputation for being evil." He sank into his chair, his shoulders curling inward as he poked absently at his ice cream. Like that, my concerns about him vanished.

"Do you think we're evil?" I asked softly. Alex might be secretly terrifying, but there was no way he was evil. I'd met evil. It didn't have a conscience, and it certainly didn't help its roommate study.

"No, but I worry the rest of the world always will. The Rebellion didn't help things."

I tried to remember the lessons from the last couple of weeks in Demonic History. "Have we covered that yet?"

"No, it's more recent. The Rebellion only officially ended a few years ago." He scraped his spoon along the body of the empty container.

"What happened? How would that affect Shadow Demons? And how come I never heard of any war?"

Alex straightened up, abandoning his melancholy, and took on his lecturer tone. "There used to be a governing body called the Regency. They presided over the supernatural world and worked hard to make sure the human world remained oblivious to supernaturals. But for all they claimed to protect supernaturals, they also did some pretty awful stuff, too." Alex shivered. "The Regency had been in control for decades and rebellions were creeping up. In their desire for absolute control, they created a specialized task force to deal with insurgents. Ironically, that group called themselves the Shadows."

I laughed. "They come up with that all on their own?"

"They were younger than us." Alex's sharp gaze flicked up to capture mine and my face fell. "Vera was actually the only Shadow Demon in the group. And truthfully, they didn't even know what she was when they recruited her."

"I'm confused. Did the Rebellion fail?" I asked, more lost than ever.

"No, they won. Eventually."

"But Vera is in charge of the class." None of this was adding up.

"They switched sides. The Shadows learned about the awful things the Regency had done, and was making them do in their name, and mutinied. They're why the Rebellion ultimately succeeded."

"How big was this group? They would need to be an army," I said, astounded at such a convoluted turn of events.

"Six people." He looked into his empty container.

I shook my head. "That's not possible."

"You don't understand, these people were better than the best of the best. And even after all the enemies they made, they held enough sway to get people to trust them." Alex didn't sound like he fully believed that.

"Is that why you hate Vera?" Granted, I wasn't too keen on her myself, but it was clear there was no love lost there.

He looked up, clearly surprised. "I don't hate her."

"It kind of seems like you do."

He shifted in his chair. "She just... she really messed things up for Shadow Demons. Before she came along and made such a mess, the world had all but forgotten we existed. You don't know what it's like to have people look at you and be afraid because of what you are." He was wrong about that, but I wasn't about to correct him.

"But if she hadn't, then we wouldn't be here." Alex seemed both surprised and pleased by my answer. "I certainly wouldn't be. Things weren't going well for me where I was. If she hadn't shown up when she did, who knows what would've happened."

I'd probably be a pile of ash.

Alex gave me a speculative look. "Are you ever going to tell me where you're from?"

I considered telling him now, but held back. Trust wasn't something that came easily to me and, as much as I liked Alex, I still wasn't ready for that. "Maybe someday." I looked around the table, unsure of where to go from there.

Alex glanced past me. "Sounds like the rain has stopped. We should probably head back before it starts again."

"We can take a stab at math," I added.

"I hope you don't literally mean stabbing the book."

"I won't lie. The thought did occur to me," I joked. "Oh, hey, will this thing ever go back to normal?" I held up the spoon, which was still darker than night, though it felt solid enough.

He laughed and reached out so that his hand was around mine and the spoon. A ripple of sensation went through my fingers and I watched as the spoon returned to its original silver.

"Eventually, it would have gone back on its own. But," he began, as he took the spoon from me once more and it faded back to black, "I would hate for it to get stuck somewhere." He calmly slid the shadowed spoon into the center of the table so that only the rounded bowl was sticking out, then returned it to normal. He spared me a mischievous grin. "We'll get it later."

"Wait," I said, as he turned to leave. He spun around, and I snatched his spoon. I leaned over the table and carefully added his beside mine so they were back-to-back. "I think that makes this our table."

Alex smiled. "I think you're right."

CHAPTER 12
STRANGE HOBBIES

Alexi

Tutoring Matt had to be one of the most difficult things I'd ever done in my life, and it had nothing to do with how intelligent he was. Now that we were talking every day, it was obvious he was actually wicked smart. He was *also* incredibly funny, observant, and outrageously charming. And *that* was a big problem... for me. If I'd been crushing hard before, I was now irredeemably smitten. Every time he asked an insightful question about the lecture, overall supernaturals, or—night help me—*me*, my heart melted a little more. Pretty sure all that was left of it at this point was a goopy puddle that spelled "I heart Matt", and that wasn't even taking into account my dreams.

I thought again about last night's dream of seducing Matt. In the fantasy, he played coy, but of course, it felt like he did that in reality. His bright, curious eyes, his full mouth slightly parted as he sat way too close for standard friendship, leaning in with every word I said, as if he was waiting for something. In my dreams, I didn't have to be strong. I succumbed to his innocent invitation every time.

I hummed to myself and debated taking another shower. The first had been wonderfully liberating as I relived every delicious second of the dream, but clearly, it wasn't enough. I gave myself a good shake and pulled on a shirt. I'd have plenty of time to indulge my ill-conceived fantasies about Matt later. As long as I didn't slip up and actually act on them, I'd be fine. Maybe. Probably.

Determined not to let my growing obsession with Matt ruin what was shaping up to be an incredible friendship, I walked into the common space. Matt glanced up from the workbook he was scowling at. I gave him a light smile and tried not to focus on how irresistibly adorable his pout was. "Good morning."

"It's about time you woke up. Sit down." He absently reached over and pulled out a chair.

I rolled my eyes and did as he bid. Matt could be bossy, yet it had nothing to do with wanting to be in charge. He was just blunt with his expectations. I examined what he was working on. "You're getting a jump start on the math, I see. You know this, you don't need me." I made to stand.

He sat up and caught me before I could get anywhere, then fidgeted like he did anytime he was anxious or unsure. Needless to say, that adorable habit had made it into my dreams.

My fingers itched to reach out and comb his hair back. He clearly hadn't brushed it yet. I mentally shook my head; this was not the place for that.

"I can concentrate better when you're here." He looked back at the vacant chair.

I suppressed an exasperated sigh.

It's like he really doesn't care how much he makes me suffer.

"Okay, if I promise to come right back, can I at least get some coffee and a book?"

He released my arm and went back to staring at the page where all that was clear were eraser marks.

I bustled about the kitchen in pursuit of caffeine. "How long have you been up, anyway?"

"Long enough to know you take excessive showers."

I almost dropped the porcelain mug. A glance over my shoulder revealed he was still focused on the blank page with single-minded intent.

"Are you going to get your book and sit down, or what?" He grumbled without looking up.

I set the coffee to start with the simple coffee maker and went to retrieve something to read. When I returned, the coffee was done. I fixed a cup, then made myself comfortable at the table, propping my feet up on a free chair. "There, are you happy now?"

"Are you really wearing house slippers?" Matt's face screwed up in obvious judgment.

I looked down at my feet. "I'm not defending my footwear to you. My toes are cold.

"They're probably always cold because of lack of blood flow," he deadpanned.

I took too big a drink and scalded my tongue. "I beg your pardon."

"Because you're so tall, Alex." He said it like it was the most obvious thing in the world.

He was going to be the end of me. No amount of caffeine could right this morning. "Shouldn't you be doing your homework?"

"No need to be so fussy about it."

I waited to glance over until I heard the steady scratch of pencil on paper. Matt hunkered over the table while he steadily scrawled out the solutions. We both knew he knew this, so why did he need me here? I shook it off and picked a spot at random in my book. I'd certainly read it enough times for it not to matter where I started.

Somewhere along the line, I must've dozed off. The book sliding down my chest startled me awake. I wasn't sure how long I'd been out or when Matt had finished his homework. All I knew was that the sound of writing was noticeably absent. When I looked out of the corner of my eye to see what he was doing, I found him openly staring at me. I quickly refocused my attention on my neglected book.

"Did you know you snore? It's not a lot, barely even there, really."

"I can't say that it's been mentioned before." I reached out for my coffee. It was still mostly full and stone cold. I spit the chilled liquid back into the cup and set it down. At this point, the only mercy was that he hadn't said anything about me talking in my sleep. That would only lead to trouble.

"What're you reading?" Matt's head was suddenly right next to mine as he looked over my shoulder.

I swallowed. He was so near I could practically taste him. "N-nothing, just an old history."

"It doesn't look like a history." He reached forward to touch the book.

I couldn't resist, he was just so close. I arched my head up and stopped just shy of actually touching him, then took a deep breath. The soft scent of sage curled in my nose, both calming and invigorating. "You really don't believe in personal space, do you?" I whispered. Suddenly, the book was out of my hands. I scrambled in my chair, nearly falling over.

Matt took a step back to avoid my flailing and continued flipping through the pages. "Are you sure this is a history? It sounds more like a love story to me."

"What? Of course, it's a history. It was written in the twelve-hundreds which, by definition, that makes it a history."

"Something can be old and still be a romance. See?" He held out the book with the page turned to the image of the Shadow Demon and the knight.

I looked at him in disbelief.

The book swiveled back to face him as he leaned against the table. He crossed his ankles and read the page. "This guy really needs to sort out his priorities, though. What do you think he means by the light going out?" Matt asked, glancing up at me from the stolen book. He looked sexy as hell standing there like that and I was having trouble convincing myself I was awake. When I didn't answer, he flipped through a few more pages. "I suppose it could be considered a history, even if it is more of a memoir." He snapped the book shut and held it out for me. "Looks interesting."

I stared at him in mute wonder. Every time I thought I had Matt figured out, he peeled back another layer. Finally, I found my voice. "It's my favorite."

"I can tell."

"How?" I turned the recovered book over in my hands.

"For starters, it's really worn. Now I know what you are going to say. It's old, of course it's worn. But it also has your name on it and no bookmark. You literally just opened it and began reading, which means you know it well enough not to have to pick up at a certain point."

I was completely flabbergasted. He'd gotten all of that while doing math? I glanced down at the book again. "Why do you think it's a love story?"

His brow dipped in confusion. "You don't? Look, if you think I'm going to judge you because you're reading a romance, I won't. They have some great pointers in those." He flashed a devilish smile. Now, that you're masquerading it as a history book, that I will judge you for."

"You've read romance novels?"

"Hey, check the judgment. There weren't a lot of options where I was. I made due. Besides, some of them weren't half bad."

I smiled wistfully, rather enjoying this latest revelation. "You're just full of surprises."

"Yeah, yeah. What're you doing today?" he asked, in an obvious attempt to change the topic.

"I'm doing it." I gestured to my lazy attire.

"Seriously?" He made to dump me out of my chair.

I hurriedly got up before he could deposit me on the floor.

"We need to get out of here. What would you say to some more practice?"

I rolled my eyes. "You don't need any more practice."

"I didn't say I *needed* it." He shuffled his feet. "But the first exam is coming up and I really don't want to blow it."

"It's not really an exam. More like a make sure you're trying quiz."

"Same difference. Now go put on some real clothes so we can go." He pushed me towards my room.

I stubbornly dug in my heels, making him work for it. "You know, I actually have three *interesting* books if you wanted to read something."

"Shut up and get dressed."

He went to give me an extra shove and I let myself become one with the shadows, causing him to fall right through. I laughed, and he spun around to grab my leg.

"That's cheating!"

I moved it out of the way just in time and his hand closed on empty air, then squatted down to look him in the eye. He pouted back at me. Any other time, any other person, I knew exactly what I would have done. That mouth was practically begging to be kissed. Instead, I simply said, "I have to get my kicks where I can. Besides, I thought you wanted to practice."

He narrowed his eyes, then went all black and disappeared.

I quickly stood and scanned the room. He was already way better at shadowing out than I was. Almost immediately, something slammed into my back and I went crashing into the couch. I thought he'd thrown something at me, but it turned out to be Matt himself. I struggled and ended up flipping both of us over the furniture. We landed with an epic thud that knocked the wind out of me. As I regained my breath, I could hear him wheezing his own laugh.

"You're messed up." I snagged a fallen pillow and smacked him.

"Oh please, that was fun and you know it." There was a loud banging on the wall and we both fell into fits of laughter.

"Okay, you win. It was fun," I finally managed. "But maybe we should keep it to the training rooms."

"Then hurry up." He snatched the very pillow I'd just used in order to smack me back.

I scrambled to my feet to do as he asked. After changing quickly, I snagged the small stack of books I'd brought with me. Without thinking, I placed them on the counter and gathered my things so we could go. As we made our way over to the training rooms specifically set aside for our class, we continued to chat amicably.

"What exactly were you wanting to work on?" I glanced at Matt.

"I don't know. What do you think will be on the test?"

"Practicum," I corrected.

"Whatever. I just don't want to look like an idiot."

"You won't look like an idiot," I said, opening the door to an empty training space.

He flipped on the switch and tossed his things to the side. "You say that now, but I never do well in class. Working with you is one thing, but having to perform like some monkey in front of everyone..." He trailed off and ran his hands through his hair, oblivious to how hot he looked when he did that.

"I think you've been doing better during the lessons," I said, trying to school my renegade thoughts.

He spared me a glance full of earnest hope. "You really think so? You're not just saying that?"

"What are you really worried about?"

He hesitated before answering. "What if I mess it up and Vera decides I can't stay?" He stared down at his shuffling feet, looking more adorable than ever.

I snorted. "There's no way she'll ever send you packing."

His gaze rose to meet mine. "That's easy for you to say. You're great. You get all of this school stuff. I... I can't go back. This is the only real opportunity I've ever had. I can't afford to mess this up."

The sad statement hurt my heart. I really wished he'd tell me more about his past. It would be so much easier to comfort him if I only knew what he was so afraid of. But if he didn't want to tell me, then there was nothing I could do to make him. In lieu of real answers, I would just have to make sure he felt confident enough in his own abilities.

"Then I guess we should get to practicing." I tossed him a sphere of shadow.

He caught it with no problem and lobbed it back. "Catch, Alex? Really?"

"It still requires concentration and you're the one who wants more practice."

"Yeah, but I was hoping for something a little more intense."

I caught the sphere and juggled it between my hands. "Intense, huh? How about this? I'll make this more interesting if you help me shadow out better."

"What're you talking about? You did it just fine not half an hour ago."

"For the record, I had no idea that would work. It's still pretty hit or miss for me."

"Deal. But I don't know how you expect to make throwing a ball more interesting."

"Who said it was going to stay a ball?" I gathered more shadow material and willed the simple sphere into a large spiked morning star, sans handle. It would be a lot harder to catch if he couldn't touch it.

Matt's eyes widened as I sent it sailing over to him. Rather than even try to catch it, he dodged. "Are you out of your mind?"

"Who can really say? Now hold still and catch it."

He spun out of the way again as it veered straight for his head. "I can't catch that!"

"That's because you aren't even trying."

"You're insane."

"Just catch the damn thing."

Matt's back pressed into a corner of the room. He had three options left: he could shadow out of the way, take control and eliminate the spikes, or stop it. The sphere sailed towards him. He held out his hands defensively, and the ball stopped in midair. He cracked open an eye and let out a relieved breath.

"I wouldn't have let it hurt you, you know."

Matt looked between me and the floating weapon. "What? Did you stop it?"

"You tell me." I held up my hands. The sphere stayed put.

He reached out carefully to touch one of the spikes, then yanked his hand back and glared at me. "Those things are sharp."

"It had to be believable." The spikes instantly vanished into a perfectly smooth sphere.

He took hold of it, removing it from where it was hovering above the ground. His voice filled with wonder as he bounced the over-sized ball in his hands. "Never in a million years did I think I'd ever be able to do something like this."

My traitorous heart fluttered. Sometimes he really looked like some innocent kid eager to see the wonders of the world. I was too busy staring at him to realize the sphere was now hurtling right at me. I blinked in alarm and it blasted into streams of shadow. When the room cleared, Matt was almost right in front of me. Again, with the lack of personal space.

"You checked out a minute there," he commented.

I played at smoothing my hair to hide my blush. One of these days, I was going to get caught for real and my goose would really be cooked.

Matt shifted his weight. "So, how do you want to do this?"

"Do what?" I asked, still trying to pull myself together.

"Shadowing out. That was the deal."

"Right. I mean, however. You're the expert."

"I wouldn't say expert. Okay, let me think." He tapped a finger against his bottom lip thoughtfully, which did absolutely nothing for how I wasn't supposed to be thinking about how plump that lip was or how incredible it would feel between my teeth. "The way I do it is all instinct based. It's like what you told me before with the spoon trick. You just *need* to be somewhere else."

"But I'm not really motivated like that."

"Then I guess we'll need to motivate you." Without warning, he swung at my face.

I caught his hand before he could actually hit me. "What do you think you're doing?" I asked, incredulous.

He gave an evil grin. "Motivating you." His fist shifted in my grasp and suddenly he was holding my wrist.

I didn't even have a chance to react before he sent me flying. My feet barely got under me in time to spin around and catch another swing. He seemed genuinely surprised that I'd caught him and his smile grew. His leg swung out to kick me and I shadowed out before I could lose my stance. He struck again, and I dodged. Every move he made was lightning fast, without restraint. If he hit me, it was going to hurt like hell.

I shadowed out of the way just in time to avoid another smart punch and materialized a short distance away. I braced myself, expecting him to slam into my back like he had at the dorm, so was completely unprepared when he came at me with a frontal assault. He slammed into my chest and I grunted as we both went down.

When the stars cleared, I was staring up into ice-blue eyes. Laughter danced in their chilly depths and my hormones started doing their own jig at realizing Matt was on top of me. Mercifully, he rolled over to lie on the floor, where he chuckled to himself.

"See, you don't need practice." The back of his hand smacked my stomach and I let out an oof. "You've got it just fine."

"Sure thing, Matt," I wheezed, sitting up. I looked down at him.

He blinked back and smiled.

It would have been so easy to lie down beside him and pretend for just a moment that we were more than roommates, more than friends. Instead, I started getting to my feet. I was going to have to start a list of things we couldn't do together.

"Wanna go again?" Matt asked, still a tad breathless.

"I think I'm good on the near death for one day." I extended a hand to help him up. He took it and surged to his feet. I misjudged where he would land and his face stopped right in front of mine.

"I wouldn't have hurt you, Alex," he said, catching my eye.

Matt really didn't have any sense of personal space. He was inches away, if that, and my entire body was screaming at me to do something. But I couldn't seem to move. I was stuck in a trance, drowning in blue. I wasn't even sure if I was breathing anymore. My only saving grace was that I seemed to literally be frozen in place. Desire for Matt smashed violently against all of my control. Abruptly, I released his hand like I'd been burned and took a step back. Air finally found its way back into my lungs. I braced my hands on my knees. It felt like I'd run a marathon.

"Are you okay?" He sounded confused.

"I'm... I'm fine." I struggled with steady breaths. "Just got the wind knocked out of me, is all."

"I'm sorry, I didn't mean to..." He stepped closer.

I quickly held out a hand to stall him. If he got any closer, I was going to be in even more trouble than I already was, and I wasn't sure what I would do if he touched me again.

"You didn't. I just wasn't expecting it is all. It's been a while since I saw stars." I glanced at him. He didn't need to know that two of those stars were his eyes.

"I feel bad anyway. You know what you need?"

To get laid.

"Ice cream."

That could work, too.

Chapter 13
Fighting Chance

Matt

I didn't know how Alex did it. One day I was in danger of flunking out altogether, then a few later, I felt like I actually stood a chance of turning this around. My grades still weren't anywhere as good as his, but they were undeniably climbing. Turned out, I was actually good at math, and while Demonic History would probably never be my favorite subject, it was Alex's. He could go on for hours about ancient wars and demonic battles, and most of the time, I let him. I found it surprising, however, for someone who was so clearly a pacifist to revel in such violence.

Of course, I had no room to talk. I was getting in more than enough practice for Battle Tactics at the fight club. Though I wasn't using shadow nearly as much as I probably should have been able to. Alex naturally had theories about my inability to consistently control my powers. He still held that somehow, I was the one preventing me from using them. Either way, all of my frustrations from class went into the ring. Or, at least, I tried to take them all there.

Alex and I walked into Battle Tactics together, as we'd been doing since he'd started tutoring me. We automatically veered to our designated corner of the room to prepare for class.

"Look what the cat coughed up," George snickered to his cronies.

Alex tensed beside me, but kept his focus straight ahead. "Just ignore them."

"Easy for you to say. He doesn't give a shit about you," I hissed back.

"That's because I don't give him the satisfaction of a reaction."

"Hey, Matty, come on little guy. Don't worry, I won't bite. Unless you ask." The barb needled under my skin and my fists tightened of their own accord.

Alex gave me an anxious look out of the corner of his eye. "Don't do it, Matt. You know the rules."

I knew the rules probably better than he did. The real question was if it was worth potentially getting expelled to punch George in the face. Having my powers bound—which I finally understood meant basically taking them away—that I could handle. I'd lived this long without powers. What was the rest of my life?

"Does little Matty need permission from his keeper?"

Alex must have seen the look in my eye. "Matt, don't," he cautioned again.

"That's right. Heel." George laughed.

I threw my bag down. "Fuck the rules." I shadowed in front of George before he realized what was happening and gave him a good shove.

"You son of a bitch," he roared and swung at me. He may have been bigger, but I was faster and actually knew how to fight.

Up 'til now, the only other shadow demon I'd sparred with had been Alex. But for some reason I didn't understand, he wasn't interested in sparring outside of class. Right now, that kind of sucked. I could have used the practice. My assumption that George would be slow and awkward fell flat as he shadowed out, only to cuff me in the ear a moment later.

He was supposed to be bad at that. But he wasn't the only one hiding a few tricks. The club manifested in my hand.

"That the best you got? Bring it on, bottom feeder," he goaded.

I charged George, fully prepared to smash his face. I should have known better. How many hard lessons growing up had it taken for me to learn "never make the first move"? A thread of darkness came out of nowhere. Unlike when Alex used shadow on me, this hurt. The normally ephemeral substance coiled around my neck without forgiveness.

My club vanished as I clawed at the shockingly firm whip of shadow. Blood roared in my ears and my breath came in fitful gasps. Dark spots swam across my vision and my body shook violently as panic took hold. This was just like when I'd gotten cornered in an alley. It had been right before I'd gotten scooped up and hauled to Superno House. The rope had burned as it cut across me then, and this burned nearly as bad now.

"That's enough."

The cord winked out of existence, and air poured into my lungs. I looked over to find Vera standing a few feet away and Alex only a few paces behind her.

"Don't look at me like that. The rules are here for a reason. They keep us safe." She rubbed her forehead like the mere act of talking to me was giving her a headache. "And as for you, George Cartwright, this is not your first offense."

He sneered back at her and gave me a look that promised pain.

Just fucking great.

"That'll be private study for the both of you. Maybe next class you can keep your tempers long enough to learn something new." The entire room seemed to hold its breath, frozen in anticipation. "Move!"

I snatched my bag off of the floor and slunk out of the room, passing Alex along the way. I didn't know whether to thank him or hit him for interfering... again. One of these days, he was going to get me killed.

I was swinging away furiously at nothing in a secondary training room when the door slammed. I spun around, expecting to find Vera ready with a tongue lashing. What I got was a face full of shadow. I quickly cleared it away, only to be shoved backwards without getting a good look at my attacker. Before I could regain my bearings, there was another sharp shove behind me that made me stumble. I barely caught myself when that same someone ripped me back to my feet. That someone turned out to be a very angry-looking Alex.

I freed myself from his grip and rounded on him. "What the hell!"

"Yeah, what the hell, Matt? Are you out of your damn mind? Fighting in class? Are you trying to get expelled?" He shoved me again.

I shifted and spun out of his way as he continued to advance. "Cut it out, Alex."

"Do you know what they're going over right now?" He paused, but not long enough for me to guess. "The subject of the practicum. Newsflash, it's one of the few things you're not a natural at."

"What?" I shouldn't have stopped moving. He came at me full force. "What's your deal?" I asked, grappling with him.

"What's yours? You're stronger than George. Fucking act like it."

"He's twice my size."

"It has nothing to do with that. Why won't you believe me? You should have knocked out his entire attack, no problem, but you just stood there and let him beat you. It's ridiculous."

I took it back. I didn't want to spar with Alex. He was freaking me out. "I won't fight you, Alex."

"Why not?" He held out his arms like some demented invitation to take a swing at him. "You were going to fight George. We're about the same power-wise. If you can beat me, then you can beat him."

"You two are nothing alike," I insisted, trying to put more of the room between us.

"You're right. I'm much better at this." He spun a disk of shadow into his hand, then sent it shooting at my head. It looked like a damn razor blade and sliced cleanly through the chair I'd been standing behind.

My eyes widened in alarm. I scurried away from the destroyed chair, but when I looked up, Alex was gone. A quick scan of the room revealed nothing. Suddenly, I caught sight of the disk of death whizzing towards me. I ducked in time only to get gut-checked.

The next few moments were a flurry of trying not to get sliced in two while simultaneously avoiding Alex popping out of nowhere to smack me.

When did he get so good at this?

Finally, I sensed him before he could strike. The disk spun harmlessly past my ear and I just barely managed not to flinch. Right as Alex materialized, I caught him and forced him against the wall. He squirmed like the devil and I had to use my full weight to keep him there.

"Alex. Enough." I tightened my hold on his biceps; he was definitely going to have bruises.

At last, he stopped struggling and glared back at me. As close as we were, I was a little afraid that the fire in his eyes might actually set me alight. I gave him another small shake, still keeping him firmly trapped. The last of the fight went out of him and I relaxed my grip, but didn't completely let go. He'd been absolutely wild before, this could be a trick.

"Enough," I said again for emphasis.

"Matt," he panted, his breathing ragged.

When I looked at his eyes again, the green fire was gone, replaced by total darkness. For a moment, I was afraid the disk of death was going to return.

"I need you to get off of me," he said, absurdly calm.

"Right. Sorry." I released him and stepped back. A glance around the room showed that the disk had wrought some very real damage. "What was that about?" Alex stood there looking like he was trying to pull himself together.

I hope it wasn't a mistake to let him go.

He shook his head, an obvious look of disappointment on his face slicing through me more efficiently than the disk would have. "I'm tired of you always acting like you're not enough. You're more demon than half that room." When I said nothing, he stalked across the space towards the door.

"Alex. Alex, wait."

When he picked up his bag, I grabbed his arm. He turned to look at me and his eyes were still black. He blinked, and they returned to normal.

"Are you alright?"

"I'm fine," he said, refusing to meet my gaze.

I didn't know what to say about what had just happened, so I fell on something more familiar. "Are you gonna show me what the practicum is about or not?"

His eyes seemed to search mine for an answer. Then he closed them and dropped his bag. "Fine."

The following lesson was awkward, not the least of which because it turned out that the disk of death was the lesson. That I could deal with. What I couldn't handle was that something was clearly bothering Alex and he wouldn't tell me what. It didn't matter how I tried to approach it; I got the same stonewall every time. By the time we finally called it, I was immensely grateful it was Tuesday.

I excused myself after the painful lesson and made my way to the warehouse. Already, I could feel the now familiar sensation of excitement and trepidation. I provided the password to the gatekeeper—now chimera's revenge—and was admitted into the underground scene.

The place crawled with the usual oddities and terrifying creatures straight out of legend. I was proving to be a crowd favorite and Neese's golden boy, which afforded me at least a modicum of respect when I arrived.

Otto walked up and clapped me on the shoulder hard enough to make me stumble. "About time you showed up. I was beginning to think we were going to have to track you down." He gave a full belly laugh that grated on my nerves.

I shrugged him off. "What's on tonight's roster?"

"Let's see, we've got a Spiculo in the house, if you're interested."

"A what?"

He gestured over to some guy that was about my height and covered head to toe with barbs.

I flashed to the sinister Khima. "I'll pass. What else?"

"Picky, picky. Something certainly has you all fired up. Alright, if you aren't up for Andy, how about Singe?"

"You mean Carl? He's a fire demon, right?"

"You better believe it. And unless you want to end up with third-degree burns, I don't recommend using his day name."

"He'll do," I said, removing my shirt. Things got burned when you played with fire and I liked this shirt. I shoved it into my bag and dropped it to the side.

"Yo, Neese! Your boy is raring to go tonight!" Otto called out over the crowd.

Neese stepped into the ring as the current fight ended and hissed for me to join him. I cracked my neck and rolled my shoulders while Otto retrieved my opponent. Before coming here, I would've never dreamed of taking on anyone that looked like Carl. He may have only been five-foot-something, but he looked like he'd been forged in fire. Which, to be fair, was entirely possible. I had no idea how fire demons came about.

He walked into the ring and snickered. Most people here still didn't know what I really was besides fast and slipperier than the devil himself. It was hard to hold a shadow unless you actually were one. I smiled in anticipation and waited. He didn't keep me waiting long.

Almost as soon as Neese announced the fight and cleared the ring, fire shot from Carl's hands toward me. I shadowed out, only to reappear completely untouched in the same spot once the flames cleared. Fury clouded his face. Perfect.

I'd started doing research on the supernaturals I saw here after that first fight with Granite, who'd turned out to be a type of golem. Fire Demons were notorious for their temper and lack of control. The angrier he got, the more mistakes he was liable to make. Of course, it also made him infinitely more dangerous, because there was no telling which way the flames would go. While he focused his attacks mostly through his hands, the ability wasn't exclusively limited that way. Get him mad enough and he could literally blow.

I danced out of the way of another assault. I had to at least make it look like I was trying. This was going to be way too easy. Across the ring, I could see Neese and Otto's smug grins. Carl may be strong, but he was still no match for me. I stepped in closer, forcing him to use shorter blasts. It clearly wasn't his style, and he didn't appreciate being forced to do it.

"Come on, Carl, is that the best you've got?" I goaded him as I shadowed out of the way of yet another blast, except I cut it a little too close and the heat of it washed over me.

Flames shot from his head and he swung wildly, abandoning the flame-thrower attacks. One moment his fists were normal, the next, they were coated in orange fire.

"There, you go. Now you're getting warmer." The pun only infuriated him more.

The flames disappeared, and he reached for my neck. Too late. In a blink, I was behind him. Less than a second later, I drove my elbows into the back of his neck. He dropped like burnt out coal, his flames extinguishing as he hit the ground. A cheer went up and Neese walked forward to retrieve me.

"You could have made it last a little longer," he scolded under his breath, even as he raised my arm up as the victor.

"Is it my fault he lost his temper?"

"I wouldn't say he got away Scott-free. Looks like our little Matty got caught by some after burn," Otto said, thumping me in the chest. A pain very much like the fire I'd been avoiding spread across my torso.

"Shit." I hadn't even noticed. I'd been reckless. Distracted.

"At least it shows the crowd you're not completely untouchable. You keep fighting like that and no one will want to challenge." Neese squeezed the back of my neck to the point of pain. "We certainly wouldn't want that, would we?" He released me with a shove. "Put something on that. After-burns can get nasty and I want you in top shape for the next meeting."

I walked over to my things and then to the corner that held what constituted as medical. While they didn't have healers to take injuries away like they never happened, they couldn't afford wounds getting infected and bringing unwanted attention to the club.

The girl manning the table tilted her chin at me as I approached. "Not bad." She unscrewed a container filled with some kind of goo. Even from six feet away, I could tell it smelled foul. "Well, come here," she snapped impatiently and indicated for me to walk around the table.

I eyed her warily. She had dark liner on and magenta hair worn in a choppy style that paired with the rest of her obvious bad-girl look. Normally, the medic on duty gave you whatever it was and left you to fend for yourself.

"The name's Misty," she said as she smeared the affected area with the ointment. "Okay…" she added when I didn't respond. "Everyone knows you're Matt, but what are you?" Her hand slid smoothly along my torso. The salve was definitely working, and already the feeling of fire sitting on my chest was dissipating.

"Are you finished yet?"

"Yeah." She quickly removed her hand and wiped it off on a spare towel, then replaced the lid.

The salve had yet to soak in when I put my shirt back on. I probably should have waited, but I didn't like her questions or the way she'd gotten handsy. I slung my bag up and turned to go.

"Hey, you didn't answer my question."

"If Neese wanted you to know, then you would."

Her jaw dropped, and I left. I could've stayed and watched some of the other fights, normally I would have. Yet something about Misty made me nervous. She wanted something, and I didn't trust the way she'd eyed me like I was something to pick apart and eat. Besides, I still needed to figure out what was up with Alex.

Chapter 14
Assumptions

Alexi

"You've come a good ways, Ed." I smiled and handed him back the writing assignment we'd been working on.

His face crinkled, and I assumed he was smiling. Always difficult to tell with Jotunn. Even with an amulet to make the Ice Demon appear more human, it didn't quite meet the mark. "I had nice help," he said with a thick Swedish accent.

"Help, maybe, but you put in the work to make it happen." I turned to his polar opposite, sitting on my other side. "Same for you, Fiadh. I'm really impressed with how much both of you have progressed."

The Merrow smiled, revealing sharp teeth and illustrating that she was as deadly as she was beautiful. "You are very generous." She brushed long strands of moss green hair back from her face with an iridescent blue arm, freckled with darker spots of navy.

"Just giving credit where it's due."

Fiadh made a pleased humming sound deep in her throat that instantly captured Jotunn's attention. She flashed him a coy smile that she then switched to me. It was easy to understand how Merrows had developed a reputation for luring men to watery deaths. Though her charms didn't have quite the same effect on me.

I pushed back from the table to signal the end of our session. "Thank you both again for coming. I'll see you next week and we can review the course's weekend homework."

"Sounds lovely, Alexi." Fiadh slipped her paper between books and rose abruptly, as if she was used to having more resistance than air.

Ed scrambled to his feet. "Yes. Good things." He reached for Fiadh's books. "Help?"

She gave him another toothy smile that might as well have been made of honey for the way Ed beamed. "That would be nice. Thank you, Edzard."

I buried my smile and focused on packing my things while Ed followed Fiadh like a happy puppy. As much as I worried Fiadh would ultimately break the poor guy's heart, I envied her as well. At least she had options. Meanwhile, my one-sided pining was getting worse by the day.

"You've got quite a way with them." Rubio pushed off from the wall he'd been leaning against and moved to help me with the last of my books. "I gotta hand it to you. When you suggested group tutoring sessions, I was dubious, but it seems to be working out just fine."

"As long as you don't count the fact that I'm not sure whether Fiadh plans to eat Ed in a good way or in a bad way later, yeah, I guess I'm doing pretty good."

Laughter erupted out of Rubio. He shifted the books to one arm so he could wipe away tears with the side of his hand.

"Oh no, the new guy has gone and broken our fearless leader." Mariah clucked her tongue while the other tutors chuckled.

I walked up to her and rolled my eyes. "How was your session with Jahzara?"

She let out a heavy sigh and placed a hand on an ample hip. "I swear, she tries my patience more every time. I don't care if she is some kind of heiress or whatever, she's still flunking rudimentary spells."

I bumped her shoulder. "You'll figure it out. You're the best."

"From your lips to Jahzara's ears. If she tells me one more time about her social position, I'm gonna kill her."

"No, you won't," Rubio said as he stepped between us. He looked around at the gathered group that had quickly all become good friends. "Great job everyone. See you later. Oh, and a friendly reminder not to kill our paying customers."

Mariah grumbled under her breath, but followed suit with everyone in leaving the study space Rubio had acquired for general meetings and now my group tutoring sessions. I might only have two in the group now, but Rubio had confidence that would change as word about me got out, and he liked to plan ahead.

I shielded my eyes as we stepped outside. Our little cluster of study rooms was off the west side of the main library, and the evening sun was brutal. A few blinks put me back to rights. I waved goodbye as the others broke away, leaving me and Rubio alone on the sidewalk.

Suddenly, Rubio let out a low whistle and shoulder checked me. "Would you get a load of that beauty? Mmm... the things I'd like to do to him."

I searched the area he was not so subtly hinting at until my gaze fell on who he was undoubtedly talking about. "Oh, that's my roommate. Matt." I was tempted to add that I was right there with him, but Matt was already walking our way with that radiant smile that kept my heart in a constant state of upheaval.

Rubio's head snapped around to give me an incredulous look. "That's your roommate?" he hissed almost quietly.

I let out a sigh. "Yep."

"And you're not hitting that. Why?"

I tore my gaze away from the stunning masterpiece that was Matt's pouty face and divine eyes to scowl at Rubio. "One guess."

"Fuck." He nodded with knowing commiseration. "The straight ones, am I right?"

"You have no idea."

Rubio gave me a sidelong look before returning his attention to the ever-approaching Matt. "He know you're gay?"

"Nope."

He raised an eyebrow. "Gonna tell him?"

"Not planning on it."

Rubio shook his head and took a deep breath. "I don't envy you. That's gotta be torture."

"Eh." I shrugged. "It's not all bad. We're friends at least."

"Sure you are."

I scoffed. "Just friends. He's straight."

"You seem awful sure of that. Have you asked him? I mean, you haven't told him about you. Seems like you're assuming to me."

"Pretty sure I would have picked up on it by now if he wasn't."

Rubio tilted his head to the side and gave me a considering look. "Does he talk about other people—girls—bring any by the dorm?"

I shifted my weight. "Well, no. But he also seems kind of new? to all of this. Could be he's trying to get settled."

"You say so." Rubio stepped closer and passed me the books of mine he'd been holding. "Just saying, you miss a hundred percent of the chances you don't take."

"What are you, a feel-good poster now?"

He laughed. "Fair. But if you tire of chasing after the straight guy, my offer still stands. And my roommate is more than game to play. He's a wyvern, you see, and he's got this wicked long tongue and when he—"

"Whoa, I'm gonna stop you right there. That's more about your personal life than I need to know, boss."

"Pft. None of that 'boss' shit. We're a casual thing, nothing serious, and you're absolutely my guy's type." Rubio gave me a slow once over that gave me chills. For an outrageous second, I was actually tempted to take him up on the offer. Maybe not the threesome part, but at least the hooking up. It would be nice to kiss someone, to be touched, craved the way I craved Matt.

"Alex!" Matt picked up his pace, quickly eliminating our space for this conversation.

"Really," Rubio deadpanned.

I shot him a look and waved to Matt so he'd know I heard him. "Shut up. As for the other..." I hesitated.

Rubio squeezed my shoulder. "Hey, no pressure, really. I like you, but if you're not into it, you're not into it. Just know you've got options if you give up on your 'probably straight' roommate."

I relaxed and offered him a smile. "You're a good guy. Thanks. I appreciate it. That's just... not quite my speed."

"Understood. Good luck with your day, Alexi." Rubio gave me a warm smile before turning on his heel and walking off. I watched him go, biting the inside of my cheek while debating whether I'd made the right choice.

"Hey, who was that?"

I turned my focus to Matt, per usual, standing a little too close. Rubio's assessment that I might be jumping to conclusions about Matt's sexuality played in my mind. Would it be wrong to ask? Would it scare him away? Or bring him closer? Fully prepared to throw caution to the wind, I opened my mouth. "That was Rubio. He's in charge of the tutoring group I joined." And... totally chickened out.

"Huh." Matt stared after Rubio, then shifted his gaze to the books he'd handed me. "He seems... nice."

I pushed any lingering temptation to delve into Matt's preferences away. "He is. The whole crew is. There's about eight of us, including Rubio, though only five were here today. I confess, I'm really relieved we all mesh so well. I was kind of worried given I'm the newest member and the youngest. Not exactly vetted."

"They're all older?" Once more, Matt was staring off in the direction Rubio had vanished.

"Uh... yeah. I'm not exactly sure of their ages, but they're upperclassmen, at least."

Matt seemed to shake off whatever funk he'd fallen under. "That's cool, I guess. You done for the day?"

"Yep. Just need to drop these by the dorm, and I'm a free man. Why? Were you wanting to study together?"

"No. I figured we could grab dinner together."

Why was it every time Matt talked to me, it inevitably felt like he was asking me out? I was pretty sure it was an overwhelming dose of wishful thinking, but maybe Rubio had a point. "Dinner would be nice. Where were you thinking?"

"The cafeteria is not too far. I noticed you left your dining card on the counter, so I brought it." He held up the square of plastic with a grin. Then his gaze dropped to the books I was holding. "I can carry those if they're heavy," he said as he reached for the books, his hands encasing mine.

My heart thudded loud enough I was positive he could hear it, and my breath pointblank refused to come. His hands were warm and oddly gentle, despite their coarseness. Where I should have been formulating a response, all my traitorous mind could do was think of how nice it would be to have his touch on other parts of my body. I swallowed hard with exactly zero moisture in my mouth. "They're not heavy."

"Okay." He blinked those stunning eyes at me, but didn't move.

We stayed like that for a long minute, that might as well have been a panicked eternity. What was I supposed to do? I couldn't think clearly enough while his hands were on me and I wasn't exactly eager to make him move them.

"Alex?"

"Yeah?" I croaked.

"Are you gonna give me the books?" He shifted his hold, making his fingers slide along mine.

Irresistible longing shot down my spine. He was so close. All I had to do was lean forward and I could finally taste those full lips, show him that as much as I enjoyed being his friend, I wanted more.

A shrill whistle pierced the air and shattered the moment. Matt glanced around for the source of the sound while I tilted the books into his hold. "What were you thinking for dinner?" I asked, wiping my sweaty palms on my slacks.

He followed the movement, then adjusted his grip on the stack of literature. "I don't know. Whatever you're in the mood for, I guess."

I wasn't sure I would ever understand why Matt insisted on eating the same things I did when he could literally have anything. Surely, he had different tastes.

Plus, most of the time, the dishes seemed to be entirely foreign to him, not that he ever complained. I chanced a smile. “What would you say to trying some Greek?”

“I’ve never had Greek before.” He tilted his head while he seemed to consider something. “If I’m remembering right, I’ve seen a few dishes, though. Looks tasty.” With that, he took off towards the cafeteria.

I sighed to myself and followed at a more sedate pace. If only he was talking about me and not food.

Chapter 15
Billiards & Besties

Matt

The classroom immediately began buzzing with conversation the second Professor Whittle left. I glanced around the room and fiddled with my pencil. Typically, I'd occupy myself by drawing in my notebook, but frankly, I was running out of space. That, and I didn't really feel like it. Alex sat at the front of the class—naturally—and was animatedly chatting with a girl with pink hued skin that seemed to shimmer every time she moved. I frowned. Something still wasn't sitting right with me about his new tutoring group or this Rubio guy. I wasn't about to tell Alex, but I'd seen the way Rubio had looked at him and I didn't like it one bit.

The pencil snapped between my fingers. I stared down at the broken pieces like they were somehow symbolic of my unease. With a huff, I threw them into my bag and resolved not to relocate so I could chat with Alex instead of sitting here by myself. If Alex could have other friends, then so could I. Right?

I took stock of my options. No one nearby struck me as interesting. I'd never been good at making friends, at least none that stuck. Much easier to be on my own. I hadn't even cared about having friends before. I blamed Alex.

The conversation behind me caught my attention, and I swiveled in my seat to get a look at the people responsible. Two guys, maybe a little older than me, but definitely not as old as Rubio, were laughing so hard tears were streaming down their cheeks. The one on the left had dark hair that fell around his face in jagged sweeps to frame his square face. He shoved his companion, who was noticeably paler, his skin a subtle pink where he was a rich earthy color.

"You're making that up!" Pale blond guy smacked his friend's hand away.

Messy hair shook his head. "I shit you not. The cue ball bounced off the nipple, flew into the air and landed with a huge splash in a pitcher of beer. Worst part? It was our beer. I'm telling you, that's the last time I play pool with my cousins."

I finished turning all the way around, hanging half out of my chair. "You guys play pool?"

"Sure do." Messy hair tilted his dimpled chin at me. "You?"

"It's been a while. Didn't realize there was any place nearby."

Blond guy leaned forward on his elbows. "Not too far from campus, but it's a total dive."

I smiled, recalling the hole in the wall I'd learned to play at. "I find those tend to be the best places."

Messy hair gave me an approving nod. "Damn right they are. I'm Lucas." He gestured with his thumb at blond guy. "And this disaster is Sam."

"Matt."

"Nice to meet you," Sam said. "We're actually headed that way tonight if you'd like to join us." A mischievous smile curled his lips. "The staff is hella cute, too."

Lucas elbowed him in the ribs.

"What?"

"Not everyone goes to bars to hit on waitresses."

Sam scoffed. "You're just saying that because you can't get any of them to look at you twice. Me, on the other hand..." His features blurred a moment, then I was looking at someone straight out of a movie poster.

"Holy shit. How'd you do that?"

Sam's face did the blurry thing again, then he was back to himself. He rubbed his knuckles on his shirt. "Magic's the game, illusion the name."

Lucas scowled at him. "You're so full of yourself." He rolled his eyes and shifted his focus to me. "In short, he's a witch. I'm a werewolf. What about you? Haven't seen you in any of my other classes and there's not exactly a ton of them during the summer."

"Uh..." I floundered, still trying to wrap my head around the fact that I was talking with a legit werewolf. A million questions bubbled in my mind. Was he more like the Wolfman or did he do some weird hybrid thing like that vampire-werewolf movie I'd seen eons ago? Could he shift any time or just with the moon? What could he do? Holy fuck, werewolves were real.

"Matt?"

I blinked at Sam, who was wearing a curious expression. "Huh?"

"I asked what you are."

"Oh. I'm..." I waffled on how much to say. Neese didn't like people knowing what I was, but then again, it wasn't exactly a mystery to everyone. Anyone who actually took a minute could probably put it together. In the end, I opted for total honesty. "I'm a Shadow Demon."

"Cool." Lucas grinned. "So, what do you say, wanna hang with us later, shoot some pool?"

Was making friends really that easy? "Yeah, I'm game. Where should I meet y'all?"

"I'm in Dire Hall," Lucas said, like I had any idea where that was.

"I have a late class in the witch's college," Sam chimed.

My brow furrowed. "That's the castle looking place, right?"

"That's the one. How about we meet on the quad over by that cluster of benches around seven? Then we can head over together."

"Sounds good to me," I said, flabbergasted at how easy this was.

Lucas nodded his agreement as well right as Professor Whitlow returned. She passed out the next week's assignment and set us loose. By the time I made it out the door, after confirming the time again with Lucas and Sam, Alex was waiting for me.

I smiled at him as I adjusted my pack and wondered if he'd ever played pool before. "What are you up to later?"

Alex fell in step with me. "I have a joint tutoring session with Rubio. Will probably go pretty late."

My jaw clenched so fast I nearly bit my tongue. "Didn't you see him the other day?"

Alex frowned, confusion clearly stamped on his face. "Yeah, but that was for our weekly meeting. This is for an actual session with clients." He shook his head and let out a short laugh. "That still feels so weird to say."

"Oh." It was all I could manage while I grappled with what was proving to be an unreasonable amount of anger directed at Rubio.

Concern flashed in Alex's eyes, briefly darkening their bright green. "Why?"

I reminded myself that this was why I'd struck up a conversation with Sam and Lucas. Alex had other friends. It wasn't a betrayal of our friendship if I did, too. "Going out with some friends tonight. Thought you might like to come."

A giant smile split Alex's face. "That's great, Matt! Sorry, I can't join. Maybe next time?"

"Yeah, maybe," I echoed, though my heart wasn't in it.

"Where are you all going?"

I shrugged. "Some place in town."

"Well, I hope you have fun. You'll have to tell me all about it." He stepped to the side into an adjoining hallway. "Well, this is me. I have some prep work to take care of before the group tutoring tonight. I'll catch up with you later." He waved and turned away before I could say anything. Past him, Rubio stepped out of a classroom and greeted Alex with a huge smile.

Irritation prickled the back of my neck while I squeezed the straps of my backpack within an inch of their life. I spun sharply on my heel and stalked out of the building. Looked like I'd be grabbing dinner on my own tonight.

Seven o'clock rolled around, and I wandered over to the benches where Lucas was already waiting. His eyes caught the setting sun and flashed yellow.

"Hey, you made it. We're still waiting for Sam. I'm convinced that guy couldn't be on time if he was an actual clock." Lucas chuckled.

I shoved my hands in my pockets and leaned against a nearby tree. "How long have you two known each other?"

"A year or so. Met in Language Studies our first year and sort of hit it off. This your first semester at Arminius?"

I leaned my head back and gave him a crooked grin. "What gave it away?"

"Nothing. Just a guess. I heard a lot of the Shadow Demons had no idea what they were. Made sense."

I appreciated the way Lucas had a way of asking questions without it feeling like he was prying. "I'd never even heard of this place until Vera scooped me up."

Lucas let out a low whistle. "Damn. For real? She as scary as everyone says?"

"Not by half." Lucas's eyebrows shot up, and I reconsidered my answer. "Well, not as a person, anyway. Demon-wise, she's kind of terrifying, but if you tell anyone I said that, I'll deny it."

He crossed his heart and grinned. "Your secret's safe with me."

"What secret?" Sam asked as he popped up out of nowhere. For all I knew, he had.

Lucas tilted his head in my direction. "Just that Matt's new to the whole supes thing."

"That has got to be wild, man. I don't envy you. So glad I had a coven looking out for me. Right," Sam clapped his hands together, "what do you say we get this show on the road? I've got a pretty brunette waiting for me."

Lucas snickered and leaned over to whisper. "In his dreams."

I smothered a laugh as Sam spun around and eyeballed us. "Lead the way."

A twenty-minute walk later, we approached what could have been a condemned building if it wasn't for the flashing neon sign that said "Open".

Trusting that my new friends weren't taking me somewhere to off me, I followed them inside. Luckily, the inside bore little resemblance to the crumbling exterior.

An oval bar sat in the middle of the large space, surrounded by bar-height tables and stools. On either side was an array of pool tables bustling with people. A quick count brought me maybe a dozen total. At the back of the joint was an assortment of vintage pinball machines and dartboards. Overall, I had to say; I was impressed.

"What do you think?" Sam asked over the ambient noise.

I swept the space once more, noting that all the patrons at least appeared human. "Not bad."

Beside us, Lucas took out his wallet to pay the host the cover, and I reached for the cash I'd shoved in mine earlier. He noticed the move and waved me off. "This one's on me. That way, if Sam chases you off, the night's not a total loss."

"Hey!" Sam shouted in outrage. "Why am I the one who's running him off? I'm not the one that smells like wet dog."

Lucas snorted as the host gave him his change and pointed at a table that had just opened up. "You sure about that? Because that new cologne you're so proud of is fucking awful."

"It is not." Despite his statement, Sam still pulled up his shirt and took a sniff. He frowned and turned to me. "What do you think?"

"I think it's weird you're asking me to smell you."

Sam's mouth fell open, and Lucas guffawed loud enough to grab a few people's attention. "Oh, I like you. You can stay." Lucas slung an arm around my shoulder and guided us to the table while Sam slunk off with a pout to secure three cue sticks.

I rubbed the back of my neck as Lucas adjusted the balls on the table. "Hey, uh, thanks for getting the cover."

"No big. It's nice to have someone else join besides that ham." Lucas crossed his arms and rested his hip on the table. "Don't get me wrong, he's a great guy and a better friend, but he can be... a lot." Lucas pointed subtly behind me.

I twisted around to find who I assumed was Sam, except now he had a deep bronze tan and dreadlocks that reached the middle of his back. He smiled broadly at a young woman with flushed cheeks and a high ponytail. Within seconds of me spotting him, her face morphed into blatant outrage and she stormed off. Sam sagged in defeat, then shrugged his shoulders and returned to himself.

When he rejoined us, Lucas gave him a level stare. "Striking out already?"

"Like you could do any better." Sam stuck out his tongue and bumped Lucas aside so he could break. "What do you say you and me take first round, Matt?"

I leaned against my cue stick. "Sure. Heads up, though, I'm rusty."

Sam smiled from his position laid over the table, ready to strike. "Don't worry, I'll take it easy on you." He took his shot, and the break was... less than impressive. He scowled at the balls, none of which had found a pocket. "My hand slipped."

"Sure, it did," Lucas teased as I assessed the table. "What about you, Matt? Any luck with the ladies since you came to Arminius?"

I shrugged and took my shot. "Eh, not really. But then I haven't exactly been trying either." I sank the nine, making me stripes, but missed my next shot.

Sam smacked Lucas in the chest. "What if he's not into that? Rude." He squared up with the four and sank it easily.

"Shit. Good point. Are you into girls?"

My face scrunched in confusion as I watched Sam sink two more shots before finally missing. "Why wouldn't I be?"

Sam and Lucas shared a look, but neither offered clarity. Sure, it had been a while—a long while—but I hadn't exactly had the time to pursue anything resembling a relationship lately. And if I was being honest, the interest, either.

Lucas cleared his throat. "No reason. Maybe we can hook you up. What's your type?"

"Not sure I have one."

Lucas chuckled. "So, you're like Sam."

Sam straightened from the shot he was never going to make. "What the hell is that supposed to mean?"

"I'm guessing he means anyone with a pulse." I kept a straight face for a couple of seconds, then cracked a smile.

Sam missed his shot by a mile and ended up sinking the eight ball instead. Meanwhile, Lucas was crying he was laughing so hard.

"I see how it is," Sam said as he fished out the black ball. "I'm totally kicking your ass next game and first round is on you."

"Fair." I flagged down a waitress in an obscenely short skirt with a few buttons missing from her top.

She bounced up to me and beamed. "What can I get you, fellas?"

I looked at the guys.

"Pale ale on draft," Lucas offered as he finished racking the balls, and Sam echoed him.

I turned back to the insufficiently dressed waitress and gave her my best smile. "Make that three." Color rose in her cheeks before she confirmed the order and ducked away. I waited 'til she was gone before looking back at the others, both of whom were staring at me. "What?"

"I already hate you," Sam stated without any real conviction.

Lucas shook his head and gestured for me to break. "I take it back. You do just fine with the ladies."

"Right..." I wasn't entirely sure what the hell they were talking about, but they were nice and this was fun. Honestly, the only thing that could make it better was if Alex had tagged along instead of hanging with Rubio... again. I pictured the guy's face on the cue ball and cracked the stick into it. Balls rolled in every direction with three solids sinking into separate pockets.

"Fuck. He's a hustler."

I smiled up at Sam and sank the two.

Chapter 16
Innocent Mistake

Alexi

"We should celebrate," Matt insisted as we entered the dorm.

I laughed as I closed the door behind us. He'd been on like this since Battle Tactics had let out early.

"We survived our first practicum. We have to do something!"

I endeavored not to laugh at his comically wide eyes and pleading expression. "It wasn't really a big deal." But it was kind of adorable how excited he was.

"For you maybe. Come on, don't leave me hanging. We don't have class tomorrow and we got an entire afternoon back." He gave me that puppy dog face I couldn't say no to, even if I wanted.

I held up my hands in surrender. "Fine, fine. What did you have in mind?"

"Yes!" he shouted triumphantly, and punched the air. Then he disappeared and reappeared in the kitchen.

I shook my head and started relocating the texts and papers strewn across the coffee table to our bags beside the door. I'd given up pointing out whenever he shadowed in the dorm. He never believed me anyway. "You didn't answer the question. What're we doing?"

"You'll see."

"That doesn't sound like I'm going to like whatever it is."

"Don't be so negative." He returned with a glass of yellow liquid. It was too dark to be lemonade and something told me it had alcohol.

"I told you, I don't really drink," I said, accepting it anyway.

Matt rolled his eyes. "Would you at least try it before you decide you don't like it? Besides, we're celebrating. You can suck it up and drink with me for one night.," he concluded with a wry twist of his mouth.

"I still don't know where you get all of this stuff." I took a sip.

"I have my ways. So, what do you think?" A grin stretched across his face like he already knew the answer.

I stared at the cold glass, already coated with condensation in surprise. "It's actually quite good." I glanced over at him to discover he had a matching glass and a pitcher full of the concoction. How much did he expect us to drink tonight?

"No beer for you?"

"And let you have all the good stuff? As if."

"What's in this, anyway?" I took another sip and smacked my lips at the sweetness. "Tastes like fruit."

He shrugged as he set down the full pitcher. "This and that."

I squinted at him and took another drink. "I see what you did there."

He smirked and grabbed my wrist, pulling us both to the floor between the couch and the table. "Sit down, you're making me nervous."

"Why can't we sit on the couch?" I asked, even as I leaned against the furniture in question. The deceptively strong drink coated my tongue with sweetness edged with just enough tart to make it palatable. I reached for the pitcher to top off my dwindling glass. Something told me Matt's idea of celebrating would entail getting absolutely smashed. I leaned back and relaxed. "Why aren't we sitting on the couch again?"

"Because I said we're sitting on the floor." He took a drink, and I mirrored him.

"You're such an odd duck."

"And you're not?" He laughed, bumping his shoulder into mine, and I barely prevented the liquid from sloshing out of the glass. "None of that this time, got it?" Matt gave me a serious look that belied the humor dancing in his eyes. "And no snorting it up your nose, either."

I licked off the little liquid that had escaped. "Got it. So, now what?"

"Now? We hang out." He flopped dramatically against the couch as if to emphasize his declaration.

"And do what?"

"We're doing it. Not everything has to be about school. Or studying. It's possible to just chill, you know."

My eyebrows lifted. "Are you really giving me friendship lessons?"

"Sounds like you need them." He winked and gave me another infectious grin.

My heart stuttered at that beautiful smile, the one that seemed uniquely reserved for me. I smiled into my glass and stretched out my legs beneath the table, getting comfortable, then we both took another drink.

"Mm," he began around a mouthful of liquid. "Did you see George almost pop a blood vessel trying to control his disk?"

I laughed as the image of George's stricken face resurfaced. "Yeah, but it was nothing compared to when Marcie's zipped off and smacked Thomas. If she wasn't such a petite woman, I'm pretty sure he would've throttled her."

"It can't be easy being one of only three girls in the class," Matt commented as he leaned forward to reach the pitcher. He promptly topped off his glass and mine. "Why do you think that is?"

"Maybe females of our kind are rare? I heard Vera searched everywhere, but couldn't find more."

Matt cocked his head to the side and stared off pensively. "Do you think it's a genetics thing?"

I took another drink and shook my head. "I can't believe we're sitting here talking about the genetic heritage of our kind."

Matt returned his full attention to me. "Would you rather talk about girls?" It was hard to tell if he was being facetious or serious.

"Not really," I said, sitting up straighter. "The problem is, there's no way to tell. We're kind of rare, anyway. And it's not like it takes two demons to make a demon."

His forehead crinkled. "What do you mean?"

"Most demons—any demons, really—hookup with other species. We're kind of notorious for it," I added, wiggling my eyebrows. We both laughed, and a lightness filled my chest. I refilled my glass.

This is awesome.

"Really? So, both of your parents aren't demons?" Matt stared at me in wonder.

I shook my head. "Nope, my mom is decidedly human. Were yours?"

He darkened a bit at the question. "I don't know."

Determined not to lose this good mood, I powered on. "Neither of Vera's parents were."

His eyes widened, and his beautiful mouth fell open. "No."

"Nope," I echoed.

"Then how is she a demon at all, let alone one of the strongest?"

"Genetics are weird like that. Apparently, there was enough latent potential on both sides and... viola, super powerful Shadow Demon. To be fair, she did kind of shock the supernatural community. And that's not talking about all the horrible things she's done." I took a sizable gulp as I continued to work myself up. "She can do stuff that no one's ever seen or heard of, at least not anyone who's still around can remember. She even taught her teacher a few things, and he's a level two as well. Which is absolutely wild, since he's like outrageously old."

"She said something about that before. Just how old is he?"

"I don't know. Over a thousand for sure."

Matt snorted, almost spilling his drink.

"Hey, I thought you said none of that?"

He waved away the scorn and pulled himself back together. "How's that even possible?"

"Demons, or at least Shadow Demons, live a really long time. The more we use our powers, the more our aging slows down. Probably has something to do with being part of a plane of existence that doesn't observe the passage of time. So, the good news is I'll probably look this good forever." I did my best to maintain a stoic expression, but laughter won out.

Matt quirked a half smile at me. "A little full of yourself, aren't you?"

"Eh, beauty may be a curse, but that doesn't mean I can't enjoy it."

"Let me make sure I have this right." He shifted around and put on a super serious expression that I couldn't help but chuckle at. "You're saying that because you've been using your powers for years, that you'll look sixteen forever."

I pressed my free hand to my chest and gasped in exaggerated insult. "Excuse you, I will be nineteen in a few months."

"No way!" Matt's face lit up with a joy that did a better job of intoxicating me than whatever alcohol he was plying us with. "When's your birthday?"

"Yes, way. It's in November. When's yours?"

"I can't believe you're older than me. Mine is in February. The thirteenth."

"Dang. So close." I chuckled and gave him a crooked smile. "Still, I bet you're a regular Casanova."

He tilted his head to the side before taking another drink. "A what?"

"Casanova, Matt. Notorious guy who slept with like half of France."

He scoffed. "I don't know about that."

I shrugged. "Honestly, it wouldn't surprise me if he was some kind of supernatural in real life. Maybe one of the Fae. Those guys can get around."

Matt looked at me with those absurdly full lips and high color on his cheeks. "How do you know all of this stuff?"

"Because, Matt, I want to." I finished my drink and poured another, not sure how many that made. Judging by Matt's slurring words, he'd had as many, if not more than me already.

"You seem like the kind of guy who usually gets what he wants." He finished his latest drink, then rolled the empty glass between his hands. Night, he was cute.

"Not always," I replied, casually setting my glass down next to the empty pitcher. I did a double take. When had we finished it?

"Oh really?" He laughed. "And when do you not?" he asked, turning to me.

I was waiting for him, though. When he turned, his lips met mine. I giggled to myself and sat back. I'd literally caught his laugh. Another giggle bubbled up, but he just sat there, staring blankly back.

Maybe I should give it back.

"Why are you looking at me like that? It was just-" My chest constricted.

Oh shit.

He blinked and turned to look straight ahead.

What have I done? I knew drinking with Matt was a bad idea.

He looked around at the room as if trying to figure out what to do.

"I didn't mean to do that." No response. "Matt," I tried again.

The sound of his name seemed to break whatever spell he was under. He set his glass down on the coffee table and glanced at me out of the corner of his eye. "So..." The question trailed off.

This was my worst nightmare. He could barely even look at me. I swallowed. "It was an accident."

"I'm getting that."

"Matt, please." I didn't know what else to say.

"I... I need to... Yeah." He got up none too steadily, then walked to his room. The door closed quietly behind him.

I could have screamed.

What have I done? I've ruined everything.

My breathing came in short, shallow gasps while my heart seemed determined to beat itself out.

He's never going to talk to me again. He'll hate me forever.

The thoughts tumbled over each other, each bringing a fresh wave of despair. Suddenly, his door opened, and he stepped out. I swiveled around to face him, and he looked over at me. I'd have given anything to appear calm and collected right then, but there was no hiding the panic that had to be clearly stamped across my face.

"So, you... you're..." His gaze slid away from me, much like his words.

"Matt, I can explain."

He nodded to himself, still looking lost. "How drunk are you?" he asked unexpectedly.

"Pretty drunk," I admitted.

"How drunk am I?"

"Also, pretty drunk."

"Okay. Right. And..." He didn't finish, just walked back into his room.

He couldn't even say it. There was no way I could undo this. I grabbed a pillow and yelled all of my frustration into it. What was I going to do? We were really starting to get along and I fucked it all up.

"Right, let's try this again."

I looked up to see that Matt had reemerged once again. Only this time, instead of confused, he looked determined. I got up and walked around to face him. I had no idea what I was going to say, but I had to try something. "Matt, I'm sorry, I..."

He held up his hand, cutting off my string of apologies. My mouth closed with an audible snap. He searched my face like he was trying to decide something. "Let's try this again," he repeated.

"Try what?" I asked dubiously.

"Kiss me."

Immediately, I was wary. "You're messing with me."

"No, I'm not. I'm perfectly serious."

"I don't think that's a good idea," I hedged, still clinging to the faint hope that I could come up with an adequate excuse for the first kiss.

"Alex, would you just do it already? I'm trying to figure something out." He looked at me expectantly.

I hung back, filled with trepidation, but his face clearly said he wasn't backing down. Maybe if I did something super small, it'd meet his demand and get me off the hook without making things much worse. He obviously wouldn't let me out of it.

I took a deep breath and leaned forward. In all of my dreams, this was not how I'd seen this moment going. This time, when our lips touched, I made a conscious effort to keep it minimal. Even then, my heart gave a traitorous skip. I was kissing Matt. On purpose.

It was probably the liquor that made me believe he was pressing back. I stubbornly fought the urge to slip into the easy fantasy. That wouldn't help anything. Then I felt his tongue glide along my lip. Alcohol-addled brain or not, it was all the encouragement I needed. I dropped all pretense of restraint and pulled his face closer. Then I kissed him like I'd wanted to do for weeks, claiming his mouth with mine. And it was incredible, so much better than I could have ever dreamed. Fireworks, sparklers, electric current, all of it and then some.

A distant part of me screamed that this was not the right answer. But as I felt his lips move against mine, I couldn't have stopped if my life depended on it. I wanted this, needed it like I needed air to breathe. He was every bit the amazing kisser I'd imagined, and I wanted more. I drew him closer, deepening the kiss, and he let me. The whole world teetered on its axis and I fell infinitely into Matt.

Abruptly, he pulled away, the suction of separation making an awful sound. Still in a daze, I drifted to follow him, more than willing to drown for an eternity, but stopped myself short. My heart beat like it was going to come right out of my chest. We were only inches apart, and I could still taste him on my tongue.

He pressed his lips together, and I longed to tease them free, to kiss them 'til they were cherry red and his breathing was as ragged as mine. Suddenly, I realized my hand was still cupping his face and snatched it down. He'd yet to look at me, and I could practically see his mind turning as he tried to absorb what had happened. It didn't look to be going in my favor.

He nodded as if to himself. "That's what I thought. So, you're definitely...?" His eyes were clouded crystal when they snared my own.

"Yes." The admission felt like it was being dragged from the depths of my soul. I could have lied, should have lied, but I couldn't, not to Matt, not after that.

He nodded again. "Right." He turned on his heel and vanished into his room yet again.

I stood there waiting to see if he would make a repeat appearance like he had before. After a while, though, it became clear that he wouldn't be coming back. I hung my head in my hands while the room continued to spin around me. Now, whether it was because I was exceptionally drunk, high off of kissing Matt, or because I was liable to pass out at any moment from mortification, was anyone's guess.

I stumbled over to the kitchen and fixed myself a glass of water. I downed it and two more. As inebriated as I was, all I wanted was to lie down and forget this whole thing had happened. Maybe I'd wake up on the floor having dreamed the whole evening. I recognized the empty hope for what it was. I knew this was real, and I'd pay dearly for it in the morning.

The empty pitcher sat defiantly on the table. Miserable thing had gotten me into more trouble than seemed possible. I walked over and snatched it up along with the empty glasses. I was far too strung out to go to sleep, no matter how much I wanted to. For want of a distraction, I stayed up and cleaned the entire living space, kitchen included. By morning, the place was spotless, and I was exhausted. Even then, I couldn't bring myself to retire. I wanted to be awake when Matt got up to at least attempt damage control. However, despite spending the entire night thinking about what to do, I was still coming up empty.

A faint shuffling came from his side of the dorm.

Instantly, anxiety laced with dread flooded through my veins. I quickly poured a glass of water, orange juice, and blue sports drink. I wasn't sure what his preference would be and wanted him to have options.

The shuffling got louder until, at last, Matt's door finally opened and he staggered out. His hair was a sleep-tangled nest, gray smudges sat beneath tired eyes, and his shoulders slumped forward as if trying to shield him from the light. In short, he looked rough. Somehow, though, he'd had the wherewithal to change into pajamas and stood leaning against the frame in his usual lounge pants and tee. It was a measure of how stressed I was that I didn't bother to appreciate the view.

He looked up at me bleary-eyed, then saw the glasses and walked over. He downed the water and blue sports drink in quick succession before taking the orange juice over to the couch. A miserable groan rose out of him as he sat down.

I refilled the water and brought it over to sit it on the coffee table. When I sat down, I made sure there was still plenty of distance between us.

He didn't react except to drink half of the glass and lay his head back. "You look awful," he said with his eyes closed.

"So do you," I countered.

"I feel worse. Just how much did I drink?" It sounded like a rhetorical question, so I didn't respond. He finished the OJ and the extra water before leaning back again.

"What do you remember?" I asked cautiously.

"Shh, not so loud," he admonished. He sat still for a moment before continuing. "Most of the night is a blur," he moaned, rubbing his temples.

I let out the breath I'd been holding. He didn't remember.

He cracked an eye. "Don't look so relieved. I wasn't that drunk."

Cold washed over me as all the blood drained from my face. "Matt, I..."

He held up his hand, much like he had the night before. "It's okay, Alex."

"But, Matt..." I tried again.

He opened both eyes and looked at me. There was no confusion or doubt this time. They were perfectly clear. I felt speared in place. "You're gay, Alex. It's fine." I opened my mouth to try once again to offer some desperate defense, but he beat me to it. "You were drunk. I was drunk. Shit happens." He glanced at the table. "I don't suppose I could get some more water and something for this?" he asked, rubbing his head again.

I was gone and back again in record time. My mind struggled to accept what he'd said. He obviously remembered the night before and was... okay with everything?

"Please stop staring at me. I can practically hear you freaking out over there. It's very loud."

I shifted my position so I wouldn't be looking directly at him, but it did nothing to quiet my mind.

He let out an exasperated sigh and sat up. "We're still friends, if that's what you're worried about."

I looked over at him. It wasn't quite what I'd been thinking, but it was close enough. "It won't be the same."

"Why not?" He leaned back again, the absolute picture of hungover ease. This was not at all the person I'd expected to see this morning after his reaction last night.

"Because... because..." I floundered.

"Because you kissed me?" It seemed prudent not to point out that he'd technically kissed me too.

I know I didn't imagine that. I know I didn't.

When I didn't respond, he officially turned to face me. "You're still my best friend, Alex."

I was completely caught off guard. The vulnerability on his face took my breath away.

"I... I've never had one of those before and I'm not about to give it up because of one drunken night." He kept his head down as he fidgeted with the hem of his nightshirt. "Is that alright with you?"

There were still a thousand things I wanted to ask. Were we really not going to talk about this? How was he okay with what had happened? I'd practically admitted that I was into him and he still wanted to be friends? I didn't voice any of them, instead I nodded numbly.

"Good, now can we please turn off all the lights? It's way too bright in here." Before I could get up, I heard all the switches click, and the room went dark. "Never mind, I got it. Try to take a nap, Alex. You really do look like hell."

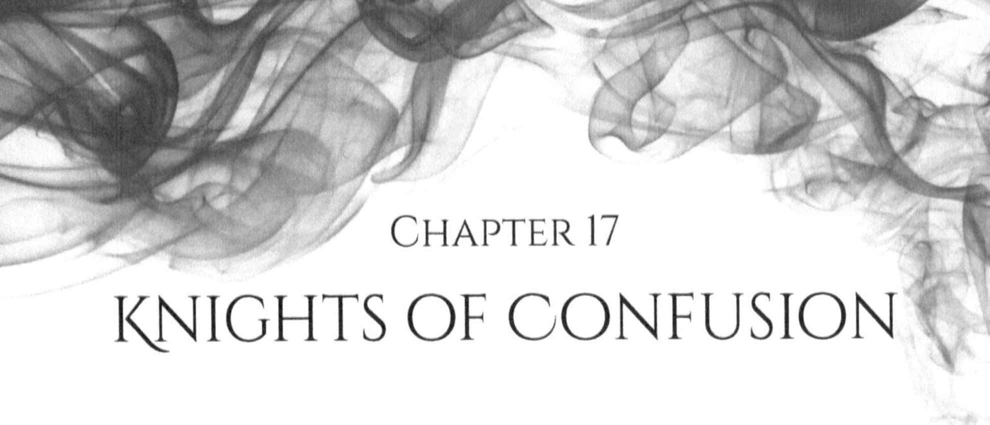

Chapter 17
Knights of Confusion

Matt

Alex was gay. The best friend I'd ever had in my life was gay, and I was pretty sure he was into me. Everything he'd ever done since we met took on a new meaning. His sudden bouts of awkwardness, why he didn't want to spar outside of class, his weird insistence on personal space, his mini freak outs he didn't think I noticed. All of it came together to paint the picture I should have seen all along. I couldn't believe I'd missed it.

Did I not want to see what was right in front of me?

It didn't matter, not really. I'd never had a friend like Alex and over my dead body was I going to give him up. So, what if he was gay? People got crushes on their friends every day, then they moved on. That was a thing. Right?

I finished changing into pajamas and was about to put on a shirt to go into the living space so Alex and I could hang out like we did practically every night. I got all the way to my door, then stalled. The shirt fell uselessly to the floor and I crawled back into bed instead. I just needed a little more time to get my head clear before I tried to be normal again.

While I lay there waiting for sleep to take me, I stared up at the ceiling and replayed every awkward moment I'd ever seen Alex have. There weren't that many, but the ones that made the list certainly stood out. Deep down, I was a little disturbed at how not disturbed I was. That I'd totally missed it and been taken off guard was what had me spinning, not the actual information.

I reached up to touch my mouth tentatively. If I thought about it, I could still feel the slight buzz of his lips against mine. I felt horrible for tricking him like that, but I also knew Alex. If I hadn't, he would've found some way to explain it all away. It would've been easy. After all, we were both exceptionally drunk.

As I trailed my finger along my bottom lip, I let the guilt sink in. I'd intentionally baited him so that he couldn't hide behind some noncommittal peck, but I hadn't been prepared at all for what I would get. No one had ever kissed me like that. It was... different. I thought about that. Why was it different? Ironically, I didn't think it had anything to do with the fact that I'd been kissing another man. No, it was different for some other reason. Even completely shit-faced, I could tell that, but I still didn't know why.

I let my hand drop and rolled over, like I could roll away from the thoughts. A good night's sleep would help me sort things out. I'd already told Alex that nothing would change. I just had to figure out how.

I should have known sleep wouldn't be a refuge. It was strange enough that I seemed to dream about Alex all the time, so I wasn't surprised to see him. Except, this wasn't like the other dreams. We didn't sit around and talk or hang out like we normally did. Instead, it was like my brain was re-writing my memory.

We were running in the rain and getting absolutely soaked. It didn't matter that people were judging us; we were having fun. The dining hall swam into sight. I already knew we wouldn't be able to stop. In the dream, I slid to a stop against the outside wall and waited to catch Alex. He immediately began laughing when he crashed into me and couldn't seem to hold his balance. His green eyes danced with humor as he struggled to get his feet under him. Something else flashed in them. You could see every thought he had in those outrageously green things.

Kiss me.

The thought was an echo of what I'd said the other night. I wasn't sure if I said it aloud in the dream or not. Either way, he leaned forward, water dripping into his eyes. When his lips met mine, it wasn't the first accidental kiss; it was absolutely the very intentional, all-consuming second one. Like that night, I kissed him back. I didn't know why, past that's just what you did when someone kissed you. In the dream, we stood pressed together, rain falling all around us and let go, drowning in water and each other.

Thunder cracked, and I bolted upright.

Trying to shake it off was pointless; there was no way I'd be able to get back to sleep with a storm rolling overhead. As I grabbed my discarded shirt from the floor, I told myself the reason my heart was hammering so hard was because the thunder had startled me, not because of the dream. I pulled open my door, then had to fight my disappointment at seeing the living room empty.

Probably best that Alex is still asleep, considering.

My gaze rebelliously sought his door anyway in the hope that he'd miraculously appear. The mere thought of seeing him had my heart rate kicking up. I strangled the sudden urge to march over there and get him. Perhaps a more sober experiment would help clear things up. I flashed to the less-than sober attempt at clarity, the way Alex had held me close, his hand on my face as he conquered my mouth in a way that instantly set my blood on fire.

A hollow crack of thunder shook the dorm and me out of the fog. I needed something to distract my thoughts, otherwise I'd just end up in the same spiral that had led to the dream. The television would certainly offer that, but I wasn't really a fan of mindlessly vegging, and I didn't want to risk waking Alex up. I glanced at his door again. It was still firmly closed. I ignored the second, sharp sting of disappointment and wandered around the kitchen, opening and closing cabinet doors as quietly as I could.

I was about to despair when I caught sight of a stack of books on the counter. The tiny pendant light flicked on with a soft click and an even softer glow. All the covers were worn with age. These had to be the books Alex was talking about. I smiled to myself as I picked each one up and examined it. They did all look interesting, though none struck me as a romance novel like he'd implied.

He must've been messing with me.

I set them back down and looked back toward the couch.

I wonder.

I searched through the mess of papers on the coffee table, then shifted to the side table. At last, I spied the worn cover beneath a notepad. I knew I'd seen it in here.

The couch groaned in protest as I took a seat. I spared a quick glance toward Alex's still closed door before settling back and opening the book. It fell automatically to the page with the drawing I'd asked about before. I ran my fingers over the illustration. A faint whiff of something tickled my nose. I inspected the tips of my fingers, then lifted the book. Soft tendrils of lavender curled in my nose and I let out a relaxed sigh. It was strange, though, that it didn't hold the typical "book" smell, given how old it was. I couldn't help but wonder why.

With a shrug, I let the mystery go and considered the virtually ancient book. Alex might be able to pick up wherever he wanted, but I actually wanted to see what this thing was about. I flipped back to the front of the book. Alex's name greeted me in his perfectly swirled letters. Before I could succumb to the temptation to trace the elegant curves, I turned the page and started reading.

My family had been fighting the darkness for as long as I could remember. Since the day the night had taken form, we had struggled to beat it back. But the darkness was all-consuming and the battle fraught with temptation. What was one soldier in an infinite war against evil? Against Darkness?

I 'twas but seven when I met my first shade. The creature stepped from the void onto our family's land. The shock of being so brazenly approached blazed through my young body, an insult to life itself. Even at such a tender age, I knew what my response should have been. This thing was a monstrosity and yet my hand was stayed. Mayhaps the creature had spelled me to forestall its demise. It mattered not. The torches came, and it fled back to the depths that had spawned it.

Thus began my crusade to ultimately capture and destroy darkness defined. I was a man obsessed. The night itself had touched me and I would not be at peace until I hunted it down once and for all. This was my destiny.

"Storm, wake you up too?"

My entire body jerked. I looked up from the book, hoping like hell guilt wasn't plastered on my face. Alex stood just outside his room, the door open behind him, looking all kinds of disheveled. "Yeah," I replied noncommittally.

He scrubbed his hands through his hair, causing it to stick up in every direction. There was another roll of thunder and suddenly he was standing there soaked from head to toe, water dripping from his hair to puddle on the carpet.

I blinked, and the vision was gone. "What?"

"I said, do you want anything?"

I shook my head, not trusting words, then swallowed and returned to my stolen reading material. In the kitchen, I heard the faucet as he fixed something to drink. When I glanced back up, it looked like he was trying to figure out where to sit. I scooted over and gestured at the couch.

"Just sit down, Alex. It's only weird if you make it weird," I said, keeping my nose firmly in the book. I squeezed my eyes shut. Ugh, I was such a hypocrite. I was making it weird.

He didn't say anything as he sat down with his water and another book.

I'd seen him notice my reading choice, but he'd yet to comment on it. Despite my dedicated effort to resume reading, the words blurred together. I couldn't focus. Alex certainly qualified as a distraction, although maybe not the best one, considering. It didn't matter. If Alex was here, I wanted to talk to him. That he actually seemed interested in what I had to say was one of my favorite things about our friendship. It was nice to feel like I had a valid opinion.

"Do you think he knows he's in love?"

Alex looked up from his own reading with a completely neutral expression.

"In the diary," I elaborated, holding up the book with my finger in it to hold my place. "Do you think he knows?"

His face relaxed, and he set his book down. "You tell me."

"What do you mean?"

"Well, someone put notes in the margins about what they thought. It could've been the author or someone else who knew the situation.".

"I haven't seen anything." I reopened the book, and he leaned over to get a better look at where I was.

"Oh, that's because you haven't gone far enough. It starts showing up everywhere." He made to turn the pages.

"Wait, I don't want to lose my place."

He frowned, then leaned across me to grab the notebook that was still lying there. The distinct aroma of lavender floated up to curl in my nose. He tore out a page and handed it to me before sitting back. I stared at him and he got fidgety. He cleared his throat. "Sorry, I—"

"You smell like lavender."

He blinked, clearly not expecting the comment, then scooted back to his corner to retrieve his own book. "Yeah... I had trouble sleeping when we moved to England, so my mom started putting sachets of lavender under my pillow. I guess I just kept it going. Anyway, you'll eventually see handwritten notes. Full warning, I don't agree with most of them." His smile felt a little forced, but I wasn't really paying attention. If the book smelled like lavender because Alex did, that meant he probably slept with it... regularly.

I looked down at my hands curled possessively around the book. The thin piece of paper sticking out was a stark white in contrast to the aged binding. With a force of will, I loosened my grip. "This is about a Shadow Demon. That's why it's your favorite."

His mouth twitched with the start of a smile that didn't fully form, then he looked away. "I suppose you're right."

"Does he kill her?" I didn't want to read any book where that was the outcome, especially one that read like a love story.

He lifted an eyebrow. "That would ruin the ending, now, wouldn't it?"

I scowled, and he returned to his own reading material.

Such a typical bookie answer.

"Do you think it's true?"

"Do I think what is true?" he asked, once again putting his book down.

"That there was a family dedicated to wiping out Shadow Demons."

He sighed and rested against the back of the couch, his dark hair a stark contrast to the red fabric. "Honestly, it wouldn't surprise me. Fear is a really powerful motivator. Back in those days, we were more common, and like any demon race, making a mess of everything." This time, his smile felt more genuine.

The tightness in my chest eased, and I returned the smile. It was nice to see my friend again. "How many times have you read this, anyway?"

He looked sheepish. "A few."

"You know, some of this doesn't make a damn bit of sense." I waved the book around. He laughed like I hoped he would. See, we could be normal.

"Well, it was written a very long time ago."

My smile widened as he shifted to face me more squarely. "And I bet you've looked up every arcane reference."

"Maybe," he smirked.

I smiled back, feeling lighter than I had in days. "You really are a know-it-all."

"Are you going to ask me to explain parts of it or just wait for me to volunteer?" he asked, then promptly smacked me with his book.

"Watch it. I will come over there."

"Empty threat." He made to smack me again, and I snatched the book right out of his hand. His mouth fell open with an indignant cry. "Come on, Matt, you've already stolen one."

I tossed it back. "Then stop hitting me with it. And for your information, I have a better idea than swallowing my pride and asking for more help than I already have." I picked up the notebook still lying on the side table. "I'll just write my own theories and you can correct me later."

"That's also not yours."

I gave him a pointed look. "Do you have anything important in here?"

"Not really."

"Then I guess you won't mind if I borrow it."

He rolled his eyes, but kept smiling. "Maybe one of these days you'll check to see if someone else's name is on something before you decide to commandeer it."

Before he could stop me, I snatched a pen from the table and opened the small notebook to the front. Sure enough, Alexi Roman was written on the cover in his perfect penmanship.

He leaned slightly toward me to get a better look. "What are you doing?"

"You'll see." I added '& Matt' then held it out for him to see. "There, now it's communal property."

"You're a regular artist."

"You're just jealous you didn't think of it first."

He shrugged and looked around. "I haven't heard any thunder for a while. Maybe the storm is finally over. I never imagined there would be so much rain when I came out here. Everything is going to be soaked tomorrow."

At the mention of the rain, I flashed to him laughing, drenched from head to toe while trying to keep water out of his eyes. It wasn't from the dream, though; it was an actual memory, complete with every tiny detail, including the soft look in his eyes as he stared back at me.

"Hello. Matt. Are you listening?"

"What?" I asked, returning to earth.

"I said, I'm going to try to go back to sleep. Maybe you should too if you're falling asleep with your eyes open."

"You're probably right." I yawned wide enough to crack my jaw. "I'll see you later."

I waited until he'd retreated to his room. While I didn't relish trying to sleep again, he had a point. I confirmed the bookmark was in place before setting the book down and marching into my room.

Chapter 18
Demon's Advice

Alexi

I went through class in a daze. Thank goodness I already had a solid grasp of the material, because not so much as an iota of the lecture pierced my fog. All my thoughts circled on replaying that night over and over again. What should I have done differently? Had it been a mistake to admit the truth? It wasn't like I was ashamed of being gay; my mother had given me all the support any kid could want. Why should it matter that Matt knew?

Of course, knowing or not knowing the answers didn't change a damn thing. Matt did know and now nothing would ever be the same again. I wasn't even sure which one of us was being more awkward. Personally, I believed Matt was acting especially weird. While he wasn't outright avoiding me, he also wasn't exactly lingering in shared spaces.

But I couldn't lay all the blame for our suddenly strained friendship on him. It was me who'd kissed him first. And if I was being honest, my behavior had altered as well. I'd stopped yammering his ear off. I didn't initiate studying sessions. Whether that was helping or hurting, though, was anyone's guess. Maybe if I—

A hand landed on my shoulder. I yelped and lurched straight into the air, briefly shadowing.

"Whoa there. Didn't mean to startle you." Rubio chuckled and dropped his hand.

I glanced around, surprised to find myself in an unfamiliar hallway.

A crease formed between Rubio's golden brows. "You okay? I called to you twice, but you didn't seem to hear me."

"Um... yeah, I'm fine." I cleared my throat and adjusted my backpack.

He gave me a curious look, but didn't pursue the lackluster answer. "What brings you around here? Meeting a tutoring client?"

"Uh, no. I actually have no idea where 'here' is," I replied, a little abashed.

Rubio's eyebrows lifted. "You sure you're alright?"

"Totally. Just distracted lately." I chose a direction at random and started walking, secretly hoping it would lead to an exit, or at least somewhere familiar.

"Uh-huh." Rubio fell in step beside me. "I haven't been loading you with too many clients, have I? Don't want to burn you out. Especially it being your first semester and all."

I shook my head, only half listening. "No, of course not. The clients are great. Really making progress."

"What about your private tutoring lessons?"

My steps faltered, and I shot Rubio a look. "My what?"

"The private lessons. The ones with your roommate." He held his hand up to nose level. "About yay tall, really hot. You know, the lessons you're not charging for."

I scrambled for words, anything that could vaguely sound like a response, but like the broken record it had apparently become, my brain stalled out.

"Ah-ha! There is something wrong."

"No, there's not. I just... just..." No matter how much I wanted the lie to come, it remained elusive.

Rubio's face took on a more profound concern. "Hey, flirting aside, you can still talk to me. I get it, you're not interested. No worries, no hard feelings. We're friends."

"It's not that. I appreciate the offer—both of them—but I..." But I felt like someone had plopped me on a possessed merry-go-round or maybe a rocket spinning out of orbit. My thoughts were a mess and my emotional state worse.

"Alexi, talk to me, man. Let me help."

The worry in Rubio's voice officially broke me. I scanned the hallway until I found what looked like an empty room. Much as I wanted to respect Matt's right to privately discover things on his own, I needed help. "Okay, but not out here." I took off for the room, with what I expected was a very confused Rubio. The room turned out to be barely more than an oversized closet, but it was mercifully devoid of people. I waited for Rubio to clear the door, then slammed it shut. Before he could say a word, I blurted, "I kissed Matt. My roommate. Whose name is Matt."

Rubio stared at me, frozen mid word. He blinked and moved his mouth, but no sound came out.

As I flopped against the wall, I groaned and fisted my hands over my eyes. "I don't know what I was thinking. I knew fantasizing about him would get me in trouble. We'd been drinking—like a lot. We were laughing and having a good time, then I had to bugger it all up by kissing him." I dropped my hands and looked at Rubio, who still seemed to be struggling to put a whole word together.

He cleared his throat and held up a finger, then paused, as if still working to wrap his head around my haphazard explanation. "So… he knows you're gay."

I rested my head against the wall and stared up at the ceiling. "He certainly does now."

"Okay, let's break this down."

I glanced back at Rubio, simultaneously relieved to have finally told someone and even more anxious because now that it was out in the world, I couldn't pretend it hadn't happened. Not that I'd been doing such a great job of that before. "What's there to break down?"

His mouth twisted to the side in a scowl. "Seriously? What's there not to break down? You kissed your supposedly straight roommate."

"He's straight, Rubio."

He snorted. "Most people aren't half as straight as they think. They simply never take the chance to consider anything else. What did he do when you kissed him?"

"Freaked."

Rubio scowled harder. "Care to be more specific?"

I sighed hard enough to stir up some dust and straightened up. "He went all quiet, gave me a funny look, eventually said he needed a minute, then went to his room."

"Ouch." Rubio winced. "Harsh."

"It gets worse. After a few minutes, he came back, floundered trying to say I was gay, then went back to his room again."

Rubio shook his head. "Yikes, man, no wonder you're in a state."

"Not done yet."

His eyes widened.

"After another few minutes, he came back out and demanded I kiss him again."

"Did you?"

I took a deep breath and let it out. "You don't know Matt. He can be really insistent. So, yeah, I did. Except…"

"Except?" Rubio leaned forward, anticipation written clearly across his face.

"He kissed me back? At least, I think he did."

Rubio smacked me on the arm. "See, not so straight after all."

"Please, the last thing I need is more confusion. And it's not like he stuck around afterward to chat about our feelings."

"Have you talked at all about what happened?" Rubio crossed his arms and leaned against the wall opposite me.

"Not beyond him saying it doesn't matter that I'm gay." The bitter sting of tears burned my eyes. "Besides, if that was true, then why is he avoiding me? He can barely be in the same room with me long enough to review his notes.".

"Hey, hey, things will be alright." He held out his arms, and I didn't think twice about stepping into the hug. "Give him time. Sounds like this might be his first experience outside of hetero-normative expectations." Suddenly, Rubio leaned back and gave me a stern look. "Unless he said or did something hurtful that you're not telling me about, because if that's the case, I'll kick his ass."

"No, nothing like that."

Rubio gave a curt nod before enfolding me back in his embrace, backpack and all. "Good."

I relaxed and rested my head on his shoulder. It really was a shame I wasn't attracted to Rubio as more than a friend. I soaked up the comfort for a few more seconds, then pushed away. "Thanks. I guess I needed that more than I realized." I wiped at my nose with the back of my hand and hoped I hadn't gotten snot on him.

He hiked a shoulder and smiled. "That's what friends are for. But now you have to tell me what I really want to know."

"Oh? What's that?"

"How was the kiss?" He wiggled his eyebrows, and I barked out a laugh.

"Sweet night, it was incredible. Beyond incredible. Straight or not, Matt can kiss." I sighed a swoon and returned Rubio's grin.

"What are the chances of getting him to do it again?"

I snorted and rolled my eyes. "Nil. I'll count it as a miracle if we stay friends."

A crease formed on Rubio's brow. "But you do want it to happen again."

"I want a lot of things with Matt. Doesn't mean they'll ever happen."

"Doesn't mean they won't, either. Tell me how I can help." He smirked. "Besides stealing a chance to feel you up."

I couldn't help but laugh. "You're ridiculous." I sobered and let out a sigh. "In all seriousness, I do appreciate the offer, though I'm not sure what you could do. Unless you have some pearls of wisdom about how I can help us move past all of this awkwardness."

"I wish. Sadly, I think it will simply take time. Try to give him space. I hate to pitch the cliche, but it's possible that you've turned his world upside down and he's working through it. That being said, if he starts acting like a homophobic wang, don't put up with that shit."

I chuckled at Rubio's colorful word choice.

"Go ahead and laugh, but I expect you to say something if he gets out of line. You've got the whole tutoring team at your back. None of us want to see you get hurt."

"Damn it, you're going to make me tear up again." I sniffled and Rubio placed a hand on my shoulder. He gave it a good squeeze, then met my gaze.

"I know you're really hung up on this guy, but don't let that give him a free pass to be an asshole. No one deserves that."

"Who says I'm really hung up on him?" I asked, even as his words warmed my heart.

Rubio scoffed. "Pretty sure the only one it's not blatantly obvious to is your oblivious roommate."

I opened my mouth to argue that Matt wasn't oblivious, then I recalled his genuine shock at realizing I was gay, and promptly shut it.

"That's what I thought. Now what do you say we skip our next classes and grab some coffee in town or something?" He immediately held up his hands. "Promise I'm not asking you out. Just think it'd be a good idea to get off campus for a bit."

I smiled and felt myself truly relax for the first time in what felt like days. "Yeah, I'm not the skipping sort." Rubio's face fell into an exaggerated pout and I bit the inside of my cheek to keep from laughing. "You're in luck. My next class isn't for another couple of hours." Normally, I'd meet up with Matt for lunch, but given how he'd conveniently already eaten or not been hungry the last couple of days, this seemed a better alternative than eating by myself.

"Sweet. Let's sneak out of this closet like we've been up to no good and head for the main entrance of the campus."

"Really? You had to go there?" I snickered as he pushed open the door and glanced around, looking sketchy as hell.

"And miss this beautiful opportunity? Never." He held the door for me and I slipped into the hallway. "Besides, it could have been worse. I could have made a dozen different closeted jokes."

I laughed loud enough to catch someone at the far end of hall's attention and clamped a hand over my mouth. "You're the worst," I hissed as I let him take the lead.

"I think you mean the best." He slung an arm around my shoulders and dragged me even with him. "You're going to love the place I have in mind. Not only do they have amazing coffee, but rumor has it that's where your notorious teacher met her mentor."

I gasped and nearly gave myself whiplash turning to look at him. "No way."

"Yep. Not that anyone in town realizes the significance of the quaint spot, everyone being human and all."

"That's true, then. The town really doesn't know that it's sitting next to an ancient university for supernaturals? How is that even possible?"

"One word, my friend." Rubio waved his hand and wiggled his fingers. "Magic." He pushed open a set of doors and we stepped out into a cloudy afternoon. "That, and people have a tendency to see only what they expect to see. Long as we don't do anything extra supernaturally, then no one pays us any mind."

"But don't they think it's odd that none of their residents are ever accepted at the university?"

Rubio gave me a sidelong look. "Who says they're not? You should know as well as anyone that supernaturals are everywhere. Not to mention you don't have to look like a supernatural to be one. Unless, of course, you took one look at me and knew I was an incubus." He lifted an eyebrow and my jaw fell.

"You're taking the piss."

"Nope. Granted, I'm not exactly a high-level Carnal class, but I'm one hundred percent sex demon."

I laughed so hard my shoulder shook, which in no way encouraged him to let go.

"What's so funny? I'm serious."

"No, no, I believe you. But that explains sooo much."

"Not sure what the hell that's supposed to mean," he grumbled to himself.

I looped an arm around his waist and squeezed lightly. "It means you're incredibly charismatic and clearly have a way with people. You're also a pretty great friend, though now I'm a little worried I've wounded your Incubus pride by not being interested in being more than friends."

"Don't be. I'm all about the casual, and I strongly suspect you are not."

"You would be correct. It might sound a little silly, but I really do believe in true love and soul mates and all that other mushy stuff."

Rubio graced me with a soft smile, gave my shoulders a last squeeze, and released me. "Not at all."

Chapter 19
Roommate Trouble

Matt

For a supposed hole in the wall, the still unnamed pool hall Lucas and Sam frequented was incredibly well kept. Everything was clean. No one was abnormally surly. Even the food was decent. I shoved my hands in my pockets and brought my attention back to where Lucas was currently beating Sam's ass in a game of Nine Ball. He missed the seven and waved for a scowling Sam to take his shot.

Lucas glanced over at me, not remotely concerned about whether Sam could make the shot—we both knew he couldn't, not with the nine so perfectly boxed. "You've been awful quiet tonight. Not that you're much of a chatter. Is something up?"

I flashed to the image of Rubio's arm thrown around Alex's shoulders and Alex's wrapped around his waist. The anger I'd been fighting all day seethed in my stomach. Sure, I'd fucked up. Maybe I should have made more of an effort to talk about the drunken kiss, but actively blowing me off for that guy? And it wasn't like I could look at it any other way either. When class let out, I'd made a beeline to grab Alex for lunch, eager to regain some normalcy in our friendship, but he'd been nowhere to be found. It had taken thirty minutes of wandering around the building and getting lost—twice—before I'd stumbled across the pair of them.

"Matt. You still with us?"

I blinked away the memory to find Lucas and Sam both staring at me with concern. "Huh?"

They glanced at each other, then Sam spoke up. "Lucas was asking if you were alright, and you sort of... spaced."

"Shit." I wiped a hand over my face like it could somehow scrub away any of the millions of thoughts that refused to leave me alone. "Sorry, guys. My head's not really in it."

Lucas shrugged and rested his cue stick against the high-top to grab his beer. "Anything you want to talk about?"

"Not really, just roommate trouble."

Sam slammed into a chair, nearly toppling it and himself to the ground. "Tell me about it. Mine is a total slob, and he eats all my food. Never replaces any of it either. Does yours do that?"

"Uh, no... Alex and I share pretty much everything and take turns replenishing the fridge. Though we eat at the dining hall more often than not." Now that I said it out loud, I couldn't help but wonder if that was normal.

Lucas downed the last of his beer and wiped the froth from his mouth. "Lucky bastard. I'm like eighty-five percent positive my roommate is a supe of the aquatic variety."

"Like a mermaid?" I frowned as I tried to make sense of that.

"Maybe, but there are a lot more aquatic supernaturals than merfolk. Could be any of them. But whatever they are, they clearly prefer their air more wet than not. I swear the humidity in our dorm room gets so bad, it's like walking through soup. And it's murder on my hair. I have to keep an extra fan in my room just so I can sleep."

Sam rolled his eyes. "You could try talking to them. I don't know, ask what they are. Maybe if you knew, you could find better middle ground."

Lucas snorted. "Last time I tried to hint around, they stared at me while a film covered their eyes before sliding back in a weird double-blink." He shuddered, and I was right there with him. Neese did something like that and that was on top of his long tongue and hissed consonants. "I know supes come in all shapes, sizes, colors, and what have you, but you gotta understand. They didn't say a word. And I could hear the film move across their eyes. As much as I love being a werewolf, there are some perks I could do without."

Sam leaned forward on the table. "I'm guessing your roommate doesn't do that."

"Definitely not." I chuckled, feeling slightly easier. "We're both Shadow Demons, though he clearly knows more about that than I do."

"So, what's the deal? He a snob or something?" Sam tilted his chin.

I shrugged a shoulder and shifted to relax my stance. "I thought he was at first, but that doesn't seem to be the case. He's actually really nice, even been helping me with some of my classes."

Sam's lips twitched in an almost smile. "Sounds like he's a really great guy."

Lucas shot him a glare. "Did something happen?"

My heart rate quickened like it did right before a fight or when I was about to snatch and run. Did I dare tell them about what had happened? I certainly could use some solid advice, like if either of them had ever kissed a guy and what it felt like. Was it different to kissing other people? Was it all the same? Why did I feel like it was different? And why did I want to try it again?

"You don't have to talk about it if you don't want to." Lucas squeezed my shoulder and there was no way he could miss how tense I was.

Problem was, I did want to talk about it... with Alex. Then there was the whole hang up of appearing weak in front of my new friends. What would they think when they realized I clearly didn't have my shit together? Not to mention I didn't know whether or not Alex was out. But now I was going too long without talking again and I had to say something. "We got drunk together the other day."

Lucas and Sam frowned, but it was Lucas who spoke. "Okay... Someone puke or something?"

"No, no," I repeated with a forced laugh, "nothing like that. It's just now things are... weird. We may have gotten a little too honest."

"That'd do it." Sam leaned back in his chair, clearly believing he had one up on gravity. Given he was a witch, heck, maybe he did. "I can think of a few drunk truth-spells I wish I could undo. Never," he angled his hand at me, "I mean never tell a girl her dress makes her look like a cow. Even if it is cattle print."

I snorted into my drink and subsequently choked laughing. "You didn't."

"Oh, he definitely did. But he hasn't even told you the best part," Lucas said with a smirk.

"You're never going to let me live that down, are you?"

"Not on your life."

I set the remnants of my beer aside. "What's the best part?"

"This dumbass," Lucas pointed his thumb at Sam, "proceeds to create an illusion of himself as a cow-person."

Sam groaned and dropped his head to the table. "It really sucks, because I was pretty sure that was going somewhere until I went all drunk magic."

"Is that a thing?" I asked at the same time Lucas said, "That's not a thing."

"Well, it should be. I shouldn't be held liable for what my magic does when I'm shit faced," Sam huffed.

"You're ridiculous." I shook my head and straightened up. Maybe my current conundrum with Alex wasn't so bad in the grand scheme of things. "Thanks for listening, but I think I'm gonna call it a night. Hopefully next time I'll be in a better frame of mind."

"Anytime." Lucas smacked me on the back, not bothering to check his werewolf strength. I coughed out air in a big gust.

"Geez, man, what are you trying to do, kill the guy?" Sam asked.

"It's cool, I'm fine. Trust me when I say that's nothing. Caught me off guard is all." I glanced between the two of them. "You sure y'all are okay if I bounce?"

Lucas shrugged. "To be honest, I have a paper I should be writing, but I didn't want to miss a chance to hang. And someone has to make sure Sam doesn't get us all banned from here."

Sam stuck out his tongue and hopped free of his chair. It tilted alarmingly before coming to rest miraculously without falling over. Magic. That was the only word for it. "If you two are bailing, then I'm hitting up the witch bar."

I glanced at Lucas, who shook his head. "Trust me, it's better not to ask. You think he's a handful? Imagine an entire bar filled with people three times as bad." We waved to Sam as he headed deeper into town, then angled toward the university.

"I get the impression you're not too keen on witches."

"Eh, they're not all bad. Sam is one of the good ones. But they've done their fair share of harm to the supernatural community, to demons in particular." Lucas gave me a wary look. "So, you know, be careful if one seems to take an unusual interest in you."

I thought back to Misty, the goth witch from the fight club. Maybe that was why she'd given me the creeps. "Noted. Thanks for the heads-up."

"No problem." We paused at where the sidewalk diverged to the different dormitories. "And, you know, if you ever want to talk about anything, Sam and I are pretty good listeners. I mean, obviously me more than him, but you get the gist."

I laughed. "Thanks. See you around."

"See you." Lucas waved and wandered off.

With a sigh, I trudged toward Starling Hall. I opened the door to our dorm and my shoulders immediately sagged when I found no trace of Alex. So much for trying to talk to him. I flung my key on the coffee table. It settled with a loud clatter that chased me into my room. It wasn't until I finished changing into a pair of loose sweats and a relaxed shirt I realized Alex was likely with Rubio at one of their joint "tutoring" sessions.

I flopped onto the bed with a creak of springs and an irritated grumble. So much for going out to get my mind off of things. I stared up at the ceiling as silence settled around me, my thoughts already orbiting around Alex. Was he in a relationship with Rubio and that's why he was avoiding me? Because he'd never meant to kiss me in the first place? Did Alex kiss Rubio the way he'd kissed me?

I swallowed hard and licked my lips. I'd certainly never kissed anyone the way I'd kissed Alex, but it had been kind of hard not to. The way his lips had perfectly fit mine wasn't anything I'd experienced before. My eyes fluttered shut as I remembered what he'd tasted like—sweet, rich mango from the tangaroa cocktail we'd been drinking. It had kind of been like an Amaretto Sour, but I'd wanted something sweeter in the hope Alex would like it. There were plenty of other things in the drink that should have been there, but on Alex's lips there was only sweetness.

My thoughts took on a life of their own as I stopped remembering the way his tongue had curled around mine in a delicate invitation to explore and imagined doing it again... on purpose. I wasn't alone in the dorm, moping in my room. I was with Alex, leaning over him to taste his smiling lips. My breath hitched as his long fingers curled in my hair and pulled me closer. A distant part of me wished I'd had the courage to touch him back that night, then I'd know what he felt like beneath my fingers, too.

Between one heartbeat and the next, I was suddenly the one on their back with Alex hovering over me. His grin was confident as he closed the distance to capture my mouth once more. Everything Alex did was confident, it was intoxicating. I couldn't help but wonder if he knew that, even as the fantasy kiss deepened and stole my breath. But it wasn't enough. I wanted more, wanted to know.

Thankfully, this was all in my head and my imagination was more than happy to supply me with exactly that. Alex's lips abandoned mine to trail along my neck. All I had to pull from were past make-out sessions with other people for what it might feel like to have his lips pressing against the tender skin, and I suspected the experiences would pale to the real thing. That didn't stop me from indulging, though. As if sensing my wavering focus, fantasy-Alex shifted to look down at me. An apology was already on my tongue—I shouldn't be doing this. It was wrong—then I saw the wicked gleam in his emerald eyes.

He lowered his mouth once more to capture mine with a kiss that had my fingers and toes curling in the sheets. Aching want pumped through every vein so hard it was a wonder I didn't explode. Then Alex's hand slipped beneath the band of my sweatpants. I gasped as I mirrored the movement and nearly came undone. He teased my lips, but didn't relent. Release danced closer and closer with each stroke, making my extremities tingle and my mind fuzzy—everything except Alex. His name became a needy chant in my mind as he—I—we, kept going.

"Hey, Matt, did you call?" My bedroom door opened to reveal a confused Alex.

I squeaked out a yelp and yanked a pillow over my crotch so fast it was a wonder I didn't break something important. "What the hell!"

Alex echoed my squeak at realizing what he'd interrupted. "Shit." He tried to back out and ran into the doorjamb. "Fuck. Sorry. I could have sworn you called my name." He attempted unsuccessfully to leave again and muttered more curses. "Clearly, I was, uh, wrong. I'll just... leave you to it." Finally, he righted himself enough to leave, and the door slammed shut.

For one insane moment, I contemplated calling him back. Maybe if I could see the fantasy all the way through, I could finally get the answers that eluded me. Like was this something I really wanted? Why now? Why Alex?

I smacked the spare pillow beside me so hard it made my palm sting and flopped back, forgetting that my main pillow was now sitting on my lap. My head bounced uncomfortably. I covered my face with the pillow and screamed as hard as I could. People said letting it all out could help make you feel better. But I didn't feel better. I felt as lost as ever. I dropped the pillow back and stared up at the ceiling, almost exactly like I had when this horrible night had started.

"What the hell is wrong with me?"

Chapter 20
Talking in Your Sleep

Alexi

I was at a complete loss for what to do with Matt. The first few days had been beyond awkward. Then I walked in on him. Where I'd expected the weirdness hovering between us to get infinitely worse, he acted as if nothing had happened at all. It wasn't like he acted like he didn't know I was gay, more like he was going out of his way to show that nothing was different, nothing had changed. But it had, everything had. Try as he might, there was no way to put the genie back in the bottle.

I looked up at him across the library. The light filtering through tall stained-glass windows fell in dappled patches on the cluster of deep mahogany tables. Within the cathedral-like building, Matt looked more like an angel than ever. He was sitting with a group of people that seemed vaguely familiar. He'd talked to them before and I was pretty sure he'd hung out with them beyond class as well. Which was great. I loved he was making friends; he needed more friends. The trouble was, I was almost positive he was only branching out to give me space.

Even from half a room away, I could tell he didn't want to be talking to them. I knew Matt. Any normal day, he would've been right next to me, making jokes and getting us endless rebukes to be quiet. I hated that I'd taken that from him. My heart ached with guilt, and I refocused my attention on my own work. I'd caught him glancing over here enough times to be sure that if he saw me looking, he'd come over.

Only the muffled sound of distant voices disturbed the bubble of silence I'd cocooned myself in. I turned another page of the text I was perusing, still undecided on whether I wanted to use it for the Demonic History research project. At the muted scrape of a chair, I glanced up to find Matt sitting less than two feet away, watching me.

"You know, we are allowed to do the project in groups." He rested his head on crossed arms. The move put him squarely within arms' reach, his head practically in the book I was currently eliminating.

I checked the impulse to run my hand through his hair. That I had such a strong desire to do that even after everything that had happened, was exactly why everything was so strained, whether he wanted to admit it or not. "It looks like you have a group," I said as casually as I could, moving the book farther away from his face and temptation.

He scoffed and leaned back. "Them? They still think they can get away with the class text. You and I both know there's a perfect book sitting in the dorm." He wanted to use my book. For some reason, that hurt.

"Then use it, Matt. I'm still looking."

"Alex."

I scanned the next page. I'd lost count how many times I'd read it since he'd pulled up.

"Alex, look at me."

I took a deep breath and did as he asked. Ice-blue eyes snared me, just like they always did. I felt like a fly caught on a web and I didn't even have the luxury of pretending that he didn't notice anymore.

"I won't use the book without you."

"Matt, I don't think-"

"You know what I think?" he cut me off. "I think you need to get your head out of your ass and start acting like my friend."

I was completely taken aback. "Why do you want to do a project with me, anyway?"

"Because you're my friend and you're the only one worth doing a project with. Now get off your ass." He hooked my arm and hoisted me out of my chair. "If we're going to use that book, then we're going to need some reference materials," he declared, then commenced dragging me over to the stacks.

His grip was like a vise, as if he was worried I'd bolt if he let go. Truthfully, I might have given the opportunity, but by the time towering shelves of books surrounded us, I'd given up fighting him. He finally released me and started thumbing through spines.

"You're more familiar with the memoir. What sort of references do you think we'll need?" He pulled out a dusty tome and flipped through it. "Translators for sure. Maybe even genealogy texts." When I didn't move or respond, he glanced over at me out of the corner of his eye. "Are you going to help or just stand there? Come on, what do we need?"

"You know, you can be really demanding."

"Are you saying you don't want to be my partner?"

I hesitated. That was a loaded question if I'd ever heard one. "No," I replied awkwardly.

"Good, then get to work."

I rolled my eyes and started perusing the options. At least we were in the right section of the library. "We'll definitely need an old English translator and Latin, of course. I'm a little rusty," I added.

"Of course, you know Latin," he mumbled.

"I didn't say I know Latin. It's just been a while since I looked up some of those passages."

"Whatever you say, Alex."

I scowled at his blatant sarcasm, which he pointedly ignored. "You know what," I looked around at the faded titles, "I think we're in the wrong aisle. These are translations. We need translators."

He swiveled around and began marching down the aisle. At the end, he hooked a right to go to another row.

"Wrong way," I called after him. Almost immediately, he crossed back the other way. "You are absolutely ridiculous," I said when I caught up to him.

He spun to face me, his blue eyes holding a touch of heat. "Look, we both know that Demonic History will never be my best class. It is, however, yours. So, if you could stop being selfish for one minute and give me a hand, I would really appreciate it."

I was thoroughly ashamed of myself. Here I was, being so stuck in my own head that I couldn't even be there for my friend. He wasn't exaggerating that history wasn't his best subject. He'd need a stellar project if he had a hope of doing anything more than scraping by with a pass.

"You're right. I'm sorry." I glanced around at the books surrounding us. "This seems more promising. Now, if I'm looking at this right, the old English should be on this side." I indicated the shelves closest to Matt. "See if you can find one that has old English and middle English. I'm going to go a little further down to see if I can scare up a decent Latin one that's not overly convoluted."

"Okay." He instantly turned to inspect the bindings for a relevant title.

I left him to it and walked away to see if I could accomplish my task. After about half an hour, I had a couple of hopefuls, but the sounds of Matt's frustration were only increasing.

"What's the matter?" I asked in too loud a whisper. The noise earned me a shush from someone sitting at a nearby table. I grabbed my small assortment and walked back to where he was. Knowing Matt, he would shout and get us both scolded, or worse, kicked out.

"Are you sure we need middle English?"

"I feel like it would be prudent."

"Prudent or not, I don't think it's here." He huffed.

I stepped up behind him to get a better look and started scanning titles. "This is the only place it would be." I adjusted my focus to search the next shelf up.

"I'm telling you, I've checked like three times. It's not here."

I smiled and reached over him to grab a book that claimed to have both translations. "You're such a dork. It's right here."

"It's not my fault I'm short," he grumbled. "You're just freakishly..." He turned around and trailed off.

I hadn't considered how close I was, and the move brought us face to face. He looked up at me and then immediately down. From a distance, I probably looked like I had him caged, with my arm still extended for the book. The smell of sage enveloped me. I'd kissed him before and the desire to do so again was overwhelming. I was pretty sure he'd kiss me back. That was, if I hadn't imagined it the other day. It wouldn't take much, maybe another half inch.

The roaring in my ears was so loud, I thought for sure it was going to draw another reprisal to be quiet. It looked like he was breathing hard, but I couldn't hear over the noise, only feel his breath on my lips. "This is a bad idea," I whispered.

His lips parted, and I wanted more than anything to taste them again. He wet them and swallowed before responding. "It'll be fine." He shadowed out, materializing behind me.

My hand not holding the book fisted by my side. It just wasn't possible to be friends with someone you were in love with, but Matt was refusing to take no for an answer.

"Do you think we'll need all of these?"

I took a deep breath to steady myself before facing him. "Let me see what you've got."

He passed me his stack. After a quick look, I put three back on the shelf and gave him the one I'd retrieved and one other he'd found.

"That should be good for now. If we need something else, you can come back." I ran my hand through my hair absently.

I don't know how I'm going to make this work.

There wasn't really anything else to say, so I grabbed my stack and headed for the checkout.

"Alex."

I stopped, but didn't turn around. It was bad enough he couldn't even look me in the eye a minute ago. Why was he so damned determined? "Yeah?"

Suddenly, he was in front of me, the reference books tucked beneath his arm. "We're still doing this together, right? Partners?" He held out his hand.

I looked at it skeptically, not sure I trusted myself to touch him.

At least he didn't spit in it.

"Partners," I finally said, accepting the hand. When I went to let go, though, he refused to release it, tightening his grip instead. I looked at him, a little alarmed. The blue of his eyes was like glass and sharp enough to cut.

"And friends. Best friends. I'm not going anywhere, Alex, so you might as well get used to it."

The rush of cold air on my hand said that he'd finally dropped it. I stood rooted to the spot as I watched him go down to the end of the aisle. He looked back to see why I wasn't following, and I quickly hurried to catch up.

The walk back to the dorm was relatively quiet. We made a pit stop at the dining hall for snacks and immediately got started when we got in. I set up things on the breakfast table while he plopped on the couch. He could say things were normal all he wanted, but his position did not invite company. His legs stretched all the way across, barring anyone from joining him. I sat down at the breakfast table, expecting to work in silence. I should have known better.

"What should our topic be?" he asked.

I fought back a groan. "You mean you didn't already have something in mind?"

"Well... no. I figured you would."

I rubbed my forehead. He was going to be the death of me. "Let me get this straight. You bullied me into doing this project with you and you don't even have a thesis?"

"When you say it like that, it sounds awful. And I didn't bully you. You agreed."

I scoffed. "After you dragged me across the length of the library and made me feel like a selfish prat."

"I don't recall doing any of those things."

"That's because you have a selective memory," I mumbled to myself.

"I heard that."

"And hearing," I added louder.

"Okay, what if we did the research project on the knight?"

"I don't follow. It needs to be a history project. We can't do it off of one person. Especially when we don't really know anything about them... like their name."

"No, but we could do it on a whole family. It's the first thing he says. 'My family had been fighting the darkness for as long as I could remember'. I could be wrong, but that sounds like it's an entire family that's been doing this for generations."

Okay, that idea held water. "You're not wrong, but how do we prove it?"

"First, we'll have to translate all the odd bits, and of course, I need to finish reading it. That would probably help."

"You have got to be kidding me. You haven't even finished it yet?" I stared at the back of the couch in disbelief.

Judging by the shuffling sounds, he was fidgeting. "I've been a little distracted, okay? I'll work on it now."

"And what am I supposed to do while you have the book?"

He snorted. "I know you're not going to pretend that you don't have this thing virtually memorized."

I made a face at his back. "Cheater."

He didn't respond except to turn another page. I saw him pick up a pencil and heard the telltale scratch of graphite against paper. At least he was taking this seriously and taking notes.

I pulled over an empty notebook and started making notes about the things I could remember needing translation. It was rough going, but I was confident that I was getting at least a good chunk. I'd never tried to see how much I could recall on my own before and was intrigued by how many pages I filled.

Suddenly, I realized I couldn't hear the scratch of writing anymore.

I swear.

I extricated myself from the table and walked around the side of the couch to see his head resting on his chest. The bugger was out cold. I let out a sigh. He may be hell-on-wheels awake, but asleep? All the innocence he didn't want the world to know about was plain to see.

My fingers itched to comb through his hair, but I really didn't want to risk waking him. I reined in the impulse and looked at the book propped against his knee. If he wasn't using it, then I certainly could. I leaned over, careful not to disturb him. One episode was enough for today. By some miracle, the pencil was still in his hand. I squinted at the paper in the book.

Cheeky bastard hadn't been taking notes at all, he'd been sketching on the bookmark.

I leaned a little further to get a better look. The image was still mostly unformed, but I had a sneaking suspicion it was a Shadow Demon. Even unfinished, I could still tell he was quite good.

Surprises everyday Matthew Duncan.

I shook my head and ever so slowly reached for the book. I was debating whether to pull it up in one swift motion or try to ease it from his grasp when he shifted in his sleep. He took a deep breath that brought him alarmingly close to where I was hovering just overhead.

"Alex." My name was barely even a whisper.

I looked down at him, not sure if I'd heard right, to find his eyes still squeezed tightly shut.

He shifted again, his face taking on an anxious expression. "Don't."

With one word, my heart broke to pieces.

I straightened up, abandoning my quest for the book and tried not to lose my shit right there in the living room. Matt might not say anything to my face, but it was clear he was struggling. I wanted to run to the safety of my room, to escape this unfolding nightmare, yet my feet stayed rooted. There wouldn't be any comfort for me there, just more misery when he eventually woke up and demanded my presence yet again, despite everything.

His face took on additional levels of anxiety. "I'm sorry."

I blinked.

What?

He shifted restlessly. The dream seemed to go from bad to worse. Seriously questioning my life choices, I squatted next to him. My hand hovered above his arm. Did I really want to do this?

He groaned and his face twisted in what could only be pain. Strained as our friendship had become, I couldn't sit here and watch him suffer. In a moment of bravery, I reached out and touched his shoulder. When he didn't react, I gave him a light shake.

"Matt. Matt." Another shake.

Stubborn even in your sleep.

"Matt, it's okay. Wake up." At the next shake, he startled up, eyes wild and nearly stabbing me with the pencil clutched tightly in his fist. "Easy, it's alright. You were just dreaming."

Finally, his alarmed gaze focused on me. I was surprised to see the fear almost instantly be replaced by relief. "What happened?" He broke the contact and pushed himself up.

"You fell asleep reading." I gestured to the still open book.

He looked over at it, confused, then snapped it shut, hiding his sketch.

I ignored the unusual behavior. "Maybe you should go to bed."

He nodded his head. "You're probably right. I haven't been sleeping well. Should have known it would eventually catch up with me."

A sharp pain lanced through my chest. I couldn't help but feel responsible. He was lying about coping, that much I could tell. I got out of the way as he swiveled his legs around to get up.

He set the book on the side table and scrubbed at his face. If I hadn't been such a mess myself, I might have laughed. He didn't say another word, just stood and shuffled off to his room, looking very much like a zombie.

I eyed the discarded book. After seeing his reaction, I was now keen to get a better look at that drawing. I was just about to pick it up when he shuffled back into the room substantially faster than he'd left.

He looked around like he'd already forgotten what he was searching for, then stepped over to retrieve the book. Again, in perfect silence, he disappeared into his room, closing the door firmly behind him. So much for me doing more research.

Chapter 21
Back to Normal

Matt

The dreams were steadily driving me insane. Gone were the days of reliving our day. Now it was always Alex kissing me. Alex kissing me in the rain, in the stacks, on the couch, in the kitchen, on the floor, in the training room. Anywhere we'd had a close call, my sleeping mind followed through with the natural conclusion. No interaction was spared. And it didn't matter what I did or how I acted when awake.

If I pretended nothing was wrong, that nothing had changed, we inevitably ended up too close. I was starting to think that was actually my fault. But if I tried to give us each some space, I was absolutely miserable, and he got sullen, not that he'd never admit it. I continued hanging out with the guys from our math class. They were cool, albeit a little preoccupied with picking up chicks. I'd tried that too, but hadn't shared their single-minded focus.

As confusing as the dreams were, they were better than the nightmares. Without fail, if I didn't spend at least a good part of the day talking with Alex, then horrible visions of him leaving, of never getting to see or laugh with him again, plagued my nights. I needed to figure this out. Preferably before my nightmares became self-fulfilling prophecies. Why was I having any of these dreams in the first place? I'd never dreamed before I came here, not with any level of detail anyway. But even that first night in the dorm, I'd been accosted with vivid dream after vivid dream. And now they'd all escalated. For fuck's sake, he'd walked in on me rubbing one out thinking about him.

I shook my head and finished packing my bag. Was it me? I could always get Alex to kiss me again. But there was no way he'd do it on his own. He was already tiptoeing around me like I'd turn on him any minute. That made me sad. I'd never hurt him, at least not intentionally. I walked into the living room with the bag slung over my shoulder. Alex, of course, was already ready, though I was a little surprised he'd waited for me.

"Good morning," I said, trying to sound cheerful.

"Morning," he replied without looking up from the research book.

I sagged. He wouldn't even look at me. I'd hoped that getting him to do the class project with me would help to resume some normalcy, but that wasn't looking to be the case. "You ready to go?" I shifted my pack.

"Of course." He shut the book and stood up in one fluid motion. I couldn't help but notice the grace with which he moved. I certainly wasn't graceful like that.

"Alex."

He looked over at me. Did I have the same circles under my eyes as he did? "What?"

I stalled out. What could I say? That I missed my friend? How things used to be? That I was having terrible nightmares about him disappearing? Or even better, that I was dreaming of making out with him and it was confusing as hell? All of these things I should have been able to talk to my best friend about and yet, I couldn't seem to say anything. "Nothing, we should get going. Don't want to be late."

He opened the door. "Since when do you care about being late?"

I caught a faint hint of teasing and glanced at him hopefully. "Since we have an actual test coming up."

"After class today, do you want to go to the dining hall and compare notes?"

I smiled. He was actually acting like his usual self. "Is that when you'll point out that I've been taking notes on all the wrong things?"

"Probably." He gave me a crooked grin.

The tension coiled inside of my chest loosened ever so slightly.

"Of course, this assumes that there are actual notes in your workbook and not just a bunch of doodles."

My grin faltered. It had been stupid to hope he hadn't seen the bookmark. I wasn't even sure why I'd started sketching him, and now he knew. I scrambled to come up with some kind of explanation that wouldn't dig me in any deeper than I already was.

"I didn't realize you were such an artist. It's a Shadow Demon, right? Self-portrait?"

My feet froze. He didn't know. He must not have seen the whole thing. Sure, it was nowhere near being done, but I'd thought for sure he'd seen both sides of the folded page. "Um, yeah..." He could assume whatever he liked.

"Have you always been a drawer?"

"I don't know, maybe? I've scribbled forever, though all it's ever done is get me into trouble."

"I can imagine, especially after you've tricked your friend into doing all the hard work." He bumped me with his elbow.

He'd made it a point not to touch me at all for days and my entire body was viscerally aware of the contact. My heart beat a little faster and my palms instantly started to sweat. I scanned him for any sign that the touch was anything more than a friendly nudge, but there was nothing. He was the same Alex he always was. The bitter taste of disappointment filled my mouth. I swallowed it down and forced a laugh.

"I'll try to be a little more focused." Which would be a lot easier after I could figure out what was going on with me. I was even getting sloppy at the fight club. Neese didn't appreciate that his golden goose suddenly couldn't perform as advertised.

"It might also help if you weren't holding the book hostage. I could use it for those translations, you know."

"Right." Of course, the book. That was why he was looking at me funny. Not because I was acting weird. "I'm almost done." There was no way I was letting him get his hands on that book with the bookmark still inside.

The day's lessons were a blur. Most of the classes focused on review since the most weighted exams were coming up. Alex said that was normal, but I thought he was fibbing. Granted, I didn't exactly have stellar attendance where school was concerned, so maybe it was? It didn't really seem possible to have already gone through an entire semester. Though I supposed summer semesters were a little shorter. At any rate, it was more difficult to focus than usual since all I could think about was studying with Alex afterwards.

"Do you know what classes you'll sign up for in the fall?" Alex asked when we settled in the cafeteria. Unsurprisingly, the oval building was bustling with students.

I shrugged. I hadn't really thought about it. Honestly, I'd assumed we'd just take all the same again.

He gave me a considering look. "You should sign up for Advanced Spells."

"Why?" I asked, pulling out my notes, which mercifully were without too many sketches.

"I think you have a knack for it. And it's one of the few classes where you didn't really need any help."

"Yeah, but intro is basic and advanced..."

"Is not?" he finished for me.

I rolled my shoulders. I supposed it was a little excessive to take all the same classes together.

"I can't believe Vera is making everyone continue taking Battle Tactics," Alex continued in the wake of my silence. "She didn't even make it optional."

I let out a sigh, grateful for the topic change. I didn't want to take different classes than Alex. While it was nice that he'd be able to tutor me if we had the same course load, I knew the real reason had nothing to do with school and everything to do with the dreams keeping me up half the night. I pushed that line of thought away and cleared my throat. "I'm pretty sure she knows you don't like her. Maybe if you weren't so focused on that, you'd like the class more."

"I told you, it's not that I don't like her or that I don't like the class. I just don't see the point. The Rebellion is over. Why do we need battle training?"

I plucked at the frayed edge of a notebook and thought about all the ways a class like Battle Tactics could have helped me over the years. "Battle Tactics is more than training. It teaches you to trust your instincts. You never know when you might need to defend yourself, and if you do, you need to have confidence in your powers and your reactions." Which I currently did not.

"Wow, Matt, that was really enlightened." He stared at me for a minute that felt like an hour, his green eyes looking into me as if they could see every wayward thought I'd had over the last few weeks. When he finally blinked, it was as though a tether had been snapped. "Fine, I guess I can try to be a little more open-minded about it. Besides, it's not like I can do anything about it, anyway. Now show me what you've got."

I maneuvered my notes around the spoons stuck in the table. It was kind of awesome that this had become our spot, a place that was purely ours.

"Let's see," he mused aloud as he scanned through them.

I watched as his emerald eyes roved over each page, patiently waiting for him to make a pronouncement of deficiency. Suddenly, I realized he was on a page with no notes at all, just a picture that took up most of the space.

His fingers brushing lightly over the penciled sketch. "This is really impressive. Did you do this from memory?" He lifted his head to look at me and I got a better view of what he was referencing. It was a replica of the illustration from the book we were doing our research project on.

"What do you think about the extension of the report?" I asked, trying to shift the conversation back. The last thing I needed was him recognizing the similarities between the illustration and the bookmark sketch.

He turned to the next page and held back a relieved sigh. "I suspect it's because no one's taking it seriously. I overheard the TA say that they might just turn it into a rollover assignment."

"That wouldn't be too bad. I had no idea how difficult it was going to be to find information about that family."

"Same here, but I wouldn't get too excited. That would mean they expect a full-on research thesis. As in, not a few pages."

I didn't bother stifling my groan.

"It'll be fine, Matt. Trust me, the paper will be epic."

"I hope you're right. But that also means that I'm going to have to dominate this final."

Alex sat back and laced his fingers behind his head, his usual picture of self-confidence. The position made him look absurdly tall and relaxed. I envied him that, not just the height, but that it seemed like he'd had an easier life. "That's what you've got me for," he said with a smile.

It was nice to see him acting normal. Which made what I had in mind to figure my shit out that much worse. I tried not to think about it too much as we resumed studying. Apparently, my notes weren't as abysmal as I feared, and we made some good headway. Still, I wasn't taking any chances. I actually liked it here and wasn't ready to get booted. Plus, I still had to figure out my deal with Alex.

The week of finals, I stayed up every night studying until I went cross-eyed. I even skipped the fight club Tuesday and Thursday—I was too distracted to be any good. By the time I actually sat down to take the test, I was positive I was going to blow it. Alex naturally wasn't concerned and kept trying to convince me not to be as well, but I couldn't help it. True or not, it felt like a lot was riding on this one grade. Rather than join him back at the dorm, I lurked outside the classroom and waited for the grades to be posted. Alex had tried to explain that it could take days, if not weeks, to get the grades; mercifully, Vera had announced she'd be getting them to us by the end of the day of our last exam. No one wanted to talk about why she would do that, but her threat about failing loomed heavy on my mind.

I feared I'd put a groove in the ground as I paced the short stretch of hall. The door across from our Battle Tactics classroom opened and Vera walked out. I caught sight of someone in the room behind her, and for a moment, I thought it was Alex. Except it couldn't be: he hated her, and I knew for a fact he'd gone back to the dorm. The door swung shut with a thud and she walked over.

"I'm impressed, Matt."

I scowled at her. Just because I was here didn't mean I'd forgiven her for locking me up. I'd like to see how funny she thought it was if I warded her in a room for two weeks.

She let out an aggrieved sigh. "Let it go already. You were a flight risk. I'd already lost so many others. I couldn't take the chance that you'd bolt before I could get you here. Especially since you're doing so well." She held up a stack of papers and shuffled through them. "Here we are. It looks like you've brought up all of your grades across the board. Math and literature seem to be doing well. I'm a little surprised you didn't do better in Battle Tactics. I would have thought that was right up your alley."

She peered closer at the page with unmasked surprise. "Yet you are doing spectacularly well in Shadow Magic. I hope you consider enrolling in Advanced Spells." She winked. "Don't worry, I won't tell anyone. But I imagine you don't want to hear me prattle on about your classes."

I shuffled from foot to foot, eying the stack of papers, curious if anyone would be sent home.

"Here, this one is yours and I imagine Alexi won't mind you bringing him his." She held out the papers.

I snatched them and surveyed the page for the only grade I was worried about. I couldn't believe my eyes when I saw the 'B' next to Demonic History.

She glanced back at the room she'd left before saying, "History wasn't my best subject either, though I hear you have a killer thesis for Demonic History II next semester." She gave me a warm smile, I was tempted to return. "Congratulations, Matt. What are you going to do now?"

"Celebrate." I couldn't believe it; all of our hard work had paid off. I'd get to stay. Alex would be pleased.

Alex.

I switched the pages to see how he'd done. All As, no surprise there. Even then, I knew he'd want the paper.

"Any plans in particular?"

I narrowed my eyes at Vera. "Why?"

"There's no need to be defensive. I was just asking." She shook her head. "Go celebrate with your friend, Matt."

I took that as my dismissal and ran. When I opened the door to our room, Alex was sitting upside down on the couch with his feet over the top. Man, he was weird, but he was mine.

Chapter 22
Truth or Dare

Alexi

Sitting upside down on the couch was undoubtedly odd, but it was what I usually did when left to my own devices. Plus, it made for some pretty hilarious views. Like Matt standing on the ceiling when he was actually standing in the doorway. I smiled at him, echoing the grin on his face. "I take it you got the grades?"

"Yep." He waltzed into the room with a box under one arm and a couple of papers poking out.

"Well, how did you do?"

He pulled out the papers, and they floated down onto my stomach. "See for yourself."

I picked them up and read over the first page. "These are mine." I wasn't too surprised at the final grades, though I certainly hadn't expected to get an 'A' in Battle Tactics.

"The other one, Alex."

I switched the pages and immediately spun so I was right side up again. The move was far too fast, and my head swam for a moment. "Matt, this is amazing! I knew you could do it. I told you you'd knock out the Demonic History final."

He zipped around the couch holding a bottle and two glasses, as well as a few beers. "Which is why we're celebrating." He set the items down and started filling the shot glasses.

All of my happy, relaxed feelings vanished. "This didn't go so well last time."

He passed me the shot anyway. "Drink," he ordered.

"But, Matt..."

"Drink."

I did as I was told, and he refilled the short glass. "I'm serious, Matt, we can't just sit around and drink," I argued even as I knocked back what turned out to be tequila.

"You're right." He passed me a third shot. He held up his glass, and we downed them at the same time. "We'll just have to make sure we're doing something this time."

"Like what?" I scoffed, accepting the beer he passed me.

"We could play a game," he suggested before taking an additional shot and sitting on the couch.

"What sort of game? I swear if you say drinking, then I'm out."

"Okay, fine." He laughed. "What would you prefer?" He leaned into the cushions, looking completely relaxed, his dark hair fanning over his eyes.

"How should I know? It's not exactly like we have anything lying around." I scanned the room for the games we definitely didn't have. "I'm not really a fan of cards, not that I have any. That doesn't really leave much. I suppose there's always truth or dare." I chuckled, because no way were we playing that.

Matt leaned forward with a gleam in his eye. "Okay."

I did a double take. "Wait. What?"

"I said, okay. We can play truth or dare. You can go first."

My mouth opened and closed uselessly. He was serious. I noticed another shot sitting patiently on the coffee table. I tossed it back and shook off the burn. "All right, but rules." My tongue was already feeling a little fuzzy. There was also a noticeable lack of snacks by the alcohol, which was odd, considering Matt seemed perpetually hungry. If I didn't know any better, I'd swear he was intentionally trying to get me drunk.

"Rules," he mimicked, giggling.

Great, he's already tipsy.

Then I realized I was giggling, too.

"Enough. Focus, Matt." He put on an air of intense concentration and it took me a moment to pull it together enough to continue. "Okay, we can play, but you can't choose the same thing more than twice in a row. The third automatically has to be the other."

"What do you mean?" His face squished in confusion. It was adorable.

"I mean, you can't just choose dare. I know you, Matt."

He frowned. "That also means you can't just choose truth."

I stuck out my tongue, earning a cheeky grin.

"You go first."

"Does that mean I ask first or I pick first?" I took a sip of the beer he passed me.

He rolled his eyes. "Truth or dare."

"Truth." I laughed when he gave an even more exaggerated eye roll.

"What is the dorkiest thing in your room?"

I shrugged and swirled the half empty bottle. "I guess that depends on who you ask."

"I'm asking you."

"Um, I don't know." I went through a mental inventory of the things in my room for something he would deem dorky. "Oh! I have a poster of the university from when I was like seven."

He snorted. "You do not."

"I totally do. Okay, you: truth or dare."

"Dare"

"Of course." I fought the urge to roll my eyes right back at him. Maybe I could dissuade him from constantly choosing a dare by making the first one awful. I noticed he'd already kicked off his socks and shoes. I shifted and looked him dead in the eye with as straight a face as I could muster. "I dare you to lick the bottom of your foot."

He didn't even hesitate, just grabbed his ankle and dragged his tongue from heel to toe.

I cringed and gave a full body shake. "That's disgusting."

He coughed through a grimace. "No kidding." He washed away the taste with another shot of tequila and a swallow of beer. "Another?"

I accepted the fresh beer but declined the shot. "Truth."

"You didn't even let me ask. Fine, you want to play like that." He gave me a serious look, his eyes squinted and his luscious mouth pursed with intensity. "When was your first kiss?"

"Oh, goodness," I gasped and sat back. "I don't even remember."

"Liar."

"Busted. Alright, my first technical kiss would be Carla Rushing when I was ten." I ducked my head at the confession.

Matt spit out some of his beer. "No shit."

"But, the one that I would consider my first was Brandon later that year. For the record, I never saw it coming. What about you?" I asked.

He scowled behind his beer. "Hey, I didn't choose anything."

"You're choosing truth." I poured him a shot. "Come on, cough it up."

"Fine. I was twelve. Shut up," he added when I snickered. "It was Michelle Carter, and she told me I was terrible."

"You are definitely not terrible."

"Thank you," he said, clinking his bottle against mine. "I believe you are up for a dare."

I groaned. "Please have mercy."

"I don't know. You look pretty hungry."

I cocked my head to the side, dubious about where this might be heading.

"Go into the kitchen and pick whatever snack you want."

If feeding myself was the dare, then I wasn't going to complain. I vacated the couch, grabbed a bag of crisps from the cupboard, then plopped back down.

"Now, open it without your hands or feet."

I gaped at him. "How am I supposed to do that?"

"I don't know, it's your dare. Get creative."

I thought about it a moment and then tried to use my teeth, but the damn thing wouldn't hold still.

"Ah-ah. No hands."

"Curse you, Matt. I actually am really hungry." In a stroke of inspiration, I dropped the bag and caught it with my arm, then used the air already in the bag to force it open. The bag made a loud pop and crisps went everywhere.

Matt fell off of the couch he was laughing so hard.

"Shut up," I said through my own laughter. "Go get me another bag while I clean up this mess."

He returned with a couple as well as a few other snack items, which were a little more substantial. "I believe I'm up, and since you hijacked my last one, I'm going with dare."

"Alright, Mr. Daredevil, I dare you to do a body shot," I challenged, waving the half full bag of broken crisps.

He looked genuinely surprised. "Did you really just... Okay." He walked to the kitchen then returned with the salt shaker and some limes I didn't know we had. "Lift your shirt."

I clutched the bag to my chest. "What? Why?"

"So, I can do the body shot."

"Yeah, so? What do I need to lift my shirt for?" He reached out to lift it for me and I forced it back down. "Cut it out."

He gave me a scornful look. "You can't dare me to do something and then refuse to let me do it." He pointed at me. "That's cheating."

I dusted crumbs off, glad I hadn't sat back down yet. "I still don't see what my shirt has to do with this."

He stopped trying to move the article and looked back at me. "You have no idea what a body shot is, do you?"

I shifted uncomfortably. "No."

He shook his head, laughing to himself. "Well, you're about to learn. Quit being such a prude."

Stunned, I stopped holding the fabric down and let him lift the shirt to reveal my stomach.

"Damn," he whistled. "This just isn't even right. I mean, come on." His hand glided warmly over my exposed skin, and I flushed from head to toe.

"Matt," I tried to admonish, though I sounded more strangled than anything.

"I'm sorry, but it's not fair. Some of us have to actually try if we want to look like this." His finger traced along my abdomen while my breathing devolved into shaky panting.

"You look fine, Matt."

"Not like this, I don't." If he didn't stop touching me, we were going to have bigger problems than his lack of self-esteem.

"Would you just get on with it?"

"Alright." The flash in his eye was positively wicked. He grabbed a lime and squeezed it enough to get the juice out, then rubbed it on my abdomen. It seemed unnecessarily low to me, but then I didn't really know what this was supposed to entail. "Lean back a bit," he ordered.

"Why?"

"So, the salt doesn't just go on the floor." Curious about what he meant, I did it. He sprinkled salt where he had rubbed the lime and reached back to grab the shot he'd already poured.

Oh, no. Please don't do what I think you're going to do. Please no.

It was all wishful thinking. In one expert move, Matt tossed back the shot and then licked the salt right off of me. My eyes rolled into the back of my head and I prayed my knees wouldn't buckle.

Of all the things to dare him to do...

When I wasn't afraid I'd simply fall over, I looked down at him. He was sitting, just finishing the lime, and he still had that look in his eye. "You did that on purpose," I accused.

"You're the one who chose the dare. If it's any consolation, you would've liked the other version even less." The cushions puffed out air as he flung himself back, clearly unconcerned about what he'd put me through. "Truth or dare," he asked.

"Truth," I said by rote, almost instantly regretting the choice.

Please don't ask me what that was like.

"Have you ever cheated on anyone?"

"Absolutely not," I replied heatedly, then promptly knocked back another shot to settle my nerves.

"Have you ever been cheated on?" he followed up, no doubt registering my anger.

"That is technically a different question, but I'll give it to you. Yes, my ex cheated on me. It's one of the many reasons we broke up... again," I added belatedly. "Your turn. Truth or dare."

"Truth." He was definitely throwing me a bone.

"Where are you from?"

He only hesitated a moment. "Nebraska mostly. Ask another, it's only fair."

I thought for a moment. The answer didn't really give me what I'd hoped for, but I wasn't about to waste another question on it. "Tell me something you don't want me to know."

"The drawing isn't a self-portrait. Truth or dare?"

My head spun. If it wasn't a picture of him, then who was it supposed to be? He smacked my leg. "Fine, dare, since I technically had two truths."

There was nothing remotely sweet or innocent about the grin he gave me. "I dare you to do a body shot."

"You can't be serious. Choose something else." I scrambled for any way to stop this. "Isn't daring someone to repeat a previous dare against the rules or something?"

He shook his head. "Nope. A dare is a dare. Let's see if you were paying attention."

I snatched a lime off of the table and the salt shaker while he poured the shot. "You're one sick pup. Give me your arm." He looked skeptical, but did it. Faster than he could stop me, I repeated the process on his forearm. The lime was worse than the tequila. "There, happy?"

"That's not how you do it." To his credit, he looked properly scandalized.

"Body, by definition, includes the arm."

"There is a spirit of intent that you've violated. You can either do it right or your next dare is going to be worse. And don't think you can avoid it altogether by just choosing truth. By your own rules, you'll eventually have to choose dare."

I had zero desire to find out what his obviously demented mind could come up with that was worse than what he'd already dared me to do. "Matt, I can't," I pleaded.

"I could lie down if that would help."

I had a very clear picture of me licking his stomach and then just not stopping until I'd licked every part of him. I vigorously shook my head. "That won't help."

He gave me a small mercy by lifting his own shirt, which helped stave off my desire to do exactly as he'd done. I wanted to get it over and done with like I had with his arm, but I couldn't seem to force myself to go any faster. The smooth lines of his stomach and the way it moved as he breathed captivated me.

He flinched when the lime touched his skin. I added the salt and took the shot. His abdomen shivered as I tasted the crystals. It was only through an active force of will that I stopped at that. I ached to keep tasting him, to feel his soft down on my face, to kiss every inch of him, to...

"You're supposed to do the lime next." He sounded breathless.

I tossed the wedge straight up, and he caught it. "You do the lime." I sat back on the couch and rubbed my face. I knew this evening would end up being a mistake. The temptation, the want, was just too great.

He passed me a new beer and sat back down as well. "Dare."

"Tell me a joke." I was in some serious need of levity.

He chuckled. "Have you heard the one about the broken pencil?"

I looked up at him from behind my hand.

"It was pointless."

The awful joke was so unexpected I couldn't help but giggle. The harder I tried not to laugh, the more I did. "That was absolutely terrible. Where did you find that? A cereal box?"

"Actually, it was a piece of candy. Now you, Truth or Dare?"

"Truth." Maybe I could trick him into forgetting I'd eventually be due a dare.

"Of course." He tapped his bottom lip, and I couldn't help but envy his finger. "Okay, what's your greatest fear?"

"That no one will ever love me for all of who I am," I responded without really thinking.

"What do you mean?"

I sighed into the cushions. "Shadow Demons have a terrible rap, Matt. Sometimes I think the world will never be able to see us as anything more than monsters."

His face clouded over. "You can't think like that. It'll all get sorted eventually. Stop being so melancholy."

"You asked about fears," I reminded him.

"Yeah, but I didn't think you were going to get all sullen on me. Now snap out of it. We're having fun, remember? Dare."

"Fun, you said?" I raised an eyebrow at him. "Do the worm for twenty seconds. And don't pretend like you don't know what I'm talking about, everyone knows the worm."

He shook his head; the sun shining once more in his smile. "I don't know if I've ever actually done this before. Here goes nothing." His attempt at the worm was even worse than his joke, but he tried it. When he was done, he was laughing every bit as hard as I was. "Please, let's never talk of that again," he said as he resumed his seat. He poured us each another shot and leaned back.

I had to scoot closer to the middle in order to get it, though, because he'd overfilled it. We chinked glasses, making an even bigger mess, and drank together. "Dare."

"Balance what's left of the bottle on your head for ten seconds in a row." He snagged the half empty bottle and handed it to me.

It took three tries, but I finally got it positioned so it didn't immediately topple back over. Even then, I almost didn't make it because I started laughing. I removed the bottle and let it slide to the ground, then rolled my head to face him. He was curled up beside me, still smiling from my pathetic attempts at balance. I loved looking at him. I loved everything about him, even his stubborn nature and the way he seemed to constantly torture me.

"I guess it will be truth," he sighed, looking at me with those perfectly blue eyes.

"What do you want, Matt?"

"For you to kiss me."

I shifted so that I was fully facing him. I couldn't have heard that right. "What? Why?"

"It's not your turn. Truth or dare."

"Truth," I replied quickly. I wanted to get back to the other thing.

"Ugh," he gave an exasperated sigh. "Why does it matter?"

"Because I want to know. Now answer the question. Why?"

"Except I choose dare," he replied maliciously.

I knew exactly where he wanted me to go with that and I refused to give him the satisfaction. "Then I dare you to tell me the truth."

"That's cheating," he argued.

"The truth, Matt."

"Because I liked it, okay? Are you ha—"

My mouth was on his before he could finish. He felt even better than I remembered, and I easily fell into the desire I'd been avoiding for the last few weeks. None of this is real, I thought distantly. I'm actually passed out drunk on the floor and having a really good dream. He tasted amazing.

"Definitely not a terrible kisser," I said between kisses as I shifted to get a better angle. I didn't care if this was a dream. Or if I woke up and had to explain myself. I kissed my imaginary Matt deeper.

Then his fingers curled in my hair. He pulled and, at the sharp pain, I realized I was still awake, but he didn't pull me away. He pulled me closer.

"Matt." His name was scarcely more than a gasp. My heart beat frantically as it tried desperately to keep up with what was happening right now. He arched into me and I pulled him tighter. Kissing Matt was like kissing fire and the burn was so good.

"Alex."

I moaned at hearing him say my name. He was still giving as good as he got, his tongue dancing with mine and addling whatever was left of my senses. I couldn't get enough of him. I abandoned his mouth to kiss along his neck. The smell of him was driving me mad.

"Alex." This time, it was more of a groan.

I recaptured his mouth, and he fiercely returned the kiss.

His hand released my hair and drifted down to my chest. He gave a solid push and forced me back a few inches. "Alex, wait." He swallowed, his lips a delectable cherry from the fervor.

"What?" I felt delirious. The world was fuzzy and intangible. The only real thing in it was Matt.

"I need a minute." His breathing came in shallow pants, every bit as labored as mine.

I so wasn't done with him, not after a confession like that. I leaned forward, still completely lost to desire. How long was a minute?

"Alex, wait," he said, his voice stronger, less of a whisper. "I think... I think... Shit." He scrambled back, failed to get up, and shadowed through the couch to land with a solid thud on the ground. I watched as he staggered out of the couch, solidified, then raced to his room. He flung the door open and vanished inside, leaving me with nothing but my confusion.

Fog continued to cloud my mind as I followed him. With his door hanging open, it was practically an invitation. I flicked on the bedroom light. I'd never been in his room beyond that first day, and not much differed from then. Where mine had books and posters, his was bare walls. The only book was the one we were using for the research project, and it was sitting on the nightstand. Other than that, there was nothing, not even Matt.

Then I heard someone being sick. I looked towards the source. The bathroom door was cracked enough to show a strip of white light. I opened it the rest of the way in time to see him retch again. He saw me come in and rolled his head on his arm, which was propped against the seat.

"How you doin'?" I grabbed a towel and wet it with cold water.

"You mean besides being absolutely mortified?" He accepted the towel, and I shrugged. "I feel like I'm dying." He laid on the cold tile floor while I sat on the rim of the tub and watched him. He looked up at me, his blue eyes swimming. "Why don't you look as miserable as I feel?"

"I'm pretty sure you had twice as many shots as me."

"That would do it. Well, I've made a complete ass of myself. Thank Nyx we don't have class tomorrow."

"Can I get you anything?"

"Water would be great."

I left to get him a cup of cold water, but when I got back, he was out. Wasn't that just perfect? Now my drunk ass had to figure out how to get his drunk ass off of the floor. The good news was, it didn't matter how awkward I was, no amount of anything was likely to wake him up.

It was far from graceful, but eventually I got him on the bed. I briefly contemplated stripping him down and putting him under the covers, but dismissed it as an exceptionally bad idea. Instead, I grabbed the other side of the comforter and rolled him up like a burrito. I was having a good laugh at myself tucking him in when he grabbed my wrist. A look at his face said he was still sound asleep.

I tried to extricate myself, but he wasn't letting go. The harder I tried to get away, the tighter his grip got. On a whim, I leaned down and planted a kiss on his forehead, lingering a moment. Instantly, he relaxed, releasing me.

What I wouldn't give to understand your secrets, Matt.

Finally freed, I made my way out, quietly closing the door behind me. The event had sobered me but, I still wasn't ready for bed. The dreams would never compare, anyway.

I looked around the dorm. The room was a total disaster. With a sigh, I set to putting it right again. When it resembled its usual state of disarray, I sat down on the couch to take stock.

How had any of this evening happened? Despite the truths I'd accumulated, I felt like I had infinitely more questions to the riddle that was Matt. But I knew one thing for certain—he'd absolutely kissed me back.

CHAPTER 23
GRANITE

Matt

My head pounded so hard I felt it in my eyeballs and my mouth tasted like something had died in there while I slept. Groaning, I shifted to get up and met resistance. I struggled to free myself from the constricting cocoon and toppled out of the bed fully clothed, followed by a mountain of comforter.

Alex.

Just thinking his name brought back memories from the night before. The game had been hilarious and fun, but the kiss had been absolutely epic. I was officially convinced that my dreams weren't some weird manifestations of finding out my best friend was gay. No, I wanted Alex to kiss me. I still wanted it. And I'd made a total and complete ass of myself.

I groaned again to the agony of my throbbing headache. How could I ever apologize for my behavior? My only saving grace was that I hadn't actually thrown up on him. Still, what I did do was bad enough. I'd cut that far too close, but I couldn't stop myself. I wanted more. Even now, I could feel it like a hunger growing inside. It was right next to the actual hunger that said my dumb ass hadn't eaten anything substantial last night.

I quickly changed and went out to the living room. All evidence of the night before was completely gone. The glasses, the bottle, even the chip remnants. Nothing remained. Then I saw Alex asleep on the couch. I walked over to see that he was still in the same deep purple shirt and gray pants as the day before.

He must've stayed up to get this place looking normal again.

What did that say? Was he upset? I felt cruel now for the body shot fiasco. It wasn't his fault he didn't know what it was, and it was wrong to force him to do it. I was a terrible friend. A terrible friend that dreamed about making out with their best friend and tricked them into kissing them.

Shame kept my feet moving. Rather than wait for Alex to wake, I quietly fixed myself a cup of water and set one out for him as well. My gaze lingered on his relaxed face. He seemed so peaceful with his quiet snore and messy hair. Then my focus dipped to his mouth. I licked my lips and fought the impulse to kiss him awake. With a soft sigh, I let the fantasy go. After one last glance back at his sleeping form, I slipped out, barely remembering to grab my key before quietly shutting the door.

Alone in the hall, I was just as lost. The only thing I was absolutely sure of was that I liked Alex kissing me. I liked it a lot. None of it made sense though. I'd never been even vaguely interested in any other guy before. But that was it, he wasn't any other guy. He was Alex, my Alex. Determined to find clarity before facing him again, I wandered off.

What I really needed was a way to clear my head so all of my thoughts weren't on top of each other. The way his hair had felt between my fingers. How his mouth molded to mine. The overwhelming mortification of puking after the most intense kiss of my entire life. I'd have gone straight to the fight club—fighting always gave me a single-minded focus—but given it was Saturday and they only met Tuesday and Thursday, that wasn't really an option.

Eventually, I found myself in the library. The massive building reminded me of a tomb some days, but now that summer semester was officially over, it was mercifully empty... and quiet. I weaved past several heavy tables until I found one that was nestled up by some shelves about halfway through the room. The chair didn't even squeak when I pulled it out and flopped down. I took a deep breath and let it out slowly. Distraction. Maybe I could make some headway on the Demonic History report for the fall class.

I took out our research book—Alex's book—and ran my fingers over the worn cover. The rough edges of the corners contrasted with the front and back, smoothed from years of loving hands. I knew now why Alex didn't want to tell me if the knight killed the demon. He didn't know. There were pages missing and everything before that was too vague to be certain.

The bookmark fell to the table. Without enough pages at the end, there was nothing to hold it. Alex was right about the image—it was a shadow demon. In fact, it was practically a modern adaptation of the illustration in the book. I unfolded the page to reveal the half that he apparently hadn't seen. Technically speaking, this part of the drawing was a self-portrait. I'd never been all that great at drawing myself, but there was no denying the figure across from the shadowed demon was me. He certainly looked every bit as lost as I felt.

With a frustrated growl, I replaced the bookmark and shoved the book back into my bookbag, angry at myself for being too much of a coward to be honest with Alex and basically sneaking out. He deserved better. Finding information about his favorite book wasn't much in the way of an apology, but it was a start.

The cavernous room seemed to swallow what little noise my footfalls made as I wandered through the stacks in search of answers. I walked past several daunting displays of books until I found the genealogy section. Surely, a family dedicated to hunting down an entire supernatural race would be mentioned somewhere.

After an hour of searching, all I had to show for my efforts was an absurd stack of ancient families and hands so coated in dust they looked gray. I flopped onto the floor and began methodically going through each one. Names like Guerreros del Sol seemed promising, but their order didn't start until the fifteen-hundreds. Then there was the Danai family, which seemed to have been around since the dawn of time. They were a twisted bunch, but they were necromancers, or at least I thought that's what the text meant. I couldn't imagine anyone being able to bring the dead back to life. But then I couldn't imagine a lot of what had happened in the last few months.

I let out a huff as I surveyed my collection. None of these had what I was looking for. But how did you find an obscure family that kept to the shadows? I was sliding the last book onto the return cart when I had an epiphany. If we were right and it was a love story, maybe something came of it—marriage, kids, something. I raced back to the genealogies with an eye for family trees on the Shadow Demon side this time. There wasn't much in the way of Shadow Demon lineage, so I grabbed them all and returned to my table. The librarian on duty eyed my haphazard collection skeptically, but didn't intervene or comment.

I stayed there well into the night, searching the books. It was rough going. The first couple of layers were full of countless demons, but as the timeline progressed, more and more holes showed up. I wasn't sure if that was because of deaths or because literally no one knew. I traced each line from an Original, careful not to skip lines or pages. It would have been much easier if the lineage behaved anything like a normal family tree. That would have been too easy. Across time, demons skipped in and out of relevance. Some disappearing for decades only to show up again in a different branch of the history.

I was getting a headache from reading the tiny script, and I desperately wanted a shower. Then I saw something that didn't quite fit with the rest. Next to some demon's name I didn't have a prayer of pronouncing was a very simple

Matthias. No last name or descriptor. Just a name and a symbol. Except I'd seen that symbol before.

I slid open books aside until I found the only one I cared about—Alex's book. There on the cover was the same symbol: a torch topped by the sun, surrounded by what appeared to be black flames. I knew better though, those weren't flames, they were shadow.

My eyes sought the link again. There had to be more. I scanned the page repeatedly until, at last, I found a reference for the symbol in a footnote. The chair almost toppled to the ground as I launched out of it to go find the matching reference, earning me a reprising look from the librarian. I was pretty sure if the library had hours, she would've kicked me out by now. Yet I was the only one there and it was pointless to exact wrath on one lowly student. I gave her my best smile and continued on my way.

Quest accomplished, I took the book back to my ridiculous display of notes. The chair screeched against the floor and I flinched at the harsh sound. It felt like days since I'd heard anything above a whisper. But no way could I leave now. I was on the verge of a breakthrough. I could feel it. The matching reference book turned out to be a compilation of symbols and coats of arms. I scoured images until I found the one I was looking for.

If I'd thought the Denai family was old, these guys put them to shame. There was no family name listed though, just a translation of the coat and their creed. The Order of Light: Where there is darkness, there is light, and the light will prevail. It sounded similar to what Alex had said to me at the start of school, except it was all backwards. There is always shadow: where there is light, there is darkness.

It was fitting, really. The light that battles the darkness, the darkness that tempts the light. Which reminded me of my earlier thought. If there was a connection listed between a Shadow Demon and a supposed knight of this order, had anything come of it?

Like so much of demon genealogy, it was difficult to determine the path, but at last I found what I was searching for—they had a child. I gasped so loud it echoed back at me. The librarian appeared around a corner and gave me a scathing look. I offered her a sheepish smile and sank into my seat, my gaze once more fixed on my miraculous discovery. Alex was going to lose his shit.

At the thought of seeing him again, my chest tightened. I couldn't face him, not after what I'd done. Mortified didn't even come close. I needed more time. Now that I'd got my mind off of things for a little while, I could tackle how to go about apologizing to Alex and making sense of why I wanted to kiss him until I passed out.

I scrawled down the information from each book, including relevant passages and page numbers. He'd kill me if we couldn't ever find the information again. Then I set about putting them all back on their appropriate return carts.

When I was done, I glanced out the large window. Bright rays of morning light pierced the tall windows to create a stunning rainbow of color. Was it possible I'd only been here twenty-four hours? It felt like so much longer. I considered asking the librarian exactly how much time had passed, but dismissed it. I'd caused enough ruckus in her domain already. Besides, it couldn't possibly be all that long, right?

The cheery chirps of birds and the soft babble of morning people replaced the quiet hush of the library. Besides the fact that I wasn't sure how much time had passed since I'd last slept, I definitely did not qualify as a morning person. Upside, at least my head had stopped hurting. I made a beeline for the cafeteria, grateful that I'd remembered to pack my dining card. However, no one had ever mentioned how much was on it or if it expired with the summer semester.

I held my breath as the cashier slid the card and eyed my outrageous pile of food. To be fair, it was a lot. I thought I'd gotten better over the last few months about not eating like it might be the last thing I'd have in a while, but once I'd started grabbing things, I hadn't been able to stop. It could have been because I was legit ravenous... or it could have been another excuse to put off returning to the dorm. Either way, I wasn't leaving until every bite of my meal was gone.

It was well past noon by the time I popped my last bite and ventured back outside. Even after all the stalling though, I still couldn't figure out what to say to Alex. I'm sorry didn't really seem like enough. I tightened the straps of my bookbag with all its treasures. Maybe distracting him with my mind-blowing discovery would help soften him up.

Or... I could kiss him.

Like karma for the renegade thought, something hooked my book bag and yanked me backward. "Hey! What the—" The angry retort died as my gaze fell on the blue iridescent scales shining in the sunlight.

Neese gave me a toothy smile. "Otto said I might find you here. You sure eat a lot for a scrawny thing."

"Who are you calling scrawny?" I snarled, jerking my backpack to no avail.

"Easy there, runt." He scowled and lowered his voice to a sinister hiss that made my spine crawl. "There's a fight tonight. You in?"

Judging by his tone and the scary look he was giving me, it wasn't so much a request as a demand. Suddenly, I regretted wasting so much time. If I hadn't of been such a coward, I would've already been in the dorm. Now I'd have to wait even longer to see Alex, to tell him what I found... to tell him how sorry I was for everything.

I nodded, and Neese finally released my backpack. He stepped to the side so we could walk next to each other. Clearly, he didn't trust that I wouldn't make a break for it. If I had any measure of faith in my shadow walking abilities, I wouldn't have hesitated. But I wasn't Alex. Guilt stabbed at me. Just how long had I been gone? My optimistic belief that it had only been a full day and night seemed unlikely now.

I cleared my throat and glanced at Neese out of the corner of my eye. He may have had two legs, but it still looked like he was slithering. "I thought the fights weren't starting until next week."

He stopped and stared at me. "What day do you think it is?"

I frowned, but kept my peace.

Neese shook his head and let out a hissing laugh. "You must've raged pretty hard after finals to lose a whole day."

I let out a breath of relief. I'd been right. Only a day. Well, two now.

"Today is just for members. Thursday we'll bring in the fresh meat." He waved a dismissive taloned hand and resumed walking.

My steps faltered. "What? I thought you said it was only Saturday."

"Saturday? Oh man, you did hit it hard. I've done a lot of wild shit, but I can't ever say I lost three days." He gave me a skeptical look, but didn't stop.

I groaned. Alex was going to be pissed. I didn't know how to explain one night. How the hell was I supposed to explain three days?

"I hope you enjoyed your siesta, because you're in it now." Neese opened the door to the warehouse without a password. Then he pulled me through.

The club was absolute chaos. Otto must have been riling everyone up while Neese tracked down renegade members. Noise buffeted my ears, a stark contrast to the quiet I'd apparently been living in for the past few days. My thoughts from before about needing a fight to clear my head vanished. I didn't want to be here, and I didn't want to do this. I needed to talk to Alex.

"Yeah, Neese, this is great and all," I took a tentative step back toward the exit, "but I really gotta get going."

"What, you got a hot date or something?"

"No." I had a roommate that was probably gonna tan my hide for making out with him, then disappearing without so much as a note.

"Then you can fight." Neese grabbed the front of my shirt and jerked me deeper into the warehouse.

I tried to pull his hand off, but only managed to put holes in my shirt. "I have other things I have to do."

"Like what?" he asked, dragging me towards the ring.

Digging in my heels wasn't helping in the least. I thought about trying to shadow, but that wasn't as consistent as I let Alex think it was. Someone ripped my backpack off. Panic spiked through me, and I fought harder to get free. I couldn't stay here. I had to get back to Alex. Why had I ever joined this club in the first place?

"Alright, you little shit. What's the deal? Where do you have to be that's so important?"

"I... I..." I couldn't say it. My issues with Alex were none of his damn business.

"That's what I thought. Give you a few days' reprieve and you go soft on us. Just for that, you get to go first."

I shouldn't have swung at Neese. I knew better. He easily avoided the assault, and I fell forward. The people I bumped into were more than eager to help me the rest of the way until I landed in a heap of limbs in the open space and left to my fate.

"Hey Granite, you ready for a rematch?" Neese called, his voice rising over the jeers from the crowd.

"You bet your scaly ass I am."

The distinct rumble of knuckles made of stone cracking came from behind me. I spun around and cursed. Granite looked more imposing than ever as he stepped into the ring with a leering smile. This was so not going to be my night.

"I've been waiting for you, you little brat." He walked around me and I kept turning to keep him in sight. "Let's see how you do when I actually know what I'm up against."

Double—no—quadruple shit. He'd finally figured it out. I spied the metal door behind him, having gone full circle, and my pack beside it. The only way out was through Granite and I needed out. I walked to the edge of the ring and Granite's rumbling laughter followed me. At the edge, I heard Neese's own hissing chuckle. I ignored both of them and reached out to push people out of the way.

Inches from the nearest person, my fingers met resistance and the air between us flashed a brilliant blue. Mind-numbing electricity ripped through my arm. I yanked back the appendage and cradled it against my chest while Neese, Otto, and pretty much everyone roared with laughter.

"What the hell?" I flexed my hand and winced against the pain. This definitely hadn't been here before.

Neese ran his long tongue over his pointed teeth and smirked. "We had a feeling you might run, especially after you no-showed on Thursday. So, we invested in a witch." He glanced over his shoulder at a girl dressed in spiked boots with black lipstick. "The spell may not be demon-specific, but it'll hold just about anything. Even you."

I swallowed back the bile crawling up my throat and hoped like hell terror wasn't written all over my face. The last time I'd been this scared, I'd been trapped in an alley with a bunch of masked guys wearing white, military-like jackets. "Please, Neese. Let me go." Despite my best efforts, my voice still shook.

Neese rewarded my desperate plea with a grin straight from the deepest depths of hell. "You can leave after the fight."

I stared at him for a long second in which neither of us blinked. He might as well have issued a death sentence. Granite knew I was a Shadow Demon. Whatever advantage I had before was nonexistent now. Braced for defeat, I turned toward Granite and a fist like an avalanche plowed into my face. The hit sent me reeling into the electric boundary so hard I bounced back and fell to the ground. I struggled to my feet and intentionally did not touch my face. The cheap shot had definitely broken my nose.

Angry, I raced towards him. He easily danced out of the way, and his fist crushed into my side. The bile I'd swallowed earlier threatened to return with a vengeance as pain washed through me and a disturbing crack filled the air. I grunted and stumbled, clutching my aching side and swinging wildly with my free hand.

If I could focus, get my head in the game, I might stand a chance, but with every hit, all I could think about was Alex. The way he smiled when I got a question right. How he always had an encouraging word no matter how down I was feeling. The hint of lavender that infused his skin. How his hair always did whatever it wanted. The soft press of his lips as he kissed me in a way I'd never known I needed.

Granite grabbed me by the ruff and threw me into the barrier again. The electric charge surged through my body and I curled into a ball as I hit the ground. Without focus, I was nothing but a rag doll. Small, inconsequential. Nothing. All the things I'd been before Alex.

Ringing filled my ears as I pushed up from the grit covered floor. No sooner was I upright, then yet another solid wall of rock knocked me back down. I shadowed out before he could kick me in the ribs. When I re-materialized, though, it was in exactly the same spot and just in time for the second attempt.

Pain ripped through my side yet again and I fell to my hands. I wanted to tell him to stop, that he'd won, I just wanted to leave. But I could barely breathe, let alone beg. I tried once again to stand, only to have an elbow crack into the back of my neck. The world went dark as I slammed into the ground.

When I came to, someone had dragged me over by the door. Feeling like a giant bruise, I pulled my backpack closer and carefully slipped it on. I eased my way up the wall while waves of pain threatened to make me vomit right there on the floor. I forced the nausea down and staggered out of the warehouse. If I could've shadowed to the dorm, I would've, but that was substantially beyond me at the moment. So, I walked. It was slow going, but one way or another, I'd get back to Alex.

Chapter 24
Tequila Straight

Alexi

One of these days, I was going to learn not to drink with Matt. All it did was make sure I made a fool of myself. I still wasn't sure how much of the night had been real and how much imagined. Had he really said he wanted me to kiss him, or had that just been a product of wishful thinking on an uninhibited mind? That I hadn't seen hide nor hair of him in days suggested the latter. He could be pretty bad with avoiding things he didn't want to talk about, but this was taking it to a new level. At least when he was avoiding me before, he was still coming back to the dorm.

Whatever his issues or reasons, though, I needed to talk to him. We couldn't go on like this. It had been hard enough pining for him in secret. That was gone now. He knew I was interested in him beyond friendship and we'd kissed... passionately. Just thinking about how he'd pulled me closer made me uncomfortable in all the best ways. We were definitely overdue for a conversation.

There was one glaring problem, however. I couldn't find him. After I'd woken up Saturday, the only sign of Matt was the rinsed glass by the sink and the fresh cup of water he'd left on the coffee table. I searched everywhere, but he was nowhere to be found. Not in his room. Not at the cafeteria. Not in the training rooms. I'd even bumped into a few classmates that hadn't gone home after finals, but they hadn't seen him either. Apparently, wherever he'd holed up didn't have prying eyes, or at least none of the places I thought he might be hiding.

Exhausted after yet another fruitless day of searching, it was time to face the truth I'd been avoiding with every cell in my body. Matt was gone. He wasn't coming back. And it was my fault. There was always a chance that I was wrong, that this time when I returned to the dorm, it wouldn't be empty. Despite the hopeful thought, I wasn't really optimistic. A couple of days I could understand, but four was decidedly intentional. Honestly, I wasn't sure why I was so determined to find him. He clearly wanted nothing to do with me. Maybe Daniel had been right all this time, and I was the problem. I swallowed past the sudden lump in my throat and realized I was staring at the lush green carpet outside our... my dorm room.

The door opened as silent as ever. My gaze instantly fell on Matt's pack sitting by the couch like it did every other day. It looked like it had been slung there and some of the contents had spilled out. I frantically sought his door. It was closed. I didn't care about respecting his privacy, I just wanted to see him. I was halfway there when the door slammed shut behind me.

"Alex? It's about fucking time."

I froze and looked around. At last, I found him stretched out between two of the kitchen chairs. His head was tilted back so I couldn't make out his face. However, I could clearly see the almost empty bottle of tequila on the table beside him.

"Where have you been? I need your help," he grumbled.

"Me? Where have you been? I've been worried sick." It was only when the words were out that I realized how true they were. I'd practically been beside myself when no one seemed to have a clue where he'd vanished. I walked over as he casually dismissed my concern with a wave of his hand.

"'Mere. Need you to make sure my nose is straight."

"What?" I stepped close and stifled a gasp at seeing the state of his face.

He rolled his head slightly to look at me, but his blue eyes were murky and lacked focus. "Make sure the damn thing is straight. I've gone this long and I'm not about to let one cheap shot land me with a crooked nose."

I battled with my shock and floundered for words that wouldn't come. Who had done this to him? Why was his nose broken? What did he expect me to do about it?

"Are you just going to stand there? Isn't it bad enough that I had to set the damn thing myself? Which hurt like hell if you were wondering."

"What even happened?" I asked, still perplexed about how we'd gotten here.

He scoffed. "Someone hit me in the face, obviously. Just look at the blasted thing."

"I don't even know what I'm looking for." I leaned over to get a closer look. Whoever had done it had not been small. The bruise around his nose looked like it would cover half of his face at least once it set.

"All you have to do is see if it is smooth. You know what my nose is supposed to look like. Make sure it does."

I leaned in more, stopping just shy of actually touching him, and squinted to inspect the damage. I could see where the break must have happened by the thin red line. As far as I could tell, it looked just as straight as ever.

"Matt I..."

His lips brush against mine and the words drifted off. I looked down at him just in time for him to crane his neck and steal another. After all of my anxiety over the last few days, I couldn't help but kiss him back. I hadn't imagined it, he really wanted to kiss me. The kiss grew more aggressive, and I pulled back.

"Matt, I don't want to hurt you." There was no way kissing was pleasant with an injury like that.

"Alex, I haven't been able to feel my face for the last twenty minutes." His hand slid through my hair and he pulled me back down so our lips could meet once more. Michelle Carter was a fucking idiot. Matt was an incredible kisser.

Every cell in my body was hyper aware that this was the first time Matt had initiated a kiss. It didn't even matter that he was drunk yet again. Alright, it mattered a little, but I was too busy drowning to properly care. I loved kissing Matt. There was a whole other world there waiting to be discovered. Would there ever be a day that I wasn't totally lost in him?

The chair screeched as it threatened to slide out from under him. I wrapped an arm around his waist to make sure he wouldn't fall. At the contact, though, he let out a pained hiss.

My worry returned tenfold. "What?"

"It's nothing," he mumbled, "just my side."

"Your side?"

"Yeah, but really, it's nothing. Don't worry about it." He dropped his propped legs to the floor and shifted to get up.

I forced him back down and lifted his shirt. His side was a mass of bruises, black, blue, yellow, purple, pretty much every color but normal skin. "What the hell happened?"

"I lost. It's not a big deal." This time, he succeeded in straightening, but remained seated. He snatched the tequila from the table and took a swig directly from the bottle. Small wonder he was three sheets to the wind.

"Lost what? A fight? When were you in a fight? How many fights have you been in? That doesn't look like one fight, Matt. How often are you getting into fights?" And how many times could I say fight in ten seconds?

He squinted at me, confusion evident on his bruised face. "Where did you think I went every Tuesday and Thursday?"

"I don't know." I threw up my hands. "Hanging out with your friends. WHy the hell would I think you were fighting?"

His gaze dropped to the floor. "I do hang out with friends... sometimes... after."

Anger that rivaled how furious I'd been when I'd discovered Daniel had cheated on me burned in my veins. I'd been literally sick with worry and he was voluntarily traipsing off to get his ass handed to him?

Matt must've recognized the mounting rage on my face, because he rose to his feet, holding onto the back of the chair for balance. "Look, can we talk about this later?" He took a shaky step and stopped when I blocked the way. "Unless you're planning on joining me while I pretend to take a shower, you'll have to excuse me."

I quietly fumed as he slowly made his way around me and hobbled towards his room. No matter how I felt, there was no point in trying to talk to him in his current state. Days of worrying about what was going on and this is what I came back to? If he wasn't already such a disaster, I'd have throttled him myself. I glared at what remained of the tequila. Without a second thought, I dumped it out and trashed the bottle. Then I yanked the chair Matt had been sitting on around so I could watch his door. I didn't know how long he'd be gone, but I'd be damned if I wouldn't be ready to give him an earful when he reemerged.

I stopped watching the clock as yet another hour crawled by. Three cups of coffee in and I was wired. There wasn't a chance I'd fall asleep this time and miss him. Even after several hours of waiting, I wasn't sure what I wanted to say to him. All of my rehearsed conversations from Friday night were distant compared to the anger that refused to abate. Fighting regularly? I couldn't fucking believe it. And I hadn't had so much as a clue until now. Livid didn't come close, and I didn't even know which part made me the angriest.

Matt's door slowly swung inward, and he made his way into the living room. His eyes sought me out right away, and while decidedly uncertain, at least they were clear now.

"How are you feeling?" I asked, doing what I could to maintain some level of calm.

He swallowed and darted an anxious look at me, like he'd caught the edge I was trying to hide. "Better."

"Still drunk?" I didn't bother to temper my clipped tone.

He winced. "No. Alex, I—"

"Are you out of your damn mind! Fighting on campus? Do you have any idea what the school would do to you if they found out?"

"It wasn't on campus. It's not for that reason."

That he already knew about the consequences somehow infuriated me more. "You can't be serious. So, this is like a real thing? You just traipse off every Tuesday and Thursday to some... some... bruiser club."

"I don't understand why you're so upset. It's not like you got your ass beat to a pulp," he snapped.

I gawped at him. "Upset? I'm not upset, Matt. I'm way past upset. How could you not tell me?"

"Why would I? It had nothing to do with you."

"Because I'm supposed to be your best friend! That's the sort of thing you share."

His face crumpled. "I didn't think."

His obvious hurt pained me, but I pushed it aside. I was hurt too, and I felt used, something I'd never expected to feel from Matt. "Of course not. You're just off in your own world and I'm collateral to use whenever it's convenient."

He took a step toward me. "That's not true."

"Where have you been the last few days? Have you been fighting the whole time?"

He shook his head, then seemed to regret the move. "No. I was in the library."

"Why?" I didn't bother to hide my disbelief.

"I needed somewhere to figure things out, and I lost track of time."

"For four days? You can't expect me to believe that." I crossed my arms and fought the urge to clench my jaw. "Did you at least figure out whatever apparently required absolute solitude?"

He shuffled his feet like he did any time he was anxious. "Sort of. I found something about the research project. I was coming back to show you when—" He took a step towards his discarded bag.

"Would you forget the damn book!" I couldn't remember the last time I'd yelled so much. I hadn't even yelled when I found out Daniel was cheating.

Matt stood there looking like some lost, injured puppy.

I couldn't do this. I hated seeing that I was hurting him. I hated knowing he was already in pain. And I hated how much he'd hurt me. I dropped my arms. "I'm not having this conversation anymore. You can do whatever you want. Get kicked out of school for all I care."

"Alex."

I ignored the plea in his voice. There was nothing he could say that would make this better. "Don't." I turned to go to my room. I needed space. I couldn't breathe. Then a fresh wave of anger flashed through me and I spun back around, startling him. "And another thing, try not getting totally smashed the next time you want to kiss me." With that, I slammed my door and finally lost whatever composure I had left.

No amount of deep breathing could alleviate the tightness in my chest. The whole episode smarted of a breakup, except we weren't dating. We weren't even anything close to resembling a couple. My deep breaths turned shaky. I couldn't do this. I'd never been in love with my best friend before, and it was proving impossible.

That brought me up short. When had I started thinking of Matt as my best friend? I knew I was completely head over heels since day one, but this was an entirely new level. Was that why the betrayal hurt so much? The worst part of all of it was that there was no one to talk to about it with. Who could understand? Lacking any better option, I called my mom. She picked up, eager as ever to hear how things were going.

"It's so good to hear from you, Lexi." Just hearing her voice helped relieve some of the pain that had taken up residence in my chest. She knew how I felt about Matt, though I hadn't shared any of the recent fails. "Tell me about finals. Surely, you're done by now. Have you gotten your results?"

I struggled to keep my tone light. "Um yeah. Finals were fine. All As."

"I'm so proud of you, honey."

"Thanks, mom. I admit I didn't expect to get one in Battle Tactics though."

She tsked. "I still don't understand why you need that class. I thought you said the war was over."

"It is. Think of it like a just-in-case class. Plus, it teaches us to trust our instincts and our powers." I almost choked. The words were nearly identical to what Matt had said to me.

"Alexi, are you alright?"

I was too busy holding back the beginnings of a sob to answer. Why did it hurt so much? I'd known nothing would ever come of my hopeless infatuation, and yet, some deep part of me had foolishly dared to dream.

"How did Matt do? Was he able to pull up his grades?"

I hadn't even made it five minutes. A sob that sounded like it'd been torn from the depths of my soul broke free.

"Alexi, honey, what's the matter?" Between heartbreaking sobs, I told her everything—from Matt finding out I was gay, to him disappearing for half a week and our horrible fight.

"I just don't know what to do, Mama," I blubbered.

"Shh, shh. It'll be okay, sweetheart. I know this is hard. It sounds like you have some tough choices ahead of you. Like you both do."

"And what choice is Matt making? He's not gay. If anything, he's too drunk half of the time to even be confused."

"You don't know that."

I scoffed, bitterness filling the hollow space left by my tears. "Please don't. Wishing it won't make it true."

"Then I guess you'll be deciding for yourself."

"I don't know if I can." I glanced toward the closed door I was positive he was hovering on the other side of. "He... he... doesn't take no for an answer." I dropped my voice and added in a whisper, "And I don't know if I can live in a world without him in it." I expected her to say I was being melodramatic. What I didn't expect were the options she laid at my feet.

"Ultimately, it's your choice, Alexi. You can stay and be miserable just so you can be near him or you can leave and try to find happiness again. But don't decide now, you're too worked up. Give it a few days, see if things settle down. Just putting it out there, but you could try actually talking to him."

"I yelled at him. Does that count?"

"Alexi Roman, you did not."

I flinched at the scandalized rebuke. "But-"

"No buts, that does not count. I mean a reasonable, level-headed conversation where you both lay all your cards on the table."

"Except Matt doesn't talk about things," I argued, "at least not personal things. He keeps everything bottled up. Mama, I don't even know where he's from. The most I got him to admit is 'Nebraska mostly'."

"What does that even mean?"

"That's what I'm talking about. Anything else and he's a bloody open book with the words written right on his face. But when he shuts down, a crowbar couldn't get in there."

My mother let out a heavy sigh. "I'm sorry you're going through this, Alexi. It breaks my heart to hear you're hurting. I wish I could be there for you, or better, we could afford for you to come home for a little while, get some space before the fall semester."

My shoulders caved inward. "I didn't mean to make you feel bad, Mama."

"You're not, Lexi, I promise. I'm just worrying and wishing I could do more like any mother would."

"Thanks for listening."

"Always. You know I love you and I'll always be here for you. I'm sorry I don't have more guidance to offer. But I really do believe you need to have a genuine talk with Matt. Try not to assume it will go as bad as you think. He might surprise you," she said, infusing her voice with more blind optimism than any voice had a right to have.

Surprising me was one thing that Matt was very good at. They just weren't always good surprises.

Chapter 25
Ice Cream Forgiveness

Matt

Alex was mad, like really mad. In the months since I'd known him, he'd never raised his voice like that, and that included when I'd gotten kicked out of class. But as much as the shouting had shaken me, it didn't compare to hearing him sobbing in his room. And it was all my fault. I hadn't even gotten a chance to show him what I'd found about our knight—which really felt like a half-baked apology now. To top it off, my body hurt like hell. I was tempted to seek out the healers on campus, but couldn't bring myself to follow through. I deserved every agonizing second it took to heal for what I'd done to Alex.

Everything he'd said played over and over in an endless loop. I'd been so preoccupied trying to figure out my issues that I never stopped to consider how it would affect him. He was absolutely right—I'd betrayed our friendship. Why hadn't I told him about the fight club?

It took me days to admit it to myself, and the answer only solidified how horribly I'd messed up. I hadn't told him, because I didn't want him to know. I knew he'd disapprove, and I didn't want to feel guilty. The joke was on me though. I felt guilty anyway.

I dragged my backpack into the kitchen and flopped into a chair, where I fingered the torn strap. It wouldn't last much longer thanks to whatever asshole had taken it from me at the club. Thankfully, everything inside had escaped the rough treatment unscathed. I pulled out Alex's book. My vision blurred as I caressed the worn cover. I swallowed thickly and blinked back the sting of tears. Since he'd blown up at me—justifiably—I'd barely caught so much as a passing glance of him. Forget whether I could come up with an adequate apology. How was I supposed to give it to him if he was avoiding me?

Considering I hadn't actually come up with a way to atone and I wasn't much for talking, I opted to use being physically present as my mode of communication. I'd told him before that I wasn't going anywhere and now I felt like I had to prove it. But the silence was driving me mad. I missed Alex's constant chatter, his physical presence. It didn't take much to realize his persistent absence from my days was why all of my dreams had taken a hard right. Gone were the toe-tingling intense dreams with the power to make me squirm. Now there were only nightmares of Alex leaving... forever. I couldn't bear it if he left. Everyone always left. And though I tried not to think about it, beneath all of my fear and guilt was still the overwhelming desire to kiss him again.

I thought hard about what he'd said about my always being drunk. He was right. I was too scared to admit what I wanted and had used alcohol to get it without taking any responsibility. So, I was not only was I a terrible friend but also a total coward.

My grip tightened on the pages of notes I'd pulled out of my bag. The crinkle of paper filled the oppressively quiet room. I let out a sigh and set them down, determined to organize the jumbled mess into something that actually made sense. I'd just finished straightening them back out when I heard the soft snick of a door opening.

I glanced up from my carefully chosen seat at the breakfast table. By some miracle, I caught Alex's eye, but he immediately looked away to gaze aimlessly around the room. Without school papers everywhere, the dorm was disturbingly clean. While he was distracted, I took stock of his overall appearance.

Smudges of gray darkened his normally bright eyes, making his face appear gaunt and sunken. Even without the massive bruise on my face, I could tell they matched the circles under mine. His shoulders sagged like he'd somehow shrunk, which seemed an impossible feat for someone so tall. And yet, he seemed smaller, more fragile. The sound of his broken sobs haunted my dreams and were definitely taking their toll on him. Clearly, neither one of us was sleeping.

I wanted to say something, but was afraid that talking might scare him back into his room. So far, this was the longest we'd been in the same general space in a week. He sighed and tilted his head back to stare at the ceiling. He was always fantastically lean, but it looked like he might be even thinner than normal. I was afraid he wasn't eating, though of course, I wasn't really, either.

Alex rolled his head to the side to look into the kitchen, and I quickly resumed my study of the papers in front of me. I heard him grab a glass from the cabinet and fill it with water. Then, to my infinite surprise, he pulled up a chair. I glanced up, daring to hope that today might actually involve words. Time stretched on, filled only with the sound of pen on paper as I continued to transfer the notes to a clean page.

"I'm still mad at you," Alex said, breaking the silence.

I glanced at him. He only caught my eye for a moment, but it was enough to feel yet another stab of guilt. What had I done to my friend? "Okay."

I was debating whether to say something else when he let out a sigh that caused his shoulders to fall even more. He stood without another word and returned to his room, leaving the empty glass. It wasn't much, but it was progress. There was hope. I could still fix this. What I needed was a peace offering. Something totally neutral that wasn't likely to get me into even more trouble. Normally, the research I'd gathered probably would've been perfect, yet after his callous comment about the book, it seemed best not to press my luck. No, I needed something totally mundane and not remotely supernatural.

I packed up my notes and went in search of my nameless item. All I could hope was that I would know it when I saw it. There were plenty of possibilities to choose from that might have worked. But I didn't want mights and maybes. I needed a ringer.

After what had happened the last time I ventured out, I was substantially more cautious. The last thing I needed was to get snatched again. My ribs had mostly recovered, and I wasn't eager for any other rematches. Accelerated healing was great and all, but it didn't make the process any more comfortable. After all of my years trying to avoid fights, I still wasn't sure what had possessed me to keep going back to that damn club. Sure, earning money was nice, but I didn't actually like fighting for my life.

I wasted the better part of the day wracking my brain for something to show Alex how sorry I was. Then I remembered Alex believed ice cream fixed everything. I swung by the dining hall and loaded up with our favorites—including every carton of strawberry they had—then headed back to the dorm as fast as I could before they all could melt. It wasn't until I was in the hall leading to our room that I wondered if it would all fit in the freezer.

A few doors away from ours, I had to stop when a guy stepped out of his room carrying a precarious stack of metal and cables. He squatted down to sit them on the floor and I shifted to go around. A thin plastic case tumbled free as he straightened up to close the door.

I squinted to make out a title. "What do you have there?"

"Oh this?" The guy pointed to the heap of electronics. "It's my old gaming unit. My grams just sent me a new one. Why?" It was perfect. Neutral. Normal. Distracting.

"What do you want for it?"

He checked out the bag I was carrying. "What do you got?"

"Ice cream."

"Sold. Here, there are even some games."

I traded him half of the ice cream and accepted the console. He probably would have given it to me for free, but it didn't matter, it was mine now. Now all I had to do was get Alex to play it.

Inside our dorm, there was no clear sign of Alex. I successfully put away the frozen goods and install the unit before he emerged from his cave again. He ghosted around a few minutes before finally settling on the couch. It was the first time he'd done that in days, so I chose to see that as yet another sign of hope. I quickly retrieved two pints from the freezer.

"Hey," I called. As he turned, I tossed him the strawberry. He wasn't expecting something to be thrown at him and almost dropped it. For a couple of shimmering seconds, it was like nothing was wrong. He was his usual self. I walked over and sat on the back of the couch, cracking open my container.

"You know a spoon would be—"

I held out a spoon for him, and he looked from it to me before accepting it.

He scooped up a bite and paused without taking it. "Matt—"

"It's fine, Alex. You have a right to be angry. I should have told you about the fight club." I stared into my frozen treat and mustered up the courage to be honest. "I… I didn't tell you, because I didn't want you to know."

He narrowed his eyes and slowly took a bite.

I rushed to elaborate, realizing too late how that must sound. "Because I didn't want you to think less of me. I don't even know why I kept going. I guess it was just nice for people to be afraid of me for a change." I bit into a frozen chunk.

He sighed, looking pensive as he scooped another spoonful. As apologies went, it wasn't the worst one I'd ever done, but there was really no way to make it right. It was already done. All that was left was to be honest about it.

Alex gestured with his spoon at my recent acquisition. "What's that?"

"Some kid down the hall was getting rid of it because he has a new one."

"That's wasteful."

"Agreed. He said nothing's wrong with it. Even gave me the controllers and some games."

"Should we see if it works?"

I diligently schooled my face from erupting into a grin. It was working. "I'm game if you are."

He hesitated a moment, then gave a small laugh under his breath. Joy surged inside of me at yet another sign I was making progress. While he inspected the selection, I put away what was left of the ice cream, then joined him on the floor. The cords for the controllers stretched over the coffee table, which he'd pushed out to give us more room.

"So, what are we playing?" I asked, sitting close enough to be present without crowding him.

He gave me a crooked grin that made my heart stutter. "Since we're apparently doing puns today, I went with Demon Crusader. It says it can have two players, though I'm not really sure how that will work."

"One way to find out." The console fired up no problem, and before long, the sounds of the game filled the room.

We played in silence, though it was substantially more companionable than the quiet I'd endured over the last week. The mechanics of the game were fairly simple, and after a while, I was confident enough to glance at Alex. He looked like he was actually having fun. That made me happy. Maybe I could fix this mess I'd made after all. Of course, there was still one more thing I had to take care of: I had to prove to Alex that I didn't have to be totally smashed to want to kiss him.

We paused at a checkpoint. While the game saved our progress, Alex excused himself and I grabbed a beer. I popped it open and sat it on the coffee table.

"What do you think of the game?" he asked, giving the beer a sidelong look as he resumed his seat. I wasn't even sure why I'd grabbed it. I didn't really want it, and it completely contradicted what I was trying to prove. My nerves were getting the better of me.

"It's not too bad. Though you would think someone would tell the creators that's not what demons look like. I mean, we don't have horns or wings and none of the other demons I've met do either."

Alex shrugged. "I don't know. Every myth has its roots in the truth somewhere. Maybe there was a time we did." He picked up the controller, and we resumed playing. He continued to glance at the neglected bottle throughout the game. Maybe grabbing it wasn't such a bad idea after all, he could clearly see that I wasn't drinking it.

I watched him, waiting for some comment or opening. There was only one thing I could think of to do to show him I didn't just want to kiss him with alcohol eliminating my inhibitions. Except I was so nervous, I could've really used that drink. Even nervous, though, the desire to kiss him was overwhelming. As much as I'd fought it before, there was absolutely no denying that it was exactly what I wanted.

I need to quit being such a chicken and just go for it.

"Alex." I shifted to face him.

"What's up?" he asked, turning to me.

I caught him in a kiss before he could say anything else. There was a moment when I thought he wouldn't kiss me back. Then there it was. I cupped the side of his face and kissed him deeper. He needed to know this was intentional, not some half-assed accident. At the feel of my hand, he relaxed into it a little more. I fought to hold myself back from completely drowning in the sensation. This needed to be as different as possible from all the other times.

The sound of something suffering on the screen invaded my concentration. I pulled away and leaned back against the couch. Alex sat there a moment looking a bit dumbfounded. I could have giggled with delight. I'd done it. I'd actually done it. And not a drop of alcohol. "You're dying," I said absently as I tried to regain control of my own character.

He turned blankly back to the game and rescued his demon before he could be fully minced.

I felt incredible. Kissing Alex sober was a thousand times better than I would have expected. It hadn't been nearly enough, but it was a start. I was probably grinning like a fool, and I couldn't have cared less. I'd done it. Suddenly, Alex's character abandoned the current mission and raced towards the next glimmering check point.

I frowned. "What are you doing?"

"Damn it, Matt." He vehemently threw down the controller.

Alarm shot through me. Somehow, I'd still made things worse. I set aside my controller and immediately started trying to apologize. "Alex, please don't be mad. I—"

He cut me off with a kiss I felt all the way in my toes. I gave in completely, melting into the soft press of his lips, his tongue confidently twirling with mine, the warmth of his hand on my cheek.

Kissing Alex sober really was like falling into a world of color I'd never even known existed. It was a drug, and I was absolutely addicted. My body reacted on its own, leaning into him, craving more, always more. His fingers slid through my hair as he pulled me closer. I moaned. This was everything I'd been dreaming about for weeks. Even more than his forgiveness, I'd wanted this, wanted it to the point it physically hurt. And now, I felt like I was spiraling out of control in a world of sensation.

I slipped and braced myself against the ground. Alex's free hand drifted down my side until it found bare skin where my shirt had ridden up. I hadn't been expecting that and broke off with a muffled gasp.

"What? What's the matter?"

What is wrong with me?

He looked me over frantically, concern clouding his face. "Are you still hurt? I would have thought by now..."

"It's not that." My heart hammered so hard I thought it might burst right out of my chest like one of the minions in the game.

His emerald gaze caught mine and I could clearly see my panic shining back. Fear flashed in his eyes to quickly be replaced by anger and then, worst of all, hurt. "Oh." He sat back, putting distance between us.

I could have screamed with frustration, but I couldn't seem to force my tongue to make words.

"Of course." He barked a laugh that sounded forced and bitter.

No, no, no.

He pushed himself to his feet, shaking his head. I leaned forward, but he refused to look at me. "I'm such a fucking idiot." He raked both of his hands through his hair while his gaze stayed firmly focused on the ground. "I can't do this." Without another word or even a glance in my general direction, he grabbed his key and left.

I stared at the door long after it had closed behind him. What did I do? Why did I freak out? It wasn't like I didn't want him to touch me, so why did I react like I didn't?

I snatched the bottle from the table with the full intent of chugging it. Instead, it flew across the room to smash against the wall by the door, sending glass and beer flying everywhere. I hung my head in my hands and let out a miserable groan. I'd ruined everything. Alex would never forgive me now.

CHAPTER 26
BLACK EYES

Alexi

I wandered around the dorm, not really sure where to go. My shoes were still in my room, so it wasn't like I could go far. Classes would start back up again soon, and already I could see the campus milling with activity beyond the dorm windows. I wished I could've taken the opportunity to go home, at least for a couple of days. My mom was right, the distance would have been good for me. Maybe if I'd taken on a few more tutoring sessions, I'd have been able to save enough. But should-of's and could-of's wouldn't help me now.

Now... now I was stuck in yet another impossible situation with Matt. I'd been a fool to believe that he could ever want me the way I wanted him. Seeing the doubt and panic in his eyes had hurt more than I'd ever imagined was possible. Even hours later, the ache was still there, right beside my excruciating love for him. If the last few weeks had taught me anything, it was that I'd never be able to stop loving Matt.

The longer I roved the halls, the more I felt like there was really only one option left. I couldn't live like this. I'd tried. Maybe someday I'd be able to just be friends with Matt, but not now. Something told me that would never happen, though. It wouldn't be enough to tell him we couldn't hang out anymore—he'd never let it be—I'd have to leave.

My chest tightened at the mere thought of not seeing him every day. It hadn't exactly been easy when I'd left Daniel, but by the end, I'd felt liberated, like I was finally free to be me. This was different. The pain went way deeper. This wasn't some band aid I could rip off. It felt more like giving up a part of myself than trying to move on with my life. But that didn't change what needed to be done.

I took a deep breath to steel my resolve and made my way back to the dorm. Whatever happened, I couldn't let Matt steamroll me. I would be strong... for both of us.

When I opened the door, it was to an empty room. There was no sign of Matt or anything else. For a moment, I was a little put out. He wasn't even waiting for me to come back? I checked my disappointment and forced myself to see this as a mercy. I'd get farther along in packing my things if he wasn't around to stop me.

As I walked past the table, I saw my book was there, along with several notes and the bookmark. It looked like the sketch he'd been working on was almost done and, contrary to what I'd originally thought, it took up the whole page. I resisted the urge to take a closer look. It would just be one more thing trying to keep me here. Without really paying attention to the other things on the table, I grabbed the book from amidst the clutter and the others I'd left on the counter. A few more feet and I'd be safe in my room.

"You came back."

I gave an involuntary flinch. He sounded so relieved. Now that I'd been spotted, it was pointless to ignore him. He'd bulldoze his way into my room if he had to. I couldn't take that, so I turned to him.

"Alex, please. I'm sorry. I-"

"No, Matt." Even saying his name was painful. Damn it, I would make it through this without falling apart. "I can't do this anymore. I won't do this anymore."

His mouth fell open, and it seemed to take him a second to recover. "What are you saying?"

"I'm saying I can't be your friend. It's too hard. I'm going to pack my stuff up and request to switch dorms in the morning." I had no idea if it was even possible, but I sure as hell was going to try.

Panic that bordered on terror exploded across his face. "You can't. You're my best friend."

"Well, I can't very well stay here. Can I?" I snapped. At least if I was angry, I wasn't a teary mess. "You won't have to worry about anything. I'll go see Marquis in the morning and get the room assignment changed. Maybe you'll luck out and have the whole place to yourself for a semester."

"Alex, wait. Just tell me what to do." He took a half step forward. "How can I make this right?"

"There's nothing you can do. It's... it's not you." That was only partially true, but it got his ire up.

"I swear, if you try to pull some it's not you, it's me bullshit..." The threat hung unfinished. "There has to be a way to make this right. We can go back to the way it was. We won't drink together anymore and... and..." he floundered, clearly not sure what he could do to fix this.

"Just stop. I know you want to keep being friends, Matt, but I just... can't. It's too difficult for me."

"I don't understand why. What's the big deal?"

"Because I'm in love with you," I replied with a little too much force. I hadn't meant to tell him that, but I felt better now that it was out. Despite his obvious surprise, he still didn't back down.

"I can fix this. You just have to tell me how."

"How? This isn't something you can fix. I've already tried. I can't do both. It hurts too much."

"But I can't lose you." He might as well have plunged a knife in my gut and twisted. "There has to be something. We... I... There has to be some way I can fix this." His voice threatened to break.

"There's nothing you can do."

He shook his head like it could somehow dispel what I was saying, a stubborn set to his mouth. "I don't believe that. There has to be a way to make this better. I won't let you go. I can't." His beseeching plea only made me angry. This was hard enough without him being selfish.

"What's it going to take for you to understand? These aren't just words, Matt. What can I do to prove that to you?" I set the books down hard enough on the counter that he jumped. I needed him to understand why I couldn't do this, why this was impossible for me.

Without warning, I stalked over to where he was standing. I grabbed his face with both hands and kissed him. He seemed unsure of what to do, but I didn't stop. I needed him to understand that loving him wasn't some passing fancy, or college crush; it had completely eaten me up so that I couldn't even breathe. I poured everything into the kiss, all the heartache, all the wishful thinking, even my desperate hope that someday he might love me back. This was probably the last time I'd ever get to do this, and I'd be damned if I wasn't going to make it count.

The longer I kissed him, the more I was in danger of losing what remained of my resolve. I loved kissing Matt; it was unlike anything else. I tried to rein it in, but he was still kissing me back.

"Matt, I've been completely wrapped up in you since the first time I saw you." I rubbed my thumb over his swollen lips. Perfectly kissable. I needed to stop.

I placed a lingering kiss, reveling in how his mouth molded to mine. I needed to go. Even having decided hours before, the decision felt like agony. I didn't want to leave Matt. I had to. I resisted the urge to steal one last kiss and released him. Already I could feel the ache spreading painfully across my chest. I quickly turned to retrieve the stack of discarded books.

"Like I said, don't worry about anything."

"Alex."

"I'll take care of everything. Student affairs will be open tomorrow pretty early and I should be able to get this sorted."

"Alex." I couldn't let him stop me. If I stopped, I'd never leave. I kept talking to drown him out.

"If I end up leaving something by accident, don't worry about getting it back to me. You can keep it."

"Alex," he said with enough force to pull me up short.

"What?" I looked at him. I knew I shouldn't have, but this was part of the problem: I couldn't seem to tell him no.

He swallowed. It looked like he was going to shuffle his feet. He didn't. He stared firmly back. "Let's try this."

I let out an exasperated sigh. "What are you talking about?" I already felt drained, and I hadn't even made it to my room yet. What was it going to be like getting my things out?

"This." He gestured between the two of us.

I crushed the stubborn hope that blossomed in my chest. "Don't. We both know you'll say or do just about anything to keep me. It's not funny, it's cruel." My voice cracked. I paused to gather myself. "I'm going to finish getting my things. I'll stay mostly out of the way."

"For crying out loud! Would you stop talking and listen?" He glared defiantly at me, heat shimmering in his eyes. "You're right, I would do pretty much anything, but I'm serious. I... I want to do this."

I shook my head, determined not to fall for it, no matter how much my heart wanted to believe. "You don't know what you're saying."

"Would you shut up? You don't understand, Alex." He paused as if not sure how to go on.

I waited patiently; he'd made it abundantly clear I wasn't getting into my room without him saying his piece.

He took a deep breath and let it out slowly. "I don't dream, not ever. Before I came here, I couldn't tell you the last time I so much as had a daydream. But I dream about you every night. Every single night without exception. And ever since... ever since that night, they haven't been the same."

This was news to me, but it didn't mean anything. We spent a lot of time together. It was bound to happen. I mean, I dreamed about him all the time too, but that didn't make them equivalent. I opened my mouth to stall him. This was only making things harder for both of us, but he beat me to it.

"And that kiss," he began with a lopsided smile. His eyes went black, catching me off guard. It didn't look like he was shadowing anything, but they were perfectly midnight just the same. "That kiss is certainly going to keep me up." He blinked, and they were back to their usual ethereal blue.

Shaken by both his words and what I'd witnessed, I didn't really know what to say.

"At least let me try." Matt stepped forward, and I danced backwards.

None of this was going at all like I'd expected. Of all the things I thought he'd say, this hadn't even made the list. Finally, I found my voice. "I need time. Can you give me that?"

He looked unsure, but nodded anyway.

Feeling out of sorts, I retreated to my room. Even with the door closed between us, I could still feel him on the other side. I pinched myself and was rewarded with a very sharp, very real pain. Not a dream then. I wanted to believe his proposal was genuine, but I couldn't bring myself to trust it. Not that I thought Matt would lie. It was that I knew he really would do anything not to lose me as a friend. Though I never dreamed he'd go so far.

My mind struggled to make logic out of the whirlwind of doubt and hope. Where did I even start processing what had happened? And his eyes. What was that about? Nothing had been shadowed, not even him. I was sure of it. It was as if he'd checked out, but I was at a loss for a time I'd ever seen him more intense.

Answers. I needed answers. There had to be an explanation for why his eyes would do that. Something I was missing. Something I didn't know. Deep down, I recognized that hyper focusing on the mysterious detail was really a way to avoid making a decision or thinking about what his suggestion. But that didn't prevent me from obsessing. But where could I go to get answers? Who would possibly know what that might mean? One name came to mind: Vera Scry. If anyone could tell me what or if his eyes turning black without evidence of shadowing was even a thing, she could.

I checked the time. It was definitely getting late, but there was a chance she'd either be in her office or in the classroom getting ready for the new semester. I glanced at the closed door where Matt's presence continued to hover. There was no way I was getting out of the dorm that way without him at least saying something.

I considered my bedroom wall. In theory, the hall was at worst twenty centimeters away. That wasn't far, right? Except, I'd never shadowed through anything before. Then again, Matt did it all the time... by accident. How hard could it be?

I slipped on my shoes and stepped up to the plaster where I let out a slow breath. The important part was not to overthink it. I just had to make sure I remained in a shadow state until I was positive I'd cleared the wall or risk getting stuck. My heart rate ticked up while I stared intently at my chosen point of passage. This absolutely qualified as advanced shadowing, and we hadn't really covered more than the concept. I shook off my mounting nerves. I could do this.

I let out another steadying breath and let my body become one with the shadow realm. The world appeared muted, both in color and sensation, but was more unnerving was the way my awareness expanded. I could easily sense even the smallest shadow in my room and Matt was basically a pulsing beacon of Shadow energy. That energy shifted as if he was aware of me too and fear that he would storm in here before I was ready to face him again got my feet moving. In two steps, I was on the other side. I made sure all of me was actually in the hall before returning to my physical form. My sensory perception of Matt shifted, betraying his realization that I was no longer in my room. I sprinted down the hall before he could investigate.

The sun sat like a molten ball on the horizon, its amber glow flooding the campus. I almost turned back at realizing it was even later than I'd thought, but that would mean going back to the dorm, which I wasn't ready to do. All the way to Mysterio College, I kept telling myself how ridiculous my fixation was. His eyes changing like that was probably nothing. Maybe he had shadowed something, and I'd been too distracted to notice. Besides, odds were that Vera wouldn't be there at all. She hardly ever was anyway. Why did I think she would be in her office now? Because I needed her to be?

When the oversized doors swung open, I gained a bit of optimism that at least someone was here. My footsteps echoed in the empty corridor as I made my way to Vera's office. To my dismay, her door was closed and the opaque window dark. I glanced around at a loss. Then I realized the classroom door was cracked open and noise was coming from inside.

I slipped inside, expecting to find one of the TAs. Much to my surprise, Vera looked up at my entrance and her face lit with surprise.

"Roman, what are you doing here? Is everything alright?" She put down the posters she was organizing, giving me her undivided attention.

"No, I mean yes, everything is fine. I… I have a question and I couldn't think of who else to ask," I stumbled.

She smiled and waved me over. "Why don't you give me a hand with these and I'll see what I can do about answering your question?"

I gently closed the door behind me. She noticed the move, but didn't comment. I plucked up the next poster and held it where she indicated while she pinned it down. "Why are you using push pins? Wouldn't a spell be easier?"

She shrugged. "Probably. But just because we have powers, doesn't mean we should use them for everything. Sometimes it's nice to do things the long way." She pressed in another pin and passed me the next poster. "So, what did you want to ask?"

"It's… uh… kind of personal."

"Oh? Is it about Matt?"

I looked at her in shock, but she didn't turn from her task of righting the poster. "Why would you assume that? Never mind, it is about another shadow demon. They did something I've never seen before. I mean, I've seen it, but not like this."

She finally stopped what she was doing to look at me. "Let's hear it then." She put her hands on her hips.

I swallowed, suddenly anxious about what I wanted to ask, not the least of which, because it was about Matt. "Have you ever heard of our eyes going black without us doing anything? Wait. That doesn't make any sense. Let me try again. Like, we aren't actually shadowing, but our eyes are black like we are. It's nothing, right?"

Her light curiosity vanished behind a cloud of dark seriousness. "Who did you see do this? Did someone say something to you?"

"What? No! No one has said anything to me about it. I just, I was just wanting to know. It kind of freaked me out." I glanced between the fresh poster in my hands and her, not at all liking her reaction. "So, you're saying this is a real thing? What does it mean?"

Her intensity slipped to be replaced by what looked oddly like embarrassment, but that couldn't be right. Vera had conquered nations, had helped overthrow an entire supernatural government. She was fearless. What in Nyx's name could have her looking so....awkward? "Well... it's... I mean..." she fumbled, which only ratcheted up my anxiety. "Good grief, of all the questions for a student to ask. I'm not old enough for this shit." She gave me a sidelong look, her mouth turned down in a resigned frown.

"I take it this is actually a really personal thing?"

"You could say that. So," she paused, taking a deep breath, "you know how Fire Demons can have flare-ups? Like when they get too worked up or emotional?"

I nodded, though I failed to see how that related.

"Consider this the Shadow Demon equivalent."

My face scrunched as I tried to make sense of what she way saying and came up empty. "I'm not following."

"I can't believe I'm saying this out loud." She ran her hands through her red hair, causing it to frizz. "Alright, here goes. Black eyes are a manifestation of a Shadow Demon's true nature and their true desires. It's not contingent upon manipulating shadow. It usually happens when we're exceptionally worked up and in the moment."

I shook my head, still confused. "Like angry? I've seen that plenty of times. This was different."

"Think other extreme emotion." Her face turned red, and she looked away.

"What? Like...." I trailed off. I thought about what had happened and what Matt had said about the kiss keeping him up tonight. "Oh." High emotion, and he'd given me that grin like... "Oh!" I repeated, the information settling. "Well, um..." I cleared my throat. "Alright then."

"Yeah, so be careful with that. Having a poker face doesn't do much good when it's literally stamped in your eyes."

I nodded numbly. Well, at least I knew I could trust what Matt had said about wanting to try. Now, to figure out what I was going to do about it. But not tonight. I'd had enough life-altering revelations for one day.

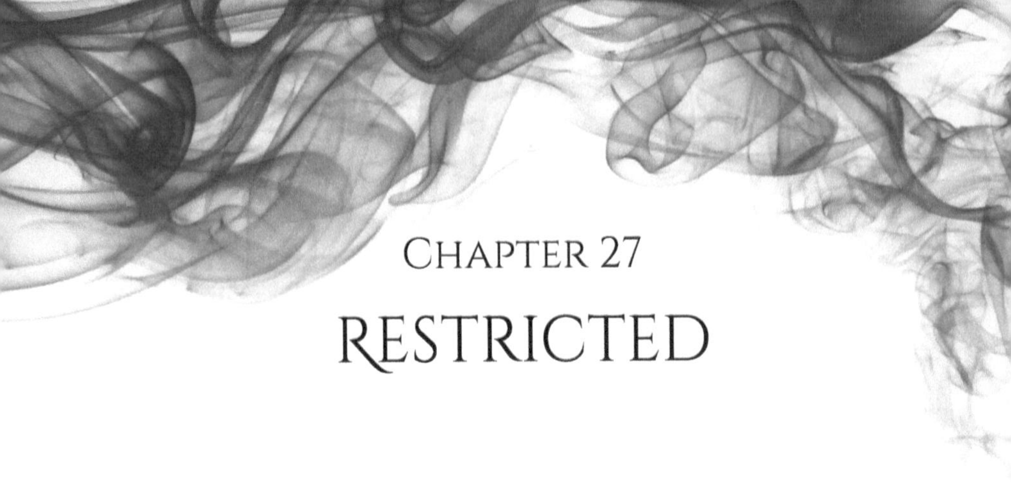

CHAPTER 27
RESTRICTED

Matt

Alex had fled the coop… again. I sank into one of the kitchen chairs, feeling absolutely miserable.

He'll come back. He did last time.

But the last time he hadn't said he couldn't stand to be here with me. I wasn't sure why I'd said we should try things his way. I didn't even know if I could. Yet, as I thought back, I'd say the same again, and it was more than just wanting him to stay. Some part of me wanted to see what would happen. Alex was unequivocally my best friend, and I'd do anything to keep him, but what if he was actually more? That would certainly explain the dreams. Maybe being… a couple was exactly the fix we needed. Except he'd left. Again.

Not left-left, though, or at least that's the hope I was clinging to. He'd asked for space and I'd do my best to give it to him. Yet, here I was, staking out both doors. If he'd gone through the wall, though, there was really no point in sitting here. I tried to think of something to do while I waited to see if he really would come back. Distantly, I considered heading to the fight club, but quickly dismissed the fleeting thought. It wasn't worth it, especially not if I was concerned about whether Alex would even agree to my outrageous idea.

I looked at the table covered with notes and realized his book was gone. Pain lanced through my chest as I shuffled through the papers in a panic. Nothing had been disturbed aside from the missing book. He'd taken it. No way I'd lost it.

He wasn't coming back.

I launched out of my chair, and it clattered to the ground. I spun in a circle, taking in the empty space. The dorm felt hollow without him there. I didn't want a new roommate or no roommate at all. I wanted Alex. Except I'd messed everything up so badly. He was never going to come back. He'd slip quietly out of my life without so much as a goodbye, and I'd be left alone. Again.

My chest tightened. I couldn't seem to catch my breath. I struggled for air, but only managed quick gasps. I couldn't do it, not again. Everyone always left. Even my bright, shining Alex, who saved me from the darkness. That's all there was, all there ever would be for me—darkness.

It felt like the lights in the room were dimming, like the hollowness of the space had been given life and was coming for me. Air refused to stay in my lungs and black spots swam across my vision. I'd be consumed by it. No one would ever care enough to rescue me, to keep me in the light. The room was closing in around me, crushing me with the overwhelming weight of emptiness.

This had happened before. The memory was distant and insubstantial, yet I knew with certainty this was not the first time this had happened. I needed to escape, to run, to hide. I needed Alex. I was drowning in darkness. It was going to swallow me whole.

Alex wanted space.

Alex wasn't coming back.

The room only got darker.

I begged my feet to move. Rather than to the door, they took me to the sink. I turned on the cold water and stuck my head under the frigid stream. Gradually, I regained my breathing and the oppressive darkness receded. I stayed beneath the spray for a few minutes more, letting the icy water run over the back of my head. Then I reached up and turned it off. It wasn't until I was drying my hair with a dish towel it occurred to me what I'd done.

I blinked and looked around the room. Everything appeared normal enough now, but I'd felt that sensation of darkness moving before: Vera had done it, and so had Alex. In my panic attack, I'd shadowed the entire room... and targeted myself. I swallowed hard. Yes, Shadow Demons were very dangerous and not just to other people.

Now that I was properly terrified of myself and everything else in the room, I couldn't stay here. It was getting late, and my options were limited. Wherever I went, I didn't feel safe enough to be on my own. What if next time I didn't snap out of it? The darkness was something that couldn't be escaped. What happened if the very darkness a Shadow Demon summoned consumed them? Could we come back from that? Or did we just become darkness?

I shook myself, fearing that the morbid thoughts would trigger another episode. I scraped the notes into my bag, not caring that half of them got crumpled yet again. My gaze fell on Alex's forgotten key as I went to grab mine.

Darkness crept along the edges of my vision. I quickly exited the dorm and made a bee-line for the library. It was slim that there would be other students there this soon before classes or this late at night, but there was at least one guaranteed soul—the librarian.

I got there so fast that I couldn't help but wonder if I'd shadowed part of the way. It didn't matter. I was here now. I dropped my things on my usual table with an audible thud, earning me a reproachful glare from the librarian, who seemed to materialize out of nowhere. I'd been secretly toying with the idea that she was actually a ghost. However, I wasn't brave enough to test the theory, and couldn't think of anyone I wanted to talk to enough to ask. Her appearance was timely though, because I had a question for her.

Quickly, before she could disappear to some other part of the library, I pulled out one of the pages. Thankfully, it was the one I needed. I smoothed it out and presented it to her. She eyed me and the page skeptically.

"I need to find this guy's last name." I pointed to where I had notated the reference books I'd found and their connection, as well as my copy of his sigil. "How can I do that?"

She contemplated the page without touching it, then silently walked away.

"Hey wait!" I called after.

She spun and gave me a stern look, holding up a finger to her lips. When it was clear I got the message, she waved me to join her. I followed a few paces behind as she quietly considered each row we passed. After what felt like an eternity of wandering, she turned down an aisle.

I'd never been in this part of the library. A glance at a dusty plaque said that it was restricted. Considering how much of her ire I'd earned over the last few months, not to mention weeks, I was impressed she was allowing me anywhere near this section.

She walked down the tight row and paused several feet away while I lingered in the opening.

I eyed the tall stacks of shelves situated practically on top of each other that seemed to reach toward the top of the vaulted ceiling. Dusty tomes lined the shelves, giving me an idea of the last time they'd been touched—a solid never. The more I stared at the imposing display of forbidden knowledge, the less I wanted to follow her. As it was, she seemed to be encased in shadow, the narrow space getting even darker farther on. Rather than urge me to hurry, she waited patiently for me to conquer my fear.

I thought about how close the darkness had come a short while ago. Did I dare risk walking into its embrace willingly? I took a deep breath and stepped forward. Almost instantly, my trepidation doubled.

This was a mistake. I'll never escape.

I took another deep breath. I could do this. It was only ten feet.

Ten months.

The thought came unbidden. Did I even care anymore? The only thing I really cared about was Alex. And if he didn't come back, ten months—seven now—meant nothing. Alone on the street or alone in the dorm, it wouldn't matter. I'd never live long enough to find out.

The sensation of darkness pulling at me got stronger, yet the librarian remained completely unfazed. Eight feet.

I did this to myself. I let all of my issues and hang-ups ruin the only friendship I'll ever have.

Five feet.

Slipping into the night might not be so bad.

The pull got stronger. Three feet. I was close enough now that I could see what the librarian was pointing to.

Two.

It won't matter what I find out about this mysterious knight whose family had decimated my kind. I'll never get to tell Alex.

One.

My hand shook as I reached up to grab a tome easily the size of my head. Like all the others, it looked like it hadn't been disturbed in decades. The gray leather binding felt like it might flake away in my hands. I carefully opened the book. Right at the beginning was a list of crests and sigils, and there among them, my knight's. The Latin beside it I knew said the name of his order, but past that, I had nothing. Everything was in Latin. Not a single word was in anything I could read or even pretend to understand.

I glanced at the librarian, who gave me a knowing smile. She walked past me towards the exit and I followed quickly, eager to leave this ominous place of darkness behind. She hadn't mentioned anything about replacing the book, so I took it with me.

As we left the confined space, the feeling of despair lifted. Maybe this book would have the answers we needed. Maybe Alex could forgive me long enough for me to share. Knowing more about his favorite story would mean the world to him.

I continued to follow my strangely silent guide to an old table with a lamp attached to it. She gestured for me to sit. I did so, placing the fragile book before me. When the binding touched the table, the lamp blossomed to life, creating a perfect pool of yellow light in which to read.

"This is great," I said, "but I already have a table."

She raised an eyebrow and looked at the book. I mimicked her and watched in amazement as the scrolling Latin transformed into a language I could actually read.

"Holy shit! It's a magic lamp."

She frowned at me.

"Oh, language, sorry."

Unfortunately, the cover was far too faded and abused to make out the title. I could only hope the inside was in better shape. I carefully turned the page. Slowly, the letters shifted and moved until I could understand them. Demon Wars: Volume Six 1100-1350. This was a history spanning two hundred and fifty years, and my knight's story fell right smack in the middle. This was everything we'd been searching for and then some. I glanced at the librarian and fought back the sudden stinging in my eyes. Even if Alex couldn't forgive me, I could still give him this.

"Thank you."

She shrugged, offering a small smile.

"Can I...?" I wasn't really sure she'd let me leave the library or even this section with the book, but I doubted I'd make it back down that aisle.

She gave the barest nod and turned to leave.

"Wait." I didn't know what possessed me, but I had to know. "Are you a ghost?"

She smiled again and gave me a wink before gliding silently away.

I shook my head and returned to the ancient volume, handling each page like it might actually crumble at the touch. The material was surprisingly thick, though, and resilient. Perhaps, like the light, the book had also been spelled. I'd read of spells that could make items resistant to time. At last, I found a page that looked like the start.

The war on Darkness was led by the Wardes, Guardians of Light. They alone held the power to harness light itself and burn the Shadow Horde.

In two sentences, I'd learned more than I could have hoped. I'd never heard of a war against darkness or even demon wars like the title suggested. I knew from Demonic History there had been plenty of "demonic wars", but nothing like this suggested. This seemed to imply that this war had been going on for ages. I couldn't help but wonder if it still was.

I gently touched the elegant letters that proudly proclaimed the Wardes as the destroyers of night. This was the first time I'd ever seen the name mentioned. The crest I'd found a few times, but never any names. Most of the time, the sigil wasn't even labeled. And here, on one page, I had an entire list of names and coats of arms, listing the families responsible for culling the demon race.

I closed the book, and the light went out. It was a shame there wasn't a way to take that with me. We'd have to come back. Assuming, of course, Alex was willing. I clutched my prize tightly to my chest and made my way back to my original table. Fortunately, no one had bothered my things, and I could add the book to my pack. I still couldn't believe the librarian was going to let me leave with it. Maybe she also didn't want to venture down that awful aisle.

I shuddered, then swung my noticeably heavier bag onto my shoulder. With exaggerated care, I made my way across campus, very aware that the last time I'd made a similar journey, I'd gotten grabbed. Luck was with me, though, and I didn't run into any unwanted faces.

I stopped in front of the door to our dorm and hesitated before opening it. What if Alex was on the other side with an answer? What if he wasn't?

I took a deep breath and stepped inside. The room was a soft dark that reached out Like a gentle caress. The door closed behind me without a sound. Subconsciously, I pushed my awareness into the darkness. It didn't feel threatening like it had in the library or like it had earlier in the day. It was warm, like a friend, and there, back in his room, I sensed Alex. I let out a breath I hadn't realized I was holding.

He came back.

I was tired from the exhausting day and my draining experience in the library, but I was just as afraid that if I went to sleep, I'd wake up to a world without Alex. For a moment, I debated sleeping on the couch. Except that wouldn't do any good. He'd already proved he didn't need the front door to come and go. Besides, it wouldn't bode well for agreeing to give him space.

I shrugged off my pack and walked to my room. Once inside, I changed and lay on the bed. I had no idea how I'd ever sleep with so much anxiety clamoring in my mind. Yet it seemed in hardly any time at all that I fell into a deep slumber and dreamed about being swallowed whole by the night. The only thing that prevented me from waking up in terror was that I knew Alex was in the darkness, waiting for me.

CHAPTER 28
LAVENDER & SAGE

Alexi

I dallied in my room. While I had a better idea of Matt's sincerity, I still couldn't bring myself to trust it. A subconscious response just wasn't the same as someone telling you outright that they wanted to be with you. Even more than my distrust of Matt's motives—subconscious or otherwise—was my distrust of myself.

I wanted it to be true so bad I was afraid I might be deluding myself. There was no way this could end in anything but disaster, and yet, I desperately wanted to hope, to believe that this could work. That we could work. Before I could, though, I needed Matt to answer a few questions. When I walked into the living room, I wasn't surprised to find him sitting on the couch.

"I wasn't sure you'd come back," he said without looking up, confirming my suspicion the other night that he'd known when I left.

"I would never leave without saying goodbye, Matt. You should know me better than that." No matter how much doing so would hurt. I walked over to join him. The cushion shifted beneath me, but everything else remained perfectly still, including Matt. "Where did you go yesterday?" If he said the fight club, I was done.

He glanced at me out of the corner of his eye, but didn't turn. "The library." It was looking like that was his go-to place to think.

"Find anything?"

"Yes." His gaze flicked to his pack. I expected him to reach for it, but he stayed still, like he was waiting for something. Then it hit me.

He's resigned himself that I'm leaving.

I studied him closer. He looked like a child lost in the woods that had given up trying to be found. My heart ached. I took a deep breath. Here went nothing. "Tell me about these dreams of yours."

Matt still didn't face me. He did, however, turn bright red. Well, that was something. Whatever they were, they weren't innocent.

I didn't prompt him. If this was going to be a thing, then I needed him to volunteer information without me dragging it out of him.

He twiddled his thumbs as if trying to decide how to start. "They began simple enough. Aside from the fact that I was dreaming at all, there was nothing particularly unusual about them. You were just there, something permanent that never changed." He almost looked at me and let out a heavy breath. "That's a really big deal for me." He paused, like admitting that out loud was especially hard.

"After the practicum, that changed. It wasn't just memories of our time together, they were... different. Do you remember that day we ran in the rain?" He looked over briefly and I nodded. How could I forget? I'd almost kissed him right in front of the dining hall. "The night of the practicum, I dreamed of that again. Except this time, when I caught you, we didn't laugh about it and go inside. Instead, we stayed outside and kissed in the rain." He plucked at the hem of his shirt, worrying a thread loose. "It was like my mind was trying to show me how that moment should have gone. Looking back, I realize that it's right. Then all of my memories of us changed. Every time we were too close, anytime I thought you were being awkward, all of them." He took a shaky breath.

I had so many questions, but it seemed best not to interrupt. This was the most personal information he'd ever shared at one time.

"As it went on, I had to admit that they weren't happening because I found out you were gay. I think I actually knew the whole time and was willfully ignoring it. That doesn't matter though. The bottom line was that I kept dreaming about us kissing because... I wanted to." His face flushed a deep pink again. "And it's not just in the dreams. No matter what we're doing, that want is there, and I don't know what to do about any of it." He let out a frustrated huff, then regathered himself. "All I'm asking is that you let me try. I'm not promising I'll be perfect. I'll need patience, but... I do want this."

I felt like the entire world had been suspended. Through his speech, he'd yet to face me. Meanwhile, my heart was somewhere between wanting to race and being too afraid to beat at all. "Okay." The word popped free, and it was like someone had finally pushed play on the world around me.

Matt turned and really looked at me. Doubt shone in his blue eyes like he was searching for the other shoe. So I gave him the clarity he needed.

"We'll do this."

A spark of hope brightened his worried gaze. "Are you sure? I know I've already made a real mess. I don't expect you to forgive me for what I've done."

I sighed and gave him a small smile. "I've already forgiven you, Matt. But I need to know that you understand I love you, that I'm in love with you. It's not some teenage crush on my roommate. Is that going to be okay?"

His eyes were wide, but he nodded. He licked his lips. "I'll make mistakes. This is very... different for me."

"I know." I leaned forward to caress his face. He didn't flinch or pull away. He simply stared back and waited. How was it possible to love one person so much? "We'll just have to take it slow." I closed the distance and gave him a soft kiss.

He let out a faint sigh, and his lips pressed back against mine. The pure intimacy of the moment shattered every romantic notion I'd ever had. This was everything our first kiss should have been. I rubbed a thumb over his bottom lip. "You have a fantastic mouth by the way." I felt him smile against my finger and kissed him again. There was a lingering heat that felt like it was clearly being held in check. I thought about his eyes the night before and what that apparently meant.

I wonder if I could make him do that on purpose.

I pulled back slightly to get a better look at him. They were still decidedly blue, albeit a bit dazed. "Also, you smell like sage."

He blinked. "What?"

"You once told me I smell like lavender. I thought you might like to know what you smell like."

"Oh. Is that okay?" He frowned.

I leaned forward until my nose brushed the sensitive skin beneath his ear, then inhaled deeply, appreciating the pure scent that was Matt. "I like it," I whispered before leaning back again.

It took a moment for me to shake off my fog. When I opened my eyes, I was rewarded with two perfectly midnight ones looking back at me. My lips twitched. I'd never been the seducer before and already I could tell I liked it immensely. I stole a more chaste kiss.

He blinked, and the blue returned.

"Now, are you going to show me what you found in the library or not?"

He blinked a few more times, then glanced around like he was trying to regain his bearings. "What? Right. The library." Without standing, he used shadow to bring his bag over.

I shook my head. He really was impossible, but he hadn't run away yet, so we were already off to a better start. When he pulled out a dusty tome and a handful of papers, I stared in shock. The book looked older than the university.

"Here," he said, passing it to me. "Almost all of it's in Latin, but there's a special lamp in the library we can use to translate."

What he was saying didn't make a bit of sense. I accepted the book, terrified it would crumble in my hands. "Where did you get this?"

"It was in the restricted section."

I looked up at him sharply.

He shrugged as if it was nothing. "The librarian showed me."

I didn't know what was more surprising, that the librarian, who never said a word to anyone, had helped him or that she'd let him take the book out of the library. "Matt, the restricted section is spelled. How did you get in?"

His brow furrowed. "What kind of spell?"

"It's an avoidance spell that makes you face all of your greatest fears." His eyebrows shot up. I'd only heard about it, but it was apparently pretty potent stuff. You had to get special permission and everything. No one simply walked into the restricted section.

Matt gulped. "No wonder I almost didn't make it."

I carefully opened the ancient book. "How did you?"

"I wanted to get it for you."

I glanced at him. "Beg your pardon?"

"I asked the librarian where I could find what we were missing and she took me there. Pointed it right out. Here, look at this." He reached over and began turning the pages.

I thought about telling him to be careful, but I was too busy staring at him in disbelief. He'd faced down his greatest fears, just to get me a book?

He stopped fussing with the pages and started riffling through the crumpled notes in his backpack. "That book, plus this, gives us our knight." He pushed a piece of paper at me. "This goes way deeper than we ever thought. I think your romance might actually be a forbidden affair."

I finally looked at what he was showing me. In the miraculously whole book was a page with a family crest and a name. I recognized the staff encircled with shadowed flames from my book. On the handwritten sheet Matt had given me were reference notes to yet another book, only this one was a Shadow Demonology.

He pointed at the page. Beside two names was the symbol once again. "Meet your knight—Matthias Warde of the Order of Light."

I gasped and nearly dropped the relic. "Mother of Night, Matt. I could kiss you."

"No one's stopping you," he quipped.

I ignored the invitation. He was right about the old book. Every scrap of it was in Latin. "Do you have any idea what this says?" I turned to the title. He looked a little put out, but produced another page. "Demon Wars: Volume Six 1100-1350." I squinted at it, not sure if I was reading it right. "Demon Wars? The only demon wars I know about are the original Wars of Power, but that was way before any of this. And was demon against demon."

"I know. Same here. I haven't read of anything about people and demons fighting. There's more, though. This book specifically references a war against darkness. This was how our kind almost became extinct."

I suddenly felt like I was holding the Holy Grail of Shadow Demons. "Why does no one know about this?" This was definitely something that should have been covered in Demon History.

"I don't know. I thought the same thing. But, Alex, there's another thing."

"How can there possibly be more?" I looked around at his pages full of notes now scattered everywhere.

"The missing pages."

My head snapped up. "You found them?"

"No, I found something else." He drew my attention back to the page with the two names. There was a line connecting them and another that went down to make a 'T'. "They had a child, Alex."

The page swam before me and I feared I might have fainted. "This, this... it's incredible. How did you ever...?" I looked up at him. Per usual, he was watching me. "This is what you were doing for four days." I didn't even need his nod of confirmation. "And..."

"I got snatched on my way back to show you. They wouldn't let me leave without going at least one round. I tried to anyway, but... you saw how that worked out."

I searched his face. I was the reason he'd gotten beaten to a pulp. He didn't have to say it, I knew it. "I'm sorry."

He averted his eyes, his shoulders hunched inward as he studied the carpet.

"Matt, there's one condition to us trying this dating thing." He looked back at me and I saw the fear in his eyes. "No more bruiser club. I can't do this if I know you're fighting all the time."

"Done," he replied faster than I would have expected. "I doubt they want me back anyway after my last performance."

"Have you healed up alright?" Concern colored my words. I'd been so worried, even while I was beside myself with anger.

He raised his eyebrows. "Do you need to check?"

I laughed. Cheeky bastard. "Slow, remember?"

"I remember." He swiped a kiss before I could react, then bounded off to the kitchen, leaving me speechless.

That little devil. Oh, this is going to be fun.

When Matt returned, he had an ice cream in each hand. He held out a carton of strawberry with a smile that warmed me despite the cold now suffusing my hand.

I popped the lid free to discover it was a fresh carton. "Just how much of this stuff did you buy?"

"Enough to be prepared." He extended me a spoon. "You were really mad."

"Who says I'm not anymore?"

He leveled a look at me.

"Alright, alright. I'm clearly not. No need to be smug about it." I shifted to a more comfortable position on the couch. "Now, show me everything you've found. Walk me through this."

He flashed me a dazzling smile and discarded his ice cream to reach for the pages. Then he folded his leg under him and joined me on the couch. He began by laying out each of the pages so he could straighten them and then sorted each into its own stack. The leather-bound monstrosity he left where it was at the edge of the coffee table. I didn't know why, but that book made me nervous.

As Matt bustled about, I couldn't help but think he was every inch his usual, carefree self. I'd known that finding out I was gay had affected him. I just hadn't realized how much until now. Without thinking, I reached out and brushed his hair with my fingertips.

He turned to look at me, his gaze curious yet unconcerned. "What's the matter?"

"I'm sorry."

Instantly, anxiety flashed across his face. He was so sensitive and would never admit it. I'd missed him.

"You weren't the only one so wrapped up in their own thoughts they couldn't see what was happening right in front of them."

His gaze shifted back to the papers, and he seemed to shy away.

I gave him a gentle push on the shoulder, prompting him to meet my gaze again. "I missed my friend, too." His smile started nervous and grew to a brilliant one that shone in his eyes. "I knew you were struggling, and I assumed I knew why."

"Alex, I'm not sure there's anything you could do that would ever make me not want to be your friend anymore." Despite all his protests to the contrary, Matt really had a way with words... when he used them. He squinted at me. "What?"

I shook my head, mirroring his smile. "Just you."

"What about me?" A shadow of the fear I'd caught earlier darted behind his eyes.

I couldn't very well have him doubting his conviction now, not after he'd finally admitted to being interested in pursuing something between us. So I set my ice cream aside and waved him over. "Come here."

His breath caught, and for a split second, his eyes turned solid black. Then I blinked and the distance between us was gone. I refused to let my joy at his instant reaction get the better of me and leaned forward to capture his mouth once more. He melted against me, making my heart soar. I cupped the side of his face and kissed him deeper, slipping my tongue past his parted lips. I'd gotten the sweet first kiss we deserved. Now I wanted the all-consuming ones that had driven me to torment.

Matt sucked in air through his nose, pressing back just as fiercely, but refusing to break away. His fingers scraped against the fabric of his jeans as he clenched and unclenched his fingers.

Smiling against his mouth, I reached down with my free hand to grab his wrist, then moved his hand to the small of my back. I didn't restrain my hum of contentment as his fingers unfurled and warmth seeped past my shirt. No sooner did the sound leave my throat than his hand clenched once more, bunching the fabric.

Matt kissed me harder, like he was starving. If I hadn't been so concerned that he'd freak out like he had before, I would have pushed him back and taken this make-out session to another level. With a restraint I didn't even know I possessed, I pulled away. His tongue flicked out to taste his swollen lips, and I smothered a groan.

There was a decidedly wicked gleam in his stunning blue eyes as they met mine. And said, "You have an interesting definition of slow."

I took a deep breath and let it out slowly, then scooted away from him enough to see the red fabric of the couch between us. "I may have gotten a little carried away."

He shrugged. "Don't hear me complaining."

I laughed and smiled back at him. "You're going to be nothing but trouble."

"So, I've been told."

"Now about these notes of yours..." I arched an eyebrow at him.

Matt's face fell. "For real? But... what about... we..."

I placed a hand on his knee and gave it a gentle squeeze. Instantly, his fumbling ceased. "There's no need to rush. We have time."

He grumbled incoherently to himself and reached for his forgotten papers. When he sat back up, though, an air of excitement had replaced his obvious disappointment.

I left my hand where it was, absently rubbing my thumb on his leg, while he regaled me with his discoveries. Everything about this moment was perfect. My lips still tingled from our fevered—albeit brief—make out. Matt was letting me touch him. We had more information about a story I'd treasured growing up. There was no obnoxious voice in my head belittling me. If this was how incredible being with Matt was in one afternoon, I couldn't wait for an entire semester.

BOOK TWO

ORDER OF LIGHT

S BOLANOS

CONTENTS

Chapter 1
Here We Go Again

Alex

Walking into Battle Tactics on the first day of fall semester was just as surreal as it had been in summer. I glanced to the side and smiled. Only *this* time, Matt and I weren't at odds. We were... dating. My heart gave a happy skip and I couldn't help but wonder how long it would keep doing that whenever I thought about Matt and me together. My guess? Forever.

I waved to some of our classmates—Ellie and Yaren were already deep into gossiping, while Louise and Roland pretended the other didn't exist. An entire class of Shadow Demons. I doubted that would ever stop surprising me either. Though it seemed we were still waiting for a few people.

My smile broadened as Matt and I walked nearly hand-in-hand to our usual corner of the room, where it seemed some fresh faces had also clustered. Or it *could* have been hand-in-hand if Matt hadn't been too busy sulking.

"I still don't see why Battle Tactics has to be so ridiculously early now," he complained from behind crossed arms, his adorable pout on full display. A morning person, Matt was not.

"It's really not that bad." For all the fuss he was putting up, I didn't think it was really about having to wake up earlier. Unlike the previous semester when we'd shared every class, presumably for our own safety, we only had two classes together this term. I was also fairly confident that Matt would die before admitting he was anxious about navigating courses on his own. Except he wouldn't be. "You know, just because we don't share the same schedule doesn't mean we can't still study together."

His sullen expression softened with a glimmer of hope. "Yeah?"

"Of course. Who else is going to make sure you're taking notes and not just doodling?" I raised an eyebrow to forestall the argument I could already see brewing.

He laughed and rewarded me with one of his stunning smiles that had become so frequent these last few weeks.

Personally, I could have done with more of a reprieve than two weeks between semesters. It would have been nice to visit home. But spending time together without things being weird—well, *less* weird—had been nice. And all the cuddles. I was a big fan of all the couch cuddles...when I got them. I was about to ruffle Matt's hair and tease him some more when he pointed behind me.

"Do we know that guy?"

I turned to see who he was talking about and a young man with deep umber skin and twisted locks that hung just past his ears waved. "Uh... no."

"Think he's another TA? I feel like Vera's wearing her usual ones out."

I glanced at Matt. "Why don't we find out?" We moved towards the young man in his pale purple tucked shirt and crisply pressed slacks. I sensed a kindred spirit. I'd dressed remarkably similar on my first day. "Hi, you must be new."

The young man gave a deprecating chuckle and rubbed the back of his neck. "Is it that obvious?"

"No," I said at the same time Matt replied, "Yeah." The three of us shared a laugh. When it died out, I extended my hand. "I'm Alexi. This is Matt, my—"

"Roommate," Matt filled in before I could finish. I darted a glance at him, but he wasn't paying attention.

The young man shifted to take Matt's equally extended hand. "I'm Gilles," he said, with an emphasized Z sound at the beginning. "I was actually supposed to be here for the summer semester, but I, uh... How you say, *chickened* out."

I nodded in understanding at his abashed smile. "This *is* kind of unprecedented. So many Shadow Demons together in one place? And the legendary Vera herself?"

"Will she really be here?" Gilles' gaze darted about the room, his face a mix of awe and trepidation.

Matt snorted. "If we're lucky. Or not." He shrugged. "Depends on how you look at it. So, Gille," Matt began, over-emphasizing the pronunciation, "where are you from?"

Like myself, Gilles was clearly trying not to laugh at Matt's butchered attempt at his name. "Do not worry, the name is French, which is where I'm from, France. You are American, no?"

Matt squinted and I could tell he was trying to decide if he should take offense at the assumption. Before he could decide he should, I intervened.

"What part of France?"

Gilles rocked back on his heels. "I grew up on the outskirts of Paris with my papa."

Matt's face brightened. "Paris-Paris? Eiffel Tower, the Louvre, and everything?"

"Oui. Arc de Triomphe, Montmartre, and the Seine too," Gilles added with a wide smile that revealed dimples.

"That's amazing! Have you been to the Louvre? Of course, you have. Better question, is it as great in person as it looks in books? What's your favorite piece?" Matt's enthusiasm took me aback and Gilles appeared overwhelmed.

I crossed my arms and scowled at him. "Hey, where was all this curiosity when I told you I was from the UK?"

"*You* said you were from a small village in the middle of nowhere," he said with a wry twist of his lips. "If you'd have said London..."

I let out an indignant squawk, and both Matt and Gilles erupted into laughter. Before I could formulate an appropriate scathing response, Matt bumped me with his shoulder.

"If you want me to grill you about your town, I will."

I deflated. "Okay, you win. There's really not much to tell. It's a plain, old boring English village, filled with the usual array of busybodies."

Matt rolled his eyes. "Please. *Anywhere* is better than Nebraska."

"You two are obviously great roommates. Hopefully, I am so lucky." Gilles smiled and Matt shifted.

"Do you know who you're bunking with yet?"

Gilles took on an intense look of concentration. "I believe their name is Miel?"

Matt and I shared a look, then Matt said exactly what I was thinking. "That's weird. Wasn't Miel rooming with Sebastian?"

I glanced around the room for Sebastian. When I still didn't find him, I shrugged. "Maybe he dropped the class?"

Before we could speculate further, the class door opened and the TA, Anne, walked in. She waved to several of us as she made her way to the front of the room. An expectant hush fell over us. Then Anne cleared her throat.

"Welcome back, everyone. As I'm sure you've noticed by now, we have several new students." She smiled encouragingly at a few, including Gilles. "Unfortunately, Ms. Scry will not be here to greet you personally today. She is currently away on... business." Anne's face tensed, her smile slipping slightly, before she pulled it back into place. "I'd like to take this opportunity to set expectations for this semester's Battle Tactics course. Out of consideration for our newest students, we will devote the first couple of weeks to review, beginning with guided meditation."

A collective groan from everyone *except* the new students filled the room.

"I know, I know," Anne said with a placating gesture. "Promise it won't be as extended as before. Vera has made it clear that once everyone is on the same page, so to speak, your studies will accelerate drastically."

I frowned and looked at Matt. He hiked a shoulder, but that did nothing to mediate my sudden concern. My hand flew into the air.

"Don't," Matt hissed under his breath.

"Yes, Mr. Roman. You had a question?" Anne asked with a knowing smile.

I let my hand fall and ignored Matt's exasperated huff. "I don't mean to sound rude, but why? What's the urgency?"

Anne shifted her weight, clutching her ever-present clipboard a little tighter. "I'm not sure 'urgency' is quite the right word."

"Then what?"

"For fuck's sake, Roman. Who gives a shit?" George grumbled from across the room.

Matt took a step forward, already snarling, and I shot him a look that our new friend definitely didn't miss. Matt stopped, but I noticed his fists didn't unclench, nor did his shoulders relax.

I dropped my voice to be for his ears alone. "Could you two refrain from getting into it for *one* day?"

He scowled at me, but didn't advance further.

"*As* I was saying," Anne said, speaking louder to regain everyone's attention, "your studies will accelerate as your requirement to take Battle Tactics will have been met. Does that address your concerns, Mr. Roman?"

A hope I hadn't thought to entertain blossomed in my chest. I wouldn't have to keep taking a class where I was required to fight? "Yes, Anne, it does. Thank you." Giddiness fizzed in my chest as I turned to face Matt with what was assuredly an ecstatic grin. "Did you hear that?" I whispered.

The way his crystal blue eyes reflected his smile only added to my fizzy feeling. "Yeah. I did. You don't have to be so damn happy about it, though."

"Now, before you all start celebrating too much, I'd like to emphasize the imperativeness of passing this course. Retaking will not be an option. Should you fail Battle Tactics, your scholarship will be revoked, you will be expelled from the university, and you will not be permitted to return."

"Yikes. That's severe," Gilles said softly, a sentiment echoed by new and existing students. Even Matt looked a touch anxious.

"Honestly, it's not much different from the proclamation Vera made over the summer. Though Anne is being a lot nicer about it," I clarified.

Gilles grimaced. "*That's* the nice version? I'd hate to hear the not nice one."

Matt's tension faded. "Don't worry, you probably will. Vera's big into scare tactics. But she's not all *that* bad."

Gilles looked at Matt like he'd lost his damn mind and I couldn't help but laugh.

"I can't believe I'm agreeing, but he's right. She likes to look all terrible, but once you know her a little better, she's not much different from the rest of us." The admission was worth it for the pleased smile that touched Matt's lips. A quick glance around showed we'd missed the back end of whatever else Anne had said and our peers were now settling into comfortable positions on the floor. "We should probably get on with it as well," I said.

"I really hate meditation," Matt griped as he lowered himself to sit on the floor beside me.

Gilles settled into a seated position and looked at us expectantly. "Now what?"

"Just wait for it," Matt mumbled.

Right on cue, the sound of waves crashing on a shore drifted through the room. "Picture a lake in your mind's eye. A dark, inky lake with a smooth surface and endless depths. This is your essence, your darkness defined..."

Matt rolled his eyes, then closed them. I followed suit with significantly less attitude.

I wonder how long it will take him to fall asleep.

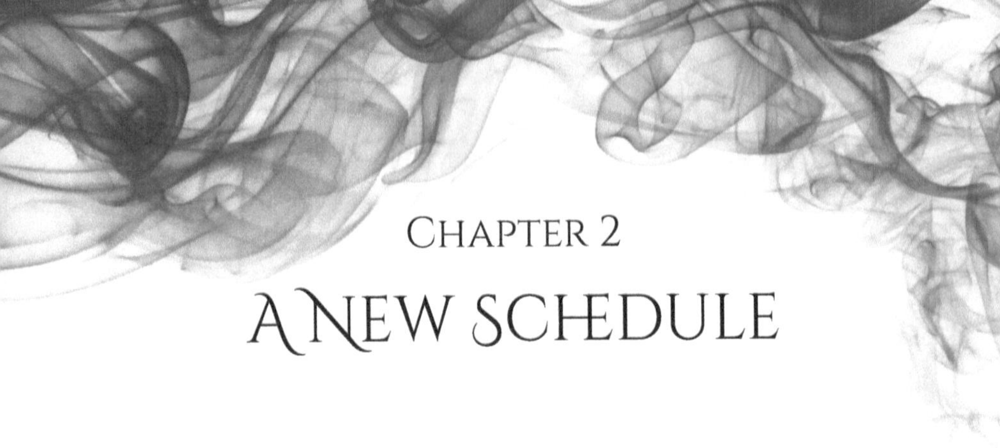

CHAPTER 2
A NEW SCHEDULE

Matt

I already didn't like the new class schedule. Demon History II was first thing in the morning, which was an obscene time to expect anyone to function. The only plus was that Battle Tactics was right after. Of course that meant you were also a sweaty mess for the rest of your classes. But the worst part was that they were the only two classes Alex, and I shared. Half of the time we couldn't even have lunch together because one of us was running off. The bottom line was it sucked. It was a good thing that I stopped going to the 'bruiser club' as Alex called it too; there just wasn't enough time or energy for it. My only concern was that they would eventually track me down, anyway. It was a constant fear anytime I stepped out of the dorm and was on my own, but thus far, there hadn't been a single sign of either Otto or Neese.

The campus was a blaze of amber as I trudged toward Starling Hall. It had only been a week of fall semester and my back already ached from all the books I was carrying. Part of me couldn't help but wonder if my back really was sore or if it was purely psychological because I was so grumpy about the extra class. Not that I had a right to be grumpy, considering I'd voluntarily signed up for it. By the time I made it to the dorm, I was more than a little tempted to shadow inside rather than climb the stairs, but I didn't trust the backpack to make the trip. My shadowing skills may have improved, but they were still inconsistent.

I walked into our dorm and dropped my bag unceremoniously to the floor. It made a heavy thump before toppling to its side, reinforcing my belief that it really was getting heavier by the day. Maybe a witch had put a curse on it. There were more than a few in my classes. That would be just my luck.

Unsurprisingly, Alex was already there and working on some assignment at the table. His dark hair swept across his forehead in stunning contrast to his flawless cool olive complexion. He looked up and smiled. "Hey, you," he said, the greeting touched by a slight British accent. The way his emerald eyes lit up made my stomach flutter.

I still wasn't sure what to make of the feelings. I'd never been attracted to a man before, but then, I'd also never had the liberty to be attracted to anyone. As uncertain as I was, there was no denying I was into Alex—*really* into Alex. Truth be told, not much had really changed since he'd agreed to date me, except he was noticeably more relaxed... and I was getting in fewer fights.

"I'm going to say it again. This totally stinks. Why do you get to be out of classes before me? It's not fair."

"Might have something to do with the fact that they also start before yours," he said, setting down his work.

"They wouldn't if we were taking the same classes," I griped under my breath. In all fairness, I *had* opted to take different courses from him.

"Oh, I don't know. I kind of like it."

I narrowed my eyes at him.

He laughed as he walked toward me, making my stomach flutter again and my skin tingle in anticipation. "It certainly makes that I get to this more special." His fingers slid around my neck and my breath caught. He hesitated only a moment before he leaned down to press his lips against mine.

All the tension in my shoulders loosened. Even my back stopped aching. Much as I hated my schedule, this was probably the best part of it, even though I had to wait all day for it. I kissed him back, tasting his lips like they were the sweetest treat I'd ever had. Yes, this was definitely the best part of my day, though his fixation on taking it easy was borderline making me manic. I had no idea when I'd become addicted to Alexi Roman, but he always left me craving more.

Alex pressed harder, and I took a reflexive step back to keep my balance, gasping when the wall brought me up short. He took advantage of my surprise to kiss me deeper, his tongue teasing past my lips, his wonderfully soft mouth holding me entranced. It always amazed me how confident he was. I, however, still didn't know what to do with my hands. They opened and closed by my side. I wanted more, *needed* it. I just wasn't sure how to go about it.

Fuck it all.

Throwing my doubts right out the window, I slid my hands around his waist. The rightness of it settled into my bones, making me lightheaded. I pulled him closer, pressing his lithe, muscular frame against me, and deepened the kiss without waiting for an invitation. There was a soft moan, though I wasn't sure who from. It didn't matter. I could do this forever. I tugged on his lip and slipped into the heat that sprung to life anytime we kissed.

He pulled back slightly and looked at me with a grin that made me want to pull him close again.

"What?" I asked, pretending to be equally confident. Thinking about what I was doing usually ruined everything.

"Nothing," he said, his smile growing. He looped his arms around my neck and claimed my mouth again.

I completely melted into it. This was more than he'd given me since this whole thing started, and I hungrily ate it up. I tightened my arms around him, determined to keep him close where I could savor how amazing he tasted. This was incredible, perfect—and it still wasn't enough. I needed more.

He sighed into me, heightening the buzz already clouding my head. Then he leaned back again and released a soft laugh. "Easy there. Slow, remember?"

Yeah, I was too far down the rabbit hole for that. "I can do slow," I responded, my voice low. I slipped my hand beneath his shirt and trailed my fingers across his lower back. His breath caught and heat flashed in his eyes. Maybe I wasn't the only one desperate for more.

"Night, Matt," he said breathlessly as he reached around to place my hand far from its wandering. "Anyone ever tell you you're nothing but trouble?"

"It might have been mentioned a few times." I gave him a crooked grin. It was definitely more than a couple.

"I bet it has." He brushed his lips against mine in a chaste kiss, then pulled away before I could steal more. "What would you say to hanging out this Friday? We could stay in, watch a movie?"

I couldn't contain my smile. "Alex, are you asking me out?"

"If I am?" He teased me with the possibility of another kiss.

"Then I only have one question."

He quirked an eyebrow.

"Are we getting Chinese or pizza?"

He laughed, stepping back and venturing towards his abandoned homework on the breakfast table. I could have groaned with frustration. He was an insufferable tease. "What would you prefer?" he asked as he resumed his seat.

"Chinese, definitely."

"Done." He pointed at the chair pulled out beside him. "Now get over here so you can actually have free time on Friday."

I rolled my eyes. "Everything is always school with you."

"School is important. What kind of homework have you accumulated?"

"You say that like you assume I haven't done any of it," I scoffed as I dragged my ridiculously heavy bag to the round table.

"Have you?" He had me there.

I plopped down and pulled out my books.

"Are the classes going well?"

"Eh." I shrugged. "Math is easy enough. I can't believe you didn't have to take the next course, though."

"It's not my fault I tested out."

"If I'd known that was an option, I might have tried harder," I complained, not for the first time.

"And now you see why it's important to pay attention during class and not just doodle the whole time," he teased.

I thought about the sketch I'd started during the summer semester—our first semester together at Arminius—when I'd started having weird feelings about my awkward roommate. It was almost done, but there were still a few details I was working on. I wanted it to be perfect. It had to be the longest I'd ever worked on any project.

"What else?" he prompted as I took out a few notebooks.

"They aren't all sketches," I said, belatedly defending myself.

He snagged probably the only folder that was predominantly drawings and gave me a look as he flipped through. "Oh, really?"

"One class." I snatched it back.

He let me have it and grabbed another one. "What's this class?" He gazed at the page curiously.

I shifted to get a better look. "That's Advanced Spells."

"You took the class?"

I rolled my shoulders uncomfortably. "Of course. You said I should."

He looked just as surprised by the admission as finding out I was taking the class. "How's it going?"

"Well, I guess. Most of the stuff so far is pretty basic in concept, though the execution seems far more complicated than necessary. I suspect it's one of those things that it's easier done than explained."

"What do you mean? What kind of magic are you learning?"

"It's still all shadow magic, kind of like our version of things that other people can do. Like manifesting something out of shadow and getting it to hold its form without constant concentration or creating a portal. Hiding a portal," I added as an afterthought.

"That all sounds really complicated."

"But it isn't. You just have to know what you're doing." I shrugged again. The irony, of course, was that I rarely felt like I knew what I was doing, especially where Alex was concerned. "What?" I asked when I realized he was staring.

"You never cease to amaze me. I can't get you to admit to being able to shadow half the time, and here you are, telling me that shadow spells are easy. Matt, only higher levels can even hope to master shadow spells. I bet you're top of your class."

I squirmed beneath his intense gaze. Alex was the smart one, not me. "Why do you say that?"

"Because, aside from Vera, I'm pretty sure you are the strongest shadow demon on campus."

I barked a laugh. "That's preposterous. There are plenty of others better than I am. I mean, look at you. Besides, the entire class isn't demonic. I think some are just there for research."

He shook his head, clearly exasperated. "I don't know how many times I'm going to have to tell you before you finally believe me. You are a more powerful demon than I am."

"You don't know that," I insisted.

"Yes, I do. I can sense it." He dropped his gaze to where he was playing with the edge of some papers. "Turns out that might actually be my specialty."

"Specialty? We have those?"

Like flipping a switch, Alex brightened, momentarily stealing my breath with the passion shining in his eyes. "Yeah, I learned about it in my Powers class. Like witches, some demons have areas they excel in. So, like a witch might have a gift for scrying or weather magic, a demon could be sensitive to power levels or exceptionally good at shadow walking. The higher up you go in levels, the more likely that you have more than one specialty."

"If you say so. If yours is sensing power levels, then what's mine? Besides getting into trouble," I added.

He chuckled. "That's definitely one of them. Who knows? Personally, I also think you're fantastic at shadowing. You seem to do it without thinking most of the time. But maybe you're also a natural at shadow magic."

"I don't shadow *all* the time."

"Maybe not in class, but when we're alone, you do. It's almost instinctive. That day I left; you said you knew. How?"

"That's obvious, because you weren't here anymore." I didn't enjoy having to think about that day. I'd been terrified my insecurities around my attraction to him had royally screwed everything up. That not only would I never get to understand these feelings, but that I'd also sabotaged the best and only friendship I'd ever had. Even a couple weeks later, I was still nervous he'd change his mind and disappear altogether without a word, no matter what he said to the contrary.

"But how did you *know*?" he pressed. "It's not like you saw me leave. The only way you would have known was by sensing the shift in my shadow presence. Instead of seeing me leave the dorm, you *felt* it."

"That still doesn't make sense. I'm not doing anything special."

"You've got to be the most stubborn person. Alright, homework can wait for a minute. I'm going to prove my point." He pushed away from the table and stood with his hands on his hips.

"We're not going to arm wrestle again, are we?" Not that I would object to getting to touch him again, even if it was for a silly game. He laughed like I figured he would. Strange to think that first interaction was only a few months ago.

"No, we're not going to wrestle. I'm pretty sure at least one of us wouldn't survive that," he replied with a smirk. "I'm going to shadow out and I want you to find me."

"Alex, really? Hide and seek? Always the kid games with you," I teased, though some of those "kid games," were my favorite memories.

"Shut up and just try it." In the blink of an eye, he faded all to black and was gone.

Damn it.

I looked around anxiously, expecting him to pop out at any moment and say boo. "Alex, this is stupid. Come on, cut it out," I said into the seemingly vacant space.

He walked out of the cabinets still the color of midnight. "Not until you actually try. Quit being so bullheaded." Once more, he vanished.

I ground my teeth.

Why can't we sit here and do homework like normal people?

I blew out a frustrated breath and attempted to focus. He hadn't gone far before. Maybe I could guess where he'd be and get lucky. I stood and walked toward the fridge. But the closer I got, the more wrong it felt. I frowned. Maybe he'd spirited away to his room. That was definitely something I could get behind. I eagerly adjusted my course, but as I got closer to his door, that also felt wrong.

What the hell?

I stopped halfway to his door and considered what I could sense. The shared living/dining/kitchen area was quiet beyond the sound of my breathing. Beyond our sanctuary, I could hear the muffled steps of someone walking down the hall. There, in the back of my mind, I could just make out the strange sensation of someone else. Close. The more I focused on it, the more it *felt* like Alex. I zeroed in on the source. I walked towards the center of the living room, then halted by the coffee table. Before I could second guess myself, I reached into the couch and pulled Alex out by his arm.

He grinned ear to ear as he returned to normal. "I told you, you could do it."

"But I didn't..."

"Now do it again." He disappeared.

"I thought we were supposed to be doing homework?" No response.

He's absolutely insufferable when he wants to prove he's right about something.

I tried to relax and get back to the state that I'd just been in, but the focus wouldn't come.

This is ridiculous. I just want to sit down and be with my friend. That's all. Why does he always have to make things so damn difficult? Isn't it bad enough that he gets to start chilling out for the day early? I knew I shouldn't have signed up for that extra class. If he's going to be pulling stunts like this, I'll never get to spend any real time with him.

My exasperation was only getting in the way. He said that this was no different from Shadow Magic. You just had to know what you were doing. But I didn't. I didn't know how any of this worked. Spells were easy. They came with instructions and rules. This was more like making it up as you went. I felt something move to my right by the front door and dismissed it. No way it was Alex. He was in the kitchen.

My eyes widened, and I turned in place. Alex was in the kitchen. Why was I so sure that he wasn't by the front door? Because I could sense him, just like the night he left.

"You can come out now. I know you're in there," I said, staring at the corner where the fridge stuck out. Sure enough, out he stepped.

"You really should have more faith in yourself. It's almost like you're intentionally ignoring all the things that make you a Shadow Demon."

I shook my head again, almost as discouraged as when we'd started this weird game. "I just don't understand how any of this works."

"Do you have to understand how your arm bends in order to catch something?" He tossed an apple from the bowl on the counter at me.

I snatched it out of the air. "Of course not."

"Or how your feet grip the ground in order to walk?" He took an exaggerated step toward me.

I placed the apple on the table. "You're being silly now."

He smiled in response and walked closer still. "What about this?" He was officially way too close.

I watched him warily. Alex had a unique ability to unsettle me. I never seemed to know what he was going to do next.

"Do you have to know how your lips work in order to kiss?" He didn't wait for another flippant response. His mouth closed on mine and I forgot what I was going to say. I wanted to wrap my arms around him like I had before, but he didn't give me the chance. After a single brief kiss, he was back at the table, looking exceptionally smug.

Insufferable tease.

"If this is how homework is always going to go with you, we're never going to get anything done," I griped, taking out the last of my notes and joining him. He laughed and picked up his pen to keep working. I shook my head and followed suit.

CHAPTER 3
DATE NIGHT

Alexi

Friday couldn't come soon enough. Perhaps it was a little childish to be as excited as I was about the date, considering we technically lived together, but I couldn't contain myself. If the week took any longer, I was going to find some spell to speed up time. It wouldn't be anything big or major or, hell, even life altering—we'd already covered most of that—just something small and simple, sweet. The big deal was that he'd said yes, had even contributed to the plan. That reminded me, I had no idea what kind of Chinese Matt would like. Of course, I knew pretty much everything else about his eating habits, so I felt safe enough guessing.

By the time the day finally bothered to roll around, I was a frantic mess. There was a good chance I'd over-ordered on the food, though I didn't see anything wrong with having options. Food and movies taken care of, all that was left was to make sure I didn't go over the top. I stopped my flurried dance around the dorm and took a deep breath.

If I made a big deal about this, I was liable to freak him out, and that was the last thing I wanted. Things were going fairly well, except, of course, for that he still hesitated with just about everything except for kissing—that was only half the time. I checked the time.

Shit, he'll be here soon.

I raced into my room and peeled off my shirt, which was sticking to me from my frenzied whirl around the dorm. I dismissed three shirts in quick succession before pausing and letting out a heavy breath.

Why am I stressing about this? Matt will probably just wear the same thing he wore to class today.

I ran my hands through my hair, unsure of what to do.

I'm definitely over-thinking this.

The shirt on top of the drawer won, and I zipped into the bathroom to freshen up. The sound of the door caught my attention, and I stopped fighting with my hair. Per usual, it was doing whatever it wanted. I scrambled out into the living room, where Matt eyed me warily.

"Hey." The greeting pitched high, and I struggled not to wince. It hadn't been *that* long since I dated.

Sweet merciful heavens, pull it together.

I cleared my throat and fought for composure. "How was class?"

He chuckled. "I'll tell you in a minute. I want to change first. They really should have showers by the training rooms. There isn't enough time to come back here *and* have lunch. Give me just a sec."

I took advantage of the delay to calm my nerves.

The only thing different about tonight is the fact that we are calling it a date. We hang out all the time.

Except, almost all of our previous attempts to hang out have ended in epic fallouts.

I shook my head to dispel the doubt and ran my hands through my hair, then immediately set to flattening it back down.

"You okay?" Matt asked, reappearing in fresh clothes. Night, he was stunning. The jeans accentuated his muscular legs and the gray t-shirt made his blue eyes practically glow.

I dropped my hands. "I'm fine." It didn't sound very believable to me, but at least my voice didn't crack. *This is only weird if you make it weir.* I took a deep breath and visualized all the tension leaving my body. Feeling much calmer, I asked again, "How was your day?"

He rolled his eyes. "Ridiculous. So, of course, today of all days, I had to get to my first class after Battle Tactics early. There was a signup sheet, and I was not about to have to choose from the bottom of the list." He walked towards the kitchen. The food was still sitting in the delivery sacks, and he began unpacking as he continued. "Anyway, so I race over for that only to find out that class had been moved thanks to a burst pipe. Then I had to scramble to another building that I swear was clear across campus in order not to miss sign up at all. All I have to say is thank Nyx we can shadow. Otherwise, bottom of the list right here." He pointed to himself with a comical scowl that highlighted his natural pout.

I joined him, grabbing plates and silverware from the cupboards. "Did you make it?"

He snorted. "Barely." He finished unpacking the last box and opened the lids. "Oh, you magical creature."

"What?"

"I'm starving." He looked at me with those puppy eyes that had gotten me in more trouble than could ever be considered fair.

I chuckled. "You're always hungry."

"You don't understand. When I say raced over, I mean I ate nothing at all."

I leaned against the counter, snagging an egg roll. "Then I'm glad I over ordered."

"You mean some of this is for you, too?" I choked on my bite and he laughed. "So, what are we watching?"

I shrugged. "There are a few options." I indicated the counter covered in movies.

He swiped the half-eaten roll right out of my hand. "You choose. Whatever you want to watch is fine by me."

I frowned as he devoured the last of my snack and turned to inspect the gathered options. While I'd hoped for a little more input, I wasn't about to make a fuss over something so small as choosing a movie. If he really didn't like it, he'd say something.

Who am I kidding? If he doesn't like it, he'll carry that secret to the grave.

I mentally shook my head and chose an adventure film that promised to have a bit of everything. Playing it safe was pretty much all I had since he hadn't offered a preference.

"Alright, movie picked. Now all I need is a—plate," I finished abruptly when he passed me a bowl already prepped. It even had a fresh egg roll. I stared at the dish in disbelief and back up at him.

How did he know this is what I would have?

He winked and relieved me of the movie. I followed numbly behind and joined him on the couch. As the movie began, I wondered if I should say something. So far, this date was anything but typical. That probably shouldn't have surprised me. This was Matt, after all.

It didn't take long for us to polish off dinner. Without a word, he collected both of our plates and came back with some water. When he sat back down, I used shadow to hit the last of the lights.

"Nice," he commented, sounding impressed.

"I've been practicing." I stretched out and crossed my ankles on the coffee table, letting my arm span the back of the couch.

In hardly anytime at all, I was sucked back into the movie. Matt, on the other hand, couldn't seem to find a comfortable position. I was about to tease him for not being able to sit still when he shifted to be right next to me. Granted, it wasn't a large couch, but there was no reason he had to be close enough to touch.

When he finally stopped fidgeting, I reached my fingers forward to brush the feathery hairs on the back of his head. That was definitely one thing I liked about this arrangement. I could touch Matt's hair anytime the fancy struck me, which was pretty much all the time. He shifted his leg and ended up leaning on me. I was immensely grateful that he was too busy looking ahead to see me grinning like an idiot. Now that he was closer, it was easier to play with his hair.

I loved his hair; it was soft like down and never seemed to be out of place. He sighed and rested his head on my shoulder. As if by magic, all of his nervous energy went right out of him. Eventually, I gave up his hair in order to finish wrapping my arm around him and languidly trailed my fingers along his arm. A part of me could not believe this moment was happening. The other part wanted me to stop jinxing it.

The movie wound down, and I realized he hadn't moved at all in quite some time. I glanced down at him. The thin light from the screen revealed he'd passed out. He really was the most beautiful thing. I stroked the side of his cheek with my free hand and he started awake.

He blinked bleary eyed, then saw me looking at him. "What did I miss?" he asked in a hushed voice.

"Most of the movie."

"Sorry," he said, shifting slightly, but not changing his situation.

"It's okay," I responded in an equally quiet tone, still caressing his cheek. If he wasn't going to make me stop, then I had no intention of doing so. I enjoyed touching him.

He stared back at me with those gorgeous blues. Even dreamy-eyed, they were enough to give me butterflies. Unexpectedly, he leaned forward and planted a soft kiss that lingered on my lips. I cupped his face and kissed him back, reveling in the drawn out slowness of it. He may have been half asleep, but he was still an incredible kisser.

I was getting the distinct impression Matt really enjoyed kissing, not even liked it so much as lived for it. He'd probably go on forever if I let him. The slow burn of the kiss continued to build until I had to consciously dial it back. It would be far too easy to drown in Matt with kisses like that. I brushed a finger across his eyelashes. "We should probably go to bed," I whispered.

He looked properly put out at the notion. He glanced over at his door, then back at me. "But I'd rather stay here." My heart swelled at the blunt honesty. Matt wasn't one for flowery words or appeasement. What he said, he meant.

"You could always sleep in my room," I suggested.

Doubt and indecision instantly clouded his eyes. He opened his mouth as if to say something, then closed it.

I gave him a small smile. "Would it have been an easier decision if I hadn't asked?"

"Probably," he admitted, shifting to a more upright position. I let him go and chose not to let the cold of his absence bother me. He had to move sometime. He looked towards his room again. "I really don't want to go to bed, though."

"Here, I have an idea," I said, smacking him lightly on the arm. "Get up."

"What?"

"You heard me. Get up." I gestured emphatically to hurry him along.

He stood, albeit reluctantly.

"Go put your pajamas on."

"Why?"

"I told you, I have an idea. Just do it." He begrudgingly did, and I quickly followed my own directions, returning with a pillow and an extra blanket.

"Alright, what's this great idea?" he asked when he reappeared, stretching his arms above his head and lifting the hem of his shirt to reveal a peep of pale skin.

I stubbornly squashed the urge to tell him to lose the nightshirt altogether and while we were at it, forget the movie. There was a litany of "date-like" things we could that did *not* involve pajamas.

"Something wrong?" he asked, his brow furrowing when I waited too long to respond.

"I meant to tell you to bring a pillow."

He tilted his head. "What for?"

"We're going to have ourselves a good old-fashioned sleepover." I moved to push the couch back, but he stopped me. My cheek twitched at being thwarted. "What?"

A darkness flitted behind his eyes. "I'm not sleeping on the floor. Honestly, after all this moving around, I'm not even tired anymore. What do you say we put on another movie?" he suggested, already walking into the kitchen to grab one.

"You couldn't even stay awake during the first one."

"That was because I'd just eaten. I've had a power nap. I'm better now." He could say that as optimistically as he wanted, he wasn't fooling me. Matt could sleep standing up after running a marathon.

"You say so," I said, trying not to grumble, and resumed my seat. To my dismay, he sat at the other end. I was debating whether or not to go over there when his legs swung onto my lap, effectively trapping me. It was like he could read minds. At a loss for what to do with my hands, I rested them on his legs. His movie selection seemed to be similar to the first in theme except more astronaut than pirate. As I predicted, he didn't even make it twenty minutes. One minute he was wide awake, the next, he was out like a light. I chuckled to myself and carefully shifted his legs to the ground.

"Hmm," he mumbled in his sleep. I took a moment to appreciate the pure innocence of it, then sighed to myself and grabbed his hands. He reflexively gripped mine, which helped me pull him up.

"Come on."

"But I don't want to," he groaned, his eyes still firmly closed.

I gave a quiet laugh. "That's great, but you're already asleep." His only response was to moan noncommittally. "Here we go." I got him the rest of the way to his feet and began guiding him to his room. I used shadow to open the door and turn on the lamp. At the side of the bed, I pulled back the covers and gently coaxed him in. I'd almost made it to the door when his voice drifted out of the cocoon of blankets.

"Wait."

"What is it?" I asked, returning to turn off the lamp, then walked around to the other side of the bed.

"Don't go," he said, his eyes still firmly closed.

My heart felt like it was going to burst. I pulled my shirt over my head and fought the covers for the right to get under them. At last, I loosened them enough to slide in beside him. "I'm not going anywhere," I whispered, wrapping an arm around him.

"Promise?" The request was barely even audible.

"I won't leave you. Promise." I placed a kiss on the exposed skin by his collar. He grabbed my arm and pulled me closer. I wrapped myself around him, grateful that he still had a shirt on. It wasn't quite the evening I'd hoped for, but I was hard pressed to complain. I placed another kiss on his neck and he sighed in his sleep, snuggling back against me.

If only he could be more like this awake.

Someday, I thought, the scent of sage strong in my nose. *Someday.*

CHAPTER 4
KISS ME STUPID

Matt

I stretched awake, feeling more rested than I had in ages, maybe ever. Part of me wondered if it had anything to do with dreaming that I'd been sleeping with Alex, though normally when I dreamed of Alex there was a lot more kissing involved. But it was hard to complain when I felt so *good.* Abruptly, I realized I was still wearing my night shirt.

Guess I was more tired than I thought.

I yawned wide enough to crack my jaw, then shuffled into the bathroom to brush my teeth. It still baffled me that some people didn't *want* to do that every morning. I ran my tongue over my teeth, enjoying the minty tingle, and made my way out to the main space. It came as no surprise that Alex was not only up, but already bustling about the kitchen. Morning people.

Alex glanced at me over his shoulder from where he was standing at the counter with a peculiar look in his eye that I was *not* awake enough to decipher. "Good morning, sleepyhead."

Sadly, the teasing greeting didn't give me anymore to go on. I stretched again to wake up my muscles and be a more functioning zombie. "How long have you been up?"

"Longer than I would have liked." Again, there was a distinct note of something else. He turned around and leaned against the counter. "How did you sleep?"

"Really well," I replied honestly, still a bit surprised.

"That's good to hear," he said, clearly trying to suppress a smile.

"What's up with you? Am I missing something?" Seriously, morning people.

His eyebrow lifted in a graceful arc, and the smile he was clearly fighting tugged at the corner of his mouth. "You mean you don't remember?"

"Remember what?" I shuffled from foot to foot, my anxiety increasing. Did the date not go well?

"We slept together, Matt." He flashed a wicked smile, then he laughed, no doubt in response to the look of utter shock on my face, and stepped in close. "Don't worry, Matt, that's all we did. Sleep. I even behaved myself." The way he said it made it sound like that was out of character for him, but he'd never been anything less than the perfect gentleman with me.

"Really?" My sleepy fog stubbornly refused to dissipate so I could make sense of what was going on. We'd slept together? Like, in the same bed?

"You didn't really give me much choice. I take it you don't remember making me promise not to go." I'd done what? He considered me, a hint of concern dimming his almost smile.

Suppose there was nothing for it now. "Guess that explains my dream," I admitted.

Both of his eyebrows shot up. "Oh really? Do tell."

"That was it. We were sleeping." It was possible there was more, but that was all I could remember. I glanced around absently, not really sure where to go from there. Passing out with ease around Alex was becoming somewhat of a theme.

"Hey."

I glanced at him long enough to note his obvious concern. Embarrassment tingled on my skin far less pleasant than the toothpaste had in my mouth. Was it even possible for me not to botch every evening with Alex? First the drinking shenanigans. Now, sleeping? What the hell was wrong with me?

"Hey, look at me." He grabbed my shoulder, and I reluctantly met his gaze. His brows knit together as he searched my face. "There's no need to be upset. I was only teasing. I promise nothing happened."

I dropped his gaze. How could he be so damn understanding? I ruined it. Given my history of ruining most things, that probably shouldn't have surprised me, but I wanted to do better for Alex.

"Tell me what's bothering you."

At the command, the truth popped out before I could temper it. "I fell asleep. Twice." I gave him a level look. "I'm a terrible date."

"Is that all? I thought the parts where you were awake went quite well. Some parts where you were asleep too," he added, tipping my chin up to look at him.

The urge to kiss him burned through me, but I held back, still uncertain. What I wanted and what was right rarely coincided in this world. Thankfully, he made the choice for me, his lips barely even brushing mine. He stayed like that until the feel of our breath mingling pushed me over the edge. I wrapped my arms wrapped around his waist and pulled him close. The feel of his body against mine was everything, and I held tighter, tangling my fingers in his hair as I claimed his mouth. He made a sound of muffled surprise, followed by a moan. Then his hands were on my back and the kiss got deeper. The heat of it was like an inferno threatening to burn us both where we stood. He pulled back and I reluctantly let him go. It wasn't enough, it would never be enough.

"I swear, Matt, one of these days you're going to kiss me stupid," he said, every bit as short of breath as me.

I wanted to trace the path his tongue took over his lips, but hesitated. He pulled back every time. I didn't know what that meant, and I already felt like I was treading water in the deep end most of the time. Was I doing something wrong? I never said I was any *good* at dating and I had exactly zero experience dating a man.

Humor danced in his eyes as he took a step back, removing himself from my arms. "What should we do today?"

I shrugged my shoulders, and he rolled his eyes.

"Come on. It's Saturday. You're already caught up with your assignments and you have the whole weekend to do whatever you like."

What I liked was spending time with him, but that felt weird to say. I wracked my brain for something we could do together, preferably something he would enjoy, too. The corner of a large tomb poking out from beneath some papers on the coffee table. I'd found it when I was trying to apologize for my horrible behavior a few weeks ago. He *did* seem excited about that. Not surprising, since it involved the author of his favorite book.

"What'll it be?" he encouraged. "We could explore town, wander campus, watch another movie."

"We could always work on translating more of Volume Six. We haven't really had a chance to do that." Though exploring the neighboring town of Sieben Hügel did sound interesting. I'd been so busy with the fight club before, I'd only ever made it to the fringes of town.

Alex's smile warmed me from the inside and helped me feel like I'd suggested something halfway decent. "See, that wasn't so hard. You get dressed, then we can go to the library. I'm curious about this mysterious magic lamp of yours."

It wasn't until then that I realized he was already dressed. He was the picture of Saturday comfort in low-slung jeans that barely rested on his hips and a dark green shirt.

"Get dressed, Matt," he said with a look that felt like I was being stripped down right there.

I flushed and quickly scurried back into my room to do as I was told, where I almost put on the clothes from the day before. Finally, I was something resembling decent. I grabbed his book about the mysterious knight and the massive book from the table, then joined him by the door. Technically, I'd finished the knight book a while ago, but every time I went to return it, I remembered the bookmark was still in it. I needed to finish that already.

"Okay, let's go," I said, after shoving everything into my backpack and zipping it.

His lips twitched like he wanted to laugh. "Lead the way." He stepped aside for me to go first.

We stopped by the dining hall for a late breakfast and then wandered to the library. It was already fuller than the last time I'd been here and I worried if I could find the lamp again. This place looked way different with the multicolored light from the stained-glass windows filling the space instead of muted darkness.

"What are you looking for?" Alex asked after we'd been standing in the same spot for a couple of minutes.

"The librarian. The last time I was here, she just sort of showed up. It was really dark when we got the book and she took me over to the lamp. I'm not sure where it is," I admitted.

He looked thoughtful a moment, then started walking with purpose across the library.

"Where are you going?" I asked, trailing after him. The overly loud question earned me several reproachful glares, including one from Alex. I quickened my pace so I wouldn't have to talk so loud.

"We're just going to retrace your steps. We'll start at the table you put your things at."

"How do you know which table I used?" I asked, mystified.

"You're a creature of habit, Matt."

"Oh." Sure enough, we stopped at the same table I'd used for my last visit, which, now that he mentioned it, was pretty much every visit. Someone was already sitting at it though, so he continued walking a little farther.

"Then from here you went to the restricted section? Do you remember which way you started?"

"I think it was this way," I said, retaking the lead. I knew I was right when I felt a sense of dread fall over me. Not far ahead was the sign that declared we were approaching the restricted section. Despite the morning light, the area still felt dark and oppressive. My previous impression that this was knowledge that did not want to be found solidified. I walked closer to the stacks, each step a struggle as the sense of overwhelming apprehension intensified. Suddenly, I realized Alex had stopped several feet back.

"I don't know how you did it, Matt. I'm nowhere near the stacks, and I don't want to get any closer. This is a horrible feeling. I didn't realize the barrier extended so far out."

"Like I said before," I glanced over my shoulder at him, "I needed to get the book for you." It was just a fact. I'd been desperate for anything to make up for my behavior, and I knew that getting that information would at least help. I shifted my shoulders beneath the weight of his assessing stare and eagerly moved on to the next leg of the journey. We didn't need to actually go *into* the restricted section; we already had what we needed. "After we got the book, I'm pretty sure we went this way."

Once more, I took the lead and walked across the space. Hardly anyone was up here. Of course, with an avoidance spell like that to contend with, who could blame them? We rounded a stack and found two rows of identical reading desks with accompanying lamps.

"Yes," I said a little too loudly, but there was no one to scold us.

"Well done." Alex clapped me on the shoulder, then swiped a chair from another table and pulled it up next to the one I'd already taken.

I pulled out his book while he placed Volume six on the table. Just like before, the lamp slowly came to life. He hadn't opened it yet and when the light touched the cover, something unexpected happened. It was almost like time was reversing. The aged binding became supple, the edges crisp and unworn. What I'd thought was flaked leather turned out to be the remains of a picture. As the image came back to life, it revealed a horrific battle scene, complete with knights, banners, and blood. A *lot* of blood. At the bottom of the picture in scrolling letters it read: *All Evil must die and to the depths returned.* I looked at Alex.

The wonder shining on his face crumpled a bit when he read the line. "Why does everyone think we're evil?"

I wanted to comfort him, but wasn't sure how. Did I say something? Wrap an arm around him? Take his hand? In my hesitation, the moment vanished.

He opened the book and the ancient Latin within transformed into something we could read and understand. Unlike when I'd last used the lamp, though, some words couldn't seem to decide what they should be.

I pointed to one. "Do you think it's because we're from different places? Is it confused?"

Alex's shine returned, and he shifted closer to the desk. "That's actually an intriguing point. I wonder what would happen if two people who didn't speak the same language used the lamp at the same time."

I let that tumble around my brain that for a moment, then let it go. That mystery wasn't why we were here. "Do you think there are other pictures?"

"Probably, but we should start at the beginning before we get ahead of ourselves. This book may contain the answers we've been looking for, but it won't do us any good if we skip around and miss them."

"You and your logic," I said begrudgingly as I withdrew my hand. What harm would it really do to flip through and see? We could always go back and read.

"One of us has to at least try to approach this scholastically."

I looked at Alex, taking in his sense of reverence as he lightly traced the calligraphy. Hope and a small touch of pride swelled in my chest. I'd done it. I'd found something to amend for my crimes.

He glanced up and did a double take. "What?"

I shook my head and returned my attention to the book. This wasn't the place to tell him how stunning his eyes were when he was excited or how graceful I thought his long fingers were. Especially not how much I wanted to feel those long fingers on me. "There are so many names. None of them look like demons, though."

"That's not too surprising. This looks more like a history written by humans, not by other supernaturals."

I pulled out the notes I'd taken on my last visit. "But doesn't it say that they held the power to harness light? That sounds pretty supernatural to me."

Alex shrugged. "Maybe? They could have had supernatural connections. This was a different world. *Before* supernaturals went into hiding." He paused as if reconsidering. "Or at least I think it is. No one can really say when *all* supes went into hiding, since each species did it independently."

We really were just feeling our way in the dark with this. What had begun as an innocent project to uncover the identity of Alex's nameless knight had instead unearthed plenty of other secrets. The involvement of Shadow Demons. The existence of a family whose sole purpose was genocide. A forbidden affair. A war against Shadow Demons that wasn't in any history book. And now, what appeared to be a conspiracy to cover it all up.

Alex sat back, and I mirrored him. "What I don't understand is how there was a war at all. I can understand that back then there were substantially more

Shadow Demons, but how could they ever have worked together to mount a defense? There couldn't possibly be enough willing to cooperate."

"What do you mean?"

He tapped his bottom lip, looking pensive. "Well, historically, Shadow Demons are known for their apathy. We don't care to get involved with the rest of the world. We're just not social like that."

I smothered a snort. "What are you talking about? You're one of the most social people I know."

He leveled a look at me. "Being social with you is not really the same thing, Matt."

"Whatever you say." He didn't have to see it to make it true. All he had to do was walk into a room and he had friends. He fell into conversations naturally, always knew what to say, how to act. That sounded like the definition of social to me. I turned the page to let the next translate. "How do you think all of this started?" I asked, scanning what appeared to be a battle strategy.

"My guess is that someone pissed off the wrong person. That's always how things like this start. Hey, look," he said.

I followed where his finger led. There was our knight's name—Matthias Warde. "That's not possible. He couldn't have possibly been born yet. How could he be mentioned so soon? Also, in your book it says that his family has been fighting the darkness for as long as he could remember. He should have been born in the middle of this war, not fully grown at the beginning." Was it possible we had everything wrong? Just great. All those hours of research wasted.

"We'll have to read more to find out then, won't we?" he added snidely. I gave him a face, and he shook his head, returning to the book. "Let's see... This says the Wardes led the campaign to eliminate darkness once and for all. That at least coincides with what we've established so far, but I think you're right. There's no way this guy is the same as our knight. Just look at how he's described. A ruthless leader who rallied his family and recruited others to the cause? That doesn't sound at all like our wavering knight." He did that lip tap again, which was incredibly distracting. "Maybe Matthias is a family name that gets passed down. Could be his grandson or even great grandson."

"I suppose that's possible." Then a wild idea occurred to me. "Random thought."

"What?" Alex asked. Faced with his open curiosity, I suddenly doubted the wisdom of sharing my idea. What if he thought it was ridiculous or it upset him?

"Um... You said you never knew your father, right?"

His dark brows pinched together. "Yeah, what of it?"

"What if you're some long-lost relative and *that's* why you have the book?"

He shook his head. "The odds of that are minuscule. Besides, while I've had this book a long time, it wasn't exactly something that was left for me. My mom found it on her quest to gather any resources she could that referenced Shadow Demons."

"Oh, well, never mind." I sagged in my chair. It had been a silly idea, anyway.

"Hey." He nudged my arm. "It *would* be cool, though. To be the long-lost progeny of a knight belonging to an ancient order."

I straightened. "Would that make you a knight by default?"

"I don't think it works that way," he said with a laugh. "Alright, come on, let's get back to this. I still want to know how or why these Shadow Demons got involved in anything that qualified as an all-out war."

We hunkered down, reading the book page by page in our tiny pool of light. Our heads were so close in order to see that it felt like swirls of lavender were spiraling around me. The world seemed to fade away as we devoured history that appeared to have been lost for centuries.

I thought again about how it felt like the books in the restricted section didn't want to be found. Was there a reason they were guarded like that? Hidden in some nameless section by a virtually impassable barrier? But I'd gotten past it. I glanced at Alex out of the corner of my eye. It was amazing what you could do with the right motivation.

Suddenly, all the hair on the back of my neck stood up. I'd had enough hard knocks and ugly surprises in my life to trust the sensation without question—Someone was watching us. I sat up and looked around. The immediate area appeared every bit as abandoned as it had been when we first arrived. As I searched the stacks around us for any sign of life, the feeling intensified. Someone or *something* was definitely out there.

Alex straightened beside me, curiosity plain on his face. Before he could speak, I held up my hand to silence him. After a minute of suffering quietly, he finally whispered, "What's wrong?"

"I thought... I could have sworn..." The feeling was slipping away like mist through my fingers. "It felt like someone was watching us."

"It is a library, Matt. We're not exactly the only people here." He had a point, but I still couldn't shake the feeling it was not that simple. You remembered the lessons you learned the hard way. Letting down your guard could prove not only dangerous, but fatal.

"I don't like sitting out in the open like this." Without waiting for a response, I reached out and closed the book. "We'll should find another way to translate the pages. Something that doesn't rely on the lamps."

Alex glanced around before he leaned close. "You don't think it's..."

"It's what?" I asked, sensing his unease.

"You said that you'd gotten... *snatched* before." Ah, *that*. He thought it might be Neese or Otto come to drag me back to the fight club.

"No, they wouldn't come here. Besides, it didn't feel like any of them. Are you ready to go?" I asked, though he was already zipping up his bag.

As we made our way out of the library, the feeling of eyes following us returned. I quickened my pace, eager to be away from the invasive gaze.

Chapter 5
COMMUNICATION

Alexi

I finished clearing the table, then swung my bag onto my shoulder. "You sure you won't be late for Advanced Spells?" Matt and I didn't get to eat together very often now that our schedules weren't identical. To say I missed it would be an understatement. Fortunately, the dining hall was near the heart of campus.

"I'll be fine. Even if I'm a few minutes late, Professor Gwendolyn is pretty lenient. Except when it comes to assignment sign-ups." He glowered at the table and I held back a laugh.

"I take it you weren't able to switch?"

He let out a heavy sigh and grumbled, "No."

I pressed a knuckle against my mouth to keep the determined laughter at bay. It was hard *not* to adore how emphatic Matt could be. For all his efforts when we'd met to be aloof and mysterious, all I had to do was ask to know exactly what he was feeling. "Dare I ask what you got stuck with?"

"A report of the social development of supernatural communities. So, like a shit ton of research."

My smile slipped free despite my best efforts. "And we both know research is one of your absolute favorite things to do."

"Shut up." He shoved me and I caught his arms.

"I'm sure it won't be all *that* bad."

"Pft. It is when I could have been making a diorama." He scowled, showing off his spectacular pout.

I used my grip on his arms to pull him closer with the intention of kissing that delectable pout until he forgot all about his writing assignment. We were less than a foot apart when he threw on the brakes.

"I should really get going." He ducked his head and extricated his arms, then stepped back.

My heart sank, and I pushed away the burning urge to steal my kiss anyway, reminding myself that this was all new for him. Though, perhaps we were overdue for a conversation about PDA. I missed being able to hold my boyfriend's hand and exchange sweet kisses when we parted. Matt had said he'd need time to adjust, had even admitted that he'd stumble occasionally, but surely those acts were small enough to be inconsequential.

"Anyway… I'll see you back at the dorm?"

"Of course, but I'll be late. I have a tutoring session followed by our weekly tutor's meeting."

A cloud briefly darkened his usually light features. "Right. I better get to class. Professor Gwendolyn doesn't like it when we're late."

I frowned at the contradiction to his earlier statement, but he'd already turned away. "I enjoyed having lunch together," I called after him.

He paused and glanced back, a hint of his usual spark dancing in his perfect blue eyes. "Me too."

My shoulders slumped as I watched him walk away. He'd die before admitting it, but he hated beating me back to the dorm, like he didn't trust I'd come back if I wasn't already there. "What's it going to take for you to relax and trust me?"

"Make an invisible friend or talking to yourself?"

I glanced to the side at the familiar voice. "Ha ha, Rubio. Just musing aloud." I crossed my arms and returned my attention to where Matt was becoming a distant, shadowy outline. Rubio bumped my shoulder, and I turned to follow him back into the dining hall.

"How was lunch with your roommate?" he asked once he'd grabbed a tray and found a seat.

I sighed and continued scratching at a spot on the table. "Exactly that—lunch with my *roommate*."

Rubio grimaced. "What happened to the whole giving things a go?"

"We are." I straightened enough to rest my elbows on the table. "Or, at least, I think we are."

"Hate to break it to you, but dating really isn't that hard."

"I *know*. It's honestly not all that different from what we were doing before. Just with a lot more—"

"Nookie," Rubio filled in with a lascivious grin complete with wiggling eyebrows.

I couldn't help but laugh. "I was gonna go with kissing, because we haven't gotten anywhere *near* anything else."

Rubio looked like I'd smacked him in the face with his sandwich. "What about groping?"

"Nope."

"Skins?"

"All clothing has remained very much on," I grumbled.

It didn't seem possible for Rubio to look more scandalized. "At least tell me you've kissed with tongue."

"*That* we have done—before, and a little now, though not as much as I would like."

Rubio abandoned his lunch and leaned forward. "Um, why?"

Okay, that was fair. "Because I don't want him to feel rushed. That last thing I want to do is push too hard and scare him off. We went through so much to get *here*. What if I screw it up?"

"Alexi, as your friend and incubus confidant, I'm here to tell you that waiting will only get you so far. If you don't tell him what you want, how is he supposed to know? He's a Shadow Demon, not a mind reader." He squinted at me. "Right? That's not a thing y'all do?"

"No, we're not mind readers. Which would come in super handy right about now. Besides, I'm not the only one not communicating."

"It's not a contest," he deadpanned. "Try talking to him."

"We talk."

Rubio sat back, his lunch completely forgotten, and crossed his arms. "Yeah? You talk about sex? Your relationship? Expectations?"

I shifted in my seat and prayed my face wasn't red.

"Alexi..." he said, his voice dipping low and a hair menacing.

I winced and darted my gaze up to meet his surprisingly judgmental one. "Yeah?"

"Have you *ever* talked about any of that with your previous boyfriends?"

"No?"

He threw up his hands. "Communicating expectations is the cornerstone of successful relationships."

"Says the guy who doesn't believe in relationships," I countered.

"Irrelevant." He waved a dismissive hand before reacquiring his half-eaten sandwich. "I don't have to believe in committed relationships to know how they work. The point is communicating is important."

"Try telling that to Matt. Getting information out of him is like trying to pry open a vault with a licorice string." I let out a huff and sat back, imitating Rubio's earlier pose. "You make it sound like I haven't tried to talk to him at all. And, sure, I maybe haven't gone into *those* particulars, but it doesn't mean we haven't talked at all."

"I'm listening," he said around a mouthful of food.

"Okay, so we had our first date-date last week. And while it wasn't a total disaster, I wouldn't exactly call it a roaring success." I leaned forward, animatedly gesturing as I worked myself up. "We stayed in and watched a movie. I ordered the takeout he requested, but that was literally the most input I got from him. And while there was cuddling, he fell asleep. Twice!" I held up two fingers for emphasis, surprising myself with how upset I actually was.

Rubio took his time licking his fingers clean and then wiping his hands before responding. "So, what I'm hearing is that he's really comfortable with you."

"I don't want him to be comfortable with me. I want him to be touching me!" My hand clapped down so hard over my mouth it made a bubble sound. I stared at Rubio looking smug as a witch, shocked at my outburst. "I... That came out... That's not..." I gave up after a few false starts with no idea how to finish them.

"You, my friend, reek of sexual frustration."

"I do not! Wait, you can *smell* that?"

"Sense it, smell it, feel it. Makes my skin itch and my nose burn. You should be glad I value our friendship so much or I'd be putting you in some seriously compromising positions." He gave me a pointed look, and I had to take a minute to absorb that.

"First off, that's kind of creepy."

He shrugged. "That's why I try to avoid mentioning it. Most people get uncomfortable when they learn you can sense their arousal."

"Yeah... second, I'm sorry. I didn't mean to be making you uncomfortable. If I'd known—"

"You'd what?" His eyebrows lifted. "Bang your roommate like you've been wanting to do for the last three months?"

I dropped my hand, temporarily at a loss. "Well, damn."

He sighed and shifted in his chair. "There's nothing to apologize for, Alexi. You feel the way you feel and you're entitled to do so without a nosy incubus getting involved. Besides, we're on a campus full of horny college students. Trust me, the smell is *everywhere*," he added with a grin that bordered on a smirk.

"Wait a second. Is that why you offered to sleep with me?"

Rubio threw his head back and laughed loud enough to attract the attention of the entire dining hall. He wiped tears from the corners of his eyes when he finally sobered. "You're a trip. No, I *offered* because you're attractive and I could see us hitting it off."

"Oh."

His smirk came back. "I *kept* offering because you clearly weren't doing anything about your attraction to your roommate."

"Rubio!"

He held up his hands defensively and laughed again. "What? I'm your friend *and* an incubus. What did you expect me to do?"

I crossed my arms with a huff and rolled my eyes. "You really know how to kill a guy's ego, you know that?"

"I know how to do a lot of things with a guy's... ego. If you're looking for some tips, I'm happy to share." Rubio's smile was nothing short of feral.

A laugh bubbled free. "Okay, I walked right into that."

"You absolutely did. But the offer stands. And, seriously, talk to your boyfriend. Bottling things up isn't healthy." He held up a hand. "Yes, that doubled as another sex joke and actual advice. Now, on to business. How are you feeling about the tutoring assignments with your course schedule?"

"I thought we were going to be covering this at the meeting tonight."

"We'll touch on it, but I was hoping to have it be a short meeting. That's why I've been making time to touch base with everyone beforehand. If there are any conflicts, then we can look at swapping clients at the meeting."

Admittedly, that was really smart, talking to the tutors one-on-one to get honest feedback before bringing any adjustments to the group, but he wasn't fooling me. "You have plans," I deadpanned.

"You wound me." He placed a hand over his heart and gave me a pitiful look. "Do you really think I'd rearrange my entire schedule and try to get the weekly tutoring meeting canceled just so I could get laid?"

"Yes."

"Okay, yeah, I would. I ran into a cecaelia at a party last semester and she hit me up. In all fairness, I did try to find a better time, but her schedule is a little more limited since she's transferring to another school."

"You could have said no."

"And give up an experience with tentacles! It's like you don't know me at all. Much as I like the group, consider yourselves collateral. If I can get out of that meeting, then I am." He rubbed his hands together, positively emanating glee. "I have a suspicion we're going to need several hours. Don't worry, I'll tell you all about it."

"Please don't."

"Suit yourself. Never know, might discover you had a kink you didn't know about. I've seen how your kind operates. Shadow could just as easily become tentacles." He wiggled his eyebrows suggestively.

"Ugh, that's an image I'm never getting out of my brain."

"You're welcome."

Chapter 6
Dating Advice

Matt

No way was I going back to the dorm while Alex had his tutoring stuff. I'd just end up wandering around the living space driving myself nuts wondering if *Rubio* or one of Alex's clients were getting handsy with him. Nope. Not happening. What I needed was a distraction.

Almost immediately, I heard Alex's voice in my head encouraging me to work on class assignments, namely that ridiculous research paper I'd gotten saddled with. I kicked at a rock that had found its way to the sidewalk. I'd meant to ask him about helping me with the paper. Truth be told, whether or not I needed the help, I... missed it. Studying felt so much easier when he was around. Besides, research was his specialty, not mine.

But was that weird? Could the person you were dating *also* tutor you? It sounded like a silly question, even in my head. What was the big deal? Then again, Alex hadn't brought up studying together at all since the fall semester had started. He'd actually taken on more hours of tutoring. And that meant more hours of being on my own. Definitely needed that distraction.

I made my way toward the pool hall. With any luck, Sam and Lucas would be there and I could kill a few hours pretending not to obsessively think about Alex. I considered attempting to shadow walk there—I could always use the practice—but opted to take the long way to eat up as much time as possible.

Garbled voices, laughter, and the sound of balls cracking together hit me in the face when I pushed open the graffiti-covered door of the bar. I searched the tables for any sign of my friends, but came up empty. Deflated, I made my way to the bar, though I had no intention of drinking. Getting drunk lost most of its appeal when I no longer needed the liquid courage, not to mention that "courage" had nearly lost me Alex all together.

I was about to snag a stool when a familiar voice caught my attention. After a little hunting, I discovered Sam struggling to contain laughter—and clearly losing. Surprisingly, the witch was his normal skinny blond self and *not* impersonating another attractive patron.

He glanced at me from where he stood a few feet from the bar as I approached and gave me a head nod in greeting before returning his focus to whatever was cracking him up by the crowded counter.

I leaned closer and raised my voice to be heard over the din. "Where's Lucas?"

Sam pointed toward the counter and bit his knuckle in another hopeless attempt to subdue his laughter.

It took a few seconds of squinting to realize that the back of the nearest person to us, who was currently leaning halfway over the counter to flirt with the bartender, was actually Lucas. "Um, what's going on?"

"*Someone*, Hera bless their soul, gave him moonshine after his run earlier tonight."

I did a double take. "He's *drunk*? I didn't even know werewolves could get drunk."

"Oh, it's not easy, that's for sure, but not impossible. Moonshine usually does the trick."

I frowned. What was so special about moonshine? It packed a punch, but was also kind of awful. "Am I missing something? I've had moonshine, and uh..." I glanced at Lucas, who was making an absolute fool of himself.

"This is not your typical moonshine, my friend. When werewolves make that shit, it's not fit for us regular mortals."

"Damn." I whistled to myself and made a mental note to always turn down any drink offered by a werewolf. "How long has he been like this?"

Sam checked his watch. "Couple hours. Given his *were* metabolism, he should sober up pretty soon. Unless..." He gave me a mischievous look that I'd learned early on always came with a side of trouble.

"Unless?"

"Unless we keep his buzz going by plying him with shots."

Considering Lucas was now openly leering at anyone with breasts who came within four feet of him, that seemed like a bad idea. "Yeah, I don't know about that."

Sam sagged and gave a huff. "You're probably right. Shots wouldn't have the same impact and would eat up all my beer money." He glanced around, taking in the bustling room. "We were waiting for a pool table, but it doesn't look like that's gonna happen anytime soon."

"This place is packed tonight. Any idea why?" I asked, slowly pushing my way closer to the bar.

He shrugged. "The early semester crowd would be my guess. Students letting loose while they still can before the pressure of classes."

I pointed at Lucas who was doing an impressive impersonation of a whistling wolf. "Do you want to or should I?"

Sam barked a laugh. "Dude, if I couldn't have pried him off the bar by myself, I'd have done it ages ago."

I thinned my lips and stared at him with a flat expression.

"Okay, maybe not, but there's still no way I can manhandle a drunk *were*."

"I've got it. You grab that high-top that just opened up." Sam ventured off as the last few people gave way and I could finally reach Lucas. I placed a hand on his shoulder. "Hey, buddy. What do you say we move to a table?"

Lucas spun to face me. If Sam hadn't already told me he was drunk, I'd have known immediately by the shine of his eyes and the potent smell of alcohol on his breath. "Matt! What are you doing here?" Without warning, he threw his arms around my neck and I stumbled under his sudden weight.

"Figured I'd see if y'all were up for a game or two."

He pouted. "We would, but there's no tables! Can you believe that?"

"That really sucks, man, but good news. Sam got us a table." I pointed to where Sam had staked his claim on a high-top in the middle of getting bussed.

"Sweet!"

I took a step toward the table, only to have Lucas jerk me back.

"Wait! Have you met Gina? She's awesome. Super friendly and extra pretty. See, Matt! Isn't Gina pretty?" He gestured with a weaving arm toward the bartender, who thankfully wasn't paying his antics any attention.

"Yeah, buddy, she's real pretty," I said, then mouthed "Sorry," before more forcefully dragging him away.

"And nice too. Did I mention she was nice?"

"You sure did. Come on, Sam is waiting for us." By now I was practically carrying a staggering Lucas, who was still determined to return to the bar.

"I should introduce you." He stopped, and I nearly fell backward at the abrupt shift. "But then what if she likes you more?" He narrowed his eyes at me. "You're too pretty. You'd just steal her."

"I'm not interested in stealing her. Besides, I'm already taken."

Lucas smacked me on the back, and I wheezed. "That's great man! Who's the lucky person?" We stepped close enough to the table, and he spied Sam shooting death glares at a bar regular that was obviously trying to steal the table from him.

"Sammy!" Lucas shouted, throwing his arms up in enthusiasm, leaving me to guide his stumbling ass to a chair.

Thank Nyx for demonic strength.

Finally, I got Lucas in a seat by Sam and heaved myself into one across from them.

Both Sam and Lucas shamelessly leered as a waitress in the usual short plaid skirt a crop-top walked up. "Hey, folks. What can I get you?"

"A round of waters. Better yet, make that a pitcher," I said before either of my companions could speak.

"I'll have those out in a jiff." She spun on her heel and melded into the crowd of bodies.

Sam scowled at me, and poor Lucas just looked confused. "What gives?" Sam asked.

I pointed at Lucas. "He at least needs to hydrate. If you don't want any water, that's fine. More for the rest of us."

"Rest of us? You not drinking?"

I shook my head. "More interested in hanging than drinking tonight."

"Suit yourself." Sam shrugged. The water arrived, and he ordered two beers, one presumably for Lucas.

By the time those arrived, I was seriously questioning why I'd come out. Playing pool was one thing, but sitting here while Sam teased a slowly sobering Lucas wasn't the distraction I'd been looking for.

"What's got you so down in the dumps?" Sam asked after taking a long drink.

Lucas leaned closer to him and not so subtly whispered, "Haven't you heard? He's *dating*." He straightened and thankfully reached for the water.

"Really now? Shouldn't that be a good thing?"

I hiked a shoulder and studied a swirl in the wood of the table. "I haven't done a lot of dating. Well, really any."

Sam snorted his beer, getting it all over himself and the table. "Like hell you haven't. You're like Mr. Charm around here. I won't believe it."

"Yeah, well, believe or don't believe, I don't think I'm very good at it. I have absolutely no clue what I'm doing most of the time."

Lucas leveled his hand at me along with a super serious expression. "What about making out? Have you at least done that?"

"A little," I answered honestly, my face heating.

He smacked the table, causing Sam and I to jump. "Well, there's your problem. Only a little," he scoffed. "Step that shit up. Face it, 'dates' are just a way to get to the fun stuff."

"I don't know if I should take dating advice from drunk Lucas," I responded dubiously.

Lucas gasped, clearly affronted. "Who says I'm drunk? I'm not drunk." He glanced at Sam, who unsurprisingly used his talent of illusion magic to transform himself into a sober Lucas.

"Dude, you're trashed," Sam deadpanned in Lucas's voice.

That Lucas didn't immediately start bitching Sam out for impersonating him—again—was more than enough to prove he was in fact trashed. He turned to face me. "Well, you definitely can't take advice from this asshole." He angled his thumb at Sam, who'd returned to normal.

"Please, I'm a wealth of good advice," Sam argued. They went on like that for a while, periodically dragging me into it until eventually I gave up.

I hopped down from my seat. "I'm gonna call it a night, guys."

Sam glanced wistfully at the queue of people waiting for a pool table. "Maybe next time we'll actually get to play."

"Yeah, drinking at a table-table isn't half as much fun," Lucas bemoaned, swirling his now warm beer.

Sam closed out their tab, and the three of us headed back toward the campus, where we parted ways.

I dragged my feet as I made my way to the dorm. So much for my efforts at a distraction. Thanks to Sam and Lucas bickering about what constituted good relationship advice, I'd spent the last three hours thinking about Alex, anyway. And I still wasn't any closer to figuring out what I was doing wrong. When I'd suggested this dating-thing, I'd warned Alex I'd stumble, that this was all new to me, but it felt more like I was flat on my face than feeling my way in the dark.

All too soon, I was standing in front of our door, the tarnished copper room number 2708 at eye level. I sighed and used my antique-looking key to open the door. No sooner did it swing open than I froze. What the hell was Alex doing here?

"Oh, hey, you're back. I was just about to turn in for the night." He closed the book he'd been reading after sliding in a bookmark and peeled himself off the couch. "You have a good night?" he asked as he stretched, highlighting his long, lean body.

I glimpsed his spectacular abs before his shirt slid back into place. "Uh, yeah. Guess so." My fingers twitched with the urge to walk up to him and feel those abs again, to feel all of him. Fall back on the couch and claim his mouth until neither of us could breathe, then kiss the rest of him.

"You guess so?"

I started at the teasing question and dragged my gaze away from where it was currently latched onto his abdomen. “What happened to your meeting? You’re normally out later when you have one of those.”

“Oh, it got canceled. Rubio had plans,” he added with a chuckle. “Anyway, I’m glad you had a good night ‘you guess’. I’ll see you in the morning.” He flashed me a smile and went to his room.

It wasn’t until his door shut I realized I’d been holding the front door open this whole time. “Of course, the meeting got canceled,” I grumbled to myself as I trudged to my bedroom, where fantasies of licking Alex’s abs were probably going to keep me up half the night. “Stupid Rubio.”

CHAPTER 7
A SIMPLE TOUCH

Alexi

Maybe Rubio had a point. Perhaps our communication *was* lacking. But communication was a two-way street and Matt wasn't giving me anything to work with. I sighed inwardly, not really seeing the notes before me. Studying should have been easy with the dorm empty, but my head wasn't there. I *wanted* Matt so much it made my skin ache any time we kissed. But I also didn't want to push him. Except... maybe I needed to? What would it take to get him to initiate contact for a change? To touch me the way I longed to be touched and to touch him?

At least the friend part of our relationship had leveled out. But Matt wasn't supposed to just be my friend anymore, he was *supposed* to be my boyfriend. I blinked at my notes for Lit II and realized they were the same ones from half an hour ago. Frustrated with my lack of focus, I closed the notebook.

I'm totally going to bomb this class if I can't get my head on straight.

"You okay?" Matt asked right beside me. It was a measure of how stressed I was that I didn't even jump.

"Why do you ask?" I returned, neglecting to answer the question.

"You just seem distracted lately, like something is on your mind." He lifted his hand as if to comfort me. It hovered a moment, then fell back down.

I resisted the urge to roll my eyes. What was it about touching me that was so difficult? "I'm worried about this class. I'm not retaining anything, and my notes are a mess." It was some of the truth, at least.

He smiled. "I'm sure you'll be fine. You always are."

Normally, his unwavering confidence would have bolstered my spirits. Today it made me bitter. Why did I have to be perfect all the time? Why couldn't he take the lead for a change?

"Let me know if there's anything I can do to help," he offered.

I considered asking for a neck rub. If I was lucky, it could lead to more... which would inevitably stop well short of what I actually wanted. Except I wasn't that lucky.

"Do you mind if I sit on the couch and work on the research project? It looks like you've got the table covered." He smiled at the terrible pun and my cheek twitched in a half-hearted response that was more like a grimace. I knew he was just trying to cheer me up, but in my current mood, I wasn't interested.

I shrugged noncommittally, and he retrieved the gray tomb from the counter. He was practically obsessed with the thing, spending more time with it than me as often as not. I watched him walk over and plop down out of the corner of my eye. I should have asked for the massage. What was the worst that could happen? My mind immediately supplied several less-than-ideal outcomes, effectively killing any desire to do so now.

By the time the silence became oppressive, my nerves were a frayed mess. I pushed up from the table and made my way towards the door. Maybe a walk would clear my head. I grabbed my key, then turned to tell Matt I was stepping out for a bit and immediately lost my breath.

He sat with his legs stretched out to rest on the coffee table and had the book open on his lap. His dark hair fell across his eyes and round spectacles perched on his nose when he glanced up.

I couldn't help but sigh with longing. Matt was beautiful, a fallen angel among mortals. I wanted more than anything to push that damn book aside and straddle him. I'd take the glasses off, taste his delicious lips as I ran my fingers through his hair.

Wait, why is he wearing glasses?

"What?" he asked, shifting on the couch like he wanted to hide.

"You're wearing glasses." He'd never worn them before. I was certain of it. Nor had he ever mentioned needing them.

"Oh." He blushed lightly as he lifted them. "They're spelled so we don't have to go to the library every time we want to read this thing. Dorky, right?" He gave a self-depreciating laugh.

"No. It's sexy as hell."

His pink cheeks turned red. "Why would you say that?"

"Because it's true." I knew I should stop; I was clearly making him uncomfortable, but the words kept coming. "You're outrageously attractive, Matt," I added wistfully.

The red darkened. "But... But I look nothing like you."

I stared blankly back at him, completely blindsided.

"What?" He squirmed beneath my stunned gaze. "Why are you looking at me like that?"

A grin tugged at my mouth. "I think you just told me you find me attractive." I had no idea a blush could go to the tips of your ears.

He opened his mouth, but no words came out. Ultimately, he closed it again without saying anything.

I cleared my throat. "So, yeah, what I was going to say before. I'm going to go for a walk and get some fresh air. I'll be back later."

"Okay." That was it. Nothing about what had just happened. No "can I come?" or "how late is later?" Nothing at all. Did he even care?

Without another word, I left. Outside, the air was indeed fresh, but it was also misty and it felt like I was passing through ephemeral curtains of water. It didn't take long for my increasingly damp shirt to add to my irritation. Not ready to turn back, I opted to put up with it a little longer. I needed to figure my shit out or *all* of my studies would suffer, not just Lit II. That meant thinking about the one thing that was irritating me most of all: Matt.

Good grief, him and those glasses.

I shook my head. Perhaps it had been a mistake to ride the breaks. Maybe if I stopped forcing things to go so slowly, everything would work itself out and we could both get what we wanted. Of course, I had zero ideas about what that was for Matt. But then, I hadn't really been clear about my expectations either. Was it possible Matt was struggling as well?

It wasn't until I was back at our door that I even realized I'd been walking back to the dorm. Resigned to more awkward silence, I unlocked it and swung it open to see Matt still on the couch. He'd lost the glasses and the book and appeared to be sketching.

He looked up at my entrance, relief in his eyes. Why was he always so afraid that I wouldn't come back?

Might have something to do with the fact that I had threatened to do just that.

"Hey," I said, closing the door behind me.

"Feel any better?"

Irritation sparked through me. "Sure. I guess." "Better" wasn't the word I'd use. My shirt was sticking unpleasantly to me, and I just wanted it off.

"Be honest, Alex, what's going on with you?"

I stopped mid-stride and turned an incredulous look on him. "Me?" The nerve. All the thoughts that had been tumbling to no avail finally found an outlet... right out of my mouth. "Why won't you touch me?"

He blinked, mouth agape.

The lack of a response only fueled the anger I'd been ignoring for weeks. "I'm serious, not so much as a little touch. Are you afraid I'll bite? You don't initiate contact. Ever." I balled my hands at my side to prevent them from gesturing wildly. "This is feeling very one-sided. Oh wait, it pretty much always has been." I knew I was being unreasonable and taking my frustration out on him. I'd known what this would be when I agreed to it, but that knowledge did little to stop me. "You can't even admit you think I'm attractive," I said, pulling off the nasty shirt as I walked towards my room.

"And what? Your solution is to do a striptease?" he responded heatedly.

I stared down at the shirt in my hand, confused, then realized what I'd done. Rather than admit that hadn't been my intent, I let my temper get the better of me. "It's only a strip tease if you like what you see." I threw the shirt down and glared back at him. What right did he have to be angry? He wasn't the one being jerked around by a string. He stared rebelliously back, and I saw the glimmer of his fighter spirit. I wished to Nyx it wasn't so fucking hot, it was not helping the current situation at all. Now I was pissed *and* turned on.

When he said nothing, I spun to go into my room only to run into him. Damn, he was fast. Just as quickly, he reached up and pulled me down to mash my mouth against his. Stubbornly, I fought him for a second. I wasn't done being mad. Then his hands shifted to my bare back, and I lost my breath. That felt better than it had any right.

"Matt," I gasped the second he released it to work his way along my jaw to my neck.

His plush lips pressed firmly against the sensitive skin, followed by nips of teeth and light flicks of his tongue. It wouldn't take much of that before I had an impressive hickey. Too soon and not soon enough, he continued his deliberate path across my collar.

"Matt," I tried again, "What are you doing?"

"Exactly what you wanted," he replied between kisses. His lips on my skin felt like a brand. I lost my response in a moan I couldn't hold back. "You wanted me to start things. You've got it."

I groaned as his hands roved over every exposed inch of me—my shoulders, waist, back—as if he couldn't decide which part of me to touch. I was falling somewhere between ecstasy and torture. The exquisite sensations bordered on torture after so long. At the rate he was going, I'd have several hickeys. At some point, my hands had fisted in his shirt. I released it to tangle them in his hair.

"Matt." His fingers dug into my hips, forcing me against him. Another gasp escaped me at finding him every bit as hard as I was. I couldn't breathe. It was too much all at once. "Matt, stop." He ran his hands up my back and curled around my shoulders. "Please. It hurts," I groaned as he continued his aggressive trail across my chest. In exactly five seconds, I was going to come in my pants. Finally, I tightened my grip on his hair and forced his head back. Two midnight eyes stared back at me and I almost lost it, anyway. "Stop."

I shadowed out and rematerialized on the other side of my door, desperately needing space to catch my breath. The heat of his ardor still burned on my skin and the distance wasn't doing anything to lessen that. I wanted to go back, to finish falling madly into him.

I need to simmer down, is what I need.

I shadowed into the bathroom, turned the water on as cold as I could get it, finished stripping down, then plunged into the icy fall. Which did absolutely nothing. If anything, the contrast made it worse. I braced myself against the wall, letting the cold water pour over my back as desire roared unchecked in my veins. Safe in the confines of my space, my control slipped away to wash down the drain. I wrapped a hand around my shaft that was still hot to the touch despite the frigid water. One slow stroke turned into a frantic pump in search of release. Just the memory of his hands all over me was enough to drive me to the edge in record time.

Something tickled my senses, and I looked up to see Matt leaning against the door frame with his arms crossed. His eyes were still perfectly black, and he was watching me, raw hunger on his face. It was the final straw. I grunted and came all over my hand and the wall. He didn't look away. Didn't so much as blink.

The water continued to wash over me as the world swam back into focus, only now feeling even remotely cold. I dropped my hand and turned it off. Silence reigned as I grabbed a towel from the rack, practically snapping it free as a spike of anger stabbed through me. I didn't even bother to dry off, just wrapped it around my waist.

"It's rude to watch, you know. Especially when you haven't been invited. That's not fair." Despite feeling a little violated, I had to admit that some part of me had liked him watching.

He grabbed the hem of his shirt and pulled it over his head. To my amazement, he followed that by hooking his thumbs in his pants and dragging them to pool on the floor. His erection bounced at his movements and I swallowed hard.

"What are you doing?" I asked in disbelief. My imagination needed an upgrade. It wasn't doing Matt justice.

"You're right, it's not fair." He kicked aside his pants and stood there, his eyes once more their startling shade of blue. "Take whatever you want, Alex."

I took a step towards him and stopped. Even after finding release, I didn't trust myself. "Get in the shower." The glint in his eye was downright devilish and paired well with his crooked smile.

"Alright." He walked brazenly past me. "But it won't be as good of a show." He stepped into the tub and turned on the water. Still cold I noticed, then raised a questioning brow at me.

Now what?

"Go ahead, bathe."

He chuckled to himself, but complied by reaching for the soap.

This is wrong, I thought as I watched his hands glide over his slick skin. That should be me. I dropped the towel and stepped in behind him, my gaze riveted on the way his muscles rippled as he moved.

"Didn't you already have one of these?" he teased.

"Put your hands on the wall," I commanded, my voice thick.

He looked at me over his shoulder.

"You heard me."

He did so without further protest, having to lean forward ever so slightly to reach.

I started slow. Tracing the contours of his back with just one finger and then expanding to both hands. He let out a sigh that sounded more like a moan.

"Tell me what you don't like about your body." I brushed my lips across his shoulders, then wrapped my arms around him so I could explore his chest. He gasped as I explored his chest and trailed my hands down his torso. How long had I wanted to do this? "Tell me," I pressed.

"It's awful. Not like yours."

"Mmm, I love your body. I don't want it to be like mine," I said, sliding my hands down the front of his hips and coming back up the sides of his legs. He let out a groan and his hands fisted on the wall. "I didn't say you could move." He drew in a sharp intake of air, but dutifully flattened his hands. "Tell me when it hurts." His body shuddered, then quieted.

He held perfectly still while my hands roved over every inch of him. He was mine to touch and I damn well was going to. Eventually, I noticed he was struggling to keep his hands flat. Still, he didn't cry mercy. I pressed against him, enjoying the feel of our skin against each other, mindless that I was once again hard. His breath hitched as my shaft slid over his ass. For a moment, I feared I'd gone too far, but he held firm.

He really is going to let me do whatever I want.

The realization came with an unprecedented amount of trust. I took my time, dragging my hand across his abdomen, then lower to wrap around his throbbing erection. It pulsed against my hand at the same time his arms slipped on the wall and he released a deep groan.

"Say it, Matt." I squeezed the base and gave a firm stroke. "Say it."

"It hurts," he finally gasped, the words falling into another groan.

"Good." I released him and he sagged, leveraging his arms against the wall for support while his breath came in quick gasps. Before I could doubt myself, I shadowed, so that I was in front of him.

His eyes widened with surprise, and his mouth parted. Rather than give into the temptation of those delectable lips, I dropped to my knees in search of a different prize. I probably could have stared at Matt's beautiful cock, jutting out from a nest of dark curls, but I wasn't willing to test how long my luck would hold. Once more I took him in hand, reveling in the feel of velvet steel beneath my fingers. I placed my free hand on his quivering thigh, then brought his swollen head to my lips. Matt cried out with what sounded like a cross between ecstasy and pain. That's all it took for me to lose all sense of self. Most guys wouldn't say no to blowjob and would rather receive one than give. Some didn't mind either way or preferred mutual reciprocation. Me? I *loved* giving head. Loved being the one to give that pleasure, control it.

"Alex," he moaned. His whole body quivered beneath my touch, like a string pulled too tight, as he panted for air he couldn't hold. "Wait. I... you have to... *Alex*," he groaned again when I pulled him deeper. There was no way I was going to be the only one to lose it tonight. His entire body tensed and he let out a moan that sounded like it had been scraped from the bottom of his soul as his release shot down my throat.

To my amazement, his hands were still plastered against the wall, though his arms were noticeably shaking, probably from the effort of holding unbelievably still while I had my way with him. I leaned forward to place a trail of soft kisses along the curve of his hip and let out a dreamy sigh. "You can move your arms now."

Faster than seemed possible, his arms fell, and he yanked me to my feet. The moment I was upright, his mouth mashed down on mine in a punishing kiss. I moaned, arching into him and well on my way to be ready for another round.

The fire of his kiss burned through us as he pulled me tighter against him. I hooked a leg over his hip, sacrificing balance to be closer.

His hands caressed my back as he continued to claim my mouth. When shifted his thigh between my legs, it was all the encouragement I needed to rub shamelessly against him. His grip moved to my waist, and he pressed me harder against him.

I broke the kiss with a gasp, tilting my head back as my second orgasm ripped through me without warning. His feather-light kisses along the column of my throat gradually brought me back to my senses. I lowered my leg, allowing the supposedly cold water to wash his torso clean.

Matt placed a tender kiss on my lips as he reached to turn off the water, his fingers trailing over my ass as he brought his hand back to my hip, where he traced lazy circles with his thumb. "You're insane," he said, his voice husky.

"So you've said," I replied, shadowing out of the shower. I grabbed my towel from where I'd abandoned it and tossed him a fresh one. "Tonight has been..." All sorts of words came to mind to describe how the evening had gone: eventful, amazing, mind-blowing. I settled for, "Exhausting. I feel like I could sleep for an entire day." At the very least, I could certainly stay in bed all day.

He looked at me like he could read my mind, but didn't add anything. He really didn't like to talk about things. For once, that was fine by me.

I walked into my room and ditched the wet towel yet again. Matt's gaze was every bit as potent as his hands on my body had been. I hid a shiver by diving under the covers. To my infinite surprise, Matt mirrored me. "What are you doing?"

"Going to bed," he said matter of fact.

I didn't really have a decent answer for that, so I lay my head back. His hand slid across my middle, and I let out an involuntary sigh. That was not conducive to going to sleep. I rolled my head to look at him. Naturally, his eyes were already closed. *You have to be the strangest creature, Matthew Duncan.*

The world was all soft darkness until mind-blowing sensation rocketed me back to wakefulness. My eyes flew open to find Matt had removed the covers and was returning the favor from the shower. I tried to hold back a cry, to no avail. Getting woken up by a blowjob was something that happened in fantasies and movies, not real life. And for someone who'd supposedly never done this before, he was doing exceptionally well.

I dug my fingers into his shoulder, desperate for something to hold on to. When that wasn't enough, I buried my fingers in his hair, moaning loud enough to wake the dead when he swirled his tongue around the head, then sucked me back into his mouth. He needed to stop. He needed to stop right now. "Matt, don't. Wait."

He listened about as well as I had and there was nothing I could do about it. The hand I hadn't noticed resting on my straining thigh shifted to caress my sac and I shattered.

"Night, holy crap, just..." The words tumbled out of me as he levered himself up beside me. I looked at him, still in a state of blissed out shock. Should have known his eyes would be crystal clear and calm as he watched me totally freak out after one of the best bjs I'd ever had. "Really dumb question, but are you sure you've never done that?"

"I think I'd remember," he said, trailing his fingers along my abdomen.

"Yeah. Right. Of course. It's just... how?" My mind refused to come to terms with his words and the reality of what had just happened.

"I paid attention."

"You paid attention," I echoed.

"I pay attention to everything you do, Alex. And people tend to do what they like." He shrugged, watching his finger trace swirls on my skin.

"So, you just... and didn't stop, because..." I just couldn't wrap my head around this.

"It seemed like a safe bet," he said, giving me a playful smile and returning his attention to the pattern he was creating.

I watched him a moment as he got lost in it. "What are you doing?" I asked softly.

"Hmm?"

"What are you doing?" I repeated, placing my hand on my stomach, just shy of his own.

Doubt flashed in his eyes, and he pulled his hand back. "Nothing."

"Why do you do that?" I asked, angling up to my elbow to be on his level.

"I don't know what you're talking about." He tried to turn away, but I caught his face with my free hand.

"Look at me." When he did, it felt like I'd been speared. There was so much hiding in those clear eyes, like a pool with no bottom. His eyes lidded when I leaned closer. "What do you want, Matt?" I whispered.

"I want you to kiss me," he replied softly.

I closed the distance a little more, savoring how our breath mingled. "No, you don't." I was close enough now that our lips practically touched, anyway.

"What?" he asked, leaning back slightly.

I smiled, my gaze still focused on his mouth. "I know what you really want." I leaned forward, passing his mouth. He gave a soft sigh, no doubt expecting me to kiss his neck. I didn't.

"If you know, then why are you asking?"

"Because I want to hear you say it," I whispered before sitting back to look at him. He searched my face, his accelerated breathing betraying his anxiety. I calmly waited, gently stroking his cheek while he struggled to find the words.

Why is it so hard for you to admit what you want?

"I..." he faltered. "I want to kiss you."

"You don't need to wait for permission, Matt."

He licked his lips, and I couldn't help but follow the path his tongue took. When he finally leaned forward, the kiss was slow and purposeful, lingering before going into another. Not at all the inferno I'd come to expect when he took what he actually wanted. The sweet press of lips had all the makings of a first kiss with none of the hesitation. He shifted so that I was lying on my back and slid his arm around to keep me pressed against him. The kiss deepened unexpectedly, searing me to the core and making me crave more. Then, just as abruptly, it dissipated back into small, lingering tastes. He shifted again and nuzzled into my side, resting his head on my chest. There, he could easily hear my heart beating way too fast.

I reflexively wrapped an arm around his waist, then kissed the top of his head. "I love you, Matt," I whispered into his hair.

"Alexi," he sighed, snuggling closer.

As surprised as I was to hear my actual name, I was really just pleased he wasn't running. I drifted back to sleep holding who I was pretty sure was the love of my life.

Chapter 8
Sieben Hügel

Matt

Something lightly brushed my face. My cheek twitched to make it stop, but it didn't work. With my eyes still closed, I ran through a list of possibilities. A bug? No, not crawly enough. Paper? Too consistent. A stick? Nah, too soft; too gentle. Maybe it wasn't a something at all, but a some*one.*

I cracked an eye and found deep emerald pools shining back.

Alex. Of course.

Now that I knew it was his slender fingers dancing across my face, the touch felt more like sparklers.

"Good morning," he said in a soft whisper that caressed my skin.

I hummed a reply and let my eyes drift shut again. For a moment, everything was perfect in the world. There was no constant anger, no pending deadline, just us. He gently stroked my cheek and I let out a contented sigh. A good night's sleep *and* Alex—the day was off to a great start.

As the fog of sleep lifted, the details of the night before rushed in to take its place. The argument. The hot make-out. The *shower.* What I did... My eyes flew open, and I saw my mounting panic reflected in Alex's eyes.

"Matt..."

I have to get out of here. What am I doing? This isn't me.

"Matt, don't."

I ignored the command and shadowed out of the bed, landing a few feet from the door.

Alex anticipated the move and launched out of the bed almost as fast as I had shadowed to cut off my escape. "Matt, stop."

"I have to... I can't... I don't..." I couldn't breathe let alone finish a thought. All I had was *run.* Suddenly, Alex grabbed my face and planted a single, firm kiss on my mouth that somehow expelled all of my anxiety, leaving me a hollow husk. I stood there frozen, not sure if I was breathing at all and not really caring. There was only Alex. Alex with his intense eyes that seemed to know all of my secrets no matter how I hid them.

"Stop, Matt. I have worked too hard for this to let you ruin everything because you're freaking out over nothing. Now, take a deep breath." He released my face and slid his hand down to my chest. I wasn't sure if it was to make sure I was doing as he said or to see if my heart was still beating. His brows wrinkled as he studied me for a few shaky breaths. "I wish you would tell me what you're so afraid of."

The passive request washed over me. I couldn't tell him I was absolutely terrified. That I didn't know what I was doing or even getting myself into. I couldn't admit that I knew if I got too invested and he left, it would utterly destroy me. Some part of me recognized it was already too late for that. I'd do anything for Alex. Anything at all. All he had to do was tell me. My breath started coming in pants again.

"Easy. I'm right here. I'm not going anywhere."

I wanted to make him promise that. Swear he would never abandon me like so many had before.

Determination flashed in his eyes, and his tone shifted from calm understanding to demanding. "Kiss me, Matt." My body jerked to obey, but his hand on my chest held me in place. "Kiss me like I know you want to," he added, his gaze sharp.

Something inside me snapped, and the rest of the world fell away. There was only Alex. I surged forward, removing his hand from between us, smashing my mouth against him so hard he stumbled into the wall and I was plastered against him. He gasped, and I used that as my opening to delve into his mouth with needy abandon while my hands explored every inch of him I could reach. Fuck, he felt incredible. I managed a gulp of air before I claimed him with another unforgiving kiss, fueled by the fire sweeping through me. That blaze absolutely terrified me, but I couldn't stop. I wanted more, *needed* more, and he was giving it to me. I kept waiting for him to pull back, to say enough that it was too much. Instead, I felt his fingers digging into my back as he arched into me. Felt his moan as I hungrily devoured kiss after kiss.

I would die for Alex. Knew it with a certainty that rang in my core. I couldn't breathe. Still, I kept kissing him and still he didn't stop me. He needed to stop me. Except he wasn't.

I braced my hands on the wall and straightened my arms. It wasn't much distance, but it was something. I had to stop touching him. He'd asked why I didn't touch him. *This* was why. Because I knew if I started, I wouldn't be able to stop. Mercifully, his hands fell away when I broke the kiss for longer than a microsecond. I closed my eyes, not wanting to see what he thought of me, and our ragged breathing filled my ears. Pain stabbed through my chest at the certainty that I'd just ruined everything because I couldn't control myself. And yet, it still wasn't enough, it would never be enough. I wasn't just addicted to kissing Alex, I was addicted *to* Alex and I had no idea how it had happened or when.

I tried to swallow, failed, and tried again. "I'm sorry," I finally managed.

"Don't be. That was... that was incredible," he said between pants.

I lifted my head to meet his gaze. A ridiculous smile dominated his face. But that didn't make sense. I was basically some possessed creature of darkness. Why was he grinning from ear to ear? Didn't he know how dangerous this was? How dangerous *I* was?

In an outrageously brave move, he leaned forward to rest his forehead against mine. I wanted to think he had a death wish, but the intimacy of the move rippled through me and I relaxed.

"I'm a demon too, Matt. I can handle the passion."

Passion, is that what this was? It felt more like some supernatural force of nature designed to incinerate the host and whatever they touched.

"It's okay. You don't have to be afraid." He wrapped his arms around me and pulled me close.

I completely melted into the embrace and him. My racing heart synced with the steady beat of his. I wasn't sure how long we stayed like that, only that I didn't want it to end. I needed Alex in a way I didn't know you could need another person. With him, I felt truly safe for the first time in my life. He finally pushed away a bit, and I looked back at him, finally feeling completely calm.

"I love you, Matt."

I searched his face. No matter how many times he said it, I didn't understand how he could.

"Does it bother you when I say that?"

"No," I said honestly.

"You look uncomfortable, though. Why?"

I thought about it for a moment. "No one has ever really told me that. I can count on one hand all the times." My face heated, and I resisted the urge to look away. "They're all you."

He looked surprised, but didn't say anything about it. Instead, he smiled and stole a quick kiss. "Then I guess I'm going to have to tell you more often. Unless you want me to stop?" I wasn't sure if that was a question or not, so I treated it like one.

"Please don't."

"Good, because I don't intend to. Now get dressed. I'm tired of being in the dorm."

"What happened to wanting to stay in bed all day?" I teased.

"There's always tomorrow," he said with a wicked smile. Then he smacked my ass and disappeared.

I shadowed to the other side of his door and walked the rest of the way to my room. Fall was already sneaking in, so I opted to grab one of the light jackets Jefferey had acquired for me. My stint under lockdown at the hotel already felt like a lifetime ago. Strange to think it was only four months. So much had changed.

Once I'd cleaned up, I wandered back to the living room. While I waited, I worked on the bookmark sketch some more. It was so close to being done that it was reaching that point of being overworked. Sooner rather than later, I'd have to let it go. I heard Alex's door open and put away the art.

"It's about time," I complained, turning to look at him and froze. Water beaded on the edges of his hair as if he'd just stepped out of the shower. I immediately flashed to last night and heat rushed through me. The look Alex gave me suggested he knew *exactly* what was going on in my head. I swallowed hard.

Out of the blue, he asked, "Why won't you tell me where you're really from?"

"Because I don't want you to look at me differently," I answered quickly, too frazzled to come up with a lie.

Surprise washed over his face. "But I wouldn't. It doesn't matter to me where you come from. I'd just like to know."

This is what I got for speaking without thinking. "You say that because you don't know," I said with a sigh. No way Alex would look at me like I was special if he learned I was really gutter trash.

"Wait, you're not a criminal, are you?" He smiled, and I recognized the question for the tease he meant it to be.

I shrugged. "Depends on who you ask. Several people have me branded at least as a juvenile delinquent." Only reason it wasn't something more was because I'd been a minor, but petty theft could still get your ass in jail.

He waved his hand flippantly as he grabbed his key and walked towards the door. "I already know about the deviant part."

"I didn't say deviant," I corrected him.

He glanced over his shoulder. "Didn't you?"

"Alex," I growled, shutting the door behind us.

"You need to learn to lighten up," he laughed. "It was just a joke." He hadn't gone as far into the hall as I'd expected and with the door shut, we were practically on top of each other. And *I* had issues with personal space.

"Didn't sound much like a joke," I said, pocketing my key and trying not to think about how close he was. Or how I wanted him to be closer.

"You're right, it wasn't." Heat curled around the words and danced in his eyes.

Desire burned beneath my skin. If I didn't get some distance between us soon, we were going to have a repeat of the shower out here where everyone could see. "So, what are we doing today?" I asked to reroute the topic. It might have worked better if my voice hadn't tipped.

He flashed a sinister smile. Alex knew exactly what he was doing to me and was enjoying it. The problem was, I was too. Before I could officially get myself in trouble, I started down the hall.

"Oh, I don't know," he mused aloud as he trailed after. "I just felt like we've had a pretty... eventful morning and could use some time outside of four walls."

"There's always the research project," I offered, except the book and all of our notes were back inside. Something told me if we went back in, though, we wouldn't come out.

He bumped me with his elbow and I nearly came out of my skin at the unexpected touch, despite how friendly it was. "What's with you and that project, anyway? You're obsessed."

"I'm surprised you're not more. It was your book that started this."

"I have something real to occupy my time." The same heat from before warmed the statement and had me wondering if I should have opted for silent study. "Seriously though, why are you so into it? I want to know."

I narrowly didn't let out a relieved breath. Academic Alex I could handle... mostly. "I have this feeling."

"What sort of feeling?

"I don't know. Like it's important. I keep hoping that eventually I'll read something and that feeling will make sense."

"Huh." He tapped his bottom lip like he usually did when he was deep in thought. "Is the feeling focused on the knight and our demon, or the wars?"

"Both?" I replied uncertainly. "I promise to let you know when I do."

"You better," he said so seriously I couldn't help but laugh.

Like that, we were back to normal. Just two friends out enjoying their Saturday. Except we weren't. We could pretend to be friends all we wanted, but we were something way past that. I now had a better idea of why Alex had said he couldn't just be my friend. After last night and this morning, I doubted I'd ever be able to be around him *without* wanting more. But was that a good thing or a bad?

"Matt."

I blinked, dragging my thoughts back to the present. "What?"

"You haven't heard a word I've said, have you?" Oops. He rolled his eyes and tried again. "I was suggesting we go down to Sieben Hügel and check it out. I've been meaning to explore, but haven't gotten around to it."

"Sieben Hügel. Is that something on campus?"

Alex looked at me like I'd grown a second head. "It means Seven Hills. It's the town right outside the university. Remember, we were going to check it out the other day?"

"Right! Sorry, I keep forgetting there's an actual town out there."

"I thought you said that ridiculous club wasn't on campus. If it wasn't in Sieben Hügel, then where was it?"

"How should I know?"

He gave me a look.

"I mean, it makes sense, but it's not like I was going down a bunch of back alleys. Plus, it was always dark, and it's in some kind of warehouse. I didn't exactly go wandering around. Class, the dorm, and there. That was it." I supposed there was the bar I went to with Lucas and Sam, but honestly, I had no clue if that was on campus or off.

Alex shook his head. "Well, now we're definitely going." He grabbed my arm and commenced dragging me outside.

Part of me said that he should be holding my hand, not my arm. I shied away from the thought. It was no one else's business what went on between us. When he let me, I took my arm back, surprising him. "I have two legs, Alex."

He raised his hands defensively. "Alright, point taken. No need to get snippy about it."

I deflated. What was wrong with me? I sighed and continued to follow him, albeit much more sedate.

Mercifully, our route didn't take us anywhere near the club. In fact, we went to a part of the campus I'd never seen. As I was looking around, I couldn't help but notice this part of campus was noticeably older than Mysterio College.

"You haven't been over here at all, have you?"

"What? No," I said, staring up at what I could only describe as a tower. I was dubious about calling it a castle, but that's what it looked like. "I had no idea this place was so big."

"And we still haven't left campus. Well, not yet. That's the exit." He pointed at a massive entryway with an arch that was easily two stories tall and at least fifty feet across.

"Whoa."

"You should see it from the other side." He walked forward and casually stepped across the invisible line that separated the town from the school. "Come on slow poke." He waved impatiently for me to join him. "What are you waiting for?"

I approached the entrance, my anxiety suddenly spiking, and tentatively stuck out my hand fully expecting to meet resistance.

Alex tilted his head as he watched me. "Uh, what are you doing?"

"I'm making sure I can actually walk through. The last time I tried to leave a place, there was a barrier spell on the door."

"What?" he asked in alarm.

I took a fateful step to join him and then let out the breath I was holding. Logically, I should have known that since I could go to other places off campus, it wouldn't be an issue. But I also didn't trust Vera as far as I could throw her. For a teacher, she had some real questionable methods for keeping her students in line... or maybe that was just me.

"Where was there a barrier spell?"

"At the hotel where Vera dropped me for two weeks before the start of last semester," I replied nonchalantly.

"She did what!"

I blinked, surprised by his outrage. "Yeah, she told Jefferey, the hotel manager, I was a flight risk and put a spell on the door so I couldn't leave. Everyone else could come and go as they pleased, but not me."

"Of all the... I can't believe she... The self-righteous..." he floundered, bordering on apoplectic.

"To be fair, she wasn't wrong. First time they left the door open, I made a break for it. At least when I ran into that one, it didn't hurt like hell. Not like the one at the club," I added with a shudder.

"What do you mean?"

"Well, the one at the hotel just didn't let me through. It was kind of like running into a wall—repeatedly, in my case. However, the one at the club felt like more like an electric fence."

"That's awful," He said, reaching out.

I shrugged and took a step back. "It happened." I looked around, eager for a way to change the topic and the fact that I'd just intentionally stepped away from his offered comfort. "So, do you know as much about this place as you do the university?"

He searched me for a moment before finally responding, "No, actually. I know a few interesting stories, though."

"Like what?" I asked, intrigued by his grin.

"Well, I can show you the cafe where Vera apparently met *her* teacher for the first time."

I frowned, worried I'd missed something. "Why would she meet him here? I thought she grew up in America?"

"She did, but she didn't actually meet her demon tutor until *after* they moved into the Manor their second year at Arminius."

"Manor...manor... Why does that sound familiar?"

"It's where the Shadows lived when everything went to pot. Actually, it's not that far from here, but they've added substantial protection spells over the years."

"So, not something we could just walk up and visit?" I asked, falling into step beside him.

He laughed. "Not really. I've heard they throw epic parties for elite guests. Though I can't really imagine Vera being the party type."

"I don't know. Maybe you just don't know her as well as you think."

"That sounds suspiciously as if you actually like her," Alex accused, giving me a sidelong look.

I shrugged. She really wasn't all that bad. I thought about how her tough-act facade had dropped outside of the orphanage and how, even as scary as she could be, Jefferey still called her Miss Scry despite her insistence to use her first name. "I think she might be a product of the situations she's been put in," I said as we continued walking aimlessly down the street.

Alex scoffed. "You *choose* to behave like a monster. That's not something you get to say people made you do."

I shook my head. I knew better. Not all monsters wanted to be that way. "You said the Shadows started younger than us, basically kids. How were they supposed to know better? They were told one thing and acted on it. When they found out the truth, they switched sides."

Alex's mouth twisted to the side. "You have a point. But look at the things she's done. None of the Shadows are blameless, yet she was the one who got the reputation of being the ruthless enforcer." He took a deep breath. "She slaughtered people, Matt. There were no trials, no juries, nothing. Just her will. No one could stop her, and now the rest of our kind will be feared forever. You asked me how I thought the Demon War started. If I had to guess, a lot like that. One rogue reminding the world to be afraid. The damage, irreparable."

"And yet, she's still trying to make amends. She knows what she did. She's not proud of it."

"How could you possibly know that?" he asked emphatically.

"When she took me to the hotel, I asked why everyone was afraid of her. She looked ashamed, Alex. *Ashamed.* She didn't want to tell me, and even said that when I found out, I probably wouldn't like her. Of course, I already didn't like her, but that's beside the point. At least she's trying. I've known plenty of real villains, Alex. They don't carry the weight of what they've done around with them, and they certainly don't make reparations," I finished hotly.

He studied me as if seeing me for the first time. "Eventually, you'll have to tell me where you come from."

"Not today, though."

He reached out like he could somehow soothe the anger that was boiling beneath the surface. I knew exactly what it felt like to be pigeon-holed. When everyone assumed they knew your motives. No one ever got my story straight, and I suspected it was no different for Vera.

I walked past him towards a quaint coffee shop. I didn't want his comfort. "Is this it?" It had to be. It was the only cafe I'd seen since we came into the town.

Sadness swept through his emerald eyes and he dropped his outstretched hand, shoving it forcefully into his back pocket before looking up at the sign. "Yeah, this should be it."

Without waiting, I went inside and up to the counter. I got him a coffee and me a hot chocolate. "Where should we sit?" I asked when he joined me.

He glanced around intently as he considered the assortment of occupied and unoccupied seats. "Here," he finally said, leading us over to a table that was a little out of the way. It was far enough off to have some privacy, without being so far as to be conspicuous.

"Interesting choice." I plopped into the wooden seat. Personally, I'd have preferred the cushy armchairs that had just opened up.

He took his time getting settled. Fussing with his drink and shifting his chair with far more excitement radiating off of him than a simple coffee shop warranted. At last, he looked at me. "*This is* where Vera and Gabriel sat the very first time they met."

I was about to ask what was so special about that when it hit me why that was such a big deal. For the first time in a couple of centuries, there had been two level two Shadow Demons sitting at a table together. One, almost an original, and the other, a miracle of happenstance. I took a nervous gulp and burned my tongue. When I looked back at Alex, he was grinning. It was hard to stay angry when he smiled at me like that. "I'm sorry," I said without preamble.

"For what?" he asked, sipping his drink far more carefully than I had.

"I shouldn't have gone at you like that about Vera. You grew up in this world and had an entirely different perspective about what was happening. This is all still new for me. I have no right to judge you for your views." I stared into my steaming mug of hot chocolate, feeling thoroughly ashamed of myself.

After a second, Alex let out a deep sigh. "No, you're right. I know nothing about her besides what I've heard or read in articles. How can I expect the world to look past the deeds of one Shadow Demon if *I* can't? I don't know what circumstances she was put in or what choices she was forced to make. She seemed to cultivate fear like it was a crop and exchange it like currency. But who knows the truth? The more people who feared her, the fewer people died. It'll take time for the wounds she made to heal, but I should be part of the solution, not the problem."

"I feel like you just signed up to be a goodwill ambassador," I said with a smile.

"Shut up." He laughed and chunked a sugar packet at me.

I caught it and promptly deposited the contents into my drink.

"I think you have a sweet problem," he poked.

"Simply supplementing the sweetness I don't naturally have."

"I think you're plenty sweet, Matt." His smile made my heart skip, and I finally understood what they meant in those romance books when they said "bedroom eyes". Then he added, "I mean, when you're not being a total pain in the neck." He winked, and we both returned to our drinks.

CHAPTER 9
CHECK UP

Alexi

I gave Matt a little smirk as we squared off to spar. He winked back, and I mentally crossed my fingers that no one else was picking up the sex appeal practically oozing off of him. Three sparring practices in and we were definitely flirting more than we were fighting.

"That's it. Everyone stop."

Mat and I straightened and turned to face the front of the room where Vera was currently rubbing her forehead. She'd been more absent than not so far this semester. Whatever was keeping her distracted was also clearly giving her one hell of a migraine.

"I think it's time we mixed things up. George, you're with Yaren. Louise with Matt. Roland and Travis. Alexi and Ellie. Gilles and Kyle. She squinted at the room as if trying to figure out who she'd missed. Finally, she waved a dismissive hand. "The rest of you figure it out." She reached for a water bottle.

"Uh, Ms. Scry?" Kyle held up a tentative hand.

Vera released a heavy sigh that emphasized how exhausted she looked. "If you don't like your new partner, you can work it out amongst yourselves."

"It's not that."

Her eyes flashed as she rounded on him, and he shrank back. "Then what is it?"

Kyle's gaze darted to those closest to him, and he swallowed thickly. "G-Gilles isn't here."

Vera's eyes narrowed while her voice dropped dangerously. "And *where* is he? Miel!" she called for Gilles' roommate, but there was no answer.

"He's not here either. Hasn't been all week," Louise said, sounding almost timid.

The tension in the room increased until it felt like electricity should be crackling between our frozen forms. Matt shot me an anxious look, then gave a nearly imperceptible nod toward Vera.

"I could stop in on them, if you like," I volunteered.

Relief ghosted across Vera's face so fast, I almost missed it. "That would be appreciated. I'll have Anne send word to your next class."

I opened my mouth to protest—I'd meant I'd go *after* my classes for the day, not now—but Matt's elbow in my ribs silenced any protest. "Thank you."

Vera nodded, though her thoughts already seemed miles away. "Resume sparring," she said absently, as she tapped her lips and stared into the distance with a thoughtful expression.

I glanced at Matt, curious if he had any insight into her present behavior, but just shrugged before walking off to join Louise. Within seconds, Ellie popped up beside me.

"G'day, stranger," she said with a smile. Her thick Australian accent had softened somewhat over the summer, but it was still as unmistakable as the first time I'd heard her speak.

"Hey. Sorry, I was thinking about Gilles and Miel."

"Wild how they're both not here. Don't suppose you have any thoughts 'bout where they might be?" Her brown eyebrows lifted as she settled into a ready position.

I shook my head. "Hopefully at their dorm." Suddenly, I realized I didn't know which one that was. We hadn't all been in the same dorm for the summer semester and that hadn't changed for fall. "Blast. I forgot to ask Vera which dorm they're in."

She blocked my attack and danced back. "Easy. They're in Agate Hall." We traded a few more practice blows.

"How do you know that?" I asked, mildly surprised, before shadowing behind her. "You... close with one of them? Maybe I should let *you* go instead."

Ellie laughed and ducked out of the way, then spun to face me again. "Not likely. Louise, however, has been after Miel since last term. She may be low-key stalking them." She replicated the same move I had, appearing behind me. "Just between us, I don't think they've noticed... the stalking *or* the mooning."

I snorted and tested out a method I'd read about, but hadn't been confident enough to try on Matt. Typically, when we shadowed, we exerted control over the shadows within our immediate vicinity. Lacking those, we used extensions of our own essence. I extended my senses to where Ellie was still behind me and in mortal form. It didn't take much to detect the thin veneer of shadow substance emanating from her. Before she could shadow away, I seized control of the shadow surrounding her like a second skin. I felt the jerk as she attempted to pull herself into the shadow world and rebounded.

She gasped and walked around to face me instead. "You have to tell me how you did that."

I spent the remainder of class walking Ellie through how to hold a shadow in place. She'd nearly perfected it by the time Vera dismissed us, vowing to "test" it on her roommate, Louise, later. I was still laughing about her scheme when Matt joined me in the hall.

"What's so funny?" he asked.

"Nothing. How was sparring with Louise?"

Matt's eyes widened. "You'd never know it to look at her, but she's a freaking powerhouse. I could barely shadow fast enough to stay out of her way."

I snorted as we stepped out of Mysterio college. "You of all people should know better than to judge people by appearances."

"Yeah, yeah. Hey, you want me to go with you to check on Gilles? Pretty sure he's in Agate Hall."

I looked at him out of the corner of my eye. "Where'd you learn that?"

"Louise," he deadpanned.

Laughter burst out of me so unexpectedly, I stopped walking.

"Glad *you* think it's funny. I'm the one who had to spend half the class listening to 'Miel this' and 'Miel that'. I wanna know why *she* didn't already know where they are," Matt huffed.

"Maybe she's still working up to it, taking her time like someone else I know."

Matt ducked his head, but before I caught the hint of a rosy blush staining his cheeks. "I wasn't *that* bad."

"Agree to disagree. Anyway, you shouldn't have to miss class too. I know you're worried about that exam coming up."

He grimaced. "Good point. Okay, I'll see you back at the dorm this afternoon."

I watched him race off to his next class, marveling at the transformation. Just a few months ago, he'd have been more than willing to skip one or all of his classes, but now he actually seemed eager to go to them. I smiled into the morning sun as I angled toward the cluster of dormitories on the east side of campus.

Thankfully, the RA was in the front office and I didn't have to track them down to find out what room Gilles was in.

"How can I help you?" the noticeably green RA asked. His name tag read "Wilke," but that didn't give me any real clue what type of supernatural he might be.

"Uh, hi, Wilke? Vera—I mean, Ms. Scry—sent me to check up on Miel and Gilles..." I trailed off, not sure how to continue from there. Luckily, the name drop did all the work.

"Say no more." Wilkes buzzed me through to the main dorm. "They're on the third floor in room 3809. Let me know if you need anything else."

"Thanks." I intended to take the stairs to my right, but the elevator fortuitously opened right as I stepped up. A thin older man with goggle like glasses stepped off, sparing me a penetrative glance that made my skin crawl as I walked past him onto the lift. The doors shut, and I gave myself a good shake before pressing for the third floor.

When the doors reopened, it was onto a hall vastly different from the one in my dorm. Where Starling Hall had a plushy velvety green carpet, Agate Hall was all modern efficiency. The floors were an ashen wood while the walls were an unassuming cream decorated with thematically appropriate depictions of geodes and other natural stones.

I at last found the desired room at the end of the hall and knocked decisively on the door. A few moments ticked by without so much as a whisper of noise on the other side. Curious, if *anyone* was at home, I extended my shadow senses much as I had in class earlier with Ellie. An initial search turned up nothing, but wary of quitting prematurely, I pushed deeper. Then I found something.

Unlike the usual vitality that accompanied Shadow Demons, this essence felt more like a shimmer, a fading whisper of shadow. Significantly more concerned, I abandoned decorum and pounded on the door. The shimmer within moved, and I faintly made out the shuffling of feet inside.

"I'm coming, I'm coming. On se calme!" The door cracked open to reveal a rather grumpy Gilles in a robe. His eyes were puffy, and he had a tissue clutched in his other hand. "Alexi? What are you doing here?" he asked, his voice noticeably nasally.

"Uh, you've missed Battle Tactics all week. I opted to see what was up so Vera wouldn't."

Gilles winced. "Thanks. I owe you one."

"It's no problem. Is Miel here as well?"

"No. Bâtard went out to get decongestant and soup, but still hasn't come back. They—" Gilles broke off with a violent sneeze he barely contained in time with his worn tissue, then groaned. "That was three days ago. Blaireau gave me this damn cold, then left me to fend for myself. Probably back home being fed chicken soup by their mommy," Gilles sneered before succumbing to another sneezing fit.

"Why do you think Miel is at home?" I asked, taking a subtle step backward.

"Because they've been bitching about how they'd rather be there for *days*. Honestly, I'm glad they're gone. Though they could have had the decency to drop off the medicine *before* they bounced." Gilles sagged against the doorjamb.

"Why haven't you gone to the University healers? I'm sure they could clear up that cold, no problem."

He snorted, then groaned again. "Tried that. *Apparently*, colds don't warrant immediate attention. 'Better for the body to fight it off naturally,'" he said, adding air quotes.

"Wow, that really sucks. I didn't even know Shadow Demons *could* get sick like this," I commiserated.

"Tell me about it. Anyway, if it's alright with you, I'm going to crawl back into bed and sleep for the next decade." He was already reaching for the door before I could respond.

"Of course. I'll let Vera know what's up, so she doesn't come bother you and drop off some decongestant as well."

Gilles grunted what might have been a "Thanks," then shut the door with a heavy clunk. I ventured back the way I'd come, making a mental note to get extra soup for me and Matt just in case Gilles was still contagious.

Chapter 10
Witch, Please

Matt

My middle name was stealth. Well, not really. I didn't actually have a middle name. But it was today I crossed the open green, doing my best not to look conspicuous. I slipped around the edge of the ivy-covered stone of the Witch's College and ducked inside. A few people gave me strange looks, but most ignored me. Now for the hard part, finding the right classroom.

I wandered down the hall and tried not to look too lost as I glanced into various rooms. One was an impressive auditorium style. Another, everyone was floating, or I guess the right term was levitating. The most remarkable looked like a chem lab. No sooner did I poke my head into it than a student looked up. Whatever they were holding dripped into the beaker and an explosion of indigo smoke erupted along with the cawing of birds. The professor shouted something I didn't quite catch, and I quickly shut the door.

On the verge of admitting defeat and asking someone, the faint notes of music tickled my ears. I spun in place until I could determine from which direction the sound was coming from. Once oriented, I took off. A few turns later, I stumbled into my destination. Not that anyone noticed. They were all too busy staring at the same thing that had immediately caught my attention. Alex... dancing.

For once, I was actually glad I was on the shorter side as I slipped into the cluster of young women openly ogling my roommate. Not that I could blame them. There was something sensual about the way Alex moved, like he was made of music instead of flesh and blood like the rest of us. The walls of mirrors offered an impressive near three-sixty view of every turn, sway, and extension... and he was only following along with the instructor.

He continued to replicate the steps she was showing him until she clapped her hands. The music cut out, and I suddenly realized Alex wasn't the only student up there.

"Let's try it together." The instructor stepped back to give the six students room to move.

One woman raced across the floor and slid into position in front of Alex, narrowly heading off another. She tossed the other woman a smirk over her shoulder before returning her focus to Alex with a beaming smile. The other woman scowled at her back, then trudged over to the remaining young man on the floor.

The music resumed and once again, all eyes were on Alex as he gracefully executed the steps they'd been covering. Despite how much I enjoyed Advanced Spells, I couldn't be happier that it had gotten canceled today. I shrank into the crowd I'd infiltrated as Alex floated by on his sweep of the dance floor.

"Switch!" the instructor shouted. The couples seamlessly split apart and came together in new pairings. The woman that had lost out before boasted a triumphant smile as she fell in sync with Alex.

My heart sped up as I imagined it was me between his arms. Alex would smile and tease, his eyes glowing as he expertly guided us around the floor. We'd laugh when he spun me out, because it was silly. But when he pulled me back, we'd be pressed close together, chest to chest, hip to hip, our bodies perfectly aligned. He'd give me that seductive smile that never failed to steal my breath, then lean down to press our lips together. Right as I got lost in it, in him, he'd pull away and spin me, because he was secretly a terrible tease.

Shame I was an awful dancer and that would literally *never* happen.

One of the women near me let out a wistful sigh. "It's just not fair."

"You're telling me," another said, a noticeably dreamy look in her eyes.

"Think he's single?" a third asked.

The first gave a quiet snort. "We're not that lucky."

"Yeah," the other two swoon-sighed.

I stole another glance right as Alex dipped his current dance partner. Good thing he had demonic strength; poor thing looked she was going to faint. Feeling exceptionally smug, I extricated myself from the crowd and quietly left the room with none the wiser of my having been there. They could look and hope all they wanted. Alex *wasn't* single and, at the end of the day, I was the one he kissed.

Back in the hall, I moseyed through the halls, contemplating what sort of date I could surprise Alex with. Movies were great and all, but they were definitely more his thing than mine. The inevitable making out was nice, though.

Okay, way more than nice. It was freaking fantastic, especially since we'd added blowjobs and handskies to the mix. I smirked to myself as I stepped into the bright afternoon sun, momentarily distracted from my quest to devise a date befitting Alex.

"Matt? Is that you?"

I spun around, glinting in the sunlight. "Gilles?" As my eyes focused, I saw it was him, his rich brown skin with burnt sienna highlights an impressive contrast to the faded stone at his back. "What are you doing here?"

He stepped closer, an amiable smile on his face. "I have a history of magic class here. Wasn't aware you had any classes in the witch's college, though."

"I don't." Gilles frowned, and I realized my response made no sense. "I was curious about Alex's dance class. Figured I'd see for myself what all the fuss was about. Still don't get why it's in the Witch's College."

He laughed. We hadn't quite become the good friends I'd hoped we would, but we got on all right. "You and, like, eighty percent of the university." He leaned closer and dropped his voice. "Just between us, it has more to do with the witch's desire to have everything in-house. Personally, I'd rather not have a generic course like History of Magic in this building."

"Why? Is it really far from your other classes?"

Gilles gave me a funny look. "Uh... no."

Now I was really confused. "Then why?"

His eyebrows furrowed. "Because it's full of witches."

"I feel like I'm missing something. Sorry, not sure if you knew, but I'm still kinda new to the whole supernatural." I spun my hand in the air to encompass the university "thing."

Gilles' eyes widened with understanding. "Oh wow. No, I didn't. In that case, you busy for lunch? I haven't eaten yet and I can fill you in on the drama they *don't* tell you in Demonic History."

Truthfully, I'd already had lunch, but he'd piqued my interest and I could always eat. "That sounds good. Student Center?"

"That was the plan."

We fell instep and made our way to the nearby commissary in the Student Center that hadn't been remodeled since the Renaissance. Probably an exaggeration, but given how old Arminius was, it wouldn't have surprised me. We each grabbed a prepackaged meal and made ourselves comfortable at a round wooden table, its surface the smooth you can only get after *decades* of use.

"Okay, fill me in on the witch dirt," I said as I removed my ham sandwich from its cellophane wrapper.

Gilles chuckled under his breath, opting to start with his potato chips. "You're really something else. We should hang out more. That's kind of on me. I got a little caught up in the uni-scene. Been going a little wild with all the sudden freedom, if you know what I mean."

If he wanted to take the blame for us not being better friends, I wasn't about to stop him, but I absolutely got where he was coming from. "Yeah, I get it. Did the same thing when I started last semester."

"Truly?" He leaned back in his chair with a relieved sound. "Thank goodness it's not just me. We'll have to swap stories some time."

Well, that wasn't happening. "Sure. Now, about the witches."

Gilles finished chewing his latest bite of chips and swallowed. "Right. So the books tell you—sort of—that witches and demons don't have the most stellar history."

"I've picked up on that. But that was like centuries ago, right?"

He snorted, then took a sizable chomp out of his sandwich. "As if," he said around a mouthful of food. He finished and took a drink. "The practice of 'summoning' demons only got banned in the last decade, give or take a few years. Not that witches care about laws that interfere with their priorities."

I spluttered, spraying half-chewed chips. "Shit. Sorry." I hurriedly cleaned the mess I'd made, though it didn't do shit for my head. "That can't be right."

"Oh, but it is. Funnily enough, it fell out of practice in smaller, rural towns before it did in the cities." He shrugged, crumpling up the empty chip bag and napkin. "Fewer places to hide, I guess. A little *too* suspect when your demon neighbor goes missing."

"Holy cow. That's wild. You, uh... ever see anything like that in Paris?"

Gilles' face fell, and he hunched over his trash, resting his forearms on the table. "Yeah. Ma tante. My aunt," he clarified when it was clear I wasn't following. "She taught me everything I know about sailing." His features softened and a sad smile graced his lips.

We'd have to circle back to the sailing, because that was *cool*, but now wasn't the right time. "What happened?"

He took a deep breath and straightened. "She'd always been an explorer, a free spirit. The year I was twelve, she promised to take me on a summer-long adventure. Back then, we lived in the city's heart. Ma tante would come over every morning and we'd work all day to gather supplies and make plans. Then one day... she was gone."

"How do you know it was a witch?"

"We didn't, not at first."

The hair on the back of my neck stood up, promptly followed by the ones on my arms. I glanced at the table to find pieces of shadow worming across the smooth surface. It wasn't quite the pull Alex could exert, but that didn't make it any less disconcerting.

"Then someone started following us. My family was leaving a movie when I got snatched."

My heart lurched into my throat and I flashed to the memory of a rope burning as it cut into my neck in a dim alley. I'd gotten away by the skin of my teeth and got picked up shortly after by the people that would eventually take me to Superno House. Weird to think that had only been six months ago.

"Luckily, my family noticed pretty quickly that I wasn't with them and found me before the witch got too far with me. They confronted him in a narrow street a few blocks from the theatre. That's where we learned that the reason ma tante was nowhere to be found was because she'd let slip to her friend from work that she was a demon. Her *friend*," Gilles emphasized, his voice raw with hurt. "The witch that had caught me had heard about the power her friend had garnered and wanted a taste for himself."

"That's... that's awful." Had it been witches that had tried to capture me?

Gilles hung his head to study his hands as he picked at his fingers. "Dad said he was the one who pushed the man into the shadow world, but I think... I think it was me. I'd recently started manifesting—part of why my aunt wanted to spend the time together—and my control wasn't great. That's... that's a big reason I didn't enroll last semester. I didn't trust myself or the fact that there'd be witches here. But it's not exactly like there are demon-exclusive universities, let alone any that would take a Shadow Demon."

"It does take some getting used to. I can't tell you how freaked I was my first few weeks here," I confessed, earning an almost smile. "So, did you, uh, ever find your aunt?"

"Now that we knew where to look, it was easier. But by the time we got there, it was too late. All we found was the holding circle and two burn marks. One in the center of the circle and one outside."

"Fuck!" Several people turned at my exclamation. I offered an apologetic expression and dropped my voice to more of a whisper. "Shit, man. For real? What the hell happened?"

"We think the witch tried to pull too much power and literally burned them both out. That, or the witch didn't know how to control shadow magic. Either way, it was a foregone conclusion my aunt was never leaving that place with her will intact. I'm just glad the witch got what she deserved." He sank back in his chair as if the tragic retelling of his aunt's untimely demise had completely drained him.

I mirrored the move, overwhelmed with the fresh supernatural horror. Magic really wasn't all it was cracked up to be. Bad people were bad people anywhere. "Damn. That's just... Wow. I don't even have words."

"Yeah. Moral of the story? Don't trust witches."

I nodded. The only witch I'd ever really interacted with was Misty from the fight club, and I already didn't trust her. Now I had whole new reasons to give her a wide berth. We solemnly picked up our trash and ventured back outside.

"I've got to get to my next class," Gilles said. "See you around."

I tipped my chin at him. "Me too. See ya." We set off, thankfully, in opposite directions. Gilles was a decent guy, but as much as I wanted to know everything about Paris, I didn't foresee us becoming more than classmates. Man could get *dark* and I'd only recently discovered the light.

"Matt!"

At Alex's voice, I spun around.

"What are you doing here?" he asked, as he jogged to a stop in front of me.

The dark cloud Gilles had left hanging over me evaporated at the sight of Alex's broad grin. "Thought I might try to catch you for a late lunch. But I've got to get going or I'll be late for my next class."

"Yeah. We'll figure it out, eventually." He bumped my shoulder. "See you tonight?"

"Yep. What do you say we go for a walk around campus after dinner? Just me and you?"

His eyes twinkled, and I knew the low-key idea had been the right move. "You asking me out on a date?"

"If I am?"

"Then, yes. I'd love to" He leaned forward and my heart hammered in anticipation. The university clock chimed the hour. We both jumped and shared a chuckle. "Better get a move on. I'll see you tonight." He winked and turned on his heel.

I practically floated to my math class already looking forward to my kiss later, my conversation with Gilles all but forgotten.

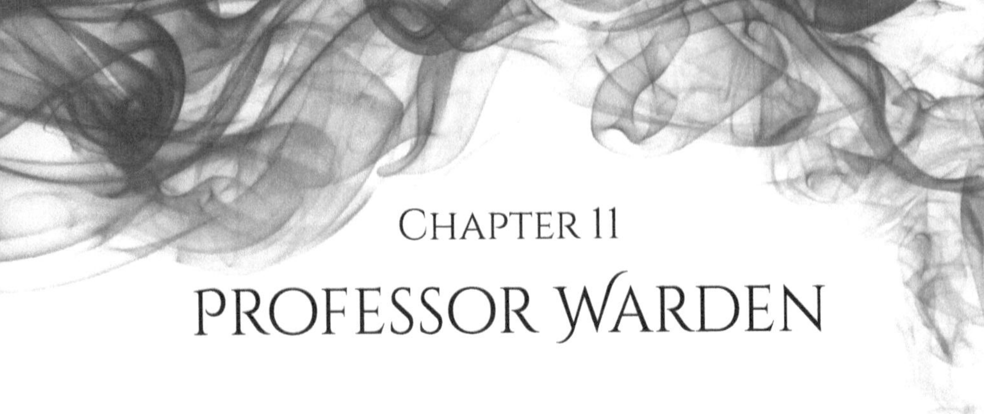

CHAPTER 11
PROFESSOR WARDEN

Alexi

"Hey Matt," I called, walking into the living room, but there was no sign of him. If we didn't leave soon, we'd be late for the seminar.

He must still be in his room.

Then I'll just have to go get him.

As I crossed the room, I spied my book on the table and stopped dead. It was so rare for Matt to leave it unattended. After casting a quick glance at his door to confirm it was still closed, I swung over the back of the couch. The book sat there with a seemingly innocent piece of paper sticking out, though it no longer bore any resemblance to the pristine, white page I'd given him what felt like ages ago. As I pulled it free of the worn pages, I realized practically every inch was covered. I'd assumed each time I caught him sketching that he was working on something different, but the level of detail suggested it had only ever been this. And it was absolutely incredible.

At the heart of the drawing were two figures leaning towards each other. It actually reminded me a bit of the illustration from the book of the knight and the demon. One character was unquestionably Matt. He'd captured that lost look perfectly and there was something in his eyes... Not fear. Yearning? I dragged my gaze across the page. Where one figure was definitely a human version of himself, the other was absolutely a demonic representation. Shadow seemed to swirl around the figure almost seductively, drawing in the knight, or in this case, Matt.

And he said it wasn't a self-portrait.

Understandably, he'd colored the demon image much darker, and I had to tilt the paper beneath the light to catch the details. Despite recognizing what it was, something about the drawing seemed off. Where the human form was replete with details that screamed Matt, the demon was not. Almost like the demon was a completely different person. Someone powerful, reaching out to tempt the young knight with darkness. Maybe this was how Matt wished he could be? Then I noticed a detail that shattered my theory. The demon's eyes were not the black they should have been. They were a vibrant green.

I reassessed the demon. The set of the shoulders, the lean waist, how his hair fell in his face. Now that I was paying attention, I'd know those features anywhere, saw them every day.

The demon is me. I'm the darkness tempting Matt.

The revelation of how Matt saw me upended my world. He'd transformed a simple piece of plain paper into a masterpiece of artwork about me... about us. It hovered on the edge of perfection, missing the smallest detail. I plucked a colored pencil from the array abandoned on the coffee table and added light blue highlights to the eyes of Matt's figure. Now his image held the same life I saw whenever I looked into his eyes.

"What are you doing?"

I turned to face him. At some point, he must have emerged. "Matt, this is... this is..." There weren't words. I could barely comprehend what I was looking at. "Can I have this?" I doubted he'd be willing to give it up, especially after guarding it so closely, but it was worth a shot.

He shrugged, his typical response when he didn't want to get into anything as messy as feelings. "I suppose. If you really want it."

"I really want it," I said, a hair too quickly and his cheeks turned a light pink. "This is stunning, Matt. I knew you could draw, but this is a whole other level. Why didn't you want me to see it before?" I knew without question that he never would have left it out if he hadn't wanted me to find it.

"It wasn't done and..." he trailed off, shuffling his feet and looking abashed. He hadn't done that in weeks. I kind of missed it.

"And it's very personal," I finished for him.

He looked up at me from beneath his lashes.

I carefully laid the picture down and shadowed over to him. He started, but didn't have time for anything else before I snared him with a kiss. He returned it haltingly, betraying his nerves. I caressed the side of his face and didn't press for more. "I love you, Matthew Duncan."

"Please don't call me that," he whispered.

"Why not? It's your name."

"It doesn't feel like it."

I was in no state to start a philosophical debate about his name, so I let it go in favor of wrapping my arms around him. "Okay, Matt." This time, his response held more of the burn as he tilted his head back to kiss me. He was everything I'd ever dreamed of and so much more. I doubted there would ever come a day that I wasn't blindly in love with him. He slid his hands around my waist and I fell into a deeper kiss. I'd gladly drown in Matt if it meant he'd always kiss me like this. Finally, I pulled myself together enough to break away.

He stood there a moment, as if waiting to see if I would return.

"Thank you," I said, my voice rough from the emotion I was struggling to keep in check.

"It's just a picture," he said nonchalantly, his hands slipping from my sides. He didn't need me to make a big deal about it. He already knew, which was why he'd kept it hidden.

I thought about what to say next. That I now had a visual representation by Matt's own hand, showing how he felt about me, was mind-blowing. However, pointing that out was likely to make him shrink away. "Still, it's nice to have something you made. I'm sorry if I messed it up."

His eyebrows snapped together. "What do you mean?"

"I added a little color. See for yourself." I gestured at the table. He may have said it was nothing more than a picture, but he sure moved pretty quick to see what I'd done. It took him less than a second.

"My eyes aren't that color."

"That's a matter of perspective. And you're one to talk," I said, walking over and picking up the pencil I thought to be the likely culprit. "It's not like mine are—what does this say—Emerald Isle."

He scowled at me, then gathered several other pencils on the table. "Actually," he plucked the color out of my hand and held it up with three others, "they're Emerald Isle, Dusty Sage, Mountain Green, and New Spring." He replaced all the colors in their case before turning back to me. "Are we going to this seminar thing or what?"

"Yeah, we're going." I fought the urge to spirit the picture into my room before he could change his mind. I'd have to trust he was actually going to let me keep it. We grabbed our keys and made our way out of the dorm towards the College of History.

"What is this supposed to be about again, and why are we going?"

"For starters, going to the lecture counts as extra credit. I would have thought you, of all people, would appreciate that." Passing Demon History I, didn't automatically make him any better at Demon History II.

He rolled his eyes. "Voluntarily doing extra work is weird," he mumbled to himself.

I held the door for him and added what I hoped would be a sweetener, "The subject is about the Wars."

"We already know about the Wars of Power. That was *last* semester."

I lowered my voice so it wouldn't carry through the auditorium style room. "Not *those* wars. Professor Warden teaches the graduate classes. He's considered the premiere authority on Demon History despite not being a demon himself. If anyone knows about the War on Darkness, he would."

Matt considered me and I could all but hear the gears turning in his head.

I gave an exasperated huff. "What? That part doesn't appeal to you either? You agreed to come," I pointed out.

"I agreed because you asked me. But, Alex, I feel like we need to be careful. I still think someone was watching us at the library and asking questions about a war we shouldn't know about could lead to trouble."

"That's ridiculous. There's nothing to say we 'shouldn't' know about it, just because no one else seems to."

He shook his head, but didn't continue arguing. To keep the peace, I let him choose a couple seats at the very back, though I'd have much preferred to be towards the front where I wouldn't miss anything. As the room filled, I worried that Matt's paranoia wasn't about the wars at all, but about me... us.

I shouldn't have kissed him before we left. It's obviously messing with him.

While we waited in silence for the lecture to begin, his obvious desire not to be here grew until it infected me to the point of distraction. I wanted to reach out to him, try to get him to relax, but I'd finally learned that would never fly. In the dorm, he would let me do whatever I wanted to him, but beyond those walls we followed strict rules of friendship. I tried not to let it bother me. I knew this was all different for him and that he was a very private person, but it would have been nice to at least hold his hand.

"Is that him?" Matt tilted his head toward the front of the room where a man with a clipped white beard stepped up to a dais. From the distance, he could have been anywhere between fifty and ninety.

I nodded, hoping that the acoustics in this place were enough to actually *hear* the lecture.

"And who's that?"

It took me a moment to figure out who Matt was referencing. "His TA maybe?"

A wiry man, wearing glasses so thick I could see the lenses back here, scurried to help Professor Warden set up his notes. His thin brown hair was both dull and made him look even paler than he already was. The assistant said something in the professor's ear, then shuffled off to the side.

Matt's lip curled with obvious distaste. "He looks like a rat."

"Don't be rude," I snapped under my breath. It may have been true, but the man was still in a position of authority and deserved respect.

He rolled his eyes and slouched in his chair.

Oh, he was going to be difficult tonight. I barely stopped myself from rolling my eyes in response and returned my attention to the front.

"The Demon Wars came centuries after the Wars of Power," Professor Warden said with a voice that easily filled the room and bellied his soldier-like posture. "They were a direct reflection of the pervasive fear and chaos of the time." He paused, scanning his audience, then with the hint of a smile, stepped away from the podium. "Now, what is often forgotten here is that while we call these wars, they were really no more than minor skirmishes scattered throughout history. Let's face it, supernaturals don't exactly play well with others."

I hissed through my teeth, and Matt cast me a quick glance.

Below, the professor continued, gesturing with his hands to encompass the room, which was, in fact, predominantly demonic. "At any given time, one race or another was constantly at odds. The witches tampered with the elementals, creating both the incident at Pompeii and the Great Flood. Werewolves fought against encroaching settlements by terrorizing the countryside. And let's not forget the demons of the sea—krakens, sirens, the ever-dreaded leviathans—that effectively stalled the exploration of the planet. Many supernatural species inspired fear and awe in their human counterparts, but none so much as the demon. With so many different kinds and no way to understand them, it's no wonder demons found their way into every religion." His smile widened, and he held his hands out by his side. "In short, Demons became the bogeymen in every story."

The room gave a collective chuckle, and I had to bite my tongue. I didn't find always being the villain remotely humorous.

"Most, over time, came to uneasy truces with mankind," Professor Warden continued when the laughter died down, resuming his circuit of the stage. "Fire demons retread to lands inhospitable to mortals. Sea demons retreated to the depths where man could not reach. In fact, the majority of the demon classes found some way to avoid the spread of humanity." He held up a finger. "Except for one. The Chaos sect. This collection of unclassifiable dark powers refused to be cowed so easily. Remember, by this point, mankind has already learned to fear the unknown, not to mention the witches summoning demons for their own misdeeds. But all of this paled compared to the sheer terror the Chaos sect instilled in man."

Several demons from the Chaos sect snickered around the room. How they'd gotten their name was no secret—trouble was all they brought. But that didn't make what the professor was saying right. Just like humans, not all demons were the same, even in the Chaos sect.

"It was this sect that was primarily responsible for what we collectively refer to as the Demon Wars."

I seethed in my seat, my fists clenching on the armrests. Lies. All lies. He made it sound like humanity was simply defending itself. That the Chaos sect had started it and other demon classes tried to avoid the fallout. That wasn't true, or at least, not all of it. We had proof that there was an actual war being waged that no one knew about and *all* the classes had taken part. My hand flew into the air.

Matt looked at me with horror and sank even deeper into his chair.

"Yes. Young man at the back. You have a question?"

"And the Shadow Demons? Where do they fit in?"

Something dark flashed across the professor's face, gone before I could place it. Behind him, the TA flipped vigorously through a notebook. Professor Warden stared at me for a long second, then let out a hearty laugh. "I'm glad to see we have some Shades in the house."

Laughter rolled through the room, and I bristled. Meanwhile, Matt looked like he was going to die of mortification. "You haven't answered my question. What about the War on Darkness?" I insisted.

"I see someone has been reading one too many fairy tales," he said with a noticeable edge that didn't prevent another burst of laughter.

I clenched my jaw so hard my teeth cracked. Suddenly, Matt grabbed my arm, and I glanced at him, fully prepared to unleash the rage bubbling beneath my skin.

He met my furious gaze with a warning glare. I tried to shake him off, but he held firm. "Look around," he hissed under his breath.

Pools of shadow swam around my feet, with more tendrils from all over the room joining it by the second. I took a deep breath and focused on regaining control over the wayward shadows. With my anger in check, I returned my attention to the professor I'd exalted less than an hour ago.

"Case in point," he said, hand extended in my direction. "If the stories around the supposed War on Darkness are to be believed, that would mean that Shadow Demons of the highest levels worked together in concert. Coordinated assaults. Lead armies." He barked a laugh and I nearly bit my tongue clean off from the effort of holding it. "As you no doubt can see for yourself, *that* is extremely unlikely. As the Shadow Demons are a fairly recent addition to our fine establishment, many of may be unaware that they are traditionally a solitary class with a reputation of not getting along with their own race, let alone others. Not to mention, their grasp on their own powers tends to be questionable at best. That lack of control is largely believed to be what almost wiped them out," Professor Warden finished, looking directly at me. I was hard pressed to determine if that last was intended to be academic speculation or some kind of threat, and I wasn't planning on sticking around to find out.

"To hell with this." Without another word, I walked out, feeling like everyone was watching me. I was still breathing hard when I ran into Matt in the outer hall. For a brief second, I couldn't understand how he'd gotten there, then I realized he must have shadowed, which is exactly what I should have done.

His blue eyes were intense as he asked, "Are you alright?"

My fists clenched and unclenched by my side. "No, I'm not." I was not a naturally violent person, but I wanted to hit that man. To be so humiliated and by someone who should have been above that.

He gave a sharp nod, as if he understood the rage flowing through me. "Come on, we're going back to the dorm," he said and immediately started walking off.

I stayed rooted to the spot, still trying to fight the urge to march back in there and give that so-called professor a piece of mind and maybe my powers, too.

"Alex," Matt said sharply, and my feet started moving. In hardly any time at all, we were back in our room and I was still fuming. "He was lying," Matt said, tossing me a carton of ice cream. I didn't wait for him to give me a spoon, instead forming one out of shadow. He gave me a face and set the spoon he'd grabbed on the table.

I chomped into a bite of the frozen treat, numbing my teeth. "Why do you say that? He certainly seemed to believe the bullshit he was spewing."

"Did you see the way he looked at us? That man *hates* Shadow Demons."

"That's absurd. He simply ridiculed us in front of everyone," I said angrily, waving my ephemeral spoon. "He clearly doesn't know shit about real Shadow Demons. I ought to report him."

Matt shook his head. "I've seen hatred before. He loathes our kind. He did a good job of keeping it in check, though. And he wasn't just ridiculing us, he was creating a distraction. Did you see what the TA started doing the second you spoke up?"

I shrugged, vaguely recalling the TA frantically flipping through papers. "He was going through notes."

"No, he was looking for something. I'd bet you anything it was our names and power levels."

"But you don't even know what you are."

"I'm a level seven."

My spoon winked out of existence, causing the scoop it had been holding to fall onto the floor. "Wha—? How did you figure that out?" A *seven*? I knew he was stronger than me. I just had no idea about how *much* stronger.

"I found a testing spell in an old grimoire. It measures potential, not just active strength."

How was he so calm about this? He couldn't possibly understand what that meant. A seven. When was the last time the world had seen one of those?

He sighed as if blowing my mind was taxing. "Try not to get too worked up. You'll always be stronger than me, Alex." With that, he got up and put away his ice cream, then disappeared into his room, leaving me to figure out what the hell had just happened.

Chapter 12
Dance Lessons

Matt

I never should have told Alex my power level. On the one hand, it certainly seemed to distract him from the horrible fiasco at the seminar. On the other, he was probably going to expect me to start actually applying myself more in class. Far as I was concerned, it was an arbitrary number. Like Scylla had told Oliver back at *Superno House Orphanage,* all the power in the world meant nothing if you didn't know how to use it. Which I didn't, not consistently anyway.

Of course, I'd done the same test on him. Being a level nine was still nothing to snub at, but it rankled that he'd *technically* been right about my being stronger. Alex was just better at everything: school, shadowing, relationships... Something soft slammed into my face, breaking my line of thought.

"Earth to Matt."

I snatched the pillow from Alex before he could smack me again. "What gives?"

"You haven't been paying attention for a while now. I'm beginning to wonder if you want to study at all."

The honest answer was no. I could think of several other things I'd rather do with Alex besides study, most of which didn't require clothes. We'd had a few make-out sessions since our *eventful* shower, but nothing as outrageously hot. Thinking about conquering Alex's mouth while we ground against each other had me chubbing up instantly. I squashed the thoughts before I ended sporting a full-on tent. If I couldn't get a handle on this, it was going to get me into trouble. As it was, keeping any measure of distance outside of the dorm was damn near impossible.

Through sheer stubborn determination, I dragged my mind out of the gutter and focused on the last thing he'd said. "Want to study and need to study are very different things." I stuffed the pillow between us with maybe a little too much force. My horniness was definitely giving me an attitude.

Alex snorted and set his textbook aside. "I seriously doubt you actually *need* to study. I don't know why you don't give yourself more credit, Matt. You act like you're some sort of dunce, but you're far from it. Then there's the whole Battle Tactics issue. I swear it's like you're intentionally trying not to get it."

"Can we not talk about that?" I groaned, flopping back. As if wanting to jump his bones wasn't distracting enough, I did *not* need a reminder about how I'd gotten my ass handed to me in the last few classes.

"Fine. What do you think of Vera shifting Ballroom from an elective to a core?"

I lurched forward to stare at him. "You mean that ridiculous dance class you have on Wednesdays?"

"Yep."

I'd stopped by once out of curiosity when one of my classes had gotten canceled. Unsurprisingly, Alex had been smooth as silk and graceful to boot. I groaned and hung my head in my hands. "You've got to be kidding me." I'd never be able to move like that.

He shook his head, his smug smile growing.

"You'll probably have to tutor me in that too," I bemoaned.

"So, at this rate, am I basically tutoring you in everything?"

"It looks that way." Which I was a hundred percent fine with. *I wonder if I could convince him to study naked... Dancing might not be so bad then.*

"You don't need my help, Matt."

I rolled my eyes and pushed away the sexy thoughts. "You've never seen my try to dance."

"We could fix that," he teased.

"Not until I absolutely have to, and not a moment before."

"Come on, it'll be fun." He leaned forward and grabbed my arm, presumably to pull me to my feet.

I resisted, pulling back, and he took the opening to tickle me. No one had ever been brave enough to try anything like that before, and it came as a complete surprise to me I was ticklish at all. "Stop it," I gasped, laughing and trying to fight him off.

"Concede," he persisted.

"No, cut it out. It's not funny," I managed through fits of laughter. No wonder tickling was a form of torture.

"*I* think it's hilarious."

Finally, I got enough leverage to push him off. He sat back, chuckling to himself and looking a bit flushed. I imagined I looked much the same. How easy it would be to close the distance between us and—

A ringing cut through the air. I looked down at the coffee table to see Alex's phone. In perfect blocky letters, it proclaimed the caller to be 'MOM'. We looked at each other, then simultaneously dove for the phone. Alex was fast, but I was faster.

I snagged the device and hopped out of reach, answering it before it could stop. "Hi, Ms. Roman," I said, out of breath. Alex stared daggers at me, and my resulting smile stretched from ear to ear.

"Hello?" The woman's voice sounded pleasant, with the same touch of British accent Alex had.

"This is Matt. I'm sorry, Alex can't come to the phone right now."

"Give it back," Alex hissed. I stuck my tongue out and moved further out of his reach.

"Matt? Matt-Matt?" his mom said in my ear. "Well, *hello*. It's a pleasure to finally speak to you. Alexi has told me so much about you."

"Oh he has, has he?" I raised a questioning eyebrow at Alex. His eyes widened and he lunged a hair too slow to catch me.

"Of course. So how are things? I hear classes are going well. Keeping your grades up, I hope."

I kept Alex in my line of sight as he stalked me around the couch. "Funny you should mention that. I was just trying to convince your son to tutor me in ballroom. He's a natural on the dance floor. You should see how the women drool."

She might have giggled, but it was too faint to tell. "I'm sure Alexi would love to teach you how to dance, Matt."

"Maybe you should tell him that." I dodged another desperate grab. "He doesn't seem too interested." My foot caught on the end table and I went flying over the side of the couch to land with a resounding thud that knocked the wind out of me.

"Everything alright dear? Sounds like quite a ruckus over there. I haven't called at a bad time, have I?"

"Of course not, Ms. Roman," I said as I stood tried to regain my bearings. Mid dusting my ass, I realized with alarm that I was standing *in* the couch. I went to take a step, but my leg wouldn't budge. Everything from my thighs down was stuck. Desperate to get free, I tried harder, each failed attempt to move adding to my panic.

Alex snatched the phone from my hand. "I'll have to call you back, mom. Now I have to tutor Matt in how to shadow properly. He appears to have gotten himself stuck." He hung up and tossed the phone on the kitchen table before swinging around a chair. He took his time primly sitting down, then stared at me.

"What do I do?" I asked, my voice bordering on a shriek.

"How should I know?"

"Come on, Alex, don't be like that. I'm sorry, okay? Just, please just help me get unstuck. I can't stay like this forever. Can I?" When he wasn't quick to answer, my panic tripled. "Oh god, can I!"

Alex fought to keep his laughter to himself... and failed. "First, you need to calm down. Freaking out is only going to make it worse."

"Worse! Worse like how?" I swiveled as much as my captive state would allow.

"Easy. Calm down, Matt. Give me a minute to think."

My mouth snapped shut to give him the quiet to come up with a solution. Inside, however, I was frantic. I'd heard plenty of horror stories about people getting stuck, but no one ever mentioned how to get *un*stuck. Alex pensively tapped his lip while the quiet drove me insane. Just when I thought things couldn't possibly get worse, black spots swam lazily across my vision.

Oh no, not this too.

"You know what?"

I looked at him, hopeful for a solution. Preferably before the darkness swallowed me whole.

"I think I'm a better kisser than you."

The black spots vanished in my surprise. "What?"

He gave a decisive nod. "Yep, I'm sure of it."

"You want to debate this *now*?" I gestured wildly at the couch.

"What? It's not like you can defend yourself. And it's hardly a debate so much as a statement of fact."

My mouth fell open in shock. *He's mad. Absolutely bonkers.* "How about you come over here and we'll see how well I can defend myself," I growled.

He surprised me yet again by flowing effortlessly out of the chair, then swayed closer with a look in his eye that had my pulse fluttering nervously, but like he'd already said—it wasn't like I could go anywhere. He stopped right at the back of the couch, leaving only a few inches between us.

"Alright, defend yourself. Prove you're better."

I opened and closed my mouth a few times before I pushed words out. "You can't be serious."

He shrugged. "It's not like you're doing anything else."

I searched Alex's face like it could give me a clue what was really going on, but he was a blank canvas. "You're absolutely insane."

"So you keep telling me. Now, are you going to prove me wrong or do you admit defeat?"

I narrowed my eyes. *Of all the hair-brained things to want to do. Fine. You want a kiss? You've got it.*

I twisted my fingers in his shirt and yanked him closer. Distantly, I heard a squeak of surprise, then it was drowned out by the pure taste that was Alex. That, plus the overwhelming smell of lavender, was enough to make me lightheaded. Kissing him really was like a drug. My heart raced as I lost myself to it. I tugged on his bottom lip with my teeth and kissed him deeper. Maybe he'd be down for no-clothes studying after all.

Alex slid an arm around my waist, and I gasped at suddenly being pressed against him. I gave up my hold on his shirt to caress his face, urging the kiss deeper. This was so much more than he'd given me in ages. I needed this, ached for it. It still wasn't enough. I wanted more. It didn't matter that I was already struggling for air.

Finally, my lungs refused to take the abuse anymore. I broke the kiss, panting for air. Even after several steadying breaths, I still felt in danger of passing out. Gradually, my wits returned, and I glanced down to see Alex's arm between me and the back of the couch. I looked back up at him with his smoky smile. "You crafty bastard," I said, snaring him with another kiss.

"For the record," he chuckled between kisses, "you are definitely the better kisser."

"I suspect that's a matter of perspective."

"Why do you have to fight me on everything?"

"Is that a real question?" The heat in his gaze was almost hot enough to melt me all over again. "Good call, by the way." I trailed my hand down the arm he was using to separate me and the couch.

"I couldn't very well have you falling back through, now, could I?"

"Well, thanks," I replied, clearing my throat. If he didn't stop looking at me like that, the couch was going to be the least of our problems. As it was, there was no hiding my erection, seeing as how it was digging into his thigh. I was tempted to create some much-needed friction and wondered if maybe now was a good time to mention that I was interested in more. A lot more.

As if reading my thoughts, he released me and stepped back.

"Um, so what do you want to do now?" I asked, suddenly awkward. Was I doing something wrong? Did he not think I could handle it? To cover the rising heat in my cheeks, I ducked my head and suggested, "Back to studying?"

"Actually, I thought we could see who really marshaled the forces in the War on Darkness. Was it really Shadow Demons? Our book hasn't been all that clear. Why don't we hit up the library? See what we can find? Who knows, maybe we'll get lucky." The idea of getting lucky sounded better than the library.

"Are you sure? I thought you weren't really into the research project, especially after the seminar and the assignment basically getting scrapped."

"It sucks that they've decided not to go forward with the original project. But we've already put in so much work and I'd like to know how it all ends. Plus, we still have to get to the bottom of that weird feeling of yours." He turned to gather his things from the table.

"Hey, wait." I grabbed his hand. Automatically, our fingers laced. He looked down, clearly surprised, and I tugged him back for one last kiss. As it lingered, I fought the urge to keep it going. "Thank you," I said sincerely, then let him go.

"I didn't really do anything." He swung his pack onto his shoulder. "You just needed to be distracted long enough to do it yourself." His smile was reassuring, but it didn't change the fact that I'd been really scared and he'd casually come to my rescue. My own personal knight in shining armor. "As for the library, I promise we can leave if you feel like anything is off. I don't want you to be uncomfortable, but that really is the only place we're going to find the missing links to this puzzle."

"You realize that there's a very good chance that those pieces are hiding in the restricted section. Right?" I pointed out, closing the door behind us.

"That is a distinct possibility. But it's not like you haven't gone in there before."

"Are you volunteering me?" I asked incredulously.

"Okay, okay, we'll exhaust other avenues first. We still need to finish that enormous history. Who knows, maybe the answers are already in there and you won't have to go searching."

"You better hope they are or that the librarian decides to be helpful again. I'd never be able to check different books before succumbing to the aversion spell."

"I meant to ask, what was it like?" He glanced at me as we walked side by side down the hall.

"Nice try. I'm not about to pour out all my worst fears for you to catalog."

He shrugged. "Worth a shot. Perhaps if I knew some of them, I could help you with whatever is blocking you from using your powers properly."

"What do you mean, blocking me? I thought you said the only thing in my way was me."

"I did, and I still think that. It stands to reason that if you have some weird fear, it could be what's holding you back." We stepped aside to let a student with balancing a precarious display pass on the sidewalk, then resumed our way. "At least consider them yourself if you won't tell me. I want to help. You could always start by telling me where you're really from," he prodded with a grin as he opened the library door.

"Are you ever going to let that go?"

"Not likely," he replied, his smile widening.

I rolled my eyes and made my way to the usual table. We could save the lamps for another time. Right now, I wanted the comfort of being surrounded by other students. "Where should we start?" I asked as he unloaded our notes.

He straightened with his hands on his hips and surveyed the stacks of books lining the library. "Honestly? I haven't the faintest idea. We could try to find more information about any Shadow Demons that were around at the time. See if there's a reference to some kind of coalition. Or we could look for the identity of the mysterious child. Then there's the matter of finishing this monstrosity." He rested a hand on the giant gray tomb that made the worn table beneath it look new. "Maybe we should split up?"

"No." I didn't want to leave that book unattended in case it magically found its way back to the shelf. Nor did I want one of us holding it while we were on our own in the stacks. "How about someone stays here to hold the table while the other checks the shelves?"

His eyebrow lifted. "And who's getting stuck with babysitting duty?"

"We'll take turns. You can choose first. Do you want to stay or do you want to go?"

His gaze softened and for a moment, it was like we were the only two people there. "I'll always want to stay, Matt."

"Okay." I was three steps towards the shelves when what he'd said registered. I stumbled and glanced back, but he was already absorbed in sorting the notes we'd accumulated so far. It was strange to think about what we'd become. Even despite all my efforts to keep our private lives private, I still wanted to go back over there and kiss him for his simple statement. He couldn't possibly know how much such a small thing would mean to me. I watched him a little longer, then resumed our quest for answers.

Chapter 13
What's in a Name?

Alexi

The door to the dorm clicked softly as it opened and I smiled to myself. Finally, four o'clock. I pushed my homework aside to greet Matt, who'd crossed the room in the scant few seconds it took me to stand. I didn't even say "hello" before he captured me with a toe-curling kiss. Most people could look forward to a noncommittal peck on the cheek or the barest brush of lips when their partner got home, but not with Matt. Every day when he returned from his classes, it was like he hadn't seen me in weeks. You'd never know it had only been a few hours, not even a whole day.

Instinctively, I wrapped my arms around him and he pulled me tighter. Some days the fire burned hotter than others and today was feeling like a scorcher. It felt good to be so wanted. I let myself fall into the feel of his lips against mine. The now familiar ache grew. I wanted more from him, had wanted it for weeks. Barely controlled desire beat relentlessly against the walls I maintained. Eventually, those needs would have to be met, but that was not something we'd ever talked about. Of course, knowing Matt, it wasn't something that *would* ever be talked about either.

Reluctantly, I pulled away, appreciating the tender feel of my lips. "Hi Matt," I said with a wistful sigh.

"Why do you always say it like that?" he asked, tempting me with another kiss.

I forcibly shook off the fog that always seemed to cloud my mind when he was around. "Why do you always kiss me like that?"

"Do you want me to stop?"

"Absolutely not," I said, leaning in with a grin.

He snared me with another kiss that I barely escaped with my senses still intact. Well, mostly intact. My heart gave a happy skip when he trailed his hands down my arms to lace our fingers together. I loved this latest development and even more that he'd been the one to initiate it. He gave my hands a light squeeze and smiled. "Why don't we watch a movie tonight?"

I extricated myself and walked back towards my discarded chair before my desire got the better of me. "Except you don't really like movies. You're only saying that because you're hoping we'll make out."

He pulled up a chair and took out his homework. "I'd be lying if I said it hadn't crossed my mind." I laughed, and he smiled, his eyebrows lifting as he waited for an answer.

"Alright, we can watch a movie tonight." His grin broadened, and I held up a finger. "*If* we finish all of our work."

His face immediately fell into a frown. "You're incorrigible."

"I see we are using our big words today," I teased.

He gave me a playful push. "Shut up and do your homework."

"What does it look like I'm doing?"

"Stalling. Talking. *Not* doing homework. Focus, Alex. We have plans."

I thought about correcting him. *He* had plans. I was just getting dragged into them. Already, he was bent over his notes, intently scratching out what looked to be spell equations. I itched to brush his hair back so I could see his startlingly blue eyes, but restrained myself and set to work.

Literature blurred into Ethics, which morphed into Lit II. I wasn't sure how much time had gone by when I felt something rubbing up and down my leg. Startled, I glanced at Matt. He at least appeared to be absorbed in his latest assignment. I subtly leaned back to peek under the table. Sure enough, he was mindlessly stroking my leg with his foot. What was even more interesting was that at some point, I must have shifted and my foot was doing the same to his ankle.

"So, what do you want to watch?" he asked without looking up, his foot continuing its ceaseless motion.

"Um..." I cleared my throat and quickly shifted my focus.

He looked up. His pen stopped, but not his foot. He blinked innocently. "What?" When I stared blankly at him, he shifted gears. "How about the one where they discover a new layer in the earth? That one looked pretty interesting."

"Sure, that sounds great. I'll order the Chinese."

He gave me one of those smiles that stole my breath and made my heart skip. "No, let me." He pushed his chair back, taking his foot with him. After so much attention, my leg immediately noted the absence. "It doesn't look like you're finished yet," he added, trailing his fingers leisurely across my shoulders as he walked behind me to grab the menu from the usual drawer.

I gave an involuntary shudder that he thankfully didn't seem to notice. I know he thought I played games with him—which, in fairness, I did—but he had no idea what he did to me daily.

"Do you want the chicken and broccoli this time or the lo mien?" he asked, his face scrunched in concentration as he considered the menu.

"What are you having?"

"I think I just want the soup," he said after a moment.

"You always say that and then you eat mine, anyway."

"So, do you want a soup?"

"I'll do the lo mien." I listened to him place the order. Sounded like I'd be sharing again, not that it really bothered me. I laughed to myself and returned to my endless mountain of homework that I'd said we needed to finish first. It was only Thursday, I still had plenty of time. But fair was fair. Yet, try as I might, there was no focusing while Matt was unoccupied. I diligently persisted until the food arrived and then gave up.

Once the table was clear, I grabbed my carton of lo mien and joined him on the couch. He's already set up the movie and was sitting with his legs crossed under him, steadily decimating his soup. "You're adorable, you know that?" I said, taking a seat. He finished slurping a spoonful and hit the lights, but not before I caught the barest makings of a blush.

We continued to eat in silence, then about twenty minutes into the movie, we switched entrees. I finished his soup, and he polished off my lo mien. When we were done, I put the dishes in the sink, then returned to the couch. He'd finally uncrossed his legs, so I took the opportunity to lie down, using his lap as a pillow. The moment I settled, he began absently tracing around my ear and gliding his fingers through my hair.

The movie played on, but I wasn't really paying attention. I shifted so I could look up at him. His fingers simply adjusted their path to trace the features of my face. He wasn't watching the movie either; he was watching me.

I wish I could freeze this moment, capture it in a picture, or a painting, or something.

His finger slid around the curve of my face to follow the outline of my mouth. My heart couldn't seem to decide if it wanted to beat fast or slow or not at all.

I pushed myself up to my elbows, and he met me halfway. The kiss was slow and languid, as if he was trying to draw out every feeling I had. Matt was very good at that. He curled a hand around my head both to support it and so he could kiss me deeper. He tasted like ecstasy, and I wanted more. I shadowed out and rematerialized, kneeling beside him. Surprise replaced his alarm at my sudden disappearance when I captured him in a kiss of my own. He pressed back eagerly, but it still wasn't cutting it. He angled his body towards me, having to move his leg onto the couch to do so. I grabbed his ankle and pulled so that he lay beneath me.

He chuckled as he reached up to pull me down. "You can be really pushy sometimes."

"It's never bothered you before." I caught his arms and moved them over his head.

"Did I sound like I was complaining?" It was likely meant to be teasing, but heat laced the words.

"A little," I said and leaned down to claim his mouth. His return was instant. That ache was growing again. I let it, devouring the kisses he so willingly gave. It still wasn't enough. I pulled back. "Take off your shirt," I commanded breathlessly.

Without a word, he complied, leaning forward and pulling the offending garment off. It barely had time to drop to the floor with a muffled thud before I kissed him hard enough to force his head into the cushions while my hands explored his newly freed torso. Then my mouth followed in their wake, tasting and teasing as I went. This is what I wanted. He let out a moan arching into me. I gave him a light bite, which earned me another delicious groan. I worked my way lower until his hand tangled in my hair. My journey slowed, and I took my time teasing his already quivering stomach with kisses while I palmed his erection through his jeans. How hot would he look with his release painted on his chest?

"Alexi," he moaned.

I snapped up. "What?"

In answer, he grabbed the back of my neck and forced my mouth down to his. The resulting kiss rocked me to my core, and I completely forgot what had distracted me. I slid my arm around his waist, and his body molded to mine. He rocked his hips up, grinding our straining erections against each other. I gasped, and he stole a kiss that snatched the rest of my breath.

There was no way I could keep on like this. We were quickly getting out of hand and my control didn't have near enough concerns about that. Clearly, I wasn't the only one aching for more. But we weren't ready for that, not yet, and I wasn't about to give in without him explicitly saying anything. Nor did I have any intention of coming in my pants, though avoiding that was becoming more impossible with each roll of his hips.

Reluctantly, I retreated from the inferno that was threatening to burn us both. I did what I could to dial it back, adjusting my angle to a slightly less precarious position and focusing on lighter touches. Finally, I got the blaze down to a low simmer.

"You're missing the movie," I whispered between kisses.

"To hell with the movie." He slid his hands beneath my shirt, then glided them along my back and sides. It was almost enough to make me toss what I'd gathered of my control right back into the wind.

I stole my resolve and pulled the cushion off the back of the couch. "Roll on your side." He made to turn, and I stopped him. "Not towards me. Face the screen."

His mouth fell open, and it took him a moment to respond. "You're really going to make me finish watching this?" He gave an exasperated huff, but did it anyway.

Without the cushion, there was just enough space for us to lie side by side. It was a tight fit, but as long as he was okay with that, then so was I. Once we were situated, I snuggled into his back and pressed his ass against my persistent erection. I fought the urge to grind against him, to reach over, unzip his jeans, and finish what we'd started. He shimmied his hips again, getting comfortable, and I smothered a pained moan. I considered telling him to stop moving around, but suspected such an order would have exactly the opposite effect and I wasn't sure how much more of this torture I could take before I completely embarrassed myself. Mercifully, he let out a sigh and stopped moving. I wrapped an arm around him, fanning my fingers across his tight abdomen, and nuzzled into his neck.

"Why did you pick this one?" I asked quietly.

"The ocean is interesting. Also, it has mythical monsters. So that's cool."

I nipped lightly at his neck. "Monster is a misnomer."

"Mythical creatures then."

"You know, *you're* a mythical creature." I blew gently on the tiny hairs at the nape of his neck. He gave a full body shiver, and I immediately regretted it. *I can do this. I can touch Matt without getting totally consumed and losing control.* He relaxed after I laid a trail of kisses on his shoulder.

"I'm nothing special."

"You're very special, Matt. You're smart and funny, sweet, thoughtful, kind of a pain in the ass, but sexy as hell," I said, nibbling his neck some more in direct contrast to my determination to keep the situation and my libido under control.

"You're biased."

"Your point?"

He turned to look at me. His eyes searched my face and for one tiny moment, I thought he was actually going to say he loved me.

When he said nothing at all, I said it for him. "I love you, Matt."

He continued to study my face, then quietly turned back to face the screen. He mercifully settled down without any more squirming, and we finished watching the movie.

When it was done, he followed me into my room, where he ditched his jeans. I tried not to stare at his toned legs or his wonderfully sculpted back as he slid beneath the sheets in nothing more than skin-tight briefs. Apparently, we weren't done spending time together.

I followed suit and joined him, dubious about how this was going to go. Heavy make outs usually accompanied our joint sleeping ventures, and I wasn't sure I'd survive another round tonight. To my surprise, he immediately curled into my side, laying his arm across my chest so that his hand rested over my heart. My hormones certainly didn't appreciate the test of their already strained control, but I also couldn't bear the thought of him moving away.

This was the side of Matt I lived for—even more than the searing kisses and heated looks—moments like this, where he was all mine without reservation. I placed a kiss on his forehead and drifted off, feeling content, albeit wanting.

Chapter 14
EXPERIMENTATION

Matt

I let out a deep breath as I pushed open the door to our dorm room. This was the night. Alex had his weekly tutoring meeting followed by some get together after. He'd be gone for hours or was supposed to be. I wasn't sure how much I trusted that after that other meeting had gotten canceled. Typically, I'd be all for more time with Alex, but tonight I needed him to be out until late-late.

A quick glance around the room didn't reveal any sign of him. No backpack by the door. No neat stack of textbooks on the dining table. Not that I really trusted any of that. I let my shadow senses expand as I dropped my bag and double checked the room, even going so far as to search Alex's room. While I was in there, I couldn't help but dally.

The smell of lavender permeated the air, subtle yet undeniable. I inhaled deeply, letting the soft scent ease the tension in my shoulders. I'd been planning tonight for a while, had gone through painstaking efforts to get everything together. But that didn't magically erase my nerves. A poster of Arminius University caught my eye, and I smirked. Alex really was a bit of a dork. It was one of the things that made him so special.

I trailed my fingers along the comforter Alex had thrown across the bed in a messy semblance of made. It struck me as funny that he was so put together in most things—school, appearance, life—and yet, things like making his bed, putting away his clothes, even cooking eluded him. With a sigh, I left the temptation of the rumpled bed to double-check the bathroom.

Once I was positive Alex was nowhere to be found in the dorm, I headed to my room. In contrast, mine was barren. I didn't have posters or knick-knacks. My bed was made like it was going to be in one of those house magazines. Even my laundry was sparse. Access to a washing machine whenever I needed one wasn't a luxury I'd had before and constantly having clean clothes—without holes—was a treasure I cherished. The only thing even mildly out of place was my set of colored pencils and sketchbooks on the otherwise clear dresser.

I walked to my nightstand and pulled open the drawer. My persistent nerves had me clenching my fists and taking another steadying breath. Putting off this little experiment I had planned wouldn't be hard; I'd already put it off twice. But then I doubted I'd get a better opportunity than this. With a sharp nod, I tossed the bottle of lube onto the bed and grabbed the anal douche, grateful I'd thought to read the directions for the strange bulb before tossing them, then made my way to the bathroom.

After scrubbing every inch of my body within an inch of life and *finally* gathering the courage to use the douche, I was as ready as I was ever going to get. But first, I wanted to do another sweep of the dorm. The last thing I needed was Alex showing up in the middle of everything. I wrapped a towel around my waist and repeated the same sweep I had earlier. Still no Alex. I let out a relieved breath and returned to my room, where the bottle of lube seemed to stare at me from the bed. I turned off the overhead light, then laid down.

This didn't have to be weird. People did this all the time. *Guys* did this. Liked it. Maybe I would too. I grabbed the bottle from beside me, removed the safety seal, then put a liberal amount on my fingers. Start slow, that's all I needed to do. One baby step at a time. Despite the pep talk, I continued to lie there frozen.

"Maybe smaller steps," I mumbled to myself. I swallowed thickly and closed my eyes. It didn't take long for my thoughts to wander to Alex, specifically our last date. The way he'd pressed me into the couch and teased my torso with hot kisses. Within seconds of reliving the memory, I was hard and aching. I trailed my fingers down my chest until they tickled my happy trail. I bit my bottom lip as I took hold of myself like I'd wanted Alex to do that night.

The familiar fantasy that it was his hand instead of mine came to life. I'd wanted Alex to touch me before, but once he had, I craved it. Needed it. No matter how I looked at it, I couldn't understand why he kept backing off. I'd thought for sure we'd go farther the other night, but just like all the other times I encouraged him, he pulled away.

What am I doing wrong?

The doubt crept in, killing my erection. I blew out a hard breath. Whatever it was, I could fix it and this was the first step to proving to Alex that I was ready for more. I brought the fantasy back up, focusing on what *had* happened instead of what hadn't. When it felt like I could blow at any second, I reached for the lube again and switched hands. My left hand now on my shaft, I let my right drift lower, spreading my legs wider and pulling my knees up to reach better.

Anxiety fluttered in my chest and I paused right as I reached the tense muscle of my hole. Maybe I was wrong and I *couldn't* do this. Just because I wanted to try, was curious even, didn't mean I could actually go through with it. I squeezed my eyes tighter and continued to slowly stroke my dick in an effort to calm myself down. Finally, I convinced my hand to move again. I got as far as circling twice, then stalled out at pressing deeper.

I flopped my head back against the pillow. I felt like a fucking contortionist and a coward. How did I know I didn't like a thing if I'd never tried it? "Ugh. This would be so much easier with Alex."

I took a second to imagine what that would be like. If it was Alex hovering over me, melting me with kisses, and guiding me. He could be one bossy fucker, but I'd be lying if I said I didn't eat that shit up. Everything was easier when he told me what to do. I trusted him more than I'd ever trusted anyone in my life. He made me feel safe, cared for...loved. He'd tell me exactly what to do and I wouldn't have to over think this, I could simply experience. I let out a deep breath and forced myself to relax as I fell deeper into the conjured image.

Alex placed kisses along my neck, working his way with agonizing slowness to my mouth. Meanwhile, my hand slid up and down my shaft with the same measured strokes he'd used before. "*That's it,*" he purred in my ear. "*Nice and easy.*" He hummed appreciatively. Or maybe that was me. "*Good. Now circle that tight hole.*"

I bit back a whimper and did as he said.

"*Slowly, my love. We're not in any hurry. There, just like that.*" He placed an open-mouthed kiss on my chest, and I moaned. The finger on my rim was slick and not bad. I had no idea the muscle could be so sensitive. Before I realized it, I'd already pushed the first knuckle of my middle finger inside.

Panic seized my lungs, but I quickly squashed it down, imagining Alex on top of me, conquering my mouth while he slid his finger inside.

"Oh." Surprise briefly took me out of the fantasy. Damn, it was hot in there.

"*Deeper,*" Alex ordered, his emerald eyes intense. I complied, and he captured my mouth. "*Do you want more?*"

"Yes," I gasped, the fantasy twisting into a weird combination of imagining it was his long fingers and him telling me what to do.

"*Slide in and out. Slowly.*"

It took a few tries and more lube, but eventually I managed a smooth glide that definitely wasn't all bad. I might even go so far as to say it was nice. My poor dick ached for more friction than I was giving it, but I was too focused on my ass to give it the attention it deserved. I let out a moan as I picked up the pace. This wasn't a terrible start, but Alex was bigger than one finger.

"*Get on your knees with a pillow below you.*"

I didn't question it, my brain too fogged with fantasy and my body too keyed up. Once I was situated, I released a loud groan at the friction the pillow provided. It wasn't much, but it was better than I'd been managing. This time, when I pressed my finger against my hole, it slipped inside with almost no resistance.

I was on the verge of release when Alex whispered, "*Now another.*"

Considering how close I was and how good this already felt, that sounded like a fantastic idea. Shame my body had other ideas. I added yet more lube and slowly worked in the extra digit. The stretch was more than I expected and took me a little off guard, as did the slight burn that accompanied it.

"*Almost there,*" Alex crooned, and I imagined his hands caressing my back while he traced my shoulder with kisses.

Finally, I had both inside. I resumed the steady glide, letting the natural rock of my hips set the pace. In a surprising amount of time, I was back at the edge and panting into the pillow beneath me that I'd never be able to look at the same way again.

"Alex," I groaned as my movements got jerkier. "Oh fuck. Alex. Alexi." I cried his name as my ass clenched and I came all over the pillow. With a shudder, I removed my fingers and collapsed into the mess. Once the haze of orgasm thinned, I let out a breath of air that might have been a laugh. I'd done it. I'd actually done it. And I could absolutely do it again. I also needed another shower.

CHAPTER 15
SAGE WISDOM

Alexi

Mariah clapped her hands together. "I'm calling it. Meeting adjourned. Time to par-tay!" Her tight red curls swished around her dark mahogany face as she did a little dance on the table.

"Hey!" Rubio shouted as he walked back into the room, not sounding the least bit upset. "I step out for one minute and come back to pure anarchy." He threw his hands out in an exaggerated pose, then gestured at me. "Come on, Lexi, you've got my back."

"Pft. I'm with Mariah on this one." I could certainly use a night out. Much as I loved spending time with Matt, I needed time with other friends. Maybe it would help clear my head.

"Damn right you are." She did another little dance, this one decidedly more victorious. "Lina! Give me a hand!" The exuberant sphinx held out her hands, still doing some happy shimmying.

Lina, our newest member and a jinn, laughed and stepped close to the table to help Mariah down. Her bright turquoise hijab offset her golden skin, which seemed to glow as she reached up. Once more, I was tempted to ask where she'd gotten the fabric. It would look incredible on Matt.

I mentally shook my head. Tonight was about hanging with my tutoring group, *not* thinking about Matt. I finished packing my things in time to catch the soft look that passed between Mariah and Lina. We were all pretty sure something was going on there, but no one wanted to be the first to say something. Not that fellow tutors dating would be an issue. The two were just so adorably sweet around each other, it was almost too much.

A spike of envy stabbed through me. Why couldn't Matt and I have that? Was it me? Had I somehow pushed him too far despite all my efforts not to? Was I just... not enough?

You never were.

I hadn't heard my ex's voice in my head in months. Daniel's derisive intrusion put my teeth on edge and I growled as I savagely pushed it back into the dark where it belonged.

"Yo, I didn't think you disliked bars like that."

I looked up to find Rubio watching me with a startled expression and realized I'd made that angry sound out loud. "Uh, no. I don't mind bars. I was just..." I scrambled for a believable excuse that didn't involve baring yet more of my insecurities to the infinitely confident incubus. "Frustrated with my notes not going into my bag properly."

His gaze narrowed as it flicked between my seamlessly aligned books and me. "Uh-huh. Come on, first beer is on me." He glanced at me as I shouldered the evidence of my blatant lie. "You drink beer, right? If not, I'll grab you a *cock*tail."

I snorted at the horrific pun.

"Maybe a Sex on the Beach? Or a Juicy Screw? Ooh, I know! How about a Dick Sucker?"

"Enough, enough," I squeezed out through side-splitting laughter. "A beer is fine. But I wouldn't mind it being a little... fruity." I wiggled my eyebrows to show I could play this silly game, too.

"Ha!" Semyon barked as he walked past us. "I knew I liked you, Alexei," he said, pronouncing my name more like its Russian counterpart. "You don't let Rubio get away with nothing." He shook his head, freeing bits of straw to float to the ground. Even after working with the man for months, I still couldn't get my head around his hair literally being made of straw, but apparently that was common for Polevoi.

Rubio waved away Semyon's snark, and we fell in with the rest of the team. While I might have grown up exposed to supernaturals—thanks again, Mom—nothing could have prepared me for the sheer variety I'd encountered at Arminius. Half the ones I'd believed were children's stories and legends were actually real. While ones I'd been whole-heartedly convinced must exist *somewhere* were not, or at least, no one could find proof of existence.

Shadow Demons were like that, I mused as we meandered our way off campus. We didn't exist for the longest time. Then, suddenly, we did, and we always had. Hell, our Battle Tactics class had fifteen people in it. Well, ten now. Didn't change that it was hard to prove something when you couldn't find it. I sincerely hoped that those that had left the class and the university eventually returned. I didn't want our kind to disappear into obscurity again.

That line of thought brought me back to Matt and what we were still referring to as "the research project". How were we supposed to prove there'd been a war, an attempted genocide, if we couldn't find verifiable evidence?

"Someone's lost in their thoughts." Rubio clapped a hand on my shoulder.

I offered him a weak smile. "Sorry. Were you saying something?"

"Just that if you didn't already know, you should definitely avoid Le Breuvage Sorcière." He pointed out a hole in the wall joint that blended effortlessly with the surrounding shops.

"Why?"

"Because it's a witch hangout."

I frowned, not following the logic at all. "Why would that matter?"

"Because you're a demon—a rare one—and some reputations have been *earned.*" Rubio's normally jovial eyes took on a steely glint. "Summoning might be banned and while the Shadows have made their stance very clear, not much impedes an enterprising witch."

I swallowed hard. I'd never had any experience with being summoned by a witch before, but I'd heard the stories. Judging by Rubio's demeanor, the uglier bits of those stories held more truth than I'd given credence.

Like someone had flipped a switch, Rubio was back to his bright, charismatic self. "Anyway, here we are!" He threw out his arm with a grand flourish.

I took in the neon sign, blinking in intermittent flashes of red, orange, and yellow, as well as the hodgepodge of guests flowing casually in and out. Judging by the crowd, the Topaz Lounge wasn't purely supernatural and equally patronized by the locals. "Have you been here before?"

"A few times. Place is an absolute gem," Rubio said, raising his voice to be heard as we made our way inside with the rest of our group. "It's got a pretty relaxed vibe, but the best part is that they only play vinyl and they have a dance floor."

"Woo!" Semyon and Rikka shouted as they made a beeline for the modest dance floor already cluttered with dancers.

I laughed at their exuberance and followed the others to a set of couches and tables. Before I could sit, Rubio touched my arm and leaned in.

"Come with me to the bar. I promised you a drink."

"You really don't have to."

Rubio hooked my arm. "Sure I do."

We wove our way to the bar and took a seat at the counter. Rubio flagged the bartender who signaled he'd be a few minutes in getting to us. I'd just settled onto the bar stool when Rubio turned to me.

"Alright, spill."

"I don't know what you mean." I fiddled with a coaster a previous occupant had left behind.

He placed a hand on my arm, and I glanced at him. "Hey, we're friends, right?"

"Of course."

His gaze sharpened. "Good, then I don't need to sugarcoat that you still smell like frustration."

"Rubio," I hissed, my gaze flitting between the various people around us that were definitely human locals.

"Don't 'Rubio' me. What's really the issue? I take it things have not really improved with Matt."

I shifted beneath his unwavering gaze. "They have... And they haven't." My shoulders slumped, and I rested my elbows on the counter. "He's definitely more willing to engage—only in the dorm, mind you—but he still hesitates. I don't know what to do. Is it me? Maybe Matt's just not that into me. My ex was right." I groaned and massaged my temple. "I'll never be enough for someone. You've seen Matt. Why the hell would he choose me?"

"Whoa!"

Rubio's abrupt response snapped me out of my spiral. "What?"

"First off, you can stop that negative self-talk shit right there. As your friend, I won't hear it. And as someone who would be more than willing to date the fuck out of you, it's not even remotely true. Second, did your shitty ex really say that to you?"

My cheeks burned with embarrassment. Normally, I was better about not vomiting my insecurities all over my friends. "Not in exactly those words."

"Well, whatever words he used, they're utter bullshit." Rubio's indignation seemed to roll off of him in waves. "As for your roommate, I've seen the way he looks at you. I've also seen the way he looks at me when I'm with you. Your boy is battling some major jealousy."

I snorted. "Not likely. Why would he?"

"Maybe because you're not the only one dealing with insecurities." He lifted a golden brow. "You may not see it, Alexi, but you are hot as sin. If he's not as enthusiastic as you would like, try asking yourself if there's a reason he's not sharing. You know, kind of like someone else."

The heat on my face seeped beneath my collar. "Easy for you to say. Getting laid for you is as easy as thinking about it." Rubio's face darkened, and I immediately regretted lashing out. "Shit. I'm sorry. That was way out of line."

He held up a hand. "No, I get it. You think I don't know how people see me? Sex is my nature, not something I chose. Hell, half the time it doesn't even feel optional or within my control. But just because I *can* get laid whenever I want, doesn't mean it offers me any kind of fulfillment. I envy you and Matt in a lot of ways."

"Why?"

Rubio's features finally softened. "Because at least you can trust that what you have is real. You may not see it, but Matt is completely wrapped around your little finger. That man would move heaven and earth if it would make you happy."

"You really think so?"

"I *know* so. I wish I could have that kind of certainty with my own partners. Being an incubus isn't all it's cracked up to be. Sure, the sex is phenomenal, but I never know when a connection is to me or what I am."

"Wow, I never thought about it that way."

He shrugged. "Most don't."

The bartender finally got around to us, giving me a few minutes to sift through my thoughts. Rubio seemed so certain about Matt's attraction, his feelings. If it was so obvious, why couldn't I see it? What was really holding him back? A beer dripping with condensation slid in front of me. I couldn't help but smile as I noticed the label on the bottle.

"What's got you grinning?" Rubio bumped my shoulder and my smile widened.

I brought the beer to my lips, savoring the first sip as it filled my mouth with flavor, a distinct undercurrent of fruity notes. "Matt got me this beer when he asked me to tutor him. It was the first drink we ever shared."

"Sounds like someone knows you."

I plucked at the label, working hard to hang onto that optimism. "Yeah, I guess so. While you're dishing out all this wisdom, mind if I ask for a little more?"

"Lay it on me." He took a swallow from his bottle and gave me his full attention.

"If Matt really is that into me, then why... Why won't he be with me outside of our dorm?" I finished, voice soft. "He doesn't... doesn't *act* like he's ashamed or anything, but he also doesn't act like he does when we're alone."

Rubio set his beer down. "That's tough, man. It's possible he's uncomfortable with PDA."

"Yeah, but it feels like more than that. He doesn't have a problem acting like we're friends. He still has zero concept of personal space. I guess you could say the vibe is off. He... shies away?" I looked askance at Rubio, really hoping he had some insight to share.

He considered his drink for a long moment, rolling the bottle between his palms. "I hesitate to say this, because I don't really know the guy, but is it possible he's dealing with past trauma? Like you have your issues because of your shitty ass ex. He could have something similar. Or entirely different." He shrugged and took a drink. "All I know is that in my experience, when people's behavior is inconsistent with what they say or feel, trauma is usually involved."

I stared ahead, catching my reflection in the mirror placed behind the bottles of liquor on display. Matt was such a private person, and I knew for a fact there were at least a couple of things about his past that he hadn't shared with me. I figured he'd get around to it when he was ready, but I'd never considered it could be trauma related. Finally, I took another drink to clear the unexpected thickness in my throat. "Thanks. That, uh, that really helps."

"Anytime." He clinked his bottle against mine. "Now what do you say we rejoin the others?" It was only then that I noticed he'd already gotten us fresh beers.

"You said only one beer."

"Eh," he hiked a shoulder, "you can get the next round."

I finished my current bottle with a chuckle, then grabbed the new cold one and followed him to where the others had started some kind of party game that looked like more laughing than any actual game I recognized.

Hours later, my body was exhausted from laughing and dancing, but my mind was still ruminating over everything Rubio had said. Talking to Matt was always a tricky endeavor, especially since he wasn't overly keen on volunteering information about himself. I was torn between taking the persistence approach where I kept asking or encouraging him to open up.

I opened the door to our dorm room and closed it as quietly as I could, not wanting to wake Matt so late in the evening. Of course, it was for naught. I turned from setting my things down to find Matt standing in his doorway, pajamas askew and a glorious case of bed head.

"Hey," he said sleepily. "Have a good time?"

"Yeah," I replied just as softly. "What did you get up to?"

His face flushed, but that also could have been a trick of the light considering the entire room was only lit by the undermount light from the kitchen. "Nothing. Stayed in."

I wanted to run my fingers through his hair and give him a sweet goodnight kiss, but also knew my breath would smell like beer and didn't want to come across as a hypocrite. Instead, I opted for a sincere smile. "Go back to sleep. I'll tell you all about it in the morning."

He rolled his shoulders and seemed like he wanted to say something, but all that came out was, "Okay." He turned to go back inside, but paused and looked over his shoulder. "Goodnight, Alex."

I smiled again. "Sweet dreams, Matt." There was definitely no mistaking his blush this time or the way he scurried into his room. Chuckling to myself, I fixed a glass of water and did the same.

CHAPTER 16
ORPHAN MATT

Matt

"There's nothing here," I said, closing the current dead end. We'd exhausted every demon history that even vaguely mentioned Shadow Demons and nothing. Forget finding snippets about the Wardes or the War on Darkness, we couldn't even find general sightings of our kind. Back in the day, Shadow Demons weren't considered rare, so where the hell were we? "You'd think we were made up. There aren't even allusions to our abilities, understated or otherwise."

"There has to be something," he said, echoing my frustration as he turned another page in the massive anthology. The pool of magical light instantly began transforming the words and reviving a faded picture to what was likely its original, rich color. "Look at this."

I leaned in to get a better view of the illustration. The yellow light made a tiny circle, so being able to see meant getting close enough that Alex's lavender scent wafted around me. Heat curled in my chest. It was getting harder not to touch him in public. It was getting harder not to touch him, period. As it was, I wanted to slide my hand along his thigh and feel him lean into me. It certainly would have been more comfortable considering our cramped seating at the tiny table. I let out a steadying breath. There was hardly a soul up here. No one would know if I placed a small kiss on the curve of his neck.

"Look familiar?" At the sound of his voice, I snapped out of it. He was going to be the end of me.

"What am I looking at?" I asked, trying to focus. There was a grizzled older man with a small boy standing next to him. Unrealistically, the pint-sized child was holding a broad sword easily twice his size.

"Don't you see the resemblance? Matt, that kid looks just like you."

I frowned at the image. "No, he doesn't."

"Come on, you can't tell me that isn't exactly what you looked like as a toddler. Just look at those eyes."

With a resigned sigh, I did as he asked. Sure enough, they painted the eyes a bright blue, but that didn't mean anything. Lots of people had blue eyes and painters exaggerated. "Maybe, but I don't actually know what I looked like when I was that little," I admitted, leaning back in my seat. The nearness of him was wreaking havoc on my concentration and I needed to be alert in case I felt those eyes watching us again.

"What do you mean? I'm sure if we compared it to a picture of you—"

"There aren't any pictures," I cut him off.

Alex floundered for a second, but didn't relent. "That sounds like an exaggeration. Surely there are a couple out there. I bet you were an adorable baby," he teased, poking me in the ribs.

I shifted away from him and glared straight ahead. "Trust me, there aren't. Just drop it, okay?"

"How could you possibly be so sure?" he scoffed. "Was there a fire or something?" His concern was the final straw.

"Because no one wants to take pictures of an orphan," I snapped.

"What?" The single word was barely a whisper, but it still sounded like a gong to my ears.

"You want to know where I come from?" I growled, turning on him. "Nowhere. I don't know who my parents were or why they didn't want me." The second the words left my mouth, I squeezed my eyes shut, if only to hide Alex's expression of shock. I willed time to go backwards, so I could hold my temper better and keep the traitorous confession from ever spilling out.

"Oh, Matt," Alex said, his voice soft with sympathy... and pity. I'd never wanted that from him. The contents of my stomach rolled, threatening to crawl their way up my throat.

"Told you you'd look at me differently if you knew the truth." I slid my chair back hard enough to make it screech and stood, not even bothering to gather my notes. The half-empty bag bounced on my back as I slung it over my shoulder and turned to leave.

Alex reached out lightning fast to stop me. "Matt, wait."

I looked down at where he had hold of my hand. Even with anger roaring through me, I had to consciously stop myself from squeezing it. My gaze rose to meet his. There was so much sadness in his eyes, I couldn't stand it. Whatever he saw in mine, he let go. His fingers slid from mine like the last drop of rain to splash into nothing on dry ground. That hurt almost as much as the way he was looking at me.

I shadowed across the room and walked out of the library. It was done. Alex officially knew everything about me. Nothing would ever be the same. All the things that I loved about our friendship and...and everything else was over. It wouldn't matter how he tried, he'd never be able to look past the pitiful orphan that no one loved. The pain in my chest welled up, threatening to drown me. He knew, and it was all my fault. I'd ruined everything.

I wandered around the campus until my feet were too tired to keep getting lost. Not that it helped. My head didn't clear, the hurt didn't ease, and I still didn't know what to say to Alex after blurting the truth I'd worked so hard to keep hidden. What *could* I say? I'd been so worried about the *world* taking him from me it had never occurred to *me I'd* be the one to take him from myself. If I'd had it my way, he never would have known that I'd literally been abandoned since birth.

Even after hours of wracking my brain about what to do, I was no closer to an answer. Was it even possible to undo the damage I'd done? Or was this it? Alex would lose interest in the loveless boy and move on. The semester would be over before we knew it. He or I could easily switch dorms at that point. It wasn't anything he hadn't suggested doing before.

I fought for breath as my chest constricted, each more painful than the one before. My steps slowed, and I stared up at Starling Hall, a sharp sting in my eyes. Walking into the restricted section was easier than voluntarily walking away from Alex. I teetered closer to completely falling apart. Deep down, I'd always known this was inevitable and that it had been stupid to expect anything else. People like me didn't get to have nice things. There was no way I could ever actually keep Alex. One way or another, he'd be gone. If years of being bounced around had taught me anything, it was that no one ever stayed. All that was left was to face the music.

Maybe it would be easier if I left before he had the chance. I could talk to Vera, see about transferring before the end of term. As much as it pained me to give up any extra time I might have with him, I didn't think I could take months of that pitying look. With a determination I didn't feel, I made my way to our dorm. A tiny voice inside said that Alex would be worried by now. A much louder one said it didn't matter; he'd be over me soon enough.

Alex immediately looked up from the breakfast table as I walked in. Notes and several other books lay scattered around him. He could have been doing homework for all I knew. That's what I got for thinking he might be worried.

I shrugged off my pack, letting it slide to the floor with a thump I felt in my stomach, and closed the door. When I looked back up, he was standing.

Here goes nothing. Just need to stay focused. Say what I have to say and get to my room.

I pushed past the lump in my throat and stepped deeper into the room. "Don't worry about trying to pretend like everything is fine. We both know it's not. I've got Vera's information somewhere. I'm... I'm going to see what I can do about getting transferred to another room."

"What? Why?"

I closed my eyes like it could block out the questions. "Because I... I can't take you looking at me like that until the term is over." The ache in my chest intensified, causing the words to come out tighter than I would have liked.

This is already so much harder than I expected. I'm never going to make it to my room.

"How am I looking at you, Matt?"

Against my better judgment, I met his gaze. He was looking at me like he always did. That wouldn't last though, not now that he knew how worthless I really was. I dropped my attention to the floor, not trusting myself to speak.

"I told you before, it doesn't matter to me where you come from. I just wish you'd trusted me enough to tell me sooner," he added, walking forward. My feet refused to obey my silent commands for them to move, so I was still standing in the same spot when he stopped in front of me. "You're still you. You're still Matt. That hasn't changed. *You* haven't changed."

I shook my head, still keeping my gaze locked on the carpet. "You're just saying that because you feel bad. No one has wanted me since the day I drew breath. Why should now be any different?"

"Ma—"

I cut him off, snapping my head up to meet his startled expression and slicing my hand through the air. "Don't. You can say whatever you want now, but I. Know. Better. *Everything* will change. You may not mean it too, but it will. It always does. You'll realize what everyone else realized, that I'm no one."

"I have *never* thought you were no one."

"Alex, just don't." The pain was so much worse than anything I'd endured in the ring. Cutting off a limb would hurt less. "I... I... can't..."

"Matt."

"You don't understand." The stinging in my eyes returned.

"Matt," he said again with more force.

"You'll never understand," I hiccupped.

"Matt, shut up and just let me love you," he demanded, and dragged me into the cocoon of his arms.

I tried to resist, but the more I fought, the harder he held me, until I finally sagged against him in defeat. I didn't want to fight Alex. I'd give anything for his words to be true, to believe that my past didn't matter, didn't define me. But history said otherwise. Too many times I'd let my hopes build, only to have them smashed.

"We don't have to talk about it if you don't want to," he said softly as the kiss he placed on my neck.

I wrapped my arms tentatively around him, fear holding me back from griping him just as tightly.

"It's okay to hurt," he whispered.

That's exactly what the pain in my chest felt like, a big ball of hurt. I finally squeezed him back and let the damn break. Soul-crushing sobs tore through me with the mercy of a tidal wave while I held onto him, the only stable thing I'd ever had in my life.

He rubbed my back in a steady motion until the flood subsided. "There's nothing you could do or be that would ever make me stop loving you." He didn't complain about the fact that I was probably close to cracking his ribs or that his shirt was now wet. He let me stay just as I was until I was ready to let go.

I buried my face in his shoulder and clung tighter. I needed those words to be true. I didn't want a life without Alex in it. "I'm sorry," I mumbled when I finally released my death hold on him.

"There's nothing to be sorry for," he replied, calmly wiping the remaining tears from my face.

I blinked at him with heavy lashes and chose to believe the sincerity in his emerald eyes. How was it possible to care about one person so much? Before Alex, I wasn't sure if I'd ever truly cared about anyone before. I took a step back and awkwardly wiped my snotty face with my t-shirt. He remained quiet while I took my time pulling myself back together. When I no longer felt like I'd burst into tears again, I took a deep breath and glimpsed the table behind Alex.

"What's all that?"

He didn't need to turn to know what I was asking about. "I found something." That got my attention. "Come here, I'll show you." He grabbed my hand without waiting for a response and led me to the table.

When we sat down, I shifted so that I was still touching him and laced our fingers to keep his hand captive. He didn't comment beyond giving my fingers a light squeeze.

"Here, you'll need these." He passed me the spectacles I'd acquired from the witch in my Advanced Spells class.

I struggled to put them on with my left hand, but refused to release my hold on his hand in order to use my right. "What?" I asked when I realized he was staring at me.

"You really do look hot in those." The heat of his words shone in his eyes and a matching heat burned on my cheeks.

"Shut up. What am I supposed to be reading?"

He gave an exaggerated eye roll and slid over *Volume Six,* which was already opened to a section. "Start here and tell me what you think."

While I took my time reading, he rested his head on my shoulder. The familiar move helped dispel the last of the tension hanging on to me. Halfway through the selection he'd indicated, I looked over at him in disbelief.

He smiled knowingly. "It gets better."

I returned to the page and kept reading. Eventually, the information was too much, and I had to stop. I sat back, which also had the unfortunate side effect that he stopped laying on me.

"I know." His smile was definitely more smirk-like now.

"That's... That's a detailed description of the opposing forces. It's... it's everyone." Try as I might, I couldn't wrap my head around the sheer enormity of it. "All the different classes. I had no idea there were so many. I've never even heard of some of those. And the generals... the commanders...."

"They're all Shadow Demons of the highest ranking. No one is below a level ten."

"How does no one know about this? There should be records everywhere. This wasn't some skirmish fought repeatedly over a century. It's an all-out war between humans and demonkind."

"Told you it got better."

"The commander, the one in charge of scouts—Sop- Soap- Sopti-something."

"Sopteală?"

"That's the one. I've seen that name before." I released his hand and practically fell across the table to reach a notebook. The cover fell open to reveal the name of its owner. Once it had read Alexi Roman, now it proudly proclaimed to belong to *Alexi & Matt Roman*. For a moment, I forgot what I was doing. I hadn't realized what that would look like when I'd so brazenly added my name to Alex's notebook. An unexpected warmth along with a light fluttering filled my chest. I shook it off and flipped through to the page I needed. "There," I said, pointing to my notes about Matthias. "That was the name of his demon lover. If she was in charge of scouting parties, then that would explain his first entry."

Alex's eyes went round as the ramifications sank in. "That would mean she literally knew him his entire life."

I peered at the ancient history that had already provided so many clues. "You don't suppose there's any mention of that in there, do you?"

"I don't see how there couldn't be. Matthias Warde was literally sleeping with the enemy. Someone was bound to notice eventually."

"I wonder who caught them," I said at the same time Alex said, "I wonder how it started." We shared a look, then burst into laughter, bringing a reprieve from the earlier seriousness.

As the laughter subsided, I shifted my hand to caress his thigh and glanced up to see his stunning eyes staring back, completely absent the pity I'd expected.

"I love you, Matt."

My heart felt like it might burst. I wanted to tell him the same, but didn't know how. For lack of words, I leaned forward and kissed him. What I couldn't express in words, I could this way. I was Alex's for as long as he'd have me.

Chapter 17
Advanced Spells

Alexi

It broke my heart to learn that Matt was an orphan, and it made me even sadder to realize he'd never intended for me to know. His issues with authority, the anger, his quiet nature, why he didn't like to talk about his past certainly made a lot more sense now. But knowing the truth didn't change how I felt about him. If anything, it helped me understand him better. Matt wasn't a private person by choice; it was by necessity.

How many times over the years had he had his heart broken? Demons did not do well in foster systems unless someone specially placed them. To think, he'd only known about being a demon two weeks before arriving at Arminius University. I couldn't even begin to imagine the pain he must have gone through as family after family rejected this strange child they could never hope to understand.

More than anything, I felt like a total jerk for threatening to leave all those months ago. I had a pretty good idea what he'd likely faced when he ventured into the restricted section. Matt could take anything, and had proved it more than once. What he was most afraid of, was being alone, being abandoned yet again. That was why he always looked at me like he was surprised I'd returned and why he kissed me like he might never see me again. It would take time, repeatedly showing up, to convince him I wasn't going anywhere.

I loved Matt with every fiber of my being and could feel that love growing every day. Every instinct in me wanted to take away the hurt he kept bottled inside, but to do that, I needed to understand him, how he grew up. Not prying into his childhood would be difficult. Either way, pushing him to share would likely only result in pushing him away.

"He'll open up in time," I told my reflection in the bathroom mirror. Until then, I refused to behave any differently than I had before I knew the truth. I squared my shoulders, strengthened my resolve, then left to join him.

When I walked into the living space, he was sitting on the couch studying something with intense concentration, hair still wet from his own shower and looking sinfully attractive as he worried at his bottom lip. Had I ever been so attracted to someone in my entire life? Anytime I saw him, I had to remind my heart to beat. Even him sitting there innocently reading was enough to make it stutter.

On an impulse, I moved behind to stand behind him and massaged the back of his neck. He immediately let out an appreciative sigh that bordered on a moan. I bit back a chuckle. It amazed me how he responded to things and I was positive half the time he literally had no idea how those reactions came across—it was part of his charm. I peered over his shoulder to see what held his focus. To my surprise, it wasn't *Volume Six*.

"What are you working on?" I asked, digging a little deeper and making him groan.

"A shadow spell."

"Oh? What's it supposed to do?" I worked my way out to his shoulders, kneading the knots of muscles, and was rewarded with another inaudible sigh.

"It's *supposed* to cloak a portal from other Shadow Demons—since we're the only ones who could see it anyway—but so far, all I'm getting is a faint shimmer."

"Portal. That sounds like third year studies. And since when is your class book in calligraphy?"

He shifted beneath my hands, which had gone still. "This isn't the class book. The grad student sitting-in lent it to me."

"Why would a TA loan you a vintage grimoire?" I asked, because what else could it be? "You must have made quite the impression on him." First spelled glasses, now a book easily worth both our weights in gold? No one was *that* generous without an ulterior motive.

Matt reached back and squeezed my hand as if he could sense my thoughts. "She's a fifth-year witch who's studying under Professor Hallow. I think Vera was involved somehow."

I pulled my hand free and stepped away. "Why would the Dean of Witch Studies have anything to do with Vera?"

He tilted his head back to look at me, a wrinkle between his furrowed brows. "Because the dean is Kyra Hallow, as in Kyra Hallow of the Shadows. Pretty sure

Vera knows she's still not my favorite person after the ordeal with the hotel. Makes sense she'd get someone else to do her dirty work."

"Vera taking a personal interest in you isn't surprising, though how she's going about it is questionable. "

"Still don't see why," he scoffed, closing the frustrating book and tossing it on the coffee table.

"Because, Matt," I walked around the couch to face him, "you're a level seven. Aside from her, you're probably the strongest Shadow Demon to manifest in ages."

"Fat lot of good it does me. I can't even get this stupid spell to work."

I crossed my arms and raised an eyebrow. "You mean a highly advanced spell that most third years probably wouldn't be able to do? That one?"

He gave me a crooked smile. "Yeah, that one."

"Walk me through it." I plopped down beside him, causing the cushion to bounce.

"Do I have to?"

I bumped his shoulder. "It's obviously bothering you. I promise to make it worth your while."

He raised an intrigued eyebrow. "When you put it like that... Okay, but we'll have to start with a portal."

I shook my head, unable to suppress my smile.

"What?"

"You're incredible. You're sitting here bemoaning that you can't do a cloaking spell and, in the same breath, you just casually mention you have to make a portal first. Like it's no big deal. I've been practicing with manipulating shadow for years and *I* still don't know how to make a portal. I'm not even sure I can."

His frown bordered on a pout. "Of course you can. I'll show you. Give me your hand."

More than a little dubious of how he planned to "show me", I offered my hand.

Matt stroked down the length of my arm before grabbing my wrist. My heart did its usual putter at the touch. I expected to see a mischievous smile, but found focused sincerity.

"Feel for the shadow world. You're looking for where this world meets that one. Got it?"

I nodded. Sensing the shadow world was easy, I'd been doing for as long as I could remember.

"Now, you're going to reach into it just enough to break the barrier without actually crossing over. Don't worry about not having an anchor on the other side. You don't need one for this."

"Where's your anchor?" I asked absently while I did as he said. I had little doubt that he would have been playing with portals without creating both sides.

He turned to look at me. For a moment his eyes searched mine, then he returned his attention to where rippling shadow surrounded my hand. "The anchor is in the freezer."

"The freezer?"

He shrugged. "How else do you think I get your ice cream so fast when you're in one of your moods?"

"I don't have moods."

He snorted, sparing me a derisive look before returning his attention to the ripple of shadow. "Focus, or you're going to lose it. Now, exert your will into the circle so that it'll sustain itself and stay open."

"Uh... That sounds hard." We'd already sailed way past the things I knew how to do. Matt may believe I was better at all things shadow, but he was the real savant.

He smiled at me enthusiastically. "Not for a nine." He stared intently at the pool of shadow, then declared, "You've got it."

I wasn't a hundred percent what I'd done, but I definitely felt the breach solidify. Curious, I stuck my hand in and it didn't reappear on the other side. "Huh."

"Okay, now for the spell to hide it." He retrieved the book and held it open for me on the same page he'd been agonizing over. "Go slow. The spell doesn't need speed, but it requires pronunciation. It may take a few tries before you're comfortable with all the words. Place your hand over the portal you've made, but don't touch it. If you do, then the cloak will be on the other side. Then we definitely won't know if it worked."

I nodded, still not convinced I could do any of what he said. Before attempting to pronounce anything, I read the lines several times. When I felt confident enough to try it, the words sounded like shadows slipping past my lips and tasted of smoke. The air shimmered faintly beneath my palm, then... Nothing. I let out a disappointed breath. "So much for thinking I could do it when you couldn't."

"Did you drop the portal?" He squinted, then scowled. "I could have sworn you had it stable. We'll just have to start over." He shifted the book out of the way to retake my hand.

I looked from him to the portal, floating exactly where I'd left it. "What are you talking about? It's right there."

Now he looked really confused. "No, it's not. One second it was, then it wasn't. It must have collapsed. That's fine. It was your first go."

"Give me your hand." He begrudgingly placed his hand in mine, then I slowly pushed his hand through the portal.

Understanding illuminated his face. "You did it!"

"I suspect you did, too. The spell doesn't hide it from the *creator*, it hides it from everyone else."

He quickly summoned his own portal and repeated the spell. Some of his inflection could use work, but the moment he was done, the portal winked out of existence. He looked at me for confirmation.

"I don't sense anything." Matt's smile could have conquered the world. It had certainly already conquered my heart. I extended my essence and collapsed my cloaked portal. Without waiting to see if he'd do the same, I leaned forward and kissed him on the cheek.

He blindly swiped at the air and turned to me. His lips met mine and the rest of the world disappeared. I cradled his neck and urged him deeper. He certainly didn't feel tense now. He slid an arm around me and pulled me closer until I was practically on top of him.

Unbelievably, the kisses stayed slow and purposeful, a steady burn versus the blinding inferno. The smell of sage enveloped me as I kissed and nipped along his neck, adding flicks of my tongue to soothe any pain. He let out a groan, which only encouraged me. His breathing turned ragged and I could feel his heart racing beneath his shirt.

"Alex."

"Hmm?" I inquired noncommittally while I continued to taste his skin. His sigh certainly sounded like he was enjoying it.

"I need more. I... want more."

I pulled back to look at him. Where I expected to find his gaze darkened to midnight with lust, I found the blue crystal without so much as a stray cloud of doubt. Was he really saying what I thought he was saying?

He cupped my face, then gave me a kiss that had my heart stuttering. "I want you, Alex."

I was too shocked to breathe. I stood and pulled him up after me, catching him with a bruising kiss. "Are you sure?" I didn't want to jinx it, but I needed to know. Needed him to say it.

"Hell, yes," he said, wrapping me in a kiss that burned away any lingering doubts.

He's going to incinerate me right here.

I pulled away after giving him a slightly more chaste kiss, then grabbed his hand and led him to my room. My heart pounded so hard, I couldn't think straight. I released him by the bed and yanked open the nightstand drawer. After a few moments of digging, I only came up with lube, which I tossed it on the bed. "Um, give me a minute?"

He seemed a little confused, but nodded. "Of course."

I scrambled into the bathroom, where I promptly fell against the closed door. Sweet mother of midnight, we were actually going to have sex. *Finally.* The thought alone had me tenting my pants. Now all I had to do was find some fucking condoms. I nearly let out a triumphant shout when I found a pack under the sink along with another essential. Trusting Matt to be patient, I freshened up. Then, after a deep breath that did nothing to calm my errant pulse, exited the bathroom.

"You're going to want these." I placed the string of foil wrapped condoms in his hand and gestured at the thankfully full bottle of lubricant. "And a lot of that. No such thing as too much lube."

His mouth twitched like he was fighting a laugh. "This isn't exactly my first time."

"Have you done this exactly?"

The almost smile vanished. "No."

"Then forgive me if I care about my body."

"Your—" He cut himself off, though it took a moment for the confusion on his face to fade. He stared at the condoms in his hand, then placed them on the bed. "I understand."

Before I could press my point, he captured me with a slow kiss that sent tendrils of desire curling through me. I was way past wanting Matt. I needed him on a level I couldn't begin to comprehend. He slipped his fingers beneath my shirt, trailing them up my torso until my shirt was so bunched, he had to pull it over my head. I reached for my pants' button, but Matt gently waved my hand to the side and guided me to lie on the bed. The cool sheets against my back had me gasping while he decorated my chest and quivering stomach like he was trying to map my body with his lips. By the time he released my erection, I was floating in a sea of ecstasy.

"Don't forget the—" The reminder about the lube died as he licked my dick from base to tip with the flat of his tongue. I dropped my head back with a moan, getting lost in the incredible heat of his mouth. Then his hands were back, gently caressing my calves and tickling the fine hairs on my legs. When he straightened to remove his clothes, I felt like I'd had a full pitcher of that sweet concoction he'd made last semester.

Finally, he crawled on the bed to join me, repositioning us in the middle. I cradled his face while he bestowed sensual kisses that threatened my grasp of reality. Then a slick finger brushed my entrance, and I released a pained moan that bordered on a whine. I'd expected to have to walk him through prepping me, but he didn't need any guidance as he slowly stretched me with deliberate movements. By the time he slid inside, there wasn't even a hint of a burn, only pleasure tingling in every cell of my body. Even then, he continued to move like we had all the time in the world, combining tender kisses with soft caresses and long thrusts. One thing was for certain: I'd never had a lover as thoughtful or sweet as Matt.

I hummed contentedly, tracing the contours of Matt's back while he peppered my chest and shoulders with light kisses. His lips drifted lower, and I laughed, feeling lighter than I had in months, maybe years. There was no chance of going back now, though I doubted there ever had been. My heart and soul belonged to Matt, without a doubt.

"What are you doing?" I asked playfully, tilting his head up to taste his lips.

"I told you. I want you."

I laughed again and ran my fingers through his hair. "You have me. Though I wouldn't be opposed to another tumble," I added with a wicked smile.

He licked his lips and swallowed. "That's not... I mean..."

I sat up fully and held the side of his face, worry killing the last of my afterglow. The sex had been incredible for me, but maybe it hadn't been for him. "What?"

"I want... I want you to top me," he finished in a rush, his cheeks burning a dark pink. "Is that the right term?"

Swallowing suddenly became impossible. "Yeah," I croaked. "But, Matt, this isn't... You don't have to bottom if you don't want to."

"I know." His blush darkened until it reached the tips of his ears. Despite his embarrassment, his voice gained strength as he continued. "I'm... curious. I want to know what it's like. With you."

Oh.

"If you're sure..."

"I'm sure," he said at the same time he tackled me back to the mattress and captured my mouth in a searing kiss I felt to my toes.

It took an effort, but I pushed him back. "Would you like a few minutes to... um..." How did I ask this delicately? "Freshen up?"

He shook his head, already leaning down for another kiss. "No need."

I dodged his lips, and he made a noise of frustration when they landed on my cheek. "Matt, I really think—"

"I already did." He laid a trail of kisses down my neck. "Grabbed those too." He gestured at a new box of condoms sitting on the nightstand. "Since you're bigger than me."

"When did you..." I trailed off as I recalled that he'd taken an exorbitant amount of time retrieving water earlier. "You're really serious about this."

"Why wouldn't I be?" He stared at me without blinking, then doubt crumpled his face and he retreated. "Unless you don't... If you're not interested..."

I quickly reached for him before he could decide to shadow away. "I'm interested. Very interested."

A tentative smile lit his face. "Yeah?"

"Oh yeah. It's just... been awhile since I wasn't expected to bottom."

His face darkened again, this time with malevolence. "Your ex better pray we never meet."

I laughed, taking him off guard, and cupped his face with both hands. "You, my love, are an absolute treasure. We can try this, but you have to promise me, if you decide at any point, you don't like it, you'll tell me." He nodded, and I shifted my hands to grip his chin. "I mean it, Matt. Promise me."

"I promise," he whispered.

I brushed my lips over his and gave him a gentle push. "Lay back and try to relax. I want to make you feel good."

"I know you will."

The trust in Matt's eyes nearly undid me. Fortifying my nerves, I grabbed the supplies, noting with surprise that he'd sprung for the high-end barely-there condoms, and placed them close by. Then I layered his body with kisses until he was writhing with impatience.

"Alex," he moaned, as I slowly stroked his erection.

"I just want to make sure you're relaxed."

"I'm relaxed," he gasped, hands and feet digging into the mattress.

Not entirely convinced, I put a liberal amount of lube on my fingers and situated myself between his legs. I couldn't even remember the last time I'd topped, but it didn't diminish how keyed-up I was to be doing it now. "You're sure?"

"Sure. Very sure."

I spread his cheeks and placed a slick finger on his rim. He released a hiss that turned into a little moan as I circled the sensitive muscle. I took my time working in a finger. When I could slide with no resistance, I pushed deeper, getting lost in the tight heat.

"Fuck."

I went stiller than if I'd just come face to face with a gorgon. "What? Is something wrong?"

He arched his back, causing my buried finger to glide again, and released a deep groan. "Why does that feel so much better when you do it?"

I blinked a couple times, not sure if I'd heard him right. "Wait. You've... On yourself?"

He lifted his head, revealing pupils blown wide. "Of course. I wanted to make sure you knew I was serious."

All other thought fled as I imagined Matt fingering himself and thinking of me. "How many?" I asked, voice suddenly raw.

"Huh?"

"How many fingers?"

"Two," he confessed, just shy of sheepish.

I nearly choked on my surprise. He was going to be the death of me. Banishing the filthy images that had sprung to mind in favor of the one in front of me, I pulled myself together. "We'll need a little more than two." I resumed moving my hand and his eyelids fluttered. "You'll tell me if it's too much?"

"Yeah. Yes," he repeated clearer.

By the time I had him sufficiently stretched, Matt was clawing at the sheets and I wasn't sure if I'd even make it inside of him before I blew. Doing my best to avoid his hungry gaze, I rolled on the condom, added more lube, and lined up with his clenching hole. I pressed his knees closer to his chest and worked my way in with shallow thrusts, then had to stop or risk exploding. He felt so good. His body was a tight vice of the most delectable heat.

Matt made a noise that sounded suspiciously like a whine. "Move already," he groaned so hard I felt the vibrations.

I slid nearly all the way out and slammed back in. Once. Twice.

He bowed off the bed. "Yes. More."

All the control I worked so hard to maintain shattered. I recaptured his mouth with a ferocity that surprised me. There was only his body and mine. There was nothing gentle about the way I rode him to a chorus of panting moans. Any hope of regaining some semblance of restraint vanished when he wrapped his legs around me, his heels urging me deeper. Then he tightened around me to the point of pain. I struggled to remain coherent as I came hard enough to see stars.

I collapsed on top of him, devouring his mouth, though I had zero air to spare. Not that he seemed to mind, given how his hands roved over my body like he could pull me inside forever. Then round two became round three, and I stopped counting.

I disintegrated into exhaustion, rolling away to stare at the ceiling. When my breathing and heart rate returned to normal, guilt sprouted. I'd behaved like some kind of depraved animal. I wasn't sure when I'd stopped checking in or when I'd started manhandling him into different positions, each one somehow better than the last. Anxious, I glanced over at him. He was the picture of sedation, his head pillowed on his arms with a dreamy smile.

I rolled onto my side and kissed his shoulder. Decency evaded before, but I could try to make up for it now. "Come on."

"Pretty sure I did. A few times," he added with a chuckle.

"Very funny."

He smirked and burrowed deeper into the mattress with a contented sigh. "I thought so."

"Get up. We're taking a bath." I stood and stretched.

He let out a groan of put upon despair. When I looked back to encourage him, hunger once more shone in his eyes. It was almost enough to get my blood going again. I mentally shook myself.

Care first, more later.

"You heard me."

He continued to bellyache, but got up. "I don't want to take a bath. I don't even like baths."

I snared him with a kiss, and he melted into me. With a force of will, I checked the heat I could feel building. The word insatiable came to mind, but I wasn't sure which one of us it applied to. "You'll thank me later."

He gave me a look. Explaining to him that this had nothing to do with believing that he couldn't handle this and everything to do with taking care of him was pointless. He would do it, because I told him to, even if he whined about it the whole time. Just in case, I grabbed his hand and led him to the bathroom. I filled the tub with steaming water and got in.

"Now you."

He eyed the steaming water. "Maybe I'll get the next one. It's a small tub."

"Matt."

"Alright, alright," he said, then carefully stepped in. He leaned back into me and the hot water immediately did its work, every muscle relaxed.

"See, not so bad," I said after a while. When no quippy comeback was forthcoming, I shifted to look at his face.

Of course, he's completely passed out.

Ever so slowly, I shadowed, careful not to let him slide further into the water. Once I was dry, I leaned down to scoop him out, for once grateful for demonic strength. With the help of some manipulated shadow, I got him back into the bed, then returned to drain the tub.

When I was done, I slid in beside him and brushed back the hair that had dried on his face. As if by reflex, he reached out to wrap his arm around my waist. I relaxed into the possessive embrace and drifted off, watching my perfect angel sleep.

Chapter 18
Uneven Ground

Matt

When I woke, Alex filled my vision. Warmth filled my chest, along with happy flutters. Damn, he was beautiful. With those pronounced cheekbones, slender nose, and complexion most people would kill for, he was more art than mortal. I resisted the urge to trace his features, kiss him awake. It was rare for him not to be up first, buzzing around teasing me for wanting to sleep the day away. I ached to touch him, but he'd earned the right to catch a few extra Zs.

My stomach growled, and I checked to make sure the sound hadn't disturbed him. Reluctantly, I shadowed out of bed. I grabbed some sweats, not really sure who they belonged to. They fit well enough and that's all that mattered. Rather than risk the door creaking, I shadowed directly to the kitchen, where I searched for something more substantial than cereal. When it turned out we had everything to make egg sandwiches, I felt like I'd struck gold.

Humming to myself, I pulled out a mixing bowl and set a pan on the small stove. The eggs gave a satisfying sizzle when they touched the heated surface, and my stomach growled again.

"What are you doing?"

I chuckled to myself—so much for worrying about the door—and turned to look at Alex. Like myself, he hadn't bothered with a shirt. My heart stuttered as I took in his lean frame and ridiculous waist. Nyx, he was stunning. He must not have seen a mirror yet, though, because his hair was everywhere. I tried not to laugh. No matter how much he messed with it, it never seemed to do any good. Suddenly, I realized he was still waiting for an answer.

"I'm making breakfast. I don't know about you, but I'm hungry."

"I didn't know you could cook." He rubbed his arm, then joined me in the kitchen, his usual air of confidence notably absent.

Anxiety shot through me. Had I done something wrong? He'd called me out last night. He was right. I'd never done anything like that before. What if I'd messed up somehow or didn't do something right? I tried to squash the insecurity, but it lingered like a gnat buzzing in my ear.

"They're just eggs. Not too complicated." I gave a casual shrug to hide the fear now ricocheting inside.

"How are you feeling?" he asked, his voice betraying a note of anxiety.

I shifted the eggs so they wouldn't burn. "I'm fine."

"Are sure? I just wanted... You might be..."

I removed the eggs from the burner and killed the heat. I could finish the toast in a moment. This clearly needed to be handled first. "Would you stop asking me if I'm okay?"

He looked like he was about to ask again, anyway. What was he so nervous about? I'd *asked* for this.

"I'm good. I promise. No tenderness or anything."

"But I—"

I stepped in close, rubbing my hands along his arms. "If anything, I should ask how *you* are feeling." His eyebrows scrunched together, and I ran my fingers through his messy hair. "Seemed like you needed that more than I did."

He swallowed and looked away. "I'm sorry."

"Why? I'm not." I offered him a crooked smile. I was about as far from sorry as you could get. "So, how *do* you feel?"

Finally, he cracked a smile of his own. "I feel great, Matt."

"Good." I stretched to give him a sweet kiss, but my small kiss good morning got lost in the sweeping command of his own.

There's my confident Alex.

"I've wanted that for so long," he said between kisses that were already stoking the fire inside.

I leaned into him, enjoying the way his arms wrapped possessively around me. "I could tell."

"Shut up." He laughed and kissed me hard enough that I stumbled backward and nearly sat on the table. The resulting twinge had me second guessing my optimism of not being sore. Maybe a marathon of killer sex was not the *best* way to see if I liked bottoming.

"I can't believe I'm saying this, but probably best to wait at least a short while," I said with another kiss.

He smiled, lighting my world more than the sun ever had. "Of course." He pulled me tight and the feel of the table disappeared.

I molded against him, melting into the embrace and getting lost in the way his tongue swept along mine. It'd be so easy to suggest going back to bed, which was not at all conducive to waiting. I pulled away, though it was possibly the last thing I wanted to do. "The eggs are getting cold."

"How can I help?"

"Start the toast? I'll warm up the eggs and get the plates." I hated giving him the instructions, because it meant he let me go. I wanted to stay lost in those kisses, to feel his touch everywhere. After last night, I'd have thought the inferno that burned inside would have diminished at least slightly but, it felt closer to the surface than ever. I reigned in the fire and tried to focus. Once we finished eating, we sat in companionable silence while Alex finished his coffee.

He peered at me over the rim as he took a sip. "What would you like to do today?"

"Honestly? I'd be happy just spending it with you."

His eyes widened, and his cup hovered at his lips. I wasn't sure why that surprised him. I always wanted to spend time with him. That wasn't new.

"We could go into town," I suggested.

He gave me a smile that made me feel tingly all over. "In that case, we should probably clean up."

"That reminds me." I couldn't believe I was actually about to ask this. "Did I fall asleep in the tub?"

His smile got bigger. "Yes, and it was *not* easy getting you out."

"In fairness, I told you I didn't need a bath."

He walked around the table to grab my plate. As he reached forward, he placed a small kiss on the curve of my neck and I gave an involuntary sigh. "Thought you said you weren't sore," he whispered in my ear.

"Oh," I squeaked, grateful he was behind me and couldn't see my face burning. "Right, so, getting ready."

"I said get cleaned up."

I turned to face him and prayed my face wasn't scarlet. "What do you mean?"

"I'm going to take a shower. You're welcome to join me," he said with a perfectly straight face. Alex could give people lessons in maintaining a poker face.

His casual invitation effectively obliterated all of my efforts to rein in my blush. "But we already took a bath."

"Sitting in scalding water hardly counts as getting clean." He waved a dismissive hand as he walked toward his room.

I continued to sit there at a total loss. A shower together was about as far from waiting as we could get.

He stopped in the doorway and turned back to me. "Are you coming?" His eyebrow lifted, giving the question a more commanding tone.

All the moisture in my mouth vanished and my heart started doing double time while my ass remained glued to the chair.

"It is possible to just take a shower, Matt."

I seriously doubted that, especially where he was concerned. Still, his words finally got my feet moving. I drifted after him, feeling like he'd caught me in some kind of spell. When I arrived in the bathroom, he'd already stripped down and was adjusting the water. He turned around and caught me blatantly staring.

His emerald eyes flashed. "I thought we talked about watching."

Yep, we did and you pointing that out is not helping. There is no way I can do this.

He tested the water temperature, but didn't get in.

"Just a shower, right?"

"Sure." He stepped under the cascade. That sounded dubious at best and the polar opposite of convincing. He gave me a look that fell somewhere between curious and commanding.

I swallowed thickly. If I didn't hurry, he was bound to make another crack about watching. Quickly, I ditched the sweats and stepped in, keeping my back to him. Maybe if I couldn't see him, I'd survive this.

Get a grip. It's not like this is the first time you've ever taken a shower with Alex. Except not much cleaning had happened then either.

My pep talk was not helping. If anything, it was making matters worse. Then Alex's hand slid around my waist and I about near jumped out of my skin.

"You know, for someone who says they're fine, you're awful jumpy." He chuckled and removed his hand. "I told you, just a shower."

I turned to fuss at him for messing with me, but the words never stood a chance. Before I could open my mouth, Alex captured me with a kiss. Barely suppressed desire roared to life. I kissed him back and groaned when his fingers dug into my hips.

Just as suddenly as he'd caught me, he released me, giving me probably the sexiest smile ever seen by demonkind. "Just a shower, right?"

"Damn you, Alex," I said breathlessly. We both knew I was his to do with as he pleased. Apparently, I was his personal plaything this morning.

"Turn around," he ordered.

I immediately obeyed.

"Pass me the soap."

My heart hammered loud enough that it eclipsed the spray hitting the tub and probably could be heard in the dorm next door. "What are you going to do?" His laugh tickled my ear, reaffirming my belief that he was definitely toying with me.

"I'm going to wash your back. You asked for just a shower, so that's exactly what I'm going to give you."

"For the record, I never asked for this shower," I said over my shoulder.

"Didn't you? At any rate, you made it very clear that is all it would be," he said as he worked the soap into a lather.

I barely didn't gasp when his hands glided across my shoulders. I squeezed my eyes shut as if it could somehow dull the ecstasy of sensation.

Sweet merciful Night, he won't need to do anything else. The feel of his hands alone is threatening to undo me.

Right when I thought I wouldn't be able to take a second more without turning into a puddle, the touch vanished to be replaced by a waterfall of hot water.

"Your turn."

I turned to face him in disbelief, and the growing suspicion that this was some kind of payback. I flashed to daring Alex to do a body shot.

He held up the soap like a challenge. "You don't have to if you don't want to."

I glared at him before snatching the soap, and he turned around to reveal the perfect canvas of his back. A whimper caught in my throat. Alex knew I had problems touching him, namely that I couldn't seem to stop once I started.

Unsurprisingly, the second I touched his skin, I got totally lost in the feel of him beneath my hands. The soap became a medium in which to paint the contours of his body. He sighed, though it sounded more like a moan.

What is it about being touched that feels so special? Is it because, as Shadow Demons, a good part of our essence is technically intangible and touch creates a connection to the physical plane?

Abruptly, I realized I wasn't washing his back anymore. In my musings, my hands had wandered around to his chest and now he was leaning against me. My senses clearly already having fled, I bent to kiss his neck, earning another sigh. "You are absolutely impossible," I whispered, my lips brushing against his smooth skin.

"What else?"

"Far too attractive for your own good."

He snickered. "That so?"

"Yeah, that's so." Thanks to entirely too much soap, he easily spun within my arms and I found myself looking into an emerald that seemed to define the color.

"I love you, Matt." The following kiss seemed to devour everything I still couldn't find the words to tell him. I got lost in the world that was Alex. He could have whatever he wanted from me; I'd never stop him. "I think we're clean enough. Don't you?" he asked, nipping at my swollen lips.

"You're a regular comedian," I said, stealing another kiss for good measure.

"I'm glad you think so."

"Does this mean we are or aren't going to town?"

"Definitely going," he replied a little too quickly.

I gave him a cheeky smile, finally feeling like I was getting the upper hand for a change. "Alex, are you afraid to be alone in the dorm with me?"

"I don't know if afraid is quite what I would say."

"And what *would* you say?"

"That you're right, and we should wait. If we stay here, that won't happen." He cleared his throat, no doubt realizing that his words were having the opposite effect of getting us to leave. "Go get dressed, Matt."

"Are you sure that's what you really want?" I purred.

"Matt, please, just go." His breathing had turned into pants and I could see my desire reflected in his eyes.

Rather than argue, I shadowed to my room, creating a sizable puddle where I landed. There wasn't a doubt in my mind that he was still standing in the shower, trying to pull himself back together. I was tempted to shadow back and see for myself, but if I did that, we wouldn't leave at all.

See, Alex, you're not the only one who can play games.

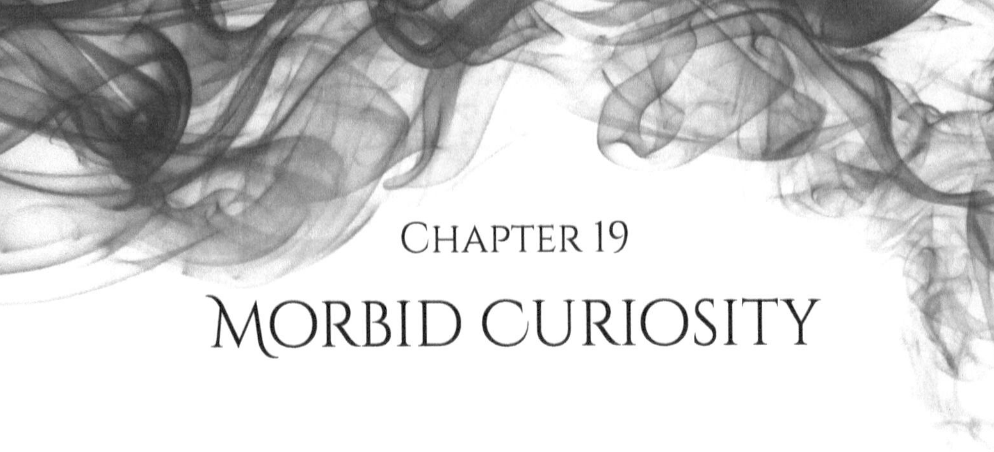

Chapter 19
Morbid Curiosity

Alexi

I never could have imagined how easy being in love with my best friend would be… Or how difficult. Making love to Matt was a life-defining experience. The way we fit together made me realize how incompatible I'd been with previous boyfriends. We'd all but perfected the art of silent communication in the bedroom, easily reading the other's needs. If only that same understanding extended beyond the physical… and beyond the dorm.

A series of giggles caught my attention, and I glanced over to find the latest couple to have entered the coffee shop. Envy that I struggled to keep in check blossomed in my chest at seeing the way the couple leaned into each other, doting smiles, and laced fingers. They probably took for granted that they could hold their partner's hand in public and be obnoxiously cute. Of course, I doubted their bedroom passions could hold a candle to mine. I smiled to myself as I drank my fresh cup. Night Matt's hands. Half the time I felt like an instrument and he knew all the right notes. Like last night. The way he'd…

"What are you thinking about?" Matt's hallmark angelic expression accompanied the unexpected question, making me wonder for the thousandth time if he could secretly read my mind.

My sip went down the wrong way and ended coming partially up my nose. Man that burned. He casually passed me a napkin, his face still deceptively neutral. "What do you think I'm thinking about?" I asked, stalling for time.

"Obviously not about swallowing."

My choking fit returned with a vengeance, while the barest hint of a smile played at the corner of his mouth. How anyone could buy that affected look of innocence was beyond me. Matt could be an evil imp whenever the fancy struck him.

I need to get a handle on this before it turns into one long series of innuendos that ends with me needing a healer.

"Tell me about your childhood." Matt's smile vanished and I could have kicked myself. Much as I wanted to know about his past, bluntly asking wasn't the way to go about it. Already his jaw had tensed and his shoulders might as well have been carved from stone. Before I could utter an apology, though, he started talking.

"I was literally a baby—maybe a couple months old—when they found me on the steps of a Catholic church in Norfolk, Nebraska. No note, no explanation. I don't remember the name of the place, just that I wasn't there very long. Makes sense now that it didn't last." I could definitely see how a demon baby in a Catholic church might not go over very well. "Anyway, after a brief stint there, I got sent to my first orphanage."

"First?"

"I've been in eight." He spared me a quick glance, then returned his attention to his almost empty cup and forgotten muffin.

I schooled my shock. Eight was downright obscene.

"I was five when they placed me with my first foster family. They were really nice until I started having fits. I don't know what started them, but no family wants to put up with a toddler that goes off the rails at regular intervals and has fainting spells. At least not one they can send back. So they did." Matt let out a long breath, his shoulders pulling closer together as he hunched in on himself. "The next family wasn't so nice. They thought they could beat it out of me. That didn't go over so well. I was stronger than they expected for a child and I broke his arm. That was the first time I ran away," he added, his muffin turning to crumbs beneath his fingers. My heart broke into pieces, much like Matt's dry muffin. Rejected, passed around, beaten—no wonder he was so reserved.

"When did the fighting start?" I asked.

He looked up at the ceiling. "Let's see, after I broke Mr. Jefferson's arm, I got branded as violent. They like to keep those kinds of kids together. Which doesn't make a damn bit of sense. That's like asking for trouble, which is exactly what they got. Lewis was the first kid I ever hit... on purpose. I was seven and in Lincoln by then."

"I thought you said Omaha."

"When I exhausted the orphanages with room, I got shipped to a neighboring city. Anyway, Lewis had been on my case for months. I don't know what about me bothered him so much, but I was definitely his personal punching bag. I did everything I could think of to avoid him. Even told an adult. That was an epic mistake." Matt rolled his eyes and his lip curled in a silent snarl. "Not only did they not help, but Lewis beat me to a pulp for being a snitch. As much as I didn't want to get moved again—it got worse every time—I finally couldn't take it anymore. One day when he went to hit me, I got out of the way in time. He didn't even realize I'd moved until my fist slammed into his face. That's when I figured out how fast I could be. I didn't have to get hit if I didn't want to."

"Sounds like your true nature was trying to manifest."

"Wish I'd known that then. Certainly would have made some of those fights easier. After Lewis, they became a blur of faces. My reputation seemed to precede me, and at each new place, the self-appointed top dogs sought me out. I did what I could not to provoke them, not that it ever did any good. As I got older, the kids got meaner... and bigger while I stayed on the small side."

Understanding from our initial meeting dawned. "That's why you started weight training."

He nodded. "Figured if I could hit them hard enough they never thought to retaliate, I'd be golden. But even when I won, it didn't end. There was always a fresh set to take their place. I was the only thing that ever stayed." His voice hitched, a veil of anguish casting a shadow over his face. "I ran away at least a dozen more times... or tried to. They always caught me. Longest I stayed on the street was a month before I got picked up in an alley in Omaha. They took me to a halfway house and then almost immediately turned around and shipped me to Superno House. I wasn't even there twelve hours before I got dragged outside by four of the strangest things I'd ever seen." He paused, and I wondered if I should say something. Did I ask what Superno House was? From the Latin I knew, it was obviously a home for supernaturals. "Sometimes, I wonder what would have happened to Oliver—a fire demon—if Vera hadn't shown up when she did. I wonder what would have happened to me," he added, playing with the empty cup again.

The defeat in his voice wounded my soul. This was the world that my beautiful Matthew had come from. My Matthew, who loved to smile and laugh, who was wicked smart and funny, who didn't think he was attractive, and believed in fairness to a fault. I ached to kiss him, hold him, tell him that all of that was in the past. He didn't have to fight for the right to be alive anymore; he deserved to be happy. I placed my hand on the table near where he was still holding the empty cup. I knew the unspoken rule. Much as I longed to touch him, to reassure him I'd never leave, never abandon him, I couldn't. Not here.

"All that matters is that you're here now. Vera did come, and she brought you to—" I wanted to say "me", that she brought you to me, instead I said, "The school where you could learn what made you unique."

Matt didn't respond, just sat there staring at my hand, my fingers less than an inch from his own. He released his cup, causing it to slide a short distance and leaving his hand on the table beside mine. Electricity arced between the hair's breadth of distance. The battle of whether to accept the comfort I'd extended or not warred on his face. A few heartbeats went by in silence, then he curled his fingers inward.

My heart sank. Forget envying other couple's ability to display affection publicly, I just wanted to comfort my boyfriend. He deserved to have that comfort, to be told constantly how much he was loved. A sudden shock rippled through my finger and I glanced down to discover Matt had reopened his hand and closed the fraction of the distance. The touch was nothing more than our fingertips grazing, but it was touch. I'd take the win. In a stroke of inspiration, I shadowed his hair back from his face. The move was light enough that it could have easily been a breeze from the door. Yet he looked up, snaring me with indescribably sad eyes.

"Anyway, enough about me." He withdrew his hand to resume picking at the crumbling mass that used to be a muffin. "What about you? Tell me about growing up in the UK. I know you at least grew up with your mom." He gave a half smile, no doubt recalling having spoken to her briefly himself.

"Okay," I began and leaned back, painfully aware of the distance between us. "I never knew my dad, and that's fine with me. I'm not sure I want to know anyone who could do what he did to my mom. She was completely devoted to him and he still left her all alone and pregnant. So, it was just me and her. But I couldn't ask for a better mother. You'll have to meet her sometime."

"I'd like that," he said quietly, staring into his empty cup again.

"Things weren't always easy, though. I know people think I've had a charmed childhood, but she worked really hard to give us a good life. It's difficult being a single mom in this world, especially with me as a son."

He snorted. "I refuse to believe you were some sort of terror growing up."

"I was a terror in other ways," I said with a playful grin. Something flashed in his eyes, but he said nothing. "What else? I've never been in a fight aside from the time I tried to get Kyle Stanton to stop pulling on Karla Lott's hair."

"What happened? Did the teacher yell at you?" he teased, clearly not believing I'd ever been in trouble a day in my life.

"No, she did."

He laughed. “You sure you’re not a knight? You seem to have a habit of coming to the rescue.”

“I do not ride around rescuing people,” I huffed.

“Sure you do,” he said warmly as the last of the ice thawed from his eyes.

“Are you telling the stories, or am I?”

He held up his hands in surrender and gestured for me to go on.

“It wasn’t until I was nine that my mom told me about my dad.”

“Why did she wait so long?”

“I think it was really hard for her. She loved him. What’s worse, she started by telling me I looked just like him.” My sigh ruffled the napkin beneath my cup. “It can’t be easy looking at someone every day that reminds you of the person you loved most. Honestly, if I hadn’t been in the picture, I wonder if she’d have continued on at all. She talks about him like he was the greatest love of her life.”

“Do you believe in that?”

"I believe in forever.” I traced the pattern on my mug while I wrestled with the resentment that typically sprouted when I spoke about my father. “He must have loved her back at least a little, because he told her what he was. Good thing too. I started manifesting early. Not as early as you apparently, but enough that she needed to take measures to keep us safe. We moved a few times until she found a place with a near enough supernatural community that I could get exposure to both worlds. Before that, I’d never met another supernatural. I might have been a little too eager.”

Matt’s lips twisted like he was fighting back a grin.

“Shut up.”

“I didn’t say anything.” His suppressed grin broke free, and he laughed.

“You were thinking it.”

“What was I thinking, Alex?” That was a double-edged question, and I was not about to dignify it with an answer.

"At any rate, it was awesome meeting all of those people, or it was until they found out I was a Shadow Demon. Then they started avoiding me like I caused the war, not some faceless demon none of them had ever met."

"How long have you known?"

"I mean, I guess forever. But my mom really helped with that because she knew what to look for."

"Not that."

I frowned, not following. Then I realized he was staring at the spot our hands had touched. "Also, pretty much forever." I was about to launch into how there were so many other sexualities besides gay or straight when he cut off my train of thought.

"Tell me about what's his face."

"Daniel?" I instantly regretted saying the name out loud.

A darkness passed behind Matt's eyes and his jaw tightened.

"I'd rather not talk about him. There are some betrayals you don't forgive." Matt knew very well that Daniel had cheated on me. "If you really must know, he's a narcissistic jerk and a bully," I finished hotly.

Matt's eyes widened before his gaze dropped to the massacred remains of his muffin and his shoulders caved inward.

Guilt itched beneath my skin. Of course, Matt would be curious about my ex. "I'm sorry. I shouldn't have snapped. It's just, he was never much of a friend and he made me feel weak. Ironic, considering he's only human."

Matt looked up sharply. "You're not weak. You're one of the strongest people I've ever met." The force of his words took me aback. I didn't realize Matt thought so highly of me.

"Let's get out of here before you break that muffin down to the molecular level." I indicated the pathetic remains of his half-eaten breakfast.

He chuckled and dusted his hands. "You're right, we should head back."

We both disposed of our trash before making our way back to the dorm. As we walked, we talked about the town and classes. Despite pointedly veering away from anything too heavy, I couldn't shake the feeling that our conversation at the coffeehouse was still bothering him. To be fair, it was still bothering me. I didn't like the idea of Matt comparing himself to my ex.

My thoughts must have been showing, because as we walked up to our door Matt asked, "Are you alright? You seem upset."

I glanced down the hall to make sure no one was around, then grabbed his wrist and shadowed both of us through the door. He was still holding his key ready when we appeared on the other side.

"Whoa, that was different," he said before I pressed him against the door, claiming his mouth with a hunger that had turned acute when I'd shadowed us. His key clattered heavily on the floor. Then his hands were on me, sliding beneath my shirt, clawing at my back, pulling me closer.

"You are nothing like Daniel. You're warm and tender and caring," I said between kisses. "I didn't know it was possible to love someone as much as I love you." He may not be willing to say it back, but his body responded with an alarming passion at the confession. There was a need in Matt that I'd happily spend the rest of my life trying to fulfill.

I yanked him away from the door and dragged him toward my room, shedding our clothes along the way. We slammed into the closed door, panting for breath, while I fumbled for the knob. Then we were stumbling to the bed, mindlessly bumping into anything and everything. The nightstand shook when we landed on the bed, bringing me out of my stupor long enough to grab supplies. Matt pulled me back for more devouring kisses, his tongue sweeping boldly into my mouth while his hands branded my skin.

I tangled my fingers in his hair and pulled his head back, not remotely surprised to find his eyes solid black with lust. Mine likely looked the same. "Top or bottom," I asked, my voice so husky it was nearly a growl.

"Bottom," he panted, without an ounce of hesitation.

I mashed our mouths back together, nipping at his lips before venturing across his jaw and down his neck. His resulting groan spurred me on and in seconds, I had lubed fingers pressing against his hole. He released a strangled whine that turned into a deep moan when I slipped inside and intentionally rubbed his prostate. "Damn, you're tight," I said through gritted teeth, adding another finger.

Matt clawed at my shoulders, bringing me closer until we met in another bruising kiss. He attacked my lips with a ferocity I echoed in my core while I continued to stretch him. Then he was gasping for air and shoving a condom at me.

I rocked back on my heels and held his gaze as I rolled it on. "Touch yourself," I ordered as I positioned myself at his entrance.

Gazes still locked, he wrapped a hand around his erection and stroked firmly. His back bowed off the bed as I thrust in one long drive, but he didn't release his hold. He managed a few faltering strokes before I removed his hand to lace our fingers and laid over him. Completely in sync, Matt wrapped his legs tightly around me while I relentlessly drove into him. Sweat glistened on both our chests, our breaths came in ragged gulps, and we still kept snatching at each other's lips.

Matt convulsed, and the warmth of his release surged between us. His ass clenched in time with his orgasm, and my ungodly pace faltered. I rammed into him a final time, then went still as my own ecstasy crested. I gave a couple half-hearted thrusts as I rode out the wave, then sagged on top of him. Rather than complain at the undoubtedly uncomfortable position, he peppered my sweat coated shoulders with kisses.

Once I'd caught my breath, I retrieved an abandoned shirt from the floor to clean us up. No longer sticky, we curled up, facing each other. "I think we might have a problem," I said jokingly as I brushed his gloriously mussed hair from his face.

His smile twinkled in his eyes. "Who says it's a problem?"

I chuckled and dropped my hand to the mattress between us. "Touche."

His hand joined mine, fingers intertwining. He lifted our joined hands to place a kiss on the back of mine. "Thank you."

"For what?"

"For being you."

I caressed his face with my free hand, heart melting. "Matt, I am more myself with you than I have ever been in my entire life." I leaned in to kiss him and to add weight to the words. He met me halfway, kissing me back, slow and deep. "I love you," I whispered against his lips. His only response was to hold me tighter and kiss me deeper.

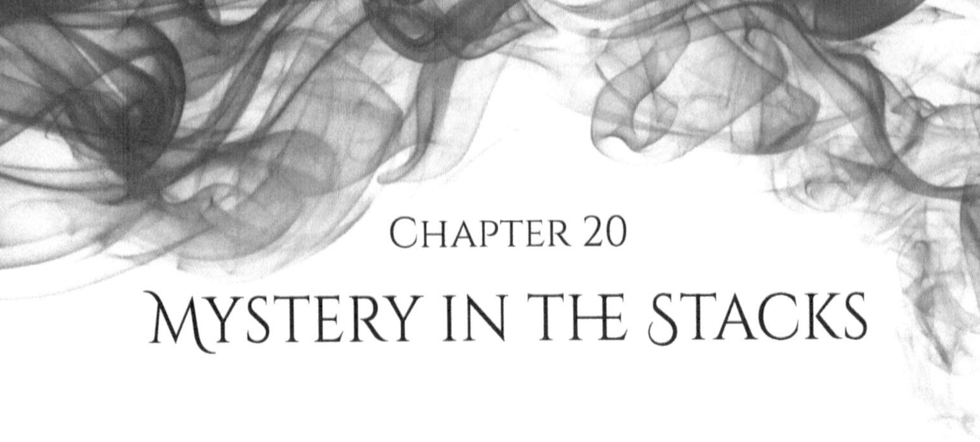

Chapter 20
Mystery in the Stacks

Matt

One of these days I was going to have to figure out how to tell Alex how I felt. Eventually he'd ask, and I had no clue what I was going to say. Unsurprisingly, that led me to the library. Much as I worried about being watched, it didn't change that I needed room to think and I seemed to do that best here. Maybe it was the quiet. Or perhaps it was the soft light. Could be that books didn't judge, didn't care who I was or where I came from.

My mind wandered as I trailed my fingers over spotless and dusty spines alike. For all that I hadn't wanted Alex to know about my past, I should have known better than to assume he'd reject me over it. But then, a lifetime of being told you were worthless, of having anything you held dear taken from you, didn't vanish overnight. I reached the end of the current stack and sighed before aimlessly wandering to the next.

It *was* nice to learn a little more about him. I was never sure how to ask people about themselves when I wasn't interested in reciprocating. Luckily, Alex didn't have that problem. I wondered if he was serious about me eventually meeting his mom. If I was being honest with myself, I didn't exactly have an outstanding track record with moms, but for the first time in years, I was actually... optimistic? Maybe I *would* get to meet her and maybe she'd like me. Alex seemed pretty positive she would.

I smiled to myself as I recalled the way his face lit up anytime he talked about his mom. Anyone that could inspire that kind of reaction from him, I wanted to meet. Not like Daniel. My nails scratched the wooden shelf. I had zero desire to ever meet him. He sounded like a total dick. Asking Alex about him had been a mistake.

My shelf hit its end, and I glanced around to see where my musings had taken me. The sign on the stack across the way read *History - Demons 1300-1800.* I thought again about the wild idea I'd shared with Alex before, about him being part of the Warde line. It wasn't wholly impossible, considering the only thing Alex knew about his father was that he was a Shadow Demon. If his dad *had* been a Warde, then maybe he'd left to protect Alex's mom. Fanatics were always bad news, *especially* when people thought they were gone.

I chewed on my lip while I considered the stack across from me. Maybe I could find more information on what became of Matthias Warde and his demon lover today. Thus far, I'd only uncovered the demon's name, nothing else. Even the demonology where I'd first found her was vague about her origins and there was nothing after. That part made me a little anxious. Typically, when people disappeared like that from history, they were dead. Of course, demons were a little different. It wasn't uncommon for demons to fall off the grid for whole swatches of time, only to reappear somewhere else.

Finally, I veered away from the stacks toward the rows of study tables. A few were occupied, though not as many as I would have expected. Fortunately, my usual one was vacant. I slid into the chair, my mind still whirling with potential places to search for answers, or at least clues. I wasn't even sure why it mattered so much, except I had this burning *need* to know. Maybe Alex was right, and I *was* obsessed. I'd already searched through several demon histories and come up empty. I could always return to the dorm where both the ancient history and Matthias Warde's journal were... and Alex.

I groaned inwardly and dropped my head in my hands. This couldn't possibly be as hard as I was making it. *Normal* people didn't have a problem telling their partners how they felt. Why was it so hard for me? Alex made it look easy, like it was the most natural thing in the world. But how could I admit to him I was absolutely terrified about how strongly I felt without sounding like a total basket case?

Frustrated with myself and the whole situation, I surged out of my chair and stalked back toward the *Demon History* shelves. I was nearly there when I had a better idea than combing back through books I'd already searched—I'd search the records for the Wars of Power. It wasn't until I was standing before the truly massive collection of history that I realized I'd never been over here. Where the hell did I even start?

With an agitated growl, I snagged a couple of volumes from the start of the war and some from the end. Maybe I'd get lucky and find a decent thread to follow. It wasn't like I needed detailed accounts of the various factions or how they tore each other apart. I needed a list of the key players, starting with the originals, which had been noticeably absent from my other research.

Rather than heft my stack all the way to my table only to have to come back when they didn't work out, I plopped on the floor. I cracked open one book at random, then almost gave up right there when I spied the heading of the first section—*Primordial Power.* How could I have forgotten that demons didn't even have a set race until *after* the Chaos Wars? Before that, they were basically masses of energy wreaking havoc, mostly with each other. And why the hell were there so many "wars" in the Wars of Power? Wasn't one enough?

My irritation growing, I swapped the volume for one that covered a later period. If I could just find a reference point that made *sense*, I might actually get somewhere. But with each ancient volume I scanned, that task felt more impossible. One thing was evident—the original demons got *around.* Five useless books later, I shifted my focus to volumes that covered the conclusion of the wars. Maybe I could find a list of surviving demons instead.

Fairly confident in my new tactic, I resumed scanning with renewed gusto. I'd finally found a promising thread when nearby voices broke my concentration. I picked myself up, body sore from sitting on the floor for so long. For once it seemed like I was going to be doing the shushing instead of the other way around. Holding my place in the book with a dusty finger, I abandoned my nest of books and made my way toward the noise with a scowl. As I approached, the voices got clearer until I realized they were in the next aisle over parallel to where I was standing.

"Are you sure he said Warde?"

I froze and stared at the shelves separating us.

"For fuck's sake, I don't know what the old coot called him. He said someone was snooping around the library, so we're in the library."

Curiosity and vindicated paranoia thawed my limbs. Careful not to make noise, I kept pace with them.

"Be quiet," a familiar voice hissed. "We don't want anyone knowing we're here."

"Why not?"

"Because, you idiot, they might be the one we're looking for."

I struggled to place the two voices, but wasn't having much luck while they were whispering.

"Is it true he's in our class?"

"That's a really dumb question." Recognition tickled at my senses so close I could touch it.

"Oh, right." They were silent a minute, then asked, "Can you believe there's been someone hiding who they really are?"

"Would you keep it down? You want everyone to know?"

"I was just asking. To think, we've been training next to someone playing for the other team this whole time." *Alex.*

"Don't get me started. I still haven't decided whether to take them to Thomas or take care of the abomination myself." The distinct sound of knuckles cracking had fear spiking through my chest.

Barely controlling my panic, I carefully shifted books to get a look at the owner of the hateful statement. *George.* Why was I not surprised?

"You don't suppose it's Ellie, do you?"

I shifted my gaze. *And Kyle. Of course.*

"You better hope not. There aren't enough female Shadow Demons as it is, and they'll kill whoever it is when we find them."

They don't know who they are looking for. I was almost too scared to breathe as I put the books back. One at a time, they slowly resumed their rightful places.

"But why?"

"Something about purifying the bloodline. It doesn't matter what Thomas' reasons are, we can't stand for something like that either. It's not natural. Honestly, I'm glad that he'll kill whoever it is rather than try to convert them. We can't tolerate someone like that in our ranks."

I nearly swallowed my tongue. In my mounting anxiety, I misjudged the angle of my current book and an adjacent book landed on another with a muffled thud. I grimaced and held perfectly still.

"Did you hear that?" George hissed, barely loud enough to be heard.

"You're letting Thomas get to you. He's a conspiracy nut if you ask me," Kyle sneered.

"Watch it. That conspiracy nut can—"

I was too busy making a dash for the exit to catch the rest. The campus whizzed past me in a blur of color, making me regret not practicing shadow walking more. I wasn't sure why I was in such a hurry. I knew for a fact that Alex was in the dorm. At least, that was where I'd left him. But I needed to see it for myself. Needed to know he was safe. George had more than one lackey and any number of them could be on the hunt. My stomach churned, and I ran faster.

By the time I shadowed through our door, I'd forgotten about why I'd gone to the library in the first place and nearly pitched face first when I came to an abrupt halt in the living room. Relief flooded through me at seeing Alex standing safely in the kitchen. Thoughts raced through my mind faster than I could grab them. *We needed to be more careful. I needed to tell him how I felt. We should run. I couldn't lose him. I lost everyone I cared about.*

"Matt?" Alex finished drying his hands and set the dish towel on the counter. "Are you alright?" He stepped toward me.

"I..." The words died. My heart felt like someone was trying to tear it apart. Why couldn't I tell him he meant everything to me?

His eyebrows pinched together. "Hey, what's wrong?"

"I..." Why couldn't I say it? It was three damn words.

He took another step, worry now clear on his face.

"I'm happy," I blurted. A smile teased his lips and the knife in my heart twisted. My world would be so dark without him.

"O-kay, I'm glad to hear it," he said, laughter teasing the edges as he reached for me.

I grabbed his hand. "*You* make me happy." My heart was going to beat itself out. His eyes softened and his concern melted away into a smile determined to steal what little breath I had left.

"You make me happy too, Matt," he said softly, continuing his reach with the captured hand to cup my face.

I closed my eyes and leaned into the caress. When his lips brushed against mine, I returned the gentle kiss while a renegade tear ran down my cheek. He couldn't know. If he did... I broke the kiss and wrapped him in my arms, holding him close.

"Are you sure you are alright?" He tried to pull back, but I tightened my hold, using the movement to wipe away the traitorous tear, and buried my face in his neck. "O-Okay."

The scent of lavender flowed around me as he squeezed back. I'd do anything to keep him safe. Literally anything. If Alex knew there was danger—real trouble—he'd want to do something about it. He wouldn't lie low. Wouldn't wait for things to blow over. He'd want to confront them or, heaven forbid, *tell* someone. I knew George's type. He'd absolutely kill Alex if he found him and it sounded like this mysterious Thomas would do the same. I couldn't let that happen, wouldn't let that happen.

"I'm fine. It's just been a weird day." I swiped another kiss, then made my way to the couch.

He sat beside me, worry once again in his eyes. "Do you want to talk about it?"

"Um..." I floundered for something believable. As it was, I was dubious about my ability to lie to him. He seemed to have a gift for ferreting out my secrets. "I went to the library."

"Need to think about something?" He gave me a knowing look.

Shit. I'm already failing miserably.

"I... found something about our demon."

"Sopteală?"

"Yeah, her." I took out the last book I'd been holding before I heard George and Kyle talking. "Turns out she's a direct descendant of an original. At first, I thought she might actually *be* an original because I couldn't find anything at all. Then I found this." I passed him the book.

"What made you think to check in these old things?" he asked, scanning the page.

I shrugged and slid my hand onto his lap beneath the book. I didn't even realize I'd done it until he laced our fingers together and gave mine a gentle squeeze. "The only wars anyone seems willing to talk about are the Wars of Power. We know the Demon Wars took place after that. I just back-tracked. Starting with a survivor list from the last great war just made sense. All the commanders and generals were substantial levels. Those would definitely be mentioned if they'd been around," I added, leaning into him. Here, at least, we were safe.

He snaked an arm around me as he leaned back, the book still in his other hand. "You would tell me if something was bothering you, right?"

"Of course." The lies kept coming. I needed Alex to be safe, and I was willing to do whatever it took to make that happen. The real question was how. I needed to find out what those jerks knew. Figure out who the hell the Thomas was and what his beef was. I couldn't protect Alex from an enemy I didn't know.

The thought of intentionally spending time with George brought the taste of bile to my mouth. I shoved it down and tried to determine the best way to go about it. Worming my way into their group after Battle Tactics was probably my best bet. But it would have to be after Alex left. Which would make me late for my next class. Others would likely suffer as well. While I was enjoying my classes and might actually be *good* at some of them, keeping Alex safe far outweighed my desire to stay enrolled.

It felt wrong to be thinking about how to deceive Alex while curled up next to him. Logically, I should work on putting more distance between us. Already, we were slipping up whenever we went into town for the day. I'd been stupid to think no one would be watching us there. Even the casual touches would need to stop. I couldn't risk me doing something stupid, because I couldn't keep my hands off of him. Not when it could get him killed. As for at the dorm... I couldn't, not yet. There was no way I could quit Alex outright; it would break me.

"Huh, I never realized Vera's husband was a Xiander. That makes more sense," he mused while he steadily stroked my arm.

"I think I'm over all of this." I scooted closer, though there wasn't anywhere else to really go. "We found what we were looking for. We don't need to keep searching."

"You don't want to so see what happened to their child?" He tried to look at me, but I refused to cooperate. If he saw my face, there wasn't a doubt in my mind he'd know I was lying.

"I'd rather..." I started, then changed what I was going to say. "I just don't want to go to the library anymore. You were right. I was obsessed. But all these people are long gone. It was silly to get so wrapped up." I tightened my fingers around his hand.

I couldn't do this. Of course, I wanted to know what happened. We'd discovered a massive cover-up, and the child was proof. Plus, being part demon, the kid could even still be alive or have children of their own. But if giving up this ridiculous quest meant Alex would stay here where it was safe, then it was a no-brainer.

He chuckled. "So *that's* what all of this is about." I fought his attempts to make me look at him, but per usual, he won. "You know you're allowed to have hobbies, Matt. Our relationship doesn't have to be all or nothing."

The merriment in his eyes made me want to scream. I wanted to shout at him to stop being so damn understanding. It wasn't like that at all. Maybe it *would* be easier to tell him. He'd just keep pressing til I caved.

"I love you, Matt," he said unexpectedly.

The knife in my heart drove home.

Chapter 21
Awkward Answers

Alexi

The main entrance to Mysterio College shut behind me with a clang. I groaned as I realized I'd forgotten all about the question I'd been dying to ask Vera. If I thought it could wait any longer, I'd have risked asking her during our next Battle Tactics class, but there was no guarantee she'd be there. As it was, she'd missed all of last week. It was now or never. Resigned to being late for my next class, I turned to go back inside.

Mere yards from her office, I heard voices coming from the classroom we'd been using this term. Worried someone had snagged Vera's attention before I could, I peered through the open door. To my surprise, Matt was still there, though I could have sworn he'd hightailed it out first thing and more alarming, he was talking with George and company. Concern blossomed in my chest and I took a step towards the room, fully prepared to intervene before talking could turn into fighting. Then Matt laughed. I froze, not entirely sure what to do.

"Roman?"

I jumped and spun around. "H-hi, Ms. Scry."

She rolled her eyes. "For the love of Nyx, call me Vera, or I'm telling Matt you were spying on him."

I blanched. I wasn't spying. Was I? Matt was free to do as he liked. My gaze slid toward the voices still emanating from the room behind me. But since when did that include spending time with George?

"Can I help you with something?"

"Um... yeah." I wanted nothing more than to march into that room and demand to know why Matt looked downright chummy with the trio of bullies. But at Vera's implication that I was spying, that didn't strike me as the wisest course of action.

"And that would be..." Vera prompted.

I cleared my throat and returned my attention to her. "I had a question about shadowing."

"You're going to need to be a little more specific. Why don't we talk in my office?" She lead the way down the hall and stopped a few doors down at her office.

I looked back into the room one last time and followed, closing the office door behind me.

"So, what's this question?" She plopped into a leather chair that looked rarely sat in behind a heavy desk riddled with papers. Despite her name on it, she didn't really look like she belonged there. Vera was a warrior, not a scholar or diplomat, a *warrior*. She'd done equally incredible and horrific things. But seeing her now, with her red hair in a frizzy ponytail and her casual attire the furthest thing from professional, it was difficult to reconcile the horror stories she'd inspired.

How could someone who looked barely older than *me* be responsible for such heinous acts? Perhaps Matt was right, and she really was only a product of her situation. It was also entirely possible that the stories had intentionally been exaggerated to cultivate an aura of fear and mystery. My mind strayed back to Matt laughing with George.

What's he doing?

It wasn't until Vera spoke again that I realized I'd been standing there, lost in my thoughts. "It hasn't been long." She leaned back in her chair, causing the leather to squeak, and steepled her fingers. "Frankly, I'm just glad they aren't at each other's throats anymore. I believe I have you to thank for that."

"What? Oh, sure."

"Now, what did you actually want to know?" she asked again.

I'd considered a thousand different ways to ask, but the most logical was also the most direct. "What's it like shadowing someone else?"

"Considering how adept you are and the fact that you are well ahead of the rest of the class, I'm going to assume you're not asking for the theory of how. You've already done it and want to know why it's not always the same."

I nodded. While I hadn't exactly shadowed as many people as she believed, shadowing Matt that day definitely qualified as different.

"Gabriel would tell me I need to let you come to the answer on your own, but I always found that trying and a tad tedious when he did it, so I'll spare you." She leaned forward to rest her arms on the desk, mindless of the papers beneath. "The experience is unique depending on how intimately you know the person being shadowed. For example, if you shadowed a family member, it might feel like a reassuring hug, whereas a stranger wouldn't really feel like much at all. Then there's shadowing lovers. That feels a bit more like..."

I held up my hand to cut her off. I got the picture, and it definitely answered my question. "But why?"

She shrugged, reminding me of Matt. "Who can say really? When it comes down to it, we're using our own essence to fold someone else into the shadow world. It's possible it correlates to the level we would want to protect them, but I suspect it's much deeper than that. Sadly, a lot of what we do and why is still a mystery, even to ourselves. There's no science behind this, only instinct and inclination."

It sounded a lot like how Matt talked about using his powers. My thoughts strayed back to him in the other room. Was he still there? Why was he there at all? Would he tell me the truth if I asked? I had a very strong suspicion the answer to that last one was "No".

"You shadowed Matt, didn't you?" I blinked at the sound of his name and looked at her. She smiled knowingly. "I'd like to say I saw it all on my own, but apparently, I can be dense with things like this. Gabriel's actually the one who pointed it out."

"Gabriel Xiander has been here?"

A malicious smile curled on her face. "He won't be pleased at all that someone figured that out. He's actually been here several times to check in on how things are going. It seems he could relate."

I looked at her, confused. *Why, in Nyx's name, would the son of an original be interested in some lowly students?* "Relate to what?"

"Pining after someone who doesn't have a clue."

I shifted in my chair. Matt wouldn't like this.

"It's okay, Alexi. I'm glad to see he came around. Like I said before, you've been an exceptionally positive influence on him. Granted, when I assigned the rooms, I *was* hoping that you'd rub off on him. I just wasn't expecting it to be so literal," she added with a crooked smile.

My jaw dropped. This was *not* how teachers spoke with students.

The mischief left her face, and her expression softened. "I'm not sure how much he's shared with you, but he's had a very rough life. The world has not been kind to Matt. Admittedly, when I dropped him off with Jeffrey, I despaired that he'd ever find peace." She looked down at her hands. "It's hard to let go of the anger, especially when most of it's aimed at yourself." Seemed Gabriel wasn't the only one able to relate.

"Why did you do it?" The words were out before I could reconsider them.

She took a deep breath, and it came out a sigh. “At first, because I was told to. We didn’t know better.” Her gaze flicked up. “That’s not an excuse, it’s a fact. Namas was the only one of us who’d grown up in the supernatural world and he had his own evils to fight.” She shook her head. “After a while, we suspected something was off. The orders became more aggressive, more final. By then, though, the damage was done. Then, of course, there’s the whole matter of demons don’t do well with heartbreak.”

“I thought you loved Gabriel.”

Her smile turned warm at the mention of her husband, then sad again. “I didn’t always. My break up with Dorian, while mostly mutual, was not exactly pleasant. I fell into the darkness and had no desire to come back out. The darkness is a living thing that can reach back. Never forget that.” Her look speared me to the chair. I’d never considered that my essence could hurt me. “The things I did are unforgivable, and the only person I have to blame is myself. I enjoyed being the Terror of the East. There was power in that. And I had the rage to carry it through.”

I wanted to ask how she did finally come back, but chose a different route. “Backing up a bit. Dorian—as in—*Dorian Valens?* The greatest healer of our time?”

"Yeah. We actually went to school together—we all did. Except for Namas. I'm still not sure where he crawled out of." She laughed like it was an old joke.

Well, that was a surprise. I’d always thought the Regency had pulled the Shadows from around the world.

"I can see you thinking how preposterous that is. Agreed. To hear the Regency talk about it, power attracts power. Guess that's how they found us." It was weird listening to her so casually mention the organization that had oppressed the supernatural community for decades. Then again, she’d just admitted her perspective on the entire thing was very different.

"Sounds like a mixed blessing."

"I suppose. Hey, do you mind if I ask you some questions about Matt? You don't have to answer, but I hope you will at least consider it."

I looked at her warily. "What *kind* of questions?"

"He still seems to struggle in class. I don't understand. I've seen him in a fight and he's a natural, yet in class, he's a totally different person. It’s almost as if he’s suppressing his own abilities."

I was inclined to agree with her, but then the full nature of what she said sunk in. "You've seen Matt fight?" I didn't care if I told Matt I would be more open to forgiving Vera, if she was complicit in that damnable fight club....

"He was fighting several supernaturals when I went to pick him up. I confess, I may have let it play out longer than I should have, but I was curious to see how he would handle himself."

"Oh."

Her gaze narrowed. "What did you think I was talking about?"

"Nothing. I was just surprised, is all."

"You and me both. He took out a Spiculo, a Sprite, and an Ick Demon. There's no telling what would have happened to that third-rate fire demon if I hadn't intervened."

I swallowed past a sudden tightness in my throat. Matt hadn't mentioned Oliver was a fire demon or what any of the others had been. Sprites were no joke and could put demons to shame for cruelty.

"Anyway, I wanted to know if he was doing better with shadowing outside of class. The classroom environment isn't really conducive to every type of learner."

"Yes," I answered honestly. "He shadows around the dorm all the time, though he never believes me when I tell him."

"Huh. What else?"

"He has a particular knack for shadow spells."

"That's surprising." She tapped a finger against her chin.

"Why?"

She shrugged. "It isn't common that demons are good at both physical manifestations *and* spells."

"He is *very* good. He's already mastered portals and how to hide them." I considered her a moment. "My turn to ask a question. Did you convince some fifth year to loan him a Shadow Grimoire?"

She gave me a sheepish look. "It's actually mine, but I didn't think he'd take it from me. Am I right in assuming that he still hasn't forgiven me for abandoning him in a warded room?"

"Wow, you really did that? Matt told me, but I wasn't sure I fully believed it."

"It wasn't my finest moment, and it really was for his own protection. So I take that as a yes?"

"Definitely, but I don't think it's the warded part he's still upset about."

She snorted. "He seemed pretty pissed about it to me."

"You took charge of him and then left him *alone.*"

It took her a moment, then understanding dawned. "Ah, I see. I'm not really sure how I can make that up to him."

"I'm sure you'll find a way," I said. And I had no doubt that she would. Vera Scry was a persistent woman if she was nothing else.

"Thanks for the vote of confidence." She rolled her eyes, but didn't seem totally put out. "One more question, then I'll let you go. How did you ever quiet his rage?"

"I kissed him." I clapped a hand over my mouth, but it was too late. She released a genuine laugh, and I started to understand how she'd accumulated so many allies, despite her notoriety.

"Relax, Roman, this room is warded. No one can hear anything we say." She stood. "I appreciate your honesty, and I'm glad Matt finally found a friend. Something tells me that's a first for him. You really are good together."

I gave her a shy smile. There was something to be said for someone recognizing our relationship outside of our four walls. "Thank you."

"I only speak the truth. I'm also pretty sure you're the only reason he passed his classes that first semester. If you ever have other questions, just call. Office hours aren't really my thing." She winked, then held out her hand. I passed her my phone, and she quickly keyed something. Her phone vibrated against the desk from where she'd set it earlier and she snatched it up, simultaneously silencing it. "There, now I'll know who's calling me."

I reclaimed my phone and pushed up from the chair. "Thanks for the uh... conversation."

"Anytime," she said, waving her phone.

With a smile, I turned to leave. If Matt was still around, maybe I could walk him to his next class.

"Oh, one more thing." Vera stood and walked around the massive desk to lean on it. "Gabriel wanted me to warn you. Demons can get a little... obsessed when we're into someone. It's normally pretty manageable if uncomfortable, but things get a little dicier when it's with another Shadow Demon."

I adjusted my backpack and frowned. "How so?"

"Remember how I said the darkness was a living thing? When our control slips, we can subconsciously reach out to the other person with our essence." She rolled her eyes and added, "It can make for some pretty uncomfortable situations. Not to mention how the line between fantasy and reality can get a bit blurred. So, you know, watch the lucid daydreams, unless you want to accidentally manifest your boyfriend or other things..." Her face reddened.

"I'm not sure what—"

Her phone rang, cutting me off. "I need to get that. I'll see you in class next week."

"Next week? Does this have something to do with Cara missing class?" I might have been inclined to think she'd just skipped, but she was the type of person to show up to class with the plague.

Vera's face pinched. "I really need to take this."

I nodded. No sooner did I turn to leave than she'd answered the call.

"What have you got? *Nothing* is not an acceptable answer," she growled.

My pace quickened, her blatant frustration chasing me out the door. With a sigh of relief that her ire wasn't directed at me, I shut the door behind me. As I walked back to the classroom, I wondered f Matt had ever experienced pulling at another Shadow Demon's essence. I certainly hadn't. Except the room was empty. Dejected, I made my way with dragging steps to my next class.

Chapter 22
Chimera's Grave

Matt

George Cartwright was a disgusting creature, and his goons were worse. Once again, I toyed with the idea of simply beating all of them to a pulp and calling it a day. The only problem with *that* was I still didn't know who this mysterious Thomas was or how he fit into everything. Until then, my options were limited to worming my way into their group.

It took a full week of staying after Battle Tactics, blowing off lunch with Alex—*twice*, and being late to class four times before I *finally* made headway. I wasn't great at lying to Alex about what I was up to, which left me doing something I hated even more—avoiding him. But it was that or risk spilling the truth and possibly getting him killed. The sooner I had what I needed from George, the sooner I could leave his foul sense of humor behind and return to Alex.

"So, what are we doing?" I asked as I joined Kyle and Travis at the end of the new fraternity row.

They shared a look, then said in unison, "Waiting." Their creepy smiles made my skin crawl.

I barely didn't shudder. "Cut the shit. I thought we were actually *going* somewhere." Given the meet-up spot, I was worried it was going to be a kegger. Given how long it had been since I'd done any kind of drinking, I didn't see that ending well for me.

"Quit your bitching." George joined us, his hair combed back like some old-school greaser and hands shoved into his jean pockets. "We're going somewhere all right. Taken me months to get the invite for this place. Real exclusive."

"You really got it?" Travis asked, practically beaming at George.

His mouth stretched into a toothy grin. "I really got it. Password, new location, and all."

"Fuck yeah! You're the fucking king!" Kyle shouted, pumping his fist in the air. A sentiment, Travis echoed equally enthusiastically.

I mentally rolled my eyes. The two were worse than leeches the way they sucked up to George; it was a wonder they hadn't bled him dry yet. Suddenly, George's words registered, and I narrowed my eyes. "Where *exactly* are we going?"

"I believe you're familiar with the place," George snickered without elaborating.

The unease in my gut grew. If I asked again, this time with more details, I risked being ejected from the group or being jumped by the three. Neither got me the info I needed. So I kept my trap shut and diligently trailed after him when he set off... away from the frat houses. With each step we got closer and closer to the edge of campus, my trepidation increased. I debated for the zillionth time if I might have better luck beating Thomas's identity out of the three, starting with George. Did I already know him? Was he in any of our classes? Was Thomas even his real name? Sadly, I didn't expect hitting George would provide any of those answers. Far more likely it would blow up in my face. The smart course would be to stick to the plan of infiltrating them.

Abruptly, I realized we'd officially left university grounds. Distant lampposts made bubbles of yellow in the night that didn't come close to touching our path. I glanced around for any kind of clue to help get my bearings without success. Then a large door came into view, illuminated by the saddest excuse of an overhead light I'd ever seen. The buzzing of the struggling bulb grew louder and revealed the door to be made of rusted metal, much like what you'd find on... a warehouse.

Alarm cleaved into my chest like a great axe, and I nearly tripped over my feet in my hurry to stop. This wasn't happening. No way had George gotten an *invitation* to the bruiser club. That wasn't how it worked. They recruited you. He might pick fights twenty-four-seven, but that didn't make him a fighter. Not like me. Cold that had nothing to do with the chill in the air slithered through my veins. *Like me.* They must have learned that I used to come here. Likely from Eric. Any chance that I might have been wrong went up in smoke the second George pounded on the metal door and a slot slid back to reveal a pair of yellow eyes.

"Password."

George opened his mouth and stalled. Then he whirled on Kyle and Travis, hissing under his breath, "Fuck, I forgot it."

"It wasn't written down?" Travis asked, earning himself a scathing look.

“No, I didn’t fucking write it down, dumbass. It’s against the rules.”

Stupid rule, if you ask me,” Kyle chipped in unhelpfully.

“It started with a C-H.” He turned back to the door and waiting eyes. “Cherub's Noose?”

The yellow eyes blinked without answering, then the slot started to close.

Somehow, I kept my exasperated sigh to myself as I stepped past the trio of morons. The eye still visible zeroed in on me, and though I couldn’t see anything else, I still registered their surprise. I may not have known the club was going to relocate, but I *did* know the cycle of passwords. “Chimera's Grave.”

The door swung open, but my feet remained rooted while I fought the urge to vomit. Then hard claps on my back, coupled with cheers, forced me forward. Never had I expected to find myself in this horrible place again. Alex wouldn't forgive this. I closed my eyes and took a fateful step into the chaos. I was doing this *for* Alex.

George gave me an appraising look. "So Otto was right. You *have* been here before. Hey, Kyle, go find him. He said he wanted to know when we got here."

Knowing I’d been right about Otto being the one to approach them didn’t make me feel any better. If anything, it made me feel worse. If Otto had seen me with these assholes, what else had he seen? Had he been the one watching me and Alex in the library? Did he know who Alex was to me? I tried to block out the trio’s triumphant cheers and the blood lust filling the room so I could think. Then I heard the last voice I wanted to hear.

"Well, well, well, what do we have here?" That hiss could only belong to one person.

Reluctantly, I turned to face Neese. The wyvern—because I’d finally figured that out—did that weird slithery-walk thing until he was right beside me and far too close for comfort. “Looksss like our ssscraper has returned to usss after all.”

"Hey, man. Kyle just went to find Eric." George angled his thumb at the crowd currently cheering around the ring.

"Ssso, who's fighting tonight?" Neese shifted his gaze to me and I glared back. "You look like you've healed up. Though you are sssmaller than I remember."

"We just came to watch," George whined.

Neese gave him a toothy grin that sent shivers down my spine. "Oh, you can, but sssomeone has to participate. Those are the rules."

George's brow furrowed. "Otto didn’t mention anything about that."

"I didn't? Funny. Must have slipped my mind." Otto joined the group, looking every bit as imposing as I remembered, and gave me a sinister grin. "But, yeah, them's the rules."

I wanted more than anything to be back in the dorm with Alex, curled up on the couch and watching a boring movie. My heart ached for it just at the thought, but that didn't look like it was going to be happening anytime soon. George was a night forsaken imbecile, and they'd tricked him to get me here. The only upside was that if I was with George, then George wasn't looking for Alex.

I pulled my shirt over my head and tossed it at Travis. He nearly dropped it as I stepped forward. "You got what you wanted. I'm here. Who's it going to be tonight, Neese?"

It didn't seem possible for him to look any eviler. "I'm pretty sure Singe has been eager for a rematch since last time."

It would have to be fucking Carl. I'd have to be extra careful; I couldn't afford to get any marks on me if I had a prayer of keeping this from Alex. That meant not getting cocky and keeping my guard up. Given how much I'd improved in my abilities since the last time I'd been here, staying out of reach shouldn't be too difficult.

"Fine. When?" I asked, rolling my shoulders to loosen up.

"How about now?"

Without a word, I made my way to the center of the room with George and the others trailing after me, sounding so excited it made me nauseous. I doubted they'd be so excited if Neese demanded one of *their* hides. But then, this had never been about them. That much I knew. It was about getting me back under Neese's thumb, officially making me collateral in my quest to keep Alex safe.

"Yo, Singe, get your molten ass out here! Your favorite person is here to see you," Otto called out in his booming voice. The crowd erupted into a cacophony when I stepped into the ring. The golden goose had returned.

I eyed the perimeter warily while I waited for Carl. I'd be staying far away from that. Last thing I needed was electric shock on top of everything else. At last, the Fire Demon pushed his way into the arena. By now, the audience was practically foaming at the mouth, including my own unfortunate companions. My jaw tightened at seeing all the eager leers. I hated this place.

"Thought you'd never come back," Carl snickered, cracking his thick neck.

"What can I say? I missed your sparkling personality." I didn't really want to rile him up, but it'd be stranger if I didn't goad him at all. Everyone would expect me to live up to my former reputation. A task made doubly tricky because I couldn't afford to be reckless, couldn't risk returning to Alex covered in evidence of my broken promise.

The Fire Demon cracked flaming knuckles together. "I'm going to enjoy this."

"Just make sure you don't finish too soon."

The resulting chorus of 'Oohs' rippled around us and a column of flame shot from the top of Carl's head, followed by two more from his hands directed at me. I calmly shadowed out and waited for him to stop. This wouldn't last nearly long enough if he was already losing his temper. Another spurt of flame, this one lashing out like a whip. I sidestepped the misguided attack and shadowed again for good measure. The feel of after burn still fresh in my mind from our last encounter.

He abandoned the whip tactic and reverted to the columns. People around us shouted as the inferno got too close for comfort. Blood on their clothes was fine, just not actual burns or marks. They were here for other people's suffering, not their own. I shadowed closer to him while he focused on controlling the attack.

"Stand and fight, runt!" he roared, manifesting a club of fire. I dodged the wild swing and buried my fist in his gut. He grunted, and the flames sputtered as his concentration wavered.

"What's the matter, Carl? I would've thought you'd have practiced more after I whooped your ass last time." I spun and kicked his feet out from under him. He went down in a heap reminiscent of smoldering coal.

Many of the onlookers here would've kicked him while he was down. No doubt including my current choice in company. Carl may have been a terrible fighter with no control, but *no one* deserved to be beaten when they were down.

"Come on. Are you going to get up or are you taking a power nap?" I danced a couple of steps back in case he blew his top again. "Maybe you should change your name from Singe to Burnout."

"I'm going to incinerate you, you mouthy bastard." He recovered faster than I expected, and a stream of fire shot across the space, searing my side.

"Son of a bitch!" I bellowed. Besides the fact that it burned like hell, Alex was *definitely* going to notice that. Furious, I warped the surrounding shadows, cutting off his flow of oxygen, and extinguished him.

His jaw dropped as the flames abruptly guttered out, then released a grunt when my foot plowed into his side. He stumbled and tried to get his arms up, but without his fire to keep me at bay, there was no stopping me from wailing on him. It wouldn't take him long to recover and relight. Then he'd be a wild card, making it imperative that I kept him unbalanced.

Thankfully, I was a lot faster than even he realized. I landed blow after blow in a relentless fury, shadowing out at least half of the time. His forearms turned black, although I couldn't tell if it was from bruising or because that was all I could see. He still hadn't landed another shot when I gave him the final hit that sent him sprawling.

I stood in the center of the ring, panting more from rage than exertion. Sound gradually seeped into my awareness, followed by colors other than obsidian. The deafening roar pushed against the rafters. Someone snatched me out of the ring and I stumbled to a stop a few feet clear of the raucous crowd.

"When Otto told me you were the club's prize fighter, I didn't believe it. But damn! I've never seen anything like that. You were incredible."

"Why would you ever stop coming here?" Travis asked, looking a little high. He might be, for all I knew. I didn't really *know* any of them, nor did I want to.

I scanned the far wall until I found the stall where salves could be had and made my way over. To my surprise, it was the same witch as the last time, Misty. She eyed me just as appreciatively as before, and I barely restrained from sneering.

"Fancy meeting you again. Thought that fight with Granite would be the end of you. I guess you found someone else to play doctor with," she said with what I was sure she thought was a sexy smile that did nothing to eliminate my scowl. "Fine, have it your way." She reached for the familiar container of burn salve. Before she could hand it over, though, Neese joined us.

"No healing for the prodigal bruiser."

I looked up at him sharply.

He narrowed his slitted eyes and curled his lip. "Consider it the price of admission after your last terrible performance. As for you three, the deal stands. So long as he fights like he's supposed to, you can keep coming without stepping in yourselves."

I ripped my shirt from Travis and slipped it on, causing the burn on my side to flare angrily. I'd have to hide it as long as possible so it could heal more. That and come up with a reasonable explanation for when Alex inevitably discovered it.

George grabbed me by the neck and led us all over to the side. "Hear that, boys? We get to come back and Matty here gets to pummel everything in sight."

"Hey is that skanky witch here every week?" Kyle asked, nodding toward the healing stand.

Travis guffawed. "Oh man, she was practically begging for it."

"I'll give her something to beg for," Kyle responded, grabbing his dick through his jeans.

I did my best to tune them out. This was my worst nightmare. Neese had found a way to get me back in the ring, and George had unwittingly played right into his hands. There wasn't a chance in hell I'd get out as easily as I had the last time. And I had a sinking feeling that Neese would make sure I paid dearly for every fight I'd missed.

Travis shoved me, and I shot him a glare. "Easy, man. I was just asking if you'd ever tap that. She's obviously into you."

"Yeah, coming back might give you a shot at redemption," George chimed in. "She seemed pretty eager to *doctor* you up." They all snickered.

I didn't care what they expected of me. That was one line I wouldn't cross. Rejoining the fight club was one thing, but there were some betrayals you just didn't forgive.

Chapter 23
Dream a Little Dream

Alexi

I took my time packing up the books from my last tutoring session of the day, then headed into the early evening. With fall in full swing and winter fast approaching, the campus grounds were already swathed in darkness punctuated by strategically placed lamps. I trudged along the path in no particular hurry. Wasn't like there'd be anyone waiting for me at the dorm.

My chest tightened, but I ignored the ache. It wasn't like I could really be upset about Matt not being there, not when it was because he'd joined a study group. Though going nearly two weeks of only seeing him in Battle Tactics and Demonic History II and passingly in the dorm didn't exactly leave me thrilled.

Tempting as it was to stop by the dining hall, it wasn't the same without Matt. Dry cereal would suit my melancholy just fine. I adjusted my course to head for the dorm and tried not to think about how much I missed my boyfriend. Maybe I could convince him to have lunch with me, not that my last attempt had gone well. Finally in front of our door, I fingered the old-fashioned key. There had to be some way to get him to spend time with me that didn't involve him quitting the study group. When I opened the door, I blinked twice, not sure I trusted my eyes.

Was Matt *really* in the kitchen or had Vera's dire warning about lonely Shadow Demons hallucinating finally come to fruition? I stepped deeper into the room to get a better look at what he was doing, letting the door thump shut behind me. Judging by the jars on the counter, he was making a peanut butter and jelly sandwich. He pushed aside a plated sandwich and began another.

"About time you got back," he said without turning around.

I refrained from pointing out that he'd been coming back in the wee hours of the morning and put my stuff down. "Did your study group get canceled?" I asked, stepping up behind him.

He tensed, then let out a sigh as I rubbed my hands down the length of his arms. The defined muscles of his shoulders and biceps had me questioning if I'd already forgotten how he felt. Was it possible he'd started working out again? I dismissed the thought as I absently stroked his exposed skin. He'd have told me.

His hand clenched around the butter knife he'd been using, then he set it aside, his shoulders slumping. "I'm sorry. I know it takes up a lot of time."

"Nothing to apologize for. I'm proud of you for taking your studies so seriously." I leaned my head down until my lips brushed the shell of his ear and added in a low whisper, "I just hope it's worth it." He shivered and desire unfurled like a living thing inside of me. Night, how I missed him.

"It wasn't canceled. I just... I wanted to be here tonight." The admission made me giddy. Seemed I wasn't the only one feeling the absence. "I made you a sandwich," he added.

"I see that." I kissed lightly along the back of his neck, teasing the sensitive skin with the tip of my tongue and tiny nibbles, the scent of sage intoxicating.

He attempted to stifle a giggle and squirmed against me. "Someone's feeling frisky."

If I hadn't been hard before, I certainly was now. I dug my fingers into his hips and he groaned. "You aren't the only one who burns." Night, I needed this, needed him. I spun him around, eager for more, barely catching his startled expression before I claimed his mouth.

He melted against me, looping his arms around my neck and giving himself wholly over to the kiss. His moan filled my chest as he slid his fingers through my hair, urging me deeper. He broke off long enough to steal a breath, then resumed trying to steal mine while he ground his growing erection against my thigh.

I mindlessly reached behind him to clear the counter, shoving aside jars, plates, and bread, then slid my hands beneath his shirt and guided it over his head. No sooner was he free than he was scrambling to be rid of mine. My shirt hit the ground, and I hoisted him onto the counter, earning myself a surprised gasp that I promptly swallowed. "I've missed you," I said between kisses, working my way down to his neck.

"Alexi."

The whispered moan drove me wild. I glided my hands over his thighs and he tightened them around my hips. His eager response was almost better than hearing my name on his lips. I palmed his straining dick and his head dropped back with a sharp cry. My fingers tingled in anticipation as I coasted them along his sides. He flinched slightly, and I leaned back, fully prepared to tease him for being ticklish. But when I glanced down, my fingers hovered over the remnants of a gruesome burn that spanned from his hip to his ribs.

"What's this?" I asked, kissing gently along his shoulder to distract myself from overreacting.

"It's nothing." He took a moment to steady his breathing, which faltered when I nipped at his neck. "J-just a spell gone wrong."

"Why didn't you go to a healer?" I asked, doing my damnedest to keep my tone neutral.

"It's almost healed."

My jaw twitched as I fought the increasing urge to press for clarity. But as I scanned his face, taking in his pink cheeks and downcast eyes, I couldn't bring myself to compound his embarrassment. I trusted him to come to me if something was genuinely wrong. "Does it still hurt?" I whispered, barely brushing my fingers over the wound.

"No." The resulting flinch betrayed the lie, but if he wanted to pretend it was fine, then I could do that too.

I brushed my lips softly against his. "You'll tell me if I hurt you?"

"Yes," he breathed, leaning into me once more.

"Good," I growled, palming his ass to hold him in place and grinding against him.

He swore and attacked my mouth with a vengeance while he raked his fingers down my back hard enough to leave marks. I groaned into his mouth and did it again before encouraging him to wrap his legs around my waist. Then I shadowed us to the bedroom, where we landed in a tangle of limbs on the bed. The rush of him simultaneously touching every single cell in my body was a high I'd never tire of.

"That was... that was..." he trailed off, still panting for breath.

"Incredible," I finished for him.

"Yeah, that," he said, then captured my mouth, revealing a need that rivaled my own.

"What do you want, Matt?" I managed through hungry kisses and roving hands that spread a blinding ecstasy of sensation.

He bit my lip and tugged before setting it free. "Whatever you'll give me."

"Don't I always give you everything?" I crooned, kissing him slowly. He groaned in obvious frustration at the sudden change in pace while my own need rebelled violently against my insistence on hearing him voice his desire. "Tell me, Matt. What do you want?"

"I want you, Alex. I always want you." His eyes burned like the hottest flame. He reached for my pants, flicking them open without hesitation, then slipped his hand past the waistband to free my aching dick. He placed tender kisses at the edge of my mouth while he stroked me with a firm grip. "I want you inside of me. Fucking me until the only name I can remember is yours."

I released a strangled grunt and gently grabbed his wrist. "You have exactly five minutes to get ready."

He didn't waste time walking, shadowing directly to the bathroom. While he was gone, I finished stripping and took out the supplies, setting them within easy reach. When Matt returned, he too was naked, though his erection had flagged.

"On the bed." I waited 'til he'd laid on his back, then tossed him the lube. "Get yourself ready for me."

His eyes widened, and he swallowed. He might have been anxious, but his black eyes and plumping cock betrayed his interest. Without so much as a peep of dissent, he popped the cap and wet two fingers. He set the lubricant aside, and I plucked it up. His gaze flicked to me as I joined him on the bed, positioned between his wide knees for the best view.

"What are you waiting for?" I asked, giving my revived erection lazy strokes.

A flush spread across his chest and darkened his cheeks as he reached for his already clenching hole. Rather than rush, he took his time circling the quivering entrance before sliding his index finger deep with a high-pitched whine. He worked himself open with a chorus of needy moans that bordered on whines, his abs contracting as he pushed deeper and added a second digit. Then he moved to grab his leaking dick.

"No," I said firmly.

His hand froze, and he stared at me, mouth agape, fingers still plunged in his tight ass.

"I didn't say you could stop."

He dropped his free hand to the bed, where he clenched the sheets as he resumed stretching himself. His breath hitched as I scooted closer, then turned into a strangled moan when I wrapped a slick hand around his erection. His dick pulsed against my palm while his fingers thrust.

Sensing his release was near, I squeezed his base more firmly.

"Alex," he gasped.

"You ready for me, love?"

"Yes. Yes. Oh god, yes," he panted, already looking half wrecked.

I kissed the inside of each of his knees, then pushed them toward his chest. "Hold them there." He moved so fast to comply, I couldn't help but wonder if he'd shadowed and I'd missed it. I watched his chest rise and fall in time with his quick breaths while I opened one of the several condoms I'd laid out and rolled it on. I placed more kisses on the backs of his thighs and made sure he was truly prepped.

Matt's gaze tracked my every movement as I lined myself up with his wet hole. Then I pushed forward agonizingly slowly, and he stopped breathing. When my head breached the first ring of tight muscle, air rushed back into his lungs and came out in a keening moan. I gradually worked myself deeper with steady, shallow thrusts, even though I knew he could handle more and the measured pace was killing me. I ran my hands over his legs, enjoying how the coarse hair tickled my palms and made his legs flex.

"Tell me what you want." I stroked deep and stopped moving.

Matt looked at me with pupils blown wide. "Fuck me. *Please,* just fuck me."

Eager to please and not sure how much longer I could withstand this drawn out torture, I resumed thrusting, abandoning the previous slow pace and pounded into him. His neglected cock bounced against his stomach, leaving a trail of pre-cum behind. My thighs burned as I increased the punishing rhythm. I griped his thighs, both for support and to pull him closer.

His fingers turned white from griping his ankles so tight and he pulled his legs farther back, encouraging me to go deeper still. The chorus of his grunts filled my ears while sweat beaded on his forehead. Then he cried out, "Alexi!" His face contorted to the brink of pain and his body curled in on itself. His hole pressed against me, the muscle spasming and fluttering as he tried to expel me.

I groaned at the intensity of it and kept going. Then I realized he hadn't ejaculated. My thrusting faltered, and I was on the verge of checking on him when his body convulsed again.

"Don't stop. Whatever you do, don't stop," he gasped, his head digging into the mattress.

He "came" three more times before I relented and reached for his swollen cock. I'd scarcely wrapped my fingers around him when he bowed off the bed, releasing his legs, and his hole clenched like a vise. I groaned deep down in my soul as he milked everything I had and then some, then collapsed beside him, barely retaining the wherewithal to lose the spent condom.

We laid like that in silence as we caught our breath and let our bodies cool. I glanced at Matt and debated whether to tell him how much I'd missed him these last two weeks. Part of me worried this time, this moment, was fleeting, and that I was wasting it. We should be talking, spending *quality* time together. Another part argued that getting lost in passion was an excellent way to spend time together.

Smiling, I rolled onto my side and traced the definition of his torso, spreading the smears of release along his abdomen. His eyes fluttered open as his chest expanded with a deep breath that he released in a contented sigh. I leaned in to give him a sweet kiss. "How are you feeling?"

He closed his eyes and hummed.

I chuckled. "That good, huh?"

"So much better than good." He opened his eyes, his easy smile shining in their crystal depths. "I've never orgasmed so many times. I didn't even know it was possible for a guy to do that without ejaculating."

I laughed again and rested my head on my arm. "Oh, it's possible. I'll explain the science of it to you later."

"So it's *not* magic," he said with a cheeky grin, then gave an exquisite stretch before sinking back into the mattress. "Speaking of magic, how are you even functioning right now?"

"Pretty sure if I closed my eyes, I'd pass out."

"So why don't you?"

I shifted my gaze from studying the rise and fall of his chest. "I'm not ready to stop looking at you." Pink blossomed on his cheeks. I caressed his jaw, leaning down for another kiss. He sighed and leaned into the touch. "I have a question for you," I said as I resumed tracing his torso.

"Hmm."

"Are you working out again?"

His eyes flew open, and he shifted away. "No. Why do you ask?"

I shadowed to the bathroom to grab a damp towel, then used cleaning him up to stall for time. Once I'd resettled, I met his worried gaze. "Because you've gained some definition." I wanted to chase down the sudden wariness hiding in his eyes, but I also didn't want to jeopardize our evening, either.

He licked his lips and swallowed. "Is that okay?"

"Did I sound like I was complaining?" I smiled and wrapped an arm around his waist, sliding him closer until he nestled in the curve of my body.

"Okay," he said with a nervous smile. "Now, I have a question for you."

"What is it?" I laughed, nuzzling his neck.

"Your eyes. Earlier they went black like when we shadow, but you weren't shadowing anything. Or maybe you were, and I was too distracted to see what," he added with a more devious grin.

"That took longer than I would've expected."

He twisted beneath my arm to face me better. "What do you mean? What is it?"

"It's a manifestation of our true nature and our true desires," I said simply, thinking back to Vera's own awkward explanation.

His eyebrows furrowed as he considered my response, then shot up in understanding. "Have mine ever done that?"

"Yes." I was tempted to leave it at that, but if I expected honesty from him, it was only right that I return the favor. "I have a confession to make." He narrowed his eyes and I let out a sigh tinged with guilt. "You actually do it all the time. I… might have been using that against you." I winced in anticipation of retribution.

"Really? How?" Matt's open curiosity once again defied my expectations.

"Yeah. As a matter of fact, the first time you did it was the night you convinced me to stay. It's why I decided to give us a chance." I placed a kiss on his shoulder for emphasis.

"Oh." I couldn't tell if the information was being well received or if he was about to be really upset. "All the time?"

I smiled. "Kind of."

He placed a hand on my chest. "Alex."

"Yes?"

"Alex, I…" Struggle twisted his face, and he didn't finish.

I cupped his cheek once more and gave him a tender kiss, our lips sticking together until the distance pulled them apart. "I love you."

His conflicted expression softened. "Alexi," he sighed as he snuggled into my neck.

I wanted to ask him about his use of my name-name instead of the nickname he used for me. Twice in one evening was surely remarkable. But there was something fragile in this moment and I didn't want to break it. I squeezed him tight and enjoyed just having him near.

It felt like forever before I finally felt him drift off, almost as if he was intentionally trying not to sleep. My sleep was much longer in coming. I wanted to relish every microsecond we had together. Gradually, my breathing slowed as exhaustion worked its magic.

Matt jerked violently, wrenching me out of a deep sleep. I shifted to give him room, but the space only let his flailing get more extreme. The sheets tangled around him, strangling his movements and mine.

"Matt. Matt. Stop. You're okay." I hastily freed an arm and switched the lamp on. The yellow light illuminated a wild-eyed Matt.

Terror flooded his blue eyes as they searched the room. The soft glow of the lamp dimmed, fading despite the new bulb. Then I realized the night itself was being pulled from all corners of the room. I looked back at Matt to find his eyes were solid black. Fear clutched my heart.

"Matt. Wake up. Matt! It's not real. Whatever you think is there, it's not. Matt, please!" I begged, as the darkness got closer and the air thinner. The very night pulled at my essence, and Vera's warning flashed in my mind. I tried again to get Matt's attention, but wherever his mind was, it was far from here. It wasn't until I grabbed his face that he reacted.

He blinked once and the encroaching darkness stalled. He blinked again and his eyes flashed of blue. A third blink and suddenly air poured into his lungs as if he'd been underwater for hours. Then he turned his panicked gaze to me. "What happened?"

"I think you were having a nightmare," I said, trying not to sound too relieved. "Tell me about it? What was happening?" I stroked his cheek in an attempt to ground him, but my anxiety returned when his eyes lost focus again.

"They were hurting you," he whispered, barely loud enough to be heard over my thundering heart.

"Who was hurting me?" I asked, confused.

His focus immediately sharpened. "No one." He shook his head and averted his gaze. "It was just a crazy dream."

I considered telling him that crazy dream had come alarmingly close to killing us. Instead, I brushed his hair back. "Matt, look at me." When he refused, I grabbed his chin and ordered more firmly, "Look at me."

Begrudgingly, he lifted his gaze, revealing the fear he was trying so hard to hide.

"I'm right here. I'm fine. I'm safe." At the last word, his face finally softened. He curled into my chest and I wrapped him in an embrace, determined to never let him go. He wriggled a hand between us so he could rest it on my heart, and that was how he fell back asleep.

I continued to rub his back and failed to dispel my growing worry. My beautiful Matthew was terrified of something and I felt powerless to help. What could I do if he wouldn't let me in? I wrapped my hand around his and fought off sleep for as long as I could. But it was for naught.

When I awoke in the morning, he was gone. The sheets were stone cold and there wasn't a trace of him anywhere in the dorm. Even his bag was gone, though it was too early for him to be in class.

Chapter 24
Pool for Beginners

Matt

After the third night of nightmares, I gave up trying to sleep with Alex. It was bad enough listening to his screams in my sleep, but lying to him when those dreams inevitably woke me up was worse. Trying to sneak out *after* he fell asleep didn't do any good either. Since I'd rejoined the bruiser club, exhaustion had become my permanent state of being. The ache in my chest doubled. He didn't deserve the constant lies, but the truth would only get him hurt, or worse, killed.

I carefully closed the dorm door and slipped quietly into my room, bypassing the kitchen despite the gnawing hunger in my belly. It was well past midnight, and I didn't want to risk a stray noise waking Alex. Safely ensconced in my room, I sagged against the door. But not even the weariness weighing me down could tempt me to seek sleep.

Memories of the most recent nightmare threatened to creep up, overlaying my barren room with a horrific image of Alex covered in blood and crying for help. I squeezed my eyes shut and violently forced them back down as I mentally chanted, "It's not real. It's not real." When I reopened my eyes, the image was gone. My shoulders slumped as I took in the empty space. We still called it my room, but it didn't feel like it. My *place* was on the other side of the dorm, back in bed with Alex.

For a moment, I considered tempting fate and just as quickly dismissed it. I was one intense nightmare away from spilling everything, consequences be damned. It wasn't worth the risk. My gaze fell on the sketch pad Jeffrey had given me eons ago. I grabbed it and a couple of pencils, then headed back to the living room. After a quick glance at his door, I started sketching Alex the way I imagined he looked right now. Snuggled deep beneath the comforter, hair in wild disarray, lips parted ever so slightly.

The mindless task worked its magic, and I settled into a kind of trance that both kept me awake and too focused to think about the dreams. When I finally looked up, the page was almost completely covered and hours had slipped. Mercifully, it was Wednesday, so I wouldn't have to go to the club tonight.

I let out a sigh and rested my head on the sketch pad. I missed Alex so much. Not just the kisses and killer sex. I missed my *friend.* I took a deep breath in a vain attempt to shake off the melancholy thoughts. At least it was late enough now that it wouldn't be strange to be on campus. I tucked the sketchbook safely beneath my mattress before grabbing my backpack.

The rest of the week went by in a blur of misery. Thursday's fight turned into *fights* and thanks to my lack of sleep, it was a total shit show. Everything hurt, even the parts of me that *hadn't* gotten hit. Normally I'd look forward to the weekend, but George had developed an irritating knack of monopolizing all of my free time. Then the impossible happened—George went home for a family event. Suddenly free, I was determined to enjoy my reprieve by spending as much of it as possible with Alex. I just had to figure out how.

By the time Saturday morning arrived, I was no closer to an answer. We couldn't risk an intimate outing at the coffee shop and no way were we going to the library. I was still desperately wracking my brain when Alex walked through the main door. Confused, I looked towards his room and back at him. He'd been in there; I was sure of it. How had he left without me sensing it? I sat there at a loss as he waltzed into the kitchen and began preparing an early lunch.

"Don't have anything better to do today?" he asked in a deceptively neutral tone, turning to glance at me.

I flinched inwardly. "I thought we could spend it together."

Guilt flashed across his face, then his eyes hardened and he turned back around. "Then I guess you should have said something sooner. I already have plans."

I sat in silence, not sure if that was actually true or not. Then he wrapped his sandwich to go. Disappointment wrapped around me and tightened until there was only pain. I couldn't even be mad; I deserved this. He chunked the food he'd put together into his backpack like it had offended him, then slung the strap over his shoulder and stalked toward the door.

"Alex." I don't know what possessed me to call out. Him being mad and avoiding me was probably for the best.

He stopped, tilting his head to listen without looking directly at me.

"What are you doing tonight?"

His shoulders sagged, and he was silent a moment before finally admitting, "I'm not doing anything."

"We should go out."

"Out?" he asked, finally meeting my gaze. I never wanted to go out.

"Yeah, somewhere different," I said with a spark of hope. "I've got a place in mind."

"I should be back around four." With that, he walked out of the dorm, leaving me with nothing better to do than wait for him.

I alternated between sketching and catching up on past due homework, while I kept a close eye on the time. Finally, it read four… and no Alex. I struggled not to assume the worst, that somehow, despite George's absence, Alex had been discovered and wouldn't be coming back. By the time five o'clock rolled around, I was seriously considering going to look for him. There was just one problem: he hadn't told me where he was going.

The door opened, and I paused in my pacing. Alex looked from me to the table covered in notes, then shut the door. "Um… hey."

"Hey," I replied, for want of something more inspired.

He set his bag down. "So, someplace different?"

"Yeah." I took a hopeful step toward him. "Ever play pool?"

A smile twitched on his lips. "No."

"Then I think it's about time you learned."

His grin stretched to fill his face, lighting the entire room. "That could be fun."

"Come on," I said, leading him back into the hallway. "If we get in before seven, there's no cover." He eagerly followed, peppering me with questions about the game and where we were going. As we walked up to the pool hall, though, his wariness returned.

He eyed the peeling paint and crooked neon sign. "This doesn't really look like my scene."

"Well, your scene is the library and you need to get out more. Besides, it looks worse than it is on the inside." I nudged him in the ribs, then walked into what, in fact, was a total dive bar. "Relax, have a drink."

He stalled in the entrance. "The last time you said that, it didn't end well."

I rolled my eyes and dragged him inside. Fortunately, the place wasn't overly crowded this early, and I spotted an open table toward the back. "Do you really foresee that being a problem here?" I asked, flagging down a waitress.

She eyed us with a grin and sauntered over, swaying her hips to emphasize her barely there skirt. "What'll it be gents?"

I gave my best play-nice smile, not at all appreciating the once-over she gave Alex. "Two beers for me and my friend."

"You're really good at that," Alex said once she'd gone.

"What do you mean?" I asked, grabbing us a pair of pool cues.

"She's completely smitten. We're going to get amazing service," he added, staring at the cue I gave him.

I shrugged. "I've found a smile can go a long way if you want decent service."

The waitress reappeared with excellent timing, dropped off our drinks, and moved on to check on other nearby patrons.

"Right, take a drink so you can stop looking so weird and come over here."

He eyed the beer like it was a grenade that could explode at any second, then took a drink. "Not bad. Not as good as that fruity beer, but not bad either."

"Glad you approve. Now get over here before someone tries to take the table because we're not playing."

He set the beer on a nearby high-top and joined me at the end of the table. "Now what?"

"Mimic what I do." I positioned the cue between my fingers and held it level.

He leaned down to imitate the posture.

I shook my head. "No. Look at how I have both of my hands, not just the leading one. When you strike, it needs to be in one smooth motion. This game is about finesse, not power." It would have been easier to stand behind him and correct the errors that way, but I really didn't trust myself or what it would look like. We may not be on campus, but that didn't mean we were safe. "Drink some more of your beer. It's getting warm."

Huffing, he grabbed the bottle and made a big show of polishing it off.

I gestured for our waitress to bring us another round and repositioned. "I'll break so we can work with a real layout." The cue ball made a loud crack as it smashed into its brethren. The balls rolled in every direction, with two dropping loudly into the pockets.

"I feel like that was impressive," he said, looking clueless.

I smiled. I kind of liked the fact that he was impressed, even though he didn't know why he should be. A walk around the table revealed I'd sank two opposites. "Okay, it's still open. Do you want to be stripes or solids?"

He frowned. "Is that a trick question?"

"No." I laughed. "Just preference. Because I got one of each, I'll let you choose."

His eyes danced with merriment. "Stripes."

"Then here's what you're going to do."

I walked him slowly through our first game. He was absolutely deplorable, but that didn't make it any less fun. We were halfway through another round when a familiar voice called over. I glanced up from sinking the eight to find Sam and Lucas walking toward us.

"Hey!" I shouted, while Alex stood patiently waiting to be introduced, steadily nursing his fifth beer. "Guys, this is Alex, my roommate."

He held up a hand in greeting.

"Alex, this is Lucas and Sam from my math class."

Sam clapped me on the back. "Haven't seen you here in a while."

"Yeah, studies have gotten in the way of a lot lately." I shot an anxious glance in Alex's direction.

"That's no excuse for blowing off your friends," Lucas said as he grabbed his own cue stick. "How long have y'all been here?"

"Not too long," Alex offered. "What about you?"

Lucas and Sam laughed and shared a look. "Long enough to know this is definitely *not* your game."

"I know. Why don't we play doubles? Loser buys the next round," I suggested.

Lucas narrowed his eyes at me. "Matt, you're a hustler. I know better than to play against you by choice."

"Yeah, but you've seen Alex play. It'll be like having a handicap."

They looked at Alex, who was giving me quite the sour face. I simply smiled and passed him a fresh beer. He drank it absently. They looked back at each other and I knew I had them.

"Deal," they replied in unison.

The table got reset, and Sam broke. I still had to coax Alex through a good portion, but by the second half of the game, the beers were finally working their magic and he was making somewhat decent shots. I dragged it out a while longer, then cleaned the table.

"I knew it!" Lucas cried after the second such game. "You tricked us. He's not a newb at all. When did you see us come in?"

I shook my head. "I promise, I had no idea you guys were here until you walked by. As for Alex, it's beginner's luck." I clapped him on the shoulder, nearly knocking him over. Alex was definitely tipsy by this point. Lucas continued to glare at me, suspicion rolling off of him, until the server arrived with the next round. Alex excused himself as we reset for the next game.

"You guys see those girls over there?" Sam said, indicating two young women a few tables away. One had long blonde hair and was wearing a pink top, while the other had short, brown hair that curled around her ears and was wearing blue. Both were shooting curious looks our way.

"What about them?" Lucas asked. "It's not like you stand a chance with either."

"You're an ass," Sam grumbled. "I know! You go, Matt. You always have luck with the ladies."

"What? No." I fervently shook my head, glad that Alex was missing this conversation.

"Pretty sure it has something to do with looking like some tortured puppy," Lucas mused.

"Shut up." I spied Alex coming back and inspiration struck. "Send Alex."

"What?" Sam asked in high-pitched disbelief.

"Yeah, he's terrible at talking to girls."

"But look at him. He could bugger the whole thing and they'd *still* go home with him. That's not even fair," Sam whined.

"What's not fair?" Alex asked.

I pointed at the women. "You see those two over there?"

He nodded in a fair imitation of a bobble head and confirming my hope that he was definitely tipsy enough to do this.

"Go talk to them."

Lucas and Sam looked borderline apoplectic. But they weren't about to go and this was a great opportunity.

"Why?"

They released groans of dismay in unison. I tried not to laugh as I leaned over like I was going to give him advice. "Because you need to blend in better and it'll make their night. Just go do it," I added louder.

He rolled his eyes and trudged over.

Watching Alex pretend to hit on women was the last thing I wanted to see, but it needed to be done. The women had the expected reaction to someone that looked like Alex approaching them. Even from over here, we could make out the giggles.

Lucas smacked me in the arm, and I laughed. "Just wait for it." Alex looked back at us with a lost expression and I snickered. "Told you."

"Oh gods, he has no clue what he's doing," Sam said in awe.

"Like it matters. Look at them, they're eating it up." Lucas wasn't wrong; the blonde was leaning in and the brunette was playing with her curls. After a while, Alex headed back to us. Disappointment flashed across the women's faces as he left them to their night.

"They were nice," Alex said, grabbing his drink.

"And?" Sam prompted.

"And what?" Lucas looked like he might strangle Alex.

"Please tell me you at least got *one* of their numbers," Sam said desperately.

"No. Why? Was I supposed to?" Alex looked at me questioningly and I hid my laugh behind taking a drink.

"That's it—for sheer shame. The next round is on you guys."

I smacked my bottle down. "Double or nothing."

"No chance. You and your roommate's 'beginner's luck' have already taken us to the cleaners. If that's what we're playing, then I'm out."

"Yeah, I think I'm done for the night, too. You're an expensive person to play with, Matt."

"You could always try not losing," I commented as we all said our farewells.

Back in the dorm, it was clear Alex was definitely still tipsy if not outright drunk. "I don't see why we had to leave too," he griped as he fixed himself a glass of water.

"Things can get a little rough there on a Saturday night. I'd hate to get into a bar brawl over something as stupid as someone spilling a drink." Or making a real pass at Alex.

He snorted. "Please. You'd love that. What are you doing?" he asked when he noticed me clearing the table.

"I'm going to show you how to play. Properly." I put the last chair in place and created a shadow billiard table. A spell later, and I didn't have to maintain it.

"Damn, you really have gotten good."

"Thanks," I said, creating a cue stick and indicating for him to do the same. "Set up like I showed you. We need to work on your form."

"Wouldn't this have been easier at the bar?"

"Not really."

He frowned and set up. While his playing had slightly improved, he really was terrible. I walked up behind him and reached around to fix the placement of his hands. "Little close, don't you think?" he asked.

I chuckled in his ear, and he shivered. "For the record, this is typically how most people teach their date how to play." I guided his cue, then had him reset. He was better, but still needed some additional direction. Once again, I leaned down to correct his positioning, enjoying the way his body fit against mine. This was much easier than trying to talk him through it.

"I think you're just messing with me." He giggled as I brushed my nose along his neck.

"Promise, just like this," I whispered. "You should see how people really play."

"What do you mean?"

"I'll show you. We'll play one game."

"Just one?" he asked.

"For now. Remember, it's about follow through," I added as he leaned his lithe frame over the phantom table.

He snickered. "Pretty sure I've never had a problem with follow through." His break was nearly perfect, albeit eerily silent. "How are we supposed to know who does what? They all look the same."

"Everybody's a critic. This is just for fun. Play until you miss." I waited until he made a few successful shots and his confidence increased. Much as I enjoyed hanging out as friends, there was no denying the desire growing inside of me. I wanted Alex in a way that sent heat coursing through my entire body. I walked up behind him once more and leaned down as he set up for the shot.

"That's a little distracting," he said calmly.

"That's the general idea." I slid a hand down the front of his thigh.

He scratched so badly I was concerned for the actual table beneath. "Shit, Matt."

I chuckled and removed the hand to take my shot.

"What was that?"

"I told you. People play differently than you think." I sank a couple, then missed.

"I think you're lying," he said, relocating to a spot at the opposite end.

I considered what he'd said about my eyes always going black and wondered if I could do it on purpose. All it would really take would be admitting how much I wanted to feel Alex beneath my hands, against my mouth, moaning...

Alex looked up and did a double take that resulted in another scratch. "Seriously, how am I supposed to focus with you messing with me?" He stubbornly went to try the shot again, and I shadowed behind him.

"You're not," I whispered, nibbling on his ear. He squeaked and his cue disappeared as I spun him around, then pushed him against the very real kitchen table. I claimed his mouth, and he eagerly returned the fiery need. "Alex," I sighed, removing his shirt without preamble. I missed this, missed him.

"What?" he responded breathlessly.

"Are you drunk?"

"No, maybe a little tipsy still, but that's all."

"Good." My mouth covered his once more while I slid my hands down his sculpted torso to undo his buckle. He moaned in anticipation and I forced him hard against me before moving my kisses lower. I pushed his pants down until his erection popped free, then licked him from base to tip before greedily swallowing him down.

"Oh fuck," he groaned, gripping the table until his knuckles turned white.

His moans of pleasure combined with the weight of him on my tongue was absolutely intoxicating. I freed him with a pop and mouthed his balls while my own erection pressed painfully against my zipper. But I couldn't be bothered to give my dick the attention it needed when that would require removing my hands from Alex. I teased the veins along his shaft and twirled my tongue around the tip. He shuddered as I sucked him down again, betraying how close he was. I pulled away. "You aren't going to tell me to stop?"

"Absolutely not," he gasped, tangling his fingers in my hair and guiding me back to his leaking dick.

I hummed in contentment as he controlled the bob of my head. When he let out a loud groan and tensed, I was more than ready to take everything he had. When he was done, he pulled me to my feet and captured me with a searing kiss.

"How are you doing, love?" he asked, palming my throbbing dick.

I choked on a groan at the same time my heart fluttered.

He squeezed my straining erection, then gentled his hold. "Tell me what you want, what you need."

"You. I want you so fucking bad."

"That so?"

"Yes," I gasped. Need bubbled in my veins, making me lightheaded and weak.

He grabbed my chin and forced me to meet his fierce emerald gaze. A hot poker of fear stabbed my heart. "Do you need a minute?" I shook my head, not trusting words, then he claimed me with a kiss so intense I forgot everything else.

We stumbled to the couch, leaving a trail of abandoned clothes. He pushed the coffee table out of the way and placed the couch cushions on the floor while I secured the condom and lube I'd hidden in here earlier. Alex plucked the supplies from my hand with a lascivious grin.

"Someone was optimistic."

"Hopeful," I corrected, as I pulled him down to the floor with me.

He kissed me deep, forcing my head into the makeshift bed, then moved on to lay a trail of open-mouthed kisses along my neck, chest, and stomach. I was shaking by the time he reached for my dick. "You are so hungry for it," he rumbled.

"Yes," I agreed eagerly. I'd been hungry—starving—plenty of times in my life, but never like this. I didn't even notice he'd opened the lube until slick fingers circled my hole at the same time he took me in his mouth. The intense sensation had me bowing off the floor. His free hand cradled my hip as he made a meal of me and sank his finger past my rim. My release danced closer. A couple more sweeps of his tongue, another press of his finger, and I'd come apart.

Alex relinquished my dick, and I let out a moan of frustration. "Not yet, love." I whimpered as he traced my freed dick with his lips. He added another finger, which slid in with almost no resistance.

I took deep gulping breaths, aching for more and already so close. He spread his fingers as he slowly thrusts them and I thrashed against the cushions. "Alex, *please*."

"You sure you're ready for me?" he crooned, peppering my chest with light kisses and tiny nips.

"Fuck yes," I gasped, and he chuckled. Too blind with lust, I didn't see him open the condom, but I heard it. Then he was pressing his head against my hole and I was positive I'd die if he tortured me with shallow thrusts. To my relief, once he'd breached the outer rim, he drove deep in one long thrust. I made a garbled sound, part gasp, part groan, at the combination of fullness and burn.

Alex's fingers glided gently along my jaw as I found my breath. "Still with me?"

Rather than respond, I hooked my ankles behind him and rolled us. It took some situating, but at last, I had him perfectly straddled. I gave an experimental roll of my hips and released a stuttering sigh.

"Night, Matt," Alex gasped, digging his fingers into my sides until his nails bit flesh. The hint of pain somehow grounded me and shot me into a whole other stratosphere. He released his grip and coasted one hand up my chest while the other encircled my erection. He gave me a firm stroke that I echoed with another roll of my hips. "That's it. Ride me. I want to see you fall apart."

I leaned back in search of that perfect angle, bracing myself against his upper thighs. He shifted his hand to the top of my dick and I thrust up to follow him before crashing back down with a grunt.

"That's perfect. Keep doing that."

I did. Again and again, getting lost in the incredible feel of Alex stretching me, owning me. My hands slipped, and I shifted them to the floor. As soon as his thighs were free, Alex thrust up hard and my head fell back in ecstasy. His hips pistoned off the floor, slamming into that spot I still didn't have a name for, but felt like pure fucking magic. Then, just like he wanted, I completely broke apart. With a grunt, I shot ribbons across his abs and chest. Alex gave a few more hard thrusts, then curled off the floor, holding me tight as he found his own climax.

I wrapped my arms around him and nuzzled his sweaty hair. This. This was all I wanted. The rest of the world—all the bullies and the bigots—could rot in hell. All I needed was Alex. *My* Alex. The light trail of his fingers along my back gradually brought me back down, grounding me in a way only he had ever managed.

"We should... we should get cleaned up," he panted against my chest.

I grumbled incoherently and held him tighter. Who needed to be clean? This moment was perfect exactly the way it was.

Sometime later, I blinked my eyes open to find Alex's emerald ones staring back. "Hey," he whispered.

"Hey," I replied with a sleepy grin. "Sorry. I must have dozed off." I combed my fingers through his hair, which was a wonderful mess, and gave him a gentle kiss that made my lips tingle. He was my absolute everything. I only wished I could find the words to tell him that.

"It's nice to see you acting like your old self."

Anxiety froze my limbs. I didn't want to think this had been a mistake, even though I knew better.

Concern darkened his eyes. "What's been going on with you?"

"Alex, please. Not tonight. I just want to appreciate being here with you." I stroked his cheek and hoped desperately he would agree. We'd found a small bubble of happiness and I wasn't ready to give it up.

He searched my face for a long minute before finally saying, "Okay, we don't have to talk about it right now."

I let out the breath I'd been holding and snuggled closer. "Thank you." He'd demand the truth eventually, and I prayed I'd be strong enough to keep it from him, but not tonight. Tonight, we were just us, like we had been before.

Chapter 25
CUTTING TIES

Alexi

Matt was a bottomless well of frustration. First, I didn't see him for weeks, then he takes me out on a date. Pool was... interesting. I chuckled to myself as I replaced the last pillow on the couch. I'd never had anyone teach me how to do something like that before. Though I was still dubious about his methods. Matt was just secretly a scoundrel. Not that it bothered me in the least. I missed feeling the fire inside of him. It let me know he was alive, that he cared.

I finished moving the coffee table and paused. If Matt *did* care, then why had he refused to tell me what was going on with him? Why had he been so distant lately? His small request to drop the subject last night had seemed reasonable, but had done little for my worry. Was he preparing to leave Arminius like so many of our classmates and didn't have the heart to tell me? If I could just get him to confide in me, then we could work through things together. I would do long distance if that's what it took. Or... was it something entirely different? I sank onto the couch and closed my eyes against the headache forming.

"You sure you got enough sleep?" Matt teased from behind me. His hand rubbed along the curve of my neck as he placed a sweet kiss on the other side.

"I don't really think sleep was one of the things we did last night," I said with my eyes still closed. His resulting chuckle made my heart hurt. When had that beautiful sound become so rare?

"I thought the other things were pretty good too," he said, his voice low, then lightly bit my neck before soothing it with another kiss.

"That so?"

"Yeah." The heat in his voice sent corresponding waves coursing through me. Was it even possible to get enough of him?

I grabbed his hand. "Come here."

He didn't resist and walked around to face me, a playful smile tugging at the corners of his mouth. He really was quite the devil. I pulled him down and he came without hesitation. This was a wonderful side of Matt. He straddled my hips like he had the night before and leaned in to kiss me without having to be encouraged. I curled my fingers in his downy hair and arched into him, reveling in his slow, methodical exploration of my mouth.

"You know, I had a fantasy like this once," I said between kisses.

"Oh really?" He ground against me and I couldn't have stopped my moan if I wanted to.

"Yep," I said, snaring him again.

He broke off breathless and pulled his fresh shirt off in one fluid motion. I ran my hands over his chest and the niggling suspicion that he'd resumed working out resurfaced. Not that I was complaining. I flicked my gaze up to find him watching me appreciate the view. A few faint bruises caught my attention, but it was entirely possible that I'd done those last night. Not dwelling on maybes, I slipped my hands around to caress his back and he slid closer.

"And how's it measuring up?" he asked, his mouth returning to mine. My fingers dug into his back as I urged him on. I loved how he felt and how he responded to the slightest touch.

"No contest. Then again, it didn't actually get this far."

"No?" he asked playfully, rubbing against me again. I gasped, and he mercilessly did it again. "Wouldn't have anything to do with the fact that I suddenly showed up half-dressed out of my room. Would it?" He nipped my lip.

"How could you possibly know that?" I asked, my shock momentarily overriding the tide of ecstasy he was creating.

He gave me a truly wicked smile. "I'm pretty sure you're the reason I fell through the bed that night. Scarred the crap out of me too," he added, before stealing another kiss.

"How would I do that?"

"Easy really." His eyes went dark and the shadows in the room thickened. They reached toward us, not menacingly like when he'd had that awful nightmare, more like they wanted to be where we were. As they got closer, I felt a similar pull on myself, a need to be as close to Matt as possible, nudging me towards my shadow state.

I drew in a deep breath as the sensation vanished. "Oh, my."

"There was that… and this." He suggestively rolled his hips.

"Thought I managed to keep that to myself," I tried to say, though it came out more strangled than anything.

He laughed low and sexy as hell. "I told you, Alex, I pay attention, *especially* where you're concerned."

Unable to stand the torture any longer, I shifted so that he fell in the open space beside me and rolled to cover him. His mouth greedily found mine as he arched against me and locked his legs around my waist. "You have to be the most impossible person I have ever met," I said, digging my fingers into his thigh. He groaned and I could feel what control I was pretending to have slip away.

"It's never bothered you before." He punctuated the statement with a tantalizing kiss. No, it hadn't, but something else was bothering me now. The words were out before I could stop them.

"What's going on with you, Matt? What are you hiding?"

He pulled back so sharply I thought he'd taken my lips with him. He searched my face while confusion and anger warred for dominance on his own. Anger won. "Is this some sort of trap? Was that your plan? You'd ply me with sex and kisses to get what you wanted?" He pushed me away, and I fell against the armrest.

"What? No. I just want to know what's going on with you. I'm worried, Matt." Now, *I* was confused. Where was this coming from?

He sat up and yanked his shirt back on. "And you thought *this* was the best way to find out? You'd bait me and I would just tell you everything? Nyx forbid you actually just fucking ask." He stood abruptly, nearly toppling me off the couch.

"Bait you? *You* started this," I said hotly. "And I *did* ask. Multiple times."

"I'm not doing this with you." He turned and stalked off to his room.

I followed close on his heels. "Maybe if you would just talk to me, you wouldn't feel baited!"

"You can't use sex to get whatever you want, Alex. It doesn't work that way."

"What!" I shouted in furious disbelief.

He crossed the threshold to his room, slamming the door behind him.

"No, you don't." I reached for the handle to find it locked. Rage washed through me as I jiggled the handle uselessly. "Open the fucking door, Matt." I shook the knob violently. "Do it or *I* will!" I could feel him just on the other side. He was less than a foot away. The lock snapped beneath my persistence and I ripped open the door.

Just as I'd suspected, he was standing literally on the other side. He looked up at me, anger burning in his eyes and his jaw clenched so tight it was twitching.

"What the hell, Matt?" I stepped forward and ran into a wall so hard I staggered back. I scanned the opening, which, for all intents and purposes, looked perfectly passable. Except it wasn't—he'd put up a boundary to keep Shadows Demons out. My fury found new heights as my fist slammed against the spell.

He took a step back as if unsure the invisible wall would hold.

"Drop the fucking barrier," I demanded, pounding on the spell.

"Let it go, Alex. Just leave me alone."

I narrowed my eyes at him, silently demanding he drop the spell. Then inspiration struck. Just because I couldn't get in through the door didn't mean I couldn't get in at all. He must have realized the same thing, because he darted to the wall to keep pace with me, barely getting the rest of the boundary up in time to prevent me from simply shadowing right through the wall. I spent several frustrated minutes searching for cracks in the defensive barrier. My essence reaching out to feel for any gap, even a hole the size of a pin, would be sufficient. I found no such opening and returned with a vengeance to the open door.

He stood on the other side, looking more determined than ever and breathing hard. Putting up a spell like that so quickly could not have been easy. The flat of my hand smacked into the barrier spell and he jumped.

"If I can't get in, then you can't get out!" I yelled at him.

He simply stood there, staring back.

"Damn it, Matt, let me in," I ordered, but already I could feel my anger waning into hopelessness. This was it; he'd made his choice to keep me out. I didn't know what that meant, and that frightened me more than anything. I rested my head against the spell, surprised to find it was cool, like a heavy mist. "Please, Matt, drop the wall. Talk to me. Just let me help." I hated the sound of despair in my voice and didn't have the energy to look up. I didn't want to see how resolute he was in denying me. My hand fell, and I turned to lean against the spell, sliding to sit on the floor. "I'm not leaving," I promised quietly. There was only silence and the sound of my breathing. I sent out feelers so I'd know the moment the spell failed and resigned myself to wait.

At some point, I must have dozed off. My head snapped up in alarm and I fell backwards, the resistance of the spell gone. Panicked and not sure how long the spell had been down, I spun around, positive Matt was gone. To my surprise, he was sitting on the floor, leaning against the bed, completely passed out. My tortured angel looked exhausted. I couldn't even fathom the amount of energy or power it would have taken to sustain such a high-level shadow spell.

Distantly, I realized my feelers had created a perfect box around the room. I released them and bent to pick up Matt, then carefully laid him on the bed. "What can you not tell me?" I whispered into the quiet. For a moment, I considered letting him rest in peace—he certainly needed it—but I'd made a promise. I wouldn't leave. Part of me was afraid that if I let him out of my sight, I'd never see him again. So I crawled on top of the covers beside him and pulled him close.

I wasn't sure when I fell asleep again, but I knew exactly what woke me. Matt was struggling in his sleep, almost as if he was fighting for his life. His heart raced beneath my hand so hard it felt like it might give out. He mumbled something, sounding distressed. I leaned closer to make it out.

Suddenly, his eyes flew open, and he gasped for air, his whole body becoming a taut string that could snap at any moment. His hand covered mine, and he spun to meet my worried gaze. The panic in his eyes slowly receded. But anger quickly replaced the relief. He threw my arm off and swiveled his legs over the side of the bed.

"What are you doing here? I told you to leave me alone." There was anger and something else in his voice that took me a moment to recognize—fear.

"And I told you I wouldn't. Something is obviously wrong. Why won't you tell me what it is?" I asked, trying to remain calm as I shifted to sit beside him.

"Because I can't," he said, his voice raw and his body shaking.

"You can tell me anything, Matt. I'm still your best friend. If nothing else, I'm still that." I reached out to him and he flinched away from the contact, his shaking intensifying.

"Please, stop. Just... stop," he sobbed. He wasn't *just* shaking, he was crying.

Desperate, I took a stab in the dark. "Does it have to do with the dreams? We can fix those."

He shook his head violently from side to side, doing what he could to keep the growing sobs silent. "You don't understand."

"I might if you told me."

"I can't. I can't tell you, Ale—" He cut himself off. "I can't lose you." It wasn't the first time he'd said it, but this was the first time he'd ever sounded so hopeless.

I wrapped him in a hug before he could stop me. "You won't. I love you, Matt. Nothing will ever stand in the way of that."

The shaking stopped dead. He pressed the palms of his hand to his face and forcibly removed the evidence of his melt down. When he finally turned to look at me, a hollow anger that bordered on apathy filled his eyes. "You need to leave." The statement was quiet, but crystal clear without so much as a hiccup or waver.

"Matt," I said uselessly.

His eyes hardened, turning to unforgiving ice. "Get out, Alex."

I stood, feeling as if someone had scooped my insides out with a spoon. I paused in the doorway to look back. He sat there still as a statue staring at the floor, then he was gone in a blink of shadow. My heart shattered into a thousand pieces and I clutched my chest at the overwhelming agony of it.

I lay staring at the ceiling for hours until the pain of it faded enough that I could think again. How I'd actually gotten to my room was a mystery. Someone or something was taking my Matt from me. I had no idea what could have that kind of sway over him or if it was even something I could fight. There was one thing I did know for certain though: I *would* fight. Whatever it took, I wouldn't give up on Matt.

Chapter 26

Bad Decisions

Matt

It took days to figure out how to tie off the barrier spell so it wouldn't drain me dry. Unfortunately, the max I could get out of it before it failed was maybe five hours. If I could find a power source, I could make it stretch longer, days, maybe even weeks, like Vera had done. But I didn't have time for that. Much easier to wait until Alex was definitely asleep to return to the dorm. The image of his stricken face when I'd demanded he leave swam in front of me, obscuring the sidewalk leading to fraternity row.

I pushed away the painful memory as I caught sight of George. Per usual, Kyle and Travis flanked him. The horrid trio had their heads bent together, their voices lowered. Travis's gaze wandered past George, and he clocked me. Abruptly, the three went silent, but not before I caught a name—Thomas.

"You look fucking terrible, man," Kyle said, stepping away from the others. He clapped me on the shoulder and I shrugged him off. I really didn't have the energy for his lackluster banter *and* the fight later. Between not eating, sleeping, or talking to Alex, I was barely more than a husk these days.

"Still looks better than you," Travis snickered. Kyle punched him in the arm and George stepped in.

"What took you so long?"

I squinted at him, knowing damn well I was perfectly on time. "Sorry, won't happen again. Got caught up by some teacher I passed wanting to 'save me'," I said sardonically. They laughed as expected. Humorless twits. I shoved my hands in my pockets and aimed for an air of casual indifference. "Who's this Thomas guy? Heard y'all mention him a few times now. He a friend of yours? Seems strange I haven't met him yet." I snuck a glance to find Kyle and Travis sharing an anxious look while George appeared speculative.

"You know, I think it might be time for little Matty to meet Thomas," George said at last, eying me like a butcher weighing meat. He cut his gaze toward the other two. "What are you ass hats looking at? Let's get a move on."

Kyle and Travis had the wherewithal not grumble, but continued shooting me furtive glances the whole way to the fight club. George gave the password at the door and we slipped into what promised to be an exceptionally rowdy night. As expected, my name topped the roster. Upside to fighting so early in the night was that I could get it over with. Down was that there was a better chance I'd get tossed into the ring again.

I gritted my teeth, determined not to give George any reason to second guess his decision to introduce me to Thomas. If that took fighting twice or more in one night, then I'd give every round my all. Without a word, I passed my shirt to Travis, then walked over to Neese.

"About time," he said in his slippery voice. "You're facing a sprite tonight. His name is Titus. Don't fuck it up, kid." He pushed me toward the edge into what amounted to a waiting block.

I hadn't fought a sprite before. I couldn't help but think back to the sprite siblings at the orphanage. They'd look terrifying, but Christian had been small, almost fragile looking. Surely a sprite wouldn't be that bad. I'd handled worse.

The previous fight ended. Once they'd finished carrying out the unconscious fighter, I took my place center ring. A couple minutes passed by, filled with the familiar sound of spectators placing their bets, then the electric buzz of the barrier hummed to life. It hadn't been used in the previous fight, but then, I'd never seen it used for anyone but me. Neese, guarantying his pound of flesh.

I glanced over my shoulder toward the evil wyvern. The barrier was still in force, but no one else was in the ring. His toothy grin said I was wrong. Something slammed into my face and knocked me into the electric barricade. A sizzle filled my ears, and I leapt away just in time to avoid a crushing blow to my spine. Dust drifted into the air as I spun to find my opponent. Except there was no one there. I glimpsed a light mote no bigger than a penny and recalled how the siblings had transformed into points of light. Fucking sprites.

I shadowed out before he could force me against the ropes again and rematerialized farther away. This was going to be exceptionally difficult if I could barely see my opponent. I gathered shadow into the shape of a fly swatter. The crowd ate up the implied insult, and Titus finally made his appearance.

Titan would have been a better name for the guy. He was easily the size of Granite and just as broad. I swallowed. Hopefully, his size was an indication that he wasn't as good with his psychic abilities. *Those*, I painfully remembered from the when Scylla had forced me to the ground and sucked all the air from my lungs.

I took a step to avoid the roundhouse coming my way, only find that my left foot refused to leave the ground. Before I could think to shadow, the kick hit me square in the side, leaving sparks of blue magic to swirl in the air. I gritted my teeth and sank into the darkness. Titus's next kick passed through me and the crowd erupted in boos. Bloodthirsty bastards loved it when I took hits, even more when I wailed.

I shook off the attack and grabbed his leg after it passed through me. It took more effort than it should have, but I managed to throw him against the electric barrier. Just because it was there to keep me in didn't mean I couldn't use it to my advantage. While he was struggling to regain his balance, I used his own shadow to reappear behind him. I locked an arm around his neck and clung for all I was worth. Unfortunately, I was nowhere near peak strength.

He elbowed me beneath my ribs hard enough to knock the wind out of me. I lost my hold, and he staggered forward, flailing out with a psychic push that knocked me toward the barrier. I skidded to a stop millimeters shy of the electricity now sizzling the hairs at the small of my back. broke free and staggered forward, using his abilities to knock me into the barrier myself. Not really sure how much I could actually take in my current state or what other tricks Titus might have up his sleeve, I used shadow to propel myself forward. The sooner this was over, the better.

As Titus rushed me, my biggest concern became a reality. Air was yanked out of my lungs. No matter how I gasped and gulped, I couldn't get it to stay. Stumbling to a halt, I held out my hands, palms facing each other. I ignored the bursts of color spotting my vision from lack of oxygen and formed the shadows into massive walls of darkness, then clapped my hands together. For a moment, Titus hovered in place, frozen mid-lunge. I dropped my hands, and he crumpled to the ground with barely a sound.

It took every ounce of willpower I had not to sag with relief as air found its way back into my lungs. I hated using my powers so much in the ring; last thing I needed was anyone realizing how strong I'd become. As it was, I was pretty sure George believed he was more powerful than me. I wanted to keep it that way.

At last, the barrier fell, and I could work my way over to the trio. When I'd fought during the summer, people had stepped aside, patting me on the back and congratulating me as I passed. Now, I had to push my way through the onlookers until I emerged on the other side in time to see Neese walking away from the others. It still rankled that they didn't have to fight at all.

I didn't bother asking if they were ready to leave. They never were. While the fights continued, I stole the opportunity to rest against the wall, letting the cool concrete ease some of my aches. Off to the side, Travis tried unsuccessfully to pick up the resident witch... again. I eyed the poultices and salves with envy, but Neese had made it clear that I wouldn't get so much as a bandage.

The witch glanced over at me while trying to avoid Travis's roving hands. She at least knew what was going on here. To her credit, she didn't seem to like it. Travis said something, and she laughed noncommittally, swatting at him. Schmuck couldn't take a hint if it bulldozed over him. Finally, George made his way back over to where I was sitting against the wall. I rolled my head to the side to look up at him.

He glowered at me, and I wondered what exactly Neese had said to him earlier. "You ready yet? I'm starving."

Kyle appeared out of nowhere. "Did someone mention food?"

"Little Miss Sunshine is a real piece of work," Travis said, joining us with a dramatic huff.

"You're probably not her type," Kyle said a little too helpfully.

"I know what her type is. The kind that wears a skirt," Travis said bitterly. I only barely didn't roll my eyes.

"Disgusting is what it is," George said, hocking a glob of spit that landed inches from my foot.

"Just because someone isn't interested in you doesn't automatically make them gay," I said, instantly regretting opening my mouth when George swiveled a venomous look on me. To my surprise, Kyle came to the rescue.

"She probably thinks you have a little pecker." Kyle laughed, and I let out a sigh of relief as George guffawed. Next time, I'd keep my opinions to myself. Travis hoisted me to my feet while simultaneously trying to slug Kyle and nearly clocking me in the process.

"Alright, bozos, let's get out of this dump." George opened the over-large metal door and I cast a surreptitious glance behind us. He better hope Neese never heard him talking that shit.

We wandered into the town proper to grab some food. Even starving, I could only finish half of my burger. I gave the rest of it to Kyle as a silent thank you for unintentionally saving my bacon. As we meandered our way back to campus, a neon sign turning off for the night caught my attention. I squinted to get a closer look, my vision still burning with the afterimage, and my heart constricted.

The coffee shop. Longing for Alex welled up, making my throat tight and my eyes sting. I quickly averted my gaze and found George eying me. "What's your deal?" I asked defensively. Not even thinking about Alex was safe anymore.

"So you want to meet Thomas, huh?"

I shrugged. "Sure, why not? You guys talk about him enough." That wasn't entirely true; they didn't talk about him around me, at least, not on purpose.

"Then you should probably know a few things. Thomas is a pretty intense guy. He has brought it to our attention that there's an impostor in our midst; a disgusting creature that has been *contaminating* us with its presence." I held my breath and forced my expression to remain disinterested. This was it, the answers I'd been looking for. "If you were interested in helping, I think I could persuade Thomas to meet."

"Depends. What sort of disgusting creature? If we're talking boils, I'm out," I said with another shrug.

Kyle and Travis laughed so hard they snorted. George, on the other hand, had gone nearly purple, his eyes swelling with rage. "We're not talking about *boils*," he spat. "We're talking about one of our own masquerading like they're one of us, an abomination that needs to be taken care of. Permanently." He spat on the ground for emphasis.

Suddenly, my path was clear. If I could get this mysterious Thomas's approval to join the hunt, then I could ensure they were always looking in the wrong direction.

"Why the miserable thing hasn't taken its own life is beyond me. So that leaves us." George gestured at my heinous companions. Travis and Kyle leered.

My stomach rolled. Alex had never done anything to any of them, was hands down the best person I'd ever met. How could *who* he was be such an unforgivable crime in their eyes? I tightened my jaw and strengthened my resolve. Whatever it took, I wouldn't let them within spitting distance of Alex. "I could do that. What do we know?"

"Eager, aren't you?" George's searching gaze made my skin itch.

I shrugged again. "It's something to do." And there might even be a chance we'd stop going to that damnable club.

George resumed walking. "Suppose you're right. We don't know much. That's the biggest reason we haven't already found them. Thomas doesn't want us wasting his time and getting it wrong. We *do* know that they're at least a level ten, not easily intimidated, fairly intelligent, and good with orders."

I struggled to take deep breaths while panic strangled my lungs. All they were missing was that he was six-one, had dark hair, and green eyes.

Kyle walked up beside me. "You okay? You don't look so good, Matty."

My stomach heaved, and I forced the bile back, focusing on breathing slowly through my nose. "I think it's the burger," I managed, bending over just in case my last meal made a reappearance after all.

Kyle eyed the wrapper in his hand and quickly tossed it, wiping the grease off on his pants. George had stopped walking and was once again watching me curiously.

If I didn't pull it together fast, I was going to blow this whole thing. I took a deep breath and straightened back up. "Maybe it's whatever that damn pixie did to me."

George's face immediately lightened. "Why don't you call it a night, Matty? We'll catch up tomorrow. In the meantime, I'll talk to Thomas, see what he thinks," he said, then vanished, leaving Travis and Kyle scurrying to disappear as well.

Some friends. What if I really was sick?

Rather than shadow walk across campus, I took my time and ruminate over what I'd learned. George had confirmed pretty much all of my fears. The only mercy was that they didn't know who they were looking for or what they might look like. It wasn't much, but I'd take it.

When I arrived back at the dorm, all the lights were out. I left them that way and walked to my room in the dark. Hand on the doorknob, I paused, glancing toward Alex's closed door. One look couldn't hurt. In a heartbeat, I'd shadowed across the living room, then hesitated. What if he was awake? I cautiously shadowed my head through the door. Darkness greeted me, along with Alex's slight snore. I walked the rest of the way in and tiptoed to the bathroom. Fortunately, it wasn't closed. I created a mock door of shadow and laid it over the opening. Then I reached inside and flicked on the light. I winced at the click of the switch and darted an anxious glance toward Alex. Reassured I hadn't woken him, I thinned the shadow door to a thin veil, careful not to brighten the room too much.

Even in the faint light, I could make out Alex's perfect features. By some miracle, his hair was behaving and, for once, not angled in every direction. His hand slid out from the cocoon of covers towards the edge of the bed, as if he could sense me standing there.

Night, I missed him. I didn't even feel like a whole person anymore. The urge to go to him, to trace his beautiful face, to run my fingers through his hair increased until I could hardly stand it. I wrapped my arms around myself, lingering a moment longer, then shadowed straight to my room. I fell onto the bed, too tired to even attempt the boundary spell, while silent tears streaked down my cheeks.

Chapter 27
Broken Promises

Alexi

I stared at the back of Matt's head in our Demon History II class. There was no telling if he was passing or even doing the assignments. Still, he was here, which was something, and more than I could say for the dorm. What I couldn't figure out was why he kept leaving the bathroom light on in my room. And why not stay if he was already there? It had to have something to do with his nightmares, which undoubtedly had something to do with whatever he didn't want me to know.

The professor dismissed the class with a wave and I lurched to my feet. I pushed past some slower movers in my rush to catch Matt before he could pull his usual disappearing act and nearly ran into him. His sharp gaze snared mine and my heart skipped. Then it darted to something behind me and he shadowed out, avoiding the crowd altogether. I looked over my shoulder in search of what had made him bolt. When I realized George and his goons weren't far, I snarled. Tempting as it was to demand answers about why my boyfriend was spending so much time with them, I didn't want to hear what they had to say. I wanted to hear it from Matt.

I all but sprinted to Mysterio College and, for what might have been the first time, was actually grateful for Battle Tactics. It was a sorry state of our current affair that I was actually looking forward to sparring. Considering how long it had been since he'd last touched me, any excuse to touch was a good one.

In a surprising twist, Vera waltzed into the room. Her gaze swept over the assembled students and I couldn't help but notice that yet another two were missing. Who the hell dropped a class two-thirds of the way through the semester? Then a possibility occurred to me—maybe it hadn't been by choice. My glance slid to Matt. Given how many classes we had together he'd missed, he was likely flirting dangerously with expulsion. At Vera's heavy sigh, I returned my attention to the front of the room.

"Today, we'll be using multiple training rooms to allow for ample space to spread out. I'll be checking on each group periodically to offer guidance and advice. You'll be in your usual pairings for sparring. Depending on how much... correction is needed, we'll be mixing up the groups next class." She crossed her arms and stared at the class. "Well? What are you waiting for? Go."

Her demand got the class moving with purpose and in short order, I found myself in the farthest training room with Matt, Ellie, Louise, Ronald and Yaren. I stood across from Matt, where he still had yet to meet my eye. Better at fighting or not, he'd have a bloody hard time holding his own if he refused to look at me. "You ready for this?" I asked, in an attempt to get his attention.

He finally glanced up from his study of the floor. His eyes glinted darkly with anger and something else. Hesitation? Fear? Why would he be afraid of me? He was substantially better at sparring than I was, if for no other reason than he was perfectly okay hitting someone. Finally, he shrugged and looked away.

I clenched my fists and fought the urge to yell at him to get over himself, to let me in. But I'd done that already, and it hadn't done an ounce of good. With no kind of warning or formal start to the match, I surged forward.

His eyes widened in alarm, and he shadowed out of reach.

I growled and spun to face where he would likely manifest. At least one of us had been paying attention in class and it sure as hell wasn't him. When he reappeared, my swing was already in motion.

He barely caught the hit before it could land and promptly followed through with his own. His fist collided with my jaw before I could even register mine had been stopped.

"Really? The face?" I snarled.

Matt looked at his hand in horror and jumped backward out of reach and kept jumping. Despite the growing ache in my jaw, I didn't relent. He could avoid me all he wanted outside, but here, he had no choice but to face my wrath head on. The sensation of someone shadowing prickled my skin, and I gripped the shadows around Matt without mercy. Shock exploded across his face, no doubt at discovering he couldn't shadow away from the hold. His demeanor slowly shifted to something akin to panic as I unleashed and he struggled to parry my attacks. Yet despite my ferocity or the shrinking distance, he didn't strike back.

The door to the classroom opened and closed, signaling Vera's arrival. "Good form, Ellie. Remember, keep your senses open so you can tell when your opponent is about to move. Yaren, try to take this seriously."

As her voice got closer, my frustration with my own sparring partner increased. Even with Matt solely playing defense, I'd yet to land a single blow. I redoubled my efforts and our motions became a blur. Then he caught my fist once more and froze. My gaze slid past where he held my hand captive to meet his. To my surprise, his eyes were black, though he'd given up attempting to shadow a while ago.

"Alex," he panted, his voice strained.

Undeterred, I shifted gears, and he caught me again. "Damn it!"

"Alex," he said again, his voice shaking.

Suddenly, worry eclipsed my frustration. I reassessed his body language. Something was wrong. I looked at where he had hold of my arm, but he wasn't holding it like he was preventing an attack, more like he was hanging on for dear life.

"Alex, I can't." This time, I recognized the tone—desperation.

I spied Vera approaching out of the corner of my eye. "I'll get you out of here, Matt."

His eyes flashed blue, and I glimpsed a spark of hope. My poor Matt was breaking.

"I'm sorry about this." I shadowed out and grabbed him in a headlock from behind. He didn't fight me, but I caught the moan when I touched him, sensed his essence bleeding into mine. That was bad. Really, really bad. Already, I could feel the pull as he reached out to the shadow world subconsciously for help.

Vera must have as well. She adjusted her course to make a beeline for us.

I looked at her and fought to keep the mounting panic from my voice. "Something's wrong."

She took one look at him and didn't hesitate. "Get him out of here." A portal opened up beside us, as big as I was tall.

I eyed it warily.

"Go," she hissed, "before anyone else notices that he's warping every shadow in here."

I didn't wait for her to tell me a second time. I pushed him through the portal and followed. It deposited us just outside of the college.

"Alex—" Whatever else he'd intended to say devolved into one pained sound. The surrounding shadows warped and twisted with a life all their own in direct defiance of the morning light.

I glanced toward our dorm clear across the lawn and down at Matt sagging against me. He looked like he was desperately trying to pull himself together and failing miserably. His eyes flashed rapid fire between blue and black. Much longer out here and we'd have significantly bigger problems than our lack of communication. I took a deep breath and grabbed his hands. The shifting stopped, landing squarely on black.

I walked us into the shadow world and raced to the dorm. We emerged on the wrong side of the door and Matt shadowed us through. I wasn't even fully materialized when his mouth closed over mine. The intensity of it forced me the rest of the way into the physical world. My shoulders dug into the door as I crushed him against me. I'd been terrified that day he'd told me to leave that he'd finally changed his mind about being together. But whatever this was, it proved that he still wanted me.

His fingers dug into my sides and I couldn't tell if he was trying to push me away or urge me on. It didn't matter. His mouth was still hungrily on mine and I was too far gone to stop. I pushed us away from the door to get to the bedroom. We made it halfway when he started pushing back. I tried to shadow us there, and he used the same trick I had earlier to keep us rooted. Fine, neutral territory it was.

The couch slid away from our less than graceful fall. It wasn't until I was holding the shredded remains of his shirt that I realized my own clothes were equally in tatters. I violently shoved the coffee table further out of the way. This wasn't about being tender or sweet. Something deeper had hold of us, a fire that left no room or breath for questions. No chance to voice doubts.

I pulled him close against me, desperate for the skin-to-skin contact I'd been denied these last few weeks. He groaned and wrapped himself around me. This was going to be rough, and I didn't care. I needed more of him. I needed all of him.

"Matt," I moaned between kisses. "I love you. I can't... I don't..." There was no way to finish that. I couldn't live without him. It was a truth deep down that wouldn't let me give up on him. I worked my way along his neck and shoulder, gripping him like he might vanish at any moment.

He arched into me and tangled a hand in my hair. "Alexi," he moaned.

I scrambled for our supplies, but barely had a chance to roll on the condom and apply lube before he drove himself onto me. The world went white. It felt frozen in place and I thought I might pass out from the sensation. Neither of us moved, and I worried that Matt actually had. He shuddered and everything shattered. Matt was mine, body and soul, whether he could admit it or not.

With a growl I didn't even recognize as mine, I drove into him, pistoning my hips until the world fell away. Matt met me thrust for thrust, his intense heat fluttering and pulsing around me, while he raked his nails across my shoulders. Not even climaxing could satiate the need dominating us.

I shuddered through a third orgasm that threatened to disintegrate me and collapsed beside Matt. Despite feeling wrung out, there wasn't a doubt in my mind that we could keep going. I was dubious if that was an upside or a downside to being a demon. Once my heart rate and breathing returned to normal, I glanced over at Matt. His eyes were closed, but he was definitely still awake. He still hadn't said a word since he'd cried my name hours ago.

Hours!

I sat bolt upright, a move my spent body immediately protested. "I can't believe you got me to skip my classes."

He cracked his eyes, revealing a pair of perfect blue crystals, a hint of merriment swimming in their depths. "You should play hooky more often," he responded with a short laugh.

I raised an eyebrow. "Is this what you do when you're skipping class?"

"No," he said simply. I didn't think he was, but the sadness in the answer implied that there was something else. But I expect asking to result in answers.

I slid down beside him, rolling so I could hold him more easily, and placed a gentle kiss against his lips. Even after our marathon, he reacted, tilting my hips closer and leaning into me. My stomach grumbled, and he smiled against my mouth. I pulled away with a groan. "We should probably eat something."

"Certainly, sounds like it," he replied playfully, a small smile tugging at the corners of his mouth.

"Are you hungry?"

"Not really."

"Liar. When is the last time you ate something?" I asked, sliding my hand over his sides, unable to deny how prominent his ribs had become since the last time I'd seen him.

He shrugged. "I haven't been able to eat." His choice of words concerned me. I'd seen how much food Matt could make disappear; he was always hungry.

"Bet I can fix that." Hope shone in his eyes and my heart broke. I glanced towards the kitchen. The phone and takeout menu were both in there, but I was petrified if I got up he'd vanish.

"I won't go anywhere," he said quietly.

I looked back at him, not sure if I dared to take him at his word.

"Besides, I'm too tired to move," he added with a devilish smile, closing his eyes as if feigning a nap. He squeezed my hand, though I hadn't realized he was holding it. "I promise," he whispered.

Waiting wouldn't get us fed, so I shadowed to the kitchen and ordered entirely too much food. In a moment of bravery, I slipped into my room to grab some lounge pants and the comforter from my bed. When I returned, Matt's fake nap had turned into a very real one. I bundled him beneath the blankets and settled beside him. He stayed curled up until a knock at the door. He blinked, as if surprised to find that he'd fallen asleep.

"Food's here," I said in explanation, standing up.

"In case you forgot, I'm still naked down here," he said snidely.

I smiled back at him. I most definitely had not. "Then I guess you should stay quiet," I said, tossing the comforter over his head. I could just make out his faint chuckle as I opened the door.

"All of this for you?" the delivery guy asked in disbelief.

"No," I replied calmly. Matt snickered behind me, and the guy's eyes widened knowingly.

"Got quite the evening planned, eh?" he asked, wiggling his eyebrows suggestively as he passed me the bags.

"Who said it was just the evening?" I returned. "My partner is very hungry after... our day." Matt's snickering was nearing outright laughter. When was the last time I'd heard that sweet sound?

"Don't do anything I wouldn't do," he added with something bordering on a leer.

I gave him my most sinister smile. "I'm sure I will."

Matt finally erupted into all out giggles beneath the comforter. The poor guy didn't even register what I'd said until I closed the door on his shocked face. The second the latch clicked into place, Matt threw off the comforter, gasping for air between bursts of laughter.

I brought the bags over and arranged their contents on the coffee table. "You doing alright?"

He struggled for air. "Have I ever told you that you're really funny?" He wiped tears from the corners of his eyes as he finally sobered and eyed the spread. "That's a lot of food for one person."

"I'm hoping you'll share." I passed him a fork and an entire carton of beef lo mien.

"I told you I wasn't hungry," he said bluntly.

I stroked the side of his face. "Yes, you are. Now eat."

He looked into the carton with a longing that broke my heart. There was no way he wasn't starving. "You're the one who should eat. You're getting too skinny."

Weren't we the pot calling the kettle black? And did my ears deceive me, or was that a note of concern? I wasn't about to argue with him, though. I leaned forward and grabbed a carton at random that turned out to be chicken and broccoli. He watched me as if making sure I would actually eat while still not having taken a single bite himself.

"I'll make you a deal. I'll eat, if you do."

He looked from my container to me and then back at his own. He let out a deep breath, then slowly swirled some noodles and took a bite. I mirrored the action, and he took another. After a few bites, he stopped checking to see if I was still eating. I finished mine and nibbled on some rice while he continued to devour container after container. It reminded me of when we'd first met and he always eating.

I leaned against the couch and went for broke. "I'm going home next weekend."

He turned at the declaration and the noodle he was slurping tossed broth on his nose.

I chuckled and wiped the sauce away. "The Harvest Fair will be in town. It's usually pretty interesting. You should come with me, get out of this place for a while."

He swallowed his latest bite and actually seemed to consider the proposal. "I guess I could see what I can do." It was more than I had dared hope for.

"It'll be nice. We'll go somewhere that we won't run into anyone or anything relating to school. Almost like a mini vacation." I smiled and mentally crossed my fingers.

"No one from school, huh?" he mumbled, more to himself than me. Then he took a deep breath that came out in a tremendous sigh. "Whoa, I'm stuffed." He eyed the devastation he'd wrought. Of the vast quantities I'd ordered, only three small cartons had survived. He glanced at me nervously.

I cupped his face, gently turning it so he was looking at me, and he met my gentle kiss with one of his own. "I love you," I whispered. This whole day had proven to me he wasn't nearly as far away as I'd feared. Maybe there was hope for us yet.

"Alex, I..." Emotion shimmered in his eyes. A longing that reminded me of the sketch he'd done. "I think it'd be great to see your hometown." He leaned in again and the feel of his mouth against mine was pure ecstasy.

We disintegrated into cuddles and kisses until at last we both drifted off. When I awoke hours later, he was gone. My heart fractured into a thousand pieces at seeing the empty space where he should have been. Not again.

I curled into a tight ball and cried myself into oblivion. Had I just imagined the whole thing? It had been so vivid, so real. Matt, my Matt, had returned to me for a few glorious hours and now it was like he'd never been here at all.

In my misery, I lashed out at the cartons on the table, except they were gone. In their place was a single piece of paper. I wiped my face and tried to focus. It was too dark to make it out properly, so I shadowed the lamp on, revealing a sketch and two words.

I picked up the page and held it up to the light. It was a picture of me sleeping with "*I'm Sorry*" scribbled next to it. So it hadn't been some dream. Matt had been here, and he'd left—again—even though he'd promised not to.

CHAPTER 28
THOMAS

Matt

My inability to stay away from Alex was going to get him killed. It didn't matter that he was like life itself to me or that even an hour in his company could restore my spirits. If I couldn't stay away long enough to eliminate the threat, I'd lose him... for good. Even knowing that, I couldn't stop myself from considering his invitation. The danger was in Arminius, not in his hometown.

Alex's home. I'd get to see the place—the people—that had made Alex, well, Alex. I'd give anything to see that. Decided, I quickened my pace. If I was going to go, I'd have to really show up until then. Sadly, that included being more engaged at the fight club. I suppressed a groan as I approached the usual meeting spot.

"You look better," Kyle said, eying me skeptically.

"What's that supposed to mean?" I crossed my arms, not appreciating his sudden interest in my appearance.

Travis walked up behind me and grabbed my shoulders. "Ease up." He released me and moved around to get a better look at me. After suffering his gaze for several seconds, he snapped his fingers. "I've got it. You look like you got laid."

I scrambled to hide my surprise, but judging did my Travis and Kyle's smirks, I was doing a piss-poor job of it. Was I really so transparent, or did I just look that bad before?

Travis's gaze narrowed abruptly. "It wasn't that witch from the club, was it? Because you said you weren't interested." He bared his teeth at me in a snarl and I rolled my eyes.

"Trust me, I'm not the reason she's not interested in you. Besides, she's not really my type."

He pulled his shoulders back and puffed out his chest. "What the hell is that supposed to mean?" It was an empty bluster. We both knew I could put him down without even trying. Still... I'd seen smarter people make stupider mistakes. I braced myself in case he took a swing after all. Getting into a scuffle with Travis might not be the wisest thing, but I was in no mood for his antics. Abandoning Alex in his nest of blankets had felt like cutting off a limb, and the wound was still fresh.

"He's saying you're an ugly ass. Now stow it. Thomas is expecting us." At George's interjection, my head snapped around. It was about time I got to meet this mysterious figure. He sneered at me. "That's right, little Matty, the big boss is intrigued enough to want to meet you. Best not to keep him waiting."

Travis and Kyle shared a look and shrugged, then ambled away from fraternity row... in the *opposite* direction of town.

I did a much better job of stifling my surprise this time. I'd suspected "Thomas" might be in charge, but hadn't been able to confirm it without raising more suspicion than it was worth. And bonus: if we were seeing Thomas now, then that meant no fight club for me tonight. I felt downright smug as I moved to follow the duo.

I'd only gone a few steps when George grabbed the front of my shirt and yanked me to his face. I mentally berated myself for letting my guard down and smothered the overwhelming impulse to tear him apart.

"You better not embarrass me, gutter rat. I went out on a limb for you." He shoved me back without giving me a chance to offer any empty reassurances, and I gained another useful tidbit. Whoever this guy was, he frightened George. He glared at me, then spun on his heel.

I jogged to catch up and fell in step. When they finally slowed their brisk pace, we were in a part of campus I'd never been, if we even *were* on campus anymore. The surrounding buildings resembled the stone of the main entrance. But where that was shiny and warm, the stone here was worn and blackened. Not even the foliage seemed to want anything to do with it beyond a smattering of stubborn weeds. One word came to mind: desolate.

"Where are we?" I finally asked, as I peered through a crumbled wall into the maw of an equally derelict building.

George held out his arms. "This is old fraternity row."

"Why does it look empty?" I asked, taking in the choking vines slowly pulling apart the ancient masonry.

"Because it is," Travis offered unhelpfully.

Kyle picked up a broken piece of stone and chunked it into the night. "We pretty much have the run of the place."

"Why?" I asked.

George rounded on me. "You sure are asking a lot of questions."

"Excuse me, if I don't want to wander off into some vampire blood cult," I snapped, getting in his face. I didn't even know if that was a *thing*, but it did the trick.

George resumed walking as if nothing had happened. "Something happened here during the Uprising.

I frowned and searched my knowledge of recent events, limited as it was. "You mean the Shadow War?"

George's face twisted with a snarl. "Leave it to that bitch to get a whole war named after her."

I wisely bit my tongue and refrained from pointing out that the war was actually named for the whole group and not Vera specifically.

"*Anyway*, like I was saying. Something happened here. Something bad. The witches won't go anywhere near this place."

I wanted to ask what had happened, but I'd already asked too many. Undoubtedly, Alex would know. If we ever got through this, I'd have to ask him. We continued picking our way through the ruins until we came to the building at the end of the row. Massive columns rose into the sky to end in broken edges. Their missing halves littered the ground in yet more broken pieces all around the entrance. I'd been in some pretty sketchy places in my life, but even *I* thought this place was a dump.

"Are you coming?" George snapped.

I scurried up the crumbling steps, dubious that they wouldn't disintegrate beneath our combined weight. Of all the rotten places to have a hangout, these assholes would find the rottenest. Not that I was truly surprised. People like George inevitably found themselves on the fringes where there were fewer people around to judge their depravity.

George and the others confidently worked their way through the rubble, and I followed sedately in their wake. The inside didn't look to be in any better repair, though magical orbs clung to the walls offering ambient light that nothing to illuminate the foreboding dark. The deeper we ventured, the more my skin crawled. Something about this place wasn't right. But beyond present company, I couldn't imagine what that might be.

Kyle peeled away from the group. "I'll let Thomas know we're here."

"I already know." The disembodied voice seemed to come from nowhere and everywhere all at once. I contemplated shifting the darkness to illuminate him, but doubted the others knew that was even something that could be done.

"Do you always have to do that?" George asked, sounding more like a whiny brat than the leader of a gang determined to hunt down and murder my best friend.

The voice laughed without humor and stepped into the light. Its owner was older than I'd expected. He could have been a teacher, and he definitely wasn't a Shadow Demon. He came closer and a sense of familiarity washed over. Try as I might, though, I couldn't place the short, dark beard and soldierly face. His gaze narrowed to a predatory slit. "You certainly took your time."

George angled his thumb at me. "The recruit was gawking at the front door."

"Recruit, eh? We'll see about that." He walked leisurely around us, his gaze picking apart every detail like he was dissecting rats in a lab instead of young men. "What makes you so sure that he's not the one we're looking for?" The man's gaze snapped to George.

"I'm not an idiot, Thomas. We vetted him. Nothing weird or nothing," he spluttered. "Plus, I'm stronger than he is."

"You have a very high opinion of your power. Come here."

It took me a second to realize Thomas was addressing me. I shoved my increasing anxiety down and took a step forward. I'd certainly faced opponents far more imposing than this guy. Sure, he had wide shoulders and looked like he could take out a stone wall by himself, but that wasn't what had me worried. I couldn't shake the growing sensation that I should *know* him.

"What's your name, boy?"

I gritted my teeth and ground out, "Matt." His eyes drilled into me until I added, "Matthew Duncan."

He raised a bushy eyebrow. "Matthew. Interesting." Despite the assessment, he sounded bored. "So, *Matthew*, what makes you think you can help with our little... quest?"

"I'm observant and better at going unnoticed than your current—" The term lackeys came to mind, but I didn't expect that would be well received. "Recruits," I finished instead.

Thomas considered me without blinking, then pointed into the distance. "You see that wall over there?"

I followed the path of his finger. A light blared to life, revealing a wall adorned with pictures of people from Battle Tactics, as well as classmates that hadn't returned for the fall semester. Some of them had giant X's drawn across them, including present company. I squinted at the X-ed out image of myself. It was an unusual shot from the side and a little blurry, as if I'd been moving when it was taken. I eagerly sought the only picture I cared about, praying there was already an X on it.

Alex's picture was significantly better than mine, boasting a stunning shot of his emerald eyes and a half smile on his lips. But no X. My heart seized, and I fought to keep the reaction from showing on my face. I shifted my gaze higher to see who else was on the chopping block, but my focus got snagged by someone unexpected.

Above the photos was a picture of Vera herself. She wasn't sporting the amiable smile I'd become familiar with, though. No, she was absolutely terrifying in full battle regalia and charging forward. The picture was too far to tell, but I'd bet good money that her eyes were the color of midnight. She might have even been shouting some sort of war cry, but it was hard to tell with the dagger sticking out of her face.

I swallowed my trepidation and forced my voice to remain neutral. "George mentioned y'all were looking for someone in class. But he was a little vague on the details."

Thomas shot George a nasty look before walking over to the wall of photos. It seemed appropriate to follow, but I made sure to stop in front of a photo a suitable distance from Alex's. "Not just *someone*. We're looking for an abomination of nature. Something that cannot be permitted to exist in this world." Spittle flew from his lips to pepper the image before him. He regathered himself and glanced at me as if to gage my reaction to his outburst. "We've been able to cobble together a few clues, but admittedly, we *are* much farther from our mark than I would like."

"What do you know?" I asked, giving him a level stare in return.

He waved a dismissive hand, but I didn't miss the tightening around his eyes. "As far as *demons* go, they'll make the top ten for sure. We suspect they've perfected the art of passing. Undoubtedly, how they've remained undetected for so long." He tilted his head and added in a more musing tone, "Moderately attractive."

"They eliminated Travis, right out the gate," Kyle snickered, only to be silenced by what sounded like Travis hitting him in the gut.

I didn't turn to look, far more focused on Thomas and his witch hunt. "What else?" I prompted, needing to know just how much they had.

He gave me a curious look. "Graceful, a natural at movement. Fluid. Like a..." He paused, as if debating how much to reveal. "Like a dancer."

Travis snorted. "You mean queer." The others laughed, but Thomas didn't.

"This stain must be wiped from the earth. Do not belittle the severity of this with your inconsequential labels." His intensity silenced the others and sent a shiver down my spine.

"How can I help?" I could have thanked Nyx herself that my voice didn't shake. Thomas' smile turned evil.

"Let's see how *observant* you are about your classmates. Perhaps you *can* be of use in eradicating this contamination of the blood."

"You're friends with Roman, right?" George asked, stepping up and yanking Alex's picture off the wall. "He's an odd one, for sure."

My stomach sank. I wasn't sure I could answer without retching right there on the floor. "Alex?"

"Yeah, what do you know about him?"

I shrugged, painfully aware of how closely Thomas was watching me. "For starters, I'm stronger than he is. He's a total bookworm. Even got him to tutor me last semester. It comes in handy knowing an egghead."

"Well, I guess that's one strike. If you're stronger than he is..." My heart slowed as the marker George held hovered over the picture of Alex.

"What about other people? Who does he spend time with? If you catch my drift." Kyle asked, and I could have killed him on the spot.

"We don't really talk about girls," I said, barely managing not to snarl.

"Oh?" George stared at me like he was second guessing my usefulness. "He never brings anyone back to the dorm or anything?"

"I haven't seen him bring anyone around. But who can say?"

"He's in ballroom, right? Who voluntarily signs up for that?" Travis asked with a grating guffaw. My murder list was getting longer, and I was increasingly more alarmed at how much they knew about Alex.

"Yeah... It's weird alright, but I think he might know something the rest of us don't. The chicks in that class practically drool every time he comes around. It's a little disgusting honestly," I added with maybe a hair too much conviction.

"And he hasn't brought any of them to the dorm?" George insisted.

What the hell was wrong with these people? Who *cared* who he brought to the dorm? "I think he's hung up on someone else."

"Who?"

"I already told you, we don't really talk about girls. He's odd for sure, but nothing special." It was the first outright lie I'd told all night, and I prayed no one would catch it.

George sucked his teeth and pinned the image back. He did not add a red X, however. Apparently, it would take more than my word to clear Alex and I already felt like I'd run a gauntlet.

"Got anything to drink?" I asked to direct their focus away from the fact that my composure was seriously cracking.

Kyle and Travis let out a whoop and waved for me to follow them. As I ventured after, I heard Thomas catch George. I slowed to listen, but didn't dare look back.

"Your little friend better not disappoint. I grow weary of your failure," Thomas said gruffly.

"Ease up, old man. We'll find your poser."

At the whisper of shuffling, I quickened my pace. George brushed past me as he followed his goons. I chanced a glance over my shoulder to see Thomas glowering at all of us like he'd rather skin us alive than trust us to find who he was searching for. His glare itched between my shoulder blades long after I was out of sight.

As I followed the trio back outside, my resolve strengthened, along with my conviction that I knew Thomas from somewhere. But where?

BOOK THREE

THE KNIGHTS OF NYX

S BOLANOS

CONTENTS

CHAPTER 1
DENHAM

Alexi

My hope that Matt would accompany me to the Harvest Festival in my hometown shriveled with each day that went by without so much as a glimpse of him. It officially died as I packed my bag. Perhaps the time away from each other was for the best. Maybe I'd even extend my stay beyond the weekend. I'd completed all of my assignments and had no pending projects. Missing a few days of class wouldn't hurt.

That I was contemplating skipping classes—intentionally—was enough to give me pause. It also reminded me of how I'd unintentionally played hooky with Matt the week prior. When I'd invited him to go with me. For all his enthusiasm about seeing my hometown, he'd vanished faster than water in a desert. Not even the sweet picture of me sleeping made up for the lackluster apology scribbled next to it or the fact that he'd left. What he was apologizing for, anyway? Leaving? Being an ass? Lying about wanting to come?

I nearly ripped the zipper of my bookbag off its track as I slammed it home with a little too much force. A glance at the clock on my nightstand confirmed what I already knew—time was up. He wasn't coming, and no amount of stalling would change that. Tears pricked at the back of my eyes. Would he even tell me we were over or would he keep ghosting me until I got the hint? I willed my eyes to dry as I carried my bag into the living room.

"Good, you're still here," Matt said, appearing out of nowhere. His gaze flicked from me to the stuffed backpack. "You still going home?"

I fought to keep my glimmer of hope at seeing him from flourishing. If he truly wanted to go, he'd have been here this last week. "Um... yeah," I said, hating how raw my voice sounded. Was this it? Had he planned to wait until the last second to break up with me so that he wouldn't have to deal with the fallout? I braced myself for the inevitable, carefully keeping my gaze fixed on the carpet, so he wouldn't see the hurt threatening to swallow me whole.

"Still want me to come?"

My head shot up. "What?"

He took a tentative step closer, that same hint of sheepishness to his features that I'd once found so endearing. "I'd like to go to the Harvest Festival with you. If you'll have me."

"Of course," I said too quickly.

Despite my over eager reply, the biggest grin I'd seen from him in a long time stretched across his face. Then a tide of words flowed out. "When do we leave? Where exactly are is Denham? How are we going to get there? What's a fair like? I've never been to a fair before. How long does it last? Do I need to bring anything? How many people will be there?"

I held up my hands to stem the rush, unable to hold back the laughter at this unexpected energy. "One at a time, please."

His mouth snapped shut with an audible bubble sound while the rest of him appeared to vibrate in place with the force of keeping his questions restrained.

"Okay, one question."

He took a deep inhale that puffed his chest, then let it out in a burst. "What's Denham like and how are we getting there?" He winced. "Oops. That was two."

A laugh burst out of me, bringing forth the tears I'd been fighting before.

Panic flashed across Matt's face as I dropped my bag and doubled over in my fit. "What? Did I say something wrong? I know I should have been here sooner. But I had a thing I had to take care of and—"

I held up a hand once more to stop his babbling. I barely even cared that he said "a thing" instead of whatever he'd actually been doing. He was here. He wanted to come with me. And he was excited. "You didn't say anything wrong. I just... missed you," I said as I straightened and wiped my eyes.

A light pink stained his cheeks. "I-I've missed you too."

My heart soared. He didn't want to break up. I cleared my throat and picked up my bookbag again before the emotion had my crying... again. "Denham is nice, if quiet. Like most small towns, everyone knows everyone. As for how we'll get there, I made a portal."

"Really?"

"Yep. It's on the roof." I neglected to mention that it had taken nearly every day since I'd invited him to make the damn thing and get it to stay open. Much as I'd have liked to keep the portal for future visits home, I wasn't sure it was quite worth all the effort to keep it maintained. Abruptly, I realized we were staring at each other and smiling. "We should get going if we don't want to miss supper. Do you need to pack anything?"

He smirked and reached into the couch. When he pulled his hand out, he held a small duffel bag.

My eyebrows shot up. "How long has that been there?" And did I need to check the rest of the dorm for other "hiding places"?

"I've... uh, been packed for a few days." His smile slipped. "I didn't mean to cut it so close."

I searched his face, but the answers I wanted weren't there. "The important thing is that you made it. Now, let's get out of here before my mom calls to ask where we are."

Matt brightened and slung the duffel across his body. Without warning, he stepped forward and planted a chaste kiss on my lips, then dashed to the door. "What're you waiting for? Let's go, slow poke. I could use a break from this place," he said, though that last bit was more to himself.

My head spun as I situated my bookbag on my shoulders and moved to join him. Who was this person? He bore no resemblance to the Matt I'd had to endure the last couple of months.

Unbridled joy danced in his eyes as he flashed me a wide smile and reached for the door. I flattened my palm on the door to keep it closed and his eyebrows pinched into a V. "What—"

I cradled his jaw, cutting him off with a kiss. It was truly a shame we didn't have more than the lingering press of lips, but if we waited much longer to leave, my mother would start calling. "I love you, Matt," I said, then opened the door. We smiled at each other, neither of us making a move to leave. My heart felt like it might burst as I waited for him to say it back.

"Alex."

"Yeah?" I whispered, anticipation making my voice thin.

Wickedness darkened his crystal blue eyes. "Race you to the top."

He took advantage of my stunned state to turn and bolt. I shadowed to catch up while the door slammed shut, automatically locking, but didn't shadow again. Our feet pounded against the lush carpet that absorbed the sound of our frantic race. We careened around a corner, nearly taking out one of our RAs, pushing and shoving each other to get to the stairwell first. We burst onto the rooftop, laughing and panting for breath. Matt caught my gaze, and we shared another smile. Then he straightened and looked around at the flat—noticeably empty—roof.

"Uh... Where is it?"

I gestured to the side of the maintenance room.

Matt looked from me to the innocuous wall, then a knowing smirk spread across his face. "You cloaked it." The pride in his voice filled my chest with a warm glow. He held out his hand for mine. "Well, what are we waiting for?"

I wrapped my fingers around his and led us through the portal. The cool mist of the barrier brushed over my face until it encompassed my entire body. Then the infinite darkness of the Shadow world gave way to bright sunlight and a crisp autumn afternoon. A light breeze ruffled my hair as we stood at the edge of a forest with nothing but open field between us and Denham. I took in Matt and his expression of awe and knew I'd made the right decision not to put the exit by my house, or even better, in it.

"That's..." He dropped my hand and took a step forward before stopping to look back at me. "That's Denham?"

I walked up beside him and wrapped an arm around his shoulders. "Sure is. And if you look over there." I pointed to our right where you could just make out the Ferris Wheel and some low-lying buildings. "That's the fair."

"It looks as big as the town."

I chuckled and squeezed him close. "Denham is small even compared to Sieben Hügel. But the Harvest Festival Fair is actually for all the surrounding parishes."

"Parishes," Matt repeated like he was tasting the word. Then he wrinkled his nose. "Why does the UK have to have such weird names for everything?"

I snorted. "You mean the right names? You know, since the UK was here before the US."

He rolled his eyes, but leaned into me. We stayed like that for a few minutes, soaking up the sunshine and appreciating the view. Then Matt tilted his head back to look at me with half-lidded eyes and whispered, "I really like it here. Your home is beautiful." He stretched his neck, and I met him halfway for a kiss sweeter than cotton candy.

Seconds from turning to him and deepening the kiss, my phone rang. I groaned and Matt chuckled into my shoulder. "Hello, mother," I said without checking the caller ID.

She sniffed indignantly. "Don't 'mother' me. Have you left the university yet?"

I glanced at Matt, failing to smother his grin. "We're actually at the edge of the forest. Should be there in fifteen to twenty minutes."

"We? Matt came along after all? That's wonderful, sweetie! I can't wait to finally meet this boyfriend of yours."

"He's my friend too, Mom," I countered, cringing at her loud enthusiasm.

Matt leaned toward the phone. "Looking forward to meeting you too, Ms. Roman."

My heart exploded. Or maybe it froze. Whatever it was doing, it definitely wasn't beating anymore. Matt had basically labeled himself as my boyfriend, in public, to another person. Granted, it was my mom, and there wasn't really anyone around to witness it, but it was also the first time he'd acknowledged our relationship extended beyond friendship out loud.

"Lexi. Honey. Are you still there?"

"Huh? Yeah. I'm still here. We'll be there soon." I glanced at Matt, whose lips were twitching in a repressed smile. He knew damn well what he'd done.

"Excellent. I'll make sure the guest room has fresh linens. See you soon. And don't dally!" she admonished before hanging up.

Matt raised an eyebrow. "So, guest room, huh?"

I ducked my head to hide the burn on my cheeks. "My mom has some very strict rules about having boys in my room."

"Almost like she doesn't trust you to keep your hands to yourself."

I looked up in time to catch his cheeky grin. "Well, it might be warranted in this case. I've always had trouble keeping my hands to myself where you're concerned." The blush that stained his cheeks was beyond adorable, but Matt didn't pull away. In fact, he leaned in closer and I wrapped an arm around his waist to keep him there.

"Are we going straight to your house?"

"I thought it'd be nice to show you around the village a little before heading that way." I released my hold on him and resumed holding his hand to make walking smoother.

"Your mom won't be upset?"

Sweet night, Matt's consideration of my mother was melting my heart, but it had been so long since it'd just been the two of us, I wasn't willing to forsake the time. "As long as we're home in plenty of time for dinner, we'll be fine. It doesn't take long to get to my house from town."

"Your house," Matt whispered beneath his breath with an unmistakable twinge of awe.

My heart constricted, and I couldn't help but press my lips against his temple. "Come on, we'll start at the community center. If we're lucky, we'll run into some familiar faces, but I imagine most of them are already helping with the fair."

CHAPTER 2
MS. ROMAN

Matt

Alex's House. I was standing inside Alex's house. Where he'd grown up. Where he'd made countless memories. And where his mom was currently staring at me like I was an alien. I waved at her, not really knowing what else to do. She positively beamed. Her eyes were like his, albeit with a striking circle of hazel around her irises and a halo of curly blonde ringlets. She was still staring. I was beginning to wonder what Alex had told her about me. He stood there watching me, as if waiting to see what I would do. I wished he would say something.

"Mom, this is Matt. Matt, this is my mom."

"Hi Miss Roman. It's nice to meet you," I said nervously, thinking about the last time we'd spoken. Stealing the phone to talk to some faceless woman hundreds of miles away had seemed hilarious at the time; it was less so now that I was standing in front of the real person.

She waved her hand. "There's no need to stand on such formality. You can call me Yanessa." Well, that wasn't going to happen. "It's so nice to *finally* meet you." She took two steps forward and swept me up in a tight hug.

I looked over her shoulder at Alex in a silent cry for help. What was I supposed to do? I'd never met anyone's mom before. Rather than come to my aid, he smothered his laugh and left me to fend for myself. Eventually, she released me, and I staggered as I tried to regain my balance.

"You do have very nice hair," she said, absently fixing it.

I looked at Alex in confusion, but his laugh appeared to have gone down the wrong way.

"Did you need any help with dinner?" Alex asked once he rediscovered the ability to talk.

"Lexi, my love, I doubt you've learned how to cook in the short time that you've been away."

"Mom."

Miss Roman blatantly ignored his deadpan. "But you and Matt can certainly set the table. I assume you still know where everything is kept?" He barely didn't roll his eyes and motioned for me to follow. When I stepped through into the dining room, Alex was already opening cabinet doors to acquire what we would need.

"She seems nice," I said, accepting the stack of plates he passed me.

"She *is* very nice. Though I fear I'm going to regret most of what she says." He grimaced. "I'll just go ahead and apologize. Things could get...weird."

I chuckled and stepped closer to him. "She's your mom. Pretty sure that comes with the territory."

He released a stuttering sigh when I placed my hands on his arms and leaned forward until our foreheads touched. "Yeah. I just..."

"Just what?" I leaned slightly back to study his face and was more than a little surprised to find it clouded with uncertainty.

"I just really want you to like her."

I snorted. "I'm a little more worried she won't like me, not the other way around."

Despite my self-deprecating statement, Alex's features softened, and he cupped the side of my face. "There's not a doubt in my mind that she's going to love you. Possibly almost as much as I do."

My breath caught, and words failed me. No one had ever made me feel as special as Alex did. I leaned into the caress and let myself get lost in his emerald eyes and the promise of a future I'd never imagined. "Alexi," I whispered as our lips drifted closer.

"Lexi, honey, why don't you go get cleaned up?" Miss Roman called from the kitchen.

We both chuckled. "I'm telling you, that woman has a sixth sense," he said as he stepped back. His hand sliding from my cheek was a painful reminder of just how much I missed his touch. "Don't worry about my mom. She can be embarrassing, at times, but she's been Team Matt the whole time." Alex brushed a kiss across my cooling cheek and flashed me a smile before venturing out of the room into what appeared to be a hallway.

"You're welcome to wash up in the kitchen, Matt."

Startled out of my fuzzy cloud of Alex, I turned to find Miss Roman leaning against the doorway, wiping her hands with a dish towel. "Of course." I scurried past her to the kitchen sink and immediately began washing my hands like I could scrub off every dirty sin from my past... and present.

"Easy, dear. You'll wash the life right out of them." She passed me the same towel she'd been using.

As I dried my hands, I could feel her eyes on me, scrutinizing, weighing. Did she find me wanting? Did she know I was lying to her son? I'd never had the pleasure of experiencing mother's intuition, but if anyone had it, I'd bet Miss Roman did. I awkwardly hung the towel, not sure what to do with myself now. A silence that I was probably supposed to be filling settled between us.

"I hope it's alright that Lexi shared the details of your past with me."

My head jerked up both at the unexpected statement and the overwhelming softness of her voice. "It's fine," I croaked, my throat suddenly tight.

She placed an equally soft hand on my shoulder and held my gaze with eyes that were every bit as intense as Alex's. "I'm truly sorry for your loss. However it came to pass, no child should have to endure what you have."

Great, now my eyes were stinging and swallowing was out of the question. Was this what a mother's love was like?

"Why don't you explore a bit and make yourself at home while I finish up here? And after dinner, we can look at Lexi's baby pictures." She winked and hip-checked me back toward the dining room.

"That would be great. Thanks, Miss Roman, for... everything."

She placed her hands on her hips, her lips twisting into a scowl. "There's no way I'm going to get you to call me anything but Miss Roman, am I?"

I smiled and offered a shrug before doing as she suggested and wandering off. While I'd been in quite a few houses during my stays with foster families, I was no judge of quality. There'd been fancy houses without a scrap of personality and some of the meanest people you'd ever meet, and houses that barely constituted more than a decaying shack with equally cruel foster parents. But Alex's house was different. There was an energy here that wrapped around you like a warm blanket and invited you to stay a while. Rather than art, the walls held photographs, and while nothing looked obviously new, everything was clean and cared for. My eyes stung again as I realized what made Alex's place so different from all the others—this wasn't just a house, it was a home.

Clearing my throat, I made my way into the hall. What was likely the living room caught my attention, but I was more interested in seeing Alex's room. Would it feel the same here as it did in Arminius? Two false stops later, I cracked open the door to a third room and smiled. I flicked on the light and stepped inside.

There wasn't a doubt in my mind that I'd found my destination. Everything about the room screamed Alex, from the historical books piled everywhere to the posters of famous figures from history on the walls. I even saw the bare spot where the poster of the university used to hang. And it did, in fact, feel like his room at the dorm. I glided my fingers over the spines of various books. The most remarkable thing about them being that they were Alex's, though I was sure he would disagree.

"There you are. I was going to give you the grand tour myself, but I see you've gone and done it without me."

I turned as Alex walked in and dropped a hand towel on the end of the bed. "Is it my imagination or are some of these posters *also* in your dorm room?"

He shifted to stand in front of an identical poster of the Roman Colosseum that graced the wall by his window. "I don't know what you're talking about."

My gaze dropped to his lips, and I thought wistfully of our denied kiss. With a significant amount of effort, I brought my focus back to his eyes. To my surprise, he was scrutinizing me much as his mother had done in the kitchen. Before I could question the look, though, he stepped toward the door and slowly closed it. I glanced from him to the now shut, though not locked, door. "What about the rules?" I asked, as he eliminated the distance between us. Each step he took had my heart skipping that much faster.

"What about them?"

The pure ecstasy of Alex's mouth on mine silenced any argument I could have voiced. I broke off long enough to drag in a lungful of air, then returned to devouring his kisses. He slipped his hands around my waist, tugging me flush against him so I had to wiggle my arms free to wrap them around his neck. Our tongues danced together in a perfect balance of give and take that at once grounded me and made me want to fly. I tangled my fingers in his hair, eager for everything he was giving me, yet aching for more.

"Dinner is ready!" Miss Roman called.

I reluctantly released my hold on him, though he refused to do the same. When he leaned down to claim another, even sweeter, kiss, I couldn't help but melt against him. "We should probably get out there before she comes looking for us," I sighed.

"Alexi Roman, I know that's not a closed door, I see!"

Alex groaned and gave my sides a squeeze before letting me go. "I suppose you're right."

As my head cleared, Miss Roman's promise for after dessert had a smile blooming on my face.

"What's that look for?" he asked with a frown.

Excitement continued to bubble in me like candy dropped in soda until it felt like I might explode. "Your mom said we'd look at your baby pics after dinner."

"Oh no we won't!" He spun on his heel and raced for the door.

Rather than compete with his long strides, I shadowed into the hallway where I stuck my tongue out at him before taking off for the dining room. "Miss Roman! Alex says he can't *wait* to share all his baby pictures!" I shouted as I skid into the dining room with Alex hot on my heels.

"He does, does he?" Her eyebrows lifted in twin arcs. "That's quite the interesting hairdo, oh rebellious child of mine."

Alex's hands flew to his hair. His cheeks darkened to a dusky peach as he tried unsuccessfully to smooth it back into submission. I coughed to cover a laugh, and Miss Roman's penetrating gaze swiveled to me.

"Be a dear and grab some napkins from the kitchen."

"Yes, Miss Roman." I quickly bobbed my head and shadowed to the kitchen. By the time I returned, they'd already sat. I took the seat across from Alex. There weren't any dishes to pass around, as Miss Roman had already plated everything. I was about to take another bite when something nudged my foot. Alex gave me a soft smile when I glanced at him.

"You should tell mom about how you figured out that nifty cloaking spell." He looked at his mother. "A third-year level spell."

She, in turn, leaned forward, green eyes alight with curiosity. "That sounds like quite the accomplishment."

"Really?" I frowned. There really wasn't much to it. "I mean, Alex helped."

He shook his head while she scoffed. "Don't sell yourself short, dear. My Lexi has shared some of his struggles and successes with your Shadow courses. You seem like a natural."

What I now realized was Alex's foot bumped mine again before rubbing along my calf. "You should be proud of yourself, Matt. I know I am."

Proud? When was the last I'd been proud of anything I'd done? Despite my doubt, though, warmth spread through my chest at Alex's words.

"Right. Who's ready for pictures?" Miss Roman plucked the stuffed scrapbook from the chair beside her and Alex groaned. All I could do was laugh at how perfectly normal it all felt.

CHAPTER 3
DANIEL

Alexi

Being forced to sleep in my room when only a wall separated me from Matt was torture. It was a wonder I got any sleep at all. But when morning came, I popped up fresh as flowers in spring. To my surprise, Matt was already up and studying the contents of the pantry.

"Would have thought you'd sleep in what with their being no classes or assignments," I said, leaning against the wall behind him.

His shoulders tensed, betraying that I'd startled him, then he he turned around and mimicked my pose. "Sleep and I aren't really on good terms these days."

I fought to keep my expression neutral. Was he still having nightmares? Why wouldn't he talk to me about what was going on with him? Much as I wanted to know, demanding answers while he was cornered was not something I wanted to do. I'd seen how well that had gone last time. "You ready to check out the fair?"

"Did you not want to eat first?"

"Figured we could pick up something on the way." I stretched, shamelessly dragging it out and basking in the feel of Matt's eyes on me. We might be in a rocky place, but he definitely still liked what he saw. "To be honest, I'm not all that hungry." Not for food, anyway.

His gaze flicked back to me when I dropped my arms. "It's important to eat breakfast."

"Oh yeah? That mean you've been eating breakfast?" I challenged, because I knew damn well he wasn't.

He broke eye contact and shuffled his feet. "Where were you wanting to grab something?"

"It's a little out of our way, but there's a decent bakery." I pushed off from the wall and helped myself to a glass of orange juice from the icebox.

"When did you want to go?" Matt asked as I rinsed the glass and set it on the rack to dry.

"Now's good."

He glanced beyond me. "What about your mom?"

"I'll leave her a note. She might join us later, but I doubt it. After years of me dragging her there, you could say she's over it." I smiled at Matt and was pleased to find him smiling back. Once I'd scribbled a quick note, letting her know we'd left, but would return in time for dinner and placed it conspicuously on the counter we made our way to town.

To my chagrin, I'd forgotten that the bakery was a major vendor at the fair. While the shop was open, options were slim. We nibbled on our day-old muffins as we wove through streets that were largely empty even at this hour. By the time we reached the edge of town, I was vibrating with excitement. Then we cleared the last ridge that obstructed our view of the fair.

Matt's sharp intake of breath snatched my attention away from the rows upon rows of stalls, the flashing lights of spinning rides, and the enormous Ferris Wheel presiding over it all. "You okay?"

"Yeah. I..." He trailed off, his eyes wide with wonder. "I've never been to a fair."

"I think it's time we fix that. Don't you?" I squeezed his hand, then let him go. He had just enough time to give me a questioning look before I made a beeline for the fair.

"Hey!" His laughter was all the confirmation I needed that he was following full tilt. He crashed into me just as I passed the first booth and it transported me back in time to that day we'd run in the rain. Everything in the world felt so right with Matt in my arms. He smiled up at me, then seemed to register the voices around us and, most importantly, that we were no longer alone. I didn't fight him when he took a step back and awkwardly ran his hand through his hair.

"So, uh, what do we do first?" he asked, once more sounding uncertain.

"Whatever you want. This event is a pretty big deal and there's no end to the things we could do, but first, I want to make sure you're okay."

His hand dropped, and he turned a suddenly anxious face to me. "Huh? What do you mean? Of course, I'm fine."

I stepped closer and took his hand. Immediately, he tensed up, his gaze flitting around us. "You sure about that?"

"You're not... worried?"

I squeezed his hand. "No." Despite my reassurance, he still looked uncertain, and that was okay. I'd grown up with all the support in the world. My sexuality hadn't even registered on the list of things to be worried about. Now, accidentally fatally wounding a guy while making out because of my demonic strength... *that* had made the list. Matt had already shared he hadn't experienced the best humanity in his formative years. It would take time for him to feel comfortable being openly affectionate with another man, but I had faith he'd get there.

"This place is a lot bigger up close. I wouldn't even know where to start."

"I vote we wander the booths, see if we can find any of the people from DAPS, then we can cap things off with Ferris Wheel."

Matt did a double take, and I barked out a laugh at his twisted expression of confusion. "Did you say 'DAPS'?"

I started off down the nearest row of booths. He fell instep, and I quietly told him all about the Denham Agrarian Poets Society. Sadly, we didn't come across anyone, though that might have been a blessing in disguise. I wasn't entirely sure how Nemo would take seeing *two* Shadow Demons in one place. We did bump into Robbie, but thankfully she'd been in too much of a hurry to give me grief about bringing a guy back from school after her advice to "Mind all them boys".

We spent hours wandering the grounds. To my surprise, Matt wasn't interested in the rides, but the Ferris Wheel was a success. It was worth giving up the other rides to see his face when we stopped at the top. It didn't escape my notice that he continued to be drawn towards the craft and other art-centric booths.

We were walking past a series of gaming booths when something caught my eye. I pulled him up short. Today had been going so well, perhaps I could try my luck with something else. "Do the photo booth with me."

He looked at the curtained box, hesitation written all over his face.

I laced our fingers. "Please, Matt. I don't have a single picture of us. They'll just be for me."

He licked his lips and searched my face. "Just for you?"

"Just for me." I silently willed him to say yes.

"Okay."

I quickly dragged him into the booth, which was thankfully unoccupied before he could change his mind.

"A little small in here, don't you think?" he grumbled, squishing in.

"That's half the fun," I laughed. "Now just watch the camera." I pressed the button to start us off, and it began counting down. The first shot he had a skeptical face. "You're supposed to smile." I jostled him and he laughed. "Okay, a funny one."

"A what?" The camera snapped.

"Try again. Make a face."

He crossed his eyes and stuck his tongue out. We both laughed, and the machine began whirring. So far, so good. Time to really test my luck. I turned to face him and he looked back, a smile still playing around his mouth. Then I leaned forward and kissed him while simultaneously reaching out to push the button again. He hesitated a fraction of a second, then kissed me back. I cupped his face, loving how sweet his lips tasted. When I pulled back to see how many images we had left, it was just in time to get my goofy grin caught on camera for the last slot.

The whirring resumed, and I shoved us out of the cramped space. Once we were both out, I swiped and pocketed the prints before he could realize there were two unique sets. "See, that wasn't so bad."

"Fine, it wasn't torture," he admitted with a laugh. "I'm gonna run to the restroom real fast. Be right back?"

"Sure thing. I'll just be over there." I indicated an open space off to the side of the booths, away from the crowds. He nodded and walked off.

I made my way over to the empty area and waited until he was out of sight to pull out my prizes. As adorable as Matt's clueless expressions and silly face were, my actual interest was in the second set. Had I caught the picture I really wanted? To my amazement, the camera had caught the whole kiss from beginning to end. In the first image he clearly was holding back, but by the second he'd given into the kiss completely. But it was the last image that stole my breath. While I'd been grinning at the camera like a lovesick fool, Matt hadn't turned. I ran my finger over the tiny picture, overwhelmed with the way his soft gaze made me feel. He'd yet to vocalize how he felt about me or us, but a picture was worth a thousand words, and this one held volumes.

The soft brush of lips on the back of my neck tickled as they ventured over the exposed skin above my collar. Today was just full of surprises. First the photo booth and now this. The tickle became unbearable, and I shied away with a giggle. "Matt, what's gotten into you?"

"Who's Matt?" The smoky response sent a ripple of shock through me. I knew that voice.

I spun around, eager to eliminate the unwanted contact. "Daniel." I felt dirty, like I could scrub for hours and still not be clean.

He gave me the same crooked smile that had worked in the past. "Nice to see you too, Alexi. So... who's Matt?"

"None of your damn business," I said emphatically.

"What do we have here? The famous Matt maybe?" he said, his gaze riveting on the strips in my hand. Before I processed the eminent danger, he'd already snatched them away.

"Hey!" I lurched for pictures with an indignant squawk, to no avail. Matt would never forgive me if I didn't get those back.

Daniel feigned looking at them, enjoying keeping me at bay far more than what was on his stolen treasure. "You look good, Lexi. Nice to see you finally gave up those last few pounds."

Mortification heated the skin beneath my collar. "Shut up. Give those back."

"Come and get them," he taunted.

I reached again. Matt would be back any second and I wanted Daniel long gone. It would have been easy enough to shadow rather than try to retrieve them by force, but we weren't exactly on campus. Irritated and fuming, I surged forward in a desperate move, only for Daniel's arm to snake around my waist, effectively impeding my efforts. Now, instead of retrieving the pictures, I was struggling to free myself without causing excessive harm or outing the entire supernatural world in broad daylight. What I wouldn't give to let loose and use demonic strength, but I didn't trust that I wouldn't accidentally tear his arm clean off.

"Alex?" The sound was so small, I almost missed it in my struggle.

This is not happening.

I looked up to see all of happiness I'd worked so hard to cultivate drain from Matt's face. "Matt, it's not what it looks like." The moment the words left my mouth, I knew they were an epic mistake. Daniel turned to see who I was shouting at, finally releasing me.

"*This* is Matt?" he asked incredulously. "A little short for you, don't you think, Lexi?"

Matt's jaw tightened, and a familiar steel entered his sharp blue eyes.

No, no, no. I took advantage of Daniel's distraction and made another swipe to snag the photos. He laughed at my futile attempt, stretching his arm higher. "Give them back, Daniel," I growled, on the verge of shadowing. Consequences be damned.

At the mention of Daniel's name, unfiltered rage flash through Matt's eyes.

A new worry shot through me. I knew full well the violence Matt was capable of, and he didn't have the practice of experience to temper his relatively newfound demonic power.

His focus zeroed in on the two small strips. "Those don't belong to you." His disturbingly calm tone made my skin crawl. While I'd never considered him a danger to me, he was dangerous.

"And what are you going to do about it?" Daniel turned to face Matt, oblivious to his now tenuous hold on life, and tucked the stolen pictures in his front pocket. "Lexi, babe, you can do better than this. But I guess that's the point of a rebound," he snickered. Of all the people to run into today, why did it have to be Daniel?

A muscle twitched in Matt's cheek. "Give them back," he demanded, the calm cracking enough to hint at the promise of retribution.

"Matt," I said, trying to infuse his name with a note of caution. He needed to remember where we were. Had anyone ever talked to him about the importance of blending with the human world? I knew I hadn't.

"That's right, little Matty. Run along. The big boys are talking." Daniel's snide comment rolled over Matt with no visible effect. Then he did probably the dumbest thing he possibly could have—he reached back and grabbed my arm. For a moment, I just stared down at Daniel's hand in shock. "Come on, Alexi. I think it's time we had a proper chat."

"Let go of him." The sheer menace coming off of Matt was enough to make me nervous.

I tried to tug my arm free, but Daniel pulled unexpectedly and I stumbled forward a step.

"Or what?" Daniel challenged, pulling again.

In the blink of an eye, Matt became a creature of pure violence. An aura of darkness hovered around him and I was more than a little surprised not to see the nearby shadows reaching towards us. Daniel made as if he was going to drag me after him. I dug in my heels and he looked back at me, clearly taken aback at my ability to halt his momentum.

"I wouldn't do that if I were you," I offered, in final caution.

"You aren't honestly telling me I should be afraid of your pint-sized rebound?"

I saw Matt's fist clench by his side. Daniel did as well and finally released me. I rubbed my arm and watched in alarm as Daniel advanced on Matt.

"I don't know what you've been smoking at the ridiculous school, Alexi, but I have never, nor will I ever, be intimidated by some scruffy rat half my height."

Searing anger burned in Matt's eyes. If Matt had been a fire demon, Daniel would be a pile of ash right now. Daniel took another step, stopping square in front of him. Arguably, the height difference between the two was laughable, but nothing about Matt's demeanor was funny.

"Matt don't," I pleaded. Too late, I realized saying anything at all was a mistake.

Daniel's mocking laughter poured out into what was feeling disturbingly like an arena. Time stood still as Matt's fist collided with his smug face. Daniel's evil laugh cut off, then he was flat on the ground. He didn't even twitch. Matt squatted down beside him.

"I said, these don't belong to you." He reached forward and calmly reclaimed the pictures, then stood. My knees crashed into the ground by Daniel's face, kicking up clouds of dust. Tentatively, I reached out, stopping shy of actually touching him. I'd never seen Matt really hit anyone before. Knowing he was capable of violence and seeing it firsthand was very different.

"You broke his face," I said numbly, looking up at him. There was still anger simmering in his eyes, only now it didn't seem to be directed at Daniel.

What have I done?

Silently, he turned and walked away, following a path that took him behind a row of stalls. I looked from Daniel to Matt's receding silhouette and back again. Daniel was still breathing, but his nose was definitely broken. I quickly scrambled to my feet and raced after Matt, finally catching up with him several yards into the gloom.

"Hey," I panted, reaching for his hand.

Without warning, he spun around, slamming me into the back of the stall with an audible thud. Before I could panic or attempt to say anything, his mouth was on mine. I could taste the fire that still burned white hot inside of him and felt completely claimed. That was fine by me. I'd made my peace with belonging to Matt a long time ago. I kissed him back fiercely. He needed to know that I was his without reservation. Some part of my mind was in absolute shock—Matt was kissing me in public. Anyone could turn the corner and see. I kissed him deeper, wanting to wrap my arms around him and keep him this close forever. Before I got the chance, he pulled away.

"Try to keep a better eye on these," he said, so close that each word was practically a kiss. His hand slid briefly into my back pocket, then he was several steps away.

"Matt, wait." I thought about apologizing for the whole disaster, but was a little worried that would make it worse, not better. "Give me your hand."

He flexed the hand that he'd used to knock Daniel out cold. For a moment, I didn't think he would. Then he held it out. I gingerly took it into my own, holding it close to see where his knuckles were almost red from the impact. Softly, I rubbed my thumb over them.

"Does it hurt?" I looked up at him through my lashes.

"I don't really feel it anymore," he said, pointedly avoiding my gaze. The way he said that didn't sit right, but pursuing why wasn't likely to help anything. I brushed my lips lightly across the pink skin and he twisted to look at me, surprise evident on his face.

"We should leave," I said, straightening. His shoulders sagged and I could practically see the gears turning; he knew how I felt about him fighting. Before he could jump to too many conclusions, I added, "We'll go back to the house. We'll just be a little early for dinner."

CHAPTER 4
JEALOUSY

Matt

We walked to Alex's house in strained silence that made my shoulders itch. I didn't know what to say to make it better, though. I could barely make sense of my emotions, let alone put words to them. Easier to shove them down. Forget about them.

"Are you still upset?" Alex whispered as we finished setting the table, no doubt so his mom wouldn't intrude and want details.

I absently rubbed my knuckles. Daniel's face had offered next to no resistance, and it had been difficult to hold back. "Upset about what?" I asked, my voice completely neutral.

He searched me a moment more, but didn't pursue it. I debated speaking up, trying to find the words to express how seeing him in his ex's arms had made me feel. Why had he been with Daniel at all, let alone hanging off of him? As if that wasn't bad enough, he'd let his ex-boyfriend manhandle him. I couldn't reconcile Alex being in an actual *relationship* with someone who treated him like that? And why did that person have to be the direct opposite of me in every way? As much as I didn't want the things his ex had said to bother me, they'd cut to the quick of virtually all of my insecurities.

His mom walked into the dining room, taking the decision out of my hands. "While I certainly wasn't expecting you two back so soon, I can't say I mind the extra pairs of hands."

"Is there anything else I can do to help Miss Roman?" I asked as Alex exited toward the hallway, likely to wash-up before his mom could tell him to. Either that, or he couldn't stand to be in the same room as me. I *had* decked his ex. It wasn't my fault the asshole had a glass jaw.

"Matt, there really is no need to be so formal. I feel like I already know you."

I shuffled my feet, a little concerned at how much she could know. Alex may not see any cause for concern being openly together, but I knew better. We may not be in Nebraska or even at Arminius where I knew about the threat to his safety, but people were people wherever you went, and experience had taught me most of them were bad.

"Snapdragon!" Miss Roman exclaimed, startling me out of my nihilistic spiral. "I forgot all about dessert. I'm going to run down to the corner store real quick and pick up some ice cream. Be back before you know it." She glanced in the direction Alex had disappeared, then left.

I stood there a moment wondering what on earth I was supposed to do now. The *right* thing would be to find Alex and try to make amends. But, then, I'd never been very good at doing the right thing. I wandered through the house, keeping an ear out for him, until I found myself in the den. Pictures covered the mantle, most unsurprisingly of Alex. Alex in a cap and gown. Alex about ten years old. Alex with his mom. One in particular caught my attention. He was leaning against a wall with his hair in his eyes. It looked like he'd been laughing. He really was stunning with those bright green eyes and easy smile. There was a noise down the hallway and I resumed my search. We nearly collided as he came out of what I assumed was the bathroom.

"Oh, hey," he said in surprise, his wet hair dripping in his eyes.

My jumble of emotions crystallized. Had he done the things that we had with Daniel? "Let's go to your room."

"My room?" he echoed uncertainly. He glanced behind me back towards the front of the house, no doubt where he thought his mother still was. "I know making out yesterday kind of contradicts what I said about not having boys in my room, but my mom really is strict about funny business in the house."

"I just want to go to your room, Alex."

His anxiety didn't seem to decrease. "O-okay." He walked the short distance down the hall and I followed a few paces behind. "Yeah, so you pretty much saw everything yesterday. Nothing special. Looks just like my room at the dorm, honestly. So I guess you got me there. It's silly, I kn—" I closed the door closed quietly behind me, but at the look on his face you would have thought the latch clicking was a gunshot.

"Alex, what happened at the fair?" I walked toward him, only stopping when I was definitely too close for comfort.

He swallowed hard before stuttering, "N-nothing happened."

I raised an eyebrow.

"He snuck up behind me while I was looking at the pictures." So there *were* two strips instead of one. "I didn't know. I thought he was you." There was something in that, something he didn't say.

"What do you think I saw?"

His eyes went wide with fear as I confirmed he was defending something I likely hadn't even seen. It took him a few tries to get the words out. While he struggled with the answer, I advanced. He took a step back and ran out of room. The bed squeaked in protest as he fell on it. He attempted to scramble back as I followed, though he didn't get far before I had him laid out beneath me.

"Tell me."

"He kissed my neck, that's all. I swear. The second I realized it wasn't you, I put an end to it," he said, the panic in his voice reflected in his eyes.

I considered him for a moment. That he'd thought it was me, didn't really make what had happened any easier to swallow. "Is it that easy to confuse our kisses?" The question sounded dangerous even to my ears.

"Absolutely not."

"Perhaps you need a reminder."

His eyes flashed black, then green, and his breathing turned shallow. I leaned forward like I was going to kiss him, and he arched up to meet me. I didn't. Instead, I trailed my nose down the long curve of his neck. He shuddered, and I placed a kiss in the hollow. There wasn't nearly enough to work with, though. I slid my hands down and slipped them under his shirt. He gasped at the touch, but didn't stop me from pulling it up. I placed another kiss on his now much more accessible chest. He moaned.

"Matt, wait. There really are rules in this house," he panted. I placed a more aggressive kiss and he let out a gasp. "You really don't care, do you? My mom is just in the other room. If we don't go back soon..." His words faded out as I forced the shirt over his head, causing his arms to go up with it.

"Didn't I say? She went to the store. She's not here," I said, stopping just shy of kissing him.

"W-what store?"

"The corner store."

"You don't even know where that is. She could literally be back any second." He tried to move, but I used the shirt to keep his arms captive, knotting it in my hand and pushing it back into the headboard, then used shadow to keep it there. I was quite proud of my handiwork. Having Alex stretched out before me like this was rather nice, I could see why he was so fond of it. There was a distant sound like that of a door closing. He looked anxiously over at his own closed one. It wasn't locked.

"You're right. I think I hear her now." I shifted to stand and Alex pulled on the bond I'd made. When it didn't immediately give, he looked surprised, then flustered.

"You don't honestly think this can hold me?" he said as he attempted to shadow out of the tie. The spell held though, and he reformed with his arms still stuck above his head. Realization spread across his face. "Matt. Let me go. You can't...she'll..." He struggled with more determination before sagging in defeat. "What do you want from me? Do you want me to apologize? I'm sorry, okay. I'm a complete idiot and I didn't handle any of that very well. Now please undo the spell."

The apology was nice, and I briefly considered it. But if I was being honest, I was still mad. "We wouldn't want your mom to worry about what we've been up to in her absence, would we?" I said, leaning down to look him in the eye. He visibly relaxed. "Best not take too long," I added, then made my way to the door.

"Matt," he hissed, struggling against the spelled shirt. It was useless. The spell would hold with or without me maintaining it. I'd gotten plenty of practice with that while perfecting the barrier to keep him out of my room, or more realistically, me out of his. "Matt."

I opened the door and walked out. Admittedly, I was a little curious about how he was going to get out of that, but was still preoccupied with what had happened at the fair. I found Ms. Roman in the dining room with the table perfectly set and plates served.

"Where's Alexi?" she asked when he didn't materialize behind me.

"He's a little tied up," I said and took a seat.

She frowned and took one as well. "That man is entirely too vain. I don't know what he's so worried about. Well, it would serve him right if his food gets cold. Go ahead and eat, Matt. There's no reason we should have to eat cold food simply because he's dallying."

We were several bites in when he finally joined us. I glanced up to find that he was wearing a different shirt and a scowl. It would seem he *hadn't* figured out how to undo the spell.

"And where have you been?"

The chair screeched as he pulled it up. "I was a little tied up," he grumbled.

His mom glanced from Alex to me, then back at her plate, before letting out a huff. The rest of the meal was awkward, if it was anything. She attempted to fill the strained silence with light-hearted conversation and inquiries about school. Alex stayed sullen through it all, and guilt weighed on me. After dinner, we helped clear the table and nibbled passively at the recently acquired ice cream.

"Alright. It's time for bed. I'm going to assume by the lack of chatter that you two are simply exhausted from your day." She pointedly looked at Alex, who was typically much more talkative. "So, off to bed, the both of you. And Alexi," she called after him, "separate rooms. There are rules in this house." The face he gave her was priceless.

My increasing guilt tempered my desire to laugh. I needed to make this right. I caught up to him just before he got to the hallway. "Alex, wait."

"I told you."

"Rules, yeah, got that, but that's not what I wanted to talk about."

"What is it, Matt?" he sighed, leaning against the wall. The pose was reminiscent of the one I'd seen on the mantle, and for a second I forgot to speak.

I took a deep breath and a step closer so that I was right in front of him. Apologizing really was the worst, but I'd messed up. "I'm sorry," I said, looking up at him. Surprise glinted deep in his emerald eyes. "I shouldn't have embarrassed you like that in front of your mom. That was wrong." I looked down, unsure of what else to say.

He tilted my face back up to look at him. "Thank you for taking the pictures. I'm sorry I almost lost them." I tried to look away, but he held me in place. "He deserved it, you know. I don't know how I ever put up with such a horrid person for so long."

"He is pretty awful," I said, earning me a half smile.

"Not like you at all," he said, stroking the side of my face. Then he leaned forward and gave me a tender kiss that made my lips tingle. "Goodnight, Matt."

"Goodnight, Alex," I whispered back. He shadowed out, presumably to go to his room and leaving me to make my way to bed.

I put on my pajama pants and considered the sleep shirt I'd brought to cover the bruise still healing on my side. In the end, I didn't bother and turned out the lights. As expected, sleep proved elusive as the events of the day played on repeat in my head and the most I accomplished was a semi-wakeful dream state.

Out of the darkness, phantom lips touched mine, and I welcomed them. The sense of Alex was undeniable. There was a noise like the rustling of sheets and a sudden rush of cold air followed by a weight sinking me into the bed. As I felt skin against skin, I realized this wasn't just a good dream. This really was Alex.

I wrapped my arm around his waist and kissed him back. Now that I knew this was real and not another hallucination, it was all too easy to get lost in the world that was Alex. Here we were safe. Here we could be together without putting him in danger. I pulled him closer, deepening the kiss he'd started. Our tongues tangled as I mapped the planes of his back with my hands. Night, I loved Alex. In all my life, I never wanted anything as much as I wanted to drown in his touch and never come up for air.

His hands coasted up my thighs, ghosting over my erection on their way to my stomach. I arched into him, releasing him enough to give him room to explore. He angled his hips to fit between my thighs. We both moaned at the resulting friction. I ground against him as I brought his mouth back to mine for another hungry kiss. Then his hand slipped to my side and I just barely didn't flinch. Once more, I was hyperaware of the mottled black bruise that dominated my left side—the one I'd neglected to hide in the misguided pursuit of comfort. If he touched it any harder, I wouldn't be able to hold back the reflexive cry.

With a force of will, I pulled back, taking my hands off of him so they couldn't betray me. "Alex."

"What?" The sultry heat in his voice threatened to strip my resolve. I wanted to roll us over and press him into the bed, feel him wrap around me, and moan my name as I claimed what was mine.

"What about the rules?"

"*Now* you care about those?" he hissed.

"Alex," I tried again, but he snagged me in a kiss that took all of my focus not to get totally lost in. He gripped my side and nausea rolled through me. Biting back a pained moan, I pulled away once more.

"Shit. You're serious."

"I want your mom to like me," I said as he raised up to look down at me. I didn't have to see his face to know he was doing the sexy smile that always made me forget how to breathe.

"We've been through this. I'm pretty sure my mom loves you." He chuckled huskily before trying to kiss me again.

"Then I'd like to keep it that way."

He made a sound of pure exasperation. "What's the point of fighting if you can't at least have makeup sex?"

I winced. This was not how I wanted to apologize for my behavior earlier. But how could I convince him I wasn't all for makeup sex when all evidence pointed to the contrary?

He shifted. "Fine. Have it your way. I'll go back to my room."

"Wait." I reached up to find his face in the dark. Thankfully moved too far. "Stay. Please." This time, when he leaned back down to kiss me, I let him. It was long and slow and substantially deeper than it should have been. It took me a few moments to find my breath again. "But you have to behave."

He made a choked sound and abruptly his weight settled beside me, mercifully not on the bruise from the hit I'd been too slow to avoid. "You are absolutely incorrigible," he said as he snuggled into my side.

"I know," I responded softly as I rubbed my hand along his back. He gave a huff and relaxed into me.

I had no idea how on earth I was supposed to sleep after getting so worked up. Telling him no physically pained me, but I couldn't risk him asking why I was injured. He wouldn't understand that my returning to the fight club was to keep him safe, that I'd endure every hurt in the world if it meant he wouldn't have to. The sooner I dealt with Thomas, George, and the others, the sooner I could come back to him, could finally stop lying.

I held Alex close and tried to clear my thoughts. Sleeping was going to be hard enough with him there without adding those to the mix. Gradually, I slipped into a deep sleep, my ears filled with Alex's soft breathing and the hint of a snore. And for the first time in months, I didn't have a single nightmare.

When I woke, I knew it was early, but I was determined not to get up until he did. The most he'd moved all night was to drape his arm and leg over me as if they could somehow hold me in place. If only they could.

"Alexi Roman, you better be wearing shorts under there." The sharp voice cut through my fuzzy daze.

My eyes flew open in a panic to see Miss Roman standing in the open doorway, her arms crossed over her chest and scowling. Heat flooded my face, and I silently cursed my hammering heart. Alex stretched beside me beneath the covers, seemingly unconcerned that his mom had caught us in bed together. And *I* was supposed to be the troublemaker?

"Good morning, mom. How'd you find me?"

"It was an easy bet when you weren't in your own bed."

He gave a wicked smile, totally unfazed.

"I mean it about the shorts, Alexi. You know the rules." He sat up, waving away her scolding, and she gave a put-upon sigh.

Eager to be anywhere else than right here, I swung my legs over the side of the bed. It didn't escape her notice that I was wearing pants as I reached out to grab the cotton tee that I was now seriously regretting not wearing.

"At any rate, breakfast is ready," she said before finally leaving. The door intentionally left open in her wake.

I looked back at Alex, who was wearing an exceedingly smug grin, and shook my head. "Are you getting out of bed or what?" He flashed me a devious smile, and it clicked. "You aren't wearing anything under there, are you?"

"Nope," he replied, casually using shadow to close the bedroom door. While the sudden click distracted me, he shadowed out from under the covers to be in front of me. I tried to take a step back, but he caught me first. "What happened to your side?"

"Don't worry about it," I said, trying not to sound anxious. What I wouldn't give to be in the dorm right now. My eyes were undoubtedly black with want.

"I always worry about you," he said, claiming me with a kiss that sent heart curling throughout my body. His hand slid down my backside, and then he forced me hard against him. He was definitely not over last night and there was no stopping my groan. "Still glad you said no?"

"I was never glad." I wanted to steal another kiss, but it seemed wiser to restrain myself. We were already in danger of dissolving into each other and getting into even more trouble.

"I'll meet you in the kitchen," he said, swiping a quick kiss before disappearing into shadow.

I stood there a few more minutes trying to gather myself, then ventured out. My journey slowed as I passed the mantle covered in pictures again.

"That's my favorite one too," Miss Roman said as she reached across and grabbed the picture of Alex laughing. He couldn't be much younger than he was now. "I took it shortly before we found out about the new classes from the Arminius community." She flipped the frame over and started taking it out. "You should have it."

I looked at her in disbelief. "I couldn't."

"Sure you can," she insisted, forcing me to accept the picture. Everything about the image was perfectly Alex. "He really loves you."

"He's said."

She blinked. "He has? Huh, imagine that. Guess he's growing up after all." She shook her head as if clearing something away. "It has been very nice to get to know you, Matthew."

"Mom, I told you not to call him that," Alex bemoaned, suddenly walking past us. It was fascinating to see how he interacted with her. At school he was always so self-confident and assured, but here, here he was just her son. I smiled at his back as he made his way into the kitchen. "Am I the only eating?" he called back.

"Thank you, Miss Roman," I said, pocketing the picture.

"I'm glad for you to have it. Take care of my boy, Matt," she added, brushing my hair back from my face in a way that could only be described as motherly. I'd never had anyone mother me before. Suddenly, sadness welled up inside of me. If something happened to Alex, I wouldn't be the only one devastated.

"I'll do everything I can to keep him safe," I promised, then made my way in the direction where Alex was still bellyaching about our absence.

Chapter 5
Betrayal

Alexi

I stared at the strip of pictures from the photo booth, much as I had every day since we'd returned from Denham. They were the only proof that the weekend with Matt had happened. Them and the fact that my mom wouldn't stop asking when we were coming back for another visit. I didn't have an answer for that and I certainly wasn't about to tell her he'd all but ghosted me the second we'd rematerialized on the roof of Starling Hall.

Frustrated, I put the pictures back in the dresser drawer where I hoped they'd be safe from Matt should he decide he didn't want me to have them after all. When I walked out of my room, I wasn't even surprised that there wasn't any trace of Matt or his things. I thought back to when I'd learned he was an orphan, how he'd said he'd find another roommate, get all of his things and go. While I was fairly sure he *hadn't* done that...yet, he might as well have for all that I saw of him.

I grabbed a bowl for cereal, then noticed it was the one he usually used. With a sigh, I put it back and grabbed another. This push and pull was killing me. It was as if the closer he got, the farther he would drift afterwards. I glanced around the space and finished my last bite. To think, only a few months ago, this room had been filled with fun and laughter. Now it felt like a tomb. Rather than dwell on the depressing thoughts, I rinsed the dish and grabbed my things. I'd be early to my next class, but it was better than wallowing in misery here. On a whim, I cut through the Witch's College on the chance I might bump into some of my friends from the tutoring group. If memory served, Lina had two classes here and Mariah at least one, despite not being witches themselves.

I'd gotten turned around when I heard a familiar laugh. I immediately oriented towards the sound, my eyebrows furrowing. While there was plenty of overlap between disciplines, Shadow Demons most definitely did *not* have any classes in the Witch's College. And for good reason. Curiosity peaked and more than a little concerned, I followed the laughter to its source. No sooner did I round the corner of a long stretch of hallway, then I ducked back out of sight.

As I'd suspected, Matt was here. Thankfully, he was further down the adjoining corridor and didn't seem to have spotted me. I carefully peered around the corner and tried to make sense of what I was seeing. Matt's stance was about as relaxed as it ever was outside of the dorm, and he wore an enthusiastic smile. Across from him, a startling pretty woman with dirty blonde hair that fell in a perfect sheet to her waist smiled back. Her laughter drifted down the hall, mixed with his deeper chuckle. I couldn't make out what they were saying, but it didn't stop my heart from sinking.

They're just friends. He probably knows her from his Advanced Shadow Spells class. He did say there were witches sitting in.

I pressed against the wall and willed myself to believe it was true.

Face it, it was only a matter of time.

I slammed a hand over my mouth to stifle my squeal of outrage at hearing Daniel's voice intrude on my thoughts.

Seriously, how long did you think it would last? He's not me and you're certainly nothing special, Daniel's diatribe continued, despite me adamantly shaking my head. But there was no silencing him. *Did you think that because he let you fuck him, he'd wake up and decide to be gay?* The mental Daniel that existed solely to torture me snorted. *He's not and he never will be.*

Mocking laughter filled my ears. He was wrong. Matt wouldn't do that to me. He knew Daniel had cheated on me, how he'd gaslighted me.

You're so pathetic. He was simply curious and used you to explore that curiosity. It's all you're good for, anyway.

I squeezed my eyes shut and covered my ears like it could somehow stop the voice coming from inside my head. Not even the pounding of my heart or my stuttering breaths could drown him out.

Fighting it won't change a damn thing. You were an experiment and now he's going back to what he really wants. See for yourself.

Against my better judgment, I snuck another peek at the pair just in time to see Matt take her hand, then snare her in an embrace that nearly knocked her to the floor. My vision went dark, bathing the hall in night as anger washed through me with sickening force. With a snarl, I reigned in the shadows, winking out along with them.

"Where the fuck is it!" I shouted, tearing the dorm kitchen apart. Matt once had a fully stocked liquor cabinet, and I seriously doubted he'd simply poured it all out. He didn't believe in being wasteful. No, it was here somewhere.

The cabinet door nearly burst off its hinges as I ripped it open yet again. I took a step back and considered checking his room, then dismissed the thought. It wouldn't be there. Plus, I doubted I'd be able to step foot in there without ripping the place to shreds. If it was anywhere, it would be hidden in here somewhere.

Think, Alexi, if Matt wanted to hide something, what would he do?

I snapped my fingers as the glaringly obvious answer came to me—he'd put it in the shadow world. Which meant there was a portal hiding in plain sight. I yanked open the freezer and sure enough, there was an unmasked portal staining the side next to a veritable mountain of ice cream. I stuck my hand through it with no concern for what might be on the other side. Judging by how the air felt, I had a serious suspicion my hand was actually floating disembodied above the couch. A quick look confirmed it. Beyond pissed and increasingly frustrated, I slammed the door.

I just wanted to numb the fury and hurt washing through me. But it was like I was stuck in a riptide of heartache, the crashing of waves, the relentless breaking of my heart. That damnable stash had to be here somewhere. I went back to the most likely place to keep liquor bottles—beneath the sink. Except the cabinet doors already hung open, none of the desired spirits were to be found. I got down on the ground and felt around in the barren space, only pausing when my fingers hit something. I carefully extended my arm further under the sink and discovered the smooth glass neck of a bottle..

"Found you." I pulled every bottle out until I was sure there was nothing left, then deposited the obscene assortment on the counter. I mixed a concoction that I hoped would be palatable. It wasn't. I downed the tall glass and tried again. This one was a little better. I polished it off as well and made a few adjustments. Recipe in hand, I made a batch large enough to fill the pitcher and grabbed the almost empty bottle of tequila as well.

As I took a swig straight from the bottle, I tried not to think about the last time this bottle had been out. The anger I'd felt then couldn't hold a candle to the hurt I felt now. Every time I closed my eyes, I saw Matt flash the young woman that dazzling smile—*my smile.* Could hear her giggle as he took her hand. His laugh that had become so rare.

The pain in my chest grew as I remembered how tight he'd held her. When was the last time he had held me like that? Did he ever plan to again? I sank artlessly onto the couch, more interested in drinking myself into oblivion than going to the rest of my classes. Even half a pitcher in my mind still couldn't reconcile my sweet Matt with this heinous betrayal.

How could he? He had to know what this would do to me.

Probably never expected to be caught.

I snorted derisively at the likeliness of that. Certainly wouldn't be the first time. I polished off another glass, leaving the liquid to curdle in my already sour stomach. I just couldn't understand. If he was done and moving on, then why string me along? Why go home with me at all? Be sweet? But then, he'd also tried to prevent me from sharing his bed. Perhaps that should have been my clue in a long line of clues I'd willfully overlooked.

I eyed the nearly empty pitcher and debated if I had enough motor control to make another. Then the door opened and in walked Matt. The fact he was here at all was a bit of a shock and not doing anything for my current state. But to have the audacity to smile? Not that he was anymore.

His greeting died as he took in the scene before him. He scanned the kitchen, clearly noting the counter covered in bottles, then his gaze returned to me. "What happened?"

"How could you?" I asked, the words slurring a bit.

"How could I what?"

"You fucking son of Dis. Don't lie to me. I saw you!" Doubt flashed across his face. "That's right. Your secret is out," I said, surging to my feet. The room tilted, and he rushed to steady me. "Don't touch me!" I ripped my arm away from him, effectively spilling what remained of my drink. I felt like I was going to be sick. Actually, I was pretty sure of it.

"I don't know what you're talking about. We need to get you to the bathroom." He reached for me again.

"I told you not to touch me."

"Alex, I'm just trying to help."

I barked a laugh. "Help? You mean like you let me help you?" He looked like I'd slapped him, which actually sounded like a damn good idea, except I couldn't get my arm to cooperate. "She's pretty. No wonder you didn't want my help. You had someone else to lean on." Tears streaked like acid down my face.

"What are you talking about?" His eyebrows pinched together, his forehead crinkling.

"Stop. Lying. To me. I saw you with her. What *else* have you lied about, Matt? Did you ever even quit that stupid bruiser bar? Is that where you met her?" Understanding lit in his eyes, and my stomach heaved.

"That's enough," he declared. "You can yell at me in the bathroom." He gently but firmly grabbed my arm.

"I said..."

"I know what you said, Alex. Now you can either walk or I can drag you. Your choice."

I pulled my arm away, and he had to catch me in order to prevent me from crashing to the ground. My stomach couldn't take this abuse. The world blinked black, and it felt like he touched every fiber of being. I opened my mouth to shout at him and threw up my life instead. Conveniently, it was into the toilet.

"Take it easy," he said soothingly while stroking my back.

I waved my arm behind me to smack the comfort away. It was about as effective as it had been earlier. I heaved again. "Who is she, Matt?" The question echoed creepily in the porcelain bowl.

"Her name is Misty and yes, I met her at the fight club. I don't know what you think you saw, but nothing is going on."

"Stop lying," I groaned. How much was it possible to hack up before you died?

"I'm not."

"She's into you." Even half a building away, I could tell that.

"I know. That doesn't change that nothing is going on." He pressed a wet cloth on the back of my neck. The cool was welcome except for the part that I was still furious with him.

"But I saw you with her. You were laughing, and you hugged. You looked happy." I couldn't hide the misery in my voice.

"She was helping me with something."

"What?" I asked, finally looking at him. Little shit was barely containing his amusement.

"A birthday present."

"Birthday? Whose?" I asked, the words sounding muffled to my ears, like someone had stuffed my head full of cotton.

He quirked an eyebrow. "Yours. It was supposed to be a surprise."

"Mine?"

"Your birthday is next week, Alex." He flipped the towel over and a fresh wave of cool kissed my skin.

"How do you know that? I haven't..."

"I asked your mom." He brushed the hair out of my eyes. The touch was so tender, it was all I could do not to sigh with relief. "You proud of yourself yet?"

"No," I replied miserably. Quite the contrary, I felt like a total ass.

"Come on, let's get you in bed. I'm pretty sure you're all puked out."

I groaned as he tried to help me to my feet.

"Can you walk?"

"We'll see," I quipped.

He made sure I was steady, then shadowed out, only to reappear a moment later holding a glass of water.

"It's warm," I remarked after taking a sip.

"The cold would just upset your stomach again. I can put a few cubes in if it really bothers you."

I drank some more, trying to clear the foul taste of sick from my mouth. The cool towel made a reappearance as he wiped my face. I hated how good it felt and that he was being so sweet after I'd been such a complete jerk.

"I'm sorry," I whispered, feeling thoroughly ashamed of myself. I'd been so desperate for an explanation for his odd behavior that I'd jumped to the first and worst conclusion.

He paused in his ministrations, looking deep into my eyes. "I would never do that to you, Alex. There are some things you don't forgive."

My heart constricted at his sincerity. I wrapped him in a hug and he carefully squeezed back. I couldn't think of a time I'd ever been so happy to be wrong.

"Alright, alright. To bed with you." He guided me out to the room, keeping a firm arm around my waist to steady me. "She's not really my type anyway," he mused aloud when we approached the bed.

"Really? What is?" I asked as I burrowed under the covers.

"Let's see," he began as he laid next to me, "tall, absurdly small waist, dark hair, green eyes. Something along those lines."

"Are you trying to butter me up?"

"Maybe." He nuzzled my neck. "Is it working?"

"Maybe," I giggled. Despite having lost every liquid I had drank ever, I was definitely still drunk. "Ugh, this is why I don't drink," I moaned, thinking about the headache that would be waiting for me in the morning.

"I don't know. You drinking has led to some pretty interesting things."

I snorted. "And what about now?"

"Got me in bed, didn't it?" he replied, wrapping an arm around me. That was a good point. "Now be quiet and try to get some rest."

"Will you be here when I wake up?"

"No, but I'll stay as long as I can." He placed a small kiss just beneath my ear. It was the last thing I remembered before the world slipped away.

Chapter 6
A Day Off

Matt

I slipped into the hall, careful to shut the door behind me so it wouldn't make any noise. Sneaking out while Alex was in the dorm was always so much harder than when he wasn't. Not risking anything to chance, I waited until I was at the end of the hall before stepping into the shadow world. The usual quiet descended along with the all-encompassing dark. I wasn't entirely sure when, but at some point, the shadow realm had stopped scaring me. Not that it wasn't still eerie as hell, but that sense of familiarity, of belonging, had come just like Alex promised.

Alex.

The dark swallowed my sigh. Of all the things for him to accuse me of, I never would have thought it would have been cheating. Sure, I'd been absent, and I *was* keeping things from him, but it was for his own protection. He'd understand that, eventually.

Hopefully.

Sound returned in the form of crickets and the distant babble of students talking animatedly when I stepped out onto the quad. While it would have been easier to materialize *on* Old Fraternity Row, I didn't want to chance leaving a trail Alex could follow. He was far too smart for his own good. The last thing I needed was him showing up unannounced at one of these ridiculous "check-in" meetings with Thomas. Shaking my head, I took off at a brisk pace. Being late wouldn't do me any favors either.

Gradually, the impressive antiquity of Arminius faded into the skeletal remains of a forgotten past. Almost as if the campus was shrinking back from the poisoned grounds of the old row. I still couldn't fathom what could have possibly happened here to have caused such permanent destruction. The place had an ominous air that stuck to it like an unpleasant smell, and it wasn't just because of the damage that had been caused. I shuddered and quickened my pace. Small wonder George and his goons enjoyed coming here.

By the time I reached the crumbled pillars at the end of the row, I had my game face on and my thoughts were as clear as they were going to get. I stepped across the threshold and the spell there tingled faintly across my skin. Once again, I wondered if the others noticed it. Considering they were a bunch of fools on a good day, I'd hazard a no. I'd tried to find a way around it, but the rest of the house was sealed up tight—there was no other way in or out. Again, I doubted that George, Travis, *or* Kyle knew that. But there wasn't a doubt in my mind that it not only alerted Thomas when one of us arrived, but was specific to Shadow Demons. How the others couldn't see the man's obvious detest probably shouldn't have surprised me.

I followed the cleared path past the rubble deeper into the ruined remains of the fraternity house and wondered how much longer I could keep this up. Aside from missing Alex so much, it physically hurt—and now this accusation of seeing someone on the side—my skin crawling anytime I was near George, plus the fight club that was absolutely taking its toll. Yes, all that aside, Thomas made me anxious in a way I couldn't ignore, like when I was living on the street and it felt like eyes were always on me. He was dangerous even if he didn't look it.

"Matty! My man," Travis hollered, slinging an arm over my shoulders. "Where you been?"

I showed my teeth in a forced smile and shrugged him off. "Are you still on about that weekend?"

"You didn't miss your buddies?" Kyle chimed in.

Another forced smile, this one bordering on a snarl. They weren't my "buddies" and never would be. I took a deep breath and focused on the way Alex had held me that night at his mother's house. My smile settled into something more genuine as I slowly let out the breath. "I'll meet up with you guys after my report."

Travis snuck up behind me to squeeze my shoulders. "Just don't take too long. We've got a fight to get to." He released me and trotted along behind Kyle and George to an adjoining room.

"You look pleased with yourself," the disembodied voice of Thomas floated into the room. It could have been coming from the right, but I knew better. That was also a spell. Thomas used a lot of those. Some he seemed to use like breathing, and others... others made my hackles rise. To say I couldn't trust Thomas as far as I could throw him wouldn't do it justice, considering I could throw him quite far, given my demonic strength. "I hope you have some more information for me." This time, the voice came from behind me. I didn't react, nor did I look up to where I knew he still stood on the landing overhead. While this trick hadn't worked on me since that first day, he didn't need to know that.

"Don't I always?"

"You've got a smart mouth for someone spying on your friends."

I hid my flinch. "They aren't my friends."

"Oh? I thought at least one of them was," he said, appearing by the wall of pictures. "Frankly, I would have thought you'd try harder to eliminate him." He touched the edge of Alex's picture.

I quickly checked the urge to tear his hand off and settled for a bored shrug. "He's weird and keeps to himself. I can't help it if there isn't much to work with." I bit the inside of my cheek and decided to roll the dice. "But, uh, something did happen the other day." This gamble would either go a long way toward clearing Alex or completely blow up in my face.

"Do tell." Thomas released the picture and faced me.

Here went nothing. I forced myself to remain casual and hiked a shoulder. "Apparently, he saw a girl with some guy in the Witch's College."

Thomas's eye narrowed, unimpressed. "That doesn't say much, Matthew."

"Considering he was stupid drunk by the time I got to the dorm, it actually says a lot." I stubbornly pushed down my own feelings at having arrived to find him in such a state and moderated my tone. "He never drinks, not even socially. He kept asking where she'd met him and how this could be happening."

"Ah, I see. And you're surmising that this is the elusive girl that he's been hiding from you. Who is the girl? Do you know her?"

Now the really dangerous part. "Yes. She's the resident witch at the Bruiser joint."

Thomas' eyes lit up with surprise. "Well, well. Why do you think he didn't want you to know about her? Surely that is information a friend would share."

Forgive me, Misty.

"She's into me and he knows it." It was one of the few things I'd said that wasn't twisted in some half-truth.

Thomas inspected his short-clipped nails, his gaze flicking to the image of Alex pinned to the stucco wall. "I see. Did he say anything else? Do you know if they broke up?"

I shook my head. "I know his last partner cheated on him. There are some things you don't forgive."

He plucked up the red marker from the dilapidated desk and I nearly forgot to breathe as he drew a red line across Alex's picture. "You've done well, Matthew. Certainly better than my other 'recruits'." He cast a withering look in the direction the others had disappeared before turning a more appraising one on me. "You are very good at this."

"Thank you sir," I said past the bile steadily clawing up my throat. Why hadn't he completed the X? I needed Alex in the clear, needed to know he was safe. What more would it take?

He recapped the marker and set it aside. "You can report back when you have more information for me. Your... colleagues are waiting." Without so much as a wave, I was dismissed. At least he hadn't called them my friends. But then, maybe that was a bad thing.

I was all set to book it straight out of there when I hesitated.

"Was there something else?" Thomas asked, his expression an unnerving cross between bored and suspicious.

"This Thursday..."

His expression turned decidedly more grim. "What about it?"

"I won't be able to check in as usual. I'll be unavailable the whole weekend, actually."

It was hard to miss the waves of suspicion coming off of him. He glanced once more at Alex's picture with its half an X. "I suppose you've earned yourself some time off."

Careful not to show my relief, I spun on my heel to join the others.

"Matthew."

I froze, every muscle in my body taught, torn between the desire to stand and fight and to flee as fast as the shadow world would let me. "Sir?" I called back, grateful that my voice didn't betray my nerves.

"Be sure this doesn't become a habit. And I'll expect your efforts to reveal the traitor in our midst to double. Understood?"

"Understood," I echoed, my blood turning to ice in my veins as I walked slowly out of the room. I was on the verge of exhaling when Travis stormed up to me, fire burning in his eyes.

He shoved his finger into my chest hard enough that I stumbled back a step. "Why didn't you tell me your roommate was dating that bitch from the club?"

I suppressed a groan and smacked his hand away. Great, now Alex and Misty had an entirely different target on their back. "I only just found out myself."

"Liar," he snapped, getting back in my face. "You knew the whole fucking time. How am I supposed to compete with that?" He flung his arms wide, and I bit my tongue from telling he didn't have a chance in hell with either of them.

"You could be less ugly, for starters," Kyle said, unintentionally coming to my rescue. He propped his elbow on Travis's shoulder and smiled, though it was more of a sneer.

Travis shrugged him off and went to skulk in a corner. I really couldn't take spending *more* time with these assholes. Exhausting didn't even come close, and that didn't factor in the fights at the club. Fuck. That reminded me, I needed to tell Neese I wouldn't be present for the usual pummeling Thursday. That was gonna go over like a ton of bricks, assuming he didn't just hold me hostage like he had the *last* time I'd tried to duck out of a fight.

"What's this I hear about you skipping out on us? Again. Isn't it bad enough you blew us off the other weekend?" George asked, catching the other two's attention.

"I'm allowed to have other plans," I replied, just short of a snarl.

"Like what? What's better than hanging with us?" Kyle asked, plopping on the dilapidated couch they'd dragged in here. Not even fleas would touch that monstrosity, and I sure as hell wasn't planning to either. I'd slept in nicer gutters.

"Some of us are able to get laid every now and again, but it requires actually showing up."

The look on Kyle's face went slack with shock and Travis doubled over laughing. Truthfully, getting laid had nothing to do with it, but it was a language they understood.

"Why Thursday?" George's question blanketed the room in abrupt silence. They swiveled to face me. Shit.

"I can't control the calendar," I said. Now all I had to do was pray that he didn't ask what a calendar had anything to do with it.

He sucked his teeth. "Well, you're telling Neese. I'm not gonna be penalized just because you want to put your dick in something." It took every ounce of control not to bare my teeth at him or, even better, break his face like I'd broken Daniel's. Despite my best effort, though, George noted the reaction and snickered.

"I'll talk to Neese tonight," I managed through gritted teeth, my anger in danger of finally boiling over. I needed to get out of here before I did something I would regret.

"Just be sure not to get too distracted by a pretty face, Matty. We still have a mission to finish."

I froze, damn near white-knuckling with the effort of keeping my fist from burying itself in his smug face. "It's one fucking day, George. Maybe if you spent a little more time focused on the mission instead of blood sport, you could provide some useful information for Thomas yourself." His features twisted into an ominous scowl and I instantly regretted lashing out. This was totally going to bite me in the ass.

Chapter 7
Friendly Advice

Alexi

A shadow cast over me, heightening the chill that had sneaked up on the campus. Though maybe sneaked wasn't the right word. It was November. Mother of Night, how was the term already over? And where the hell was my boyfriend? Did I even still have one?

My stomach rolled unpleasantly, and a cough came from above. I glanced up to find Rubio standing over me.

"Took you long enough. Mind if I sit?" He joined me on the bench without waiting for a reply. The late afternoon sun hit his blond hair, momentarily blinding me.

I blinked rapidly a few times, then cautiously glanced at him. "So, uh, what brings you here?"

He leaned back, spreading his arms along the length of the bench. "Figured since you couldn't be bothered to make it to the meeting, I'd bring the meeting to you."

"Shit!" I immediately reached for my bag. "I'm so sorry. I'll head right over."

Rubio placed a hand on my shoulder, stilling my movements. "The meeting was yesterday, Alexi."

I groaned and slumped against the bench. "I'm sorry."

"You said that."

"My head's been a little... messed up lately."

He angled his body to face me better. "That's actually why I'm here."

I tried—and failed—to hide a wince. "Judging by that tone, this is about more than missing a meeting. And... I can't really blame you. I've been a horrific friend and tutor."

Rubio sighed and moved his hands to rest on his lap. "You're not a horrific friend and you're one of the best tutors I've got." He paused, then added, "When you're on point, which you haven't been for a while."

"It's just Matt..." How did I even come close to explaining everything that had been going on between us?

He nodded knowingly. "I suspected as much."

I gave him a sharp look and straightened. "What's that supposed to mean?"

"I get it. He's hot, occasionally sweet, probably fucks like a demon—no pun intended, and he's convenient. But he's not exactly what I would call reliable."

My face burned, though it was a toss up if it was from humiliation or outrage. "You know nothing about him."

"And you do?" he countered with zero mercy.

I held onto my indignation for all of point-five seconds, then shrank back into the bench. "I thought I did."

"Wanna talk about it?"

I scrubbed at my face. "I love him. But he's not talking to me. We were really good there for a bit. Something... changed. I think... I think he's in trouble." To my chagrin, Rubio didn't look even remotely surprised by this revelation.

"You care about him." I opened my mouth to correct him and he held up a hand. "And I care about you. Anyone could take a one look at the guy and know he's got issues longer than the river Ebro. It's not your responsibility to fix them. Please don't punch me, but are you sure he's not just a project?"

I'd push Rubio into the Shadow Realm before he could shout if I didn't value him so much as a friend. Since I wasn't about to potentially murder my friend, I settled for a glare. "Matt is *not* a project."

"I'm just putting it out there. My main point still stands. I'm worried about you." He looked down at his hands. "I think it might be a good idea if you stepped back from the tutoring group for a bit. Take some time to sort yourself, get caught up with classes, prepare for finals."

"What about my clients? They have finals too."

"Let me worry about them. I've already talked to Mariah, Semyon, and Rikka. They've agreed to take on your clients to give you some breathing room."

Despite his comforting tone, I bristled. "You already... So my taking 'time'," I said with air quotes, "to sort my shit isn't a suggestion at all. You've already decided." In a huff, I lurched off the bench, nearly flinging my bag across the lawn.

"Alexi, please."

"I don't want to fucking hear it, Rubio. You pretend to come to me as a friend, but you're really just here as my boss. And instead of supporting me, you just... just..." I threw my hands up. "Cut me off."

He surged to his feet. "Don't you dare. Maybe if you'd come to the meeting yesterday, this would have felt more amicable, but that's on you. Not me. As for supporting you, that's *all* I've done. Seems to me that your so-called boyfriend isn't the only one who's absolute shit at communication."

I gasped, my righteous anger abruptly fizzling into shame. My eyes burned, and I wiped at them brusquely. "I... I don't know what to do."

Rubio's gaze softened, and he rested a hand on my upper arm. "Why don't we go somewhere a little less public and talk through it? The Topaz Lounge? Less chance of campus looky-loos at least and there's booze. But the first round is on you."

I nodded and placed a hand over his, then looked at him with wet eyes. "Don't let go." Before he could speak, I stepped us both into the Shadow Realm. A couple of minutes later, we emerged in an alley across from the retro bar. Walking-walking might have been smarter, but I was on the verge of a full meltdown.

"Whoa, that was..." Rubio swallowed thickly while he continued to look around at the faded bricks and stucco around us. "Different," he finally finished.

I blinked in sudden realization. I'd only ever shadowed Matt before, and that was a heady experience all on its own. But shadowing Rubio had been nothing like that. When he finally looked at me, I gave him a sheepish smile. "Sorry, probably should have warned you a bit more. Now you can say you've walked in the Shadow Realm."

"Is *that* what that was?" He looked behind him as if he could see some kind of doorway.

"You, uh, get used to it. We should probably get inside, though, before someone wonders how we got here." Especially considering the alley dead-ended behind us.

"Right." He quickly checked that the way was clear, then walked across the narrow road. We found a relatively secluded booth and placed an order for two Tequila Sunrises with a passing server.

Once the drinks arrived, my excuse for putting off explaining ran out. I took a sip of the colorful drink and sighed. "I really don't know what happened. We really were doing well. Great, even. I'm not imagining or exaggerating that. He'd finally shared his past with me, and, yes, the sex was incredible. Now, I don't know where he is most of the time. He's certainly not in class, or at least not in the classes we share." I paused for another drink.

"Do you think he's-"

I quickly held up a hand. "Please don't say it. The thought crossed my mind, but when I confronted him about it, he was so earnest that he wasn't." I rolled the glass between my hands and watched the colors blur. "That he would never," I added in a whisper.

"I won't insult you by asking if you believe him." Judging by Rubio's tone, *he* certainly didn't. "When do you think things shifted?"

I abandoned my study of my drink to stare up at the ceiling. *This* I'd had plenty of time to consider. "It wasn't just one thing, not at first. There were lots of little, random bits that didn't add up."

"Like," Rubio prompted.

"Like he came back to the apartment in a state. When I asked what was wrong, he fed me a line. I believe part of it was true," I added quickly in his defense, glancing at Rubio. "But he was clearly holding something back."

He took another drink, keeping his focus on me and my pathetic tale. "Anything else?"

I sighed and finished my drink, then pushed it away. It glided across the table and would have fallen off if I hadn't halted its trajectory with a bump of shadow. "He wanted to stop working on our research project. Not that it really mattered for class, because they ended up scrapping it altogether, but he was so... passionate about it. That he would randomly want to call it quits, especially after we'd made so much progress, was odd."

"If that's the case, why did you go along with it? Why not press for more answers?" Rubio flagged the server and signalled for another round.

"Matt can be cagey. Don't look at me like that. He has his reasons, and they were valid. Plus, he was clearly very upset about it and I didn't think it was worth riling him up further."

He snorted. "And what were these 'valid' reasons?"

I rolled my eyes at his dismissive tone. "Some of them were personal and the other..." I straightened and turned my full attention to Rubio. "Do you know anything about a Bruiser Bar near campus?"

"A what?" He frowned and took a healthy swallow from his fresh glass.

"A fight club. Matt used to go to one before we got together and I'm almost positive he's started up again."

"So, you think that's where he's sneaking off to when he's not with you?"

His word choice was less than stellar. I was positive an actual knife to the chest would have hurt less. "Possibly. Probably." I sagged in defeat. Of course he was. All the signs were there—the unexplained bruises, the late nights. But that still didn't explain his peculiar behavior the rest of the time. And why miss class?

Rubio sat back in the booth. "Well, I can't say I've heard anything about a fight club. Could always ask my roommate."

"The wyvern with the tongue?" I teased, finding a modicum of merriment thanks to the alcohol and an empty stomach.

He chuckled. "Don't knock it 'til you try it. Guy can do truly magical things with that...appendage." He wiggled his eyebrows salaciously.

I barked a laugh, nearly spilling what remained of my drink, which turned out to be not much. We both signalled the server at the same time with Rubio adding an order of chips.

"I'm serious. Neese knows a shit ton of people. Even more than me. If anyone has heard of this Bruiser Bar your man's been popping off to, it'd be him," he offered again before devouring several chips in one go.

I shook my head. "No reason to get your roommate tied up in my mess. I appreciate the sentiment, though." We clinked glasses and fell into an almost comfortable silence. Finally, I let out a heavy sigh. "I just really miss him. We were even sleeping together."

Rubio snorted into his drink. "I knew *that*."

"That's not what I meant!" I shoved him in the shoulder. "Well, I mean, yes, that too, but sharing a room. Sort of." I glanced at him and started. "What's that look for?"

"I think I just threw up a little in my mouth. You're so freaking adorable. I think I might actually die." To lend credence to his ostentatious statement, he mimed a very dramatic death.

"Get off it. Judge all you like, but he was—*is*—very sweet and an absolute cuddle bug."

He pointed at himself. "Seriously, me, dead. Riddle me this, if it was *so* sweet, then why did you stop?"

I worried my lip, then downed the last of my drink, waving off the server's inquiry for another. "Okay, so it might have something to do with the nightmares."

He sat straighter. Even with the shine of inebriation in his eyes, I had his full attention. "This is a new wrinkle. Go on."

"So, um, they were really bad—mumbling in his sleep, thrashing about, the usual stuff. And he maybe, kind of, almost...killed me," I finally finished with a grimace.

"He did what!"

I grabbed Rubio's arm and gave him a severe look. "Would you keep your voice down?"

"Okay, well, way to bury the lead. That sounds as good a reason as any for your beau to ghost you."

"It would. If he knew." I held his gaze until understanding glowed in his eyes and he deflated.

"You didn't tell him?"

I couldn't help but groan at his incredulous tone. I dropped my head into my hands. "No," I mumbled through my fingers.

"Shit, Alexi. How could you not tell him?"

"I don't know. Okay? It just... he'd already been acting weird and even though I was absolutely terrified, I was more afraid *for* him than *of* him." I was regretting declining another drink.

As if reading my mind, Rubio flagged the server. However, the waiter placed two tall glasses and a pitcher of water on the table instead of more tequila. He poured us each a glass and encouraged me to drink. Only once I'd downed half did he ask, "You think he found out?"

"Maybe? But then why not talk to me about it?" And what about the bruises and the rest of the shit he was obviously hiding? "I think you're right about me taking some time. My classes could sure benefit from the extra attention."

He rubbed my back while I watched the condensation slide down the glass. "And your spot with the tutors will be waiting for you next term. Just..."

I glanced at him. "What?"

"Call if you need something. Okay?"

"I will. You're a good friend, Rubio."

He threw his hands up and gave me a wry smirk. "*Now* he says it."

Chapter 8
Birthday Promises

Matt

Fight club was a fucking disaster. Telling Neese I wouldn't be at the club Thursday went about as well as I expected. In hindsight, I should have known there would be immediate retribution. After not one, not two, but *four* fights in one evening, I was dead on my feet. At least I hadn't gotten any marks on me, though my body still felt like I'd subjected it to a meat tenderizer. Too exhausted to even pretend to try, I slept... and slept... *And* missed waking up in time to wish Alex a happy birthday before he left for classes. Determined to make the best use of his absence and glad I'd had the foresight to get everything I needed beforehand, I got to work transforming the dorm.

The spell I'd laid in the hall to alert me when Alex returned tripped. I did a quick scan of the table, making sure everything was in place before laying a cloaking spell. My heart beat a nervous rhythm as I turned to face the door just in time to greet him with a wide grin. He must have had a presentation today, because he was dressed to the nines in a deep blue button down and tan slacks. And just *wow.* He looked stunning. Somehow, he'd tamed his hair, though it looked like it was starting to fight back. In true Alex form, everything was perfectly crisp and well put together. Even frozen in the doorway, he exuded an aura of confidence.

"Why are you looking at me like that?" he asked, setting his things down by the door.

I blinked, realizing I was staring. "Happy Birthday, Alex."

"Oh, uh, thanks."

"Got anything planned?" I pushed on despite his obvious surprise that I'd remembered, crossing my fingers behind my back. I didn't know what I was going to do if he said he was already doing something.

"Um, not really. I was going to go home this weekend to see my mom, but other than that..." he finished with a shrug. I fought to temper my grin into something a little less manic. This was absolutely my best-case scenario.

"In that case, I have a surprise for you." His eyes brightened and my heart gave a little skip. I shooed him toward his room. "You get cleaned up and I'll change."

His brow furrowed. "Why do you need to change?"

"Because it's your birthday, and that warrants something nicer than a sweaty shirt and ratty jeans." Before he could argue, I walked toward my room, dragging my feet just enough to make sure he did the same. Eventually, he rolled his eyes and moved, mumbling under his breath. I shadowed the rest of the way and changed into a gray button down I didn't know I had until the other day and even darker slacks. Then I shadowed back, undid the spell hiding the table, double-checked everything once more, and dimmed the lights.

He was already talking as he came back out. "I guess dressed up means we're not playing pool." He sounded a little disappointed. If that was what he wanted, we could always do that tomorrow, but tonight I had other plans. "You're acting really weird, too. What's..." he finally turned and saw the room. "Up?"

"A tie? Really, Alex?" I laughed, finally feeling relaxed for what felt like the first time in weeks.

He absently straightened it. "You said nice." He glanced past me at the table ladened with plates and the candle in the middle. "Did you do all of this?" I didn't bother to hide my smile.

"You didn't honestly think I wouldn't go all out for my boyfriend's birthday, did you?" His focus shifted back to me. It looked like he wanted to say something. Instead, he shadowed across the room and caught me with a kiss. I sighed into him, loving how he held me so close. The kiss deepened, and I chuckled. "That's supposed to be later."

"Later, huh? What if I said I didn't want to wait until later?" He ran his thumb along my bottom lip, his eyes an intense emerald.

I swallowed thickly. "It's your birthday. I can't exactly tell you no."

He swiped a smaller kiss. "That so? I like the sound of that." He glanced at the spread. "It would be a shame to let this go to waste, though," he said, releasing me.

I joined him at the table, still buzzing with so much excitement it was hard to focus on anything except Alex. Would he like the food? Was everything still warm? Did I remember to turn everything off?

After a while, he waved his fork at me. "I thought you said you couldn't cook."

"Actually, I said that eggs weren't exactly complicated."

"That may be true, but *this*," he gestured at the various dishes, "strikes me as very complicated. And it's good. *Really* good, Matt." My face heated, and I attempted to cover it by taking a drink of water. I'd intentionally left alcohol off of the menu. "Where did you learn how to cook like this?"

That was a fair question, especially given my history. "One of my brief stints in a foster home got me started. There was this grandma that would watch us during the afternoons. She wasn't what I could motherly or even nice, but she was one of the few people who bothered to teach me something. When it was clear I had a knack for it, she taught me more. I even learned a little baking."

"Does that mean I get a cake too?" he asked, as if already knowing the answer.

I bit back the automatic "No". "Do you want a cake?"

"Not particularly." That was a relief. I wasn't exactly sure where to get one on such short notice.

"There's ice cream though."

"Of course there is." He laughed, undoing his tie. It made a soft whisk as it slipped free of his collar. He looped it around his hands so the silk slid through his fingers again and again in a kind of hypnotic dance. When he glanced up, his eyes were the color of midnight.

Heat surged through me. Being able to see how much someone wanted you was downright intoxicating, and there wasn't a doubt in my mind that my eyes were now equally dark. I watched entranced as the tie continued to weave seductively between his fingers.

"Stand up."

I lurched out of my chair so fast I nearly toppled it over. In contrast, Alex flowed effortlessly out of his seat, the embodiment of grace. He walked closer, his eyes once more green, though no less intense.

"Give me your hands."

I held them out, palms up, expecting him to take them. What I did not expect was for him to wrap the tie around my wrists and secure them together.

"Does that bother you?" he asked, a grin teasing the corner of his mouth.

Again, I had to check the immediate "No" and find a different way to answer. "Whatever you want, Alex." He grabbed my arms and leaned close. I tried to close the distance, but he held it.

"You know what I want." His husky reply sent a shiver through me. He didn't give me a chance to respond before moving my arms above my head and then using shadow to keep them suspended. This felt oddly familiar.

"You know that can't hold me," I said with a crooked grin.

He raised an eyebrow. "Then I guess you'll have to maintain it." His slow, sexy smile had no doubts whatsoever that I would, simply because he'd told me to. My heart stopped trying to beat altogether.

"Don't you want your present?"

He hooked a finger at my collar, then traced a line of shadow all the way down my chest. My shirt fell open in its wake and I gasped. "I get more than one?" My breath caught when placed his hands on my bare skin.

"Y-yes. It's still on the table. Are you sure..."

"Matt," he said with a stern expression. "Stop talking."

My mouth closed with an audible snap. Already maintaining the strip of shadow was becoming difficult. It didn't get any easier as he continued his slow, methodical exploration of what he was deeming to be his present.

"I love your body, Matt. I'm glad to see you're taking better care of it."

The earth itself seemed to shatter when he finally kissed me again. I moaned and arched into him, desperate for more. Apparently, I had too much slack, because he casually willed the strand shorter, bringing me to a point where my toes barely scrapped the ground. I stifled my alarm and tightened my hands on the strand, now relying on it to keep me from falling in a puddle at his feet.

"Still good?"

I managed the barest of nods, not trusting myself to speak.

"Good." His fingers danced down my abdomen until they reached my pants. With deft movements, he had my fly undone and my pants pulled free, leaving my arousal completely exposed and entirely at his mercy. His gaze roved over my body as he methodically removed his own clothes, draping them with care over the back of the chair. By the time he was naked, my dick was leaking like a firehose and he hadn't even touched me.

He stepped closer, and I was so enthralled by the way his cock bounced with each step that I gasped when he wrapped his long fingers around my shaft. I struggled to maintain the thin strip of shadow as he lazily stroked me. His thumb glided over my slit, stealing the latest bead of pre-cum, and he brought it to my lips. I obediently opened my mouth, but rather than feed it to me, he sucked his thumb clean. My entire body shuddered and my tentative hold on the shadow binding my arms took another hit. He brushed his hands over my straining shoulders and kissed me again.

I wanted to beg him to let me down, to let me feel him, or at the very least, let me talk. I also didn't want to disappoint him. Not ever if I could help it. And definitely not tonight.

Alex coasted his palms down my quivering sides. He hooked his hands behind my thighs and lifted me higher. I reflexively wrapped my legs around his waist, taking the pressure off of my arms. It seemed to be the appropriate response, because his fingers dug into my hips, causing me to groan. Unwilling to pass up having him within reach, I leaned forward to capture his mouth. It wasn't until I felt a slick finger at my hole that I broke the kiss.

He rubbed his finger in a slow circle along the rim and I worked diligently not to squirm *or* drop my hold. By the time he slipped the digit in, I was positive I'd pass out from anticipation. I moaned as I tried to bear down on him, craving so much more. But the more of him I tried to get, the more he pulled away, until I was whining pitifully.

"That's it, love. I wanna hear how good you feel." He pressed against my prostate as he glided his fingers in and out of my clenching hole. My moan turned into an undignified sound of disappointment when he pulled them free. Then, with no warning, Alex tipped my hips at an angle and speared me in one thrust.

I cried out, immediately tightening my legs around him to keep him there. If he pulled out now, I was positive I'd die. Thankfully, he only pulled out partially, before thrusting back in again and again, until he was fucking me in earnest. I didn't care that I couldn't feel my arms anymore or that I'd yet to touch him. With each thrust, my dick rubbed along his abdomen and the multitude of sensations were unravelling me. He slammed home once more, and I shattered, groaning through an orgasm that seemed to carry my soul.

He caught the sound in a savage kiss that dominated me and stole what little breath I had. Then he panted into my neck while he continued to piston his hips. His fingertips dug into my ass and his breakneck pace faltered. Then he grunted, his body stiffening as his release slammed through him. Finally, he reached up and pulled my arms down. If it hadn't been for already clinging to him, I likely would have crashed to the floor, my legs too unsteady to hold me.

It wasn't until he laid me on a makeshift bed of sofa cushions that he tugged the tie loose. The moment my hands were free, I pulled him to me, every fiber of my being vibrating with need. There was no way to get enough of Alex, but I'd be damned if I wasn't going to try. An exhausting round or three later, plus a break for leftovers, Alex finally gave me leave to talk again.

"Don't suppose you want your actual present now?" I asked, while he trailed his fingers lazily across my abdomen.

"You mean this wasn't it?" He laughed, sending wisps of heat spiraling beneath where his fingers played. "I don't need anything else, Matt." He placed a tender kiss on my shoulder. "Just you."

I smiled, my heart full near to bursting. Had I ever been enough for anyone before Alex? "I apparently got myself into some unnecessarily hot water getting this for you. The least you could do is let me give it to you." He looked away, embarrassment clearly written on his face. I tilted his head up to look at me. "Please."

"Okay, let's see it."

Unwilling to give up the glorious tangle of limbs to retrieve the small box, I shadowed it over. Not exactly easy when I couldn't see it. Thankfully, my selfishness didn't backfire, and I retrieved the delicate box without incident.

Alex shifted as if to sit up.

"Wait," I stalled him and created a thick sphere of shadow around us, making the space extra dark.

He laughed. "How am I supposed to see to open it?"

"Good point." I thinned the sphere enough to let some of the candlelight through. "Lay down." He gave me a look, but I refused to back down. "Trust me."

He shimmied back down into our nest and opened the box. "What's this?" he pulled out a piece of paper covered in colorful words.

"Hold it away from you and tear it in two."

He glanced at me, uncertainty clear on his face. "Matt, what is this?"

"Just do it," I said impatiently. I already knew what was coming, so I watched him to see his reaction instead. After another moment of hesitation, he tore the paper perfectly in two. A series of miniature fireworks leapt from the torn paper to explode above us in tiny pops. I re-darkened the sphere to make the contrast more stark. The reflections of the bursts shone in his eyes. "Do you like it?"

"This... this is incredible." He turned to look at me.

"You're missing it," I scolded. He quickly adjusted his focus. I scooted closer, resting my head on his shoulder so I could watch as well. His arm tightened around me, and I sighed contentedly. "What do you want, Alex?" I whispered between the muted bangs.

He glanced down, catching my eye. "This. I want this feeling to last forever."

I stretched up to kiss him. Someday I'd be able to give that to him.

"Will you be gone in the morning?" he asked sadly.

I barely stopped the "No" before it sprung forth. "I'll be here."

"What about the morning after that?"

"Still here."

"And after that?" he whispered.

"For the next five days, I'm all yours." I saw the disbelief in his eyes, like he was too scared to hope.

"I love you, Matt," he said, rolling us and capturing me in a kiss I'd gladly spend eternity drowning in. My heart felt like it would burst as we made love beneath the fireworks that had been conjured in our living room.

Chapter 9
Blending

Alexi

Not even a whole day after what was likely the best birthday weekend of my life, everything was back to usual. Matt resumed his disappearing act and left me to wonder if he was attending *any* of his classes, let alone passing them. Apparently, loving him would only be on his schedule, which at the moment was full up with Nyx knew what.

Losing my tutoring job stung, but it meant I had more time to study before the end of term and winter break. It also gave me entirely too much time to think, namely about Matt. If he would just talk to me, then I knew we could sort this out together. But he clearly didn't trust me with whatever had him so preoccupied and that hurt almost as much as the avoidance.

I couldn't fight the feeling that time was running out for us. Which meant I needed to play Matt's game by his rules. I already knew he wouldn't like it, but I needed answers. Despite the pristine condition of his body on my birthday, the bruises had made an almost immediate reappearance. The question was, was he fighting again or had he never stopped? Neither made me happy, but at least the former meant he hadn't been lying to me the *whole* time.

It took some research, but I eventually learned how to set replicate the perimeter alarms he used. They were incredibly handy for determining when he returned to the dorm, as infrequent as that was. Unfortunately, he could give a ghost a run for their money and often had disappeared by the time I realized he was around. At some point, I was going to have to stop letting the distraction of seeing him for the first time in days prevent me from doing what needed to be done. Until then, I practiced the spells until I was sure I had them down. Not that it did me any good—he never tripped them. Considering how outrageously good at practical shadow spells he'd gotten, it was entirely possible he was sidestepping my feeble attempts. Refusing to be deterred, I expanded my web in the dorm, practicing the spell until I could do it effortlessly in my sleep. I also figured out how to mask the spell like the portal-cloaking spell he'd taught me and placed the "trip wires" in creative places. Now, I just had to wait.

I sat on my bed appreciating the pictures from the fair. It had quickly become the only way I could see him for longer than five seconds. They'd found their way into a keepsake box along with the sketches he'd given me, as well as the remnants of the spell for the fireworks. I couldn't help but smile as I fingered the torn paper. That had been such a thoughtful and original gift. It spoke to how he thought and the caring soul I knew was still inside of him, no matter how he hid it.

A wire tripped, and my head shot up. As I suspected, he was sneaking into his room through the wall. I quickly put away the treasures, then rushed into the living room, careful not to shadow despite my urgency. Shadowing would only trip more wires and alert him I knew he was here. When I pushed his door open, he spun around in surprise. He was mid-change and there was no hiding the mottled bruises covering his torso.

"I knew it. You're fighting again." I tried and failed to reign in my anger.

He sighed and finished pulling the shirt over his head. "Alex, not now."

"Then when? You won't talk to me anymore. What happened to being best friends, Matt?" He flinched. "No matter what, remember? You said that no matter what, we would always be best friends. If you've changed your mind about other things, that's fine," I lied, "but at least have the decency to tell me to my face instead of sneaking around, barely even able to look at me. We don't even hang out as friends anymore."

"*Now* you want to be friends?" he scoffed.

"I never did anything you didn't ask me to," I bit back. There were a few liberties with that statement, but the spirit was true.

He opened his mouth, but it took a moment for the words to come. "You and I both know that being *just* friends is out of the question. If I recall, you said it pretty much always was." He turned his back to me and reached to grab his shoes. "Why are you here, Alex?"

"Because I miss you. I miss us. And you won't talk to me about anything. You haven't even denied that you're fighting again."

He shook his head. "What do you want from me? Do you want me to lie to you and tell you everything is fine? I can't do that, Alex."

"You seem to be lying plenty of late." Shock exploded across his face like I'd backhanded him. I softened. This isn't what I'd intended. "I want answers. I want you to trust me again."

"I never stopped trusting you."

"Then why are you hiding things from me?"

"Because I know you. If you knew what was really going on, then you'd try to march off and save the day. I can't let you do that. You'll only get hurt." He clapped a hand over his mouth and groaned. "Damn it, Alex. Just go."

"Why are you so convinced that I can't handle whatever it is?" I closed my hands into fists at my side. "Matt, I'm not a wimp. I can take care of myself."

"I know you can, but this is different."

"Why?"

"I can't tell you that."

"Can't or won't?" I asked angrily.

His shoulders sagged, and he dropped his head back to stare at the ceiling. "I shouldn't have let you spell the dorm."

"Let me?"

"I thought I could avoid them all, but apparently you're getting creative. How many are in here?" He didn't wait to see if I would answer. I reeled from the backlash of all the tripwires disintegrated at once.

"Maybe I wouldn't have to go to such lengths if you would stop avoiding me altogether. Tell me what's going on," I demanded, stepping up to him. I'd avoided outright ordering him to tell me what I wanted to know for a reason: it was practically my last card and if it didn't work, I didn't really have anything else. Much to my shock, he stood frozen in place while a war of indecision and doubt played across his face. Risking it all, I pushed. "Tell me, Matt."

He grimaced. "You don't understand. It's not that simple."

"Then explain it to me." He went to shake his head, and I stopped him. If I lost eye contact, he'd be gone. His eyes widened and I could see the panic as he realized he was caught. "Tell me."

"No." It didn't seem possible to infuse a word with more pain. "They'll hurt you," he added in a whisper, then closed his eyes, clearly having said more than he'd intended. And just like that, I lost him again. When he reopened his eyes, the apathy was back and more solid than ever.

"Stop pushing me away!" I shouted, even though he was still standing there.

Without another word, he shadowed out of the room.

I yelled all of my frustration into the space, resulting in a series of angry knocks on the wall. Despite his slip, I had no more answers than when I'd started—not if he'd been fighting this whole time, *why* he was fighting, were we even together anymore, and who did he think would hurt me? Defeat weighed me down until I sat on the edge of his bed and cradled my head. What was there left to do besides give up, let him go?

My heart gave me a painful reminder that it would never happen. But I didn't know what to do. It felt like I was slowly dying without Matt. Was that possible? It sure felt possible, and honestly, it didn't look like he was faring any better. How much heartache was it possible for someone to endure before there was simply nothing left?

I went to stand when an edge of paper poking out between the mattresses caught my eye. Without a thought for how I'd be violating his privacy, I swung around and investigated. Sandwiched between the mattress and box spring was his sketch book. I glanced at the door before slipping it free, though I don't know why I bothered. He wasn't liable to come back soon, nor was he likely to use the door. I resumed my seat and carefully began turning the pages.

To my amazement, nearly every page was covered edge to edge with precise detail. I now knew why the light was always on—nearly every sketch was of me sleeping. I flipped faster through the pages. None of this made any sense. In my frenzy, something fell out of the book and drifted to the floor. When I picked up the photograph, I saw my face smiling back at me. It was a picture from the house. But how had *he* gotten it? Judging from the state of the edges, he looked at it often.

My level of understanding diminished even more. What did all of this mean? Matt was definitely lying, but now I wondered who he was really lying to. Was it me? Someone else? Himself? I gently closed the nearly full book and replaced it and the picture where I'd found them. One way or another, I was going to find those answers and if he wasn't willing to tell me himself, then I'd have to find them on my own.

Days passed without so much as a sensation of Matt near the dorm. Not that it surprised me after our fight or after he casually undid all the spells I'd spent days placing and hiding. Clearly, he'd gotten far more advanced with his Shadow magic than seemed possible for someone only going to class half of the time.

As I made my way to ballroom class, my trepidation increased. I'd only taken this course because I thought it'd be enjoyable and suspected that it'd be required in the future. Now it was simply a hassle, a drain on my time and annoying on top. I had more important things to do than get fawned over by people I wasn't interested in—like finding out the secrets Matt was trying so hard to hide.

"What's the matter, Roman?" my current partner asked at the end of the set. Amber, that was her name. She was nice enough and one of the few who didn't expect me to grope her.

"Sorry, Amber, just a lot on my mind."

"Girlfriend troubles?" she asked in an unsettling tone.

I looked at her warily. "I guess you could say that." We practiced a few more turns, and she continued the conversation.

"You sure that's all? Your dancing is usually much better."

"I'll try to improve," I replied sardonically.

She shrugged as if it was no big deal to her and spun out. "Anything I can do to help?" Where was this coming from? Sure, Amber and I were on decent terms, but I'd never shared anything about my personal life with her.

"I doubt it."

"Oh, I'm sure there is *something* I could do to at least cheer you up. You seem so melancholy lately." She pouted and while the expression undoubtedly helped her with others, I was unphased.

"Don't trouble yourself," I said as we tried the turn again. This time, when she spun back in, she landed practically on top of me. She really needed to work more on her footwork, but I was in no mood to point that out.

"It's no trouble," she said. Again, there was that hint of something else. Before I could chase it down, though, she reached up on her toes and placed her mouth against mine.

Shock rippled through me. I had to restrain myself from pushing her off. She was just a witch and demonic strength could send her sailing clear across the room. Then, I thought about what Matt had said to me when he forced me to go talk to those girls that night. I needed to blend in. Is this what he meant? That he was perfectly okay with us behind closed doors, but out in the rest of the world he needed me to be more like everyone else? Maybe just me wasn't enough for him. Could I do this for Matt?

Something heavy hit the floor, the sound of it echoing in the open space. Startled, I pulled back. Amber had an almost evil grin and there by the door was Matt. His face was a mix of shock and something he was trying desperately not to let show—hurt.

My heart fell somewhere in the vicinity of my stomach. I looked back at Amber, who was now evil *and* smug. I didn't know what game she thought she was playing, but I wanted no part of it. What was worse, now Matt was leaving. I struggled to disentangle myself. "Let me go. Matt, wait!"

"Come on, Roman, maybe just one more," she teased.

Beyond irritated with Amber's sudden antics, I shadowed out of her clutches, barely remembering to grab my backpack before barreling through the door. I caught sight of his back before he turned a corner and silently thanked Nyx that he hadn't simply shadowed away.

"Matt, please," I called after him. I could clearly see him now, though even at my shout, he didn't turn back. Instead, he made his way into what appeared to be an empty classroom. I followed him and jumped when the door slammed shut behind me. "Matt, I can explain." Actually, I had no idea how to explain what he'd seen. When he rounded on me, I was reminded of when I thought he was going to kill Daniel at the fair.

"I would be very interested to hear that," he said, his voice low and suspiciously calm.

"It wasn't what you think; she kissed me." I could practically feel his rage intensifying.

"It didn't look one sided to me."

"I..." I didn't have an answer for that. "I thought that's what you wanted. You're the one who told me to blend." Something flashed in his eyes. It wasn't anger, but it was gone too fast for me to pinpoint what it really was.

"And you choose now to experiment?" he asked, just shy of shouting.

I flinched. "It's not like that," I tried again, reaching out for him.

He shadowed out and my hand went right through him, causing me to stumble. When he rematerialized ice was warmer than his frigid glare. "I know we've been having issues, but this... this is low even for you. There are some things you don't forgive."

My jaw fell open. I was struck dumb as he angrily walked past me and left. If I'd been confused before, I was even more so now.

CHAPTER 10
THE BREAK

Matt

I couldn't breathe. The tightness in my chest wouldn't let air in. I needed to find a safe place before I passed out in the hallway. A place far away from Alex. My chest spasmed. I spied another empty room and made a beeline.

I sank to the floor the moment the door was closed, bracing against the wall for support as my legs gave out. I stared at the ceiling, but it did nothing to stop the hot tears from falling unhindered. Even though I'd orchestrated the whole thing, I couldn't stop the pain from welling up. When I'd approached Amber about this, she'd seemed more than enthusiastic. That should have given me pause—hadn't Gilles warned me about witches?—but at the time it had only convinced me it was the right choice. That the ploy would work. I was desperate to get the X completed on Alex's picture, and rumors of him making out with a cute witch from his ballroom class would certainly go a long way toward accomplishing that. But I had no idea that I'd have to witness it.

There was no doubt in my mind that she'd made sure that I'd see, if only so I'd know she'd held up her end of the bargain. But never in a million years did I ever think he'd kiss her back. I bit hard on my knuckle in some vain attempt to hold back the sob threatening to tear me apart.

Why did it hurt so much? This had been the plan—my plan. If anything, he'd made it more convincing. But knowing that didn't change the sickening thud of my heart against my ribs or that every time I closed my eyes, I could see his arms around her, see the moment he kissed her back. It was certainly believable, and that's what I'd needed. Then I'd almost ruined everything when I dropped the backpack. I'd been so surprised that it had just slipped from my fingers. Of course, when I ran, he followed. All I could do was hope that the fight had been enough to put him off of trying to pursue anymore answers from me.

Something tickled at the edge of my senses, and that small hope evaporated.

He doesn't believe I've left. He knows me far too well.

My reprieve over, I pushed to my feet, the abrupt change nearly making me sick. There was no way I could look at him right now, not without completely caving. I stepped into the Shadow World, not caring that doing so would likely result in him opening the very door I hid behind. An actual portal could be tracked, so I walked to another area, stepped out, and opened another breach. It would be harder to follow me if I was playing hopscotch through the Shadow world.

With each step further away from him, I reminded myself that this was the plan. That we'd fought would help to solidify the break. I stumbled, barely catching myself, before crashing into a wall. It felt like I was being torn apart from the inside. My deep breath was less than steadying. I'd do anything to keep Alex safe, even if that meant giving him up. That conviction didn't make it any easier, though.

Unsure of what to do with myself, I returned to the dorm. If this was going to work, then it needed to be believable. I packed a bag full of clothes and a few other items. There was no way I was about to stay at that miserable house Thomas lurked in, but I was no stranger to the streets either. I'd figure something out.

I was already lifting the mattress to retrieve my sketchbook when I thought better of it. If I got caught with literally pages of nothing but Alex, that wouldn't help anything. Then again, I couldn't leave it here either. I'd have to hide it somewhere it couldn't be found. I reached under and, to my surprise, found two books instead of one. I fell to the bed in disbelief. Alex had already found it. I opened the fresh book to the first page. There in his perfect handwriting, was a message. My heart constricted as I read.

> *It looked like you were running out of room and I thought you could use another. Perhaps I'll even be awake for some of them. You really are a talented artist. I miss you and I want you to know that I'm not done fighting. I love you with all that I am and one way or another, I'm going to get to the bottom of this. Come back to me. I'm not going anywhere; you are my forever.*
>
> *~ Alexi*

I barely got the barrier up in time before I completely disintegrated into sobs.

No. After everything I've done, he's still going to pursue this.

He's going to get himself killed.

The sound of my heartache echoed back to me in the bubble I'd created to contain the sound. I clutched the precious gift to my chest as I tried to rein in the pain. What more could I possibly do to keep him from following? I looked down at the empty book. Setting it on the bed felt like ripping off my arm, but I couldn't keep it. Leaving it here would look like rejecting it. Perhaps that, combined with what had happened today, would convince him to let me go.

A quick check showed that he still hadn't returned to the dorm. That was good. I needed to be gone before then. I carefully eliminated all evidence of my breakdown. My hand hesitated when I reached for the other sketchpad with the photo. It was too dangerous to leave those behind. Destroying them would be the smart thing to do, but I couldn't bring myself to do that either. This was already hard enough.

I opened the nightstand and took out the box that had held his present. For a few shining days, things were like they had been before all of this had started. Another sob tried to escape, but I forced it down. I grabbed the book and shadowed it down into a compressed sphere. It would be impossible to maintain it that way, though, which is where the box came in. I willed the inky substance into the box and placed a shadow lock on it. Now the book would stay suspended until the box was unlocked. As an added measure, I put the box in a pocket of the Shadow world inside the drawer, then cloaked it.

I spared one last look at my room. This was the most at home I'd ever felt in a place and I was abandoning it. The book sat on the bed, a clear declaration of my leaving. I considered putting it in the kitchen instead, but that would mean venturing into a space dominated by memories of happiness. I shook my head. There was zero doubt in my mind that he'd check my room when he finally returned. Here was as good a place as any to leave it.

Now I just have to figure out where to go.

After some deliberation, I decided to check out the other forsaken houses on old fraternity row. Then at least I could see anyone they brought to see Thomas. While I hadn't been privy to this event, it was inevitable. Thomas was absolutely the type of guy who'd insist on meeting his target face to face. With over half the class eliminated, options were running low. It was only a matter of time until the stragglers were brought before him to be eliminated.

My stomach heaved. Despite all of my efforts, Alex still made that ever-shrinking list. Not even offering up Gilles and his sketchy past with witches had done any good. Asshole had gone and dropped out, taking my best shot with him. Hopefully, my latest endeavor would be the final piece to clear Alex once and for all.

Resigned in my decision, I laid tripwires much like Alex had. If I couldn't resolve this quickly, I'd likely have to return if for no other reason than to get fresh clothes or shower. Satisfied that it at least *looked* like I'd left permanently, I shouldered the duffle bag. It felt light compared to the weight in my heart as I shadowed out of the dorm.

The first house I checked was in such a sorry state that even desperate, I couldn't bring myself to camp there. Sadly, several of the other options fell into that same category, forcing me further from my ideal vantage. Not that it really mattered if I was at the first house or the last; I'd be spending enough time with the others that I wouldn't be likely to miss anything.

Eventually, I found a place that sufficed. A sweep of my final stop resulted in some halfway decent bedding, surprisingly not infested with fleas or other vermin. That was an unforeseen plus. No running water though, which meant I'd either have to go back to the dorm or find somewhere else to bathe. But that was a problem for later. The day's events had me bone weary and as I laid down on the lumpy bed, I couldn't help but long for the warmer bed clear across campus.

Alex would be back by now, likely have found the left behind sketchbook, and hopefully drawn the right conclusions. He hadn't tripped a wire though, so I could be wrong. As I lay there struggling to sleep, I couldn't help but wish I had brought a sketch or something. Even pretending that I was with him would help. Gradually, the night reached out to claim my abused body. I wasn't surprised when the nightmare started. That's all there ever was now.

> Alex was standing in the kitchen when I came in from class. He turned like he always did, and I smiled in anticipation. This was my favorite part of the day. I closed the distance, eager to touch him. Lavender encompassed me like a blanket. I loved that. Lived for it.

> He was close enough now that I could practically feel his breath. Just a little further. He stopped just shy, denying me. I caught his

eye. There was no happiness or laughter playing in them, just a sadness that made them infinitely dark.

Why Matt?

Why what? I thought, confused, reaching out for him. There was only smoke. Panicking, I tried again.

Why do you want me to hurt you?

Because I have to keep you safe. I can't do that if you're chasing me.

Why Matt? Tell me why. Why? Why? Why? Why?

I jolted awake. All around me, shadows flailed, inching across the floor and climbing up the walls, as if looking for something. I quickly reined them in. I knew exactly what they were questing for—they were looking for Alex. I'd heard of demons unintentionally summoning others. This was the last thing I needed. Now I was going to have to find a way to limit my powers in my sleep lest I wake up and find Alex beside me.

Fat lot of good convincing him to let me go will be if I'm fucking summoning him.

I grabbed the grimoire the fifth year had given me and flipped through in the vain hope I could find something. There had to be a way to keep me from reaching out like that. Finally, I found something halfway promising. It was like the ward Vera had placed in the hotel. Hell, it was possible that it was the same one. There was no real way for me to know beyond asking her, and that wasn't going to happen.

I worked on perfecting the spell throughout the night, leaving me bone-weary by the time morning light streamed through the boarded windows. Once it was cast, I wouldn't be able to leave or affect anything outside of the sphere of influence until I properly broke down the barrier. With a heavy sigh, I stood and cracked my back. A little sleep would've been nice, but I had a job to do.

I shoved the grimoire into my bag, lacking the reserves to hide it like I had the sketchbook and unwilling to leave it lying around. While I hadn't seen signs of anyone else attempting to squat in the ruins, I also knew better than to trust what I couldn't see. Shouldering my bag, I stepped into the Shadow world and minutes later emerged on the green, shading my eyes against the unforgiving light.

A quick glance around revealed it was still a little early for the majority of students to be out and about. I briefly debated actually going to Demonic History II. Maybe not into the class itself, but enough to glimpse Alex. My heart constricted. Even thinking about seeing him hurt and it had nothing to do with the contrived fight about Amber.

I shook my head to free the wayward impulse and caught sight of one of my Shadow classmates. A single step back put me firmly in the shadow of the large tree I'd emerged beside and out of sight of Ellie as she walked by. We shared almost no classes together these days, so she'd been a little harder to get a handle on. Maybe this was the universe's way of helping me out. The sooner I could get intel on everyone in class, the sooner I could stop this awful business.

She continued on the path leading to the Witch's college and I fell instep a few paces behind. Close enough to monitor her if she made a sudden turn, but far enough not to raise suspicion. It was honestly scary how good I'd gotten at tracking my classmates. I'd even figured out how to follow them when they'd shadowed somewhere, which was how I knew it left a trail for anyone looking. Luckily, Ellie didn't shadow, as I doubted I'd have the energy to follow.

It wasn't until she was in the castle's shadow that she looked around. I flattened against the side of an adjoining building and kept her in sight. The way she paced combined with the way she kept adjusting her hair struck me as nervous, but I'd yet to deduce why. Then her face lit up suddenly. I followed her gaze and spotted a guy slightly older than us walking toward her. His brown hair was pulled into a bun and his ruddy complexion begged him to spend more time in doors. But his smile appeared genuine as he gathered Ellie into a hug, then planted a kiss on her. When she stepped back, she was equal parts flushed and smiley and oddly still anxious.

I inched closer to hear what they were saying.

"Good morning, dark heart," he said, tucking a stray hair behind Ellie's ear.

She beamed at him. "It's still too early to decide if it's good or not."

"Cheeky minx." He chucked her under the chin. "You ready?"

Ellie's face momentarily fell, then she squared her shoulders and gave a curt nod.

"You're so perfect." He wrapped a hand around the back of her neck and kissed her soundly. I was so wrapped in my own memories and daydreams of kissing Alex, I nearly missed that he'd removed a palm-sized glass vial from the bag at his side. When he broke the kiss, he flicked the mysterious vial open at the same time he seemed to... What? No.

I rubbed my eyes, but the scene remained the same. That was *Shadow* he was pulling out of Ellie. It drifted from her parted lips and into the glass until darkness filled it to the brim. Abruptly, the tendril of Shadow essence vanished. Ellie staggered and braced against the moss-covered stone while he stoppered the bottle.

"Such a good girl," he said as he replaced the now full vial back in his bag.

She gave him a weak smile. "Anything for you." Ellie paused as she struggled to regain her bearings with no assistance from the guy. "Uh, how much more do you think you'll need?"

The guy stepped in close to wrap his arms around Ellie and place a swift kiss on her lips. "Not much, dark heart. I promise. You're so good to help me with this. What other witch in the entire college beside the acclaimed Kyra Hallow herself could lay claim to such an... intimate relationship with a Shadow Demon." The way he trailed his index finger along her cheek made my skin crawl.

I'd seen a lot of questionable shit following my classmates around, but this took the cake. Gilles warning not to trust witches had alarm bells blaring in my head. Even if the guy wasn't a witch, I'd met his type before. A user. Someone who saw others as a commodity to be taken advantage of for their own ends. Thomas would definitely want to hear about this. And maybe, just maybe, this would bring me that much closer to getting Alex cleared.

Chapter 11
Surprise Appearance

Alexi

After being led on a wild goose chase, I returned to the dorm. I wasn't surprised that he wasn't there, but he clearly had been. I didn't even hesitate to go into his room and immediately wished I hadn't. There on the bed was the new sketch book I'd gotten him. I knew it had been a risk to leave it with the other, but I'd stupidly hoped that it could act as a kind of peace offering. Seeing it so intentionally left out sent a lance through my chest. I walked into the room and picked it up with the vain hope that he'd written something back or left another picture or *some* sign that he wasn't totally lost to me. Nothing. In an inexplicable wave of panic, I yanked back the mattress—the other book was gone. I looked around, a terrifying realization taking hold: everything was gone.

This wasn't be possible. All this over Amber? I shook my head. No. This was something else. While his hurt had been genuine, that fight had been fabricated. Matt was clever, and I was only now realizing just how clever. Everything had a purpose. Every single thing he did had a reason. It might not make sense outside of his own mind, but he definitely had one. Suddenly, I knew he hadn't taken the book or the picture. They were still here. Somewhere.

I reached out with my essence, searching for a pocket of shadow in which he could have hidden the wayward items like he had the liquor bottles in the kitchen. But no matter how many tendrils of shadow I sent exploring, I kept coming up empty-handed. Frustrated, I kicked the nightstand, and the drawer flew open. Almost instantly, I noticed a strange... absence, a void of sorts. I leaned over to investigate, reaching with shadow to determine the confines of the space. The drawer was just that—a drawer. Except for one spot. Curious, I reached into the peculiar spot of nothingness.

My fingers brushed over something small. I pulled my hand back, not sure if I wanted the answer to this riddle. Why couldn't I feel this space? Then it hit me. When I'd cloaked my portal, Matt had instantly lost all sensation of it, but it was still there, still an opening to the other side.

Cautiously, I reached back in to the undefinable space and closed my hand around a small item. In the light of the room, I knew why it felt familiar. It was the companion to my present. I'd wondered where the little box had gotten to, but had been too distracted to care. A smile tugged at my lips.

I scrutinized the box. It should have just opened at a simple touch and yet it resisted. Then I realized there was a faint spell keeping it locked. Refusing to dwell on why it would need to be, I pressed against the spell until it broke. The box sprung open and I just barely caught the oversized item that exploded out of it—his original sketchbook. If I wasn't convinced of the fight before, I was even less so now. And now that I knew what to look for, it was time to uncover any other secrets he might have squirreled away in the dorm.

I reached out, searching for the absence that I now recognized as a cloaking spell against Shadow Demons, and found two more spots. The first was in the middle of the doorway to the hall, the second, my room. I didn't need to break the cloaking spell to know what they were. Tripwires to know when I was here... and when I left.

After several days, I figured out how to remove the cloak. It took asking Vera, who was no less than shocked that I even knew the spell. I neglected to mention where I'd picked it up as well as dodged questions about the location of her secret prodigy. That one I couldn't answer if I wanted to. Wherever he was, he came back twice for clothes and to lay more wires.

I sat on the couch and casually removed the cloak on the latest one. It was in the walkway, in a direct path from the door to the kitchen. At this rate, my only hope was that he'd misinterpret me tripping the wire as leaving and accidentally return while I was still here, either that or grow tired of this horrible game. Final exams were officially here, and it wasn't possible for him to pass Demonic History II or Battle Tactics if he didn't even show up for the test.

The feeling of dying had subsided somewhat at realizing that however much distance he tried to put between us, he still couldn't completely let go. There was still hope. I'd get through to him, eventually. With a resigned sigh, I stopped staring at the latest tripwire and made my way to the kitchen, carefully avoiding three others. I opened the cabinet with no apparent purpose beyond moving. After a few moments of mindless searching, I turned and leaned against the counter, feeling lost.

Abruptly, every shadow in the room warped and twisted, spiraling in on the center of the room. Then, with a painful snap that left me gasping, the inky pool imploded. I blinked several times, not sure I trusted my eyes. The darkness had vanished and now Matt stood in its place looking like he'd been dragged through hell backwards.

"You're here." His voice was like music to my ears, but it couldn't override my concern.

All questions of where he'd been vanished in favor of the most prescient one. "What happened?"

"That's not important." He took two long strides and captured me with a kiss that stole my breath. I tried to put some distance between us, but he was persistent, a blinding firestorm of need.

At last, I managed to at least steal a breath. "Matt, wait. What's going on?" Aside from the obvious looking like hell, something clearly wasn't right.

"Alexi," he whispered, once again ignoring my question, and pressed me against the counter.

"Matt, look at me." When he did, one eye was perfectly blue while the other was midnight. Something was definitely not right.

He leaned forward to kiss me again, and I pulled back as much as our positions would allow. He delicately cupped my jaw and looked up at me entreatingly with his mismatched eyes. "Please, I need this. I need you." His lips ghosted over mine and, much as I knew I should, I couldn't deny him.

"Oh, Matt, I've missed you." I succumbed to his demanding kiss, sweeping my tongue past his parted lips while I tangled my fingers in his hair and wrapped an arm around his waist to pull him closer still. Maybe if I could hold him tight enough, he wouldn't slip away.

Matt moaned into my mouth. But unlike his usual moans of pleasure, it was tinged with pain. He pulled away, wincing as he dragged in a deep breath.

Before he could stop me, I reached down and pulled up his shirt to reveal his side. "What happened?" I shrieked at seeing the condition of his torso.

"I lost," he said matter of fact before snaring me with a kiss that refused to be denied.

Reflexively, I wrapped my arms around him, then caught myself. "Matt, this is wrong. I can't... I won't... I don't want to hurt you." I tried to hold him at bay, but he was having none of it and my desire to have him close again was weakening my resolve.

"I do. I want it to hurt." He leaned in and kissed me again while intentionally putting my hand on his battered ribs. The pain only seemed to spur him on harder.

"But Matt..."

"Alex, please, just give me this," he implored. I could feel myself giving into the inferno that was Matt. No mercy, no prisoners, just pure burning desire.

Against my better judgment, I caved. The feel of him against me felt like summer after an eternal winter. I grabbed his hand and started dragging him to the bedroom. His fingers laced through mine and he came willingly. I'd barely got my trousers off before he yanked me onto the bed. He must have shadowed out of his clothes, because he was already gloriously naked. The lurid bruises on his beautiful body gave me pause, then his hands were on my body, coasting, caressing, kneading. He rolled us so I was beneath him and spent a few minutes conquering my mouth and grinding against me, then stretched across the bed to grab supplies from the nightstand.

Before I could ask if he needed a minute, he'd already rolled the condom on my aching cock and slicked it up. Then he shifted so his back was to me and slowly guided my length to his hole.

I placed my hands on his hips to slow him. "Matt, wait. You need prep."

He glanced over his shoulder, both eyes now mercifully blue. "You're all I need."

The sincere statement threw me for such a loop that my grip slackened and he finished lowering himself. His breath caught repeatedly as he slowly worked me deeper. We both groaned when I was fully buried in his tight ass. Then he moved. Each roll of his hips sent arcs of pleasure up my spine until taking things slow was no longer an option. I shifted so I could wrap an arm around his torso and pressed his back flat against my chest. His needy whine urged me on as I thrust into him again and again.

The rest of the world melted away. There was no room for fear or doubt or worry. Just this impossible connection we had when we were together, our essences bleeding together, uniting us in darkness. I reached for his cock and he twisted to capture my mouth while we writhed together.

At some point, I blinked and had the distinct impression that hours had slipped past. The sun had long since set and the quiet of night blanketed the campus beyond our bubble. I quickly turned the lamp on and looked around. The room was a mess, but Matt wasn't there. Had it all been a dream? Brought on by my desperate desire to have Matt once more in my arms and in my bed? I coasted my hand over the vacant spot beside me, startled to find it warm. Maybe it *wasn't* a dream after all.

A soft thump snatched my attention to the bedroom door in time to see the man himself shadow through it. "Matt?" I asked softly, still not sure if I was actually awake or not.

"Hey, Alex," he slurred as if he was drunk, an observation emphasized by the fact that he was walking in something more like a zigzag than a straight line back towards the bed.

"What happened?" I asked again, unable to ignore the mottling of bruises decorating him from head to toe.

He looked behind him, then back at me, and giggled. "What happened where?" he asked, his gaze sliding as if he couldn't focus.

"Are you high?"

"*That* is an excellent question." He giggled again as he crawled onto the bed and nearly tumbled back off.

I barely caught him in time to prevent the painful fall. His side glowed sickeningly in the light from the lamp. It didn't seem possible that his ribs could look any worse than they had earlier, and yet they did. "Are you alright?"

"Pft, I'm fine. Though in hindsight, *that* was probably not a good idea with broken ribs." He flopped down and continued to giggle.

"You're totally high. What did you take?"

"Oh, dis and dat. There's quite an accumlation of pain kickers in der." He dissolved into laughter at his inability to speak properly.

"How did this happen? Where did you get pain meds like that? How many have you had? Where have you been?"

He rolled his eyes. "I told you, Neese is an asshole. He made me lose." His features twisted into a sullen pout.

"Neese?" Who the fuck was Neese? And why did that name sound so familiar? "How did he make you lose?"

"He's still *super* pissed about me blowing off the fight that Thursday. Totally worth it, by the way." He winked at me and laughed. "Oh, and I'm apparently on his shit list. He bet against me. Can you believe that? Don't matter no ways, he was gonna win one way or t' other."

"Did you throw the fight?" Between the slurring and general gibberish, I couldn't believe or understand most of what I was hearing.

"Haven't you been listening? I've never lost on purpose before," he mused aloud.

"Matt, you need a healer."

"No healers," he said with a surprising amount of force.

I wanted to ask why, but left it alone... for now. "Well, rest at least."

"No can do. Can't sleep with a cunssion."

"Concussion?"

"Yeah. That." He looked at me out of the corner of his eye. "Are you still mad at me? You are aren't you? I don't blame you. I'm awful. And you kissed Amber." His face twisted into a disgusted scowl. "Should've known she was trouble. Can't trust 'itches."

I had no idea who he was talking to or even what he was talking about, so I latched onto the only thing that did make sense—the concussion. "Matt, do you know where you are?"

"Hmm? Sure, I'm... Oh no you don't." He wagged a finger at me. "I'm onto you. I'm not falling for your tricks. You always try to trick me into telling you. At least you haven't asked me why yet. That's a nice change." He let out a contented sigh and settled back down.

"What?" I asked, confused.

"See, no why. Thanks for that. It was really driving me bonkers."

I didn't have the heart to tell him I thought he was already there. "We should wrap your ribs if you won't go to a healer." He glanced down at the marred skin.

"Probably a good idea. They're really starting to hurt. Maybe I should just take the last of the bottle." He made to get up, and I forced him back down.

"I'll get them. You wait here."

He visibly sagged into the rumpled sheets. "You're so good," he whispered. "The best."

"I'll be right back. *Don't* go to sleep."

"M'kay," he hummed with a dreamy smile.

I shadowed to the kitchen and grabbed some candy pieces that I hoped would convince him he was taking the last of the mysterious pills. Then I scoured his room for anything to wrap broken ribs with. I finally found a long scarf that would do well enough and returned to find his eyes closed.

"Matt, wake up!" The candies clattered to the ground as I rushed to his side.

His eyes flew open. "Wha—? This isn't..." He looked at me and I saw true understanding for the first time since he'd appeared out of nowhere in the middle of the living room. He shadowed to within feet of the door and rage incinerated my earlier concern.

"I swear, Matt, you walk out of here and don't bother coming back." He froze mid-step, and I took a step closer. "Now get your ass back over here so I can wrap those disasters you call ribs."

His shoulders slumped, and he turned to face me. I couldn't think of a time I'd seen him look more defeated. But I couldn't give in. Without a word, I walked over to where he stood and began wrapping his ribs.

"Is it too tight?" I asked quietly.

"I shouldn't be here."

"Then why are you?" I finished tying off the last piece, hoping my makeshift bandage would suffice.

"Because I—" he stalled, searching my face. I waited. I wouldn't say it for him no matter how much I wanted to. He glanced away. "I need to leave."

"Not tonight, you don't. Get back in the bed, Matt." He hesitated. "I don't care if you are stronger than me. You're in no condition to fight me on this. In the bed. Now." He continued to stand there uncertainly, so I reached forward and cupped his face. He sighed into the touch and I kissed him. It was gentle, but sincere. He made a noise that sounded like resignation and kissed me back, melting into the embrace. I brushed the hair from his face. "Please get in the bed, Matt. Let me take care of you for one night."

He looked at the bed longingly. "What about the nightmares?" he asked, sounding haunted.

I flashed to the night he'd almost suffocated us both. "You won't have any tonight." It broke my heart to see the hope in his eyes. His resistance faded and he let me help him back into the bed. "How long do you have to stay awake?"

"When did I get here? It's a little fuzzy," he admitted.

I glanced at the clock on the stand. "Several hours at least."

He nodded slowly. "I should be fine."

"Good, now lay down." He did as he was told, and I carefully curled around him. "And Matt."

"Yeah?"

"You better be here in the morning." He didn't respond, but I suspected it was because he was already asleep. I waited a while, still not one hundred percent convinced he was really here or that he still would be come dawn's first light.

Chapter 12

The Dream

Matt

How could I have let this happen? I must've hit my head harder than I thought. The last thing I remembered was Neese telling me to throw the fight. It hadn't made any sense, but then, not much of what happened after that did. He'd told me to make it look good and not just like me giving up. While it was true that my fights had been less than stellar of late, this seemed unusually cruel even for him. Of course, that had been the point. After that, it was a blur.

I vaguely recalled my opponent looking unassuming, but nothing beyond that. I didn't remember coming to the dorm or even how. And Alex. I remembered Alex being concerned. I should have known it wasn't a dream when he never asked me why. He always asked me why.

As I laid there trying to figure out what to do, the pain in my chest intensified. One thing was for certain: I had at least two broken ribs and several bruised. I drifted my hand over my chest, fingering the odd bandage. Even after everything I'd put him through, he'd still taken care of me. Pain stabbed through a deeper part of my chest.

"I have to admit, I'm a little surprised you're still here."

The bed shifted beneath me. How long since I'd been in this bed? Days? Weeks? I turned to see Alex staring back at me, no forgiveness in his eyes, though maybe a little concern.

"You really need a healer."

"No healers," I replied by rote, my voice strained and odd to my ears.

Alex scoffed in obvious exasperation. "That's ridiculous. You obviously need one."

"They'll find out. No healers. It's a rule." Given what I'd been through already, I wasn't exactly inclined to find out what kind of retribution I'd face if I broke that rule.

"Is this the same they that apparently want to hurt me?" Alex lifted an eyebrow.

I did a double take. Had I talked in my sleep? I didn't remember having any dreams, but these days it was hard to tell the difference between reality and nightmare. "I don't know what you are talking about."

"Yes, you do. You said something about it last night when you were high as a fucking kite. Where did you get all of those painkillers, anyway?"

I shrugged. "Around." He let out a put-upon sigh. It was past time I'd left. I shifted to get up and the pain that ripped through my side convinced me I'd never broken a rib before now. This was something I would certainly remember.

"What are you doing? You need to rest."

"I shouldn't have come here."

"Why did you?"

There it was, the inevitable "Why". But I couldn't tell him the truth, that even disoriented and blind with pain, I'd run to the only person I trusted. This was why the ward I set up every night was so important. I *wanted* to be here, to be with him, and I couldn't trust myself to stay away.

"I hope whatever secret you feel is so damn important is worth it."

I struggled not to wince at his sharp tone and took a deep breath. That turned out to be a major mistake. My ribs couldn't support that level of air.

"Matt, please," he pleaded, worry eclipsing the edge of anger.

I pushed up from the bed, ignoring the pain lancing along my side. I didn't have the energy for any of this. It had been an epic mistake coming here. It was confusing everything I'd worked so hard to fabricate.

Alex slapped the mattress. "Damn it, Matt, you aren't the only one with abandonment issues."

I rounded on him. "And what would you know about that? You had a mom who loved you and supported you. I just had a long line of strangers that wanted nothing to do with me."

"I am not some stranger!" He surged to his feet. "You have *me*. I don't know how many times I have to tell you, I'm not going anywhere. If you would just talk to me, I know we could figure this out together. But I need you to share."

"I can't." Agony squeezed my heart. "If I let you in, they'll find you. I can't lose you, Alex. I wouldn't survive it."

"And what's this then? You call this surviving? You walk around like some sort of ghost. You used to smile and laugh. Now... now, all you do is lie and run away."

"It's not my survival I'm worried about," I whispered, my shoulders crumpling. Thankfully, it was too low for him to hear, otherwise, I'm sure he would've said something. He stepped closer, and I shied away. I didn't trust myself so close to him and coherent. Every part of my tired, battered body wanted the comfort he was offering, to ease into his touch and believe, if only for a moment, that everything would be alright.

"Tell me one thing." I looked up at him as he took my hands.

"What?" The word was barely more than a whisper. We were entirely too close. Already the pure scent of him was pushing back the aches and pains. I swallowed, my eyes stinging with unshed tears. I missed him so much.

He released my hands to trail his fingers lightly along my jaw, but ensuring that I was looking directly into his emerald eyes. "Will you ever come back?"

I want to, I thought, but I couldn't bring myself to say it out loud. The smart thing would have been to say something hurtful or at least a sharp rebuke, but those died on my tongue as well. I'd already hurt him so much.

"I can see you hurting, Matt." A traitorous tear slipped out. He either didn't see it or chose not to comment. Instead, he leaned forward and placed a lingering kiss on my lips. "I love you."

The ache in my heart tripled as it broke anew. Why was he so understanding? How, after everything I'd done, could he still say that? I kissed him back, unable to stop myself, wrapping my arms around him despite how much it hurt. "Alexi," I croaked in a strained whisper, the pain of it tearing at my heart. I couldn't deny him, didn't want to. I'd spend forever with him if he let me. But this had to be done first. I couldn't rest until I knew he was safe.

"Please stay." His lips were so soft against mine and I sank into the feeling I couldn't deny. I needed him, but needing him wouldn't do anyone any good if he was dead. I pulled away.

"I have to go."

"Where?"

"You know I won't tell you that."

He sighed and rested his forehead against mine. "Then at least make sure you eat. You need to keep your strength up if you intend to heal." I nodded. "Promise me."

"I promise," I said, choking back a sob. How many times was I going to have to say goodbye to him?

"Wait here, I'll get you some fresh clothes," he said and walked out of the room.

I was gone before he could return. Saying goodbye once today was enough. I'd already dallied too long. The others would look for me and I couldn't risk them coming here.

My journey to the place I was squatting was slow going and painful. I wasn't sure if I'd be able to make it in one trip, so I'd stolen a pair of Alex's pants, though I suspected that I'd regret doing so. Having anything of Alex's was a mistake. I changed as fast as I could manage and tried to clean myself up a bit as soon as I was in the hovel I was calling a room. While I couldn't remember much of last night, I had no doubt that some serious reprisals were in store. My report was due hours ago.

At least semi-presentable, I made my way over to the main house. I wasn't surprised at all to find the usual suspects as well as a couple of additional, albeit unfamiliar, faces waiting for me.

"Where did you go after the fight?" George asked. I had a sneaking suspicion he was the one responsible for me getting my ass handed to me.

I showed my teeth, lacking the energy to pretend to be polite. "I went to lick my wounds."

"You took quite the beating," Kyle commented.

"And look at him now. Still standing," Thomas added. Asshole almost sounded impressed. "I hope you didn't spend all of your time assuaging your ego. What do you have for me?"

I looked at him through slitted eyes. "It's a little hard to gather intel when you can't see straight or walk upright."

"I suppose."

"Aw come on, Matty. You still gave him a run for it," Travis chipped in unhelpfully.

"If they'd allowed me to fight, he would've received a lot more," I said, shifting my glare to George.

"Let it go. It's all for the cause." George passed Thomas a wad of cash. "That outta take care of our... dues. Just make sure we get what we're owed." The withering look Thomas gave him was wasted. George was too busy congratulating himself.

"*You.*" I took a step toward him, anger searing through my veins at this confirmation. "You're why Neese told me to throw the fight."

"Watch yourself," George snarled. "You're no match for me healed. I'd hate to see what would happen if you forced my hand while you were in this state."

I tried unsuccessfully to temper my rage. I didn't need to be at full strength to rip this son of a bitch apart. As for the rest of the room, that was debatable.

The image of Alex's concerned face flashed in my mind. If I retaliated, George would find some way to punish me. I couldn't take the risk that he'd use Alex against me. My shoulders slumped.

"That's what I thought." This was ridiculous. One of these days, I was going to teach George a lesson and enjoy every fucking second of it. "Get yourself cleaned up, little Matty. You look like shit and there's still work to be done."

I glanced over at the wall. Many of the pictures now sported X's thanks to me. But not the only one I cared about. There was still only the one red line across Alex's picture.

"What's up with you?" Kyle asked. "You look even more depressed than usual. Where'd you go yesterday, anyway? You never said."

I could have killed him right there. Curious eyes swiveled to focus on me. "I got into an argument," I said through gritted teeth.

"I bet it was this girl he doesn't want to share," came Travis' snide remark. For once, his inability to see beyond sex was playing in my favor.

"Like anyone would want to share anything with your disgusting ass."

"Shove it, Kyle. What did she say?" They looked at me expectantly.

Why did they have to be so damn nosy? "Doesn't like all the fighting. Especially when I showed up like this," I said as casually as I could, indicating my ribs.

George snickered. "You tell that bitch you can do as you damn well please."

Thomas caught the flash of anger that passed across my face. "I don't think Matthew appreciates you calling his partner a bitch. Also," he said, pulling out a vial, "you're useless to me if you can't move around. This will speed up the healing process."

I reached out to accept this unexpected gift. I'd heard of healing tonics, but didn't know where to get them. There were plenty of times something like this would've been handy. He pulled it back out of reach, and I quickly checked my snarl.

"I expect you to earn this. No more slacking." Thomas glanced at my asinine companions. "And, George, no more fight club either." I could have sighed with relief at hearing that. George, on the other hand, looked livid.

"And how am I supposed to explain his absence to Neese? The arrangement was that Matt fights."

"You could always grow a pair and step in yourself," Thomas said blankly.

My snicker popped out before I could even attempt to hold it back. Now that was a fight I would pay to see. George shot me a look, and I quickly tried to suppress it.

"I don't know what you're so damn pleased about. Neese will never let you go."

My face fell. He was right. Neese had already proven that any absences would be severely punished.

"I'll take care of Neese." Thomas returned his gaze to me. "You just make sure you stay useful."

I took the bottle of bluish liquid, unstoppered it, and downed it all in one go. Immediately, it felt like I had swallowed sparklers or maybe lightning bugs. The pain in my ribs instantly subsided. They still hurt quite a bit, but I was confident they were no longer broken, at least.

"Should be a lot easier now," I said, walking up to the remaining photos. I resisted the urge to look at Alex. "Who are we looking at next?"

"That's my boy." Thomas clapped me on the shoulder. It made my skin crawl, but I held firm.

A quick look at George showed him staring daggers at me. He was going to be a problem.

CHAPTER 13
REVELATION

Alexi

The book landed on the table, falling open to easily the most viewed page. I looked down at the picture of the knight leaning towards the demon and thought about Matt's picture safe in my room. His image felt truer than this one. Not to mention, now that we knew for a fact the two ended up together, the sword and full battle armor felt out of place.

I shook my head and scooted it forward to make room for the other books. At least two of them would need translating. Something must have triggered the lamp, because the light slowly came to life. I glanced up to see our book—my book—squarely within the illuminating pool. My eyes widened as I watched the image I'd dedicated to memory change right before my eyes. The demon became less shrouded in darkness and you could actually see her features now; she was smiling warmly and quite pretty. The weapons vanished entirely, and now the knight was holding his helmet instead of wearing it. I stopped breathing altogether as I took in his revealed features.

He was the spitting image of Matt, from the feathery hair and pouty mouth to the brilliant blues that practically shone on the page. But it didn't just look like Matt, it *was* Matt. I became faint as dozens of puzzle pieces clicked into place. Matthew was a derivative of Matthias. A family name passed from father to son. Matt didn't like his full name was because it *wasn't* his name. He was a Warde.

No wonder Matt was obsessed with all of this. Some part of him must have instinctively recognized that this was *his* history, not just some random family. It also explained his dueling nature: the light and the dark, forever at odds with one another.

Holy. Fucking. Hell. Matt was a Warde.

I quickly closed the book and shoved everything back into my bag. The last book was nearly in when I hesitated. I needed to find out what happened to that child. How many generations removed was Matt from this? I thought again about the picture. They could have been twins. The knight even had that same lost expression. The gray history practically flew back onto the desk as I yanked it back out, pages flipping past in a whirl until I found a time frame that applied to what I needed.

I stopped my frantic search when I saw a passage that said Matthias—our Matthias—had gone missing. What? No, that didn't make sense. Unless, of course, he ran off with Sopteală. But that didn't feel right either. Taking a deep breath to calm my racing thoughts and heart, I read line by line until I found something that made me pause. Matthias had been found nearly dead, protecting a newborn boy. They'd taken one look at the infant's eyes and known it to be Matthias' son. The family took the baby to raise as one of their own in the true Warde tradition and buried their fallen brother. No one knew who the mother was, only that the battle was nearing an end. The commander of the scouts, Sopteală, had been caught on the fringes of camp and her execution was to serve as the final blow to end the war.

A breath escaped me as if I'd been punched in the gut. We'd been looking for a child we assumed was missing and the entire time he'd been securely within the family's grasp. We'd searched for a demon baby. Yet, if he hadn't manifested, no one would have known that this seemingly mortal infant was of mixed lineage. And without a surviving parent, no one would be the wiser.

I skipped whole chunks of pages, seeking the resolution of this grizzly tale. Without the scout's organized efforts, surveillance fell apart. She'd apparently found the blueprints for how to make shadow lights and carried the secret to her grave. Generals and commanders on the demon front were captured and executed without mercy or distinction. As the leaders fell victim to the remaining unstoppable weapons, the rest of the gathered forces dissipated. Most notably, any remaining Shadow demons vanished without a trace. The Wardes immediately set to eliminating all evidence that any such battle or race had ever existed, determined that the world would never again know the fear and evil that resided in the night.

Matt was right. The histories were scrubbed. There was no way that humans could have possibly erased everything, though, not with so many supernaturals involved. Which meant Shadow demons had played an active part in disappearing themselves from history. They became myths, hiding in the night and never revealing their power. For the Warde family to stop hunting them, they had to make them believe there weren't any left.

I sat there, shocked at my revelation. Between this horrible family and my kind, we'd almost led ourselves to extinction. If it hadn't been for Vera forcing us into the limelight, then Shadow demons around the world would have continued to fade until we really were nothing more than a story in some long forgotten history.

The book fell with a sickening thud into my bag. I knew there was a reason I hated this thing—it was genocide told by the victors. I finished putting away my things, then glanced over at the stacks where Matt had said the librarian had taken him. Stealing my resolve, I made my way over. He'd said it was like the books didn't want to be found. As I got closer, my trepidation increase. I pushed against it until fear sprouted like an unruly weed.

Matt wasn't just acting out, he realized this was a mistake.

Another step.

He was waiting at the dorm to tell me he'd changed his mind and was leaving. This wasn't him. It never had been.

I gasped at the very real pain in my chest. How had he done it? I was still yards away from the shelves and I didn't feel like I could go on. This spell was more than any reasonable aversion. There wasn't a doubt in my mind that I'd die before I ever reached the shelf. The school would never have put such a drastic spell in a public place. That gave me pause. If not them, then who?

I took a few steps back so I could think more clearly. The only people I could think of who wouldn't want the world to know about these wars were the demons that had lost. But that didn't make sense either. If demonkind knew what the Shadow demons had faced and what they'd done, it could have been a rallying cry. That only left the humans. Of course, what better way to eradicate your foe than to delete them from history? Including any record of your own great victory. It was insane. How was it possible that the Warde line was still around? How would they even have known that they hadn't wiped out Shadow Demons once and for all? Once again, the answer was Vera. She was simultaneously our salvation and would likely cause our ultimate demise.

Suddenly, I remembered something I'd read long ago in the Shadow Chronicles. I raced through the shelves in search of a copy, earning me several reproachful glares and numerous demands to be quiet. When I found them, I struggled to remember which volume had what I was looking for. The most I could scrounge up, however, was that it was towards the end of the Rebellion.

I skimmed volume after volume in search of my elusive answer. Surely I hadn't imagined Vera being captured and tortured. There! I almost dropped the book in my excitement. The entry was small, as if intentionally understated. A pair of brothers had held her captive for weeks and tortured her. They'd used science and magic to create something they called a Shadow light which could burn a Shadow Demon's essence.

I closed the book and slipped it into my bag with the others. Only one brother had ever been caught, despite relentless searches using every available resource. I'd bet my life that those brothers were members of the Warde family, and thanks to Vera, they'd rediscovered how to make the most dangerous weapon known to Shadow Demons. My first instinct was to ask her how she'd escaped, but first I needed to tell Matt what I'd found. This changed... everything.

My journey out of the library took me back by the entrance to the restricted section. I shuddered. How had he done it? Then it dawned on me. Matt was part Warde, and Wardes had placed the spell. It was the only explanation that made sense. The spell would have recognized one of its own. But Matt wasn't pure Warde. I swallowed hard before turning away. He'd literally almost died for me.

I was almost to the dorm when I remembered he'd still be in class, assuming he'd gone. If I waited outside of his classroom, then he couldn't avoid me without drawing too much attention. At this hour, he should be at his Advanced Spells class. He actually liked that one, so I was optimistic he'd be there. That left me thirty minutes to get there and find an inconspicuous place to wait.

Luck was with me, and there was a sort of nook with a water fountain around the corner from the door. From there, I should be able to hear when people started leaving. Now I needed to figure out how to break this life-altering news to Matt. My phone ringing sliced through my thoughts and made me shadow right out. I pulled it together and answered.

"Hi mom."

"Everything alright dear? You sound a little excited."

"Yeah... everything is fine," I side-stepped.

"Alexi Roman, do not lie to me."

"Okay, everything is not fine," I corrected, almost rolling my eyes. She had a knack for knowing when I did, even when she couldn't see me.

"Is it Matt still?" *Still...*

I sighed. "Yes, I mean, no. It's hard to say."

"I take it y'all have yet to sort things out?"

"Sorting things out would require him actually talking to me, which he isn't doing at present. And don't tell me to make the first move. That's all I've ever done." She tried to offer some condolence, but I was on a roll. "I love him so much and I still don't know if he feels the same. What if this is all my fault? What if I pushed him into something he never wanted?"

"I don't believe that, Lexi. I've seen the two of you together. Matt loves you even if he can't say it."

"But why? Why can't he tell me he loves me?" I was so absorbed in our conversation, I didn't realize I had an audience.

"Aww, are we having boyfriend problems?"

I looked up to see none other than George from class. Behind him were two of his lecherous followers. My mouth went dry. I knew for a fact that almost all of them had barely passed Intro to Shadow Magic, so there was no way they could have gotten into Advanced Spells. Which meant they were here for some other reason. Maybe they were also here for Matt. He'd been spending a lot of time with them lately.

"Mom, I'm going to have to call you back." She was still trying to ask what was wrong when I hung up. My gaze darted between the three of them. Nothing about this situation felt right... or safe.

"And he's calling his mommy for advice," one of them snickered. I wasn't sure if it was Travis or Kyle. I didn't bother trying trying to distinguish between the two.

I shifted to grab my pack and stand, keeping George in my line of sight. He altered his stance, cutting off my exit.

"Told you there was a fag in our class," George sneered.

"Yeah, but is he the one Thomas is looking for?" That was definitely Kyle. Spineless weasel.

"Does it matter? One queer is much like another," Travis chimed.

"Just think how pissed Matty is going to be when he finds out we found him first," Kyle said, high-fiving Travis behind George. Matty? Matt? *My* Matt knew about this?

"First things first. We take him to Thomas." Something that resembled a thin baton slid from George's sleeve. He flicked a switch on the handle and it sprung to life with an eerie purple light that seemed to buzz with electricity. I didn't need him to name it to know what I was looking at—he was holding a Shadow light.

I shadowed to my feet, forgetting my bag and tried to knock it out of his hand, suddenly grateful Matt had never taken it easy on me in training.

The demented weapon skittered on the floor, still fully functioning. George floundered at the loss, his venomous gaze shooting to me before he lunged for the weapon. Pain blossomed on my back as if someone was searing my soul. I screamed as waves of agony forced me to my toes, then collapsed into darkness.

When I came to, they'd tied me to a chair. A look around revealed nothing more than a dark room. My lower back felt like some had beaten me with a super-heated metal pipe. I didn't see George or his crew, nor any other signs of life. No telling how long that would last. It was now or never.

I shadowed to escape the bonds and excruciating pain radiated from my wrists and ankles. My scream could have woken the dead. The agony refused to abate until I released my hold on the Shadow world. I sat there gasping for air. The pain may have relented, but the memory was still there. Fear blossomed in my chest as the gravity of my situation fully sank in.

"Good, he's finally awake. Go get Thomas." The voice could have belonged to George, but I was too out of it to investigate.

In hardly anytime at all, someone was forcing my head back. I groaned and tried to open my eyes. A light came on and I instinctively flinched.

"See, boys, it doesn't take much to teach them fear. A little more of that, and I doubt he'd ever shadow again or even crawl out of whatever abyss spawned him." That voice sounded familiar. But why? Where had I heard it before? It wasn't one of my classmates.

I tried to focus, but I didn't recognize the man who swam into focus. The one behind him, however, I did. It was the weaselly TA from the seminar that Matt didn't like. I looked back at the man in the lead. His beard was black instead of white, though it retained the severe cut, and he no longer looked to be of such indiscriminate age, now appearing decidedly mid forties. "Professor Warden?" The inquiry was barely audible.

"I told you he was a smart one, Douglas," Professor Warden said to the TA.

"But is he the one we are looking for?"

"We will find out soon enough. Carmen and Matthias were delusional to think they could hide their abomination from us. They paid for that crime with their lives. If he isn't the one we seek, I bet he knows." He picked up my bag, dumping out its contents, and I vaguely wondered how it had gotten here. Professor Warden snorted as he examined the collection of books. "This explains some of your rather impertinent questions." He picked up Volume Six. "How did you get your hands on this, I wonder? No demon should be able to go anywhere near these. Look into it, Douglas. We can't have others sticking their nose where it doesn't belong. And what do we have here?" he asked, bending down to pick up our book. I struggled uselessly against my bonds, mindful not to shadow even the tiniest bit. The book fell open to the same page it always did. "Well, I'll be. Look at this, Douglas."

"What is it, sir?" Douglas asked in a nasal voice, stepping closer.

"This is the journal of Matthias Warde himself. You know, he almost lost the war for us? I guess now we know why." He held out the picture for his comrade to see. Mercifully, without the lamp to illuminate the spell, they couldn't see the true identity of the knight. George, at least, would instantly recognize Matt.

"And only they had the power to harness light itself and burn back the darkness," I quoted to distract them from the book lest they put it together, anyway.

"Very good," Professor Warden rumbled.

"You're a Warde." It wasn't a question, it was a fact. Matt's instincts had been right about not wanting to share what we'd found. I turned to face my classmates in disbelief. "How can you be helping him? His entire family tried to wipe out all Shadow demons!"

"It's just a shame we weren't as successful as we were led to believe. As for them." The professor indicated the disgusting excuses for Shadow Demons. "They would do just about anything to ensure their place at the top of the pyramid." Naturally, the goons were busy congratulating themselves in the background.

"How stupid do you have to be? They won't let any of you live." My argument fell on deaf ears.

"Douglas, you and your... creatures find out what he knows. If he *is* the one we've been looking for, then our search is over and we can finally wipe this taint from the Warde bloodline. If not, don't kill him just yet. There's someone I want to see him before he dies." The malicious gleam in Professor Warden's eyes sent a fresh wave of fear crawling over me.

Chapter 14
Unwanted Gift

Matt

Over the following week, I became the epitome of a shadow following and reporting after my remaining uncleared classmates. With the almost perfect exception of Alex, I supplied information that would make their mother's blush. My guilt grew with each check in with Thomas, as did my suspicion that there was more going on than I was being led to believe.

As upsetting as that was, though, it wasn't what had me worried. Alex hadn't tripped a single tripwire in days. At first, it was easy to assume he was studying or taking a final or shadowing through the wall, but as more time went by, those excuses fizzled away. There was only so much I could take not knowing. I began stopping by the dorm regularly, not even caring whether I bumped into him. Not that it made a difference. Even the hope that he'd simply gone home felt like an empty dream. I'd have called his mom to find out, but I didn't have her number or even a phone. Finally, I got desperate enough to go into his room.

Bracing myself, I opened the door. The smell of lavender was like a blanket on my aching heart, but it was getting faint. That wasn't good. I scoured the room for any sign of where he could have gone. Distantly, I imagined that he'd likely done much the same when I hadn't come back. I rubbed at the ache in my chest at the thought of how hurt he must have been to see his loving gift so callously disregarded. I dropped my hand. There wasn't time for guilt; I needed to figure out where he was.

When nothing immediately sprang to attention, I tore the place apart. However, despite my frantic search, no clues were forthcoming. His things were still here, even something that looked a bit like a keepsake box. He wouldn't have left that if he'd truly gone, which meant he intended to return. I'd even stumbled across my sketchbook. Because, of course, he'd found that. I paused my search to flip through the nearly full book, wishing for more pictures with his eyes open. I loved his eyes.

Stealing myself, I took out the keepsake box and inspected that as well. It wasn't likely, but there might be a hint as to his whereabouts hidden within. Inside, I found several things that tugged at memories of a more carefree time when my only concern was passing class. That certainly wasn't happening now. Smaller trinkets, like a beer bottle cap and a spoon, got set down on the bed so I could examine the drawing I'd given him what felt like a lifetime ago. The darkness reached out like a lover's touch across the page. My heart clenched as I thought about how nervous I'd been to give this to him and how excited he had been to receive it.

I sighed and set it aside, revealing the two strips of photos from our visit to the fair. Looking at our happy faces, I couldn't help but wonder when the last time I smiled was. But it was the second strip that really caught my attention. I'd had no idea he'd started a second series when he kissed me in the booth. His wonderfully ridiculous grin looked back at me, full of joy. I just barely didn't crush the delicate material as I fought back a tide of worry. Where was he?

After days with no clear sign or trail, I simply came back to the dorm full time. I had no desire to sleep in my bed and couldn't bring myself to go into his room again, so I stayed camped in between. All the keepsakes I'd found got moved to the living room, where they remained spread out across the coffee table. They felt like my only remaining connection to him. A lifeline of sorts. I was beginning to fear that I'd grow roots into the couch as I waited impatiently for him to return. After a while, I had to turn the clock off because I kept uselessly checking the time like it somehow bore any relevance to when he'd return. Assuming he ever would.

Even though I was back in the dorm and loathe to leave it, I didn't dare risk avoiding my checks-ins with Thomas. So I continued to report, although the information I was bringing arguably became less useful in clearing anyone. The only good news was that I'd heard nothing from Thomas about people being brought in. I could feel it, though. Any day now, they'd decide questioning suspects face to face would be easier than this hide and sneak game we'd been playing the last few months. I didn't relish that day.

I opened the new sketchpad to add yet another rendition of the photos I had at my disposal. All I could do was hope that Alex really was at his mom's and that all of this worrying was for nothing. As the pencil moved across the page, my mind wandered to a better place. It always did when I sketched Alex. Focusing on his pronounced cheekbones and the curve of his mouth calmed me; although getting his eyes right was a source of endless frustration. Time slipped by with nothing remarkable to measure it and the page gradually filled with more and more details.

I was adding contours to his face when there was a loud knock on the door that shook the dorm and fractured the peace I'd struggled to cultivate. I glanced at the locked door in alarm. No one came here and Alex could have gotten in with or without his key. Anxiety and adrenaline coursed side by side through my veins. Out of habit, I shadowed to hide everything on the table before getting up.

I cautiously approached the door, sharpened pencil in hand like some sort of last ditch weapon. My free hand opened and closed nervously before I finally turned the handle. I tried to brace myself for whoever or whatever could be on the other side. But when the door opened on ever-silent hinges, there was no one there. I blinked and glanced down the hall. Not a trace of anyone. The hall appeared completely deserted. Then I looked down.

"Alex!" My anguished scream ripped through me to echo down the deserted walkways.

The entire world stopped as I stared down at his still form. I could barely even make out his face amidst the matted blood. It bore no resemblance at all to the image of him not ten feet away. How had this happened? This wasn't happening. It couldn't be. I'd fallen asleep on the couch while sketching. This was just another nightmare. A really, *really* bad nightmare.

I couldn't... I couldn't breathe.

Darkness crept in on the edge of my vision. I let it. Dream or not, I couldn't take this. What was the world, my life, without Alex? The darkness inched closer. I'd finally find out what happened to Shadow demons when they got swallowed whole. I wasn't afraid. The night could take me. There was nothing without Alex.

A tiny sound like air through a small tunnel drifted up. All the darkness fell away when I realized it was coming from Alex. He was moving.

"Matt?" My name was a barely audible rasp. I crashed to the ground, too afraid to touch him. A glance down the hall showed that my outcry had drawn attention, though, and there was no telling who else may have been watching the tragic scene. I didn't care. He was still alive.

"Alex, it's okay. I'm right here. Everything is going to be fine."

He tried to move and was racked with coughs. It sounded like there were bubbles of blood coming up, but there was no way to tell amidst the already crusted fluids. That wasn't good. I needed to get him inside and cleaned up so I could see the worst of the damage.

As carefully as I could, I slipped my arms beneath him and carried him inside. I didn't even think as I carried him to his room and laid him on the bed. His breathing resembled someone scratching up and down a washboard. At least he was still breathing. I shoved down the desire to heave uncontrollably and retrieved a cloth that I dampened with warm water. As gently as I could, I cleaned his face.

One eye was almost perfectly sealed shut with bruising, making his beautiful skin a horrible mottled purple. Scratches and breaks canvased every stretch of visible skin. He winced when I touched his cheek. It looked broken. My stomach tried to heave again as I took in the sight of the unbelievable damage covering him from head to toe. No part of him had been spared. Even in my worst fight, I'd never come out looking like this.

"Matt, I..." he trailed off, unable to gather enough air and disintegrated into coughs that made his wounds bleed again.

"Please, don't talk," I sobbed. My chest spasmed, and I dropped my head to rest beside him as agony wracked my body. Against all odds, his hand fell to the side and touched mine, where I was white knuckling the now blood-stained cloth. I broke. "Alex, I'm so sorry. I should have tried harder. I should have stopped this. I can't... I can't..." My blubbering prevented me from continuing. "I don't know what to do."

"Healer."

I looked at his face, barely even believing it. Looking back at me was a sliver of green. Of course, a healer. I sprung up, ready to track one down, then stalled.

"How?"

"Phone." He tried to move his hand, but only managed a vague indication of direction. His phone was in his back pocket. There was no way I could get to it without causing him immense pain.

"This is going to hurt," I cautioned. "A lot."

"Do."

I took a deep breath and wiped my face. The quicker I was, the less I'd have to move him. He cried out when I shifted him and my heart shattered, but I didn't roll him back until I had the device. Mercifully, it was unscathed. I shadowed to the kitchen, tripping practically every sensor in the dorm. I dispelled all of them in one sweep and ripped open the drawer with all the emergency school numbers. As I dialed the Healer Station on campus, I prayed they would answer.

"Healer Services. What is your emergency?" The voice was perfectly professional, bordering on mechanical.

"He's hurt. We need someone now."

"Sir, I'm going to need you to take a deep breath. How extensive are the injuries? Where are you? Do you know what happened?"

"I don't have time for this," I snapped. "We're in Starling Hall. Room 2708. He needs help now."

"I understand your frustration, but this is information we are going to need."

I tried to take a breath and slow down. "The injuries are bad, really bad. But I can't see the extent."

"Without better information, we can't put your case as a priority. We are completely booked. All our healers are currently out at the moment on other calls. It may be quite some time before we can get anyone there."

"He doesn't have time!"

"Sir, I'm going to need you to stop shouting. That will not help the situation. Give me your information and I will add you to the list. In the meant time, do what you can to make your friend comfortable."

I gave her the address again and hung up. Help would come—eventually. I ran back to the room, taking the last of the pain pills with me, thankful I hadn't finished the bottle. "I'm going to help you sit up. Then I need you to take these."

He groaned.

"I know, but they'll help with the pain. Someone's coming to help." I couldn't bear to tell him how long he might have to endure this pain before that help arrived.

Gently, I shifted him so he wouldn't drown trying to drink the water. He bit back a cry and I saw the effort it took on his face to keep it to himself. Finally, I had him more or less propped up. The faint sound of bubbles punctuated his wheezing breaths, and there was blood on his lips again. The unfeeling machine was right. I needed to know more about the injuries, and cleaning him up would go a long way towards that. In a move I would come to regret, I peeled back the sticky mess that was his shirt. Beneath the oozing wounds were burn marks, but they didn't look like any burns I'd ever seen. It looked like some kind of acid or allergic reaction had literally disintegrated the skin, leaving it puckered.

"What... what are these?"

"Shad—shadow," his words gave out as did his breath. It looked like he was going to be sick. I shouldn't have moved him so much, I fretted. Then what he was trying to say sunk in and I knew.

"Shadow lights." It felt like the world around me imploded. He'd been beaten and tortured within an inch of his life with nothing less than a mythical super weapon. Unadulterated rage swept through me, burning away any doubt or hesitation in its path. "I'm going to kill them," I snarled. They'd pay dearly for what they'd done. When I finished, there'd be nothing left of their miserable corpses.

"Don't," he said, the word barely a whisper.

"I'll be right back." The lie came easily. An iron grip held me back when I attempted to stand up. A look down revealed Alex's hand encircling my wrist. I caught his eye and held firm. I was practically vibrating with anger. They had done this to him.

"They'll kill you." Already I could tell that his strength was waning. An inkling of doubt tried to worm its way in. Then he coughed and blood seeped from the vicious cut on his lip.

"You need to rest. A healer is on the way." His grasp slipped, and I shadowed out.

CHAPTER 15
SHADOW LIGHTS

Alexi

My world became one long series of painful breaths. I gave up trying to see, but that could have been due more to the fact that my eye wouldn't open. My only reprieve was when I passed out, though that never lasted long. Shadow lights were truly an impressive weapon and exceptionally effective. I could see why generations of Shadow Demons had chosen to hide rather than risk facing them again. Douglas was ruthless in his pursuit of answers. But try as he might, I wouldn't let them have Matt.

My throat became raw from the screaming until it became apparent that I lacked the ability to talk at all. That's when they started tipping drops of what had to be healing tonics down my throat. Never enough to repair any actual damage, only enough so they could start again. George and his minions lost the stomach for outright torture early; however, Douglas seemed to relish in his work. He'd used the searing agony of a Shadow light against my abused flesh many times, without even asking a question. I was coming to peace with the knowledge that I'd likely die here when he inexplicably stopped. Someone cut my bindings, and I slumped forward without any support.

"You know where to leave him?"

"Yeah, we've got the just the spot. He hasn't left the dorm since his last report." That sounded like George, but who was he talking about? The question evaporated in the blinding pain that consumed me when I was picked up and the world fell once again into darkness.

It wasn't until I heard a scream that any level of awareness returned. Something about the sound struck a chord. I struggled to focus, but all I could see were fuzzy feet. Then a face came into view. Matt? Absolute devastation twisted his angelic face and though his lips were moving, the only sound I heard was my labored breathing. The world swam back out of focus again.

When I next opened my eye, I was in my room. The soft bed beneath me was a stark contrast to the pain. Something touched my face, bringing the distant aches back to the surface full force. Finally, it stopped, and I returned my focus to just trying to breathe normally. One plus to the fresh wave of agony was that it had caused one of my eyes to crack open. I was rewarded with an image of Matt. Seeing him made my heart hurt every bit as much as my body. His eyes were bloodshot, his nose was red, and I could just make out tear tracks. He was falling apart. But I needed him to pull it together. The Order of Light was real, was still active. And it was only a matter of time before they came for him. I needed to warn him, but the words didn't want to work.

"Healer," I finally croaked. The suggestion seemed to surprise him. Of course, Matt never went to healers. Now that he knew what needed to be done, there was just one problem: I was lying on his only way to reach them. No amount of care could diminish the flood of agony when he moved me. Pain defined every aspect of my being and, like so many times before, death felt a hairsbreadth away. Except this time, there weren't any healing tonics. Not even the dribbles they'd afforded me. My only consolation was that at least I was with Matt.

Abruptly, I was moving again. I gritted against the excruciating pain. As suddenly as it started, I was still once more. Then he held a glass to my lips. I reflexively refused to drink.

"I know, but they'll help with the pain. Someone's coming to help."

Tears I didn't think I had left welled in my eyes, making the already hazy image of Matt even harder to distinguish. I parted my lips as much as I could, given the swelling in my face. He pushed small somethings—pills maybe—into my mouth and I fought the urge to spit them back out. By the time my throat stopped throbbing from swallowing, I was spent.

A squelching sound had bile clawing up my throat. Unable to stop myself, I glanced down to find Matt had pulled back my blood-soaked shirt. Compared to the rest of the pain I'd endured, breaking the seal on my open wounds barely even registered. I shifted my gaze to Matt's face to find him looking as green as I felt.

"What... what are these?" The horror in his voice broke my heart, but also lent me a renewed sense of urgency.

I needed to warn him they had Shadow lights. That the Order was real. That they were coming for him. "Shad-dow," I wheezed. I watched his horrified disbelief turn to understanding, then into a fury that frightened me.

No. Matt, no. You can't. They'll kill you. You're the one they want. If you go, they'll know it's you.

He looked at me as if he hadn't gotten any of that. It was getting harder and harder to focus, to feel. As if the world and I were suddenly made entirely of cotton. It could have been the painkillers he'd forced upon me, but I suspected something far more sinister.

Before I could try again to convey my worry, Matt disappeared in a blink of shadow. I shouted in dismay at the place he'd been standing and surged forwards despite the debilitating pain. There was no way I could bring him back myself, but there was someone who could. Unfortunately, my lurch had caused the phone to tumble to the floor. I fumbled for it as best I could, ignoring how my arm didn't to want to work properly or that hot blood was seeping into the comforter. At last, my fingers closed over the tiny piece of salvation. Now she just had to answer.

The ringing sounded overly loud and harsh, but it had to be the most beautiful sound at that moment. "Hello?" a man's voice answered and all of my hope crumpled to dust. Had I really just used the last of my strength to dial the wrong number?

I struggled to get my words together and hoped against hope that I hadn't. "Vera there?"

"May I ask who is calling?" he asked absently. I didn't know how long I'd be able to talk, so I needed to make this count. Already, darkness crept along the fringes of my limited vision, reaching up to drag me back down. I longed to give in, but fought it back the best I could.

"Matt in trouble. Shadow lights. Old fraternity row. Needs help... can't... please..." I dug deep to stay conscious for a few more precious moments. "Please... don't let him die." The darkness won, and I fell into oblivion.

When I came to again, it was to the distant sound of arguing. As I gradually regained awareness, I realized they weren't far away, just lowered.

"I already told you. Gabriel didn't say anything else." The woman's exasperation was palpable and her voice was eerily familiar.

"Get a healer is pretty cryptic, even for him," an unfamiliar man responded sardonically.

I struggled to make sense of the hushed conversation. Gabriel... That rang a bell. But what did Vera's husband have to do with anything? Then it hit me— *The phone.* I shot forwards and immediately cried out as I was reminded that virtually every part of me was beaten, broken, or burned.

"Oh my god."

I cracked an eye at the declaration of disbelief. Unliked the muffled conversation earlier, the voice was crystal clear... and close. The man standing in the doorway seemed vaguely familiar, like someone I had seen a picture of. Maybe in a book? Try as I might though, I couldn't push past the throbbing in my head to place the tanned open face, hazel eyes, or sandy brown hair. However, I absolutely recognized the fiery-haired woman attempting to push past him.

"You can't come in here. Doctor/patient confidentiality," he declared, forcibly shoving Vera back.

"Dorian Valens, I know you are *not* pulling that bullshit with me. He is *my* student and I have every right to be in there." Dorian? *The* Dorian? I had no idea when Matt said a healer was coming how well he would deliver.

"Unless you're a spouse or a parent, you wait out here." He scowled, contorting his otherwise stunning features, and pointed back into the living room. "I mean it, Vera. Sit." He closed the door, then walked to the side of the bed. "Jesus Christ." A gentle touch on my forehead accompanied the whispered exclamation. Then a warmth spread through me as if I was sinking head first into a bath. "You'll need more for sure, but this is going to take a while. But first, I need you able to talk to me. Do you think you can do that?" He peered at me with intense hazel eyes and waited.

"Yes." My eyes widened with shock at how easily the word had come, and without blood bubbling up either. The rest of me still hurt like hell, but my face and throat were at least tolerable. This revelation in hand, words rushed out of me. "You have to help him. They'll kill him as soon as they know. He's walking right into a trap. Why isn't Vera with Matt? Is he here? Have you seen him?"

"Easy, easy." Dorian made soft shushing sounds and placed a hand on my shoulder that made me wince despite how feather-light the touch was. "That was only a minor healing and you overdoing it is just going to make this take even longer than it already will," he said, then did a double-take. "Wait, you're not Matt?"

I nearly shook my head, then thought better of it. "No. I'm Alex, I mean Alexi."

"If you're Alexi, then where is Matt?"

A keening sound I didn't even recognize came from my throat. "I told you on the phone. Matt went to the old fraternity row. You don't understand, they have—"

"Shadow lights," he whispered, cutting me off. He glanced quickly at the door. "And keep your voice down. Vera can*not* know. Understand?" I nodded numbly. "And you didn't talk to me," he said as he carefully removed the rags that used to be my clothes. "You talked to Gabriel. He's with Matt."

"But..."

"Don't worry. He'll keep him safe."

"What if he can't find him?" I asked, terrified that he'd never get there in time.

Dorian shook his head, as if musing to himself. "If anyone can find your missing friend, he can. And he's dealt with," he paused and glanced at the door again, "what they have before. He'll keep him safe."

I relaxed slightly; it wasn't like there was anything I could do about it now. "So, um, why are you here?"

He looked at me like that had to the most ridiculous question he'd ever been asked. "Gabriel told Vee to bring a healer to the dorm. All he told her was that Matt was in trouble. She assumed he was the one who needed a healer."

"But why you? She could have brought any healer."

"She always calls me first," he sighed before stepping into the bathroom to grab some towels and hot water. "This won't be pleasant. The last time I had to do this, it took days. To be fair, I think you might actually be in better shape. Also, I doubt you're pregnant."

I frowned at him, not really following. "You have a strange bedside manner."

"What is it with Shadow Demons and constantly criticizing my methods? I'll have you know that no one else ever complains."

"That's probably because you're attractive." He looked up sharply, and I gave a sort of shrug. "Plus, you're healing them."

He shook his head. "Back to the task at hand. We're going to focus on the more severe burns and open wounds first, then move on to breaks and bruises. I say 'we', because this is going to take from you as well. While normally I could use just my energy, your injuries a far too extensive for that and I imagine when the others return they'll need help as well. Shadow Demons always need help, bunch of troublemakers makers," he mumbled under his breath. "Anyway, that means the rest of the energy has to come from somewhere. I'm not about to let Vera in here, which leaves you." He paused and softened his voice as he met my gaze once more. "I understand you're tired and in a lot of pain, but I'm going to need you to be strong. The good news is, as bad as this is going to hurt, you're not dying anymore." I tried to ignore the casual implication that I would have died if he'd gotten here any later.

"You're still in love with her," I said as a way of distracting myself from the awful feeling of his fingers probing the wounds on my chest.

His jaw tightened, and he didn't respond.

I fought the urge to sick up as a blistering cold radiated out of a burn. Then it stopped, taking some of the pain with it. I gasped for breath. That was easier now, too. I no longer felt like I was trying to breathe underwater. "Is he going to be okay?" I panted.

He looked at me, his hazel encouraging. "If he's half a strong as Vera says he is, I'm sure he will be. But *you* should really be more concerned about yourself right now. I don't have time to clean every wound to find the worst. You'll need to guide me."

"Don't have time? I thought you said I wasn't dying anymore."

"Not actively dying doesn't mean you still couldn't. I suspect the drugs in your system, combined with the initial minor healing, are helping you to ignore the acute agony your body is in. Anyone of these wounds could turn fatal and if I don't get to the right ones in time then..."

I scanned his face and fought to get my sudden shaking under control. "They shoved a rod of Shadow light between my ribs."

"Excellent." He shifted around to address the wound. The sensation of ice being stabbed through my chest reached a blinding height and stopped. "What else?"

"There's a cut on my leg. It was really deep." It took him a few minutes to find it because he had to cut away the fabric first. A warmth much like the bath feeling from earlier emanated from the gentle touch. "Why... why is that different?" I asked, closing my eyes and forcing myself to take deep breaths.

"Hey, stay with me. You can sleep when we're done. It feels different because something mundane versus magical caused the damage. I've been told that the magical wounds are the worst." He saw my confused look as I struggled to stay awake. "I heal a bit differently." That made sense.

I continued walking him through as many of the major injuries as I could remember, my body becoming increasingly numb. The tips of my fingers tingled and needles raced up my arms. If I'd had the energy to move them and restore circulation, I would have, but exhaustion weighed me down. Then Dorian touched my broken cheek. I screamed and passed out. It wasn't until a fresh round of pain from him shaking me that I came back to. I blinked at him, but everything was fuzzy and indistinct. I was fairly sure he was scolding me. He really had a terrible bedside manner.

"S-sorry," I mumbled.

He let out a sigh that held a worry that wasn't present in his words. I got the distinct feeling that he was lying before and I was definitely still dying. There were simply too many wounds to get them all and without me being able to guide him, there was no telling if he'd gotten all the major ones. Not to mention that for every inch of skin he cleaned, fresh blood covered it. He glanced back at the door nervously. I could practically see his indecision to have Vera help. His mouth set in a grim line of determination and he turned back to me.

"I'm just going to assume that the worst has been addressed. Okay, Alexi, this last bit won't be easy. I'll do what I can to prevent too much energy coming from you—you simply don't have it to spare." He placed one hand on my forehead and the other on my now exposed knee. "I'm totally going to regret this," he muttered to himself before saying louder, "Brace yourself."

A torrent of ice and fire swept through me, relieving the last of the aches and pains. The tide ebbed. Then there was darkness.

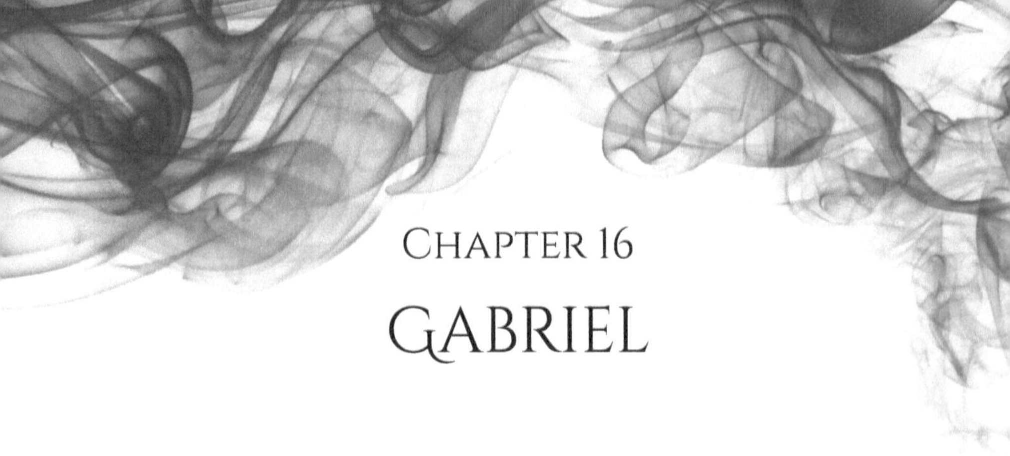

Chapter 16
Gabriel

Matt

The moment I arrived at the house I'd been squatting in, my scream ripped into the dilapidated room. The expulsion of sound felt like someone tearing me apart from the inside out. After everything I'd done, they'd still gotten Alex. Had beaten and tortured him. And shadow lights. They were real, not some really messed up fiction. All myths have roots in reality; Alex had told me that. But the truth was so much worse than the story. Just remembering what his skin had looked like made my stomach turn.

Alex—*my* Alex—they'd done that to him and I was going to kill them for it. But I had to be smart. I couldn't just barrel in, not the least of which, because I didn't know if they were actually there at the moment. I should've known challenging George would come back to bite me in the ass. Except it hadn't been me, it had been Alex, which was so much worse.

I looked around the room, trying to focus. Ideally, I'd have snuck into the house and waited, then taken each of them out as they arrived so I could draw out their agony. However, there was one huge problem: the house was shut up tight. I'd never located any entrance besides the front door. Without stealth as a viable option, that meant they'd definitely see me coming.

I glanced around the room for something clean. It wouldn't do any good to show up covered in Alex's blood. I got as far as removing my top before my frenzied movements stalled. I stared down unblinkingly at the stained shirt in my hands, a sense of emptiness rising. How had I let this happen? He'd suffered so much and it was all my fault. I hadn't protected him. I'd promised his mom I'd keep him safe and then... then.... The shirt crumpled in my hands as I fought the urge to dissolve into a sobbing mess. I couldn't live without him.

The presence of another shadow demon tickled my senses, effectively snapping me out of my downward spiral and putting me on high alert. Out of reflex,

I pulled on all the nearby shadows, prepared to rip apart whatever unfortunate soul had stumbled across my hiding place. Whoever thought that trying to sneak up on me was a good idea was going to be sorely disappointed. I couldn't help but hope it was George, though it certainly didn't feel like him. Getting a jumpstart on my retribution would be great. I tightened my grip on the darkness and settled into my customary fighter's stance.

"Easy there. I am not here to harm you. Quite the opposite."

I oriented on the deep velvety voice, but didn't see anyone. The sensation I got from the presence wasn't like any I'd ever felt before. Closest comparison I could think of was Vera, but it definitely wasn't her. Who or whatever this was, I didn't think my odds were good. I relaxed my hold on the neighboring shadows, but I didn't completely drop my guard. Just because I didn't feel confident that I'd win, didn't mean I wouldn't fight to my last breath. I owed Alex that much, at the very least.

"Who are you?" I demanded. A long, lean figure stepped from the darkness, slowly solidifying from shadow to physical. I did a double take. His dark hair and complexion reminded me of Alex, though he was decidedly older. I took an involuntary step backward as I registered the waves of raw power emanating off of him. He noted my reaction and quirked an eyebrow the same way Alex did when he thought I was doing something strange.

"Interesting that you don't know. After all, you called me." He meandered around the room, taking in its shabby state with a disinterested expression. "At least you know you are outmatched, though I suspect that wouldn't stop you from fighting if you thought I would prevent you from reuniting with your lover."

I narrowed my eyes. The only people I'd called had been the campus healers, and this guy was no healer. "Alex," I said, realization sinking in, then the rest of his casual statement sank in. He nodded in agreement. "We're not lovers," I added belatedly, though the defense sounded hollow even to my ears.

"Aren't you?" His slow, purposeful movements were making me nervous. They reminded me of a snake waiting to strike. The fluid motion was reminiscent of the way Alex moved, except significantly more sinister.

"He's my best friend."

"Does he know that? Because he is absolutely in love with you." The mysterious demon's gaze flicked to me. "He's the one who told me where to find you, by the way. Even made me promise not to let you die." He ran a finger along some dilapidated shelving, then flicked away the dust. "Says something that he never asked for help for himself, despite his obvious condition. That being said, you seem exceptionally determined to seek vengeance for someone you only deem a friend—best or otherwise. What *is* your plan exactly?" he finished, catching me with startlingly gray eyes.

I resisted the urge to shrink from his penetrative stare, squaring my shoulders. "What's it to you? Who the hell even are you?" For all I knew, he was one of Thomas' creatures.

He released a long, exasperated sigh. "I swear, they don't even pretend to teach proper history anymore. Of all the Shadow Demons in the world, I end up dealing with the two most insufferably stubborn, blindly ignorant, anger-ruled..." He stopped himself and took a deep breath. "I am Gabriel Xiander."

I stared blankly at him. The name sounded vaguely familiar, but nothing more.

"And that means nothing to you." He sighed again. "I am Vera's husband. Alex called her a short while ago. Thankfully, *I* answered. He didn't sound in good shape. I can't imagine he had very long left, and that was before he used so much energy to make that call. I suspect it is far less now."

I blanched. "Wha- What do you mean?"

"Honestly, he sounded like he was moments from death. You didn't know?" That eyebrow again.

The room tipped and swayed alarmingly. I was going to be sick. Alex wasn't fine. I'd been deluding myself. He was *dying, and* I'd left him all alone. I hadn't even told him...

"Does he know you love him?" Gabriel asked, as if reading my mind.

I looked up at him amidst the tilting room.

"What?" he inquired passively.

"I'm not..." I began.

He scoffed and rolled his eyes. "Why today's generation is so preoccupied with sexual orientation, I'll never understand. When you live long enough, it is a trivial matter. Everyone tries everything. Judging by your expression, I'm going to assume that you haven't told him. That's a shame. I'm sure he would have liked to know. I would have." He sounded so calm, so matter of fact, about something that I hadn't even been able to admit to myself.

I clutched my chest, struggling to breathe. "He's going to die, and I never told him, not once. I just... I just..." I gasped for air, darkness creeping in on the edges of my vision. Alex was going to die all alone, not knowing that I loved him with everything that I was. That I'd do anything to see him smile. That he was my whole world. That he was the reason I knew what happiness felt like. I had to get back. I couldn't let him die without knowing.

Except… it was too late. In my blind rage, I'd left him in immense pain with the vague promise of a healer that would never arrive in time. He was probably already dead. Alex was gone, and I'd never hear his laugh or teasing comments again. He'd never hold my hand under the table while we studied. Wouldn't kiss me so deep I felt it in my soul. All of it… gone. Without him, I was nothing. There was only the void opening up beneath me. An immense chasm ready to swallow me whole. Unshed tears stung my eyes as the gaping emptiness within me yawned wider. It wasn't worth fighting. What had fighting ever gotten me?

"Shit." The hissed explicative barely registered. Then hands were gripping my arms tight as if they could somehow save me from falling into the abyss. But what was the point? There was no escaping the darkness.

"I have to go. I can't…"

The firm grip forced me back a pace. "You need to take a deep breath and focus. He won't die."

I glanced back at Gabriel, barely registering his sincere, albeit concerned, expression. He really reminded me of Alex. The world steadied ever so slightly.

"I know what I said, but I told Vera to get a healer there as soon as possible. She won't dawdle, and she'll bring the best one she knows. For the record," he added, releasing me as the darkness finally retreated to where it belonged, "that was a major sacrifice on my part. Not that you care. Your… friend will be fine. Now, back to the task at hand. I can't allow a fresh cache of shadow lights to exist, not when I know where they are for a change. I've spent too long chasing these people to give up this opportunity."

"What are you saying?" The last thing he'd said that had made any sense was that Vera was bringing a healer. Alex wouldn't have to wait.

"What I'm saying is that we are already here. We might as well finish what you planned. Which was what again?" The condescension was hard to miss.

"I…I don't really have a plan. Yet," I added quickly, to which he rolled his eyes. "The use the last house on the row as a base of operations, but I don't know if anyone is there yet."

Gabriel scowled, his dark brows snapping together. "Why haven't you shadowed inside already?"

"Wards are everywhere. The main entrance is the only open way in, and even that alerts Thomas when someone arrives." He nodded, receiving the information without comment. "They know me though, so it won't be unusual if I walk in unannounced."

"That sounds like the makings of a plan that would make Vera proud." He grinned and shook his head. Something told me that wasn't a compliment. "The two of you are alarmingly similar. No wonder she likes you." That was news to me. Last I'd checked, I was nothing more than an irritating thorn in her side. "Let me make sure I have this correct. The entirety of your plan is to walk through the front gate and see what happens."

I shrugged. Sounded about right to me.

He laughed. "This should be interesting. From what I can tell, there are already a handful of other Shadow demons that have already passed this way."

My rage returned two-fold as an image of George breaking Alex's cheek came to mind. It was possible it could have been one of the others, but my gut told me it was definitely him.

"Easy," Gabriel admonished. "I take it those are likely the people who will face the brunt of your wrath. In that case, there is no need to wait any longer. Finish changing and we'll go."

At his command, I realized I was still standing there half-dressed, clutching the bloody shirt. I tossed it aside and picked up a clean one. "Pretty sure the spell on the front gate is Shadow Demon specific. If you walk in, he'll know I'm not alone."

"It's no matter." He waved a dismissive hand. "You will go in the front as expected and I will find another way in." I was about to ask how expected to do that when he once again responded to the unasked question. "There isn't much that can keep me out." Well, that was vaguely ominous. "Lead the way. I'll follow at a distance and see you inside." He slipped back into the shadows, leaving me to make my way out to the main street, where I then proceeded on foot.

I hesitated at the door. Leaving Alex had been a mistake. My heart constricted. If he died before I told him how much I loved him, I'd never forgive myself. Of course, I doubted I'd live much longer myself. I was walking blindly into a hornets' nest with little more than the distant expectation of unknown backup. If Gabriel didn't find a way in, I was fucked.

A noise from within the rundown house and anger seared through me. They were going to pay for what they'd done. I took a fateful step forward, hyperaware of the spell that would alert Thomas to my arrival. Step by step, I worked my way through the ruined building until I reached the cavern of the main room. A sense of anticipation seemed to fill the room, making the hairs on the back of my neck stand on end. I glanced around, noting the presence of too many people in the gloomy space. My anxiety spiked. When had so many joined Thomas' ranks? None of the additions were other Shadow Demons, either. The suspicion that had started weeks ago intensified. There was a lot more going on here than George's homophobia.

"Hey, Matty, you made it!"

I nearly shadowed out at Kyle's sudden speech. *Focus, this is no time to be caught off guard.* Per usual, where there was Kyle, there was Travis.

"Did you hear? We totally caught him." I could have punched Travis in his stupid, excited face. He caught the anger that flashed across my own. "No need to be bitter, just because you missed it."

I walked past him silently, barely restraining myself from throttling him right there. Striking out now would ruin everything, and I didn't know how long Gabriel would need to get inside. So I did what I could to reign in my mounting fury. Already that seemed like an impossible task as I caught sight of my true target. My feet carried me the rest of the way across the absurdly open space to where George stood on the far side. Kyle and Travis were by no means innocent, and they would certainly get what was coming to them, but George was the instigator.

"Where's Thomas?" I asked, barely keeping the sharpness from my voice.

"What's your deal, Matty?" Kyle asked, flanking me.

"Yeah, just because you didn't find him first. Though how, I don't even know. He was right under your nose the entire time." Travis was a special kind of stupid. I kept my focus on George and suppressed a growl.

"Yeah, Matty," George sneered, narrowing his eyes. "Did you like your present? We left it special, just for you." Travis and Kyle laughed like it was the best joke ever while my fists clenched by my side. "How long did you know he was the one we were looking for?" The cage on my temper thinned. "Were you hiding him this whole time?" he asked, like I'd committed a heinous breach of trust.

"I want to talk to Thomas," I insisted.

George glanced over his shoulder at someone I didn't recognize. "Tom did say he wanted to know when Matty finally got here. Go get him."

At last, the presence of extra people made sense—this was a trap. They'd been expecting me. I glanced around warily, taking stock. They wouldn't let me walk out of here in one piece. Hopefully, Gabriel was halfway decent in a fight.

"You should have heard him scream," George said, recapturing my attention. "He was a lot stronger than I would have expected from a fagot." His lip curled and the thin reign on my temper completely snapped.

"That *fagot* is my boyfriend and I'm going to fucking destroy you." The words fell with the effect of an atomic bomb, ricocheting off of the distant walls and coming back as shrapnel.

Surprised fury dominated George's face while Kyle and Travis shared a confused look. I advanced, ready to knock George's head clean off his shoulders, when the sensation of something dangerous buzzed into my awareness. I looked in his hand to see a thin baton crackling with purple energy. All I saw was black.

Without thinking, I used shadow to lift Kyle and Travis, who were advancing behind me, and slung them clear across the room. There was a loud crack as they smashed into the flaking plaster. George growled and took a step toward me, weapon in hand. I'd waited a long time for this moment. Every horrible thing I'd endured because of him—every hateful statement, how he'd kept me from Alex, how he'd left him dying at my door like some demented calling card—all of it fueled my arm as I hauled back and slammed my fist into his face. He didn't have a prayer of getting that flimsy weapon up in time to stop the assault. An immense satisfaction washed through me at feeling bones crush beneath the impact.

Unfortunately, my victory was short-lived. A searing pain the likes of which I'd never experienced in any of my countless fights spread across my back. I shouted and spun around to find that Kyle and Travis had both recovered and were wielding their own batons. The eerie purple light leapt and danced while it burned into my flesh. My teeth ground together as I fought back the shout. Someone tossed what felt like a rope around me and pulled it tight, unleashing a wave of unbelievable pain.

I attempted to Shadow away, and the agony increased tenfold. The instant I released the Shadow world, the pain subsided. Right, so shadowing was off the table. That was fine by me. I'd fought plenty of fights without it. Ignoring the burning on my hands, I tore the flimsy binding off and tossed it at Travis and Kyle. They squealed in terror as the remains fell on them. Their desperate attempts to avoid the painful material only resulted in them getting more tangled. That was perfect; I needed time to deal with the rush of people coming at me from the edges of the room.

In the gloom, it was difficult to get an accurate picture of just how many bodies were hurtling toward me. Not that it mattered. One or a million, none of them were innocent and none would be spared. Chaos and pain swirled around me, fueled by my anger and grief. I barely even saw faces as I dispatched each one. Yet for each body I sent flying away, another was already there to take its place. I leveraged the Shadow World as much as possible, but with the presence of so many shadow lights, that was increasingly difficult. Even without being physically touched by the weapons, the mere glow on my skin was like being brushed with acid.

I fought through the onslaught, but the tide was never ending. Abruptly, I realized I wasn't fighting on my own. Somewhere in the melee, Gabriel had joined me and was dispatching opponents with equal indiscrimination. A gap opened in the flood and I caught sight of George making a break for it. I barreled through two nameless faces and slammed into his back.

"Not so fast, you son of a bitch." I smashed his face ruthlessly into the ground. "You're going to suffer like he suffered." I could hardly distinguish the red painting the ground amidst the black clouding my vision.

"Tell me, Matty," he laughed through bloody lips. "Did you wait for him to die before coming here or just abandon him?"

I growled and twisted his arm.

He laughed again. "When did you realize no healer was ever going to come?" My grip loosened slightly, and he took advantage of the hesitation. Somehow, he'd kept his hold on his Shadow light and it burned ruthlessly into my stomach. "That's right, Matty. We made sure no healer would answer your call. You fucking queer. You condemned him to die miserable and alone. Just so you know, I enjoyed shoving this in him." He pressed the light harder until it broke the skin.

I gasped at the horrible feeling of my insides bubbling. If he pushed any harder, the other end would push through the other side. The thought of him doing something similar to Alex sent me over the edge. I roared and reached down, taking hold of the unforgiving light. The urge to be violently ill rose as I pulled it out. I grimaced through the pain, and at last, the light was free.

George's eyes widened as he fought and lost to keep the light where it was.

"I'm going to end you, you night-forsaken, miserable waste of life." Terror filled his eyes when I snatched the baton from him and raised it overhead, ready to plunge it into his chest.

"Matty... Matt... please. Don't. I'm begging you."

I snarled at his desperate pleas for mercy. There would be none. I braced myself to drive the flimsy weapon down with enough force to pin him to the ground permanently. A hand rested on my shoulder, not restraining, just firm.

"Matt, stop. You don't want to do this." At the sound of Gabriel's voice, I realized the din in the room had subsided. Besides the muffled groans of agony, there wasn't a single sound beyond my own harsh breathing and George's whimpering.

"He... he... Alex is dead, and it's *his* fault!" My entire body shook with the effort of remaining steady. "He deserves to suffer for what he's done. Let's how you like it, *Georgey.*" With every ounce of strength I had left in me, I drove down.

Gabriel's grip on my shoulder tightened, halting my progress. "He wouldn't want you to do this."

A sob wracked my body. "He was all alone and now he'll never know. They blocked all the healers. I'll never get to tell him." My grip on the evil baton was failing. George watched the wavering shadow light with wide eyes while the world crumbled around me.

"He's not dead, Matt, not yet. There is still time."

Was it true? Was there still a chance? I stared down at George, my desire to destroy him warring with my need to see Alex. Alex won. Alex would always win.

"Let's go," I said, flinging the baton as far as I could.

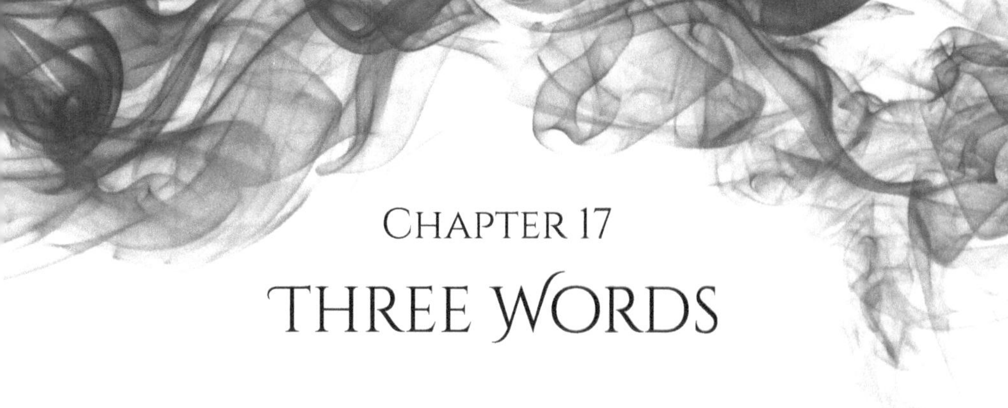

CHAPTER 17
THREE WORDS

Alexi

"I don't understand. Why did they take you in the first place? How is Matt involved in all of this? I swear that boy," Vera added, rubbing her temples.

I didn't really have answers for her. After Dorian's warning, I was afraid to say too much, but she needed to know Matt was definitely still in danger. The moment he arrived, the Order would have known he was the one they were seeking all along. Exhaustion weighed heavily on me, but I refused to rest for even a minute until I knew Matt was back safe and sound. Except with each second that passed, that seemed less and less likely.

I shot Dorian an anxious look, which he noted. He gave a barely perceptible nod. At least he understood I had to tell her something. "They're looking for someone, but they don't seem to know who exactly. They asked a lot of questions."

She raised an eyebrow. "Asked?"

"Demanded," I corrected myself. Memories of the agonizing burn tried to resurface. I closed my eyes against the phantom pains and pushed them as deep into the dark recesses of my mind as I could. There was no time to fall apart. Not when Matt was still in danger. "I'm pretty sure it's actually Matt. I didn't tell them anything, though." Nothing they could have done would have gotten me to give them him. However, that hadn't stopped them from trying.

I absently rubbed the spot on my chest where a Shadow light had forced its way between my ribs. According to Dorian, it had barely missed my heart. He said it was lucky; I suspected it was skill. Douglas had known exactly what he was doing every step of the way. He'd never have "accidentally" killed me.

I noticed Dorian watching me and snatched my hand down. He wasn't pleased at all about my refusal to rest. Vera, however, had no qualms in pursuing her inquiries while I was awake. Not that I blamed her for being confused. Thanks to Dorian, she was only getting half the story.

"Why do you think they're looking for Matt, of all people? How did he even get involved?" She threw her hands up in exasperation. How Matt got involved in the first place was something I, too, very much wanted to know.

"I think he thought he was protecting me." That much I'd been able to cobble together from his slipped comments over the last few horrible months. "As for why, I believe he's the one they are actually after—he fits the bill."

"What do you mean?" she prodded.

I gave Dorian another nervous look. Just how much was I not supposed to say? At this rate, she'd never know why Matt was in so much danger. *They'll never let him leave that house.* I smashed the dire thought down with a violence that surprised me. I couldn't think like that, not if I wanted to keep standing. The hope that he was alright was the only thing that had gotten me through the healing process at all. I took a moment to pull myself back together and attempted to answer her. "Well, they had certain criteria that needed to be met and.... I found something."

"You're being awful vague, Roman. Out with it." Vera put her hands on her hips, her eyes burning into me.

I swallowed anxiously. Did Gabriel get there in time? Did he ever even find him? There'd been no word from either of them. Yet, Vera didn't seem worried—at least, not about that. I took a deep breath and chose my words carefully. "They're looking for a missing member of their family." This subterfuge was giving me undo stress. I just wanted to know if Matt was okay and I doubted that all of this questioning was good for me after my ordeal—healed or not.

"That doesn't answer anything." Damn woman was persistent.

"Matt's a Warde," I blurted in complete disregard to Dorian's very pointed glare. Vera stared blankly back.

"I know he's a ward—he's my ward—but that doesn't explain why you were harmed or why he's in trouble."

I stood there, dumbfounded. She didn't know. All my caution not to say too much and she didn't even know who the Wardes were. Did she know anything? Surely, she of all people would know the truth. "Have you ever heard of the War on Darkness?" I asked tentatively.

"No. Should I have?"

At that moment, the door to the dorm flung open with enough force to hit the wall. I immediately stood up and nearly fell right back down from the head rush.

Matt walked in with the same the purpose he did everything. He looked a little worse for wear, but he was alive and walking. I'd never seen anything more beautiful.

"You need healing."

"I'll be fine," he argued with the voice behind him.

"I didn't say you wouldn't be," the deep voice countered.

"I need to talk to Alex." His gaze finally fell on me standing there. He froze in place, his eyes going wide as they swept up and down me in what could only be disbelief. I tried not to think about what I probably looked like the last time he'd seen me.

I gave him a small wave, inexplicably self-conscious. "Hey, Matt."

The moment he stopped, Dorian stepped forward to proceed with the aforementioned healing while who I assumed must be Gabriel followed Matt into the room. The two words seemed to snap him out of whatever trance he'd fallen into. He surged forward at the same time Dorian reached out to stake hold of him. "Let go of me. I need to talk to Alex."

"You can talk to him in a minute. We need to see to your injuries first."

"I can wait. This can't," Matt insisted, struggling to free himself from Dorian's grasp.

"Why do Shadow Demons always have to be so damn difficult?" He shot Vera an accusatory look. Though whether it was because she too was a troublesome Shadow Demon or because she wasn't helping him restrain Matt was anyone's guess.

"I need to talk to Alex," he repeated, continuing to fight Dorian, who was proving very unsuccessful at keeping him still.

"Then talk to him," he replied, sounding irritated.

"In private." It looked like he was going to resort to actually hitting Dorian if the healer didn't release him soon.

"I strongly suggest you let him," Gabriel offered, sounding bored. Vera looked from him to Matt and then to me. Dorian simply threw up his hands in total exasperation.

"Fine, have it your way. I get called out here in the dead of night and then no one will let me do my job. What about you?" He gestured to Gabriel.

He held up a polite hand. "I think I'll pass."

"Of course," Dorian grumbled, though he didn't seem surprised. I was so absorbed in the scene that I didn't even realize Matt had finally liberated himself.

"I'm going, I'm going." I laughed as he practically dragged me into my room, then closed the door. I could hardly dare to believe it—he was okay and his usual pushy self. "What did you want to talk to me about?" I asked, turning to face him.

"It's impossible. There's not a scratch on you," he said, not answering the question while he commenced what amounted to a full pat down. "I was so worried. I never should have left. They said such horrible things and I... I... " he trailed off. Meanwhile, his hands continued to rove gently over my body, presumably in search of the aforementioned scratches.

As much as I was enjoying hearing how much he cared, he really needed healing. "What did you want to talk to me about?"

His response was to snare me with a kiss, once again avoiding the question. After days of torture and then hours of wondering if he would come back alive, I gave in completely. I knew he had to be hurt and had no idea how severe those wounds might be, but his lips worked just fine. As suddenly as he caught me, he let go, returning to his ceaseless inspection. "Its incredible," he mused softly as his fingers brushed gently across my face.

"If kissing me was what you wanted to tell me, I really don't think the others would have minded."

Confusion flashed across his face. "What? No. I don't care if they see me kiss you." That was certainly news to me.

"Then what is it? You need healing." I brushed a smudge of something on his face and tried to ignore the fact that it was probably blood. My fallen angel looked like he'd walked through hell itself. He stared back at me as if searching for something. Surprisingly, there didn't seem to be a hint of doubt or trepidation in his clear blue eyes. I was about to prompt him again when he spoke.

"I love you." The world went completely still. "Alex, I'm *in* love with you. I'm so sorry about everything. I should have told you how I felt every single day. Leaving was the dumbest thing I've ever done. What if I hadn't gotten back in time?"

The tide of words flowed over me and seemed my heart had finally given out. I was pretty sure I hadn't blinked or drawn a breath since he'd uttered those three fateful words. He opened his mouth to keep talking, and I stole the next words with a kiss. Awareness returned in an explosion of feeling. I cupped his face and kissed him harder, desperate for an outlet for the emotion threatening to overwhelm me. Matt loved me. It didn't matter what I'd been through to get to this moment, that was all I needed.

He let out a sigh and melted into me. Raised voices in the other room threatened our beautiful bubble, but he didn't pay it any mind and neither did I. Matt placed his hand over mine and kissed me deeper. We were absolutely falling, and the best part was that we were finally doing it together. I wanted this perfect moment to last forever.

"I will not sit here and just twiddle my thumbs! Certainly not while someone is still in need of healing. No, I've had it with you Shadow Demons and your weird demands! Oh."

At the exclamation of surprise, I cracked an eye to find Dorian standing in the doorway, turning an interesting shade of red. Beyond him, Vera was hiding a laugh behind her hand and Gabriel looked like he was trying very, *very* hard not to say "I told you so". Reluctantly, I pulled back and found Matt's stunning eyes looking back at me with such openness I thought my heart would burst.

Dorian cleared his throat awkwardly. "I, um... I can come back."

"It's okay, Dr. Valens. Matt will sit still now," I said, without taking my eyes from Matt. Dorian gave a nod and retreated to the other room. A hint of curiosity touched Matt's unblinking gaze.

"Valens, like Dorian Valens?" he asked in a whisper. I nodded. "When Gabriel said that Vera would get the best healer she knew, I had no idea it would actually be *the* best healer. Wow. And I was so rude," he added, looking a little ashamed.

I rubbed a thumb across his cheek. I loved him so much. Him and his quirky mannerisms and strange sense of right and wrong. "And now it's your turn to get healed. I'm ready to have *my* Matt back."

His small smile touched his eyes. If he kept looking at me like that, he wasn't going to get any healing at all. Despite his assertion that he didn't care if they saw us kissing, I fully suspected he might have an issue with them being in the other room while I performed my own thorough inspection.

I smiled and turned him around. He allowed me to steer him back towards the living room, where he sat on a chair in the middle of the room. His eyes never left me, going so far as to crane his neck around when he was facing the wrong direction. He didn't even glance up when Dorian placed his hands on his shoulders, presumably to do an examination like he'd done on me. I watched, fascinated, as the minor scrapes and bruises disappeared from Matt's skin as if being erased.

"What on earth?" Dorian exclaimed. "What the hell have you been doing? You feel as if you've been in a fight nonstop for months. It's a wonder you can walk at all." He gave Vera yet another accusatory glare.

"Don't look at me like that. Tonight's the first I've heard of any trouble. Albeit, Matt has a history. Maybe that's what you're sensing?" she offered hopefully.

He shook his head. "No, all of this is more recent. Come on, I'll need to get a better look at what you've done to yourself." Dorian nudged him back towards my room. When Matt stood, I knew he had no intention of walking in there.

"It's fine. You can look here," he said as he removed his abused shirt.

Simultaneously Dorian, Gabriel, and I all shouted for him to stop. But it was too late. Matt stood there with his shirt in his hands, looking confused. The entire upper half of his body was a canvas of abuse, the shadow burns eerily clear in the yellow light.

"What?" he inquired innocently.

It was like someone sucked all the air out of the room. The moment Vera's eyes lit on the horrific marks, it felt like all the shadows began collapsing. It was as if there was a black hole in the middle of the room and she was the epicenter. The pull on my essence was so strong it was a wonder I was still standing. Everyone's eyes went dark save Dorian's, who looked appropriately alarmed. The sensation of the Shadow world being torn in two made me want to vomit. The violence of it was overwhelming. I was completely powerless to fight against what was happening.

My knees crashed into the ground, and Matt stepped towards me. It was like he was moving in slow motion or more likely, fighting a pull he had no chance of resisting. I looked at him, feeling helpless, and saw my fear reflected back. The room was quickly becoming darker than midnight and the pull was only getting stronger. Whatever she was doing, she had complete control over both of us.

Gabriel stepped towards Vera and wrapped his hands around her arms. She didn't seem aware of him at all, her eyes still riveted on the burns. "Vera, my love, you have to stop."

I'd have screamed if I thought I could. As it was, I felt captive, held in place, waiting to do the bidding of a far more superior demon. This was something for stories, not something that could actually happen in reality. Our essence forced into a shadow state, possibly never to return to a physical form. I focused on Matt, who didn't appear to be faring any better. He'd finally come back to me and now I was going to lose him forever.

Without warning, the pull and the darkness both disappeared. I fell forwards. Matt's own momentum from trying to reach me brought him close enough in time to prevent me from face planting. I gasped for air and kept my head down, too afraid to look at Vera. Matt's arms encircled me and I held onto him for dear life. One of us was shaking, maybe both.

"I... I'm sorry," Vera said hesitantly after several tense moments while she leaned into Gabriel's comforting embrace.

"I didn't know," Matt whispered shakily in my ear. I wanted to console him, but was struggling myself to come to terms with what had just happened. How was that even possible? I was beginning to think that the horror stories regarding her escapades were grossly understated.

"Right. Now that the cat is out of the bag, let's get a look at you." Dorian was the picture of professionalism, though he still sounded shaken.

"Go," I told Matt as he helped me to my feet. The world spun as if it was untethered. I took a steadying breath. "You still need healing." Even saying that much was difficult.

Matt looked back at me, his eyes clouded with concern. For a moment, I thought I'd have to march him back to the chair myself. Then, thankfully, he did as I asked. Dorian shook his head and quietly began examining his patient again. As I'd said he would, Matt sat perfectly still while Dorian began to heal, first one wound and then another.

While he still didn't have as many burns as I'd had, he had enough, not the least of which was where it looked like one had nearly to skewered him. Once again, I envied Matt his exceptional control. He didn't cry out or fidget, he barely even flinched. The whole time he kept his eyes locked on me like he was afraid that if he blinked, I'd disappear. I didn't think I'd ever be able to bear telling him how close that had actually been.

"You're strong, kid, but I'm going to need a lot more energy to take care of some of the older wounds."

"Leave them," Matt responded, clearly unconcerned.

Over my dead body, I thought, then immediately reconsidered my choice of words. "What do you need?" I asked, remembering how he'd said he could take energy from someone else.

"Absolutely not. You don't have a speck of energy to spare after what you've been through. Neither do I." Fear flitted across Matt's face as Dorian confirmed his suspicion that he almost hadn't made it in time.

"This is ridiculous, Dorian. You don't have to ask, just..." Vera said as she stepped towards the pair.

"Take mine," Gabriel said, cutting her off and capturing everyone's attention. Even Matt blinked. Vera looked at her husband like she couldn't believe what she was hearing. Then the light of understanding blossomed in her eyes and she stepped back.

"Are you sure?" Dorian asked, gazing at Gabriel with no small amount of trepidation. Gabriel gave him a level look. Dorian shook his head again, like he wasn't sure how he got himself into such predicaments to which I could whole-heartedly relate. "Fine, but I don't want to hear anything about you getting healed by proxy."

Gabriel nodded and placed a hand on Dorian's shoulder, then turned to Matt. "You might want to brace yourself."

This time when Dorian placed his hands on Matt, Matt gasped, his eyes going wide. I couldn't help but relive the acute sensation of being shoved under a bitterly cold waterfall with no apparent hope of relief insight. Matt arched back, the force of the intense healing literally lifting him from his seat. Then Dorian released him and he fell back. He swayed in the chair and tilted forwards.

I raced to catch him, but Gabriel beat me to it. I caught his gray eyes, and he gently released Matt into my care. He sagged into me, his breathing shallow. Carefully, I shifted my hold to ensure he wouldn't fall off of his perch. True to form, he'd passed out. No sooner did I realize he was out cold, then his eyes blinked open. Panic shimmered in his blue eyes as he scanned the immediate area, vanishing when his troubled gaze settled on me.

"We should let them be for the night," Gabriel said.

"But..." Vera started.

"Fine by me. The lot of you are insane," Dorian said at almost the same time.

"You can talk to them again later," Gabriel reassured Vera, who in turn pouted. It was impressive to see someone handling her for a change. "For now, I think they have earned the right to a peaceful night. They need to rest."

"That at least I can agree with," Dorian said, turning to face us. "Be sure to eat something substantial to restore your strength," he said, then promptly exited the room. Man really did have the *worst* bedside manner.

Chapter 18
Forgiveness

Matt

After some vague statement about reconvening later to debrief, Alex and I were finally alone. And I didn't know what to say. He'd almost died, and it was *my* fault. If I closed my eyes, I could still see his broken body bleeding on the bedspread. I watched Alex move restlessly about the room, putting it back in order. Not that it was a mess to start, but that didn't deter him. He'd also probably been the one to change his bloodied sheets after being healed. He silently ventured back over to where his backpack was sitting on a table. I couldn't recall how it had gotten there or even if he'd had it when I found him in the hall. The horrific image of his busted cheek and blood frothing at his lips flashed through my mind. My fault. It was all my fault. I curled inward on myself with a whimper.

Alex's head whipped around from whatever he was scrutinizing in his backpack. "Matt? Are you okay?" He stepped toward me and I nearly fell in my rush to vacate the chair. "Did Dorian miss something? I'm sure he can't have gone far. I'll call Vera," he said, already reaching for his phone on the coffee table.

"Don't do that," I said, the words thick in my throat.

His eyebrows snapped together as he looked up from the device. "Do what? Call Vera?"

I squeezed my eyes shut and shook my head, but none of it could erase the way he'd wheezed my name or the sharp metallic smell of his blood sinking into the carpet.

"Matt," he said again, softer, his bare feet making a light whisk on the floor as he continued to move closer. I took another step away, my hands tightening by my side. "Do what, Matt?"

My eyes flew open and the burn of tears I'd been fighting stung as they filled my vision. "Try to take care of me," I said with an anguished cry.

Alex stopped walking and stared at me in shock. "What... I don't—"

"No, *I* don't," I cut him off. "I don't deserve your compassion or even your love. Don't you see? I'm a *monster*, Alex. And I almost got you killed."

"Matt. Love," he said gently, resuming his approach.

I side-stepped him. "No. You don't know the things I've done. I may not have physically hurt any of the others, but it wasn't like I didn't know what they were in for. What could happen." I sobbed, no longer able to delude myself into believing that they'd been okay. "I might as well have done all of that to you myself." My hand shook as I pressed the heel of my palm into my face to scrub away the tears that kept falling. Suddenly, Alex was in front of me, holding both my wrists.

"None of that. Whatever you got wrapped up in was *not* your fault. Those people's actions are *not* yours. They used you, manipulated you."

I tugged to get free, but he wasn't letting up. "But they didn't. *I* got George to introduce me. *I* walked in of my own free will. *I*... I reported on our classmates," I finished in a whisper. "It was all me. I was so afraid of losing you I... I would have done anything, Alex. *Anything*."

He released my wrists, which fell limp and defeated to my sides in order to cup my face. His thumbs brushed lightly across my cheeks as he wiped away the latest tide of tears. "That doesn't make you a monster, Matt. *None* of that makes you a monster."

"But—"

"But nothing," he snapped, his emerald eyes flashing. "You are *not* a monster. Say it."

I stared into his eyes, eyes that had captured me the first time I'd seen them, though I hadn't realized it at the time, and tried to see what he did. But I couldn't. I'd done unforgivable things all because I'd been a coward.

"Matt," Alex sighed and rested his forehead against mine a moment before leaning back. "Say it. Say 'I'm not a monster'."

I didn't think it was possible to shed more tears, yet more spilled free.

"Say it, my love."

"I'm not a monster," I croaked, my voice weak.

He brushed the hair back from my face with such delicacy that it nearly broke me. "That's right, you're not."

I squeezed my eyes shut once more. What right did I have to this tenderness? I should be consoling him, not the other way around. But after what I'd done—ghosting him for months, lying, breaking up, leaving him to die alone—I didn't even deserve to touch him, let alone talk to him. "I'm so sorry," I whispered.

"Shh, shh, we're safe now. I'm safe. You're safe. And we're going to get through this... together." He paused, running his hands over my hair. "Speaking of which, I need to tell you something." His serious tone cut to the quick of my insecurities. We might be safe now, but it wouldn't stay that way. Thomas was still out there and after the stunt I'd pulled, I was walking with a target on my back. With any luck, they assumed Alex *had* died and wouldn't come for him.

I stepped back and looked him over for the hundredth time, still unable to accept that every single injury was gone. Sure, I'd endured the same intense healing, but my wounds had been nothing compared to his. "Are you okay?" I cupped his formerly injured cheek, now blemish free, then ran my hands gently over his shoulders and arms.

"Yes, Matt, I'm okay. In fact, I think Dorian might have even healed some of my childhood scars. That healer does *not* fool around. Terrible bedside manner, though," he added with a chuckle that was a balm to my bleeding heart.

My lips twitched with an echoing grin. "No kidding. Pretty sure he's not our biggest fans."

"To be fair, I don't think it's *us* personally."

"Oh?" I responded absently while I continued to run my hands over him. A large part of me still wasn't convinced any of this was real. Odds were higher that I'd gotten cracked pretty hard at the old frat house and this was a fever dream fueled by delusional hope.

"Yeah, definitely more about demons always getting into trouble or some such." He grabbed one of my hands and I glanced up. "I really need to tell you something."

While I heard the words, all I could see was the way his mouth formed them. Not an hour ago, I'd believed I'd lost him forever. Now, he was standing in front of me, warm, safe, *alive*, and all I wanted to do was get lost in him. I pulled him into an embrace, tightening my arms around him. He hesitated a second, then wrapped his arms just as tightly around me. I sagged into his chest, burrowing my face into his neck, where I could inhale his wonderful lavender scent. When was the last time I had just held him? It felt like something inside me was breaking, or maybe it was already broken and trying to reform. "I thought I'd never see you again," I said, squeezing him tighter.

"Hey, it's okay. I'm fine. You can't get rid of me that easily."

I'd never heard anything more beautiful or tragic. I pulled back and kissed him. His return was equally soft as he stroked my cheek with the backs of his knuckles. "I don't expect you to forgive me," I whispered, sadness weighing on my heart.

"Matt, look at me."

I lifted my head to meet his stunning gaze.

"There is nothing to forgive. You did what you thought was right. I can't fault you for that. Now that morning you left after you promised not to.... that's a different story." His lips quirked into a smile.

The band around my chest tightened. I didn't deserve this tenderness, not after what he'd been through because of me. How could anyone be so forgiving, least of all him? The memory of the shadow lights searing my flesh was still just as fresh as if it was happening now and his... his had been so much worse, and none of it would have ever happened if it hadn't been for me. "Alex, I don't know how I can make this better. There's no way to undo the awful things I've done, the people that suffered because of me. You, you suffered because of me. I'm so sorry," I finished, looking down. I couldn't bear to meet his gaze, to see that gentle understanding peering back at me.

"Matt, you have to stop apologizing." Even his voice was gentle. Guilt sat heavy on my chest, steadily gaining weight.

"But..."

"I mean it, Matt. Stop." The whispered command silenced me. His fingers were gentle yet firm as he moved my chin up to look at him. My heart stuttered. How was it possible to care so much about one person?

"How can you still say that after everything? After what they did to you? After what I did? The way you looked at me..." I could still see with perfect clarity the expression of abject horror as I shadowed away, leaving him to die alone.

He frowned, but didn't release his hold. "What are you talking about? What look?"

I took a shaky breath. "When I returned to the house after seeing... after seeing..." I squeezed my eyes shut, it was too much.

Alex's warm laugh washed over my face. "Matt, my love, shade of my heart," he punctuated each endearment with a soft kiss on my lips, my cheeks, my nose. "I wasn't afraid *of* you. I was afraid *for* you. You were so furious. I was terrified that you'd leave on a reckless suicide mission and I'd never see you again." He ran his fingers lightly through my hair and gave me a small smile.

I blinked, taken aback. He wasn't wrong: it had absolutely been a suicide mission. "Oh."

"Good. Now that we've gotten that out of the way, I need to talk to you about something." He glanced toward his discarded bag.

I nodded and caught him in a kiss. As much as it didn't make sense to me, he'd forgiven me. What was more, he didn't believe I needed forgiveness.

He pulled away slightly. "I really need to tell you something."

I loved him so much. I claimed his mouth with another kiss, letting my feelings for him fuel it. More than anything, I just wanted to drown in him. That, and never let him out of my sight again.

"I'm serious," he persisted.

"Uh huh," I replied noncommittally, snaring him again. I needed him, and I wouldn't deny that longing anymore.

"It's important," he said breathlessly.

"Tell me later."

"But Matt..." His words got lost in a deeper kiss. He let out a moan and the last of my doubts disappeared. All wasn't lost. We still had each other.

"Later. Right now, all I want to do is make love to you. I almost lost you, Alex," I added for emphasis, slipping my hands beneath his shirt.

"Matt," he gasped when I pulled him tight against me. I missed touching him and couldn't seem to decide where to start. All of him. All of him seemed like a good place to start. "I don't really think this can wait," he stubbornly insisted.

"I want to be surrounded by you, Alex," I whispered, running my hands down the length of him. He arched into me and groaned, effectively contradicting his insistence that he needed to tell me something first.

Without preamble, I shadowed us both to his room, where the smell of lavender and *home* immediately enveloped me. Shadowing us had the expected result. The control Alex tried so hard to have completely dissipated and he unleashed all the demanding passion I craved. His kiss was harsh and filled with a need that rivaled my own. I helped him pull his shirt over his head as he rid us both of what remained of our clothing. I trailed my fingers down the beautiful, unmarked canvas of his chest. For a moment, visions of shadow burns blazing across it overrode reality. Delicately, I traced the line that one of the worst had taken.

"Matt, don't." He took my hand and brought it to his mouth, where he brushed a light kiss on my palm. I stared back at him, feeling so lost. "It's okay, I'm right here. Everything is going to be fine."

My breath caught. He'd heard me. When I'd thought he was all but gone, he'd heard me.

He used my captive hand to pull me back in close, and I went. I needed him on levels that defied reason. There was no me without him. The next kiss held its own burn, sweeping through me with all the fierceness of a firestorm. There had always been an undeniable heat between us and for the first time, I wasn't afraid of it.

"I'm so sorry," I managed between kisses.

"Stop. Apologizing," he growled, then snared me with a kiss that sent heat curling all the way to my toes. It was all-consuming and seemed to claim my very essence. The force of his ardor propelled us until my back hit the wall. I gasped at the cold contrast and his mouth closed over mine again. He hoisted me up to straddle him, and I groaned as his fingers dug into my hips. I was never going to let go of him again. He abandoned my mouth to work his way along my neck and collar, each touch a brand declaring me his. "I love you." The low, heated words sent a shudder through me.

"Alexi," I moaned, tangling my hands in his hair. I arched into him, desperate for more. I'd missed this so much, missed *him.* He shifted, and I realized he was reaching for the nightstand. With a cheeky grin, I let my eyes go black and reached into the Shadow World. "Looking for this?" I asked, holding up the bottle of lube.

"You." He smashed his mouth back onto mine as he took the bottle. I twined my arms around his neck, adjusting our angle to give him better access to where I wanted him most. His finger brushed my rim and electricity raced up my spine. He pressed inside and my head dropped back with a loud moan. I rocked into each thrust of his fingers, unabashedly giving into my desire for him.

"Now, Alex. Please," I panted.

"Need a condom," he panted right back, his mouth barely leaving mine long enough to form the words.

"Fuck the condoms. I want *you.* And I'm pretty sure that whatever Dorian did took care of any and every ailment we could have had."

He laughed as he snatched another kiss. "Fair. I was going to suggest we get tested soon, anyway."

"Yeah?" I asked, squirming with impatience now that his fingers were gone.

"Yeah. I'm tired of there being anything between us." He stopped kissing me and stared deep into mine as if he was seeing my soul and not the blue looking back at him.

"Me too," I whispered, momentarily forgetting about my clenching ass and the need coiled around the base of my spine. "I love you."

Something feral entered his eyes as he shifted his grip and lifted me. "You're mine," he growled and then sank into me in one thrust.

"Alexi!" I cried, throwing my head back. I dug my fingers into the back of his shoulders, giving over wholly to the mind-blowing sensation of having him inside. He was right, I was his, always had been.

He pressed me into the wall as he continued to thrust, magically hitting that perfect spot again and again until my brain was more liquid than solid. I stole what sloppy kisses I could while he alternated between nipping and sucking on my lips, neck, shoulders. I squeezed around him and the feel of him bare was pure fucking ecstasy. Every move brought fresh sensation that conquered me, body and soul. Eventually, he gave up the wall and walked us over to the bed where he still didn't slow. I was completely his and reveled in every touch, caress, and kiss.

When we were somewhere near satiated, we simply lay there staring at each other. His green eyes seemed so peaceful as they looked back at me. For once, I felt content; a feeling I'd been waiting on for a very long time. Alex was my friend, my lover, my everything. I couldn't imagine life without him, and I hoped I'd never have to again.

I traced the contours of his back while he continued to watch me. Visions of the horrible burns kept trying to reassert themselves. Between each blink there was the brown of dried blood mixed with the bright crimson of fresh bleeding. I shuddered. There was no way to unsee the gruesome damage caused by the shadow lights, no matter how perfect his skin looked now.

"What are you thinking?" he asked quietly.

"I don't think I'll ever be able to forget the way your breathing sounded." I could almost hear it now, the way each bubble had brought a fresh paint of blood and that night awful rattling. My stomach twisted.

He snaked out a hand to cover my free one. "You can't keep blaming yourself." Yes, I could. "Matt, I mean it. You aren't the one who did any of that." He was wrong. None of it would have happened if I'd protected him better.

I trailed my fingers down his back and along the perfect curve of his ass. Then a new horrible thought occurred to me. What if they'd done more than just torture him? I couldn't even formulate the heinous thought as my hand stalled. "They didn't... they didn't..." I swallowed, pretty sure I was going to be sick. I couldn't bring myself to say it out loud. It had been a mistake to spare their lives. One I was fully prepared to rectify.

He blinked back at me, then seemed to realize what I was trying and failing to ask. "No, they didn't. Lots of other things, but not that." I looked into his perfectly green eyes. They seemed haunted by the memory of what had happened in that place. "Did you kill them?" he asked.

"No," I said, doubt creeping in. What if Gabriel had been wrong?

His face relaxed. "Good. I don't want something like that following you around for the rest of your life." Suddenly, I had a new doubt. Would he lie to make sure I didn't?

"Would you tell me the truth? If they... they..." I closed my eyes against the awfulness.

He paused a moment, as if weighing his answer. "Yes. There's no reason to lie to you, Matt, no matter the consequences. I'd tell you everything they did to me if I thought it would make you feel better, but I don't think it will."

I stared back down at him, not sure if I could trust this. Did I want to know? "Who broke your cheek?" The question simply popped out. I was pretty sure I already knew the answer, but I needed him to confirm it.

"George. He is definitely homophobic."

I flinched. I was right. He definitely should have suffered more. If Gabriel hadn't stopped me, then he would have. What else had he done to my beautiful Alex?

He looked pensive for a moment, then continued on without encouragement. "They found me while I was talking on the phone with my mom. I was actually waiting for you outside of your advanced spells class." I blinked. He'd been so close. "Unsurprisingly, I was talking to her about you. She wanted to know if we'd worked things out yet."

Guilt stabbed through me. He never would have been there at all if it wasn't for me.

He gave my hand a gentle squeeze and went on. "I'm pretty sure they missed that though, otherwise I doubt they would have just taken me. Thanks to you never taking it easy on me in training, I was able to knock George's weapon out of his hand before he could use it. Lot of good that did me." I gave him a curious look, and he answered the unspoken question. "I didn't expect his lackeys to have their own as well. They are the ones that burned my back first. I'd never felt anything like that. I'm a little embarrassed to admit I passed out. Maybe if I hadn't, I could have fought them off long enough for your class to get out. At any rate, when I came to, I was bound by shadow lights to a chair."

The thought of what he must have endured to learn that was sickening.

He sighed and continued. "Travis and Kyle lost the stomach for it almost immediately. George didn't hold out much longer. When Douglas started stabbing me with the shadow lights, he gave up as well. For all his bluster, he really is a coward."

"He said you begged for your life," I said, recalling his goading from earlier in the night.

Alex snorted. "He didn't stick around long enough to know what I did or didn't do."

I glanced down at him, seriously doubting he'd begged. Despite his self-deprecating statement of being weak, he was far from it. Alex really was the strongest person I'd ever known, certainly stronger than me. "I love you." The words seemed to find their own way out of my mouth. They were no less true now than they'd been the first time I'd said them. His face almost immediately broke into a stunning smile, and I raised an eyebrow. "Are you going to grin like an idiot every time I tell you that?"

"Probably," he said, rolling onto his back and effectively trapping my arm. Then he pulled me down for a kiss. Undeniable heat and desire curled through me. There really was no way to get enough of him. Already I could feel the fire flaring to life inside of me. "I love you too, Matt."

I sank into him, letting the kiss get deeper, and used my trapped hand to pull him in close.

Suddenly, he pulled back. "Wait. Are you going to be here in the morning?"

"Yes," I replied with a laugh, kissing his collar.

"What about the next day?"

"Yes."

"And the day after that?"

"Yes," I said, trying to hold my laughter. He opened his mouth, no doubt to add another day, and I cut him off. "I'll be here every day. I'm yours as long as you'll have me."

He scanned my face. "Are you sure? Forever is a long time." There was no suppressing the smile that dominated my face. My heart felt like it was flying.

"Not long enough," I replied, pulling him back to me.

Chapter 19
Legacy

Alexi

The next couple of days slipped uneventfully by and Matt hadn't let me out of his sight for more than a couple of minutes. It was wonderful. After waiting for him to come back to me for so long, having him be his old self again felt more like a dream than reality. Every morning that I woke up to him curled beside me, I had to pinch myself to prove I wasn't still asleep. Aside from the random times when he would look at me and I could tell he was actually seeing the wounds, things were wonderfully normal. I didn't know how to help him with that besides giving him time. Then there was him telling me he loved me. Every time he said it, I felt giddy. Shamelessly, I'd been counting how many times he actually said the words and I was running out of things to count on. It was incredible, like telling me had opened up a whole new side of him, like all of his reservations and hang-ups disappeared over night.

But our perfect bubble couldn't last. Selfishly, I refrained from telling him about what I'd discovered before I was taken. We deserved this feeling of happiness and I wanted it to enjoy it as long as possible. But I also knew it was wrong to keep this from him. Once again, I glanced over at my bag and considered showing him the picture. Surely the magic of the spectacles would be strong enough to see through the spell.

"What's this?" he asked, interrupting my internal struggle.

I turned to find him holding up a piece of paper he'd presumably picked up off of the table. "I don't know. It's not mine." I knew for a fact nothing had been on the table before. "What's it say?" I asked, joining him. His arm slipped absently around my waist as I leaned over to examine the page. It looked like a handwritten note, except it was in some other language.

"Grab the glasses," he said, giving me a light squeeze before letting me go.

"Bossy. Why don't you grab the glasses?" I fired back.

He laughed under his breath and kissed my shoulder. "Because I don't know where they are."

"Oh. Right." I stepped over to the bag and rifled through until I found them. When I straightened, I was holding both the spectacles and the memoir. Apparently, not telling him was really weighing on my conscience. He took the glasses and immediately put them on, briefly derailing my brain with how incredibly hot he looked in those. Then I remembered the book. I swallowed. "Hey, Matt, I still need to talk to you about something."

"It will have to wait. We've been summoned."

This was it. I was officially out of time to come up with a better way to break this to him. My heart fell. I'd hoped for a little more time, but time was not on our side. "It really can't," I said, trying not to sound like it was terrible news. He looked up at me over the glasses with a curious expression. For a moment, I forgot to breathe altogether. I didn't care what his lineage was. He was still Matt, and he was mine.

"Okay, Alex. What is it?" he asked quietly, taking the book like he knew it had something to do with it.

"I found something. Look at the picture," I said awkwardly.

He chuckled, "Alex, I can sketch this picture in my sleep. I don't know what you expect me to see that I haven't already. We've literally looked at this image at least a thousand times."

"Not with the glasses we haven't." That piqued his interest, and he opened the book. Suddenly, I didn't want him to see it, didn't want him to know. Something told me he wouldn't take the news well at all, and I couldn't bear the thought of him shrinking away again. "Wait," I said, obscuring the image.

"Alex, come on." The smile on his face suggested he thought this was a game, and it about broke my heart. I couldn't bear to lose him, not again. "What's wrong?" he asked, his face clouding over.

I stepped forward and kissed him. Once more, his hand snaked around my waist and he pulled me in tight, deepening the kiss. I easily slipped into the ever-present desire.

"We really don't have time for this," he said, his voice low as he returned several smaller kisses. Despite the statement, he didn't much sound like he cared, letting the heat build unchecked with each brush of his lips against mine. As much as I now didn't want to tell him, that didn't change that he had a right to know. Not talking to each other is what had led to this whole mess in the first place.

"I need you to know that I love you no matter what," I said with another kiss.

"I love you too," he replied, caressing my face.

My heart fluttered, and I felt sick. His eyes were so blue it hurt. "No matter what," I emphasized. There was merriment dancing in the crystal like he thought I was being silly. It would have to be enough.

"Alright, let's see what all the fuss is about."

I stepped away to give him more space.

He repositioned the glasses and looked down at the fateful page.

I held my breath while I waited. What was taking so long? Maybe the glasses weren't strong enough. This was a mistake. There had to be a better way to tell him.

Then his eyes went wide, and he looked up sharply. "What is this?" he asked with a distinct edge, as if *I* was somehow responsible for altering the image.

"That is a picture of Matthias Warde and his lover in 1218 BCE," I said as matter-of-fact as I could.

He shook his head. "This can't be right."

"Matt, what did you think George and the others were looking for?" I asked, suddenly curious and not sure why I hadn't asked sooner.

He immediately turned pink, then cleared his throat and looked down. "George led me to believe they were looking for someone pretending to be someone else. And he's... you know. I just assumed..."

I thought back to what George had said when he found me. "You thought they were looking for a gay kid in class." His blush deepened. "You do realize that would include you," I said with a smile. He finally looked back up at me.

"What? No. I'm not—"

"Maybe not gay, but also not entirely straight." I simply raised an eyebrow when he opened his mouth, no doubt to continue arguing, and his blush returned two-fold.

He cleared his throat awkwardly. "I hadn't... I didn't.... You're different."

"You think Gabriel is attractive, don't you?" I asked, taking a stab in the dark. He looked like he was going to swallow his tongue. I laughed. "At least you're consistent. We can go over the myriad of sexualities another time, but the point stands."

"He's still not you," he grumbled. "Anyway, back to what you were supposed to be telling me."

I rolled my eyes. When Matt didn't want to talk about something, he *really* didn't want to talk about something. But that was a concern for another day. Right now, we had bigger issues to tackle. "They were looking for the same thing we were. Except where we were looking for a story, they were looking for an actual person." He frowned, his face the picture of confusion, and I pointed back to the picture. "They are looking for you, Matt. You don't like your name because it *isn't* your real name. You are the legacy of Matthias Warde."

He stared blankly at the page. Unfortunately, his silence wasn't giving me any clues how he was taking this.

"You're a Warde, Matt. The Order of Light is real."

He stood there frozen in silence for a solid, tense minute, then dropped the book on the table like it had burned him. It landed with an exceptionally loud thud that seemed to echo through the room. "No, I'm not. I don't know what I am, but I'm not that. I'm not one of *them*." The loathing with which he said it tore at my heart. I reached out and pulled him close. He melted into the embrace and clung to me as if he was afraid that if he let go, he'd simply drift away. "They lost any claim to me when they abandoned me," he mumbled into my shoulder.

I hugged him tighter. "None of this changes who you are or how much I love you. Now you just know more about where you come from."

He snorted. "A line of bigots and assholes. Awesome. To think this whole time.... I *knew* something was off about Thomas."

"That reminds me. I'm surprised you didn't recognize him."

"What do you mean?" he asked.

"Thomas is Professor Warden. He must have been using a spell to make himself look older than he was, but it's definitely the same guy." His eyes brightened with realization, then darkened with sorrow. He leaned forward and rested his head on my shoulder. I rubbed the back of his neck, grateful that he was finally willing to let me comfort him.

"I'm so sorry, Alex. I was so blinded by my need to keep you safe I never even... I should have seen it. Can you ever forgive me?"

"I already told you, there's nothing to forgive." I placed a kiss on the top of his head.

After another moment, he let out a sigh and straightened up. "We really should get going. They'll be waiting for us." He looked at the book on the table. "We should probably bring all of this, too. They'll need to know the whole story, if they don't already."

"I think you're right," I said, picking it up to add it to my bag with the others. Vera, at the very least, didn't have a clue about any of it. I paused, considering the book, and smiled.

"What?" he asked, folding the missive and putting it in a pocket. The glasses he tucked into his shirt.

"I was just thinking about how I've basically been in love with you for the better part of my life." He gave me a quizzical look, and I waved the book for emphasis. His smile was small, but still shone in his eyes. Perhaps some part of me had seen past the spell and that was why I'd reacted to Matt the way I had the first time I saw him. I'd just *known*. He studied me a moment longer, then swiped a quick kiss and out we went.

It felt strange to be out in the real world. So much had happened in such a short amount of time. I was grateful for remembering to grab a jacket as the frigid air hit me. The holidays would be over soon and the smattering of people still around would grow until the place looked overrun. The day was beautiful with the sun glistening in a perfectly blue sky, which only added to how surreal everything felt. Odd how the world kept turning even when yours was falling apart.

"Hey," Matt said in greeting to someone. I looked up to see Sam and Lucas adjusting their course to meet us.

"You guys stuck here for the holidays, too?" Lucas asked.

"Yeah," Matt replied.

"Totally boring, right?" Sam said as he stopped beside his friend. "You look in better spirits," he added.

"Something happen?" Lucas asked.

"You could say that," Matt replied with a smile.

"Like what?" Sam asked, sounding genuinely curious.

Matt laughed, sounding wonderfully carefree and relaxed, then held out his hand to me. I looked down at the extended appendage not sure what he expected me to do with it. I searched his face for a clue and he quirked an eyebrow. Hesitantly, I took the proffered hand. This broke all of the rules. *His* rules. His fingers tightened around mine and he pulled me in close, where he stole a kiss. That broke even more of them.

I leaned back, shocked. "What are you doing?" I hissed under my breath.

"I won't ever let anything stop me from loving you again," he whispered and placed his lips against mine once more. I nervously returned the kiss, convinced this had to be a dream. He released me in time to see Lucas smack Sam.

"Told you so. Hand it over."

Sam rolled his eyes and took out a twenty. "I knew it was weird. You're not that good with girls and *never* take one home," he huffed, passing it to Lucas. Matt simply chuckled and released me. I caught the barest hint of a blush before he ducked his head.

Lucas admired his prize a moment, then asked, "You guys up for pool later?" Sam brightened.

"That sounds like fun. I've been helping Alex with his form, so it should be more interesting." Matt slid an arm around my waist. It was borderline possessive, and I was still struggling to believe that any of this was actually happening.

They groaned in unison at this news. "Great, but you're buying your own drinks," Sam said.

"What do you say?" Matt asked, turning to me.

I blinked, and he stared back, patiently waiting. In fact, they were all staring at me, like what was happening was perfectly normal and didn't go against everything I'd been led to believe over the last semester. At last I found my voice. "Yeah, I'd love to."

"Then it's settled. We'll see you guys later. What..." Lucas looked at Sam.

"Tomorrow?" Sam finished for him, looking back at us.

Matt nodded, and we went our separate ways. My head was spinning, and the day had barely started.

Chapter 20
The Manor

Matt

We made our way through Mysterio College to Vera's office. The note had said to take the portal. Considering how cagey Vera could be, I doubted that it'd just be sitting around for us to walk through. Thankfully, the door to her office was unlocked, so there was one hurdle we didn't have to jump. However, a glance around did not immediately reveal the promised mode of transport. I let out a sigh and began searching along with Alex, who'd remained stoically silent for the better part of the journey here.

I suspected his silence and the looks he kept giving me, that he clearly didn't think I'd noticed, had something to do with what had happened with Sam and Lucas. While I was a little surprised that they'd placed bets on whether Alex and I were together, it really wasn't a big deal. I didn't care, and neither did they. Did Alex?

"Are you alright?" I asked after checking beneath Vera's desk, which, in retrospect, was a little dumb. Who would put a portal there?

He glanced up from his search of the wall with a calendar as if he'd been caught writing naughty things on it. "What? Yeah, of course."

I sighed and walked around to sit on the edge of the desk closest to where he was doing a shit job of pretending to be okay. I hooked a finger in his belt loop, gave a sharp tug, and he stumbled into my waiting hands, letting out an "oof" as I caught him. "I won't apologize for loving you. Nor will I hide it. Not anymore," I said earnestly before he could speak. Despite my words, he remained stiff and uncertain. I shook him by the hips. "Talk to me."

"There's nothing really to talk about. I... It's just adjusting to a new set of rules, that's all."

"What do you mean?"

He let out a huff that I wasn't sure what to make of and crossed his arms over his chest. "Matt, you made it very clear from the beginning that I wasn't allowed to touch you outside of the dorm. Out here," he gestured to the general space, "we were strictly friends."

Guilt lanced through my heart. Had I really done that? "I'm sorry. I never meant to make you feel that way." He shrugged and looked away. "Hey, that's my thing," I said, tugging on him again so he lost his balance and fell against me. His lips molded with mine and I barely checked myself from sliding right into the fire. "It won't happen again," I assured him.

He kissed me deeper. "You could always make it up to me."

I groaned as his fingers dug into my thigh, positive my eyes were solid black. "I want you," I whispered against his eager lips.

"I know," he responded huskily and rubbed against me. My breath caught as he worked his way down my neck. Night I loved this, loved him and the way he made me feel. I'd gladly be his play thing forever. Just one thing was getting in the way: we were supposed to be somewhere else. As if reading my mind, he whispered, "This really isn't the best place for this." I mumbled some sort of agreement as he snared my mouth again. He pressed into me and I arched back, loving the feel of him against my body and letting out a moan as his hand left my thigh to grab my ass and pull me closer. "Or time," he said, his breathing ragged.

"Except," I said, still struggling for air, "we can't find the damn portal. It has to be here somewhere, but I can't sense a thing." Despite his declaration that this was neither the time nor the place for our... extracurriculars, he was already kissing along my neck. Definite lack of conviction in stopping. I was half a heartbeat away from sliding my hands beneath his shirt and suggesting he lock the door, when I felt him chuckle along the sensitive skin. I shivered at the delectable sensation. "What's so funny?"

"You mean I know how to do something you don't?" Laughter danced in his eyes as he leaned back to look at me.

"You usually do," I grumbled. He gave a half shrug, not disputing it. I was seriously contemplating bringing him back by wrapping my legs around him, then he spoke again, and I could have groaned in frustration. He did this on purpose. Insufferable tease.

"Think about it. If *you* had to place a portal that you didn't want anyone to find, where would you put it? How would you keep it hidden?"

"That's easy. I'd put it behind the door and cloak it."

He raised an eyebrow. "Did you check behind the door?"

"Yes," I replied, with no small measure of attitude. It really wasn't very nice to leave someone hanging. "But there's nothing there." He chuckled again, and cold air rushed between us as he added more distance. Damn it.

"Think outside the box. How do you think I found all your trip wires and squirrel holes?"

Squirrel holes? I stared back at him, waiting for him to answer his own rhetorical question.

He rolled his eyes. "If the portal is cloaked, then you can't feel anything." I nodded. We'd covered this before. "Anything at all." I frowned, but it did absolutely nothing to temper his enthusiasm. He swiped a kiss, then stepped toward the door. "It creates a void, Matt. That's how you find something cloaked."

I thought about that for a moment and focused on feeling the shadows around where I'd have hidden a passage. Nothing. Alex waited with an expectant smirk. I pushed harder and discovered a very distinct absence. There was only one spot that the shadows didn't behave normally, almost as if they just stopped existing altogether. My eyes went wide. "You're a fucking genius," I pronounced, hopping off of the table.

"I am pretty good," he said humbly.

I shook my head and reached up to feel the space where the portal must be. There was still something off. Then it hit me. "There's a barrier spell."

"Can you break it?"

I gave him a look.

"Of course you can."

"But I'm not going to—you are."

He gave me an incredulous look. "Matt, we are already unbelievably late."

And we'd have been even later if I'd gotten my way. "They'll wait. Now come here. Take your time and look for a part of the spell that feels like it's coming off. We don't want to break it, just... loosen it. Once we are through, we'll need to tie it back. Can't very well have someone wandering through by accident." He gave me a look that said I'd officially lost it. "You're wasting time," I prompted.

He huffed, but moved closer to inspect the barrier. Abruptly, he spun back to me and grabbed my hips, pulling me flush against him. Maybe he wasn't going to be such a tease today after all, I hoped, as his hand slid into my back pocket. As suddenly as he'd grabbed me, he let go.

I stumbled and wasn't able to stop my sound of disappointment. "What the hell?"

He held up the folded note with a smug grin, and I scowled.

"You could have just asked."

"Where's the fun in that?" he countered with a maniacal grin. He was going to be nothing but an endless source of frustration. I just knew it.

"So what are you thinking, then?" I asked, trying to rein in my denied hormones.

"You and Vera are both very crafty. I doubt she would have told us to come to a locked door without giving us a key to open it." He unfolded the note and held it up to where we assumed the portal was. It still felt like a safe bet, although I didn't sense any change. I shrugged and his mouth tugged down into a frown. He looked back at me. "Put on the glasses." I sighed and did as he asked. For a second he just stared at me, then seemed to shake off whatever had distracted him. "Here," he said, pointing to a word that didn't seem to fit the rest, "What does it say?"

"All it says is 'into darkness'. Doesn't make much sense with the rest of it, though."

"Huh. Maybe it doesn't need to be translated. *In tenebras*," he said with damn near perfect pronunciation.

Immediately, I felt a shift. "It's opening," I said in disbelief.

"And you wanted to do things the hard way," he said, passing me back the paper. He took a step forward and half of him disappeared. "Are you coming? I doubt it will stay open for long."

I hastened to follow and felt his hand close around mine as I stepped into a world of pure darkness. For all the times I'd ventured into the Shadow world, this felt infinitely deeper, making the office we'd just been standing in feel like a distant reality. "Now what?" My words barely traveled at all, like we were standing in a vacuum instead of another layer of the world. I felt more than saw Alex gesture to the ground where there were faint illuminations that resembled footsteps.

Without another word, we followed them. Out of reflex, I sent my essence out to explore this strange place in which we had found ourselves and could sense Alex doing much the same beside me. Turned out, the door we'd come through was one of many. Some had similar barriers that made the world look and feel extra muted from this side, while others felt like they would simply dump you out. We were heading for such a one now. As we crossed the invisible threshold, bright light from all sides greeted us.

"I told you they'd figure it out," said a familiar woman's voice.

"And you were right," a man replied.

I blinked to bring the world back into focus. It was entirely too bright.

"So, which one of you figured it out?" At last I could make out an excited-looking Vera and an exceptionally bored looking Gabriel.

"Matt knew where the portal was, but he wanted to crack the spell. I assumed you gave us the key," Alex said beside me.

I glanced around, taking in shelves upon shelves of books. We were in the library? Why not just say: hey, go to the library?

"Well done, Alexi," Vera said, walking forward. Gabriel gave me a nod, which Alex unfortunately did not miss.

I quickly adjusted my focus. "Where are we?" I asked, praying that I wasn't turning as red as I thought I was.

"Welcome to the manor." Gabriel stood from the wing-backed chair he'd been occupying and held out his hands. We both turned to look at him. As long as I didn't think about how much he reminded me of Alex, I was totally fine.

"The Manor?" Alex repeated in awe.

Vera's laugh rang out into the space. "It's just a big house."

"A big house filled with a ludicrous amount of history," he said, rushing over to one of the many tables strewn about the space. Since he hadn't released my hand yet, that meant I got dragged along in his wake. "I mean, right here is where the Shadows sat to devise a plan to overthrow the Regency."

"Only because the War Room is too crowded," Vera replied casually. "What happened to your neck? I thought Dorian healed you."

It took me a moment to realize she was talking to me. I absently reached up. "We were making out in your office," I said, still trying to take in the room. Her jaw fell open, and Alex looked mortified.

"On that note, we really should get down to business. While I'm pleased to see you've brought what notes you have, I doubt they will be of much use," Gabriel said, sinking into a seat at the table.

Alex gave him a searing look and dumped out the contents of his bag onto the table. I looked between the two of them and took a seat beside Alex. I was beginning to suspect that my apparent hickey was not an accident. Meanwhile, Vera seemed to miss the entire exchange and took a seat opposite us.

"Here's what we've uncovered." He lined up the books we'd brought and organize the notes. The history immediately caught Gabriel's attention, and he reached forward to grab it. Alex surreptitiously moved it out of his reach before he could. "During the War on Darkness, the Warde family attempted to wipe out Shadow Demons using what we call Shadow Lights." Vera's face darkened at the mention of the weapons, but she held her peace. "One of them had an affair with a general on the other side. While neither survived, their child *did.*

Somehow, over the centuries, this child grew and unknowingly passed on his Shadow Demon heritage beneath the watchful eye of a family determined to erase all existence of said heritage. Now, it seems they've realized the betrayal and are looking for that progeny." He gestured to me. "They are looking or *were* looking for Matt."

I shifted uncomfortably in my seat. Hearing it again didn't make it any easier to swallow.

"But how do you know that? And who are the Wardes? I've already asked Gabriel about this supposed 'War on Darkness'," she said with air quotes, then shot Gabriel a nasty look. "Do not get me started there."

He let out a sigh. "How many times do I have to tell you? It was a joint decision. All Shadow Demons went into hiding. We just did it for so long that many forgot what they were hiding *from*. As for the Wardes, that's the name of the family that founded the Order of Light," Gabriel offered by way of explanation.

"Douglas and Cane," she said, her voice dripping with acid.

Gabriel nodded and reached out to her. I could clearly see her anger fighting for control and braced for a repeat of what had happened at the dorm.

Out of nowhere, a small child burst into the room and raced over. Vera immediately snapped out of her fury-induced funk. "Lelana Isabel, what do you think you are doing?" Vera scolded the young girl. She couldn't be more than four. "You are supposed to be with Aunty Kyra. And where is DJ?"

The child pouted. "She's taking a nap, and DJ won't let me play with my powers."

Vera picked up the child and let out a sigh. "Sorry, Kyra was supposed to be watching her while we had our meeting. I'll track her down." The little girl immediately began squirming, her long dark hair swirling around as she fought Vera's grasp.

"She can stay," Alex said. I looked at him. His eyes were bright as he resisted the urge to laugh at the young girl's antics.

Immediately, the girl turned to Vera. "Mama, please, please, pleeeaase..." she begged.

Vera looked anxiously around the table, then she gave a resigned sigh. "Alright, but you have to be on your best behavior. Understand?" The little girl nodded enthusiastically until Vera set her back down. She then raced over to where Alex had scooted back from the table.

"What's your name?" she asked her benefactor.

He laughed, "My name is Alexi, and this is Matt."

I gave a small wave, not really sure what else to do.

"Uh-lex-e," she said, accentuating every syllable. "I like it! It's pretty like mine," she beamed up at him before scrambling into his lap. When she turned back to the others, she looked like a proper, miniature adult, complete with a super serious face.

Alex laughed again and resumed what he had been talking about. The memoir and glasses he slid to Vera so she could see the unbearable likeness between me and the infamous Matthias Warde. Then we talked at length about what to do next. Which amounted to a lot of nothing. It felt like they were really just talking in circles, rehashing things we already knew. None of it getting me any closer to punishing Thomas.

Eventually, Lelana decided it was time to share her attentions. She calmly extricated herself from Alex's lap and ventured over to me. She looked up expectantly until I picked her up. I'd never dealt with children outside of the orphanage and was a bit at a loss. Alex gave me an encouraging look, and I sat her down on my lap, much like she'd been before with him. Vera looked borderline mortified, while Gabriel looked like it was the funniest thing he'd ever seen. Alex, however, was giving me an entirely different look that I didn't understand in the least. I let it go and tried to refocus my attention on the current topic. They were saying yet again that there was no lead where the Order could be hiding or if they were even still around to be found. I rolled my eyes and tried not to look as bored as I felt.

Abruptly, I jerked and realized I'd been dozing off. Reflexively, I made sure the small child curled against me didn't fall. She too had fallen asleep and the sound of her faint breathing drifted up. Something about that innocence was reassuring. I blinked the sleep from my eyes and tried to figure out where we were at. Vera and Gabriel were talking animatedly, or maybe they were arguing. It was difficult to tell. Alex, on the other hand, was smiling at me. I returned with one of my own nervous ones.

He turned back to the others and interjected, "We should probably get going. It's getting late." Vera and Gabriel looked up, then back at each other. Something told me this battle of words was common for them.

"He's right." Vera stood and walked around the table.

I looked down at the little girl nestled like some kind of baby bird in my arms and gave Alex a beseeching look. He chuckled and moved over to help. She mumbled in her sleep as he scooped her off of my lap. She really was precious, if a bit feisty. I watched as he walked her over to her mother, looking totally comfortable holding the small child.

"I'm sorry about that," Vera said as she took the child from Alex. "She can be quite insistent. And without her powers being bound, sometimes it's more trouble than it's worth fighting her on things."

"It's no trouble," Alex whispered, gently rubbing Lelana's back. "As a matter of fact, if you ever need a babysitter, just let me know. We'd be happy to." He looked back at me. What? How had I gotten volunteered? He smiled and gave me a wink.

CHAPTER 21
PLAYING FOR KEEPS

Alexi

I finished getting dressed to go out and was trying in vain to get my hair to do something resembling decent. Matt had vanished to his own room to change and was likely already waiting for me in the living room. I let out an exasperated sigh and gave it up as a lost cause. My hair would do whatever it wanted, no matter what I did. Defeated, I made my way to the door and hesitated. On the one hand, I was super excited about getting to play pool again. While admittedly, I wasn't very good, that didn't make it any less fun. On the other, though, I literally had no idea what to expect from this evening, especially after Matt's blatant display of affection the other day. Quite frankly, I wasn't even sure what the rules were anymore. Were there rules?

I shook my head and stepped through the door, forgetting to actually open it. Startled, I blinked at the still closed door behind me. Amazing how second nature shadowing could become. And I made fun of Matt, I mentally scolded myself.

"It's about time." I looked back to the room to see Matt waiting impatiently, the hint of a smile playing around his mouth. "Let me guess," he began, walking towards me, "you were fussing with your hair. Am I right?" He ran his fingers through the rebellious strands for emphasis.

"Seriously, Matt?" I admonished as I tried without success to flatten it back down.

He chuckled and let it be. "It looks fine. *You* look fine." Heat colored his words, and I dropped my hand.

"Um, thanks," I responded after clearing my throat. "We should really get going or we'll be late."

"Pft, I feel like it's almost impossible for a Shadow Demon to be late," he scoffed, shadowing out for emphasis.

"Vera does it all the time," I countered. "Besides, while walking through the Shadow world expedites the process, it still takes time."

"Fair point," he conceded.

"At any rate, we should leave," I tried again, attempting to move around him towards the door.

"What, no kiss?" he asked, raising two curious brows. The question may have sounded innocent enough, but there was a devilish glint in his eye.

I narrowed my eyes at him. This was a trap, I could feel it.

"Just one," he offered reassuringly. I'd believe that when they brought cheese down from the moon.

"Fine. One." I gave him my best serious look, which didn't faze him in the least. I licked my lips nervously. There really was no telling what he would do. He'd been fairly unpredictable before and this new Matt was a whole other level. He was attentive, affectionate, open, possessive, and absolutely insatiable. To be fair, he had been most of those things before, only now he wasn't shying away from it. In truth, I had no idea why I was so anxious as I leaned forward to press my lips against his; I loved the way his molded perfectly to mine. However, that did nothing to prevent my heart hammering loud enough to echo in my ears. To my infinite amazement, he gently kissed me back without doing anything else. I leaned back, still feeling dubious about the whole affair. "Better now?" I asked, quirking an eyebrow at him before taking a step towards the exit. I only made it two before his hand on my arm stopped me.

"Wait a sec."

I turned back to him. "What?"

In less than a blink, he'd pulled me back to him and snared me with a substantially less sedate kiss. His arms tightened around me, pressing me hard against him. I let out an involuntary squeak, and he stole the opportunity to deepen the kiss. I instantly got swept up in the pure fire of Matt's passion. My fingers tangled in his hair as the torrent of desire poured through me. And his hands felt incredible as they roved relentlessly beneath my fresh shirt. I moaned and leaned into him. At last, he pulled back to give me an absolutely evil grin. The sigh that escaped me at the release completely contradicted my earlier assertion that we needed to go. I now very much wanted to stay.

"Just that," he said

I struggled to get my breathing and my heart rate back under control. There was zero doubt in my mind that I looked 'peeked', as my mother would say. He, on the other hand, was barely even breathing hard. "You are absolutely insufferable," I said at last.

His grin widened. "You know you love it." He took a step back, giving me more space to breathe. "Now we really should stop stalling. The guys will wonder what we're getting up to." The look in his eye suggested he already had several ideas in mind.

My jaw barely didn't drop. Who was this person and what had they done with my awkward roommate, who could hardly admit he wanted to kiss me?

I followed Matt in a daze to the pool hall and likely would have drifted aimlessly off if he hadn't been holding my hand. A part of me wasn't sure if I could handle this completely unreserved version of Matt. Another recognized that this was always who he'd been and was the exact person I'd fallen in love with. Either way, it was proving to be a little unsettling. The entrance rose unexpectedly before us, snapping me out of my fog. The place really looked like a total dive, and contrary to what he'd said our first visit, the inside *did not* look better.

"It's about time," Lucas said, straightening up from his shot as we joined them at a table. Sam looked over and waved in greeting.

"Sorry," Matt said as he grabbed two cue sticks. He passed me one and leaned on his own.

"Would someone please explain to me how people who can shadow walk can always be late?" Lucas asked aloud as Sam leaned down to take his own shot. Matt slid me a sidelong look. I didn't even want to think about what sort of disaster would result if he'd shadowed us here.

"Shadowing isn't always the best idea," Matt replied.

"Just because you have powers doesn't mean you should use them for everything," I added.

"Speak for yourself." Sam passed Lucas the cue ball, and suddenly, there were two Lucases. The real Lucas leaned down to line up his next shot. As he was working on getting his angle just right, other Lucas slid the cue stick up his leg. Original Lucas scratched. Matt snickered, and Lucas spun around to face himself.

"Cut it out, Sam. How many times have I told you? It's creepy to play with myself." It wasn't until the rest of us erupted in laughter that he realized what he'd said. He groaned and rolled his eyes, then promptly smacked Sam back to normal. Perhaps Matt *hadn't* been exaggerating when he said how people messed with each other when playing.

"Don't be such a sore loser," Sam poked, once more, his usual blond self.

Lucas soured. "The only reason I'm losing is because you're cheating."

"I am not."

"You are too."

"Alright, alright, either break it up or get a room," Matt interjected. They both rounded on him, and I looked at him in total amazement. "What? Look, how about we mix this up a bit? Which one of you is the better player?"

The question had the effect of tossing a match into petrol. Eventually, after some very loud quibbling, they resorted to flipping a coin.

"Ha!" Sam declared at winning the toss. "What's my prize?" he asked Matt.

"You're on Alex's team."

"What?" Sam and I said together.

Matt shrugged and bumped my shoulder. "You'll be fine. Just remember what I showed you." There was nothing innocent about the smile he gave me.

"Surely you don't mean *everything*," I fired right back. Two could play this game.

"You're welcome to remember that too, but I don't think Sam will appreciate you being so distracted," he responded with a sly grin. Sam immediately began having a coughing fit, and I thought Lucas was going to pass out from laughter. The devil.

"Right, so the game," Lucas finally managed. He set the table and stepped aside so Sam could break.

It wasn't bad, but I was definitely getting a better understanding of just how good at this Matt was. Luckily, I still recalled enough of the actual instruction from last time that I wasn't totally deplorable. I even sank a few shots. Once the game was truly under way, the shenanigans resumed. Matt leaned down to take his next shot. I was appreciating the view of him completely laid out on the table when he suddenly jerked his head and snatched his hand up to his ear. His intended shot went wide, and he ended up sinking one of ours instead.

"The hell, Sam! No spells, that's cheating."

"It's only cheating if you can prove it was one of us," Sam responded, gesturing between us. Matt barely spared me a look before returning to glare at Sam. I was a little offended that he didn't think it could have been me. We'll just have to see about that. Sam then confidently walked up to take his turn. I watched as Matt stepped forward, no doubt to return the favor, only to have Lucas hold him back. They smiled at each other, and Lucas stepped closer until he was almost right beside Sam. From my angle, I couldn't quite make out what he was doing, but judging by the feral grin, it was nothing good. Sam was just about to take his shot when he let out a yelp. The ball bounced off the table and Matt had to run after it as it continued to roll halfway across the room, disturbing several other patrons. Matt sat the cue ball back on the table, still laughing.

"What was that?" I asked.

"Oh, we forgot to mention. Best not to get on Lucas's bad side. Things can get hairy," Matt offered.

I looked at Sam in the hope of some clarification. "Yep, he's a real howler when he gets mad," he teased.

"Would the two of you knock it off with the cheesy puns?" Lucas griped.

"What are you guys even talking about?" I asked.

"I guess it's time we fessed up. So, Lucas is a werewolf and I'm a witch. My specialty is illusions if you hadn't already figured that part out," Sam added. Lucas glanced up from his unhindered shot to give me a smile with a few too many teeth.

A tad surprised I hadn't picked up on all the wolf puns, I shifted the shadow nearest Lucas to slide down the neck of his shirt. He squirmed wildly and sank the eight ball by mistake. Matt's jaw dropped in total disbelief.

"You've got to be kidding me! Seriously, Lucas? The hell was that about?"

"How should I know? Ask those two," he said, still trying to rid himself of the shadow that had long since dissipated.

"Don't look at me." Sam held up his hands and Matt's shocked gaze turned to me.

I shrugged. "What? I'm just playing the way I was taught."

Lucas smacked the table. "I call do-over."

"It doesn't work that way," Sam argued.

"House rules. We can call a do-over if everyone agrees," Lucas insisted. "I demand a vote."

Sam rolled his eyes. "Fine. What do you say Alex?"

"Doesn't matter to me."

"There, you have your bloody do-over. Put the ball back, but your turn is forfeit."

"Sold," Lucas said as he carefully replaced the eight ball roughly where it had been. I shook my head. These guys were a mess. "Okay, newbie, you're up."

Now that it was obvious what sort of game we were playing, I was not looking forward to my turn. My mind rebelliously kept flashing back to the last time I'd played pool with Matt. Consequently, I remembered quite a bit that had nothing to do with pool, resulting in the very distraction Matt had alluded to before. Damn him. I lined up my shot and took my time, making sure I had the form right. In a brief moment of hope, I believed I might actually make it through the turn with no one messing with me. Sadly, hope was a fickle mistress. I smelled Matt before I felt his hand on the back of my leg. But I was determined not to lose focus. I would not mess up this shot. By some miracle, I was doing halfway decent and I wanted to keep it that way. As I prepared to take the shot, his hand drifted towards my inner thigh. *Focus, Alexi.* Suddenly, his hand shifted *much* higher and I let out a squeak of indignation. Unfortunately, the cue was already in motion and there was no way to adjust the very wrong course it was now on. The stick skittered off the top of the ball and Sam gave his own indignant squawk.

"Foul play."

"You're just saying that because we got a do-over," Lucas countered.

"That's not even fair. Alex barely has a poker face, let alone the experience to stand up to—" He waved wildly at Matt, who didn't look the least bit ashamed.

"Don't be deceived. Alex has an excellent poker face," Matt calmly defended me.

I glanced at him. "What is that supposed to mean?"

"I'm just saying you're not a guileless as you're leading them to believe."

"That's ridiculous. I would never," I responded with a crooked grin.

"I'm done. Matt, it's your shot. I'm going to get a drink. Anyone want anything?" Sam asked as he walked backwards towards the bar. Matt and I declined, while Lucas requested a refill.

Matt assessed the table before choosing his intended target. He seemed to be trying to determine the best angle to take when he glanced up. Whatever he saw made him do a double take. The angle was all wrong and, while I was pretty sure he hit the right ball, it knocked into the eight ball on its skewed path. Lucas watched in horror as the black ball slowly rolled towards a side pocket, hesitated at the cusp, then fell in.

"You have *got* to be kidding me," Lucas cried.

Matt didn't seem to notice. He was still riveted on whatever had caught his attention. "What the fuck is Alex doing?" he asked, his voice dangerously low.

"I'm standing here watching you lose like a pro. What the hell do you think I'm doing?" I quipped. Matt and Lucas both looked back at me, then across the bar.

"Oh shit," Lucas said.

"What?" I still couldn't figure out what they were looking at.

"I'm going to fucking murder him," Matt hissed as he threw his cue on the table.

"Murder who? Why?"

They both ignored me. "What the hell does he think he's doing?" Matt asked again.

"I'm pretty sure he's using your boyfriend to pick up chicks," Lucas supplied, shaking his head. I reevaluated Matt's obvious anger and the direction of his murderous rage. Then I saw him—or more appropriately, I saw me—and the two girls from the first time I'd been here. I was blatantly flirting with them. Oh fuck.

"Matt," I cautioned. "Take a deep breath."

He looked at me and stuttered, unable to put words in anything resembling a coherent sentence.

I glanced back up in time to see me gesture towards our group. This had disaster written all over it. The girls giggled and turned back to the bar. I gave a small sigh of relief that he wasn't escorting them over. I had no idea how we would explain *two* of me. Another glance at Matt said I wouldn't have one for long. Sam then began walking back, looking exceptionally smug and more like himself. He made it all the way to the table before he realized we were all staring at him. He froze mid-step and glanced around at the accusatory glares.

"Uh, hey guys. What's up? Is it my turn already?" he asked nervously.

Matt made to advance, and I held him back, having caught sight of the girls now making their way over. Sam caught the move and quickly scrambled out of the line of fire. Matt barely wiped the scowl off of his face before they stopped in front of us. They both smiled and waved at me. For lack of any better ideas ideas, I did the same. I felt Matt tense, but it couldn't be helped. Hopefully, Sam hadn't promised anything too outrageous.

"Are you sure it's alright if we join you and your friends?" the girl with blond hair even paler than Sam's asked.

I looked at Matt and sent up a silent prayer that he wasn't scowling. Much to my surprise, he was the picture of confident ease. I quickly checked my own facial expression. The girls gave each other an anxious look. When Matt didn't answer right away, Sam not so discreetly nudged him in the back. I was beginning to think Sam had a death wish. Somehow, Matt refrained from reacting to the obvious prod, aside from finally deigning to speak.

"I don't see why not. The more the merrier, right?" They looked relieved. "My name is Matt, by the way." They gave him a once over that was a little too thorough for my liking. I definitely hadn't imagined that they were hoping for a package deal the last time. Now, thanks to Sam, that hope was alive and kicking. "That there is Lucas, and that dork is Sam," he finished mercilessly. Sam made a strangled sound, but I had zero sympathy for him.

"I'm Taryn," the blonde said, pointing to herself, "and this is Hannah." Hannah gave a small wave and glanced behind us at Sam.

Matt nodded at the information and gestured at me. "I'm assuming, of course, you've already met my boyfriend, Alexi," he added, cool as a cucumber. Both of their faces fell. They definitely hadn't expected that when they made their way over.

Lucas took in the situation, glancing between those gathered as if waiting for all hell to break loose. Finally, he asked in an obvious attempt to break the ice, "So you ladies play?" Their focus shifted immediately to the less hostile member of the group. The second their attention was on Lucas, Matt spun around and smacked Sam.

"What the hell is wrong with you? You can't pick up girls on your own, so you hijack *my* boyfriend?" he hissed under his breath.

"Ow. What? I thought you'd be more upset if I used you. Besides, you did it the last time," Sam tried to defend himself.

"Wait a minute. Last time?" I interjected. "What's he talking about?"

Matt waved it off. "That was different."

"How so?" Sam persisted.

"Yeah, how so?" I mimicked. I'd been exceptionally inebriated at the time, and most of the conversation was a blur, though I had a distinct memory of pink.

"I knew he wouldn't come back with anyone."

Sam blanched and finally had the decency to look guilty.

"Now get your ass over there and save Lucas before he puts both feet in his mouth."

Sam quickly scurried to obey, if only to get out of range of Matt's wrath. A glance showed the girls were sufficiently amused by their bait-and-switch partners. I shook my head and followed Matt over to the stool he'd acquired.

"Did you really put me up as bait last time?" I asked, in an attempt to divert his anger.

He gave a half smile. "We've already talked about this." He spun me around so that I could lean my back against him.

"That doesn't make it better," I prodded. "What would you have done if I'd been more successful or if they'd been more interested in you?"

He chuckled. "I think I've made it pretty clear by this point that I have no intention of sharing." His thumbs slipped beneath the hem of my shirt and began rubbing the small of my back.

I sighed into the intimate gesture. "You know what I think?"

"Hmm?" he responded as he ran his nose along the back of my neck.

"I think you're a bit possessive."

"Your point?"

"Just an observation." He placed a small kiss at the nape of my neck and the heat of his breath sent a shiver through me. I felt him smile and the next kiss was adventurous enough that I had to work to school my features.

"You taste amazing," he whispered in my ear. I shuddered as he followed the statement by tasting my skin. "All of you."

"Matthew." I straightened and turned to face him. He flashed me a wicked smile. Unbelievably, his eyes were perfectly blue, without so much as a hint of black. The damn things should have been midnight after a heated statement like that.

"What's going on over there?" Lucas asked while Hannah took her shot.

"Nothing," Matt answered, once more looking like an innocent angel.

I scowled at him. These last few days proved that Matt was about as far from innocent or angelic as it was possible to get. One thing was for certain: I needed a minute to cool down. I politely excused myself. In the men's room, I stared at myself in the mirror and wondered when our cat-and-mouse dynamic had shifted. *Probably about the time that Matt owned up to actually being in love with you,* I helpfully answered myself. *This will never do. It doesn't matter how much more open he is now, he's still Matt, and I still have his number.*

When I returned, it was like I'd lost again before I could even start. I could hardly believe my eyes. Matt was *dancing.* He smiled and laughed as he spun, first Taryn and then Hannah, much to their delight. It was clear he was trying to get the others to join, but they were pointedly refusing. Despite their earlier disappointment, the two girls seemed to have accepted the newly corrected perception with an impressive amount of ease. Even they were trying to coax the others to join them as they grooved along to the music. Though I doubted this latest turn of events was diminishing their belief that they still might walk away with both of us. I walked up and crossed my arms while I waited for Matt to notice I was there. He eventually spun far enough around that he caught sight of me. His smile stretched from ear-to-ear, and I could feel mine trying to surface. I carefully schooled my face. I loved seeing him happy and carefree, but I was on a mission.

"Come on. Don't tell me you're not going to join either," he teased.

I raised an eyebrow. "I thought you said you couldn't dance. You seem to be doing just fine to me." I swept my eyes over him, none too subtly.

He laughed self-consciously and danced closer. "I said I couldn't dance ballroom. Besides, I wouldn't exactly call me flailing about like a bobolink that's lost its tail dancing." I had absolutely no idea what on earth a bobolink was, but I didn't think he was doing all that bad.

"Didn't you say something about wanting me to tutor you in ballroom?"

He hesitated a fraction of a second.

That was all I needed. I used shadow to push him towards me and grabbed his hand. Before he knew it, I guided him through the box step, a ball change, a heel turn, and several spins before landing him in a dip. His eyes were wide with alarm as he stared back at me from his precarious position. A chorus of appreciative "Oohs" surrounded us. He gave a nervous swallow. Without warning, I spun him back up and caught him with a kiss. The "Oohs" turned to whoops. When I pulled back, he looked totally shell-shocked, his face a wonderful shade of pink and his eyes completely black.

That's more like it.

Chapter 22

Q&A

Matt

I quickly concluded that going out with Alex was dangerous. Beside the fact that now that I had no qualms about who knew that we were together, he'd made it clear that if I got out of hand, he'd very decisively set me down. Not that I minded. That was fun on its own.

I smiled up at the ceiling. My whole life, I'd never known it was possible to be this happy. Being in love with Alex was like getting to have my cake and eat it too—but like one of those really *fancy* cakes. He was the best friend I'd ever had. He was funny, understanding, attractive, and phenomenal in the sack. He was too good to be true, is what he was. I couldn't help but wonder when the other shoe would drop. Good things like this just didn't happen to me. Eventually, the universe would realize its error and that would be the end of everything.

I tried to shake off the negative thoughts. It was easy enough to do, considering the scent of lavender still surrounded me. I pulled the comforter over my head to make it more complete. Despite the warm cocoon of contentment, my mind rebelliously refused to be silenced. There was still the whole Warde issue. Vera had yet to say anything more past the absolutely nothing we'd covered at our one and only meeting. The covers flew back down. Thomas wouldn't give up. I knew that just like I knew that neither would I. He'd threatened something I held more dear than life itself and I would never forgive him for that.

"What are you scowling about?" Alex asked, flopping onto the bed practically on top of me.

I let out an oof. "Nothing."

"Liar."

I looked at him. His green eyes danced with humor, but there was an edge to them. I let out a sigh. "I'm just tired of waiting to hear from Vera. I want to know what's going on. Haven't I earned the right to be kept in the loop?"

Alex's sigh was as heavy as mine. I knew he didn't enjoy hearing about what had happened, but he'd asked, and there was no sense in lying about it. We'd already established that I sucked at lying to his face, anyway.

"I wish you could move past this," he said softly. He cut me off before I could do more than open my mouth. "I know you can't, but that doesn't change that I wish you would. Why can't you simply appreciate where we are now and enjoy our time together?"

"I *do* enjoy our time together." I sat up. "I love our time together." He smiled, and I went on before he could interrupt. "I'm just afraid it won't last. That something will happen." He reached up to cup my face and I leaned into the caress. I didn't know what I would do if I lost him again.

"Matt, together we can handle anything thrown at us. Try to remember that." He punctuated the statement with a kiss. It was small, but I caught him before he could pull away and deepened it. Colors burst to life in fireworks of sensation. The familiar burn grew until flames were actively licking up my insides. I could kiss him forever. Reluctantly, I let him go. He looked back at me, shaking his head, his eyes still clouded with heat. "I'm serious. One of these days you really are going to kiss me stupid."

I gave him a lopsided grin. "Pretty sure I already have... a couple of times."

He gave me a look and shifted to a better sitting position. "Anyway... Are you planning on staying in bed all day or are you actually going to get dressed and be a productive member of society?" It wasn't until he mentioned getting dressed that I realized he already was. By the looks of it, he was planning on actually going somewhere other than the living room.

"Where are you off to?"

"In case you've forgotten, school is due to start back up soon. I'm going to go out and get some supplies for the new semester. I was going to ask if you wanted to join, but I suspect I already know the answer."

I made a face. It didn't escape my notice that we were both pointedly ignoring the fact that I hadn't taken most of my finals. There was no telling if I was even still enrolled.

"That's what I thought. Fine, you stay here and be a laze-about and I'll get extra supplies for you." He stood and straightened his outfit.

"You're the best," I said, enjoying the view. He really was a work of art. I recalled the only semi-full body sketch I had of him. At the time, it had been almost pure extrapolation. I could do better.

"I know. Oh, there's still some breakfast in the kitchen, if you're hungry."

At the mention of food, I scrambled out of the bed and was pulling on pants by the time I heard him laughing. "What's so funny?"

"I figured that would motivate you. Maybe I should've led with that."

I frowned and stopped my flurried movements.

He chuckled and walked up to me, then snagged my belt loop and dragged me closer. "I'm not criticizing. Honestly, it's comforting to know that you're eating again." He snagged a quick kiss before adding in a low voice, "You're looking more like yourself." Familiar heat curled inside of me. My eyes must have betrayed me, because he released me and stepped away. "I'll be back in a few hours. Try not to get into too much trouble while I'm gone," he finished with a wink.

"Yeah, yeah," I said, then he made his way out of the room. The door closed behind him and I instantly regretted not stealing another kiss. I raced into the living room, but he was already gone.

I pondered what to do while I devoured the leftovers in the kitchen, which amounted to a full meal. Oatmeal wasn't really my favorite, but it was my own fault for over-sleeping. I considered the options available to me. I could read. Nah. Play a game. I glanced at the neglected console. It brought back memories that just made me wish I had gone with Alex instead of being a bum. Hmm, what else? Could always draw. But if I was going to sketch Alex like I wanted to, I'd need him here. Still at a loss, I cleaned the dishes. I could always wander around the campus. That was probably the least appealing of the options. Then my gaze landed on a small piece of paper lying forgotten on the counter. It was the note with the directions on how to get to the manor. Could always get some answers. I immediately shoved the paper in a pocket and finished getting dressed.

Rather than shadow directly to Vera's office, I opted to walk, if only to take up more time. The thought of the college being locked or under a boundary spell only vaguely crossed my mind.. Neither really concerned me. The air was beyond cold and I was seriously debating shadowing back to the dorm to add a few more layers when Mysterio College came into view. I quickened my steps. Part of me hoped she was in her office, but judging by the lack of bodies on campus, that seemed unlikely. To my amazement, the doors were neither locked nor warded. Admittedly, I was a little disappointed at the lack of challenge, but shrugged it off.

Inside, it was substantially warmer. I rubbed my hands together and wondered if Jeffrey had included some decent gloves in that comprehensive wardrobe he'd put together. How it could be so damn cold and not even snow was beyond me. At last, I made it to the classroom. Unsurprisingly, it was vacant. Sadly, so was Vera's office. Unlike the last time, the door was locked, but still no barrier. I shook my head as I shadowed through. Maybe she wasn't worried because the portal wasn't here anymore. That would really suck.

I sent out my essence, searching for the void Alex had so ingeniously picked up on before. As I explored the area, it occurred to me that was why he'd never tripped a wire. Crafty bastard played me, and I couldn't be more proud. The tendrils of my essence suddenly fell into nothingness. I let out a triumphant whoop and walked up to the portal. "*In Tenebras.*" The words felt strange in my mouth and weren't nearly as eloquent as when Alex had said them, but they worked. It wasn't until I stepped through the inky door that it even occurred to me to check for a trip wire. No help for it now.

As I followed the same dimly illuminated path as before, I couldn't help but wonder where the other doors led. I resisted the urge to explore, more determined to get answers than to satisfy a vague curiosity. No sooner than I stepped into the massive library, I felt another demon materialize out of the shadows. Definitely needed to remember to check for trip wires from now on.

"What are you doing here?" Gabriel asked as he stepped into the light, his uncanny resemblance to Alex messing with my head.

"I'm looking for Vera."

"Why?" he asked, sounding bored, though I detected a hint of defensiveness.

"Because I'm tired of waiting around to find out what's going on. I've earned my stripes, now I want answers." It was getting difficult to maintain my righteous stance in the face of his blatant apathy. He raised a speculative eyebrow at the demand. The room became deadly quiet. He continued to stare at me while I waited to see what would happen. Never had I felt so picked apart. I swallowed involuntarily. At last, he spoke, and I could have sagged with relief.

"Have a seat. I can answer your questions."

I eyed the chair he indicated, my relief vanishing. I'd come here for Vera, not him.

"Do you want to know or not?" he asked, taking a seat across from the one meant for me. This felt like a bad idea, but I needed to know. Reluctantly, I joined him.

"Why are you helping me?" I asked, not trusting this.

"You mean, aside from the fact that you just broke into my wife's house?" I could feel my embarrassment creeping up my face. It hadn't even occurred to me what this would look like. "Aside from that, I am also a teacher. Helping is kind of what I do."

"You don't exactly strike me as the helpful-type." Or the teacher-type, I mentally added.

"I helped you, did I not?" He had a point there. "You're welcome, by the way." My flush deepened, and he chuckled. It was a rich sound that started low and got louder. "You and Vera are remarkably similar. I can't help but wonder if it is a generational thing or perhaps it is the unprecedented way you two have become so strong. Of course, it's entirely possible I've just had enough time to mellow."

"Just how old are you, anyway?" I blurted, instantly wishing I could take back the impertinent question. Something told me that the way I interacted would Vera would not fly with this demon. I held my breath, waiting for the rebuke.

He sat back, giving up his speculation. "I'm not sure how well you are in history, but, to be brief, I was born in Mesopotamia." For a fraction of a second, my mind completely stalled out. He wasn't serious. History was by far not my best subject before or after Arminius, but even *I* knew that was an unbelievably long time ago.

My mouth fell open. "But wasn't that... I mean... didn't they..."

"Yes, you are thinking of the right civilization. It really is a shame they never finished the Tower of Babel," he mused to himself.

There was just no way. He didn't look a day over forty. And Vera taught *him* tricks? I didn't believe that for a second.

"I can clearly see that you're not handling this very well. What do you say we move on to why you came here? Uninvited, I might add."

"Um... I want to know what's going on?"

"So you said. Understandable really. After all, they did kidnap and torture your lover. I can certainly empathize with the desire to seek retribution." I looked up at him, surprised. "What part got your attention? The lover comment or that I'm capable of empathy?"

"Did something happen to Vera?" It was a stupid question. Obviously, something *had* given her reaction that night.

He nodded his head. "They stole her from the group in the middle of a mission. It took me months to find her."

I blanched. No wonder she'd freaked when she saw the marks.

"I am pleased, however, to see that you have gotten over referring to Alexi as your lover. I told you he would be fine." Was he really pulling an "I told you so"? "Back to what is going on. Admittedly, we aren't having much success. Of course, now we have a better idea of what likely happened to the other recruits that vanished before we could get to them." I vaguely recalled Vera mentioning something along those lines eons ago.

"Are you suggesting that the Order of Light was abducting people before class even started?" This whole thing was so much bigger than I had imagined.

"You know the Warde mission statement." He gave me a strange look. I didn't like to think I fell in that category. Yes, I'd always wanted to know who I was, but not this, not them. "However, I doubt that those poor souls were nearly as fortunate as Alexi."

Rage swept through me. "There was nothing *lucky* about what happened to Alex."

He failed to acknowledge my outcry. "Strange that you still insist on calling him Alex. I wonder why that is," he mused.

I bristled. "Alex—Alexi," I corrected myself, "endured unspeakable horrors. Tell me, what's lucky about that?"

"He's alive."

That gave me pause. "Just how many recruits went missing?"

His face darkened. "Too many. If we had known that Thomas and Douglas were involved, we would not have assumed it was cold feet. I should have listened to her when she said it didn't feel right. Knowing what we know now, it is a good thing she picked you up early. You were relatively safe in the human system, but the moment you set foot in Superno House, red flags would have popped up. Most people, even in the supernatural community, can't recognize a manifesting Shadow Demon. But the Order of Light would have recognized the signs right away. Is it true that you took on all four by yourself?"

My head spun with the horrific information. I nodded numbly, noting the impressed glint in his eye. Never in all my years would I have viewed those houses as anything other than hell-holes. To think they were keeping me safe was mind-boggling.

Without warning, he shifted the conversation back to its original track. "Regrettably, the pair seem to have vanished once again. Now, before you accuse us of not looking hard enough, know that I am *particularly* motivated to find them. The last time I was this close, I had to choose between saving my other half or exacting vengeance. Much like your own decision, it was an easy one to make." The hardness in his eyes suggested that when he finally got his hands on them, they would wish they were already dead.

"What about the others? His lackeys," I added for clarity. I already knew what he thought had happened to the demons Vera hadn't found. It was awful.

Though having been a person more often forgotten than not, I couldn't help but think someone should still look. Just in case.

"Gone without a trace. Though I do not believe they have fled the school. Not yet anyway. They are here somewhere and we will find them. I also believe Thomas is still lurking about. There is something here he still wants very much."

I squirmed in my seat beneath his hard, penetrating stare. It was difficult to determine if he was sizing me up to put me on a battlefield or to use me as bait. Suddenly, Vera's voice cut through the mounting tension.

"What the hell is going on?" I looked up to see her marching towards us. She stopped at the end of the table with her hands on her hips, her eyes filled with fire as she waited impatiently for an explanation.

"Young Matthew here was simply stopping by to see you. He had some questions, though I think I have answered most of them," Gabriel supplied more calmly than I felt.

"Is that so? And what sorts of questions did you have, Matt?" she asked, turning her fiery gaze on me. The nerve to be mad at me when she was the one intentionally keeping me in the dark. She should know better than anyone how wrong that was. I was a breath away from giving her a piece of my mind when Gabriel once again interjected.

"He was inquiring about some abilities he used the other day. You were right, my love, he is quite the natural, much like yourself." She narrowed her eyes at him. My gaze darted between the two of them. Could she tell he was lying? Despite the obvious animosity she was sporting, Gabriel remained the essence of calm.

"I think it's time you went back to the campus, Matt. Don't you?" Her gaze swiveled around and I quickly found my feet. If Gabriel didn't want her to know what we'd been talking about, that was his business, and I had no desire to stick around to see it blow up in his face.

"Alex is probably back by now anyway," I said, although I didn't know how long had passed since I'd left. She let me leave without another word and I could bet good money that the door got sealed behind me. I stared back at the portal once I reemerged in her office, tempted to test my theory, then caught sight of a clock. Shit, Alex had likely been back for hours. Without further ado, I shadowed back to the dorm. Sure enough, he was sitting on the couch organizing supplies.

"There you are," he said from where he was sitting on the couch, organizing supplies.

"Sorry, I lost track of time." That was an understatement. I was still struggling to make sense of half of what Gabriel had told me.

"What did you get up to?" The question was innocent enough, but it held a definitive undercurrent.

"I went to go talk to Vera. She wasn't in her office, though."

"And you got lost on the way back?" he teased.

"No, I took the portal to the manor to look for her there," I said, putting the slip on the table. His mouth fell open as shock exploded across his face. "She wasn't there either, or at least, not when I got there. So, I ended up talking with Gabriel."

"You what!"

I blanched in the face of his fury. "W-what?" It had been a while since I'd heard him shout.

"You mean to tell me you simply let yourself into one of the most heavily guarded houses *in the world* and then casually sat around sipping tea with Gabriel Xiander the entire afternoon?" There were a few parts of that question that should have given me pause, but they didn't seem to be the actual issue.

"Well, yeah. I had questions, and he was willing to answer them. Insisted on it, in fact. And we didn't have tea." This latest information didn't seem to help my case.

"What sorts of questions would you have for him that you couldn't ask me?" His eyes took on a dark cast and suddenly his anger made more sense.

"I don't know what you think went on, but all we did was sit at a table and talk."

"For an entire afternoon?" he pressed, his disbelief palpable.

"Again, I wanted to talk to Vera. She wasn't there. *He* was." This didn't seem to be getting me anywhere. It was almost as if...

"That's not an excuse."

"Alex, are you jealous?"

"What? No," he replied a little too quickly.

"Nothing happened. Besides, Vera eventually showed up and sent me home anyway, otherwise I'd probably still be there." Too late, I realized that was the wrong thing to say. Anger flashed through his eyes and he turned away to march into his room. "Alex, wait, that's not... Come on, don't be like this," I called as I chased after him. I eventually caught him in the middle of his room, but he refused to look at me. I didn't understand what this was about. There was no reason for him to feel threatened like this. Gabriel may look a bit like him, but past that, they were nothing alike. "Alex, please," I said, shaking him.

He intentionally kept his gaze averted.

"I love you."

He finally glanced at me out of the corner of his eye. Success.

"I love you, Alex."

He blinked.

"What do you say you tell me about your adventures in town? Were you able to find everything you were looking for?" It was clear he recognized the obvious attempt at distraction, but he allowed it and walked back into the living room. I let out a relieved breath and followed him, sending up a silent prayer that this would not become "a thing". Unfortunately, I feared it was too late for that.

Chapter 23
Future Plans

Alexi

I wasn't sure if our meeting with Vera and Gabriel accomplished anything beyond getting us all on the same page. Aside from Matt gallivanting off on his own to get answers, there'd been no communication at all. Part of me hoped the reason they hadn't reached out was because they were going to handle it themselves; we were just students after all.

I looked over at Matt sketching on the couch. Life should never have been this complicated, and he deserved some peace after what he'd been through the last few months. He wouldn't see it that way of course. He'd want to be involved right until the end, especially after what they'd done to me. I still couldn't believe he hadn't killed any of them when he'd gone to confront them. But I worried now he knew who was mostly responsible for my injuries he wouldn't stop until Douglas was dead. If I wanted to make sure he didn't, I'd have to go with him. He wasn't going to like that.

"You're thinking very loudly over there," his voice drifted back.

I shook my head and walked over to join him and his weird sixth sense for whenever I was thinking about him. "What are you working on?" I asked, taking a seat beside him.

He shrugged.

"Fine, don't tell me." He laughed under his breath and tilted the page so I could see. To my surprise, it was little Lelana. There were three images in total on the page. One was her sitting on my lap trying to look very behaved, another was her looking up at Matt waiting for him to give her permission to crawl into his, while the last was just of me looking at him. She'd been quite the adorable surprise. I hadn't expected Matt to pick her up or let her sit on his lap. Actually, I had no idea how he felt about kids at all.

"You're doing it again," he said as he added texture to Lelana's hair with soft scratches of his pencil. "I didn't know Vera had a kid. Did you?" He spared me a quick glance.

"I feel like I did, but confess I was still a little surprised. She's sweet."

He looked at me out of the corner of his eye. "What gives with volunteering us for babysitting duty, by the way?"

"What? I like kids."

"I could tell," he replied with a smirk.

"Shut up." I playfully shoved him. He gave me a scandalized look when the pencil almost made several extra marks across the page. "It really is amazing how you can do all of that from memory."

He shrugged. "It's not as much fun as a living model." He closed the book and gave me a pensive expression. "You should let me draw you sometime." he leaned forward to place the book safely on the table with the assortment of pencils, then caught me with an unexpected kiss.

I chuckled. "Don't you draw me enough?" He deepened the kiss and his hands slid beneath my shirt. I didn't resist as he pulled it up.

"That isn't the kind of drawing I had in mind." The low, sultry statement sent heat flooding through me.

My face burned. "Matt."

"You really do have beautiful skin, Alex." He trailed his fingers down my back as if to emphasize his point. "One of these days I'm going to trace every last inch of you," he whispered between kisses along my neck and shoulder. I shivered, and he returned to my mouth, where the heat of the kiss effectively banished any thought of cold. "Alexi." My breath caught. His fire was all-consuming, and I so loved how it burned. There was a brief sensation of him touching me everywhere, then we rematerialized on the bed. He fell back into the pillows, taking me with him.

I laughed, working to remove his clothes. "You're such a devil."

"I've been called worse." He raised his hips to aid in my endeavor. The moment he was free, he pulled me back down. A moan escaped as he pressed hard against me. I slid an arm under him and rolled us. He instantly set to work liberating me as well, then made to roll us back. I resisted, and he looked down at me curiously.

"Oh no, you started this, you can finish it."

He gave me that devil's grin of his, then slid his hand up my leg to grip my thigh and pulled me closer. "What do you want, Alex?"

"Whatever you'll give me," I replied, breathless with anticipation.

"Don't I always give you everything?"

I had a sneaking suspicion my eyes were black, judging by the heated look he was giving me. I wanted to respond with an equally quippy remark, but the snap of the lid on the bottle of lube distracted me. By the time I got my wits back about me, he'd shimmied between my legs. I groaned as he took his sweet time, slowly sucking me down until he'd buried his nose in my groin. I had just enough time to register his pleased hum before he popped back off to do it all over again. He nuzzled my bent legs farther apart. A hiss escaped between my teeth as a lubed finger tapped at my entrance and electricity shot up my spine. "I shouldn't need to remind you it's been a little while since I bottomed," I said through panted breaths.

He released my cock after a firm suck on the head and angled up to face me. "No, you don't," he said before snaring me in a kiss. Then his finger breached the tight ring of muscle.

I gasped at the simultaneous burn and buzz of pleasure. "Just... you know, take it easy."

"I would never hurt you, Alexi." He stared into my eyes, the crystalline blue holding me captive as he gently thrust his finger in and out. I held his gaze until he added more lube and another finger, then squeezed my eyes shut as he curled them, rubbing my prostate and stealing my breath.

"Night, Matt, I don't know how long I'll actually last at this rate." Already I could feel the imminent release building at the base of my spine and tightening my balls.

Abruptly, his fingers vanished, as did my pending orgasm. "Turn over. I want to try something."

Curious where this was going and hoping it involved at least his fingers returning if not his cock, I quickly shifted so I was on my hands and knees. At his soft sigh, I glanced over my shoulder. "What?"

"I ever tell you you have a beautiful ass?" He softly caressed the globes as he looked at them with a reverence that had my face heating.

"Can't say you have."

He snorted. "Well, you do. Eventually I'll sketch it properly, but right now..." He trailed off, and I released a long moan as his fingers glided back inside. Sadly, they didn't stay long. In short order, they were gone and the blunt head of his cock pressed against my hole.

The familiar burn of being stretched melded into waves of pleasure pulsing up my spine. I squirmed with impatience, desperate for him to move, but he continued his agonizingly unhurried pace. "Matt," I groaned. "You're killing me, love."

"So impatient," he teased, though his voice was strained. "I told you, I have an idea."

I was a breath away from telling him I'd die by the time he got around to it when he wrapped an arm around my torso and pulled me up so that my back was flush against his chest. I'd only thought he'd been fully seated before. The change of angle helped him slide even deeper. I moaned, sinking onto him, and reached for my aching cock, though I wasn't sure whether it was to stave off the pending explosion or encourage it. Centimeters from my destination, Matt grabbed my wrist and pulled it away. I let out an undignified whine.

"That can go right here." He placed the captive hand on the back of his neck, then took my other one and set it on his thigh. Once he had me positioned the way he wanted, he lightly ran his hands down my torso while he lavished open-mouthed kisses along my neck and shoulders. I reflexively dug my fingers into his thigh, pulling him even deeper, and gasped at the overwhelming fullness. His hands continued their leisurely exploration, noticeably ignoring my throbbing cock, until they eventually settled on my hips. "I love you so much," he whispered in my ear as he shifted his hips back and thrust back inside me in one smooth motion.

I moaned and dropped my head onto his shoulder. My one hand shifted higher to tangle in his hair while I used my other to encourage him. Pleasure bordered on pain with each roll of his hips, bringing me that much closer to release. But despite my needy moans, he continued to lazily thrust in and out as if we had all the time in the world. I moved my hips in counterpoint to his thrusts, driving down on him until he was groaning every bit as loudly as I was, but my orgasm still hovered just out of reach. "Matt, *please...*"

He finally took mercy and wrapped a hand around my neglected cock. The sudden stimulus had me arching into him so hard I nearly fell forward. Matt's firm grip on my hip kept me in place. He quickened his pace, matching his strokes with the rhythm. My movements faltered, and I used my hold on his hair to bring him in for an awkward kiss. We panted into each other, our breath mingling, as he continued to drive in and out with increasing speed. He adjusted his grip on my leaking cock and twisted his wrist.

My release ripped through me. I jerked against him while he milked me dry and kept pounding my ass. After several more thrusts, his grip on my hip tightened, and he stiffened as warmth pulsed inside of me. I dug my nails into his ass as wave after wave of spine-tingling pleasure washed over me. Whatever coherency I laid claim to slid into addled ecstasy. I scarcely even noticed when he pulled out beyond the slight sting and sudden emptiness. Nor could I muster more than contented happy sounds as he cleaned us up.

When I could finally think straight again, our legs were tangled, and I was at a loss for what had happened to the sheets. "What are you thinking?" he asked as he traced a finger along my arm.

I rolled my head to face him, and warmth filled my chest. "You should do that more often."

"And why is that?" he asked with a crooked grin.

"Because you're *very* good at it." He turned a light shade of pink. I chuckled, then scooted closer and stole a kiss. Almost immediately, his arm went around me, pulling me tight against him. "And apparently insatiable."

A wicked smile replaced his blush. "It's a demon's life."

"That it is," I responded, returning for a deeper kiss. His lips met mine with equal enthusiasm, and his grip tightened. This is everything, I thought as we got lost once more to the fiery whirlwind.

By the time the storm died down, I felt thoroughly spent, and he looked it. Also, the sheets had made a reappearance. In the quiet, my mind wandered back to our meeting at the manor. I prayed Vera wouldn't reach back out. If Matt didn't know, then he couldn't insist on joining. Of course, there was no telling how long he'd be willing to put with radio silence.

"Your thoughts look noisy again." I turned to face him and his serene smile. He lightly tapped my forehead. "What's going on up here?"

I couldn't very well tell him my concerns about the possible pending mission or tell him I didn't want him to go. In lieu of that, I chose a different tract. "Would babysitting Lelana really bother you?"

He laughed. "That's what all that noise is about? No, it wouldn't bother me. I just wasn't expecting to be volunteered."

"Have you ever thought about kids? I mean, like kids of your own?" I wasn't sure where the question came from, it just popped out.

He raised an eyebrow and seemed to really consider the query. "Honestly? I never really thought about it. I doubt I'd make a very good father, though. Not with my issues." He rolled his eyes to play it off, but his casual dismissal of his own life experiences made me sad. In truth, I suspected Matt would make an exceptional father *because* of his history.

I rolled to look up at the ceiling. "I've always wanted a family of my own and I know my mom certainly wants grandchildren." His chuckle shook the bed. "I'm serious. She can be very pushy when she wants something." The bed shook again, and I smiled. "For the record, I think you'd make a great dad." His hand slid across my stomach as he snuggled closer.

"I'm not opposed to having kids, if that's what you're driving at." I wrapped an arm around him and he kissed my collar. "It just depends, I guess."

"On what?"

"I've told you, Alex—whatever you want, I'm yours."

My heart stopped beating and my hand froze. "I love you."

"I love you too," he mumbled, burrowing deeper.

Thoughts raced through my head to the point I was sure he'd accuse me of having loud thoughts again. But it couldn't be helped. I couldn't wrap my mind around what he'd so casually put out there. He'd give me kids if I wanted them. All I had to do was ask. I tightened my arm tightened around him and he sighed in his sleep. How he could sleep so easily after dropping that was beyond me.

By the time morning came around, I was still just as flabbergasted and trying to get my thoughts in order when a loud curse came from the kitchen. In a flash, I grabbed some pants off of the floor and shadowed into the other room. "What is it? What's the matter?" I asked as I materialized. He did a double take at seeing my state of dress. Now that I could clearly see that there was no immediate danger, I took the opportunity to put on the pants I was still holding.

"We got a letter." He waved a piece of paper. Unlike the previous missive, this one didn't appear to be spelled. "From the devil-woman herself," he added with extra acidity. I frowned. Despite his supposed continued grudge for her initial treatment of him, I suspected he actually liked Vera quite a bit.

"Well, what's it say? Are they calling us for another meeting?" I mentally crossed my fingers.

"No," he said bitterly, and I let out the breath I was holding. "Plenty else though. Apparently, Thomas has fled the coop—not that I'm surprised—but they don't want me getting involved anymore. And not so much as a mention of the rest of them. Can you fucking believe that?" He shook his head. I could believe it and was glad that she was being an adult about this and choosing to keep Matt out of that world. "But get this, to 'sweeten' the news, she says that I can enroll in spring classes. Apparently, between our research and what Gabriel saw at the house, I have sufficient knowledge to have passed both finals."

"What about your other classes?"

He waved a dismissive hand. "I didn't miss as many of those." I frowned, and he looked up as if realizing what he had said. "Alex, I..."

"Don't, it's done now," I said, trying to shake off the pain. Knowing why he'd avoided me didn't make it hurt any less. I walked closer to him. The guilt was still plainly written on his face. I took a deep breath and let it out, trying to let the traces of resentment go as well. "What else does she say?"

He looked back down at the letter. "That's it. She doesn't say anything else. But there was this as well." He passed me a second piece of paper written in a different hand. "I won't do it if you don't want me to."

Curious, I began reading, but each line was more unbelievable than the last. "Gabriel wants to teach you. Private lessons. And something about a job after school?" I asked incredulously.

"Apparently, I bear a striking resemblance to his last pupil."

"He married his last pupil," I snapped, and he flushed beat red up to his ears. I struggled to reign in the unexpected ire, but it kept slipping through my grip.

"Like I said, I won't do it if you don't want me to."

I closed my eyes. It wasn't fair to punish Matt because Gabriel made me anxious. But still....

"He reminds me of you, you know. That's why. But he's different. He's *not* you and he never will be. I'm yours, Alex, and only yours. Just tell me what you want me to do."

"No." Guilt wriggled uncomfortably in my chest.

He nodded, calmly accepting the verdict, and my guilt increased.

"No, I won't tell you not to do it. You would probably benefit from one-on-one training. Vera obviously has her hands full with the class and whatever she's doing when she's not actually teaching. And... I agree with him," I finished with a resigned huff. "I think you and Vera have a lot in common. If he can handle her, then he can probably handle you, too." I had expected some sort of enthusiasm at hearing that I wouldn't stand in his way. Instead, he searched my face as if doubting my sincerity. To be fair, I did a little as well.

Then he surprised me by saying, "He was very concerned that I hadn't told you I loved you before I left. He's also the reason I didn't kill George. It would have been easy. He was already down and I'd taken the shadow light that he'd used to stab me. I was ready to return the favor when Gabriel stopped me. He said that you wouldn't want that."

My lingering animosity toward Gabriel softened somewhat. I hadn't realized how close he'd come. I stretched my arms out and Matt willingly stepped into the embrace. I tightened my hold around him and he melted against me.

"I love you, Alex." I doubted my heart would ever not skip when he said that.

Chapter 24
Black Rings

Matt

I was less than thrilled at being left out of plans to track down Thomas. That son of a bitch needed to face the consequences of what he'd done to Alex. The thought that he might get away scot-free made my blood boil. Alex, on the other hand, didn't even try to hide his relief that I wouldn't be involved. I could understand where he was coming from, but that didn't make it any easier. Knowing at least would be better than nothing. Maybe if I talked to Vera, she'd be willing to tell me something.

"Did you finish registering for classes yet?" Alex asked, interrupting my thoughts.

"Um, yeah," I replied absently.

"How does it work with the added lessons? Do you still have to take Battle Tactics like the rest of us, or what?" He wouldn't admit it, but I could tell he was bothered at the prospect of me spending time with Gabriel regularly. I didn't know what to do to make him feel better about it, though.

"He said that we'd train while I'd typically be in class, so to register for it, anyway. Apparently, the private training may not be a hundred percent consistent and I'll be expected to go to class like normal otherwise."

"That's thought out. How will you know if the lesson is canceled? More mysteriously appearing letters?" he asked jokingly.

"Actually..." I held up a phone similar to his. "Vera thought it would be a good idea." Probably to prevent me from showing up at her house again, I mentally added.

"That's awesome! How many times would that have come in handy last semester?" he mused aloud while reaching for his own phone.

"I've already put your number in it as well as your mom's. I hope that's okay."

"Of course, that's okay," he said, finally pulling out the device. "What's the number?"

I smiled, "It's in there already, under Matt."

He rolled his eyes. "You've been busy this morning. Wait. You went through my phone?"

I shuffled my feet. I'd done a bit more than that. I cleared my throat. Time to come clean. "I might have also deleted Daniel's number."

For a second, Alex looked really confused, then he flapped a hand. "Good riddance."

I sighed in relief. He wasn't mad. When the name had popped up, I hadn't been able to stop myself. Before I knew it, I was confirming the deletion. By then, it was too late.

"I hope his nose healed crooked," he sneered.

"Alex," I said in disbelief.

"What? Just because I'm not naturally violent doesn't mean I can't hope that your meeting left a lasting impression."

"You're ridiculous." I laughed and turned to go to my room. I really did just need to move the rest of my things over. It was basically just an over-sized closet at this point, anyway.

"Are you sure you can put up with me? Forever is a long time," he teased.

"Yes." I laughed again and stuck out my tongue. Forever wasn't nearly long enough in my book.

"Hey, wait a sec," he said, sounding unusually animated for only one cup of coffee. I turned in time to see him vault effortlessly over the couch. Damn, he was graceful. "I have an idea."

I turned to fully face him. "Oh? And what would that be?"

"Marry me."

Unsure if he was joking or perfectly serious, I chose an ambiguous response. "What, no knee?" I quirked an eyebrow, and he smiled.

"Matt, I will gladly get down on one knee if it means you will say yes."

Sweet Mother of Night, he was serious. I tried to remain calm, but my heart was racing so fast it was a wonder it didn't speed off without me. "Do you even have a ring?" I stalled.

His face fell.

"Didn't think that far did you?"

"I mean, do we really need rings? I can always get one later."

"This kind of thing calls for a ring." He looked at a loss, then I had a thought. "Hold on." I spun to go back into my room.

"But, Matt..." he called after me.

"I'll be right back. Just give me a minute." I ran in and glanced around. Now where did I put that thing? For a split second, I was afraid I'd left it in the house I'd been squatting in, then I spied it beneath several other school books. "There you are," I said, pulling out the shadow grimoire. There was a spell in here somewhere that I'd been wanting to play with more. I found the page and my notes stuck to it. I quickly scanned through the fundamentals of the spell. At its heart, it was fairly basic, but what I wanted to do with it was far from it. *Hopefully, this works.*

I took a deep breath and began pulling apart some of my essence. It was a strange sensation, but not painful, even when it officially separated from me. The small sphere of shadow—of me—easily took the shape of a ring. Now for the hard part. I examined the spell and my scribbles as I considered how to modify the spell. I didn't want to confine the essence, just make it keep its shape and not try to return to me. In a stroke of genius, I switched some notes around and the result was the perfect spell. I cast the spell and instantly the shadow in my hand stop trying to reunite with my body.

"Matt?" Alex called, the slight waver in his voice betraying his nerves.

I shook my head at his impatience and raced back into the living room with the book and my prize. "I've got it."

"Got what?" he asked, taking in the open book I was balancing in one hand.

I quickly set it down on the table. "Give me your hand." He hesitated a moment, then raised his right hand. "No, your other one."

His eyes widened. "In Europe, we wear bands on the right."

"Oh, well, in that case." I snagged his hand before he could drop it.

"Matt, what are you doing?"

I slid the ring on, unable to contain my grin. As I expected, it naturally adjusted to a perfect fit.

"What is this? It feels... different."

"It's me, Alex. Now you'll always be able to find me."

He looked from me to the ring, then held up his hand to inspect it closer. "This is incredible. But what? I mean how? This is really *you*?"

"Yep." Pride surged in my chest. "I used my essence to make it and I found a spell to keep it just like that... forever."

"Forever," he echoed. Then his gaze snapped back to mine, intensity shining from the depths of green. "How do I do it?" I picked the book back up and held it open for him. He immediately began scanning the page. "You made the spell?"

I shrugged, though it was pretty hard not to preen at the sound of his awe. "Adjusted really. It's not hard, and it doesn't hurt."

"What made you think of using your own essence?"

I blinked at him. Wasn't it obvious? "So I can always be with you."

He paused, staring at me, then returned his attention to the makeshift spell. "Okay, I think I've got it. Does it matter where the essence comes from?" I shook my head. "Of course not. Essence is essence." I watched as he repeated the same steps I had. His eyes lit with wonder as he finished the spell. "Incredible. Put the book down."

I closed it and set it safely aside. A more serious expression replaced his look of awe. He caught my eye and my heart skipped. Night, I loved him. I stood there motionless, unsure if I was even breathing.

"Matt, I love you with all that I am. I don't want to spend another minute of any day without you. You truly are my forever. Will you marry me?" I was grinning from ear to ear long before he ever finished.

"One condition." I brought up my right hand, and anxiety flashed across his face. "I get to take your name." He laughed and slid the ring on my finger. It fit perfectly and I suddenly understood his reaction. Having someone else's essence so close was strange and a little exhilarating.

"Done. You can have whatever name you want."

"I want yours."

He smiled harder. "So... is that a yes?"

"That's a hell yes." I pulled him close for a kiss. I couldn't believe it. I'd just agreed to marry Alex. "This calls for a celebration."

"In a minute. I'm kissing my fiancé." He tightened his arms around me and stole another kiss that I felt all the way to my toes and left me breathless. I could *definitely* do this forever. "My mother is going to freak."

An unwelcome punch of anxiety hit me in the gut. "You lied about her liking me?"

"No! She absolutely *adores* you. I just don't think she ever thought I'd settle down." He chuckled and leaned down to touch his lips to mine again. I gladly gave in. A forever of getting lost in Alex sounded just fine to me. "I love you, Matt."

"I love you, Alex."

He smiled against my lips. "Say my name, Matt. My *real* name."

"Alexi," I sighed into another captivating kiss.

"You know, when you say my name, it sounds a lot like when you say you love me."

I thought about that. Funny, it felt a bit like it, too.

"Now what did you have in mind for celebrating?" he asked, loosening his hold.

I'd almost forgotten. I whirled back to the freezer. "What else? Ice cream, of course." His laughter was warm as he wrapped his arms around my middle and propped his head to look over my shoulder. My enthusiasm died a bit at seeing the barren space. How was it possible for us to have run out?

"Looks like we're making a trip. Go get dressed and we'll head out." He smacked my ass, and I moved to comply. "Oh, and Matt," I turned back to look at him, "I expect the rest of your things in our room by the end of the week."

I flashed him a smile and shadowed the rest of the way. *Our room*, I liked the sound of that. Once changed, I met him in the living room, no doubt still smiling like a fool. At least I wasn't the only one. He extended a hand, and I laced our fingers. The door closed silently behind us and we were off. We walked close together to ward off the intense chill that had settled over the campus. But even with the blinding snow crunching underfoot, it was a beautiful day. We laughed as we sank into unseen pitfalls and kicked the powder up to float down in crystal flurries. Everything about it was perfect. I couldn't have asked for a better day.

"The golden boy lives." The hissing statement sliced through my wonderful bubble of happiness.

One day. Why couldn't I have just one day be good from start to finish? I looked up to see the last person I'd ever thought to see again and shoved Alex behind me.

"Who is that?" Alex whispered in my ear.

"What do you want, Neese?" I asked, not bothering to keep the sharpness from my voice. He shrugged his shoulders in that weird, snake-like way. My resulting shiver had nothing to do with the cold that fogged our breath.

"Neese?" Alex hissed behind me. Suddenly, he was pushing to get around me. "You son of a bitch. You want a fight, I'll give you one. Get your scaly ass over here so I can rearrange your fucking face!" The level of animosity shocked and alarmed me.

I grabbed Alex's arms and struggled to hold him back.

"Damn it, Matt, let me go," he demanded, fighting against the hold.

"I don't think your boyfriend likes me very much."

"Fiancé," I corrected him.

Neese's eyebrows climbed up his forehead.

Meanwhile, I was having a hell of a time preventing Alex from launching himself at Neese's face. "He's not worth it," I repeated, and he finally let me pull him back until he ran into me. I wrapped my arms around his chest, effectively pinning both arms. He'd yet to relax, though, and I was pretty sure he was still staring daggers at Neese. I let out an irritated huff. "What do you want, Neese? I'm not coming back. I'll never go back to that place."

He laughed in that awful hissing way of his. "Never is a long time. Don't worry though, you're off the hook. Seems you've got friends in high places. We got shut down." He flipped a dismissive hand, and I suddenly realized that almost none of his scaly exterior was exposed to the elements. "It's no matter. We'll find another place. Look us up if you ever change your mind. In the meantime, enjoy married life. I never would have guessed. He's cute," he added, shaking his head as he walked past us. When it was clear that he was truly gone, the tension finally left Alex.

"Why did he call you the golden boy?" he asked, almost too low to hear as he turned to face me.

I looked into his eyes, so filled with sadness, and told him the truth. "Because I was the prizefighter." He nodded like the news didn't surprise him. I felt a tug on my arm and we resumed our walk to the dining hall, albeit far more somber than it had started.

"He's the one that made you throw the fight?"

"Yes."

"How many fights?"

"A lot. Too many to count." The information clearly upset him, but I suspected there was more to it than what he was asking. "You want to know if I ever stopped going in the first place."

He glanced at me. Yep, that was it.

"Of course I did, Alex. You are far more important than some stupid bruiser club," I said, but he didn't appear reassured. I stopped in the middle of the walkway, pulling us up short. "I'm serious. Look at me." When he did, it almost broke my heart. What had happened to our beautiful day? "I know things got rocky the last couple months, but I need you to believe me when I say I never wanted to see that place again. You told me to stop fighting, and I did. The only reason I ended back there was because of fucking George and his need for bloodsport. Even then, I'm positive that Neese and Otto manipulated him into it. I love you, Alex. You are the most important thing in my life, and I will always choose you over anyone or anything else."

He gave me a half smile. "Will you still say that when we have kids?" Well, that confirmed that suspicion.

"I'll just have to save everyone."

"Like a knight?" He laughed.

"Yes, like a knight." I chuckled and pulled him in for a lingering kiss. "Whatever you want, Alex. I'll find a way to give it to you."

"How about we start with ice cream?"

"I can do that," I said, re-lacing our fingers.

We'd gone several paces when Alex suddenly missed a step.

I quickly turned to him. "What? What's wrong?"

"Neese."

"Yeah..." Fear circled in my belly.

He smacked his head. "I *knew* I recognized that name. Neese is Rubio's roommate. You know, Rubio actually propositioned me to have a threesome with them."

"Rubio's roommate? Really? I knew I didn't like that guy for a reason," I said, then the back half of Alex's statement registered. "He did what!"

Alex laughed and tugged me further along the sidewalk. "I didn't *agree*. And why do you dislike Rubio?"

I glowered at him. "Besides the fact that he hit you up for a threesome with his psychotic roommate?"

"To be fair, I'm fairly confident Rubio doesn't know Neese runs a fight club. Or, at least, I hope he doesn't." Alex paled.

"Look, you don't like Gabriel and I don't like Rubio. Fair's fair."

He squinted at me, but kept walking. "Yeah... I don't think that's how it works."

Chapter 25
Bait

Alexi

"Have you told your mom yet?" Matt asked, and I grimaced. "I'll take that as a no." His following chuckle was warm and relaxed. It was so good to have the real Matt back, *my* Matt. I felt his hand slide over mine and he squeezed my fingers. The extra bits were nice too.

"I figured we could tell her together," I offered, sparing him a hopeful glance.

He gave me a look, no doubt recognizing the stalling tactic for what it was. "She's *your* mom."

"She'll be yours too," I fired back.

His eyes widened as if I'd goosed him. "Mine?" he echoed.

"Of course. My family will be your family. It may just be the two of us, but it'll still be yours," I said, shifting on the couch to face him. Getting nervous when he didn't respond, I asked, "Is that okay?"

"I... I've never had a...." he trailed off, still looking like he couldn't quite wrap his head around this latest tidbit.

Great, I broke him. "Hey, talk to me." I jostled him. "What are you thinking?"

Suddenly, his face erupted into a dazzling smile. "I'm thinking marrying you comes with a lot of perks."

"Oh really? And what are some of these perks?" I asked dubiously. He simply chuckled and leaned forward to place a slow, lingering kiss on my lips that made them tingle. "Yeah, I'd qualify that as a perk. What else?" I felt him smile against my mouth and kiss me deep enough to steal my breath all over again. I was about to reach up and tangle my fingers in his hair when he suddenly pulled back. "What?"

"Shh." He held up a hand to stall further questions. I was about to ask again anyway, when all the playfulness left his face and he got super serious.

"Matt, you're freaking me out. What is it?"

His eyes were sharp and focused as he turned his gaze to me. "Do you feel that?"

Fear trickled through my veins. Then I felt something. A kind of... pull at my very essence, not unlike when Vera had her little freak out and unceremoniously yanked at every shadow in the vicinity. This, however, was nowhere near as intense. It was faint, like it was coming from far away, and almost like...

"Someone's calling for help," Matt said, finishing my thought aloud. He surged to his feet, nearly toppling me off the couch.

"What are you doing?"

"We have to help them."

"We don't even know where they are," I argued. Not that I didn't want to help, but we were students, not warriors. This wasn't our job.

"I do."

A horrible sinking sensation started in my stomach and worked its way up to my throat. "Matt, no."

"I can't just leave them there. You know what that place is like."

"Exactly, which is why you shouldn't go. Besides, Vera told you to stay out of it. Let her handle it."

He shook his head. "She doesn't know the place like I do."

"But Matt. Things are finally getting back to normal. It's likely a trap anyway," I floundered. This wasn't happening.

"You're probably right. And knowing Thomas, it'll be just as deadly for the bait as for the intended targets."

"At least *call* Vera first." It was a last ditch effort, and we both knew it, but he didn't fight me. He quickly removed his new device and placed the call.

"Voicemail," he mouthed, then left a somewhat detailed message before hanging up.

The look of determination in his eye left little doubt in my mind how this was going to play out, but I had to try. "We should really wait for Vera." Though at this point, I'd be willing to settle for Gabriel if it meant Matt wouldn't set foot in that awful place again.

"We don't know how long they have. I won't sit here and wait Nyx knows how long for her to decide to check her phone."

As expected. I gave a resigned sigh and stood up. "Fine, then I'm going with you."

"I can't let you do that."

I arched an eyebrow. "*Let* me? What are you going to do to *stop* me?" For a fraction of a second, I saw him actually consider it and my heart sank. Matt was stronger than me and if he wanted to, he could absolutely make sure I didn't follow him.

"But, Alex... what they did to you."

"Is nothing compared to what they'll do to you if they catch you. If you go, I go. You're not the only one who almost lost someone," I added.

"Alex, please," he begged.

I understood the pain, but there was no way I was going to sit idly by while he raced into the jaws of death, no matter how scared I was. "I won't lose you, Matt, not again," I said with enough force to take him aback. Still, he hesitated.

"O-okay. We'll do this together."

"Like we'll do everything." I held out my hand.

He took it, and we blinked into the shadow world. Normally, Matt shadowing both of us would have its usual extreme reaction, but I was far too distracted by my worry to be consumed by desire. Even then, I was still breathing hard by the time we emerged on the old fraternity row. To my credit, so was he. The horrid place was a lot farther than I'd thought.

I glanced around at where he'd brought us. We were immediately outside the last house in the row and the gloom overhead promised rain. Fitting, as how the place looked like an abandoned graveyard. Unlike the rest of the campus, here, evidence of the epic battle that had taken place at the university had not been wiped clean. Columns decorated the scorched earth in broken, jagged pieces much like the Regency that had once made this their base of operations. I shuddered. It was said that the spell used to cover their retreat had tainted the masonry so bad the not even Kyra Hallow with a team of fifty of the strongest witches at the time could purify it. Only time could do that. Until then, an undeniable atmosphere of evil permeated the area. The kind that felt like slime oozing over your skin.

"Its coming from in there," Matt said, snapping me out of my dark thoughts.

"I feel it." Now that we were so close, there was no denying it was absolutely a call for help or that we were in the right place. Something was still off. I frowned at the desolate entrance, unable to shake how much it looked like a cavernous maw ready to swallow us whole. "Why is it so faint? It's almost like it's muffled somehow."

He shrugged and walked towards the skeletal remains of the massive house.

"Why didn't you shadow us inside?" I asked, scrambling to catch up.

He paused at the threshold, looking up at the crumbling façade. "Because this place is likely booby trapped down to the studs." Trepidation rolled off of him, reaffirming my decision to come. I couldn't let him face this alone. "Whatever you do, *don't* shadow," he cautioned.

After my last experience here, that was kind of a given. I scanned the ground, toeing aside bits of rubble as I searched.

"What are you doing?"

"Looking for a weapon. If we can't shadow, I feel like it would be prudent. Don't you?" At last I found a piece of loose ironwork. I worked it free and gave it a couple of practice swipes. "This should do. Of course, I'd feel more confident if we'd actually had any training with actual weapons rather than just hand to hand."

Matt squinted at me and I looked over my shoulder, not sure what had caught his attention.

"What?" I dropped the hand holding the iron to my side, suddenly self conscious.

"Night, you're smart," he said before scanning the immediate area himself. Eventually, something caught his eye, and he walked over to tear off an exposed piece of structure, resulting in something that vaguely resembled a quarter staff. He brandished the makeshift weapon. "You ready?"

"Wait." I stepped close, then pulled him in tight, ignoring his squeak of surprise, and kissed him for all I was worth. "I love you, Matt." I didn't want to die without telling him at least one more time.

He squeezed me hard enough my ribs creaked. "I love you too, Alex." He let me go and swallowed hard, as if bracing himself for what was to come. The phantom SOS we'd followed here was still fading in and out. I doubted that bode well for whoever was broadcasting it. After another deep breath, his bright blues captured me. "Stay close. Don't wander. And for Nyx's sake, don't touch anything." I nodded, and we crossed the threshold of the main entrance.

The house was darker than I remembered. Of course, my memory was a tad skewed, having been unconscious for most of the traveling parts. Then I realized the glow spheres were gone. Between the gray light drifting through the entrance and the boarded-up windows, the creepy levels were off the charts. It felt like an abandoned crypt or some kind of tomb and it *definitely* felt like a trap. The darkness was undoubtedly intentional to encourage a sense of safety for any Shadow demon dumb enough to be there. Sadly, that list included us. I fought the urge to reach out with my essence. At least then, I'd have a better idea of what might lurk beyond our limited field of vision. The temptation was unusually strong, almost like we were being baited by the darkness itself.

I pulled up short. "Do you feel that?"

"Feel what?" he whispered back.

I wasn't sure how to explain the paranoia, so I focused on finding a solution. "We need light. Any chance this place still has running electricity or candles lying around?" I couldn't really make out his frown in the gloom, but then, I didn't need to see it to know it was there.

Abruptly, he spun on his heel and ventured to an unfamiliar part of the house. The room we ventured into was noticeably smaller than the main foyer. A distinction made more pronounced by the odd assortment of chairs and tables cluttering the space, including what appeared to be the dilapidated remains of what I hoped was a couch.

"What is that?" I asked, unable to hide my revulsion.

He glanced at the furniture without me having to clarify. His lip curled in disgust. "One guess who brought that trash in here." My money was on Kyle. Guy had no sense of personal hygiene. But then, Travis was vile in his own right. However, I couldn't imagine George deigning to dirty his hands by touching it.

"Is this where you were all that time?"

He stiffened. "Sometimes, but mostly I was out stalking our class mates like some deranged sociopath or at the bruiser club being taught a lesson." The level of hatred in his response was like a knife in my heart. The physical pains I'd suffered during those few days were nothing compared to the torture he'd endured for months. I doubted he saw it that way, though.

I took in the overturned tables and eerie sense of abandonment. While I wasn't prone to paranoia, the place felt haunted. The rest of my life might not be as long as I'd hoped. I looked over at Matt and tried not to be consumed by sadness. He needed me focused. "You think there are candles in here?" I asked, trying to sound confident.

He stopped at chest and leaned down to inspect it. "Fucking great."

"What?"

"This is going to hurt," he said and gently pushed me a couple of paces away. Before I could ask, he shadowed his quarter staff and brought it down with enough force to smash the flimsy chest. The moment the shadow touched the wood, an eerie purple lightning sprung to life. In the lurid light I saw Matt strain not to shout and then, just like that, it went out.

I rushed to his side to find him breathing hard and no longer holding onto the shadow world. "Are you okay? What was that?"

His only answer was to pass me the staff so he could lean down and retrieve a couple of torches. He flicked the switch on each, but alas, only one produced a wavering pool of dim yellow light. "That's what I was afraid of. Virtually everything in here is hard-wired to zap."

I clutched my iron bar tighter. "This is impossible. How are we supposed to get someone out when we can't touch anything?"

"We've got bigger problems."

"What could possibly be a bigger problem?" I asked, rounding on him. This was a ridiculous suicide mission and I should have tried harder to get a hold of someone more qualified to handle this than us.

"For starters, them." He angled the flashlight towards the far wall.

"Oh shit," I whispered at finding several faces leering back at us.

Matt hiked his quarter staff up while I white-knuckled my makeshift sword. I had just enough time to wonder if the iron was rusted through when the nameless faces surged towards us en masse. "Try not to shadow as much as you can," Matt said as we stepped closer to each other. I didn't need the reminder, but then I had no idea how we could hope to escape so many without it.

A loud crack echoed through the space and I glanced behind me to see that Matt had slammed his staff into the side of a snarling face. My stomach heaved. I'd never been in an actual fight before. What was I doing here? This was insane. I didn't know how to fight one person, let alone half a dozen. My panic threatened to strangle me. Suddenly, the hairs on the back of my neck stood on end. Out of pure reflex, I reached into the shadows and threw the person sneaking up on me across the room. Shadow lights filled my vision, drowning everything in that lurid, crackling purple glow. I screamed. Douglas's face hovered before me, his characteristic snarl twisting his face as he plunged first one and then another light into me. My continued screams swallowed up all the other sounds, including Douglas's maniacal cackle. I was going to die strapped to a chair, unable to defend myself or see the love of my life ever again. But I wouldn't give them Matt. More lights, more pain. Searing agony dominated every inch of my world. There was no escape. I'd be trapped here, burning into eternity.

"Alex!" Matt's desperate cry dragged me out of my personal hell and I realized I wasn't still in the chair. There was no evil torturer, and none of the lights were actually touching me, at least not yet.

CHAPTER 26
THE TRAP

Matt

Alex's scream rang in my ears. I never should have let him come. And now we were surrounded by several of Thomas's non-demon minions who were completely immune to the deadliest weapon in the room. I spun my weapon around and punched it in the gut of the latest attacker. They crumpled to the ground, only to be replaced by another. I grunted as I blocked an assault, then sent them staggering back several steps with almost no effort. If it wasn't for the overwhelming odds and presence of Shadow lights, this would have been a cakewalk on my own. A terrifying thought occurred to me—what if they were human? Suddenly, I was very grateful I'd opted for a blunt weapon. I checked my strength as I sent another assailant soaring across the room and shifted closer towards the main entrance to the room.

"Work your way towards the source of the call! Maybe if we can break through whatever is holding them, then they can help," I shouted over the melee. It was a desperate hope that they'd be in any condition to help or that someone was even here to save. Everything about this place was one big trap tailor-made for Shadow Demons. If I hadn't believed the Warde mission statement before, I certainly did now. No Shadow was meant to leave here alive.

"We need to get out of here," Alex gritted through clenched teeth as he fought off a faceless figure freely waving a Shadow light. Whatever panic he'd had at initially seeing the lights was gone now. He fought with everything he had to make sure the purple glow never so much as grazed him. And I'd brought him here. Would I ever stop doing reckless shit that put his life in danger? I quickly refocused my attention to parry an assault that almost crushed my skull. The force of the defense sent my attacker staggering back, but it didn't deter him. Already, he was running full tilt back into the fray.

"I know, but there are too many." My latest assailant went down, only to be replaced by two more. I snarled in frustration. They were multiplying.

"Then we'll have to use the dark, Matt."

That sounded like a terrible idea, but we were out of options. "I have a feeling this will not go well," I said as he turned to shadow before my very eyes. I followed suit and met him in a larger room. Outraged cries drifted from the room we had just vacated. Thankfully, I still had hold of the flashlight, a minor miracle after the chaos we'd stumbled into. I kept it off for the time being, reluctant to give away our new location.

"That went better than expected," Alex said, sounding as surprised as I felt. "Now what?"

"Now we get out of here, before those things find us again." I struggled to get my bearings, having never shadowed in here before and uncertain of our location without the usual paraphernalia decorating the space. "This way," I said with all the confidence I could muster, leading us deeper into the house. If I got Alex killed, I'd never forgive myself.

Alex walked close enough to touch me as we crept down the hallway. My skin itched with a sense of anticipation and imminent danger. I very intentionally did not touch the walls and noticed Alex being equally cautious. The hallway ended, and we stumbled completely exposed into the open. The abrupt expansion put me off balance and it took a second longer than it should have for me to recognize where we were. This space I was intimately familiar with. I didn't need to see to know that not 20 feet to my right was a wall of pictures, most adorned with garish red X's and a picture of Vera herself atop it all.

Without thinking, I shadowed to the wall, briefly leaving Alex's side. I reached for the dagger stabbed through Vera's face and regretted it the second my hand closed around the hilt. Pain ripped through my arm and I bit down on my tongue to keep from crying out. In the light of the purple flames, I could just make out Alex's expression of abject horror. I fought to relinquish my hold on the Shadow world, but kept trying to pull me deeper, intensifying the pain from the Shadow light trap. Finally, it relented, and I sagged against the wall. Still shaking, I ripped the dagger free of the wall, sending Vera's mutilated picture floating to the ground.

"Are you out of your mind?" Alex hissed, striding up to me. He snatched the flashlight from my grasp and turned it on, keeping it pointed to the ground to limit its field of light. Howls of rage drifted down the hallway.

"Come on. We need to move." Before I stepped away, I tore his picture off of the wall. Damn thing was the whole reason I'd gotten into this mess. He didn't argue or comment, just shook his head and eyed the exceptionally sharp tip of the long dagger. In retrospect, grabbing the blade hadn't been the best idea, but I'd be damned if I let those *things* have it. As quietly as I could, I led the way down a corridor that I hoped would bring us closer to the source of the SOS. "I don't understand how it can't still feel so distant," I whispered. "The house isn't *that* big. We have to be practically on top of them by now."

"Assuming it *is* an actual person, they're probably in a warded room."

I glanced at him out of the corner of my eye. "You're a damn genius."

He rolled his eyes and walked toward the same entrance I'd seen Thomas use a hundred times. As we stepped into the space, my anxiety increased tenfold. We were officially in uncharted territory. The adjoining pathways and doors struck me as unnecessarily complicated, and I couldn't help but wonder if that was real or a spell designed to confuse trespassers. Knowing Thomas' proclivity for creating confusion, I was inclined to believe the latter.

How had Gabriel found me through all of this? Hell, how did he even get in?

"Why haven't they caught up with us yet?" Alex asked.

I glanced over at him and the flashlight shaking in his hand. I didn't know, and it had me equally worried. But I wasn't about to tell him that. "Maybe Vera finally checked her phone." Even in the half light, his relief was evident. If only that were the case. I didn't expect help to come. We'd either find it inside or never leave here at all. I swallowed and once again questioned my life choices that had gotten us here. "Come on, we're getting closer. I feel like we're practically standing on the source."

He nodded and continued down the latest hall. A loud screech came from the far end and we froze. Liquid adrenaline poured like ice through my veins. It had been stupid to think that all the people in this place were behind us. On cue, two bodies rushed toward us. The narrow space wouldn't have been so bad if we could shadow, but that wasn't an option. Alex grunted as one of them made impact. There was nothing I could do to help, though. I already had my hands full with the one clawing to get at my throat. The light of the flashlight swung wildly against the walls until it landed with an ominous crack against the ancient wooden floors. Light poured down the hall to reveal several more pairs of beady eyes.

"Shit. There's more!" The thing attacking me took advantage of my distraction and outrageously sharp teeth pierced my shoulder. I shouted in surprise, dropping the dagger. Alex spun to see what had happened while his opponent was busy picking itself off of the ground. The mediocre glow of the flashlight revealed a face twisted into a savage snarl and and two perfectly spaced porcelain teeth. Dread swirled in my stomach. *Vampires.*

Ignoring the excruciating pain in my shoulder, I frantically searched the ground for the dagger. My fingers had scarcely closed on the hilt before I sent it flying. Alex's eyes widened as it whizzed past him to land with a thunk in the chest of the one sneaking up behind him. His alarm became palpable when he realized what had almost happened. I reached behind me and yanked at the creature clinging to my back. Teeth dug in deeper, and I let out a hiss. We didn't have time for this. Those eyes were getting closer, and the call was fainter. If we took much longer, we might lose the signal altogether and this whole thing would have been for nothing. I slammed into the wall, shadowing partway. The second I contacted the paneling, shadow light burned my skin far worse than the electric barricade at the fight club ever had. It wasn't nearly as potent as the free standing lights though and I could still shadow the vampire on my back into the wall, which is exactly where I left him.

"*Matt*, more are coming..." Alex's worry was palpable. We'd barely managed two. I didn't like our odds against a horde, especially without the ability to Shadow. Why they weren't charging headlong at us was a mystery though.

I grabbed his hand and veered us back the way we'd come. We had to dismiss two routes due to one being cluttered with pieces of broken furniture and rubble and the other holding yet more eyes and matching screeches. Fear clutched at my heart as I realized we were running out of places to run.

"In here!" Alex yelled and pulled me through an unlocked door.

A distinct sense of wrongness prickled my skin. "This doesn't feel right," I said as we stepped into what appeared to be a sitting room similar to the one George and his goons had commandeered. Except, the SOS was closer than ever. In fact, it felt like it was...

"They're in there," Alex finished my thought, gesturing with the light to a door that had an unholy amount of locks on it.

As he walked closer to inspect the overly-guarded door, I examined the room. Unbelievably, the sounds of angry screeches had vanished the moment the door closed behind us. While something still felt decidedly off about the space, maybe it wasn't such a bad hiding spot after all. I used the reprieve to take stock. The presence of the locks, which were undoubtedly spelled, could have been the source of my unease, but I doubted was it. Something else was in here. I just had to figure out what.

The room seemed ordinary enough. Several winged back chairs were set far back from the center, as were any other pieces of furniture, almost as if they'd been moved. Confused why anyone would need to shift furniture like that, I scanned the ground. Scratches on the floor caught the shifting light, and I squinted to make them out. They weren't just scratches; they were marks, designs. I stepped further back to put together the complete picture. It seemed familiar somehow. I stepped a few feet over to get a different vantage and realized what I was seeing. The symbol for the Order of Light was carved into the ground with additional symbols surrounding it. They'd led us into a trap.

"Alex, no!" I shouted as he stepped onto perfect likeness of the sigil.

Instantly, he went completely black and Shadow light erupted from the floor. His scream of agony reverberated through me until I thought I'd go deaf with it. Gritting my teeth, I charged the circle, aiming for where he was standing. By some miracle, I made it through and knocked him out of the sphere of deadly light. I barely registered him crumpling to the ground before the searing pain saturated every cell in my body. Pain unlike anything I'd ever known consumed me, forcing me deeper into the shadow world, all the while seeking to burn out the essence of my soul. But it still couldn't compare to the pain in my chest. Alex was dead, and it was my fault. I deserved this and so much more. I couldn't tell if I was shouting or not. There was only Alex's scream trapped inside my skull.

The world became an empty void defined by light and never-ending pain. My very being continued to reach out despite the agony, desperate for an escape from something that there was no way to escape.

I'm going to die here.

The thought was insubstantial beside my heartache. Alex was gone. Forever.

Distantly, I heard another shout and Alex swam into my field of vision.

Oh good, the hallucinations were back. Except he looked so scared. I didn't want him to be afraid. I wanted to see him smile before I finally gave into the darkness that had been trying to consume me my whole life.

"Don't look sad." My voice sounded weird, like it wasn't coming from the right place. Did I even have a body anymore? Horror flashed in his eyes, but he quickly regained his composure. Even then, he looked like he was in pain and fighting it.

"Matt, you have to fight! Focus on me."

Except you're not real. You never are. I'm still in that damn house, all alone, trying to keep you safe. Except you died anyway. You died because of me.

I crumpled in on myself. There was nothing to live for anymore. Why was I fighting it? Giving up would be so much easier, then the pain would be gone. Did demons have an afterlife? Would Alex be there?

"Damn it, Matt. I won't let you go! You want to be a Roman? Well, Romans don't give up."

That sparked something. But it was distant, and I had to chase it down amidst the tide of agony. How was I even conscious? All I wanted was to slip into the night and let all feeling go. The blinding purple light cast a lurid shadow across the face of the greatest love I'd ever known. Even as a hallucination covered in burns, he was beautiful. I very much wanted to be a Roman, but that would never happen now. Alex was dead, and I was going to die here as well. At least we were together.

"Matt," his voice cracked as he hovered just outside the bubble of pure pain that had become my world. "You promised me children. We're going to have a family. You're going to be a great dad. We're going to watch the times pass together. Forever isn't long enough. Remember? This is *not* where we end." Tears flowed down his face. He clenched his shaking hand and a thin band of black winked back. He followed where my gaze had landed and inspiration seemed to glow in his eyes. "Focus on me, Matt. Focus on the ring."

I didn't have a ring, though. I didn't even have hands.

"Quit being such a stubborn ass and do as you're told," he barked.

Clarity snapped back and suddenly I could see my hand in front of my face, complete with its own black band. That was Alex. That was why he was hurting, because he was in here with me.

He eyed my hand like it was the answer to everything. "Give me your hand, Matt," he ordered calmly, though his own still shook.

I reached for him, struggling against the current of pain until my fingers stopped inches from the outer rim. But I couldn't force my hand any further. I was trapped in this sphere of torture, a breath away from salvation. It would have been nice to touch him one more time. Abruptly, his hand closed over my wrist and the pain intensified, as if every molecule of my body had been doused in oil and set alight. Then there was only darkness.

The floor shaking and the sound of smashing brought me back to consciousness. I blinked, feeling wearier than seemed physically possible. Everything was fuzzy around me and nothing looked familiar. Where was I? Even my bones were tired and every part of me still ached from the memory of the shadow light. Could your soul hurt? There was a solid thunk, followed by the sound of splintering wood. What the hell was that? I groaned as I forced my head up and was rewarded with a vision of Alex holding an iron poker. Beneath him were the shattered remains of the sigil for the Order of Light.

Alex.

The world came into sharp focus and I surged to my feet, ignoring the immense pain it caused. He turned at the scrapping sound. The relief in his eyes made me want to sob. The metal in his hand clattered to the floor, and the ringing echoed off of the walls. In two steps, he walked over to where I was barely standing. As he got closer, I realized there were tracks in the dirt covering his face. When had he been crying? He wrapped his arms tightly around me. The embrace hurt, but touching him was worth the pain.

"You're alive," I said in disbelief.

"I thought I lost you," he whispered into my shoulder, clinging tighter. "No more Shadow lights, okay?"

"Agreed," I said, pushing him back and glancing toward the locked door. "What do you say we finish this?"

He nodded, then reached down to retrieve the poker and tossed me a splinter of wood that resembled my shadow club. I hefted it in my hand and looked at him. We walked over to the warded door and aimed for a spot just to the right of all the locks. There was no way the wall itself could hold up to demonic strength.

"Together?"

"Together."

We swung in unison as hard as we could, where the bolted locks would do no good. The frame cracked beneath our combined assault and wisps of purple Shadow light leaked out. We swung again, and the crack grew. Again. Wood splintered off, flying into the room and decorating us with tiny cuts. Again. The space beside the door imploded, leaving behind a sizable hole.

Alex quickly dropped his weapon and retrieved the flashlight. In the yellow glow, we both appeared covered in layers of shadow burns. He angled the beam of light into the room and a figure took shape. All I could do was hope that it was harmless or too injured to be dangerous. As the form shuffled closer, I noticed they were using their arm to shield their eyes. They also looked terrible, covered head to toe in their own gruesome wounds.

"Lower the light," I whispered. Alex quickly adjusted the angle of the flashlight. The arm fell, and we saw the haggard face of a girl who had clearly been through hell.

"Ellie?" Alex asked in disbelief.

She glanced from him to me, taking in our own state of disaster. "Matt? Alex? Oh, thank goodness! I thought no one would ever come," she sobbed, then promptly collapsed. We caught her together, and another voice rang out behind us.

"Dorian is going to be *pissed*," Vera said, looking every bit as roughed up as we were.

I looked back at Alex over Ellie's practically lifeless form. He seemed just as surprised as I was at her appearance. "Guess she checked her phone after all."

Chapter 27
Retribution

Alexi

As Vera surmised, Dorian looked less than pleased to be seeing us a second time. We were back in the manor, only this time we hadn't been taken to the library. I was fairly sure we were on the second level, but couldn't recall going up any stairs. In fact, how we'd gotten here at all was fuzzy. Had we used a portal? Had we shadow walked? I shook my head. Right now, my only concern was making sure Matt got healed and there was no telling what I looked like. I knew logically that I had shadow burns all over my body, but Matt's appearance was worse. He looked like he'd been left in a broiler and forgotten. I had no idea how he was standing or how he'd even survived.

Dorian and Vera's voices drifted into the hall despite the closed door separating us. Matt and I shared a look as their volume increased. Thankfully, Dorian wasn't shouting at Ellie, but at Vera.

"Just once, could you *not* to end up a shredded mess?"

"I already told you, Dorian, I don't need healing. Besides, it's nothing I haven't healed naturally from before," Vera added dismissively.

"Over my dead body are you walking out there without even a minor healing. For Christ's sake, look at you!"

"That's not funny."

"You're right. It's not. Neither is getting called up repeatedly to heal children. Children, Vera. What were they doing there in the first place? I thought you said you were going to leave them out of this?"

"I don't need a lecture and I can't control other people's actions. As for them being children, they're older than we were that first summer."

"And how wrong was what we went through?" Dorian paused in his tirade. "You know what? Forget I said anything. Let's get this over with. On the upside, none of them seem so bad that I should need to borrow energy."

"You should take some anyway," Vera insisted.

"I told you I don't need it."

"Stop arguing and just fucking take it. I know what this does to you. I'll deal with Gabriel."

"Where is he, anyway?"

"Still trying to track down Thomas and his cohort."

"He told you that?"

"No," Vera deadpanned. Silence fell.

I glanced at Matt. "He'll find them," I whispered, reaching out to him.

He clenched his charred fists in his lap, causing them to crack and reveal raw, bleeding skin beneath. "No he won't. Thomas is long gone."

"In that case, I hope we never see either of them again."

Matt shook his head. "They won't give up hunting us so easily."

"But for now, at least, we're safe. *You're* safe," I emphasized.

He opened his mouth, no doubt to argue, when Dorian stepped out. We turned to face the irate healer, who looked like he'd been sucking lemons for the last hour.

"Right, who's first?" he grumbled.

"Matt." "Alex." We said at the same time.

I glanced at my stubborn angel. "You need more than I do. You're going first."

"I'm fine. You're going," he insisted.

"Look, I don't have all day. Either one of you gets in that room right now, or neither of you is getting healed." Dorian crossed his arms and stared us down.

I suspected he was bluffing, but Matt clearly wasn't taking chances. He glowered at me and I caved. He'd absolutely refuse healing until I was seen to. We needed to have a serious talk about how little he seemed to value his own life. I took a step forward and Dorian grabbed me in order to haul me the rest of the way. We passed Vera on her way out, looking pale and exhausted. She'd obviously won the argument to give up energy after all. The door closed behind her, leaving me alone with Dorian. I glanced around the pristine room, which was set up as a minimalist doctor's office, and wondered where they'd taken Ellie. She hadn't come out with Vera and I didn't see any other exists. At a curt gesture from Dorian, I took a seat on the metal table.

"I'm sorry you had to be dragged out here again. Why do you keep coming if it's so difficult for you?" I asked to take my mind off the unpleasantness of sitting.

"I'm here because I'm a healer and it's what I do. As for the other, I keep coming because I can't seem to tell the damn woman no. This was so much easier when she thought I was dead," he mumbled under his breath.

"I can understand not being able to deny someone. It sucks. If it's any consolation, I have no intention of repeating any of this," I offered.

He frowned. "That's what they all say. Now, care to explain exactly what happened? Your friend—"

"Fiancé," I corrected.

Dorian blinked. "My apologies. Your fiancé looks absolutely terrible."

"We tripped a spell. I'm not really sure what it was. It felt like it was forcing me into my Shadow state amidst a ring of Shadow light. Matt knocked me out of it and got himself stuck. He was in it much longer." I looked at the ground, ashamed. If I hadn't just blindly walked into the room, we could have avoided it all together. "It was horrible, I thought... I thought he was gone. All of his essence was spread out. He didn't even have a body anymore. And... and he couldn't recognize me." I hiccupped as the fear I'd felt welled up inside of me.

A warm hand covered my shoulder, and the familiar rush of ice swept through me. As the tide receded, it took all the physical pain but left the heartache. I didn't think I could live without Matt and he was so determined to sacrifice himself. "He's alive. What ever you did, saved him," Dorian said gently.

I lifted my head to look at him. I hadn't said I'd done anything.

"What? You think I don't know how self-sacrificing demons can be? You guys may be reckless and a tad suicidal, but you're also loyal and honorable to a fault."

I snorted. "I'm pretty sure that no one has ever referred to a Shadow demon as honorable in the history of ever. That's not really a word you associate with the Chaos Class."

"Maybe you've been misclassified. Every Shadow demon I've ever met has behaved much the same. Now, in all fairness, I also am a firm believer that each one of you is also certifiably insane."

"You really have the strangest bedside manner."

"Yeah, yeah. Everybody's a critic. Now, send in your fiancé, so I can get on with the rest of my patients." Patients? How many did he have?

"Thank you, Dr. Valens," I said, making my way out. He simply nodded and retrieved Matt before he had the chance to stall again. Matt shot him a downright sinister look at being denied the chance to confirm the thoroughness of my healing. Dorian remained completely unaffected and dragged him off anyway. To my surprise, Matt actually didn't fight him, nor did I hear any telltale arguing.

Now I was even more convinced that Matt was experiencing more pain than he was showing. That was the problem with Matt. There was never any telling just how much he was hurting, because he kept it all bottled up. But I knew the truth.

I glanced down at the thin black band encircling my ring finger. He couldn't hide the hurt from me anymore. I'd felt it. The moment he'd pushed me out of the circle, acute agony had radiated from the small connection. The force of it had been crippling, far surpassing my experience in the ring. I whole-heartedly believed that while the spell had been Shadow Demon specific, it had been *designed* for Matt. He was a Warde that shouldn't exist. The entire house was an elaborate trap designed by someone to eradicate the last of Matthias' line once and for all. I was a collateral bonus. That either of us had escaped still breathing was a miracle in and of itself.

The door opened again, and Matt walked out. My heart swelled at seeing that the garish burns and charred flesh were gone, replaced with perfectly healthy, albeit filthy, skin. "That doesn't get any better with repetition," Matt said, looking back into the room where Dorian was still standing.

I tentatively reached up to touch his face. "It really is incredible," I whispered in awe. Before he could say anything, I pulled him into a tight embrace. He gave an "oof" then wrapped his arms around me. "I thought I lost you." He squeezed tighter, and I pulled back to look at him. The perfect crystal of his eyes shone back with their own level of concern. "Are you okay? What that spell did to you. I don't even know..." I trailed off.

"I'm fine, Alex. I'm more worried about you."

Anger sprung up unexpectedly. "I'm going to need you to stop treating my life like it's more valuable than yours."

"But it is."

"Only to you." I snared him, and he met the fierce kiss with one of his own. That fire I craved swept through us, a blinding inferno binding us together. "I need you to live, Matt. Forever will be very short if you keep up with these suicide missions."

"Okay, Alex," he sighed before recapturing me. "I really do love kissing you," he whispered, deepening the kiss. It felt like he was seriously trying to steal every breath I'd ever had and I was perfectly alright with that.

There was a faint squeak of surprise somewhere far outside our bubble of bliss. We stopped kissing long enough to see who had joined us.

"Hi, Ellie," Matt said breathlessly.

"Well, that explains a lot," she said calmly, in direct contrast to the pink flush spreading across her cheeks.

I tried to step away from Matt, but he wasn't letting go. I rolled my eyes and removed his hands from my waist. He rewarded me with a look like someone had just stolen his candy right out of his mouth. Chuckling to myself, I walked over to Ellie. "I can't believe you're awake." I said.

She blinked, dragging her gaze away from Matt, who undoubtedly still looked like a petulant child.

"Um, yeah," she replied absently, then the rest of her wits returned. "Though I wouldn't be if it weren't for you two. I don't know how much longer I had. That room was lined with... That room was awful." She shuddered.

"I know." Matt placed a comforting hand on her arm. "You're okay now, though. They won't hurt you anymore. They're gone."

Her eyes lit up. "Oh, right. Ms. Scry wants you in the library."

"You should probably call her Vera," Matt offered helpfully as he took my hand. Ellie looked at him like he'd grown a second head.

I cleared my throat. "If you'll lead the way. I'm not really sure where we are."

"Of course, follow me." She spun on her heel and we dutifully trailed after her. She was in surprising spirits given her ordeal. But then again, I glanced at Matt, so was I.

The journey didn't take near as long as I expected. Turned out the library was closer than I realized. We walked in just in time to see Vera end a call. She turned to us and gave an appreciative nod.

"Thank you, Miss Thornton. If y'all will have a seat, there are a few things we should cover." We did as we were told, clustering around a smaller version of the table we'd sat at the last time.

"Where is Thomas? Has Gabriel caught him yet?" Matt asked without preamble. He clearly assumed that Gabriel had been on the other end of the line. I squeezed his hand, but he remained hyper-focused on Vera and it didn't look like she had good news.

"Thomas is in the wind, as is the rest of his operation. None of those he coerced into waiting in that house have any inkling of where he might be. No matter the persuasion," she added darkly. I swallowed at what sort of "persuasion" had been used.

"He can't just be gone. He has to answer for what he did," Matt said emphatically, releasing my hand to gesture wildly. "What he did to Alex, to Ellie, and who knows who else." I noticed he hadn't included himself in the list of injured parties. I sighed to myself. It seemed ensuring Matt had self-worth was going to be a lifelong struggle.

"I understand your frustration, Matt—believe me, I do—but just because they've slipped away doesn't mean they'll elude us forever. I want retribution every bit as much as you do. The things I've seen and endured... There's not a question in my mind that this cruel order needs to be eliminated." Vera held up a hand to forestall the argument brewing on Matt's face. "*However*, we can only work with what we have. Is there nothing else you can remember from your time spying for him? Even the tiniest detail could be of use."

"I already told you everything I remember. It's not like he was passing out his darkest secrets. Don't you think if I knew more, I would have already done something?" He waved wildly in my general direction.

Of that, I had no doubt. It was the main reason I'd been keeping such a close eye on him. I simply couldn't trust that he wouldn't run off on some hair-brained scheme, today's adventure not withstanding. She glared back at him, clearly ready to yell herself. The both of them made quite a pair of hot heads. Meanwhile, Ellie glanced from Vera to Matt like she was watching a tennis match. Poor thing probably had no idea what was going on.

I sat back in my chair expecting a rather long evening, mostly composed of the two of them shouting at each other. Unexpectedly, a door on the far side open and a familiar TA walked into the room with three people trailing behind her. Upon closer inspection, I realized manacles connected the three. Then recognition dawned. I let out an involuntary gasp.

"What's the matter?" Matt asked. He turned to me, then followed my line of sight. Before I could react, he blinked out to reappear across the room.

"Matt, no!" I shouted as he crashed into George, nearly sending the whole grisly caravan to the ground. His fist slammed into George's face repeatedly. He struggled to defend himself against the brutal assault of rage while Travis and Kyle cowered as far away as their chains would allow. I was paralyzed with shock as I watched Matt wail on George and he'd only broken my cheek. What would Matt do when he finally found Douglas?

"Get off of me!" Matt howled as Vera pulled him off of his victim. George remained huddled on the ground. "Where the fuck did these assholes crawl out of? Why are they even still alive? Where is your master, you son of a bitch?" Matt asked furiously, spitting on George and fighting Vera's grip. Despite her higher power level, she seemed to struggle to constrain him. I'd never seen so much anger, and it terrified me.

"Are you serious!" Dorian shouted upon entering the madhouse. "Damn it, Vera, I'm not healing these people just so they can rip each other apart all over again. That's it. Do you hear? I'm done. His nose can stay broken. I'm taking the portal home."

"Dorian, wait," Vera tried to call him back, but she was still fighting Matt, who was determined to finish what he'd started. "Damn it Matt, cut it out. He's done. It's over."

Matt snarled. "It's not over until he's in a lead-lined box six feet underground." He was going to kill him, anyway. I couldn't let him do that. He may not regret it now, but one day he would.

I shadowed over and laid a hand on Matt's shoulder. "Matt, stop. We talked about this." The fight instantly left him, but the rage stayed plastered on his face. There was nothing I could do about that, but I wasn't worried he would continue the attack. George, however, did not seem so confident. "I've got him," I said to Vera. She looked amazed and dubious. After all, I wasn't even holding him. Nonetheless, she relinquished him to me.

"Get them out of here," she ordered the TA. "And get him cleaned up." She watched as the troop left the library. "Good grief, Matt. What the hell is wrong with you?" she asked, rubbing her temples.

"Why are they here?" he demanded.

"Because I had the same questions as you." Her mouth twisted to the side as she gave him a withering look. "They're clueless. Thomas kept them every bit as much in the dark as you. That idiot didn't even know that he was working for the Order of Light. There's no telling what he thought he was actually hunting. But that doesn't absolve him. He'll pay for his crimes. He didn't just hurt you two." Her subtle glance back towards the table suggested Ellie had not been spared the wrath of George.

"And the others?" I asked before Matt could launch into a fresh tirade.

"The other two are fools. Blind sheep following a wolf."

"They're just as culpable," Matt hissed angrily.

"I'm not disputing that. They have their own crimes to atone for, but the severity is far less."

"What will happen to them?" I asked.

"George is going to prison. Maybe after a century we can visit the idea of parole. The others? I'm still working on that."

"He doesn't deserve to live after what he did." Matt's words dripped with acid and I wrapped an arm around him, surprised to find him shaking. Would my beautiful angel ever be able to move beyond this rage?

Vera shook her head. "I know how you feel, Matt, I really do, but there just aren't enough of us left in the world to go around executing other Shadow Demons with impunity. Incarceration will have to suffice for now."

Matt sagged, defeated, and leaned against me. "I'm sorry," he whispered, barely loud enough for me to hear.

"It's okay," I reassured him, placing a small kiss on his forehead. "All that matters is that they've been stopped and we're all okay."

CHAPTER 28
LESSON ONE

Matt

Spring semester was officially in session. Being in a classroom felt surreal after the absolute chaos of the last few months. Personally, I was over the constant brushes with death, though that didn't seem to prevent them. I made sure that this semester Alex and I would have more classes together and intentionally signed up for as many of the same as I could. Regretfully, that list only comprised two. My over-achiever fiancé had either already taken or tested out of most of the core curriculum, which only left Demonic History III and Advanced Battle Tactics. However, despite all of my efforts, I ended up in the same class at a different time. Apparently, more shadow demons appeared out of nowhere and enrolled, forcing Vera to have more than one class. That I did take up with Vera. I'd be damned if I was going to be in a different time slot than Alex.

She conceded without much of a fight, which should have given me pause. Talking to her was never that easy. Sure enough, I got Alex *and* two parolees. Apparently, I'd be keeping an eye on Travis and Kyle, while Alex kept an eye on me. I was less than pleased about the arrangement, but wasn't willing to argue in case it meant my schedule got shifted again. Consequently, my first couple of lessons with Gabriel didn't happen. Now that I was taking Advanced Tactics in the afternoon instead of the morning, everything was out of whack. We were drawing to the close of our third week by the time I finally got the call that I'd be having a lesson.

"And you're sure it's today?" Alex asked for the fifth time.

"Yes, Alex. You saw the message yourself." I knew he didn't like the private lessons, but I couldn't seem to make him understand that there was no reason to dislike Gabriel. He was a teacher, that was all.

"And it's in the manor?" He definitely didn't like that part. Logically, though, where else would it be?

"Yes."

"And you have everything you need?"

"Alex, enough. Stop mothering me."

"I'm not mothering you," he responded with a scowl.

"Yes, you are. Speaking of which, have you told yours yet?" He frowned. I didn't know what was taking him so long and was beginning to fear he just didn't want her to know. Was it because it was me? Was that why?

"Not yet. But seriously, are you sure you don't need to bring anything?" He would not be diverted.

I rolled my eyes. "He's not exactly giving me a history lesson." The moment the words were out, I regretted them. The look on Alex's face said he was very aware I was not going for history. Without warning, he pulled me into an empty room and conquered me with a kiss that was entirely inappropriate for campus. "Damn, Alex," I finally managed, totally out of breath. He wasn't done, though. I let out a moan as I his teeth grazed my neck. Okay, there *might* have been some upsides to this inexplicable jealousy his. "I really have to get going. You do too, otherwise you'll be late." That did it.

"Fine. Go to your damnable lesson." He stepped away, releasing me from where he'd pinned me against the wall. There wasn't a doubt in my mind that I was now sporting an impressive hickey. He paused before leaving and turned back to look at me. "And, Matt, behave." There was a lot more in the quiet command than simply an order to keep my temper. I gave him a crooked smile and stepped up to him to steal one last kiss, albeit a more chaste one.

"Of course," I said before shadowing out.

When I finally stepped through the portal created specifically for these lessons, I was definitely late. I let out a sigh. Already off on the wrong foot. After stepping through the portal, I surveyed my surroundings. I appeared to be in a training room, but it didn't resemble any of those on campus.

"You're late," Gabriel's voice came from the shadows across the room. In what was proving to be his signature style, he followed his voice into the room. One of these days, I was going to figure out why they looked so similar. It could just be the area they were from, random genetics, or maybe they shared a common ancestor.

"Yeah, I got held up."

"I can see that," he replied, casually tipping my collar. I fought back the burn of embarrassment. "Is that going to be a common occurrence?" That was an excellent question and one I didn't have an answer for.

"Are we going to train or what?" I asked, to refocus the conversation.

"Yes, but we need to cover a few items of business first." That didn't sound good. I tensed. He shook his head and commented, "I swear you and Vera have to be related somewhere down the line. Obviously, not through the Warde side, but perhaps through Teala's."

"Who?"

"Sopteală. She had other partners before Matthias, you know. I would like to say that I thought their union was preposterous, but I have a better understanding of it now," he finished, glancing at the ceiling. Vera must be in the house, and we were definitely not on the top floor.

I did a double-take. "Wait, you *knew* her?"

"Naturally. There may have been more Shadow Demons back then, but we have never been a numerous species. We are not quite the rabbits our cousins are," he said, with no small amount of scorn.

"Did you?"

"Did I what?"

"Did you have other lovers before...?" One of these days I'd stop indulging my curiosity like this.

He gave me a deadpan expression. "I *am* several hundreds of years old. If you are trying to ask if I am Alexi's father, then you should just ask."

My face went cold as all the blood drained from it. I hadn't even thought of that, though it would certainly explain why they looked so similar. "The answer is no. I intentionally had no progeny. My relationship with my father was not exactly conducive to cultivating any desire to carry on the family line."

"Your father is an original." The regurgitated information fell out of my mouth.

"He is. But back to what I was talking about. Sopteală was more than just a rebel who fell for a mortal. She was also the head of the Knights of Nyx, which I plan to reconstitute. Starting with you."

I stared at him. I didn't even have enough wits to make some noncommittal noise.

"Well, you haven't said no yet, so this is already going better than Vera expected."

"Is this where you trained her?" It was a stupid question, but I was still struggling to wrap my head around the other. I'd never heard anything even resembling the Knights of Nyx. There had been no mention of them in any of the texts we'd found.

"Yes, although most of her initial training began in the library." He rolled his eyes at seeing my confused expression and elaborated. "Being raised mortal, she was seriously lacking in history. Before I could teach her how to use her powers, she needed to understand what she was, where she came from. Not so unlike yourself. Besides, it was the first time someone had ever summoned me to be a teacher, and I wasn't really sure where to begin. I was—am—a history professor, so I started there."

"You teach history?" This conversation was getting more unbelievable by the second. He nodded. "But I thought..." I trailed off.

"I am still one of the oldest Shadow Demons left, thus making me the most qualified."

"One of? There are more?"

"Of course there are more. Alright, enough stalling. Let's see what you've got."

I snorted. "You already know what I've got. You were there."

"That was different." He created a long stick out of shadow. "This is a quarter staff. You'll be training with one of these."

"Why not swords? Why a weapon at all?" I was on a roll with the inane questions.

"First, I've seen you in hand to hand as you so eloquently pointed out, and second, I have also seen that temper—you do not need anything with a sharp edge to it."

I scowled. I was here to learn how to use my powers, not get some sporadic history lesson and a beating. Which is exactly what it would be, given how severely he outclassed me. However, before I could argue, he bore down on me. I quickly summoned a quarterstaff and barely blocked him in time from sweeping my legs out from under me. My speed meant nothing in the face of Gabriel's assault. For every attack I countered, two more landed. I rubbed my rump, where the latest smack still stung like a bitch.

"Come on, Matthew, you can do better than this. If you are going to be a knight in the order, I need to know you can do more than defend. Attack me."

I parried the latest strike and danced back, narrowly evading his backswing. "Why do you want me to be part of this, anyway? Is that why you offered to teach me?" My body ached from the countless raps I'd received, and I was definitely winded from trying—unsuccessfully—to avoid his relentless assault.

"In part. Demons are over due for representation. The disaster with the Order of Light just proves that we need our own driving force to stand up for those who cannot stand up for themselves." He spun around and disappeared, only to materialize behind me. The butt of his quarter staff smacked into my back, not hard enough to bruise, but enough to knock me off balance.

I shadowed out of reach to buy time to regain my footing.

"Attack me. Attack me or I will find someone else to take your place. Perhaps Alexi would be more suited for this work." Rage swept through me. "He certainly doesn't have any qualms about fighting for what he believes in or dying, for that matter."

I rushed him and our shadowed weapons met with jarring force. "You don't touch him. Alex isn't a fighter."

"Neither are you, apparently. Perhaps if you had spent less time skulking around, you would have been able to prevent him from being taken."

I black. Our movements became a total blur as I completely unleashed. The frenzied attack came to a sudden halt in a perfect stalemate.

"Much better," he said with an evil glint in his eye. Where I was panting from exertion, he wasn't even breathing hard. "Next time, we will work on your control. Interesting that you do not use the shadows when you fight. Don't worry, I will break you of that." I bristled at the low key threat and the belated realization that he'd been playing with me. The only person in this world allowed to toy with me was Alex.

I dropped my hold on the staff, and it vanished. "I'm done."

"You are done when I say you are done." He swung his quarterstaff at me and I used shadows to halt the movement.

"Alex taught me that little trick. And just to be clear, you don't go anywhere near him." I narrowed my eyes at him. "Does Vera know about the Knights of Nyx?"

He stopped maintaining his staff and straightened. "No."

"I won't keep this from Alex."

"I would expect nothing less." His casual assumption only pissed me off more. I spun on my heel to return to the portal. "And Matthew, I will see you here again on Friday. Unless, of course, you would prefer I reach out to your friend." My steps faltered, but I kept moving.

"Fiancé," I corrected. His congratulations hardly even registered before I walked through the door.

No sooner did I emerge than I shadowed directly to the dorm. Even with anger still ricocheting inside me, I could have sighed with relief to see Alex already there. I was furious with Gabriel and myself. Once again, I'd willingly signed myself up to fight. That brought me up short. I didn't recall having agreed, but I knew I would, that I already had. Alex was going to be pissed. I doubted he'd be comforted that this time it wasn't for sport.

"You're back sooner than I expected." He stood, abandoning the mountain of papers on the breakfast table.

In two shadow steps, I was on top of him and pulling him in close. I needed an outlet for the fire inside of me. I needed Alex. I always needed Alex.

"Whoa, bad day? Did the training not go well?" he tried to ask between my relentless kisses.

I grabbed his hand and dragged him to our room, still not answering. There, I slipped my hands beneath his shirt to feel the perfectly smooth skin beneath. I couldn't believe I'd let Gabriel get to me. He was infuriating. The nerve, using Alex to get me worked up. That was cheap.

"Matt, talk to me."

"I need you."

His gaze searched mine. "I'm always here for you."

"No, Alex. I want... I *need* what you do." I didn't know how else to say it. Alex had a way, and right now, I needed that more than anything. He stared down at me and I saw the moment it registered what I was really asking for. I let out a breath of relief because I really didn't know how to say it. He captured me in a demanding kiss I felt in my core. When he released me, I was entirely out of breath. *That*, I needed that. I needed his fire to burn as hot as mine.

"Okay, Matt, but after, you *will* tell me what happened," he said with a fierce look.

I nodded, then swallowed nervously as he continued to just look at me. "Alex, please." I felt so adrift in the world. If he didn't anchor me, there was no telling where I'd end up.

He took his time with the next, teasing my lips apart and lightly sucking on my lip before gliding his tongue in. I moaned and completely melted as our tongues danced together. Then he removed my hands from his hips and pulled them over my head. My breath hitched as he left them suspended in order to slide my shirt over my head. Once it was free, he tugged them down to rest on his shoulders. I tangled my fingers in his hair as he deepened the kiss and guided me backwards. My arms fell back over me as he laid me out before him. He removed my pants and returned to claim my mouth.

"What do you want?" The sultry question sent electricity coursing through me.

"This," I groaned and kissed him harder for emphasis. It was so easy to get lost in Alex and I was quickly becoming completely addled.

"My mouth, huh?"

What? No. That didn't make any sense. But as he worked his way across my shoulders and torso, I didn't argue. His kisses really were wonderful, especially when he paired them with those light nips. I buried my hand in his hair again and arched into him, then let out a gasp when his lips wrapped around my dick. That wasn't what I'd meant at all, but that didn't stop my eyes from rolling back or my moan. He took me down to the root and I nearly passed out from the incredible constriction of his throat when he swallowed. Per usual, he took his time playing with me, slowly dragging his tongue up the shaft before lightly sucking on the swollen crown. I was afraid I'd pull his hair out when he mouthed and sucked my balls. Alex needed to not be so good at blowjobs. Already I was tiptoeing the edge and struggling to decide if it would be better to let go or keep holding on to enjoy more of the mind-blowing sensations. He returned his attention to my dick, and I got that much closer to falling over. Then he pulled off, leaving me shaking and the wrong side of completely wrecked.

I immediately sat up to capture him with a kiss, but only got the briefest one before he pushed me back down and pinned my arms up above me. "Alex," I moaned into the following kiss. Distantly, I felt shadow encircle my wrists and tighten. Trepidation shot through me.

"Don't break it again." The husky command liquefied my insides.

My heart beat uncontrollably and I squirmed in tortured ecstasy as he used his mouth and fingers to explore my body and eventually open me up. I struggled against the bond, very conscious not to snap it. Then, all sensation vanished and I could have cried with denied want, but I kept the strip of shadow intact. I lifted my head and watched Alex slowly and deliberately remove his clothing with what I was positive were black eyes. When he finally stepped closer, I desperately wanted to reach out and feel him, but dutifully remained as he'd left me. His palms tickled the hair on my legs as he caressed their full length. Then he grabbed my thighs, and he pulled me to the edge of the mattress, forcing my arms to stretch out above me. My breath came in stuttered pants as he positioned my legs so that my calves rested on his shoulders.

I heard the pop of a cap, though I hadn't seen him grab the lube. His fingers returned to my clenching hole and my toes curled as he stretched me more, taking time to rub that special bundle of nerves that drove me wild. When he was satisfied I was ready, he positioned the swollen head of his dick at my entrance. I clenched in anticipation, then remembered to relax. In one powerful thrust, he breached the outer rim of tight muscle and buried himself to the hilt. I let out a strangled cry, barely maintaining the thin band of darkness. He rolled his hips, driving me into the mattress again and again until I felt spilt in two. All thought fled as I dissolved into him. There was only Alex and his touch. I was his to do with whatever he wanted. Now, later, forever.

Eventually, I floated back down to Earth and lay there lost in contended bliss. I had no idea how he did that, but he did it every time and it was wonderful.

"Tell me what you're thinking about." The soft command felt like a caress on my already sensitive skin.

"That I rather like being your plaything." My eyes widened as the unfiltered honesty left my tongue. Instantly, my face burned. If the damn thing got any hotter, you could fry an egg on it. Meanwhile, Alex's laughter rolled out to envelop me like a blanket.

"Is that how you think of it?" he asked, laughter still playing at the edges.

I didn't even try to manage words. Was it possible to die of mortification? He shifted so he could look down at me. Judging by the heat in my face, I was likely still the color of a beet. Night, this was awful.

He slid his hand across my abdomen as he nuzzled my neck. "If it's any consolation, I've never had a plaything before. And, for the record, I rather enjoy it as well." The low, whispered words sent a corresponding heat rushing through me. I was all set to dissolve back into ecstasy when he unexpectedly changed the topic. "Now, about this day of yours. What made it so bad?"

It would have been easy to override the question and focus more on his touch, except it had been part of his terms. I took a heavy breath and released it a put-upon sigh. He starred down at me expectantly and unfazed. This wasn't exactly a conversation I wanted to have in bed, but I'd agreed. He raised his eyebrow, no doubt wondering what was taking me so longer to answer. Here goes nothing.

"I had my first private lesson today," I began awkwardly.

"I know." Something flashed in his eyes, but he said nothing past the scary monotone words.

I swallowed anxiously and searched his face. Stalling was making this so much worse. But I wouldn't lie to him, not anymore. "Gabriel knew Sopteală." Shock exploded across his face. "There's more." He sat back and waited. I shifted to a sitting position and looked back. He wasn't going to like this. "Remember that job the note mentioned? Well, it's a task force. Kind of like..."

"The Shadows," he finished for me. If I'd thought he sounded scary before, I was wrong. Dead wrong. Every hair on my body stood on end and I shuddered at the sheer malevolence in which he uttered those two words. His lip curled in a snarl as his eyes turned to green fire. "I can't believe this. He wants to fucking resurrect the Shadows."

"Not quite."

The look he speared me with made me really wish there wasn't more. Fury and disbelief warred for dominance in his emerald eyes.

"He wants to revive an ancient order. They've been disbanded for centuries. Apparently Sopteală was actually running the whole thing before she died. Have you ever heard of the Knights of Nyx?" I desperately hoped that the play on history would help soften the blow. It didn't.

"Are you fucking serious? And before you ask again, no, I haven't heard of the Knights of Nyx. But it doesn't make a difference what you call it, the result is still the same. You'd be an enforcer, a fighter, a bloody fucking peacekeeper! Your job would *literally* be to hurt other people. You just got away from all of that and he wants you to—What? Dive right back in?" His disbelief was as palpable as his anger. He threw the covers off and got up. This was already going way worse than I'd feared.

I quickly scrambled after him. "Alex, please. It's not like that. I'd—"

Suddenly, he spun around to face me. "You want to do it, don't you?" He didn't even wait for me to respond. "Of course you do," he said, throwing up his hands and turning away from me. "That's why you haven't even asked how *I* feel about it. You're not asking for permission or even a blessing, you're simply telling me. You've already decided. I knew it wouldn't end at just the lessons. Any excuse, right?" he scoffed. Already he was halfway to the door. He wouldn't listen to anything I said if it related to Gabriel.

"Alexi Roman."

He froze at the use of his full name, anger clearly etched in every line of his body.

"What are you more upset about? The job or that it's Gabriel?"

He stiffened at the name which answered that question.

"This isn't some arbitrary militant squad. This is for demons, for us, *our* kind. They are out there, Alex, and too afraid to come out." His shoulders slumped and I could tell I was getting through to him. I reached out and turned him around, but he refused to meet my eye. "On top of which, this is in my blood, my legacy."

"I always knew you were a knight in shining armor," he commented snidely.

"You've always been mine." That got his attention. I took another step toward him, effectively invading his bubble. At least he was looking at me again.

"I don't want us to fight about this," I said, cupping his face so he couldn't turn away again.

Uncertainty swam in his eyes. "I just don't understand why you'd agree to this. You don't even *like* fighting. You told me so yourself."

"That's not why I'm doing this. Plus, it's a far cry from that night-forsaken bruiser club. I'll be protecting people that can't fend for themselves."

"Bloody knight," he mumbled under his breath.

"I thought you wanted a knight?" I asked quietly, with just a hint of teasing. The question earned me the hint of a smile. "I love you, Alex."

He blinked back at me. My heart hammered against my ribs like it always did when he looked at me. I leaned forward and placed my lips against his. Time seemed to stand still while I waited for him to kiss me back. When he did, it was like the black and white of the world became awash with color. I wrapped my other arm around him and pulled him close as I deepened the kiss. His return was equally impassioned, and tendrils of desire curled through me.

"It'll only ever be you," I said breathlessly. His arms tangled around me, crushing my body against his. I let out a gasp, and he claimed my mouth with a fierce, unforgiving kiss that reverberated through my very being. Alex was possessive, overbearing, and demanding... and he was mine.

EPILOGUE

Alexi

It was surreal being back home after everything that had happened. The world barely even made sense anymore. Yet, amidst all the chaos, there was one thing I knew with perfect clarity: I loved Matt. That Matt loved me back, however, hardly felt real. Selfishly, I wanted to keep him all to myself, but as much as I was willing to wait, there was only so long I could put off telling my mom about us. Not the least of which because he kept asking if I had, to which the answer was always a vague I'll get to it.

I worried he was taking my reluctance as a sign that I didn't think this would go over very well. The truth was quite the opposite. I was wary of my mother's enthusiasm when she found out about our recent status change. Trepidation aside, I couldn't put it off forever. Today, we'd tell my mother we were engaged. However, we'd unanimously decided to omit anything related to the Order of Light. I fully expected that at some point the truth would come out, but until then, I believed we'd earned ourselves a reprieve. Besides, it'd be nice to enjoy the moment before seasoning it with all the tragedy that had led to it.

I'd opted to walk to the house from the portal in order to give us a chance to talk things through again. It seemed safest to have a plan regarding breaking the news to my mother. I had zero doubts that Matt believed it was to soften the blow of what he viewed as bad news, whereas I simply wanted to minimize the potential and inevitable chaos that would erupt. The side door appeared with its welcoming glow amidst the bronze afternoon light.

I took a deep breath. This was it. "So again, we're not saying anything to my mom about what happened last month," I repeated anxiously.

"Or the last few months," Matt added. "Having to explain it to you several times over was bad enough." The eye roll was a bit much, but I couldn't really blame him. He promised to be an open book, but I still wasn't completely satisfied with some of his explanations. But it wasn't fair to hold the decisions of yesterday against him today; that was no way to live life. At least in his own mind, he'd thought he was doing the right thing.

"Maybe next time, don't keep secrets," I said, shifting my bag and opening the door. Unsurprisingly, the handle turned without resistance. I was barely across the threshold when I was forcibly dragged the rest of the way inside by an over-eager hug. "Hi mom," I said as I attempted to disentangle myself and failed.

"Don't give me that. It's been ages since I've seen you. You don't call. You don't write. What am I supposed to think? A mother is entitled to be happy to see her child," she said, fussing with my hair and collar.

"Come on, mom, at least let me put my things down so I can hug you properly," I griped. Matt snickered behind me, capturing her attention.

"I see you two have worked things out." She gave me another once over.

"You could say that." I gave him a sidelong look. His eyes glinted with a promise of heat, and I gave him a sidelong look, wondering if the no fooling around business still applied now that we were betrothed.

"Its good to see you again too, Matthew." I gave an inward groan at her use of his full name. "Though I confess," she went on oblivious, "I'm a little surprised y'all would choose this weekend of all weekends to visit."

"I have my reasons," I said, now finally at liberty to set my bag down. Matt closed the door and raised his hand in greeting as my mom advanced towards him for his own crushing hug.

"Hi Ms. Roman."

She immediately zeroed in on his waving hand. "What's that?"

"What's what?" he asked.

"On your hand."

He looked at the appendage in question and immediately snapped it back down to his side, guilt clearly stamped on his face. Then he looked at me, which only intensified the appearance of guilt.

I let out a sigh and walked towards him.

"Alexi Roman, what is going on?" my mother demanded, with her hands on her hips.

"I didn't even think," Matt whispered apologetically when I reached his side.

"It's okay," I whispered back and slid an arm around his waist. This was as good a way as any to break the news. "So, mom... we have something we'd like to tell you."

Her foot tapped impatiently on the tile as she waited.

"Matt and I are engaged." I raised my hand so she could see the matching band. There was no denying the grin that spread across my face. I loved saying that.

Her eyes went wide and she let out an ear piercing squeal. We both flinched. Then, she clutched her chest, and for a moment, I thought the news was too much for her and she'd simply keel over right there in the kitchen. She took an exaggerated breath and her words came out in an almost unintelligible tide. "This is wonderful! I couldn't ask for better news. Oh, and here I thought... Well, never mind what I thought. I get a son-in-law and grandbabies and I'll get to use my book after all. This is amazing! There's so much that'll need to be done. And I'm so happy for both of you." She rushed us and squeezed the life out of our frozen forms, then spun on her heel, her curly hair flaring around her head, and practically raced out of the room, still rambling to herself. I had no idea what book she was referring to, but the moment she was out of sight, words bubbled out of Matt as well.

"I'm so sorry. I didn't mean to. You just wave. That's what you do. In my defense, it's typically on the other hand where I come from. How was I supposed to know it would be the first thing she saw?"

I laughed and ebbed the tide of defenses with a kiss. At last he stopped trying to talk around it and gave in. "Its okay. Now, it's done," I tried to reassure him. "Plans are great, but the only real goal was to tell her, and we did that."

"But," he tried to protest.

I shook my head and stole another kiss. He sighed and let it go. His wonderfully blue eyes searched my face, and I reached up to stroke his cheek. "I told you she'd freak out."

He gave a low laugh, and my mom made a reappearance.

"What's so funny?" she asked, struggling with her burden. She was clutching an extremely bulky scrapbook, with bits of fabric, ribbons, and paper peeking out.

"Nothing," I said, stroking Matt's side while trying to figure out where she'd been hiding such a massive book.

She gave a flippant wave of her hand, dismissing my noncommittal response. "I thought this thing would never get used. This is going to be so much fun. And the planning!" she exclaimed, opening the book. At last, it dawned on me what it was—a wedding planner.

"Mom," I groaned, releasing Matt.

"I will not be denied, Alexi. Though now I'm even more surprised that you'd wait until the day before Valentine's to tell me," she remarked positively in a tizzy.

I gave Matt a dubious smile. Astoundingly, he still hadn't put it together. "Because, mum, today is Matt's birthday." I shifted my gaze back to Matt. "I thought he might like to celebrate with his family."

Matt's jaw literally fell, while my mother's face melted into a tender expression. She clasped her hands over her heart and I prayed she wouldn't make too much of a to-do about it. Matt could be oversensitive about his past, and I really didn't want to spoil the weekend by upsetting him.

"How... how did you know?" he asked, disbelief coloring the inquiry.

"You told me. Remember? I even have a gift for you... from Vera." That bit certainly took him off guard. I reached into my bag and fished out the thick folder, then passed it to him.

He looked down at the tenuous stack of papers as if unsure what to do next.

"Go ahead, look." The words *Happy Birthday Matt* were elegantly written on the cover, but it was what was at the end that made it truly special.

"What is it?" he asked.

"It's your file, Matt."

For a second, I thought he was going to close it without flipping through at all. Then, with hesitant hands, he turned the pages. Page after page detailed the horrible life Matt had endured while living in a world that could never hope to understand. It had been difficult, but I'd forced myself to read every last incident where he'd been in fights. The earliest records were by far the worst, no doubt because he wasn't defending himself. Yet, as the years progressed, the tables shifted, and the violence increased. It broke my heart, but this was part of who he was and I wouldn't ignore it just because it wasn't pretty. His eyes glazed over as he looked at his history, and I waited somewhat impatiently for him to reach the last page. It would all be worth it once he got to that. At last, he was there. I watched his face go from puzzled curiosity to baffled amazement.

He looked up from Vera's note and I thought my heart would burst with love for him. "I don't understand."

"Congratulations, Matt. You are no longer a ward of the state *or* Vera. You are perfectly free in all fifty states and in every other country, too, for that matter," I said with a smile.

He barked a disbelieving laugh. The folder fell to the ground with a smack, sending papers and pictures sliding in every direction. Ignoring them, he stepped across the small space and grabbed me. The resulting kiss was full of all the fire and passion that defined him. And love, so much love.

I pulled him in close, not caring that my mother was watching. Matt was everything and loving him felt like the most important thing I'd ever done in my life.

"I'm not a Warde anymore," he said, his eyes sparkling with unshed tears.

I smiled, my heart on the verge of bursting. "No, you're a Roman now."

About the Author

Sam Bolanos (she/they) is a genderqueer author and founder of Chaotic Neutral Press LLC. They believe in love, equality, and the Oxford comma. When not playing with her three dogs, who you can follow on Instagram @austendogs, or spending time with her incredible husband, she's probably agonizing over edits or escaping into her latest fantasy.

Welcome to the adventure!

Newsletter: subscribe
Website: Booksbysbolanos.com
Facebook: @ Booksbysbolanos
reader group: Sam's Sunbeams
Instagram: @ sbolanosbooks

www.ingramcontent.com/pod-product-compliance
Lightning Source LLC
Chambersburg PA
CBHW030543310726
48979CB00010B/2010/J
* 9 7 8 1 9 5 6 1 2 8 5 2 9 *